WEASELS AND WISEMEN

WEASELS AND WISEMEN

ETHICS AND ETHNICITY
IN THE WORK OF DAVID MAMET

LESLIE KANE

MACMILLAN

First published 1999 by
MACMILLAN PRESS LTD
Houndmills, Basingstoke, Hampshire RG21 6XS
and London
Companies and representatives
throughout the world

ISBN 0–333–75470–0

A catalogue record for this book is available
from the British Library.

10 9 8 7 6 5 4 3 2 1
08 07 06 05 04 03 02 01 00 99

Printed in the United States of America by
Haddon Craftsmen
Scranton, PA

For my father

CONTENTS

Acknowledgments

SEVERAL YEARS AGO I traveled to the set of *Homicide* to interview Joe Mantegna for a collection of essays on David Mamet that I was editing. As I was leaving, he insisted that after traveling so far I must at least meet David Mamet. We walked into a bustling commissary where he made the introductions, and then, if memory serves, it became very quiet. I was clearly out of place and overdressed. The playwright quizzed me about the nature of my work—a dialogic paradigm that has since informed our discussions—and spontaneously invited me to the cramped set. As good fortune would have it, that was the day he was shooting the library scene in his new film. The scene portrays a Jewish police officer, investigating the death of an old Jewish woman, confronted with the fact of his conflicted loyalty, confused identity, and scant knowledge of Jewish practice, language, and liturgy. When I left ten hours later, I had in my possession an interview with Lynn Mamet, the first she had granted in ten years, a script of the film, and an ally. I had long considered writing a study of marginality in Mamet's work. Surely now a new journey had begun.

The challenging, circuitous journey of *Weasels and Wisemen* has taken me from Boston to Baltimore, New York to London, Chicago to Phoenix. I have been blessed to encounter a steady stream of individuals, academicians, collectors, curators, editors, librarians, actors, and directors, who have contributed materially and intellectually to the experience and have treated me with great kindness. Longtime admired friends and colleagues, Christopher Hudgins and Robert Vorlicky gave unselfishly of their time, energy, intellect, and warmth throughout the writing of this book. Two scholars whose trenchant criticism has immeasurably enhanced Mamet scholarship, Chris and Bob have proved ideal readers and valued friends. My work has benefited enormously from their meticulous reading of drafts, insightful options, probing questions, and astute criticism. Chris, who prompted me from the first, has gently prodded me to completion, whereas Bob's artistic sensibility has had an enormous influence on the book's shaping and vision.

Both have been unstinting in their support of the project, their guidance, and their sensitivity to the strain and isolation of writing.

At every stage, I have found collegiality and generosity, such as that of Michael and Betsy Hinden who encouraged me to stay at their beautiful home in Madison, Wisconsin, whose peaceful, wooded site and bountiful library gave me the necessary space and peace to begin my work. During that first productive summer, Robert Skloot was a fine breakfast companion with whom I enjoyed stimulating discussions about Mamet's theatre. The scrupulous scholarship of Sander Gilman has inspired my own; his discussions of discourse and Jewish self-hatred helped to shape this book. Steven Price read part of the manuscript and offered splendid advice. Robert Skloot, Hersh Zeifman, Ruby Cohn, Deborah Geis, Janet Haedicke, Al Wertheim, and Matthew Roudané have kept me honest. Harriet Voyt, David Mamet's administrative assistant, has smoothed the way in countless ways.

Yet the demands of writing and research have kept me apart from friends and family who have, each in his or her inimitable way, sustained me from afar. Five years can test the closest of relationships, for it is families that sustain the greatest burden. My deepest thanks go to my children, Pamela and David, for their abiding love and pride in me; to my husband, for his encouragement and patience with my work habits; to my mother, whose zest for living and generosity are an inspiration. My life has been enriched and nourished by the friendship of Janet Rapaport, Sandy Sirull, and Bonnie Meltzer.

I especially thank my daughter Pamela, whose legal advice has been invaluable as has her willingness to go the length in any discussion that involved points of law. I thank, as well, Rabbi Ronald Weiss, who eagerly answered questions of liturgy at every stage of this project, even when he was puzzled at their relevance to my work. Although seven years older than David Mamet, Ronald Weiss grew up in Mamet's "old neighborhood," and his recollections, as well as his archival collection from Temple Sinai, Chicago, have been very useful. Lew Foreman's scholarship has immeasurably aided mine; his love is deeply valued. Douglas Lieberman, Martin Blumenson, and David Desser were especially helpful. Special thanks, too, to Dan and Helen Levenson, Paul Sirull, Jay Meltzer, and Ellen Foreman for their confidence in me and this enterprise.

I acknowledge the enormous assistance of curators Lauren Bufferd, Special Collections Division of the Chicago Public Library, where the St. Nicholas Theatre and Goodman Theatre papers are retained; Dr. Charles Cutter at the Judaica Library, Brandeis University; and Nicola Scadding, Royal National Theatre, London; along with the Research Division of The

New York Public Library for the Performing Arts; Memorial Library at the University of Wisconsin, Madison; and to Brian Hubbard, Research Librarian, Westfield State College, who has fielded my endless requests with unflagging interest and responsiveness. Jan and David Sauer's recent bibliographic research on the work of David Mamet has been immensely useful; and to the academicians who have generously shared their scholarship with me prior to the publication of their own work, I am especially grateful. Sabbatical leave from Westfield State College afforded the valuable time to begin my work and flexible class schedule to advance it, and visiting scholar status granted by Arizona State University provided a home to continue my writing in the peace and beauty of the Southwest.

For her advice, patience, and personal commitment to this book, I thank Maura Burnett, my editor at St. Martin's Press. For his careful shepherding of this book through production, I am indebted to Rick Delaney. And for her meticulous copyediting of the book, I especially want to thank Enid Stubin.

Many theatre professionals whose work is closely aligned with that of David Mamet graciously took the time to meet with me and share their recollections and perception of these plays in performance. I acknowledge my appreciation to Joe Mantegna, William H. Macy, Mike Nussbaum, Nan Cibula Jenkins, Sam Mendes, and especially Gregory Mosher, who has generously shared his recollections, marvelous insights, and time during the entire project. Lynn Mamet was an early champion of this book, ever generous with her time; my debt to her is enormous.

Finally, I am indebted to David Mamet for the inspiration of his work, for his accessibility, for his great kindness, and for his friendship. My gratitude for the innumerable manuscripts, invitations to visit film sets or attend rehearsals for *Oleanna, The Cryptogram,* and *The Old Neighborhood,* humorous anecdotes, challenging questions, and wonderful luncheon chats without which *Weasels and Wisemen* would be a different—and lesser—work.

THE THINGS
THEY CARRIED

Weasels and Wisemen: Ethics and Ethnicity in the Work of David Mamet is the
first major study of David Mamet's work to investigate the moral vision and
cultural poetics upon which this playwright's aesthetic vision is founded. A
seminal figure in contemporary American drama whose ascendant reputation
as an innovative playwright and filmmaker demands an appraisal of his
thought and the evolution of his craft, David Mamet has demonstrated a
commitment to the dynamics of ethics and ethnicity that informs his work.
Tracing the development of Mamet's work over the past twenty years from his
early, unpublished play, *Marranos*, through his recent screenplay, *The Edge,* I
examine the subtle link between the moral vision that distinguishes Mamet's
theatre and film and its foundation in Judaic thought, values, and cultural
experience, which have been insufficiently acknowledged or understood.

Mamet's plays are analogous to great echo chambers in which the
sources of sound are magnified and distorted so that each achieves resonance
and universality through the suppression of explicit reference to Jewish
cultural and historical experience. This book will explore the impact of
personal experience upon aesthetic vision and will illustrate the presence of
substantive Jewish content and methodology. Although the subjects and
settings of Mamet's work have clearly changed since 1975, the ethos that
undergirds his work, the education that is inextricably bound to ethical
conduct, the perception that ethical (private) and legal (public) acts are
inseparable, the prevalence of marginalized figures, and the compelling role
of diction and discourse for which he is justly famous are remarkably
consistent and revelatory. Especially in those works in which complex
ironies, parody, and linguistic reticence enable Mamet to fuse identification
with Jewish cultural experience and moral imperative in texts seemingly

devoid of ethnic reference, I examine the unity of moral vision and methodology that informs Mamet's work.

Widely considered to be one of the most influential and powerful voices in contemporary American theatre, Mamet, like his prodigious canon, continues to grow in status. His sensitivity to language that defines and confines his characters, his precision of social observation, concern for metaphor and its dramatic and cinematic force, theatrical imagination and inventiveness, striking tone poems of betrayal, loss, and renewal, brilliant use of comedy that celebrates the capacity to survive—even though, as some have argued, that survival is venal—have engendered commentary that has read, approached, or deconstructed his work from a plurality of critical discourses. However, I approach Mamet's work from the perspective of cultural poetics, offering a compelling rationale for the struggle for dominance, extended and estranged families, the evocative presence of history, recurring intimidation, persecution, and betrayal, and the pivotal place of memory. I will locate cultural poetics, as well, in the marginalized figures that dominate Mamet's vast and varied terrain, in the resonant tropes of legacy, learning, and loyalty.

Significantly, Mamet's plays balance ethical ideals and moral imperative through the teaching trope by continually posing the critical question: Is there an ethical component that calls for an ethical decision? And as my closer examination of selected stage plays and screenplays will reveal, Mamet's work is dominated by pedagogical relationships that constitute an implicitly ethical contract. As the source of power struggles that characterize his canon, these relationships simultaneously serve as the site of ethical choices and the consequences of conduct, providing an apt forum for revising questions of competence and pretense and an appropriate venue for airing issues of fairness and injustice. For Mamet, "Theatre is a place of recognition, it's an ethical exercise, it's where we show ethical interchange" (Wetzsteon 1976, 103). From this perspective, I believe that Emmanuel Levinas's philosophy of ethical responsibility casts light on Mamet's aesthetic vision. To Levinas, "ethics and epistemology converge in a moral righteousness that is not the rightness of the true but that makes truth possible" (R. Cohen 2). In other words, "the ethical relation is a unique relation" predicated on "*proximity,*" that is, one is responsible to *and* for the other (5), a fundamental principle of Judaism. The playwright, however, finds an exemplar in Tolstoy. As he tells theatre critic Ross Wetzsteon in 1976, "I'm more interested in what Tolstoy said—that we should treat other human beings with love and respect and never hurt them. I hope *American Buffalo* shows that, by showing what happens when you fail to act that way" (Wetzsteon 103), a statement that underscores the ironic inversion that undergirds his work. In short, for Mamet every transaction is an act of faith or the loss of it.

The first tropological study of Mamet's body of work, this book approaches Mamet's work from a cultural perspective, exploring the diction, discourse, depiction, and disconnection of drifters, con artists, stoop philosophers, and scholars who by conduct or particularized portrayals invite identification as Jews or whose social or commercial exchanges in typically Jewish settings—commerce, entertainment, education—occasion an ethical contract. Mamet's work for the stage and screen is peopled by "weasels and wisemen"—disreputable cons, teachers, salesmen, hucksters, tricksters—who tenaciously survive solely on their wits. In language that juxtaposes the profane and mundane, the quotidian and the mythic, the vulgar and the spiritual, colloquial and sacred texts, Mamet, drawing on a six-thousand-year-old Jewish tradition of argument, paints a broad canvas of civilized arguers who dispute with each other about everything that matters: history, memory, law, connection, responsibility, justice, love, and "success as a social fact, if not as a moral dilemma" (Shechner 1979, 203).

Increasingly more vocal on the subject of his renewed Jewish faith, Mamet admits that his recent work exhibits "an *a priori* spirituality";[1] however, the thematic and metaphoric use of cons and confidence games, the rhythm, minimalism, and cadence of Yiddish, allusion to mystics and the Talmud, the teaching trope, references to the Jew in transition, and elaborate narratives that enhance, recover, and protect self-image pervade his canon—as do frequent and casual recourse to Jewish heritage—further evincing that his ethical "first principles" are informed by Jewish cultural and historical experience. Staging marginality, with a particular sensitivity to the persecuted and disenfranchised, Mamet unifies the secular with the spiritual, the past with the present, the individual and the community, the teacher and the student, the tale-teller and the listener, the actor and the audience. But he is aware that despite our need for communication and connection, unions are tenuous, transitory, even exploitive, a point he reiterates in disappointing reunions, dissolving marriages, and disintegrating values. Thus, although Mamet encourages us in essay "to change the habit of coercive and frightened action and substitute for it the habit of trust, self-reliance, and cooperation" (1987d, 27), he dramatizes men and women who want to be good people but, faced with impossible choices abandon "a sense of community and collective social goals" in their "obsessive search for success and individuality" (Ranvaud 232).

Christopher Bigsby has rightly observed that storytelling is fundamental to Mamet's work.[2] Yet his assertion that characters employ storytelling as an evasive tactic of self-justification or to create coherence in a world lacking both shape and meaning (1992, 217), while correct, fails to address Judaism's reliance on narrative as a means of unifying one generation with another, of preserving and teaching history and heritage, of reaffirming its teachings of righteous conduct, of binding one individual to another through narrative, and of establishing a fundamental mode of communication. Given that *American Buffalo* is the "break-out play" in which "a man's character is defined by his actions," everyone from petty thieves to movie producers in Mamet's canon is judged by his or her behavior and viewed through the lens of ethical choice.[3]

In fact, the narrative that we encounter in Mamet's work is aggadic, narrative that is imaginative. This literature, writes Cynthia Ozick, is "utterly freed to invention, discourse, parable, experiment, enlightenment, profundity, humanity" (175). And more than the preservation of the past. . . . [i]t is a continuing process of reintegration of the past into the present" (Schwartz 101). Or as Steven D. Kepnes explains in "Narrative Jewish Theology," "Jewish aggadah exploits the resources of language—its ability to simultaneously conceal and to disclose" to open a dialogue with the past, framing its practical wisdom in the present and the everyday world (211-12).

"I have always felt like an outsider," writes Mamet in "On Paul Ickovic's Photographs," and "I am sure that the suspicion that I perceive is the suspicion that I provoke by my great longing to *belong*" (1987d, 73). The grandson of Ashkenazi immigrants from Poland, he remembers the Reform Judaism of his youth as "nothing other than a desire 'to pass'" in American society. "We were Jews, and worthless. We were everything bad that was said against us . . ."(1989b, 17-18).[4] Indicative of what is missing in the lives that he dramatizes and the Jewish identity that was denied him by his parents in "rabid pursuit" of success and acceptance, the bonds of friendship, trust, loyalty, and memory are absolutely central to his aesthetic vision (8). This essential need to belong, to forge communal relationships, to establish a relationship to God and an ethical relationship with other human beings is extraordinarily constant in a body of work distinguished by its diversity.

A prolific writer, Mamet brings to his work, most notably in *The Old Religion,* a particular sensitivity to the ways in which language is employed as camouflage, communication, and a means of achieving one's goal.[5] "My main emphasis," Mamet told Wetzsteon, "is on the rhythm of language— the action and rhythm are identical. Our actions describe our actions—no, our rhythms *prescribe* our actions" (104). Yet in 1975, when the young playwright burst on the theatrical scene with *American Buffalo,* with its iambic pentameter, its profanity, its male cast of characters planning a heist, and its violence, the play was profoundly misunderstood and misjudged by innumerable critics in Chicago and New York who failed to recognize what Richard Christiansen lauded as a work so important that it would change American theatre.[6] Now a classic of the American theatre that Gregory Mosher has described as "Mamet's audacious stylistic breakthrough. . . . [which] was, famously to craft iambic pentameter out of obscenity-laced vernacular of the underclass" (1996, 80), whose nuances, rhythms, and pornography have subsequently intrigued, baffled, and thrilled critics and audiences for twenty years, *American Buffalo* stands alone as one of the great tragedies of the twentieth century in which a "closed moral system," as Mamet would have it, is framed by profanity. Arthur Holmberg, in fact, dubs Mamet the "poet laureate of profanity" in whose hands "language is a lethal weapon" (1997b, 7).[7]

If we characterize Mamet as the "playwright of pornography, patrism, or perversion" in what Matthew Roudané recognizes is a slippery slope, "we risk oversimplifying what precisely empowers his stage" (1992, 4).[8] Mamet's idiosyncratic use of rhetorical questions, recurrent queries, rising interrogative rhythms, elisions, inverted syntax, repetitions, and monosyllabic words, "the most striking of which are obscenities," are surely testimony of a "fecund creativity," observes Ruby Cohn (1992, 117). Notably, however, the full range of his linguistic strategies is ceaselessly directed to questions of wisdom, competence, and conduct. The language that characterizes Mamet's work reflects a Jewish sensibility, a power of the imagination that "mix[es] in a way we can call Jewish, the earthy with the grand, the sad and the comic, the psychologically real and the farcically fantastic" (Opdahl 186). It is a language typified by invective, to varying purpose, colloquialism, and paronomasia. Its ironic humor is not merely self-critical but self-justifying; it literally "discloses culture," as Mark Shechner has put it. Essentially, Mamet has, to quote Don in *American Buffalo*, the "Skill and talent and the balls" (1977, 4) to craft a dramatic language of rhetorical excess and masterful minimalism that delights us and draws light to its ethos. Typically counterpointing a laconic figure and a voluble one, Mamet's dazzling parabolas of speech beguile us on the one hand and draw us into contemplation of the typically (un)ethical interchange. For as Sander Gilman reminds us, "Language . . . play[s] a vital role as a marker of Jewish difference" (1991b, 5).

Thus, although not immediately noticeable in his work, Mamet's Jewishness, deeply ingrained, forms the bedrock of his writing. Close scrutiny of his canon from 1975 on reveals that Judaic thought and values are neither a recent focus of his work nor a digression but an intrinsic, integral element of Mamet's work fundamental to his artistic vision. Its

impact is evinced in his language, rich in complexity, skepticism, intellectu-
alism, and particularities of ordinary life, and in his bawdy, ironic humor,
dramatization of (un)ethical personal and commercial transactions, abiding
concern with learning, legacy, and compassion. Its subjects are repeatedly
the law, be it moral, ethical, or common, coupled with the analysis of or
expounding on the law, as his stunning novel *The Old Religion,* amply
illustrates. Though of varying social classes, Mamet's characters, who are
typically marginal figures, repeatedly rivet our attention to justice, what
George Steiner terms "the pride and burden of the Judaic tradition" (1961,
4). Whether confronting the past—personal, familial, or cultural—struggling to survive, or finding the means and character to behave ethically,
responsibly, and compassionately, his characters reflect a doggedness, savvy,
persistence, initiative, resistance, and above all, humanity, both in their
propensity to selfish action and their acquisition of (self-)knowledge and
need of community. As Michael Hinden has rightly noticed, Mamet's work
is typified by "nostalgia for family ties, the importance of the father-son
relationship, the brooding loneliness of the midwestern landscape, a fascination with men whose lives are dedicated to dollars. . . . [and] a continuing
quest to establish the groundwork for a vision of community that could
create the closeness of family life" (33).

In *Speed-the-Plow,* Mamet's Hollywood hucksters, Bobby Gould and
Charlie Fox, reveal the playwright's explicit examination of issues of learning
and loyalty. With integral dilemma, a dash of *chutzpah,* moral lapse, Yiddish
expression, and bawdy humor, this play would seem to signal a turning
point in Mamet's work. Yet, upon closer inspection, *Speed-the-Plow,* like
American Buffalo, which precedes it by a decade, evinces centrally Jewish
concern with behavior that places "faith in actions rather than dogma"
(Guttmann 6). Although Mamet's recent work exposes a turn toward the
spiritual, thematic and metaphoric cons and confidence games, the rhythms
and cadences of Yiddish (in which he is fluent), allusions to mystics and
Talmud, the teaching trope, marginalized figures (whether "in the wilderness" or in the junk store)[9] and elaborate aggadic narratives that enhance,
recover, and protect self-image pervade his canon from the outset.

Increasingly, in Mamet's essays—about Chicago; about his family life
in "The Rake," a painful memoir of familial abuse that frequently exploded
into rage; about his youth; about the truck factory where he worked—the
most frequently uttered words are "I remember." Reflecting a shift in
Mamet's work in the last decade toward family plays that are intimate,
personal, and painful, profanity has taken a back seat to profundity, and
recollections, stories of his youth, evocation of the Holocaust or the
American Jewish struggle with affiliation, increasingly frame the events of

the plot. Beginning in the mid-to-late 1980s Mamet has affirmed his Jewish identity in essays and reminiscences in *Some Freaks, The Cabin,* and *Make-Believe Town;* his screenplay, *Russian-Poland,* based on a Hasidic story; three plays, *The Disappearance of the Jews, Goldberg Street,* and *The Luftmensch; Homicide,* and *The Old Religion,* where, as Wetzsteon precisely puts it, the outcast Jew, "Paralyzed by his bifurcated sensibility . . . is destined to swing from a tree" (1997). These works not only find new ways to reconsider the familiar motifs of learning and legacy but privilege issues of loss and conflicted identity. Evidence of Mamet's Jewish renewal finds form in his work in the foregrounding of anti-Semitism and Jewish self-hatred, and in the continuing conflict between materialism and mindfulness. History plays a perceptibly dominant role in his work, and memory is backlit in a new and deeply personal context. "[I]t's not impossible to be Jewish [in the United States]," Mamet tells Holmberg; "it's difficult to be Jewish and to come to grips with it" (1997a, 8-9). My analysis of plays of this decade, therefore, will cast light on frequently cryptic works in which the young and the mature "come to grips" with ethnicity, responsibility, and their growing awareness of betrayal. As humor is muted, legacy, learning, and self-scrutiny assume an even greater prominence.

To understand Jewish identity in the Diaspora as it is portrayed artistically, Sander L. Gilman and Steven T. Katz posit in their introduction to *Anti-Semitism in Times of Crisis,* "one must also understand the creation, generation and the perpetuation of the negative images of the Jew" (1991, 18).[10] In *The Jew's Body,* moreover, Gilman, whose propensity to provocative, thoughtful statement is much like Mamet's, argues: "My assumption is that the Jew in the Western Diaspora does respond, must respond, to the image of the Jew in such cultures" (1991b, 4). And, further, he adds, "no one who identifies, either positively or negatively, with the label 'Jew,' is immune from the power of such stereotypes. . . . [which] reflect the relative powerlessness of the Jew in the Disaspora and the hostility which Christian society (even in its secularized form) has against the Jew" (3).

Crucial to any discussion of revealing Judaism in Mamet's work, then, is a closer scrutiny of both the rhetoric and "the specific contexts and locations in which the idea of the Jew and the reality of the Jews comes into conflict" (3). That Mamet's landscape is typified by fast-talking thieves, con artists, charlatans, and "Sammy Glick" swindlers—the sharp, often rootless, wheeler-dealers involved in schemes to line their pockets—as well as bookworms and teachers—Talmudic scholars of righteousness, moral integrity, intuitive intelligence, and questionable teachings—whose patois and narrative genius are clear signifiers of difference, compels us to consider archetypal Jews who find form in Mamet's landscape as parodic and paradigmatic weasels and wisemen. Indeed, I believe that it is in the ironic inversion of negative stereotypical representation of the Jew, the allusive link among delusion, deception, and discourse, that one gains a greater understanding of a key signifier of marginality in Mamet's plays and films.

Stereotypes, Gilman points out, are not derived from the object of prejudice but are the product and the projection of the majority's prejudice against the Other. Although they bear little or no resemblance to those whom they seek to categorize and are by definition "Janus-faced images of dichotomy," the portrayal of stereotypical Jews often serves "to define the borders of acceptability, which must be crossed into the world of privilege" (1986, 4-5).[11] From a historical perspective, then, the emergence of negative stereotypical images of the Jew in the twelfth century reflects a fundamental change overshadowing and devaluing long-established perceptions of the Jew as wise magician, teacher, and physician whose connection with his valued books was inextricable. As Gilman illustrates, the admiration for the Jew's wisdom associated with Jewish knowledge of Hebrew wanes as two tropes of the Jew emerge—that of the "blind" Jew and the "seeing" Jew.[12] This evolution from the mystical to the mendacious was engendered and provoked by a vigorous campaign undertaken to devalue and strip the Jew of any special role in life. Preceding and paralleling medieval portrayals of the stage Jew, numerous publications sought to establish that the blindness of the Jews derived from their limited comprehension of the divine text. Although rhetoric changes from religious to secular, the Jew is a threat to the body politic whether as usurer, thief, trickster, con artist, kidnapper, criminal, or alien. As Moshe Lazar explains in "The Lamb and the Scapegoat: The Dehumanization of the Jews in Medieval Propaganda Imagery," the mythicization and diabolization of the Jews that culminated in their dehumanization included representation of Jews as those who "dispute," "rage," "act as madmen," "mock," are "blind," "hard-necked," or "mad dogs" and stigmatized them as carnal, lecherous, and avaricious and possessed of monetary acumen (55, 54).

Seventeenth- and eighteenth-century portraits of buffoons and sharpers pale by comparison to the malevolent, parasitic villains that were their immediate forebears, but it was only the portrait and not the perception of the Jew that had been altered. Portrayed as gesticulating ranters in dirty clothes, their speech devalued into an apparently foreign jargon or unintelligible gibberish, these money-mad characters illustrate a fixation on the discourse of the Jew. Although Jews in these plays are transformed into the butt of the joke rather than the object of fear, it would be fallacious to assume that they represent a refinement or an enhancement of previously established stereotypic models of the Jew. Rather than enhance the image of the Jew as barbarian however, these portraits, too, reinforce the view of the Jew as an individual whose language is as repugnant as his or her speech.[13]

And even though these stage portraits sought to depict the Jew as less cunning and covetous, Christians were nevertheless convinced that the dishonest criminal nature of the Jew was inextricably linked to the use of Yiddish, the conspiratorial language of Jews and their criminal activity. Gilman theorizes that "The linkage between Jews who hide their evil deeds in a language that is not understandable" to the Christian world combined with the idea that "Jews lie," imbued Yiddish, "perceived not as a language but as the means for conspiracy, [with] its own hidden power"(1986, 73). By the eighteenth century it had become axiomatic that Jews were possessed of a language of corruption through which they concealed their inherent evil. Thus, despite the fact that criminals were neither Jewish nor Yiddish-speaking, observes Gilman, their social function as outlaws stigmatized and transformed them into mimetic Jews. As European Jews were Yiddish-speaking, it was assumed that they employed their language fluency to undermine state authority, so that Jewish identity formation in the eighteenth century inexorably bonded the speaker of Yiddish to the language of marginality and implied criminality (76-81).[14] Yet, abandoned by assimilated Jews, the "new mode of discourse" for the Jew would be "the ironic tone of the observer" (162). And it is in this position that Mamet sees himself. "[T]he world of the outsider, in which I have chosen to live, and in which I have trained myself to live is based . . . on observation. The habit of constant *acute* awareness can be seen in animals with no resource, with no option to fight, with no margin for error . . . Historically, it is the habit of the Jew" (1987d, 73).

It is not my intention to reduce Mamet to one message or to suggest that he is writing "Jewish plays" with purely literal and exhaustive meaning. Indeed, Mamet's work can surely be enjoyed without recourse to its moral aesthetic. Yet to do so, in my view, is to fail to read it backward, to understand the impact and sweep of history that inform his canon. Rather than diminish the universality that he has achieved in his dramatic and cinematic expression, *Weasels and Wisemen* illuminates the sources and scope of Mamet's body of work, thereby, I hope, enhancing our understanding of his artistic expression by intensive and comprehensive (re)viewing of the work of America's foremost contemporary playwright. As Susanne Langer reminds us in her classic study, *Feeling and Form,* in drama "We do not have to find what is significant; the selection has been made—whatever is there is significant, and it is not too much to be surveyed *in toto*" (310).

I shall examine a number of selected major works as illustrative examples of Mamet's fusion of technique and thought, range and complexity. *American Buffalo, Glengarry Glen Ross, Speed-the-Plow, Oleanna,* and *The Cryptogram,* as well as several films, *Things Change, Homicide,* and *The Edge,* will be discussed individually within a tropological and chronological context. However, emphasis will be placed on thematic and aesthetic elements that reflect continuity in artistic vision. In addition to major works, several of Mamet's shorter and lesser-known plays, sketches, and monologues, among them his unpublished *Marranos* and *The Old Neighborhood* (to which I had access prior to publication) have been included, confirming an aesthetic and moral underpinning in the minor works and exposing the reader to some of Mamet's most demanding writing. Both in major and minor keys, we are reminded that when you see a Mamet film or "you leave the theater after a Mamet play," as Robert Brustein recognizes, "and realize it's exploded in your brain. You're asking questions about the nature of our society" (Freeman 50).

In the last quarter century, questions inspired by David Mamet's extraordinarily diverse body of work have been timeless and timely. In counterpointing the demotic and the dialectic, myth and material culture, belonging and marginalization, the search for truth and the merchandising of it, Mamet's work is suffused by every aspect of Jewish cultural experience, none more obvious than that his world is peopled by weasels and wisemen for whom performance is both appearance and accomplishment.

THE COMFORT
OF STRANGERS

> "In a place where there are no decent people
> strive to be one."
>
> —Rabbi Hillel, *Pirke Avot*

The earliest example of ethnic representation in the Mamet canon can be found in David Mamet's little-known, unpublished play entitled *Marranos*. Approached in 1975 by the Bernard Horwich Jewish Community Center, located in Skokie, Illinois, Mamet was paid the handsome fee of $1,000 and "provided only with the subject Marranos—not even stipulated to be a title." Douglas Lieberman, director of the play's only production, recalls that Mamet's primary concern was the "feelings of the Jewish family as they discover they are coming unmasked."[1] Not surprisingly, Mamet sets his play in the home of a wealthy Portuguese merchant on the evening that his family, denounced to the Inquisition, is hurriedly completing preparations to flee to Holland.

Although the term "Marranos" is typically associated with the expulsion and extermination of covert Jews during the Inquisition in Spain in the fifteenth century and Portugal in the sixteenth, the practice of Judaism in disguise in the Iberian Peninsula may be traced to the fourth century when the Visigoths ruled Spain and first promulgated anti-Jewish laws. The contemptuous and derisive term, suggests Joachim Prinz in *The Secret Jews*, is believed to have been derived from "the Spanish word *marrar* meaning to deviate from truth or justice," and was employed to describe "Jews who *marran* or *mar,* the true faith with insincere conversion," namely converting to Catholicism but remaining secret, practicing Jews who transferred Jewish traditions and values from generation to generation. More likely the word, derived from the Spanish word for prostitute or swine, *marrano*, was an expression of hatred reserved for *cristianos nuevos*, "new but not real Christians" (17).

In 1348 the Seven Part Code (originally introduced by Alfonso the Wise in 1256) instituting brutal anti-Jewish restrictions throughout Spain became the law of the land, establishing the legal precedent for anti-Jewish violence, such as mob riots and the widespread destruction of temples from Cordoba to Barcelona. The legislation and pervasive violence contributed to nearly 200,000 conversions (Prinz 21-25) in what Cynthia Ozick terms "the first . . . large-scale passing" (115). Yet these secret Jews continued to exert a disproportionate influence in the society. Thus, rather than solving the "Jewish question," mass conversions effected on the rack, on the pyre, on a torture wheel, through molten lead poured into orifices, during de-tonguing, de-nailing, and skin-stripping, created a new problem. A powerful middle class comprised of secret Jews (Judaizing Christians) found security in assimilation, their "insidious" invasion of society posing a threat to the authority and purity of the Catholic Church, for *conversos,* as they were called, assimilated as monks, nuns, parish priests, even bishops and cardinals. Therefore, Ferdinand and Isabella, persuaded by Torquemada, the Chief Inquisitor, reconvened the Inquisition in 1492 to ferret out infidels and heretics. Some eighty thousand Jews fled to Portugal; their refuge, however, was short-lived as the Inquisition followed them, taking a particularly brutal form of slaughter of Jews that rivals any in Jewish history. Only those rich enough to pay exorbitant ransom demands or wise enough to plan a timely departure escaped extermination and founded new Jewish communities in Holland, France, Turkey, Brazil, and the Indies (Prinz 126).[2]

Exemplifying what Elie Wiesel terms Judaism's "great attachment to its past," *Marranos* reflects an understanding that "Jewish history unfolds in the present" and that "all events are linked" (1976, xi-xiii). Thus, while Mamet's historical play dramatizes the trauma and terror of one Jewish community threatened with expulsion and extermination, it echoes the experience of others. Drawing striking parallels between the Inquisition and the terror of Germany during the 1930s and 1940s, Mamet simultaneously links these past events to his personal experience—a wretched childhood lived in fear— and that of many other Jews of his generation, for whom Reform Judaism was an attempt "to 'pass'. . . unnoticed" in American society, cognizant that both anti-Semitism and assimilation threaten the existence of the Jewish people (Mamet 1989b, 17). Addressing such issues as betrayal, the continuity of Jewish tradition and learning, and the experience of assimilation, *Marranos,* a two-act play framed by a prologue and an epilogue, stages the past and the present as contiguous historical events. And Mamet, who has described himself as "just a storyteller," merges his story and history into the living tradition of the Jewish people (Roudané 1986a, 81).

Notable similarities to the plays of Samuel Beckett and Harold Pinter, whose work is similarly characterized by narrative and whom Mamet has credited with influencing his early work, abound.[3] Like Beckett's drama, Mamet's play is characterized by repetitions, biblical allusions, the motif of waiting, metadramatic techniques, and a profound sense of ending. Paralleling Pinter, Mamet employs images of entrapment, colloquial dialogue that leaves more unstated than explicitly expressed, a process of defamiliarization of the familiar, the suspension of specified chronological progression, and the potential for surprise. And like Pinter's plays, we note truth is unreliable or unattainable.

Yet there is nothing derivative about *Marranos*. Like *American Buffalo*, which was written concurrently, *Marranos* is a play about love, loyalty, and ethical behavior.[4] Both plays dramatize life in the family, even if the family in *American Buffalo* consists, as Michael Hinden has observed, of "three male rogues" who constitute "an ersatz family circle" (36). In both plays, energized by interrogatories and interrogations, "Mamet writes about characters whose capacity for action is limited" in civilizations that virtually seem to be approaching extinction (Bigsby 1985, 43). Admittedly, *Marranos* is a flawed, uneven, and overwritten play that pales in comparison to *American Buffalo*, lacking its poetry, its humor, its explosive tension, its tragic grandeur, and its expletives and obscenities whose "sonic resources" (1992, 111), notes Ruby Cohn, "Mamet exploits" and gathers "in bouquets at climactic moments" (118). But *Marranos* is arguably a seminal work, evidencing the scathing irony, metadramatic and aggadic techniques, ethical and moral vision communicated by common language, theatrical inventiveness, predatory characters, power plays, and dramatization of outsiders that characterize the best of Mamet's work. In it Mamet stages what Matthew Roudané terms "the *possibility* of increasing self-knowledge and honesty" (1986b, 37) coupled with the assertion that "passing" is deceptive, dishonest, and potentially destructive.

Its central themes—teaching, betrayal, and loss—are explicitly announced in a prologue in what Lieberman terms "a delicious trick." In lieu of the home of a Portuguese family in the Middle Ages that one might expect, "the first thing that the audience sees," he notes, "is a modern nun who rolls out a blackboard and begins a lecture on her wonderful work among South American Indians of the Amazon and her discovery in an Indian tent of a menorah and several pieces of silver that appear to be very old. And then the play begins in flashback."[5] An atmosphere of expectation and contagious anxiety is immediately established by the seemingly endless questions posed by a twelve-year-old boy named Joao about the mysterious and unusual absence of both of his parents and by the grandfather's evasive responses that fail to reassure him. As the child admits to knowledge "about the fireplace"—an enigmatic phrase that speaks volumes about the crypto-Jews' secret hiding place for religious items needed to perform Sabbath and holiday rituals—his incisive perceptions and persistent questions score the play's central rhythm; and as the boy begs his grandfather, Dom H, to dispel the mystery surrounding the evening's events and the family's behavior, one sees the beginnings of Mamet's brilliant *Cryptogram*.[6] Satisfied that no servant can overhear their conversation, the grandfather couches the family's motivation for hiding its Jewish identity within the context of persecution and conversion, revealing his intention—now accelerated by the evening's events—to enlighten the boy about his heritage on his thirteenth birthday, typically the age of bar mitzvah.

In Judaism, the bar mitzvah signals the rite of passage from childhood to mature religious and ethical obligations.[7] Although tradition and religious imperative are typically transferred from father to child, Martin Buber maintains that biological propagation and the propagation of values are coincident: "Just as organic life is transmitted from parents to children and guarantees the survival of the community . . . so the spirit of a people is renewed whenever a teaching generation transmits it to a learning generation" (1963, 137). Assuming the responsibility of the "teaching generation," the grandfather teaches his grandson about his ethnic identity, as well as his Hebrew name Moshe (from the Hebrew root *mashah* "to draw out" or "one who draws forth," frequently chosen by persecuted Jews in the Middle Ages for its symbolism), by spelling out the letters as if the child were free to learn Hebrew and be called to the Torah as a bar mitzvah.[8] Implicit in Mamet's choice of name for this character is the biblical Moses's role as leader and lawgiver chronicled in the Book of Exodus—or the Book of Names, as it is known in the Jewish tradition—whose compositional scheme and themes include liberation, revelation, and Covenant, notably the escape from bondage and the establishment of a holy (ethical) social and religious community.[9]

Yet, if Dom H had sought to "draw out" the curiosity of the astute adolescent who clearly knows more than he feels free to admit, he also liberates the fears and prejudices of a child raised as a practicing Catholic:

Joao: You are Jews?
Dom H: Yes.
Joao: (*Pause*) Am I a Jew? (*Pause*)

Dom H: Yes.
Joao: We'll be burnt. (1975, 6)

Despite Dom H's monosyllabic rejection of this premise, Joao's unanswered, reverberant question hangs in the air: "How could I be a Jew if I
did not know?" (6). Notably, the slipping of pronouns from "you" to "I"
to "we" concretizes the boy's fears, and reflects his alternating and
opposing loyalties of family and Church. However, before the grandfather
has had sufficient time to reassure the boy, a knock at the door terrifies
them both. Composing himself, Joao opens the door to his governess,
Gracia, who reprimands him for staying up so late at night. Quickly
covering for his grandfather and himself, Joao responds, "We are telling
stories"(8), proving that Joao, like "all of Mamet's characters are storytellers or performers—or both" (Dean 1990, 119). The lie that comes so
easily to Joao's lips mirrors the family's more elaborate deceit to protect
him by raising him as a Catholic. And it is as a Catholic that Joao is
inspired to suggest that penance and prayer, rather than escape, might be
the family's salvation. But the grandfather, having perpetuated a lie for
more than twelve years, will not allow the boy to slip back into the illusion
of security. Responding negatively to each of Joao's suggestions, he
linguistically yanks him back into the reality of his Jewish identity,
eschewing both the yoke of Christianity and its teachings of guilt and
everlasting punishment, and illustrating that when "an older generation .
. . comes to a younger with the desire to teach, waken and shape it; then
the holy spark leaps across the gap" (Buber 1963, 139).

The emotional atmosphere is so electrified by their fear that when
Diogo, Joao's father, bursts into the house, he, too, startles the old man and
the boy. Yet Dom H and Diogo are immediately engrossed in an agitated
conversation about the whereabouts and welfare of the family and preparations for its departure. Reflecting a paradigm of revelation that characterizes
this play (one reprised, for example, in *Speed-the-Plow* and *The Cryptogram*),
Joao, however, is so intent on revealing his secret that he repeatedly
interrupts his father's conversation until he gets his attention:

Joao: I know everything.
Diogo: (*Pause*) What everything?
Joao: I know we are Jews. (*A Pause. Diogo embraces Joao, who starts
          to cry. Tableau*)
Diogo: Hush. Hush. Be quiet now a while, there's no time.
          (*Pause*) How do you like being a Jew ?
Joao: We're damned. (11)

Putting a positive spin on Joao's interpretation, Diogo affirms, "It's quite a responsibility, eh? (11), his position echoed recently in Mamet's remark to John Lahr, "Judaism is not a religion or a culture built on faith. . . . You don't have to believe anything: you just have to do it" (Lahr 1997a, 74-75).

The poignancy of the moment and the pride of the father are typically undercut by the self-deprecating humor. In "Decoration of Jewish Houses," Mamet observes that being "racially Jewish" means sharing "the wonderful, the warm, and the comforting codes, language, and jokes, and attitudes which make up the consolations of strangers in a strange land" (1989b, 8). But as a stranger in a strange land who has been denounced by an as-yet-unidentified betrayer in his house, Diogo is able to maintain the mood only momentarily, distracted by the prolonged absence of his wife, the impending doom, the pressure of time, and the growing possibility that the family will be trapped and forced to face the auto-da-fé. The dangers and potential sources of betrayal are innumerable. Thus, ironically, although Diogo long anticipated disclosing Joao's Jewishness to the boy, he must now be concerned that Joao's knowledge of the family's Jewish identity could prove an unwitting source of betrayal. Aware of his responsibility as the boy's mentor, Dom H intercedes once again, emphasizing the critical life skills that he is about to teach Joao: "You must act naturally. You're going to have to learn to be an actor, and you don't get a rehearsal. . . . Curtain's up, son. (*Pause*)" (12C).

When Diogo's brother, Tonio, arrives, confirming the denunciation, he accuses Roberto, Diogo's manservant, of betrayal for no other reason than that he appears to be the most likely candidate. Lacking evidence, Tonio nonetheless seizes upon Roberto because he seems to offer him the much-needed opportunity to affix blame and identify a scapegoat in a terrifying and chaotic situation out of his control. Tonio encounters strong opposition from Joao, who desperately needs to retain belief in someone and something in an evening of exposure that has forced him to question all previous loyalties. Facing death, however, Tonio has little patience for his twelve-year-old nephew, whose protests are hilariously squelched by an exasperated Tonio: "My dear, you've been a Jew for five minutes, so shut up" (14 D). The ethnic representation of the unmasked Jewish family is most apparent, however, in the "code-switching," as Sander Gilman puts it, in this scene (1991b, 2), whereby the family's ability to speak differently given an altered social and linguistic context is evidenced in Dom H's traditional blessing to his departing son Tonio, "Shalom, Avram" (Abraham), in the ironic manner in which Dom H uses the term *mitzvah*, a meritorious act, to apply to the padre Hernandez, who is extorting the family in exchange for his expediting their escape, and the way that Diogo speaks to his son in parting, "You help your grandfather, Moshe" (16).

After the departure of his father and uncle, Joao is once again left alone with his grandfather. Given the events that have transpired, his newly acquired knowledge, and the responsibilities that have been bestowed upon him, the focus of Joao's questions shifts from the practical to the sociological. Deeply unnerved by what he has heard and surmised, Joao pleads with his grandfather to explain why Jews are persecuted. Once the grandfather clarifies the theological position from which the question is asked—"You are asking as a Jew yourself?" (25)—and satisfies himself as to the boy's sincere curiosity, he compliments Joao on the wisdom of his question and complies by telling a story. "The storyteller," suggests Walter Benjamin in *Illuminations,* "joins the ranks of teachers and sages. He has counsel—not for a few situations, as the proverb does, but for many, like the sage. . . . The storyteller is the figure in which the righteous man encounters himself" (108-09). Indeed, in *Lakeboat, Sexual Perversity in Chicago, Prairie du Chien, The Woods, Things Change,* and *Speed-the-Plow,* storytellers are so integral to Mamet's works that, as Christopher Bigsby and Anne Dean have argued, Mamet has given storytelling a central role as method and subject. The aggadic narrative tradition comprised of the storytelling, imaginative elements of Talmud has long been a method of choice of Jewish theologians from biblical times to the present to communicate halakah—the set of rules that legislates social and religious behavior—and teach practical wisdom through fable. Typically characterized by invention, discourse, parable, and enlightenment, aggadic narrative parallels the biblical story in its elements of concealment and disclosure, opening "a dialogue between God and humanity, between God and the contemporary situation and between the Jew and his tradition" (Kepnes 215-16). Hence, in *Marranos* Mamet employs stories and parables—themselves instructional and revelatory—to establish a thematic link among Jewish history, the experience of persecution, and the revelation of Law that comprises the moral teachings of the Jewish people. Employing a variation of Pilpay's ancient Persian fable, "The Scorpion and the Tortoise," as a metaphor for anti-Semitism, Mamet illustrates that the fairy tale—or aggadic parable—is not only a credible methodology for the presentation of complex sociological issues but "a solution to a problem which is nonsusceptible to reason" (Mamet 1987d, 12).[10] Stunning in its simplicity and complexity, the story that Dom H tells Joao is a microcosm of the play and an exemplar of the con-artistry that characterizes Mamet's stage and screenplays. Establishing its historicity, Dom H explains, "This is a very old story, Joao" (25); Joao, however, is merely concerned with whether or not it addresses his question. "Perhaps," Dom H admits with typical Mametic terseness and ambiguity, though his recitation of the tale provides ample opportunity for embellishment. Recounting the story of a frog sitting peacefully on the riverbank sunning himself, the grandfather relates the events whereby the frog is approached by a scorpion who coerces the frog to carry him on his back across the water. Although the paranoid frog smells danger, he sublimates his natural instinct and permits himself to be duped by the scorpion who appeals to his good nature, overpowers him with logical reasoning, and predictably, mortally wounds him. With its premise of mutual destruction engendered by deceit, an observation that will illumine all of Mamet's work, the story appears to require no explanation, and the grandfather gives none. Indeed, Mamet's modification of the tale is an example of midrash, the Judaic genre of parable in which "there is no visible principle or moral imperative." Ozick explains that in the literature of midrash "The principle does not enter into, or appear in, the tale; it *is* the tale; it realizes the tale. To put it another way: the tale is its own interpretation. It is a world that decodes itself" (246).

If Joao has questions about the story, he is offered scant occasion to ask them. Rather, dispatched to collect his mother's jewels while the grandfather opens a secret panel in the fireplace to extract religious articles, a silver lamp (probably a menorah that doubled as a Sabbath light), yarmulkes, a tallit (prayer shawl), and Torah previously referred to by Joao earlier in the evening. In the time it has taken the boy to collect the jewelry and the grandfather to assemble these items, the boy considers the story. His enhanced sense of Jewish identity, coupled with his expanding knowledge of Jewish philosophy, inspires a new line of inquiry about the ceremonial objects. Notably, as in the case of the fable, the grandfather's method of response is indirect. Rather than answering Joao's seemingly interminable questions, he begins to tell the story of Moses, in whose honor Joao has already surmised he has been named. The biblical story, however, is more familiar and understandable to Joao than the fable, and it is he who sketches in the outline of the story. The grandfather, however, drawing parallels between Moses's life in Egypt and theirs in Portugal, simplifies the story's complexity. The significance for the Jew, he explains, is that Moses "cast his lot" with the Jews. "He made a choice and was prepared to live with it. He was prepared, Moses"—and by implication so we must be—"to cast off his comfort and to live by his insights" (28). However, obsessed with whether or not Moses knew he was a Jew, Joao raises the issue that the grandfather has hesitated to discuss, namely that Moses died prior to reaching the Promised Land. Implicit and explicit references to death have informed this play from its inception, be they the fear that the family has waited too long, that Tonio has killed Roberto, that missing family members have been arrested, that they will all face the auto-da-fé and certain death by immolation or drowning. Fearful that he will expose his own fears, the grandfather short-circuits discussion, and dispatches Joao to complete another errand.

As act 2 begins, memories flood the scene. Joao has brought an heirloom to the staging area where he and his grandfather are assembling the few items that they can carry on the boat, but Dom H discovers among the papers that he is burning a silhouette of himself in his youth with a woman he can no longer remember, the reverberant emblem of the things one carries that will reappear, notably in the form of photographs, throughout Mamet's canon. Sharing the memory with Joao, the grandfather, acutely aware of the boy's unease, wisely sends him into the kitchen to keep both his hands and mind busy, but not before Joao extracts the grandfather's promise that he will help him make sandwiches for the boat and tell more stories—both of which we understand as life-affirming activities. The warmth of the fire and the promise of stories have lulled both into a false sense of security, and reality intrudes, giving form to the fears both have harbored all night. Expecting his sons and daughters-in-law, Dom H is understandably startled by the knock at the door and the appearance of an armed guard with Fra Benedetto, whose name means blessed one, further evidence of Mamet's ironic humor. Although Dom H has been telling stories all night, his fictions now become increasingly fantastic and incredible (not unlike Bernie's monologue about the broad, the flack suit, and the fire extinguisher in *Sexual Perversity in Chicago*) as he concocts a story about his gravely ill granddaughter whom the family has taken to the doctor. Clearly lacking confidence that his attempt to con the priest has been successful, but taking the advice he previously gave to Joao regarding skilled improvisation, Dom H assumes a successive series of roles. He is by turns helpful, indignant, obsequious, histrionic; finally he resorts to outright lies. He is a huge flop, his audience unimpressed. When he seems to win the moment by appealing to Fra Benedetto's humanity, the priest notices papers he is burning. "What are these papers? You burn them from anguish at your granddaughter's illness?" Although Dom H assumes an authoritarian tone as a defensive posture, threatening Fra Benedetto, "You cheapen yourself with sarcasm, sir," the priest sees the silhouette among the papers, and a vintage Mametic exchange ensues:

Fra B: . . . This is you?
Dom H.: Yes.
Fra B: When?
Dom H: Long ago.
Fra B: Who is the woman? (36-37)

Typically undercutting the moment with the granddaughter Astrud's sudden appearance, Mamet casts the grandfather in his role as fictionalizer, but with stakes measurably raised once the girl is taken prisoner by the guard. Fortunately, with Diogo's timely arrival, Dom H is relieved of his role-playing by the younger "actor" (foreshadowing *A Life in the Theatre)*, who similarly improvises without benefit of lines or rehearsal. However, this time Fra Benedetto, having all the best lines, threatens to steal the show: " . . . You are all, all of you, strongly (the word hardly suffices) suspected of heresy. Of Judaizing. Of Fautorship. Of perversion of the Young. (*Pause*) You are, of course, Jews" (40). The excessive verbiage, so typical of Mamet's male characters—Teach, Bernie, and Ricky Roma come to mind—puts Fra Benedetto in the best of company, exemplifying the kind of comedy we have come to expect from Mamet. Though it appears that the priest is holding a flush in a marked and stacked deck, Diogo decides to calls his bluff. In the Jewish comic tradition of what Mamet terms "being quick-witted and silver-tongued and rooting and tooting" (Harriott 87), Diogo asks, "What do you want of us?" A stunned Fra Benedetto replies: "What do I want of you? . . . I want to eradicate hate and divisiveness. I want the Millennium. . . . For the present, I will settle for an answer to my questions . . . "(40).

As an envoy of the Church he has come to save their souls, to take them to some place where the Church may minister to them (not unlike Goldberg and McCann in Pinter's *The Birthday Party*), to line his pockets with the Jews' wealth and, in Mamet's version of history, to have a bit of fun in the bargain. Yet Diogo, following his father's lead—though he has most certainly missed his father's act—adopts one pose after another to stall or distract the priest. Though he is as unsuccessful in trying to please his audience as was the older actor, he is undoubtedly far more hilarious. Suddenly, like Ricky Roma in *Glengarry Glen Ross,* Diogo sights his mark, and using a variation of the classic Myron Cohen joke, begins to pitch the guard:[11]

Diogo: (*To Guard*) Let me ask you, then. Let me ask *you* something. Do you have any compassion? Do you hold with this? Do you hold with destroying a man's family? How much money do you make in a year? Is your family comfortable? Let me ask you.

Fra B: This is enough.

Diogo: One second. How long would it take you to earn, for example. (44)

Although Fra Benedetto tries to quiet him, Diogo presses on, aware that he is moments away from cutting a deal. He might as well be selling swamp land in Florida, for in both *Glengarry Glen Ross* and *Marranos* the stakes are the same: the Cadillac or the set of steak knives, this time quite literally. Trying every con in the book, Diogo is playing for time and praying for a miracle, but the guard, intimidated by a direct order from Fra Benedetto, whacks Diogo with a staff. Before he can deliver the coup de grâce, however, Diogo is saved. Having trusted his instincts regarding Roberto's loyalty and understood his grandfather's lesson that to be a Jew means to make a choice, Joao has freed Roberto, whom Tonio had knocked unconscious and locked in a closet, to save his father's life. Yet, while Roberto can freely strike the guard, he hesitates to kill Fra Benedetto because he is a priest, one of innumerable Mamet men faced with impossible moral decisions. Rising from the floor, Diogo strikes and kills Fra Benedetto while Roberto, visibly shaken by the sin that he has witnessed, crosses himself, ties up the guard, and covers the dead priest. The stage instructions at this point, rare in any Mamet text, reveal how much the young Mamet was oriented to the subject of ethnic representation. Whereas Mamet has increasingly employed Yiddish (and Hebrew in later works such as *Homicide, Speed-the-Plow,* and *The Old Neighborhood*), here Roberto "schleps out the dead priest" (47).

Even when an affirmative conclusion is in sight, the padre Hernandez returns to bleed the rich Jews for more money but in the absence of ready cash is willing to negotiate for a note payable by one of their rich Jewish friends and Diogo's permission to "take a turn through the house. . . . To see . . . you know, to see . . ." some property he can confiscate (50). Mamet exploits this opportunity, as he has throughout the play but less humorously, to explode the fallacious myth that Jews are thieves, con artists, deceivers, liars, and moneylenders. On the pretense that the family's wealth will be confiscated by the Inquisition, Hernandez, arms bursting with booty, plays the part only too well. More frustrated by his impotence in the face of Hernandez's implicit threat than Fra Benedetto's explicit one, Diogo finally expedites Hernandez's departure by his not so subtle, "Hadn't you better be off for the ship?" (52) making us wonder even more than we have previously whether there ever *was* a ship. However, no sooner has he averted one threat than another appears in the person of Gracia. Changing roles and stories as each new intruder demands, Diogo once again rises to the challenge by dispatching her to the doctor using the very same story that unbeknownst to him his father had concocted earlier in the evening to deceive Fra Benedetto. Unlike the latter, Gracia apparently believes the fiction; departing as quickly as she arrived, she finally affords the family a fair chance at escape once all members have assembled.

Not unlike the action of Chekhov's and Beckett's plays, all the comings and goings of the evening have diverted our attention from the passage of time. Although no clock is evident on stage (as in Marsha Norman's *'night, Mother*), Diogo is aware that precious little time remains before the ship sails with or without its passengers. Obviously desperate because neither his wife nor his brother nor sister-in-law have returned, Diogo, faced with the impending loss of his entire family, devises a plan to save the lives of Dom H, Joao, Roberto, and Astrud by sending them ahead to the ship on the pretense that he will join them. "The habit of constant *acute* awareness" energizes Diogo to fabricate yet another fiction to conceal their vulnerability (Mamet 1987d, 73). And to maintain the illusion of an escape that is rapidly becoming evanescent, he sends Joao to find Astrud's doll so that she will be comforted on the ocean voyage. Notably, although Diogo and Teach differ markedly in intellect, social class, and circumstance, Teach's remarks in *American Buffalo* echo the practical philosophy that Diogo now implements:

> All the preparation in the world does not mean *shit*, the path of some crazed lunatic sees you as an invasion of his personal domain. Guy goes nuts, Don, *you* know this. Public *officials* . . . Ax murderers . . . all I'm saying, look out for your own. (1977, 85)

Reflecting a paradigm of surprise and exposure of betrayal that characterizes many of Mamet's plays and screenplays, such as *Glengarry Glen Ross, Speed-the-Plow, Oleanna, House of Games, Homicide,* and *The Spanish Prisoner,* the playwright surprises us by the reappearance of the predatory nursemaid whom no one suspected of betraying and denouncing the family. Entering the home with several armed guards, Gracia—the prototype for a long line of cunning but seemingly ingenuous women in Mamet's works—foils the plan for departure and directs the family's arrest. As all are herded out of the door, Gracia, recalling Hernandez scarfing up the possessions of the Jews, grabs Astrud, the one possession for which she has returned.

Only Joao, sent in search of Astrud's doll, is not discovered, though he is not spared the anguish of witnessing his family's arrest. Clothing himself in his father's traveling cloak and picking up the Sabbath lamp and the Torah, symbols of illumination and the teachings of Judaism, Joao fixes one last picture of his Jewish home in his memory and departs under cover of night. He is quite literally by fate, by choice, and by race the Jew as survivor. Empowered like his namesake Moses with a passion for social justice and a responsibility to change the course of history, Joao carries with him not only ceremonial objects—whose purpose and meaning he now understands—but a Jewish identity, heritage, and history. His is the burden and blessing of chosenness, "his fate sealed into his flesh at the moment of begetting," as

Leslie Fiedler has it (56), and *Marranos* is as much a story of loss as it is a story of Jewish tenacity and survival.

In the brief epilogue that follows the body of the play, the modern nun, reappearing, concludes her history lesson of the lost tribe. Although the play appears circular, the implication of *Marranos,* notes Lieberman, "is the big piece that's untold as the play ends. The kid goes out the window in Portugal and four hundred years later we find a menorah in the Amazon. . . . And you are left to imagine the rest of the boy's life and how he wound up fleeing to South America." In her summation, "sister-what's her name even mentions that the family of Indians preserved a coupled of garbled Hebrew prayers that they said before meals. So, of course, we're left with the implication that the family, if it still retains its heritage, no longer understands the meaning."[12]

Like Gershom Scholem, Mamet seems to be drawn by what Ozick terms "mysterious magnets to the remote heritage" that his parents, like Scholem's, who sought social invisibility through assimilation, denied him (139). Rather than a eulogy to that heritage, *Marranos* illuminates the playwright's personal quest to rediscover Jewish history and reaffirm its teachings, both threatened by assimilation and anti-Semitism. While it lacks the universality, complexity, subtlety, and artistry of much of Mamet's body of work, *Marranos* is a historically accurate representation of Jewish expulsion and literal and metaphoric extermination consistent with the Mamet canon, characterized by the themes of homelessness, hidden identity, and betrayal, by explicit reference to cultural loss, intimidation, and persecution, paradigmatic pedagogy, and the centrality of memory. Indeed, it sounds pleonastic Mametian tropes: "the sense of not belonging, the imperative of speaking out, the betrayal by authority" (Lahr 1997b, 73). The playwright's commitment to the dramatic representation of ethics and ethnicity that informs his work is most clearly articulated in *A Life in the Theatre,* written shortly after *Marranos.* Addressing John, Robert asserts emphatically, "One must speak of these things . . . or we will go the way of all society. . . . On the boards, or in society at large. There must be law, there must be a reason, there must be tradition" (1978, 67). Clearly Mamet has continued to devote himself personally and artistically to these ethical first principles that are the foundation of Judaism.

Written concurrently with *Marranos,* David Mamet's *American Buffalo* is arguably a companion piece to *Marranos.*[13] Admittedly such a comparison between the brilliant and now classic American work and one Mamet has chosen not to publish because "it's not a very good play," would appear to have little credibility.[14] However, upon closer inspection *American Buffalo* is a masterful minimalist version of *Marranos*. Whittling the cast of *American Buffalo* down to three men in a pattern of male-dominated casts that will largely characterize his canon, and side-lining offstage the much maligned and much anticipated no-shows, Grace, Ruthie, and Fletcher, Mamet rivets attention to love, loyalty, and ethical behavior. Like *Marranos*, *American Buffalo* dramatizes the experience of a family of socially marginalized characters engaged in ethical compromises and financial contracts, delineates the centrality of the pedagogical relationship, and emphasizes the destructiveness wrought by self-deception and fraud. And like *Marranos*, *American Buffalo* is a waiting play—the second act of which Steven Gale names "Waiting for Fletcher" (212)—that similarly invites correspondences to the plays of Beckett and Pinter. Exploring persecution and the imposition of power coupled with the dramatization of violence, *American Buffalo*, moreover, mirrors *Marranos*'s concern with integrity and idolatry. Its self-deprecating humor, raptorial characters, biblical references, exposure of betrayal, and ethical and moral vision focus attention on an essentially corrupt world. Mamet confirmed as much to Arvin Brown, director of the play's 1981 revival, to whom he described his vision of the thieves' dilemma: they were all striving to be excellent men but "the society hasn't offered them any context to be excellent in" (Bigsby 1985, 64).

Yet the differences between *Marranos* and *American Buffalo* are as significant as their similarities. Notably, Mamet shifts the scene from the Iberian Peninsula to the Midwest, from the Middle Ages to the twentieth century, from the home of a wealthy Jewish businessman to a junk shop in Chicago, from a family persecuted despite the fact that they have committed no crime to a family of would-be criminals that plots a crime, from a culture founded on ethical behavior and ethnic identity to one founded in Mamet's view on "Hurray for me and to hell with you" (Roudané 1986a, 74). In place of a grandfather's mentoring his grandson on the subject of his ethnic identity that we observed in the earlier play, Mamet foregrounds an endangered paternal relationship in a domestic play comprised of male characters. The most distinctive of these differences, however, is the play's discourse. "Mamet's audacious stylistic breakthrough," Gregory Mosher remarked on the twentieth anniversary of the play's premiere, "was, famously to craft iambic pentameter out of the obscenity-laced vernacular of the underclass" (1996, 80), a discourse whose vulgarity inspired Guido Almansi to dub Mamet "a chronicler and parodist, of the stag party" (191). Eschewing the home as setting, Mamet explores the devalued currency of deeds and deals in Don's Resale Shop, an example of what Roudané terms Mamet's "not-home play space," a prominent "feature of his dramaturgy . . .

calling attention to an urbanized culture and its effects on its people: the dysphoria of his heroes" (1992, 7). In theatre spaces that are characteristically workplaces, argues Roudané, "human relationships and the environments in which those tragicomic relationships come into view are devalued, exchanged, compromised: fiscal capital replaces cultural and spiritual capital" (10). And as June Schleuter and Elizabeth Forsyth observe, the play's junk shop set "with its piles of once treasured, now rejected cultural artifacts, proves to be a powerful image for an America in which the business ethic has so infiltrated the national consciousness that traditional human values have become buried under current value of power and greed" (499). The junk shop as "home," albeit unconventional, reflects the young playwright's intention not to "write about day-to-day bourgeois existence." Still, from a distance of 20 years, Mamet recently told interviewer Terry Gross, "I see that much of what I wrote under the guise of the picaresque was nothing other than a domestic play. *American Buffalo* is finally a constellation."[15]

Like the family, the junk shop—a claustrophobic ludic space whose chaos makes it all the more amazing that a mark sights a valuable coin among this detritus—proves a powerful cultural reference evoking the economic progression from junk peddler to store owner, from *shtetl* to city dweller. As Murray Baumgarten illustrates in *City Scriptures,* the modern city—as image, symbol, ethnic and historical referent—is not merely a potent "psychic geography" for the American Jewish writer but a fitting landscape for the exploration of the modern Jewish experience as stranger and cosmopolite (36). American urban centers like New York and Chicago offered immigrant Jews who congregated in them—as they did formerly in cities like Budapest and Odessa—the illusion, if not reality, of freedom, and the possibility and vital energy of the modern city (2), a pattern reflected in such classic works of Jewish-American literature as Abraham Cahan's *The Rise of David Levinsky* (1917), Michael Gold's *Jews Without Money* (1930), and Henry Roth's *Call It Sleep* (1934). Additionally, "cityscapes," as Sanford Pinsker would have it, provided the bridge from tradition to assimilation, from communal life to individual ethnic identity. Mamet's connection to the city, and to Chicago in particular, which serves as the setting for many of his plays, is visceral. Evoking the sights, sounds, smells, and what he terms "a self-respecting . . . voice of home" (1992a, 58) in such reminiscences as "Wabash Avenue" (1992a), "WFMT" (1992a), and "Seventy-First and Jeffery" (1992a), the playwright also confirms that his ethnic identity was reinforced during shopping excursions with his grandmother, who conversed in Yiddish, Polish, or Russian with local shopkeepers, by ritual visits to the "Ashkenasiac Dionysia" of the Shoreland Delicatessen, and by the "mysterious" landmark that anchored the Jewish neighborhood of his youth in "the southeastern corner of my world": a golf club restricted and closed to Jews (1992a, 126).[16]

Stripped of the overt, explicit Judaic reference, blunt depiction of persecution, and evidence of ethical choice that characterize *Marranos, American Buffalo* appears severed from Mamet's ethnic and cultural roots. Nothing could be further from the truth. Ostensibly the least Jewish of Mamet's plays, it may well be the *most* Jewish by interior design—the clearest example of his ethical first principles. *American Buffalo* is a family play, as Mamet told Henry Schvey, in which junk-store owner Donny Dubrow, whose surname is an acculturation of Dubrowski, a Jewish name of Russian-Polish origin (Kaganoff 144), "is trying to teach a lesson in how to behave like the excellent man to his young ward. And he is tempted by the devil into betraying all his principles" (Schvey 1988a, 94).

Mamet's central issues combined with an urban setting, social orientation, parodic comedy, self-deprecating irony, scatology, stereotypical businessmen-cum-hucksters, and English discourse characterized by its interlinguistic—that is, Yiddish inflected—qualities situates *American Buffalo* firmly within an ethnic and ethical framework. For Mamet, like the comic filmmaker Mel Brooks, whom he most resembles and whom he has called "the Sage of the Age" (Stayton 1985, C1), Jewish culture and heritage provide "a framework, a cultural context, for viewing the world" (Desser and Friedman 107). While Cohn has coined the phrase "Business Trilogy" to link *American Buffalo, Glengarry Glen Ross,* and *Speed-the-Plow,* this resonant, compelling play, as well as the other two, has as much to do with making a life as making a living (1992, 109). William H. Macy, longtime Mamet friend and collaborator, who portrayed the role of Bobby in the premiere production of *American Buffalo,* confirmed as much in an interview with me. "Given that *American Buffalo* is the 'break-out play,'" he observed, "all the themes that are in that are in everything."

> It's about a man is his word. If a man's word is useless, then the man is useless. A man's character is defined by his action. . . . And everyone from petty thieves to movie producers are constantly talking about their integrity—trying to find their integrity in an essentially corrupt world. Everyone is trying to answer for himself: How can I live in a world where . . . where nobody does what they say they're going to do, where everybody is capable of anything, where everybody will screw you over and most people do? . . . all of his characters want to be "stand-up" people in the Chicago meaning of the term, . . . be people who you can rely on.[17]

Discussing *American Buffalo* with Roudané, Mamet observed, "The play's about Donny Dubrow. His moral position is that one must conduct himself like a man and there are no extenuating circumstances for supporting the betrayal of a friend" (Roudané 1986a, 76). We better understand the playwright's repeated reference to the concepts of community, ethical choice, and conducting oneself "like a man" if we substitute the Yiddish term *mensch* for the word "man," notably the "excellent men" about whom Mamet speaks. Defining a mensch as a human being in the moral and ethical sense of the word, whose philosophy, character and dignity are worthy of respect, and whose actions are trustworthy and honorable, Leo Rosten employs the aphorism: "'Act like a mensch—not like an animal'" (1989, 350). Significantly, personal morality, what Buber terms the "humanly holy," is acknowledged as the supreme value in Judaism, recognizable in ethical choice and deed, *mitzvah*, that sanctifies an otherwise profane world.

Hence, if one is "confronted by an 'either-or' choice between thought and deed, intention and action," Shubert Spero explains in *Jewish Law and Ethics*, "Judaism would select the deed over the thought and the consequences over the intent as the prime moral element" (134-35). Predicated on two inextricable premises—that "moral rules are relative to the situation" and that each individual must determine his or her own conduct "guided by conscience, a sense of justice, experience, and wisdom"—Jewish teaching juxtaposes moral conduct and wisdom to instruct individuals that whosoever is possessed of wisdom can better practice moral conduct (B. Cohen 18). The key to understanding ethical behavior in Mamet's work, then, is located in the linkage between conduct and pedagogy, between words and living, that represents teaching at its fullest.

The extraordinary emphasis placed on the correspondence between education and moral conduct in Mamet's canon strongly suggests that Buber's views, presented both in practice and in parody in Mamet's work, justify a brief digression. As L. S. Dembo astutely argues in *The Monological Jew*, Buber's "conception of the ethical, as well as methodological, dimensions of dialogue" as "an indication of one's character and moral situation," is of great value when broadly interpreted to fiction and drama, "especially but not exclusively, Jewish American" (30-31). This is particularly evident in Buber's definition of education. For Buber, "teaching is inseparably bound up with doing . . . [and] it is impossible to teach or to learn without living [because] teachings must not be treated as a collection of knowable material" (1963, 140). In fact, Buber adds, "Israel [Judaism] is probably the only one [religion] in which wisdom that does not lead directly to the unity of knowledge and deed is meaningless" (140). Thus, the supreme "biblical concept of *hokhmah*," or wisdom, is best understood as "the unity of teaching and life," a pattern for living whose goal is the survival of the community rather than knowledge for its own sake (140). Rosten's explication of the term *khakhmah* (an alternative spelling for the Hebrew word for wisdom) enhances our comprehension of this concept integral to Jewish thought, which, whether secular or religious, presupposes that "wisdom, is not simply the fruit of intelligence, scholarship or knowledge." Rather, as Rosten explains, we best understand wisdom as that which "involve[s] basic attributes of character and conduct toward one's fellow men," given that the "the highest *khakhmah* (wisdom) lies in being learned *and* righteous *and* spreading loving kindness" (1972, 542).[18]

Crucial to our understanding of the confluence of pedagogy and ethical behavior in Mamet's work is Buber's distinction between the two basic ways of influencing another person of one's views and attitudes toward life: either through the imposition of idea or "dialogue in which the full personality and character of both student and teacher are engaged." In the latter, he argues that "a man wishes to find and to further in the soul of the other through the disposition toward what he has recognized in himself as the right. . . . The other need only be opened out in this potentiality of his"(1959, 180).[19] Hence, the methodology by which ideas are communicated, as well as their content—whether through imposition or mutual respect—is of central importance in *American Buffalo,* measurably enhancing our understanding of Don's moral obligation, his relationship to Bobby, and the correspondence between speech and deed in this play. Indeed, the paradigmatic trope of teaching is announced immediately in *American Buffalo,* as is Mamet's use of typically Jewish comic stereotypes: the *schlemiel,* a saintly fool; the *luftmensch,* a dreamer; and the *schnorrer,* a beggar.[20] The opening scene, moreover, reveals his celebratory (albeit implicit) allusions to Jewish innovation, individualism, paranoia, and survival. Unifying Buber's philosophy of education with the vulgarity, the scatology of workaday Yiddish, Mamet has staked out the moral and linguistic territory that he has mined for 20 years.

From the opening beat, Don, the owner of a junk shop and Bobby, a boy he has befriended, are engaged in a conversation about a stakeout for a heist they are planning (and that they will fail to execute), during which Don takes advantage of every opportunity to teach Bobby life lessons on a broad range of subjects. Their credible, quotidian conversation effectively confirms a closeness between them manifested in Don's discernible concern for Bobby that in subsequent scenes will provoke him to throw his full weight—emotional and moral—behind his ward. Moreover, his lessons reveal that the commonest acts of economic behavior are testimonials of faith or betrayal.

Citing the relationship of Don and Bobby as the best illustration of the mentor-protégé variant in Mamet's canon, Pascale Hubert-Leibler suggests that Don's comment, "You don't have *friends* this life. . . . You want some breakfast?"(8) is illustrative of his mothering and pedagogy (76). Correct in her characterization that the scene links care and pedagogy, Hubert-Leibler, however, fails to observe that the relationship is paternal, the discussion is dialogic, that in both presentation and content it is Judaic, grounding ethics in the everyday, and that its humor derives from a Jewish (Ashkenazic) tradition in which sensibility and vulgarity coexist. Rather than "mothering," Don is fulfilling a Jewish father's obligation to teach his son Torah, the Law, a trade, and "how to swim"—as in a father's advice to his son in Alan Dershowitz's *The Advocate's Devil:* "'Never swim against the current; always look for dangers beneath the surface; and always anticipate a change in the weather'" (1994, 46). That Don imparts this potpourri of information about skill, loyalty, health, self-reliance, and vigilance on the job and in the world in a chaotic manner is entirely consistent with the portion of the Torah called Kedoshim (Lev. 19, 20). Comprised of ritual, agricultural and ethical laws, Kedoshim underscores that Jewish moral behavior presupposes honesty in business, fair play in sport, and humane conduct and mutual consideration among family members (Jung 102-03). Rich in aphorisms, which because of their inherent wisdom were perceived as guides for living, the Talmud, a monumental compendium of commentaries on the Torah, reinforces this teaching. Among these are the oft-quoted axioms:

> He who does not teach his son a trade, teaches him to be a highway robber.

> If thou hast knowledge, what lackest thou? If thou lackest knowledge, what hast thou?

> A man's character is seen in three things: in his cup, his purse, and his wrath.

> To haggle without money is to cheat. (Bermant 34-35)

Traditionally, Jewish teachers have communicated ethical knowledge through introspective questions such as "Why?" "How?" and "To what end?," and through resonant proverbs, what Rosten terms "pithy sagacities," which illuminate moral dilemmas, communicate elementary knowledge, skills, and a codified system of ethics, morals, and sanctions. Historically employed for vocational training, "the voluminous output of sayings, ironies, insights and paradoxes flowed from the Jews' untiring exercise of analytical intelligence," and "their training in introspection, their need to be astute observers (that is, to anticipate the acts of tyrants or bullies or brigands)—and their literacy" (Rosten 1972, 18-19, 21). Moreover, in Yiddish, the workaday tongue of everyday Ashkenasic life, Jewish proverbs and folk sayings were "freighted with emotion, laden with ornate metaphors and purple exaggerations" (reflecting the language's propensity to invent and embrace expressions for genital organs and copulation), typified by "glutinous benedictions and fearsome maledictions," and characterized by the deployment of a single question capable of exposing stupidity (Rosten 28-29).

The opening scene of *American Buffalo,* then, with its mixture of vulgarity and moral seriousness, is Mamet's response to Sholem Aleichem's comic line: "The real 'Jewish Question' is this: From what can a Jew earn a living?" (Rosten 313). And to this question, Donny Dubrow has a series of questions, or rather, an answer: teach your surrogate son to be a mensch *and* a thief. Thus, Don's "So? So? (*Pause.*) So what, Bob?" signals a dialogue replete with Don's life lessons and displeasure (3), Bob's reiter-ated apologies, and confirmation of his failure to complete the assign-ment. Overflowing in "purple exaggerations," Don's brilliant parody of the obligations of a Jewish father covers the waterfront, replete with pithy aphorisms of his own:

> Bob: I came in.
>   *Pause.*
> Don: You don't come in, Bob. You don't come in until you do a thing.
> Bob: He didn't come out.
> Don: What do I care, Bob, if he came out or not? You're s'posed to watch the guy, you watch him. Am I wrong?
> Bob: I just went to the back.
> Don: Why?
>   *Pause.*
>   Why did you do that?
> Bob: 'Cause he wasn't coming out the front.
> Don: Well, Bob, I'm sorry, but this isn't good enough. If you want to do business . . . if we got a business deal, it isn't good enough. I want you to remember this.

Not at all convinced, Don leaves his ward with a watchword for survival: "Just one thing, Bob. Action counts. (*Pause.*) Action talks and bullshit walks" (3-4).

Concluding his lecture, whose Yiddish inflection is notable in the placement of the single word *only,* the use of *so* (in Yiddish the multifaceted *nu?*), the closing of a statement with a question, ridicule implied by an apparently innocent question, and elisions, Don emphasizes the importance of accomplishment—"don't go fuck yourself around with these excuses"—and knowledge: "The only thing I'm trying to teach you something here" (3-4).[21] Thomas L. King maintains that the thrust of Don's lesson, namely that "Action counts and talk does not . . . [enhances] the same paradox that Aristotle raised" (539), but as Lahr astutely notices, "speech becomes the doing that reveals being" (1997b, 77-78). Consistent with Jewish moral wisdom on the subject of deed, the "one thing" to which Don refers is that *only* action—that is, deed (either oral or corporeal)—talks, a lesson illustrated by his own.

The opening scene of *American Buffalo* presents Don, in the view of Schvey, "posing as a Bellovian 'reality-instructor' and paternalistic advisor to Bobby," whose instruction runs the gamut of "business, breakfast, vitamins, and most of all, friendship" (1988b, 82). Conversely, I believe, that from the first, Don's lecture on the business of life—eat well, watch your back, do a job right—sets high standards of obligation and conduct and is far more revealing, ironic, and indeed, prophetic than is his discussion on life in business. Distinguishing between business and friendship, Don explains, "'Cause there's business and there's friendship, Bobby . . . there are many things, and when you walk around you *hear* a lot of things, and what you got to do is keep clear who your friends are, and who treated you like what" (7). Even as he teaches Bob to be "a stand-up guy" like his friend Fletcher, to employ "Skill and talent and the balls to arrive at your own *conclusions,*" and that in "Everything . . . it's going to happen to you, it's *not* going to happen to you, the important thing is can you deal with it, and can you *learn* from it" (4, 6), what Bobby ironically extracts from Don's instructive lecture is the lesson that a "stand-up guy" like Fletcher is a card shark and cheat, "like when he jewed Ruthie out of pig iron" (6). Despite its blatant anti-Semitic slur, one that Mamet's father prevailed upon the young playwright to cut from the play, the stinging insult is exactly what Mamet intended as a precursor to Don's crucial lesson on confronting an indifferent, often hostile world:[22]

Don: There's lotsa people on this street, Bob, they want this and
        they want that. Do anything to get it. You don't have *friends*
        this life . . . (8)

If one reads the third sentence of this speech "as a declarative statement," without the rhythm of Jewish discourse that, as Toby Zinman posits, is a reflection of "Mamet's second-generation Jewish sensibility," Don's comment to Bob "becomes," in her view, "an utterly cynical refusal to believe in the possibility of friendship. Alternately, if read with an implied "If," Zinman contends, the sentence is far more affirmative and consistent with the play that "turns on the betrayal of friendships, the belated reassertion of friendship's claims, and the collision between the cynical amorality of Teach and the feeble humanity of Don" (212-13). Yet if one reads the sentence declaratively, as written by Mamet, with the Jewish inflection intended, we have a far more accurate portrait of the reality-based lessons that Don is teaching Bob, the practical intent and moral content of his words, and the dialogic nature of their discussion, however much or little of it Bobby retains. We also gain an increased understanding of the playwright's use of irony, which I read, from the perspective of Wayne Booth's definition of "Covert irony [as that which] is intended to be reconstructed with meanings different from those on the surface" (6). From this perspective, then, a person is his or her word, and survival is predicated on staying aware *only* if that person is not buffaloed into disregarding either his or her word or survival. Even with Don's wisdom and wariness, it's "not just people on the street" who represent a threat, it's all in the family: it's people in the shop, at the card table, and in relationships Don has characterized as friendships that have, and will, betray him as he will betray Bob. In fact, the deeper irony of Don's disregarding of his own first principles sets the tone for the actions of the man and of the play. As Mosher points out, "there are *great* speeches about loyalty in *American Buffalo*"(Kane 1992, 237), but there is precious little evidence of loyalty. That Don quickly changes the subject from betrayal to breakfast reveals not only his deeper thoughts on the former, but also on the latter—that is, that survival is predicated on staying strong. It also establishes a natural entry for Teach whose opening spiel picks up the dropped thread of Don's lecture, one that turns on breakfast and the betrayal of friendship and transforms the profound into the profane.

Teach's dramatic entrance, coupled with the linguistic circularity and vulgarity of his story, Ruthie's alleged affront, and his consequent indignation, literally announces his ethnicity, his philosophical posture, his propensity for verbal (and ultimately violent) aggression, and his marvelous capacity for dramatic narrative. No sooner does he enter Don's store than Teach's "Fuckin' Ruthie" immediately draws Don's attention, and Teach launches into his hilarious story of abuse and offense at the Riverside where he has gone for a morning cup of coffee, clearly ignorant that his own behavior has violated aggadic midrashim, specifically the moral teaching that "It's good to eat with a friend, but not from one plate" (Rosten 1972, 237):

Teach:	So Grace and Ruthie's having breakfast, and they're done. *Plates . . . crusts* of stuff all over . . . So we'll shoot the shit.
Don:	Yeah.
Teach:	Talk about the *game* . . .
Don:	. . . yeah.
Teach:	. . . *so* on. Down I sit. "Hi, hi." I take a piece of toast off Grace's plate . . .
Don:	. . . uh-huh . . .
Teach:	. . . and she goes, "Help yourself." Help myself. I should help myself to half a piece of toast it's four slices for a quarter. I should have a nickel every time we're over at the game, I pop for coffee . . . cigarettes . . . a *sweet roll,* never say a word. (10)

Although Teach reminds Don and us that he is not one to complain, we hear him in great form: "Only (and I tell you this, Don)," says Teach, "Only, and I'm not, I don't think, casting anything on anyone: from the mouth of a Southern bulldyke asshole ingrate of a vicious nowhere cunt can this trash come." And turning to Bob in the same breath, Teach calmly informs him, "And I take nothing back, and I know you're close with them" (10-11). Teach's excitability, exaggeration, capacity for vulgarity, understatement and overstatement are emblematic. His charming transition from the jocular to the solemn, anger converted to sarcasm, dismissive scorn framed as contempt and flabbergasted disgust, and his inverted syntax ("I should" rather than "Should I") are consistent with his character and discourse, what Max Weinreich terms "internal bilingualism"—the blending of Yiddish and English.[23] Evoking Teach's ethnicity in emotion and discourse, characterized by the inversion of the scatological and the idealistic, Mamet reveals Teach's brilliant narrative skill (reflecting in the telling of a tale the talent of Jews anywhere to reconstitute themselves as a community of listeners) and his own masterful use of satire.

Familiar with Teach's excitable nature, Don attempts to listen and lessen the tension, endeavoring to calm him with reasonable excuses for Ruthie's and Grace's behavior, but Teach would rather "some brick *safe* [presumably the one that does or does not exist and that they will or will not find the combination for in the mark's house] falls and hits them on the head, they're walking down the street" (11). Jews are instructed at a young age to "to feel an *obligation* to respond to the misfortunes of others with visible, audible sympathy," observes Rosten, so one cannot "possibly fail to recognize the depth and sensitivity of one's compassion." Moreover, since

Jews believe that "emotions are not meant to be nursed in private: they are meant to be dramatized and displayed—so that they can be *shared*" (1972, 51), Don meets his obligation as an empathetic person, a mensch, when he listens and responds to Teach's pain, regardless of whether Teach brought it on himself or the vulgarity and melodrama with which he relates his story. Finding words ineffective, however, Don diverts attention from the serious subject of betrayal, as he did earlier with Bob, attempting to placate Teach by pushing food. In a parody of the Jewish mother and hostess, immediately identifiable in the traditional attribute of the Jewish mother and the plays of Clifford Odets by the proffering of food, Don offers various foodstuffs from the Riverside. When Teach finally decides on a rasher of bacon, Don's mitzvah of compassion and generous hospitality reaches its pinnacle in his offer of fruit. While consistent with his philosophy of good nutrition, Don's proffering of fruit is, as Rosten reminds us, a cultural referent, as in "have a piece fruit already" (1989, 152-53). Thus the deliberately comic ethnic joke, "A cantaloupe?" undercut by Teach's punch line, "It gives me the runs" (13), implicitly calls attention to their ethnic identity and common language and unites typically Jewish generosity with the propensity of Jewish humor to the scatological.

Waiting for Bob to return from the Riverside with the breakfast order, which, like his earlier assignment, the good-natured schlemiel will fail to complete correctly, Teach characteristically initiates and subsequently controls the direction of a casual conservation with Don: "So what's new?" (16). On the surface Don's terse response to Teach's inquiry, "Nothing," would appear to short-circuit their conversation, but because Don in fact means, "What should be new?" their conversation provides the opportunity for Teach to discuss last night's game of gin rummy, in which both lost heavily; Teach's missing hat; Ruthie, whose name still inspires Teach's obscenity; Fletch's absence; the "thing," the Chicago World's Fair. Noticing a compact from "the thing," in Don's Resale Shop, Teach and Don engage in a "mock" negotiation on the price of the item—despite the fact that such negotiation without either intention or capital to purchase the item would be considered immoral, fraudulent business practice from a Jewish perspective (Mishnah *Bava Mezia,* 4:10). The scene is not only prophetic but deeply ironic, given that Don's subsequent negotiations with Teach will devalue his moral compact with his ward, "the three," in effect, "a parodic Oedipal triangle with Bobby as object-child of conflicting dynamics, which reflect Don's internal struggle" (Haedicke 1997b, 7).

As if on cue, Bob enters with breakfast and a fabricated story of his spotting the guy whom he failed to watch effectively earlier in the morning. With each detail, he earns Don's enthusiastic commendation, "Now you're talking" (23), no doubt referring to the earlier distinction that Don made that "Action talks and bullshit walks." But in this case, the action is all in Bob's mind: it is *just* talk, not deed. Demonstrating that he has the "Skill, talent, and balls to arrive at [his] own conclusions," even if in doing so he has misunderstood Don's lesson and apparently retained only the part of the lecture that concerns learning from previous experience, Bob applies that principle to this encounter, learning that fabrication plays better than the truth, as evidenced by Don's glowing praise. Bob's failure to get the correct breakfast order and his return trip to the Riverside to retrieve Don's forgotten coffee, however, provides a realistic opportunity for Don and Teach to chat about business over breakfast. And Teach's comment, "It's a one-man show" (24), like his previous observations on the wisdom of separating cards, friends, and business, reveals how different his perspective is from Don's. Whereas business in Don's view is "people taking *care* of themselves" (7), for Teach, self-reliance is the imposition of self: one man running the show. Although "The matter at issue," suggests King, "is between two points of view, embodied in words," which not only "create the terms of the engagement between the characters" but comprise "the ground of the conflict" (539), Teach's comment—"*Any* business. . . . You want it run right, *be* there" (24)—is an excellent example of Mamet's play on words. Providing a perfect opportunity for mockery of Teach, who wishes he were in business, the moment contains an allusive reference to the classic Jewish joke about single proprietorship cited in Richard Raskin's *Life is Like a Glass of Tea*. A dying patriarch surrounded by family members is revived by his own question: "Then who's minding the shop?" (206). In all its varying permutations, the joke directs attention to familial inheritance, financial independence, and responsibility. Hence, however comic Teach's pontification on business practices may appear, Mamet's ethnic referent reveals a quintessential aspect of the Jewish psyche: self-proprietorship is coincident with self-reliance and responsibility for the family.

But if Teach is not literally *in* business, he is always looking to make a deal. "[T]he people of the book were also the people of the deal," quips Mark Shechner, mindful of the "marginal hustler and jobber whose voice keens with the desperate wisdom that comes from 2000 years working bum territories: Egypt, Spain, the Pale of Settlement" (1990, 48, 44). Like the ingratiating *schnorrer* he is, Teach weasels and hustles his way into "the thing," the robbery scheme, with a question: "So what is this thing with the kid?" Attempting to cut off his inquiry and implied intrusion, Don summarily discounts the scheme, "It's nothing . . . *you* know. . . . it's just some *guy* we spotted" (25). Unlike his previous question, "So what's new?" intended to make conversation, Teach's specific and characteristically (Yiddish) inverted question is designed to extract a specific answer from Don: "What is it, jewelry?"(26). However, Don's evasion assures him that "nothing" in this case is something, and that Don is withholding information. In contrast to *Marranos,* where Dom H variously attempted to cover deception by performing a succession of roles, Teach adopts a number of poses—alternately defensive, casually indifferent, mildly interested, and insulted—to con Don into being more forthcoming. His comments dripping sarcasm, Teach plays upon Don's guilt, inducing him to reveal what he is apparently concealing. Nonplussed, Don asks, "You know?" Sounding the now familiar motif of knowledge and ignorance, Teach tries ignorance and comes up a winner. "Yeah. (*Pause.*) Yeah. No. I don't know. (*Pause.*) Who am I, a *police*man . . . I'm making conversation, huh? 'Cause you know I'm just asking for talk" (26). Fearing resistance, Teach closes with a typical zinger that puts Don on the defensive: "And I can live without this" (26).

Yet Teach, who has played Don so well that Don actually *thinks* he wants to spill the beans about the heist, has to get the last word in. "Tell me if you *want* to," he says (26), virtually convincing Don by his derisive tone that Don is freely choosing to impart the information about the impending heist to a friend. Don, however, interrupts their conversation to place a phone call to the fence, which as Christopher C. Hudgins observes, provides both a humorous moment and "ironically, a sense of communion between the two," during which an ill-informed Don can barely hold up his part of the conversation with the more astute coin dealer (1992, 206). Notably, the telephone call reveals Don to be less a money-hungry, cunning criminal than he would have us believe. But Teach, not unlike Charles Citrine in Saul Bellow's comic paean to Chicago, *Humboldt's Gift* (1975), recognizing that "in business Chicago, it was a true sign of love when people wanted to take you into money-making schemes" (176), demonstrates his love by showing his empathetic support of Don. "Guys like that," he says, "I like to fuck their wives" (28), returning the favor, as it were, of Don's earlier emotional support when he was stung by what he perceived as Ruthie's abusive tone.

Responding to the insult to his intelligence and competence by "the phone guy" by relating an elaborate story about a customer with whom Don negotiated the price of a nickel from "two bits" to ninety dollars, Don's fabrication of the event conceals his vulnerability, allowing him to maintain the illusion of internal power, even if none exists. However, paralleling Teach's "Fuckin' Ruthie" speech and subsequent references to her insulting behavior, Don fuses the earlier, galling conversation with "the phone guy" with the customer who "comes in here like I'm his fucking doorman"(31). Finally exploding, he reveals that despite his expert negotiation, he is convinced that the customer cost him a substantial profit. Reading Don's mind but always seemingly two steps in front of him, Teach quickly summarizes the shot: "You're going to get him now" (32). Before long Don, a luftmensch with a great scheme but little practical skill, has laid out the heist as conceived, but from the get-go it has all the markings of a fiasco because Don's partner and protégé, Bob, a schlemiel if there ever were one, is incapable of following even his simplest instruction, "You're s'posed to watch the guy, you watch him" (3). Teach's sympathetic, shrewd response to Don's story, however, earns him Don's appreciation, providing Teach with the perfect opening to undermine Don's choice of Bob as a business partner. Responding to Don's characterization of Bob as "a good kid," Teach's ironic " a great kid. . . . I *like* him" (33) twists the praise into tacit criticism and his advice, whose only apparent motivation is concern for his good friend, into the cleverly concealed *khakmah* of a *khukham*, given that the Hebrew word *khakham*, one who is wise, not only underwent a change of spelling in Yiddish to *khukham*, but it acquired the connotation of "wise guy," a kind of trickster anxious to acquire something for nothing (Telushkin 68-71). Expert at employing *khakhmah*, tricky, cleverly concealed ruses, double-talk, or "casuistic hocus-pocus" (Rosten 1968, 65-66), and exploiting and assuaging guilt, one of the most powerful and pervasive psychological forces in the psyche of the Jew, Teach begins his sales pitch under the guise of caring about the best interests of his friend: "But I gotta say something here" (33). And to emphasize both the intimacy of their relationship and the importance of what he wants to say, Teach suggests, "Let's siddown on this" (33).

What follows is a lecture that differs markedly in style, intent, and content from Don's. Though Teach is talking with a friend, their discourse crafted in code, Teach's presentation, specially designed to sidestep introspection (not unlike Roma's initial speech to Lingk in *Glengarry Glen Ross),* is a marvelous sales pitch cum illogical argument that persuades Don by appealing to common sense and those ethical tenets that he knows Don values. Zeroing in on a critical component of his presentation, Teach simultaneously makes a key point and then apparently downplays its centrality. As in Yiddish, which characteristically employs one expression to mean the opposite (Rosten 1968, 42), Teach advises, "Don't send the kid in," underscoring his previous remark, " *Only* this—and I don't think I'm *getting* at anything—" (33). By the use of *only* and its placement in the sentence, which in Yiddish inflection places emphasis on this word, by his controlled delivery, praise of Don's concern for Bob, and his paean to loyalty, Don is caught off guard: Teach is getting at everything, or more particularly, the only thing: "What are we saying here? Loyalty. (*Pause.*) You know how I am on this. This is great. This is admirable. . . . This is swell" (33-34).

His brilliant slip of the tongue, "It turns my heart the things that you do for the kid," which "In your mind you don't"(34), moreover, is evidence of Teach's brilliant methodology of thought control that may be summarized as: the kid is great, he's doing great, you're great, loyalty's great, and the heist is great. In other words: it needs a pro. Teach's reference to the brand name Magnavox is yet another example of ethnic coding or "code-switching" like that employed in *Marranos*. Although the allusion is hilarious in the context of Teach's argument, revealing his attempt to con Don into believing that there was a bigger prize within their grasp, it resonates with immigrant and first-generation urban Jewish familiarization with, and belief in, the cultural importance of brand-name merchandise as a signifier of acculturation and middle-class status, sharply contrasting with the traditional Jewish notion of *yikles,* in which prestige derived from education (Heinze 95-99). Referring to Teach as Walt for the first time, Don reinforces the intimacy and personal knowledge only intimated before, lending credibility to the fact that Teach's advice not to send "the kid" in, that "a guy can be too loyal" (34), and that this clearly "is not jacks, we get up to go home we give everything back" (35), will be valued by Don. Having employed the pronouns "I" and "you," Teach progressively advances in the direction of "we," as in we're a reliable team: "We both know what we're saying here" (34), or rather what *he* is saying here. Not unlike Dr. Tamkin in Bellow's *Seize the Day,* Teach seizes the moment and capitalizes on it, convincing Don to bank on and with him. Thus, having stressed their unity, Teach moves in, affirming Mamet's contention that the criminal milieu "subsumes outsiders" and "rewards the ability to improvise" (Lahr 1997a, 59) with his final derisive point guaranteed to isolate "us" from "him": "the kid's gonna skin-pop go in there with a *crow*bar . . . " (34).

Characterizing *American Buffalo* as "a play specifically about violence and loyalty and ethics," Mamet told Steve Lawson, "The violence in the second act—when he [Teach] hits him [Bobby] over the head—is the same as the violence in the first act, when through rhetoric he shoves him out of the conspiracy"(43). Mamet's explanation finds precedent in Jewish ethical law. What Teach is doing is morally unethical because the Torah (Deut. 25; Lev. 18) specifically restrains a person from being a "talebearer," thereby causing harm to another, whether in life, limb, or reputation (Spero 136; L. Kushner 1993). As Leo Jung explains in *Human Relations in Jewish Law,* "Morally . . . there is no difference between violence by fist or abuse by fraud" (114). Thus, although Don attempts to suppress Teach's words, and with them their insidious implications and allegations, demanding that "I don't want that talk, only, Teach" (34), Teach knows that Don's words are only talk. He has won Don's heart and mind, and the rest will follow. "I more than understand, and I apologize. . . . I'm sorry," he says, but obviously not sorry enough to stop talking. "'Cause," he continues, "it's best for these things to be out in the open," knowing that Don does not want Bob's addiction discussed. However, despite Don's defense that "the fucking kid's clean. He's trying hard, he's working hard, and you leave him alone" (35), it is obvious that Teach's indirect method of instruction, his duplicitous propaganda, has been effective: once planted, the seed of doubt has begun to bear fruit. Teach's most ingenious, egregious, and ultimately effective argument is presented in an abstract and depersonalized format as an appeal to Don's common sense and business sense combined with a deeply personal attack on "this motherfucker": "there's the least *chance* something might fuck up . . . you cannot afford (and simply as a *business* proposition) you cannot afford to take the chance" (35).

The beauty of this speech, among other things, is the placement of "simply," which, paralleling his use of "only" in an earlier part of his presentation, accentuates the irony of Teach's words. The enormity, rather than the simplicity of the decision, is left to Don, who, from an ethical perspective, cannot afford to take this chance. But having betrayed his own common sense and moral values, Don finds sufficient justification in Teach's lecture on which to base his affirmative answer to the ethical question that he posed several moments before and upon which the morality of his future actions hangs: "I shouldn't send Bobby in?" (33). Reiterating and inverting the phrase "Where is the shame in this?" that Teach employed earlier to convince Don that the job exceeded Bob's skill (35), Teach now praises his own initiative, ironically illuminating the correspondence between Don's rhetorical question and Teach's rhetoric. If Bob lacks the skill and talent, then Teach "has the balls" to arrive at his own conclusion that there is nothing shameful about initiative. However, the irony of initiative cuts both ways: Jewish historical experience urges that survival depends upon personal resourcefulness, which Teach, to his own benefit, encapsulates as "The freedom. . . . Of the *Individual*. . . . To Embark on Any Fucking Course that he sees fit. . . . In order to secure his honest chance to make a profit" (73), even if it requires depriving another individual of that freedom by deceptive means.

Once Don's unethical choice has been made and their partnership consummated, all that remains is to plan the heist and negotiate the split. While Teach appears to lack the wisdom to know that the highest wisdom lies in being righteous and showing kindness to others, this schnorrer's resourcefulness, imagination, and chutzpah far exceed that of Don, the luftmensch, whose pie-in-the-sky scheme, by implication, lacked adequate planning and the elements of effective implementation by its inclusion of Bobby, whose efforts at watching the mark and fetching coffee provide ample evidence of his ineptitude. Determined to illustrate his expertise and the wisdom of Don's choosing him as a valued member of the team, Teach launches into a financial analysis on the division of profits that, from his perspective, anticipates all of Don's concerns: 10 percent for the connection, Earl, a two-way split of 45 per cent for Don and Teach respectively, and for Bob, "A hundred. A hundred fifty . . . we hit big . . . *whatever*" (36), which he assumes will assuage Don's moral obligation to Bob. On a roll, Teach begins to designate responsibilities: he'll go in; Don can "mind the fort" (36), which, as Hersh Zeifman observes in "Phallus in Wonderland," lends "this pathetic band of thieves" the illusion of a "a beleaguered paramilitary unit" (1992, 128). While it appears that Don defers to Teach because he has little to say, his mind is not on the fort: it's back at the split. Since Teach has dominated the conversation and from his perspective covered and concluded all relevant issues, he responds to Don's distraction with annoyance. "I thought we were done talking," he says sardonically, because *he* was finished talking. But Don wants to "think for a second" (37). More likely, what Don is doing is rethinking. Concerned that he will be cut out of the deal or that his profit margin will fall, Teach instantly picks up on the word "think" and in a speech heavy with sarcasm gives Don something to think about: "Fifty percent of some money is better than ninety percent of some broken *toaster* that you're gonna have, you send the kid in. . . . because you didn't take the time to go *first-class*" (37). Riveting Don's attention to the potential profit and loss and the correlation between money and class, Teach, for whom accounts receivable assume a position of primacy to actions accountable, secures his position by burying Bob.

Teach's chameleonic capacity to switch from foe to friend is particularly striking at this moment, as Bob, who he has just maligned as "second-class," enters the shop with pie and Pepsi that pass for breakfast food—clearly not the health food that Don had previously recommended to his student—and is greeted warmly by Teach who has in his absence usurped his position. Don's duplicity, however, is of far greater importance, and it is in his interaction with Bob that we see how his unethical deed, his betrayal of Bob, plays out and anticipates his complicity in Teach's interrogation of his ward in act 2. Teach's efforts to illustrate Bob's ignorance and expose his disloyalty—in other words, to provide evidence to prove his previous allegations—are juxtaposed to Don's efforts to hold the fort and family together by deception and avoidance of the truth. Repeatedly, Don tells

Teach to "Hold on," when he means for him to back off so that Don does not have to deal honestly with Bob (40-41). Neither ignorant nor disloyal, Bob conducts his own negotiations to arrive at the truth that Don has attempted to withhold. Despite his desire that this negotiation obviate their previous deal "Like it never happened" (43) and by extension obviate his immoral deed and attendant guilt, Don is aware that his student and friend is no fool. Indeed, in his attempt to buy Bob out, Don has seriously miscalculated and compounded his error of judgment, because Bob has understood Don's actions more clearly than he has his words.

Finally, once Bob is expelled from the conspiracy as well as from the junk shop, and all negotiations have finally concluded, Teach is anxious to return to planning the heist, only to find Don as distracted from the planning as he was from the discussion of the distribution of profits. Irritated, he finds he must coach and coerce Don: "Don, (Can you cooperate?) Can we get started? Do you want to tell me something about coins? (*Pause.*)"(45). Despite his characterization of it as "A crash course" to familiarize him with coins, "What to look for. What to take. What to *not* take," Teach's rapid-fire questions with little or no opportunity to respond is a crash course in his pedagogical methodology (45). Indeed, rather than ask questions to inspire introspection, as Don's dialogic teaching method previously illustrated, Teach's "lesson" in coins appears to be less an effort to acquire information and inspire education than a substitute for learning. Succinctly it may be summarized: "We *take* it, or leave it?" (46). Moreover, as the following conversation amply illustrates, Teach's "teaching" is literally creative: he fabricates knowledge, preferring to coin fact, as it were, rather than master it.

Teach: All right? A man, he walks in here, well-dressed . . . (With a briefcase?)
Don: (No).
Teach: All right. . . . comes into a junkshop looking for coins.
         Pause.
         He spots a valuable nickel hidden in a pile of shit. He farts around, he picks up this, he farts around, he picks up that. (45-46)

Although Don has characterized the blue book (whose list prices typically quote prices of cars rather than coins) as a means to gain "a general idea," Teach concludes, "Naaa, *fuck* the book. What am I going to do, leaf through the book for hours on end? The important thing is to have the *idea* . . ." even if a "blue book" (49), a college-level examination book or the legal bible that specifically spells out how something can be stated, would surely reveal his knowledge of ideas as neither specific nor general. However, when Teach begins to quiz Don about the specific coin that he sold, the one that Don thinks the collector "would have gone five times" what he spent (46) and that Teach has been instructed to retrieve, Don covers up the fact that he does not know either the date or the value of the coin in question because he failed to record and research the nickel in the outdated and presumably worthless book. Changing the subject from his area of expertise (or rather incompetence) to Teach's, Don quizzes Teach about how he will get into the mark's house. "More than a conflict over different views of the world," argues King, Teach's and Don's conversation reveals the conflict and the criteria employed to evaluate their views (540). A typical schnorrer, Teach equates improvisation with skill. "Aah, you go through a *window* they left open, something" (49), he tells Don, who is increasingly more convinced that Teach lacks the skill that Teach convinced Don that Bob lacked. Pursuing the point he asks:

> Don: Yeah. What else, if not the window?
> Teach: How the fuck do *I* know ?
>   *Pause.*
>   If not the window, something else.
> Don: What?
> Teach: We'll see when we get there.
> Don: Okay, all I'm asking, what it *might* be.
> Teach: Hey, you didn't warn us we were going to have a *quiz* . . .
>   (50)

Although Don attempts to quell Teach's agitation with the placating, "It's just a question," he is nonetheless intent on acquiring a satisfactory answer, and he surmises that Teach's "We're seeing when we get there" is an evasion.

On the surface, Teach's and Don's conversation appears to be one more example of a farcical, nondirectional stand-up comic routine, but like others that precede it, it gains profundity and importance by its intertwining of key Mamet tropes. Paralleling his work in *Marranos,* Mamet employs humor to deflate the stereotypical image of the Jew as a crafty, cunning criminal, but in *American Buffalo* he further rebuts the historically negative stereotype of the Yiddish-speaking Eastern European (specifically Polish and Russian) Jew whose discourse was linked to the *pipul shel hevel.* A quintessentially Jewish mode of argument that Gilman defines as "the traditional Talmudic mode of argument . . . based on analogy and approximation" rather than "syllogism, the basis of classical logic," the *pipul,* viewed by anti-Semites as the principal "sign of the corruption of the Jews of Poland" (1986, 90-94, 101), inspired the falsehood that the Jew was a dogmatic, aggressive, illogical, corrupted liar.[24] In Mamet's parody of the *pipul,* Don's and Teach's circuitous discussion, with its allusive Judaic and pedagogical reference to "quiz"—implicit in its connotation of testing an individual's character and wisdom—simultaneously satirizes an impositional rather than dialogic manner of instruction in which only one response sanctioned by the educator has validity.

"Teachings," Buber reminds us, "must not be treated as a collection of knowable material," because for "the Mosaic man" (the Jew), whom the Jewish theologian distinguished from the Socratic man, "cognition is never enough" (1963, 140-41). Hence, Teach's unsatisfactory "answer" creates a marvelous comic moment in which Don, failing to understand Teach's response, misconstrues it as a disputatious and superficial failure to answer. However, Teach's present participle response, "We're seeing when we get there" (50), resonates with a deeper ethnic reference, pinpointing one of the central premises of Jewish survival: "never say die" (Raskin 68). Indeed, Mamet's choice is not capricious; the faith manifested in "We're seeing when we get there" may be traced to the binding of Isaac when Abraham was told, in effect, "God will provide" (Gen. 22: 7-8). The same spirit of Jewish resourcefulness, the need to retain a sense of internal power, create one's own reality, focus on practical solutions to ongoing, albeit differing challenges, doggedness, and rejection of fatalism reflected earlier in the play in the protagonists' elaborate fictions is similarly represented in the classic Yiddish proverb, "If you can't climb over, you tunnel under" (Raskin 90).

For Teach, "getting in" is simply not all that complicated: "What the fuck they live in Fort Knox? . . . You break in a *window,* worse comes to worse you kick the fucking *back door* in. (What do you think this is, the Middle Ages?)" (77). He typically finds roots and referents in the past. Yet Don, convinced neither by Teach's ingenuity nor his chutzpah, hears in Teach's defensive posture a mimesis of Bob's earlier responses that similarly failed to satisfy Don. However, having made what he knows to be an unethical choice for profit, Don, now committed to obtain that profit, is determined to bring his friend Fletcher in on the deal to achieve "Safety in numbers," a term that immediately translates in Teach's mind as a significant reconfiguration and reduction of the monetary split to "a traditional . . . three-way split"(53). Just as Teach anticipated Don's intentions in the previously negotiated deal in act 1, now no mention is made of money for Bob, because he hopes either that Don will not have heard his slip of the tongue, or that no amount of money would minimize Don's betrayal of Bob's loyalty. And whereas Teach laid out the shot in the previous agreement, telling Don to "mind the fort" (36), he now defers to him to "Lay the shot out for me" (53). Thus, having completed the planning of the heist and the bargaining of the terms, Teach makes one more attempt—and fails—to reinstate the original deal, an exchange that illustrates both the *chutzpah* and the tenacity that he formerly demonstrated. Finally assured that Don is not angry with him, Teach leaves Don to worry about both the deal and the deed.

It is in this state of high anxiety in act 2 that we find Don in the shop at 11:15 P.M. waiting for his partners in crime, Teach and Fletch, neither of whom has yet to make an appearance. Visibly agitated, Don's soliloquy echoes Teach's linguistic paradigms:

> Great. Great great great great great.
> *Pause.*
> (*Cocksucking* fuckhead . . .)
> *Pause.*
> This is greatness. (59)

Ironically on cue, Bob makes a surprise appearance, to the profound embarrassment and discomfiture of Don, whose clipped questions are expressly designed to short-circuit conversation and expedite Bob's speedy departure from the shop. Parodying Teach's "crash course" on coins, which was given in act 1, Don and Bob, in possession of a buffalo nickel, discuss the relative value of coins, for which, Don asserts, "the book is like you use it like an *indicator*." But he adds, "You got an idea you can *deviate* from" (61). Don's garbled syntax exposes not only the double-talk he espouses for what it is but the irony that Don's instruction is no longer in the realm of theory as an idea; it, like the book, *was* "an indicator," from which he has deviated by unethical behavior (61). However, when Bob explodes that the "book don't *mean* shit," Don's defense—that it provides "a basis for *comparison*"—underscores that their discussion has less to with coins than with character (62). Don knows this when he appeals to Bob to let him off the hook. "Look," he says, "we're human beings. We can *talk*" (62), which for Don means a willingness to negotiate a deal that will simultaneously pay off his former partner for the right price and buy Bob's forgiveness of Don's betrayal, a moment that underscores Mamet's view of the theatre as "a place of recognition . . . where we show ethical interchange" (Wetzsteon 1976, 103).

Don's inability to communicate with Bob on any level and his ineffectual attempts to extricate him from the shop, together with his anxiety about Teach's and Fletch's late arrival, boils over as rage directed at Teach when he arrives more than a half hour late for the heist. The issue of time keeping and Teach's "excusable fucking lateness" detracts only momentarily from the issue of Fletch's absence and Bob's presence that Teach perceives as a double-cross, not unlike Don's betrayal of Bob. Challenging Don, Teach demands, "I don't know what the fuck *he's* doing here . . ." (64). However, Don's equally threatening challenge to "Leave him alone," reiterated three times, seeks to defuse Teach and to illustrate that Don, in control of the shot, can behave like a human being, if not a mensch. Unconvinced that Bob intends to leave, Teach pushes him in the direction of the door by a parodic monologue similar to the rhetoric by which he extricated him from the conspiracy: "You're sure it isn't like the bowling league, Fletch doesn't show up, we just suit up Bobby, give him a shot, and *he* goes in?" (65). Teach's quintupled apology, in concert with brilliant variations on the initial charge, and caustic "So what do you want me to do? Dress up and lick him all over?" (65) reveal a linguistic pattern typical of Yiddish sarcasm and cursing: despite the hilarious tone of his monologue, what Teach says is the opposite of what he intends, which is, I'm not sorry and "What's going on here. Huh?" That Don has immediately understood Teach's meaning is made evident by his renewed efforts to encourage Bob to leave, but having refused to dignify Don's earlier question, "What do you need?" Bob now answers the question when posed by Teach by responding that he wants to sell his buffalo nickel for fifty dollars. Eager to precipitate Bob's departure, Teach attempts to buy him off cheaply, that is, to "jew" him down with "a fin" (66), derived from the Yiddish *finf*, five. However, only when Don kicks in another ten dollars and an additional unspecified bill, and Bob delivers his message that Don "should talk to Ruthie" does Bob finally depart, leaving Don and Teach to squabble over Fletcher's absence (67).[25] With Bob's departure Don's earlier question assumes greater significance, for what Bob needed has not been forthcoming. Rather we are encouraged to see this act, and this moment in particular, as a "mirror image" of the first act, which, as Mamet puts it, depicts Don trying to "buy his way back in" (Wetzsteon 1976, 103).

Employing a pedagogical methodology similar to the one he used earlier in the day to defame Bob and convince Don of Bob's incompetence, however fraudulent the allegation, Teach now attempts to illustrate that Fletcher, who had motivation, opportunity, expertise, and the propensity to steal, "took the joint off by himself" (75). Though his argument is groundless and fallacious, Teach maintains that "A fact stands by itself": Fletcher is stealing the shot because he is "an animal" (75), and as Bob previously noted, he "jewed Ruthie out that pig iron" (6). Mamet's repetition of this charge, merely alluded to in act 1, is not without significance. In expanding the ethnically loaded referent to a conversation in this scene, he both characterizes Fletch and Ruth as Jewish traders of pig iron—a typical Chicago commercial venture for Jews who had long been traders by profession[26]—and exposes the stereotypical accusations against Jews of odious business practice for what they are: mere allegations, differing little from those leveled by Teach against Fletcher. When Don further insists that he has a deal with Fletcher, which as Teach points out differs little from the one he had with Bob and subsequently disregarded, and rejects what Teach is saying as "nothing but poison," Teach once again assumes the role of educator: "The man is a cheat, Don. He *cheats* at cards—Fletcher, the guy that you're waiting for" (80). Underscoring and ironically inverting one of the principal motifs of the play, one's responsibility to and for another, Teach proves his point by a play-by-play of the previous night's card game, defending his silence up to this point by a basic principle of behavior: "It's not my responsibility, to cause bloodshed. I am not your keeper" (82).

However, as midnight approaches, the only cheating that Teach has on his mind is that he will not be cheated out of the heist and the anticipated payoff. In a wonderfully comic moment that plays on the eschewal of violence among Jews and the nonviolent nature of Jewish crime—historically associated with burglary, larceny, arson, receiving stolen goods, and prostitution (Joselit 1983, 33)[27]—Teach takes out and begins to load a gun. Once again Teach swamps Don with sophistry. Characterized by inference, inversion, exaggeration, and malediction typical of internal bilingualism, and implicit reference to survival, their dialogue, similar to a stand-up comic routine, hinges on wordplay of inclusion and exclusion through repetitive use of "I" and "we." As chief of this operation, Don makes a categorical decision: "We don't need a gun, Teach." But he immediately meets with resistance from Teach, who in his inimitable way wins the moment. "It's not a question do we *need* it . . . *Need* . . . Only that it makes me comfortable, okay? It helps me to relax. So, God forbid, something inevitable occurs and the choice is (And I'm *saying* 'God forbid') it's either him or us." Grounding his argument on a fictitious, but credible scenario, Teach wins the point by improvising: "I'm saying God forbid the *guy* (or somebody) comes in, he's got a knife . . . a cleaver from one of those magnetic *boards* . . .?" And in Teach's peerless playing out of the crime scene, the very presence of the cleaver, one of the innumerable iconic knives that appear in Mamet's canon, illustrates the need for preparedness. "And *whack*, and somebody is bleeding to death. This is all. Merely as a deterrent," he concludes (84-85).[28] The irony, of course, is that the shot is dead: the only one who will be bleeding to death will be armed with neither gun nor cleaver.

The triad of Fletcher's absence, Bob's "discovery" of a buffalo nickel, and his subsequent, surprise reappearance and announcement that Fletcher, mugged by "some Mexicans," has been hospitalized with a broken jaw (87), cumulatively provides sufficient evidence of the "facts" previously laid out by Teach in his lecture on Fletch's disloyalty and ultimately persuades him that they have been double-crossed. Interrogating Bob in a series of escalating questions, Don first attempts to verify his story, and when facts fail to support it, he and Teach double-team Bob to break the lie. Don, as Robert Vorlicky remarks, effectively "works for Teach at this point" (1995a, 223). Simultaneously instructing and threatening Bob that "Loyalty does not mean *shit* a situation like this," Teach expects the "young fuck" to "come clean" (93). In the original draft and Chicago version of *American Buffalo*, it is Don who interrogates Bob and delivers the caustic, crucial ultimatum, "I want for you to tell us here and now (and for your own protection) what is going *on*, what is set *up* . . . where *Fletcher* is . . . and everything you know" (94).[29] Paralleling the inexhaustible accusations that inform *Marranos*, Bob's inquisition is intensified and magnified by Teach's savage pistol-whipping of Bob, what Andrew Harris has correctly acknowledged "was a predicable and deliberate piece of stage violence" (106).[30] Despite the dramatic consistency with Teach's earlier presentation and insistence on the revolver, his brutality, coupled with an appearance remarkably like "some crazed lunatic," doubly ironizes Teach's earlier assertion that the gun's principal purpose was "Protection, deterrence" (85).

Mamet's contention that the meaning of the play could be jeopardized by changing the balance in this scene (that is, in shifting the focus from Don, the laconic figure, to the "flash" role, Teach), directly pertains to Don's role as the protagonist of *American Buffalo* and the tragedy's dramatization of his betrayal. Hence, when Don is tempted to betray his ward, suggests Mamet, "he is incapable of even differentiating between simple lessons of fact, and betrays himself into allowing Teach to beat up this young fellow whom he loves."

> He then undergoes . . . recognition in reversal—realizing that all this comes out of his vanity, that because he abdicated a moral position for one moment in favor of some monetary gain, he let anarchy into his life and has come close to killing the thing he loves. . . . [R]ather than his ward needing lessons in being an excellent man, it is he himself who needs those lessons. (Schvey 1988a, 94)

However, in subsequent drafts of the play, during which Ulu Grosbard and Mamet collaborated on rewrites for the Broadway production of *American Buffalo*, the character of Don was subtly undercut (Harris 98-101). A pattern of changes in the second act resulted in Teach's intensifying interrogation of Bob that erupts into explosive and audible violence when Teach grabs the nearest object and hits the young man viciously on the side of his head causing a fractured skull, evidenced by the blood oozing out of his ear. The swiftness of the act and the clarity of the resonant image are stunning, making it impossible to miss Don's culpability. Yet, significantly, Bob's cries to Don go unheard, as the latter's recriminatory lecture seeks to shift the blame for the beating to Bob: "You brought it on yourself" (94), he says, implicitly endorsing the punishment—an assertion adopted by Mamet men and women as varied as Charlie Fox in *Speed-the-Plow*, Edmond in *Edmond*, Carol in *Oleanna*, and Del in *The Cryptogram*. However, as it becomes apparent that Bob is critically injured, Don is motivated to express his justification and apprehension, "You know, we didn't want to do this to you, Bob." A half-hearted apology, Don's comment underscores by his use of "we" not only his complicity in the senseless brutality but his divided loyalty (95): of course they wanted to do it to him.

Employing a technique that will recur in numerous Mamet plays, especially *Glengarry Glen Ross* and *Oleanna*, Mamet breaks the tension of the climactic moment and advances the plot with the intrusion of the telephone. Counterpointing the long running gag in the second act during which Don and Teach have attempted to verify whether the mark is at home and tried to locate Fletcher all over town, the phone rings. Displacing his anxiety and anger with Teach, as well as himself, Don explodes at the telephone: "What? What the fuck do *you* want?" (95). Calling to make plans to visit Fletcher at Columbus Hospital on the following morning, Ruthie provides factual corroboration of Fletcher's mugging that only moments before would have spared Bob serious injury and injustice. "In the brutally macho and materialistic dog-eat-dog world of American business," argues Zeifman, "values like compassion and spirituality—implicitly inscribed as 'feminine' and therefore, in the figures of Ruth and Grace, devalued and excluded—are totally lacking," evoking the conclusion, he suggests that, "The world of *American Buffalo*—the world of American business—is thus *literally* ruthless and graceless" (1992, 128-29). However, in the conclusion of the play, I believe, we more fully comprehend Ruth's key offstage role and the deeper irony of Mamet's emblematic use of this character that renders this world the antithesis of ruthless and graceless. Albeit a maligned presence, Ruth is central to *American Buffalo*, and we seriously misjudge Mamet's world as ruthless if we fail to take cognizance of her role, her relationship to Grace, and of Mamet's biblical referent, the Book of Ruth.

Analogous to his use of biblical references and revelatory and instructional stories in *Marranos*, the playwright's implicit reference to the Book of Ruth forges a critical thematic link between Jewish ethical and moral teachings and contemporary experience. As Wiesel notes in *Sages and Dreamers*, the Book of Ruth is unique in Scripture: a sacred book whose focus is human events and relationships; whose three protagonists share the predicament of strangeness; whose principal focus is the benefit of generosity (1991, 50-64). A story whose primary themes are loyalty and love and its purpose essentially edifying, the Book of Ruth is the most dramatic and intimate of any biblical narrative (Sasson 322). Predominantly driven by its idiosyncratic, idiomatic language, Ruth's remarkable density is reflected, Jack M. Sasson maintains, "in the balanced proportion of its scenes," its meticulously structured paradigms that frequently rely on such "binary oppositions" as "escape/return . . . isolation/community, reward/punishment, tradition/innovation . . . life/death," by which the narrative achieves a distribution of themes and their thematic opposition over a period of time and activity (320-21). The literary, linguistic, and dramatic analogues to *American Buffalo*, however, are most clearly illuminated in Ruth's final coda. In contrast to its frequent greetings, the conclusion, Samson asserts, "anticipates a future beyond the story's immediate frame." Its lesson of ethical conduct was "of particular interest to the historically minded Hebrew: common people achieve uncommon ends when they act unselfishly toward each other," for during an historical period of moral hunger, he claims "people were constantly losing God's grace before earning it again" (321-22).

Likewise, Mamet employs the character Ruth to suggest powerfully the potential for covenant and connection, although both her absence and the myths surrounding her abusive behavior have contributed to a misreading of her role. A woman of few words, like her namesake Ruth the Moabite, we "hear" from Ruth, or rather Don does, only once during the play after Bob's skull has been cracked. Her intentions are threefold: to confirm that Fletcher is injured and hospitalized; to verify that they will visit him as a family tomorrow; to inquire about Bob's whereabouts. Clearly, if Don has forgotten his ethical obligations, Ruth's "call" to obligation, responsibility, and caring literally and figuratively jars his memory, or at least his conscience, for Ruth has not forgotten either the family or the biblical obligation of *gemilut hasidim*, acts of unselfishness that include visiting the sick (Gen. 18.1).[31] Thus, even as Don seeks to conceal knowledge of Bob's whereabouts from Ruthie, he reveals his profound mortification that his duplicity and immorality have sanctioned Bob's heinous inquisition and unjustifiable injury, which evoke, more than he would like to admit, the Middle Ages to which Teach alluded earlier in the evening. Subtly shifting from interrogator to protector and turning his wrath on Teach, who persists in talking about "the job," Don explodes, "You leave the fucking kid alone" (98). When it is revealed that Bob bought the buffalo nickel for Don, his mentor and friend is confronted not merely by Bob's loyalty and generosity but by his disclosure that he, like the others, has perpetrated a fraud, revisiting a pattern of revelations that typify *Marranos*. On some level, then, all the characters in *American Buffalo* may be labeled liars, fabricators and frauds. "The subject of Drama is The Lie," writes Mamet." And, "At the end of the Drama THE TRUTH—which has been overlooked, disregarded, scorned, and denied—prevails. And that is when we know the Drama is done. It is done when the hidden is revealed and we are made whole, for we *remember*—we remember when the world was upset" (1998, 79).

Mindful that it is not his young protégé who has deceived him but that he has allowed himself to be deceived and to deceive for profit, Don finds solace in identifying Teach as the principal fraud. "Unlike Bobby," who, Schvey rightly contends, "has remembered who his friends are, Don has allowed himself to be conned by the strategies con man, Teach, whose desperate accusation—'You *fake*. You fucking *fake*. You fuck your friends. You *have* no friends. No *wonder* you fuck this kid around'—contains, despite its self-serving aspects, a considerable amount of truth" (1988b, 83). Advancing on Teach, Don explodes, "*I'll* give you friends. . . . You stiff this one, you stiff that one . . . you come in here, you stick this poison in me . . ." (101), eager to blame on Teach his failure to rely upon his own just principles. And although "Don realizes that Teach animates lies and fear to deceive him into turning on his friends . . . more importantly," as Vorlicky recognizes, "Don knows that he *chose* to believe Teach and thereby betray Bobby—and herein lies Don's conflict of consciousness" (1995a, 225). Moreover, despite Judaism's obsession with responsibility, particularly as it pertains to an individual's responsibility "not to pass on negative information"—sharply contrasting with the principal emphasis in American society on the right of free speech (Telushkin 189)—Don is fully aware that in disregarding his own instruction to Bob to be vigilant, coupled with his failure to be Bob's keeper—to remember that from a Judaic moral perspective the continued existence of the world "depends on his deed" (Buber 1967, 86)—*he* alone bears the full responsibility for his abdication of the moral position he espoused. This is the central thesis of *American Buffalo*. While it is easier to blame Teach for making "life of garbage" (101), Don's betrayal of Bob, ultimately of his responsibility to humankind, has made garbage of life. As Mamet tells Wetzsteon, "What I was trying to say in *American Buffalo* . . . is that once you step back from the moral responsibility you've undertaken, you're lost" (1976, 103).

Finally taking control of the now fucked up fort, of himself, and of his priorities, the most important of which is the penultimate *mitzvah* in Judaism, *Pikuach nefesh:* the basic, overlying life-saving principle of Jewish law (Lev. 18: 5), Don implores Teach four times to go and get the car so that Bob, who is losing consciousness, will receive the medical attention that he requires. That Don is not angry with Teach for destroying his place of business—indeed, that they are reconciled at the conclusion of the play despite the near murder of the young man whom Don loves as a son—says much about *American Buffalo's* basis in Judaic ethics and conduct. The Wilderness and the Promised Land merge in the Book of Leviticus, suggests David Damrosch, for "that place where everything has been lost" has a redemptive potential (75-76). Just as Teach's and Don's previous discussion of depraved, vicious, and animalistic behavior anticipates the climactic violence that corporeally manifests their own capacity for savagery, it illumines the play's central tropes so that we understand with Don the humanizing values of a civilized life—of conscience, compassion, kindness, and responsibility—that are absolutely fundamental to Judaism. Thus we gain new insight into Teach's relationship to Don, and his role, mirroring that of Don, as weasel *and* wiseman.

Walt "Teach" Cole—whose acculturated surname is an Americanization of the Jewish name, Cohen, derived from the Hebrew *kohen* (priest), whose given name in Hebrew means "chief of an army" (Colodner 24)—is an extraordinarily complex character whose attitudes, philosophy, entrepreneurial instincts, and ethnicity are revealed in his discourse. At once a parody of the loud-mouthed, pushy Jew obsessed with money, whose stereotypical dramatization has long dominated the portrayal of the Jew in drama, of the dialogic and ethical teacher, and the Jewish gangster-cum-businessman, Teach also portrays the post-Holocaust American Jew, outraged equally by the Riverside's charging thirty-seven cents for coffee and the inhumanity of the Holocaust. Dean posits, "Teach can apparently conduct all the affairs in his life by means of speech alone," because "linguistically so versatile," he can continually "subsume the listener and sweep him or her along" as if what was being said was the truth, even if he doubts "the veracity of his fabrications" (1990, 100). Although Dean is apparently unaware of Teach's ethnicity or the basis of his characterization, like Zinman, who refers to him as a "goyishe hoodlum" (214), her analysis of his linguistic versatility is astute. A *schnorrer,* Teach lives on fabrications. With no visible means of support, like Don who owns the junk shop and

Fletcher and Ruthie who trade in pig iron, Teach supports himself, as it were, by talk. Indeed, in the second joint-Goodman/St. Nicholas Theatre production in Chicago in December 1975, notes Mosher, Mike Nussbaum "found something in the character of Teach that nobody else has ever figured out about him—namely, he is a poet, not a thug" (Jones and Dykes 24).[32] While it is entirely true that merely listening to Teach, Don becomes so involved in his fabrications and seduced by his promise of success that Don forfeits his own interpretation of events, he never seeks verification of Teach's allegations against Bob, Ruthie, and Fletcher, and he subsequently blames Teach for the chaos that is the direct consequence of *his* abdication of morality.

Cohn has observed that Mamet "presents himself obliquely and sardonically" in many of his plays, giving his own nickname, Teach, acquired in a pool hall while he was writing *American Buffalo,* to the "least sympathetic character" in the play (1992, 117). But if Teach is the least sympathetic, it may well be that we view him, as does Foster in Pinter's *No Man's Land,* as another marginalized Jew, as "a con artist. . . . [with] A typical Eastern contrick" (42-43). In *American Buffalo* Teach is literally that con artist, a parody of the anti-Semitic stereotypical Jew, itself a parody. And Mamet's intention, while oblique, may not be sardonic. In "The Lamb and the Scapegoat: The Dehumanization of the Jews in Medieval Propaganda Imagery," Lazar traces the depiction of Jews in medieval plays as gesticulating, shouting, ranting, raving like mad dogs, cursing and blaspheming figures. Typically regarded as noisy, brash, and obscene, Jews, whose speech was dominated by questions, were dramatized as villains, antagonists, madmen, and perpetrators of evil, specifically but not exclusively money-changers, thieves, traitors, and murderers, often engaged in stabbing activities or clothed in the abhorrent *pileum cornutum,* a three-cornered horned hat. All of this yields new insights into Teach's behavior, discourse, and interest in and use of the pig-sticker, and the absurd paper hat that he wears at the close of *American Buffalo* (54-57). Certainly Teach's speech is typified by expletives, sarcasm, threats, and defamation of character, which announce and color his famous, or notorious, "Fuckin' Ruthie" entrance, leading critics to read him in Shakespearean terms as "a postmodern Polonius" (Geis 1993, 101) or "a foul-mouthed streetwise Iago" (Schvey 1988b, 83). But if we become blinded—or deafened—by Teach's obscenities, as many critics have, we miss one of Mamet's great Jewish characterizations.[33] More importantly, we fail to see the celebratory elements of his character: his chutzpah, his entrepreneurial spirit, his quick-wittedness, his resilience, his creativity, his perennial optimism, his ability to view events from an historical perspective, his capacity to leap tall buildings, to crack imaginary safes, to refuse to play the part of victim, to bear arms, to survive in the company of friends.

One of the great comic routines in the play—and in Mamet's body of work—in which Teach pontificates on the defining issues of past centuries and the twentieth century, illuminates *American Buffalo*'s ethical, ethnic, and educational rhythms. Teach makes brilliant associational leaps from American history to Jewish and American Jewish experience, from freedom to entrapment, from profit to loss, from commerce to conduct, from campfires to crematoria, from freedom of the individual to the destruction of six million. The apparent outrageousness of Teach's monologue, punctuated by Don's rhythmic responses, prompts us to laugh and Don to inquire whether Teach has had his nap. However, Teach's musical mimicry, "Nap nap nap nap nap" in his characteristically, rhythmic quintuplet of repetitions, is perfectly timed to arouse our laughter and to set us up for his deadly serious comments characteristically undercut in the punch line:

> Teach: (Nowhere dyke . . .) And take those fuckers in the concentration camps. You think they went in there by *choice?*
>
> Don: No.
>
> Teach: They were *dragged* in there, Don . . .
>
> Don: . . . yeah.
>
> Teach: Kicking and screaming. *Gimme* that fucking phone. (73)

Teach's speech, whatever else it is, is imbued with a stunning veracity: Jews did go to their deaths "by choice"—by virtue of their choice to be Jews, or rather by virtue of chosenness. While the facts clearly contradict Teach's fiction of six million "kicking and screaming," the speech, delivered by Teach in his inimitable way, refutes both sentiment and speculation: it is a luminous statement of Jewish pride that refuses, even after the fact, to believe that Jews were victimized.[34] A macho "super-Jew" who defends his right to carry a gun ("So, God forbid, something inevitable occurs and the choice is . . . either him or us" [84]), who casts aside books despite their historical association with the Jew, Teach offers, however much we laugh at him, an image of the post-Holocaust Jew as "macho warrior" (Gilman 1986, 339-40). Rejecting the image of the Jew as scholar and as coward—and with them their attendant associations of victimhood, circumcision, and the feminine—Teach supplants images of risk with those of destruction and control, even retroactively displacing onto figures who were deprived of control some measure of it (Fiedler 56-57). Indeed, his speech rejects out of hand what Alain Finkielkraut has characterized as a "tenacious . . . legend of Jewish passivity" in which millions of victims of the Holocaust are depicted as "docile sheep" who were "led to the slaughter in resignation. . . . as if they *collaborated* in their own destruction" (42-43). Although Mamet will address the Holocaust repeatedly and with intense seriousness in his later work, Teach characteristically breaks off from his brief, empathetic history lesson to return to the moment at hand: waiting for Fletch. And empowered by his own fighting words, Teach, newly enraged by the passage of time and Fletch's apparent disloyalty, demands that he and Don go do "the job": "It's kickass or kissass . . ." (74).

That Teach kicks the wrong "ass" is consistent with both their bungled plan—in sharp contradistinction to their extensive planning of the heist in act 1—and the play's central theme, betrayal. No Hamlet he, Teach takes up arms against a sea of troubles, the *tsurris* generated by the feckless schlemiel Bob, and as Don calls Columbus Hospital, hoping to discredit Ruth's story as he has Bob's fiction, Teach confronts the reality that he has bashed in the head of an innocent man. One expects him to launch into a diatribe of expletives, but for the first time since his "Fuckin' Ruthie" entrance, Teach surprises us by launching into song. Mamet's apt allusion to the operetta *H.M.S. Pinafore* is inspired, at once ironic and incisive.[35] Bending the lyrics of *Pinafore,* he not only renders comment on the situation, he once again reveals Teach as a word man. Like *Pinafore, American Buffalo* contrasts senseless action with seemingly poker-faced words and colloquialisms. The scene in act 1 of *Pinafore* is the famous recitative and song, "My gallant crew," in which the captain and his crew (the chorus) repeatedly compliment one another on his superb leadership and their excellence, to which the captain adds: "I am never known to quail/At the fury of a gale." Like the captain of the H.M.S. *Pinafore,* Teach may not "quail . . . At the fury of a gale," but before long he resumes his inimitable obscenities, confirming by the use of the inclusive "we" that they are all "fucked up here" (97). However, the fact that he is sick at heart and wildly out of control is evidenced by his trashing of Don's Resale Shop. Teach's hotheadedness, like his hysterical logorrhea earlier in the day, consistent with anti-Semitic stereotypical imagery of the Jew as madman, inspires Don's empathy once again: "Are you all right?" he asks. Teach's response, "How the fuck do I know?" (104), assuring him that yes, he is all right, sets up the final coda of forgiveness. Although the spare dialogue belies the profundity of larger destructive issues we have witnessed and the depth of their friendship, Don's forgiveness of Teach, touchingly, powerfully, and candidly conveyed, reveals his compassionate understanding of Teach's humanity—and his own—and affirms that the former will neither be exiled from the shop nor excluded from Don's friendship. In short, we understand with Don that whereas the temptation to blame his bad judgment on Teach by expulsion might have served some immediate release, Teach's need encourages Don to remember that, as Levinas would have it, "the danger of justice, *injustice,* is the forgetting of the human face" (R. Cohen 9).

Echoing the opening moments, with its emphasis on apology, *American Buffalo* concludes with a reversal.[36] Here the redemptive apology signals the restoration of "solicitude toward Bob we noticed in Don at the start of the play" (Barbera 273). Whereas his ward's apology in the initial scene pertained to the inadequacy of Bob's skill, Don's apology to Bob, realistically achieved and pointedly underscored by Teach's departure to retrieve the car to take the injured young man to the hospital, pertains to a failure of Don's judgment and conduct. Put simply, the literal moment of truth for Don is his acknowledgment that he and not Bob "fucked up" (106). As Vorlicky notices, this is "one of the more primitive, yet strikingly compassionate scenes of male bonding in American male-cast plays," in which "men who come to value their friendship to one another . . . speak of that value" (1995a, 227-28). While Don's apology is apparently motivated by love, guilt and grief, it is also motivated by obligation: Jewish ethical law requires restitution, the pardon of the defrauded individual, effected here by Don's direct apology to Bob (Jung 112). Thus, the final words of the play echo and reverse the first, underlining Don's confession of error—a critical first step in (re)assuming personal responsibility—as well as the affirmative rhythm of tragic knowledge, what Mamet terms "the capacity for self-knowledge" (Schvey 1988a, 93). "[I]t is not the sins we commit that destroy us," Del, a family friend who similarly betrays those he loves, will assert in Mamet's *The Cryptogram* twenty years hence, "but how we act after we've committed them" (1995b, 83), reflecting a pattern in Mamet's work of loss and negotiated return.

Don learns to be an "excellent man" from Bob, whose *menschlekeit,* practical knowledge born of genuine caring and will to virtue, embodies above all the Jewish injunction to remember. But we also observe that Bob has not acquired that knowledge in a vacuum. Having learned little about how to stake out a heist from Don, it is not too much to assume that he has learned much about the teachings of Kedoshim, the code of Holiness, by the example of Don's life, his patience, his generosity, his genuinely unselfish concern, his kindness, his loyalty—however misplaced—and his humanity, evidenced by his failure to consistently make wise choices. The pairing of the father and son, of teacher and student or that of older and younger family surrogate members evokes the family, a fundamental motif in American Jewish life and art that assumes a pivotal place in Mamet's work. Moreover, the eidetic function of this relationship—as symbolic, biblical, and ethnic referent—prefiguring that of subsequent Mamet plays affords the playwright the opportunity to explore questions of guilt and responsibility, themselves biblical, not the least of which is the guilt of the individual who threatens the fabric of family. Thus, ironically, in his attempt to buy into the promise of American abundance, Don has failed to remember the central lesson of what it means to be a mensch—to choose to do good, to be a member of a community. He has failed to be a "stand-up guy," a point Bob makes abundantly clear in words that Mamet ultimately cut during the premiere performance: "Your father is a faggot."[37] Writing in 1982, Richard Christiansen perceptively recognized that *American Buffalo*'s "enduring value" lies not in its "fresh poetry and passion," or its comically bungled get-rich-quick scheme "as penetrating commentary of the American capitalist system," although admittedly both introduced the uniqueness of Mamet's artistry and moral vision. Rather, the play's "ultimate crime, [one that] Mamet was to make clear in all of his plays, was the failure to connect with and care for other human beings" (12).

Thus, when Teach taunts Don, "you're my *keeper* all a sudden?" (63), the answer is yes, not because it is "good business" but because it is the only business of human relations. "Whatever pulls the individual away from . . . the consideration of others," observes Wiesel, contradicts "The emphasis on the *other* [that] is paramount in Judaism: *Achrayut*, responsibility, contains the word *Akher* (Acher), the Other. We are responsible for the other. And first of all, for those closest to us" (1991, 184). Likewise, the key to understanding *American Buffalo*'s insistence on responsibility and the consequences of abdicating that responsibility is illustrated, above all, in human terms, for the tragic knowledge that Don and the audience acquire is not merely the futility of idolatry; it is that our moral responsibility to others testifies to our humanity, a lesson evident in the play's concluding image implicitly affirming the value of father-and-son unity and of male bonding. Commenting on a similar pattern in the work of Mel Brooks, Desser and Friedman note that "it grows out of a Jewish sense of fatality, the idea that land and wealth, power and position, may vanish in a wink of an eye or a ruler's change of heart, but personal affection remains a powerful bond that lasts beyond the whims of fortune" (153). Mamet would surely add that the threat emanates not only from a whim of fortune but from a whiff of fortune, from willful disregarding of one's identity, responsibility, and family. Don does "have friends this life" if he remembers his responsibilities to them (8).

CAUGHT IN THE
AMERICAN MACHINE

"For the Jew, exile is . . . the very essence of his
mythic-ethnic condition. . . . [He is] eternally
not at home, as those who are, in whatever place
he finds himself, constantly remind him"
—Leslie Fiedler

Increasingly concerned with issues of cultural identity, Mamet has observed
that "the greatest American play, arguably, is the story of a Jew told by a Jew
and cast in 'universal' terms. Willy Loman is a Jew in a Jewish Industry," he
writes. "But he is never identified as such. His story is never avowed as a
Jewish story, and so a great contribution to Jewish and Jewish-American
history is lost . . . to the culture as a whole; and more importantly, it's lost
to the Jews, its rightful owners" (1994, 30). Unlike *Death of a Salesman*,
Glengarry Glen Ross overtly dramatizes the story of Jewish men in a Jewish
industry, whose biblical, historical, linguistic, and cultural echoes tally the
profits and loss of the promise of America and the potential for survival in
the depersonalized world of business antithetical to Judaic values.[1] Comprised of three tightly framed dyads in act 1 and the inspired genius of the
freewheeling Roma-Levene-Lingk skit juxtaposed with the despoliation of
act 2, *Glengarry Glen Ross* stages the exploitation of the injudicious, exposes
the bending of morality on all social levels, arouses suspicion, and solves the
mystery of criminal actions perpetrated on and by the desperate. Juggling
nearly as many off-stage characters as appear on stage, Mamet literally
dramatizes a sales contest for a Cadillac or a set of steak knives, whose

metaphoric resonance is immense, in which only two of four men will survive the murderous, cutthroat competition.

In her review of the 1984 production of *Glengarry Glen Ross*, Masha Leon remarked that had Mamet written the play for the Yiddish theatre, "it would have been titled, 'Ameritchke Goniff,' that favorite expression that encompasses everything innovative, ingenious . . . and insincere associated with business" (19), which in Chicago "outstripped the pallid tribute 'Only in America'" (Rosten 1989, 49).[2] The lure of America, a golden land of boundless riches and freedom, observes Irving Howe in *World of Our Fathers*, enticed Jews to its shores and its marketplaces with the vibrancy of its optimism and its promise of a better life and living (1976, 35). Though its mythic streets lined with gold fell far short of their billing—like the grossly overrated properties promoted as Glen Ross Farms, Rio Rancho, Mountain View, and Glengarry Highlands in Mamet's *Glengarry Glen Ross*—the abundant land that had lured Jewish immigrants with its promise of gold, and "sustained a distinctly American faith in the future," transformed "a disparate populace of hopeful [Jewish] immigrants . . . into a 'people of plenty'" (12) who, as Andrew Heinze points out, believed that "Success in religious scholarship or in business was available to almost anyone with the talent and the initiative to pursue it"(95).

In no city more than Chicago, what Dreiser termed "a giant magnet," was the profit realized and the promise corrupted by what Thorstein Veblen recognized in *Theory of the Leisure Class* as "business enterprise," calculating business values.[3] Peddlers by tradition, whom Stephen J. Whitfield colorfully terms "walkers and talkers," Jews, who had engaged in mercantile occupations for centuries, discovered that sales and shopkeeping in America were appealing choices for outsiders, affording both the opportunity for independence and the preservation of family structures.[4] Mamet's sympathy for the outsider—the marginalized other—is reflected in his portrayal of characters throughout his canon. In fact, the outsider as Jew is a conspicuous feature of Mamet's work, much of which dramatizes the experiences of peddlers of one sort or another.[5]

Like *American Buffalo, Glengarry Glen Ross*, written less than a decade later, concerns itself with outsiders—their deeds and deals, promises and performance, friendships and betrayals, imagination and initiative, moral dilemma and compromise, and search for iconic gold, whether coin or Cadillac. Fierce competition, ribald language, injudicious decisions, profit margins, negotiations, and moral choice situate *Glengarry Glen Ross* within an ethical and ethnic framework whose focus on "conduct and of the consequences of conduct" Cynthia Ozick has characterized as "centrally Jewish" (164). Like the earlier play, *Glengarry Glen Ross*, a work that opposes

covenant and idolatry, is "drenched in considerations of conscience, responsibility, and love" that typify the work of Jewish writers (Shechner 1979,
212). Moreover, it explores persecution and the imposition of power
coupled with inquisitional scenes, its violence expressed verbally rather than
physically. Equating would-be criminals with working salesmen, *Glengarry
Glen Ross* dramatizes the planning of a robbery, albeit on a larger scale than
American Buffalo, that ideally will provide a measure of personal and
financial independence.

Mirroring *American Buffalo*'s urban setting, *Glengarry Glen Ross*'s
cosmopolitan locale implicitly evokes a fitting terrain for the exploration of
the modern Jewish experience. Not only is the play set in Chicago, but as
the filmed version of the play makes abundantly clear, in the northwest
section of the city, "where Mamet envisioned the real–estate office and the
Chinese restaurant that inspired the setting for the first act" (Jones and
Dykes 57),[6] whose neighborhoods, linked to the commercial urban center
of Chicago by "the El," were largely inhabited after the 1950s by upwardly
mobile Jews (Holli and Jones 282). Like the junk store that serves as a
powerful ethnic referent in *American Buffalo,* the Chinese restaurant
similarly establishes a cultural and ethnic frame that implicitly attests to
advancing assimilation in the Jewish community, whose connection with
food is integral. Increasingly attractive to Jews abandoning traditional
Jewish life, Chinese restaurants loom large in the experience of second
generation American Jews for whom they were an essential element of
community identity, "as much a fixture of . . . the Jewish neighborhood as
the appetizing store and the corner deli" (Joselit 1994, 214-15).[7]

So skillfully has Mamet universalized his themes, however, that critics
have failed to note that from its opening beat *Glengarry Glen Ross* is a
profoundly Jewish play whose familial, ethical, philosophical, spiritual, and
communal concerns take center stage, informing its discourse, locution,
tropes, and controlling images.[8] Issues of social justice, personal freedom,
and the right to express oneself are coupled with what David Desser and
Lester D. Friedman characterize as prototypical "persecution, powerlessness,
and paranoia" (15). Framed as a brilliantly conceived maze of questions—
"Do I want pity?" (22), "You need money?" (46), "What does that mean?"
(43)—that are themselves typically Jewish, *Glengarry Glen Ross*'s intrinsically
Jewish concerns are evident in its linguistic rhythms, comic irony, and
consideration of conduct in a society rarely hospitable to human aspirations
and dignity. Although this play, like *American Buffalo,* is a critique of
capitalism that exposes a failure of the American Dream, as so many critics
have averred, *Glengarry Glen Ross* shifts the focus to an examination of
choices—their wisdom, their folly, their moral and legal price—consistent

with Mamet's view expressed in "Decadence" that the appropriate subject for drama is "the human capacity for choice" (1987d, 58). Situating choice in the realm of morality, Shubert Spero tells us in *Morality, Halaka and the Jewish Tradition* that "A necessary condition for praising or condemning a person morally is his ability—choice—to have acted otherwise" (4). For "Judaism is never more sober or more powerful than when it promises to sear the spirit," opines Whitfield, "requiring of its believers that they ponder the meaning of their lives, the nature of their existence, the purpose of their creation." Indeed, there is "no more cogent expression of the dilemma of conduct" than that articulated by Rabbi Hillel in a "characteristically Jewish question: 'If I am not for myself, who will be for me? If I am only for myself, what am I?'" (1984, 274-75).

Although these questions are critical to all the *Glengarry* salesmen, what strikes us immediately is Mamet's portrayal of three Jewish men, Shelly Levene, Dave Moss, and George Aaronow, whose tenacity, principles, comic genius, and daily survival he celebrates, whose ethical compromises he scrutinizes, whose troubling temptation to iconic gold he illuminates, and whose encounter with latent anti-Semitism he deplores. These subjects were very much on the playwright's mind in 1982-1983, as evidenced by the fact that themes of personal worth, achievement, loss, and acceptance of outsiders by the majority society are treated overtly by Mamet in the one-act episodic play, *The Disappearance of the Jews*. A dyad between friends, one of whom (in a early version of the play) is a traveling salesmen who encounters anti-Semitism in business and at home, *The Disappearance of the Jews,* which Mamet recently conceived as the first of a triptych, will be treated more fully in a subsequent chapter.

While I do not believe Mamet intends for us to read *Glengarry Glen Ross* as an allegory, given its tropes of performance and promise, its preoccupation with justice and judgment, its focus on obedience and choice, and its consideration of law, the parallels between biblical figures and Mamet's most overtly developed, identifiable trio of Jewish characters are compelling. Tony Stafford has aptly noted that numerous "Old Testament images accrue around Aaronow, Moss, and Levene" who may be viewed as "modern-day children of Israel" (1996, 192). Despite their contemporary context, concerns, behavior and vulgarity, these pivotal characters, whose names evoke those of the biblical Aaron, Moses and the Levites, bear a strong semblance to archetypal figures from whom Mamet has drawn inspiration for character development and conduct, but whose profane and parodic treatment permit the playwright to distance himself from biblical models, what Leslie Fiedler, writing about a similar technique employed by Bernard Malamud, has likened to removing "the curse" of overt biblical referents (139).[9] However, their Jewishness is not in name alone, nor in linguistic facility. Indeed, they are not just so many "talking heads" whose names evoke 6,000 years of Jewish history. Rather, as the play reveals, what defines them as Jewish, as L. S. Dembo recognizes in the work of other American Jewish writers, is not their quick-wittedness or silver-tongued speech, but that the topics of survival, injustice, disloyalty, responsibility, and cultural and personal history are the subject of their speech, and that Jewishness and "moral significance. . . . pose a problem" for these characters that is reflected in their actions (55).

A closer look at these biblical characters, whom Mamet employs as a link between ancient and modern worlds, values, aspirations, and spirituality and the means to explore the doubleness of vision that characterizes the American Jewish experience, reveals fabulously rich figures that history has mythologized and Jewish tradition humanized. Modern interpretations of Moses, for example, view him primarily as a lawgiver, oracle, and teacher, ruthless in the pursuit of justice. Distinguished by a superior intellect, Moses was known as well for his profound disappointment in what he perceived as the Jews' *shesavlu,* suffering coupled with tolerance and resignation (Wiesel 1979, 188), which earned him the reputation as a rebel who resisted "oppressive orders" whose intent was to coerce human beings "to be less than they can be"—an insight central to Judaism (Lerner 66). Occupying a unique place in Jewish tradition based upon his encounter with God, Moses' "passion for social justice, his struggle for national liberation, his triumphs and disappointments, his poetic inspiration, his gifts as a strategist and his organizational genius," combined with "efforts to reconcile the law with compassion" are tempered in Jewish tradition by a portrait that reveals human fallibility: a quick temper, the hesitation to act without the counsel and cooperation of others, inability to comprise, and breach of faith (Wiesel 1979, 182).

Assigned a subordinate role to his younger brother Moses, Aaron was known as an eloquent speaker and passive associate. Absolved of the forging of the Golden Calf that was attributed to the people who both identified it with divinity and worshipped it, Aaron shared with Moses an "hostility to authority" (Exod. 16: 2-36; Num. 14:1-45, 16:3, 20:1-13). Distinguished by his spiritual strength, altruism and generosity, Aaron, however, acquired a reputation as a lover of peace who would employ every stratagem to reconcile disputes.[10] The smallest of the tribes, the Levites attained honored status as guardians of the threshold, servers of the tabernacle and teachers. Their loyalty to Moses, as evidenced by their zealous punishment of idolaters involved in the Golden Calf sin, earned them the name "men of zeal." Wanderers having no land of their own, the Levites, whose name

derives prophetically from the word *laveh,* "to lead by righteousness," were
dependent on others for support.[11] And in recognition of their righteousness, rejection of idolatry, and family devotion, they were chosen by God for
special protection, ultimately rewarded by entering the Promised Land,
unlike the rest of the Exodus generation (Num. 1:11).

The promise of a cash bonus, the promised land (Hawaii), and the
plethora of numerical details that characterize *Glengarry Glen Ross*—the
eight units of Mountain View that Levene sells to Bruce and Harriett
Nyborg, an $82,000 sale that yields a $12,000 commission, the five
thousand stolen leads, three days during which Lingk can break his contract,
$50 per lead Levene offers to Williamson raised to fifty percent of all his
sales, Roma's $6000 squandered commission, and the salesmen's numerical
order on the board—cumulatively point to the accounting and measuring
of personal performance, profit, and loss. "Behind or within the soundshape
of these enumerations," comprised of "measuring, accounting, or drawing
up lists . . . so basic a way of creating order" (39), as Geoffrey H. Hartman
suggests in another context, there "glimmers a hidden sense, a hidden world,
a history. With its hierarchical structure, unseen power, and confluence of
contract and conduct, *Glengarry Glen Ross* structurally and tropologically
evokes the Book of Numbers, a referent that unifies statistics and statutes.
Moreover, its profane iconic symbols of tangible divinity, its overt treatment
of entrapment and freedom, justice and injustice, frustration and lack of
faith similarly evoke Numbers in which Moses, Aaron, and the Levites
figure prominently."

As he has in *Marranos* and *American Buffalo,* Mamet finds telling
referents in mythologized history, in biblical context, that when glossed with
Glengarry are revelatory. The Book of Numbers narrates Israel's departure
from Mount Sinai and its journey through the wilderness to the border of
the Promised Land that modern interpretations read as the prototypical
Diaspora. In this "chronicle of the birth of a nation" magic and realism
coexist; ordinary individuals are tested, survive, accept a code of law, express
emotions for and against strong leadership, and, Hartman posits, "accept
the sense that it [Israel] has a special destiny, beyond wandering" (41-44,
45). Framed by the sin of the Golden Calf depicted in Exodus, "the profane
analogue to the apocalyptic occurrence then taking place on Sinai" (Dembo
104) on the one hand[12] and the exaltation of the Baal of Peor, an event that
"dramatizes a readiness to become like the [other] nations and to serve their
gods" (Ackerman 88) on the other, Numbers' major themes are: temptation,
human fallibility, bearing a moral burden, the threat of assimilation by
foreigners and their gods, and transfer of power to the younger generation

(90). Central to Numbers, moreover, is the attention "to legal matters and organizational minutiae," the result of which is a book characterized by its "forthright cohabitation of imagination and law" (Hartman 41).

Reiterating these tropes structurally, as James S. Ackerman suggests in his perceptive analysis, three major sections of Numbers are unified by recurring "thematic concerns that lend the epic narrative a literary unity," further supported by a resonant, echoic technique that contributes by symphonic, rather than verbatim, repetitions to narrative development (78-80). Similarly *Glengarry Glen Ross*'s echoic rhythms, discernible in recurring, nuanced references to land developments (Glen Ross Farms, Rio Rancho, and Clear Meadows), to ethnic groups (the "fucking Polacks" and the "Patels"), to powerful individuals (Mitch, Murray, and Jerry Graff), and phrases (that is, "the board," "the leads," and "opportunity") create a cohesive narrative structure that engenders comment on previously stated phrases and provides a key to varying repetition and interpretation. Thus, recalling the first section of Numbers—the counting and ordering of the multitudes in a census, precise figures for each tribe, and hierarchical and spatial structures intended to limit divine access—at the beginning of *Glengarry Glen Ross,* repetitive reference to the positioning of members of the sales force and their placement on "the board" in the real estate office similarly intensifies awareness of their ascending and descending positions of power, a hierarchy that "forms a simple moral continuum" (Tuttle 164).

We recall, furthermore, that Numbers contains some of the best-known events in the Hebrew Bible, many of which have magical appeal: water springs from the rock, manna drops from the sky, Moses's authority is contested, Aaron is reconfirmed after his involvement in the Golden Calf incident, Levi's and Aaron's staff blossoms and bears fruit (Num. 17:12), an ass speaks, and Balak, the Moabite king, a "Pharaoh *redivivus,*" as Ackerman puts it, endeavors to curse the Jews (86). The most magical of all, suggests Hartman, are words, both "pregnant with promise" and "potentially deceiving"; thus, it is not for nothing that its key word is *daber:* to speak (Num. 11: 17-25; Deut. 32.2). The analogues to *Glengarry Glen Ross* are again vivid. In fact, speech is so central to this play that David Worster characterizes it as Mamet's "speech-act play."[13] For example, retailing the word of God, Moss attempts to draw Aaronow into participation in his scheme to steal the premium leads and sell them to Jerry Graff by words that are full of promise and deception; Levene sells eight plots to the Nyborgs on the strength of "B list" leads ostensibly empowered by magical speech that bears fruit, a sale Williamson terms "remarkable" (1984, 75); and Aaronow, outraged by the abuse of authority, establishes himself as a spokesman for human rights.

Echoing its opening with a tribal census and spatial arrangement (one mirrored, as well, in Mamet's concluding scene), the Book of Numbers concludes with the revelation that the Exodus generation is to be denied the Promised Land, whereas Joshua, leading a new generation, will be permitted to cross into the Promised Land, a place that spies' reports have revealed is both exceedingly fertile and "eats its inhabitants" (Num. 13: 32-33). With the new generation poised to move into the Promised Land, Israel is reminded to "walk in the law," resist the temptation of Egyptian comforts and the pressures of assimilation by realizing that mere numbers would not suffice for survival, and to be fully cognizant that many will fail the (con)test. Indeed, the role of law is so prominent in *Glengarry* that Mamet's screenplay for the film version features a new scene and character,[14] Blake, who concretizes the enforcer power of the unseen abstractions, Mitch, Murray, and Lemkin—the Glengarry downtown bosses who "take[s] the cream," as Sam Mendes has it (3).[15] In this ancillary scene, Blake (read Balak), the inhumane emissary from the front office, lays down the law of the land in "stentorian tones," to borrow Christopher Hudgins's phrase, both expressing and ironizing the central element of choice, "Because it's fuck or walk. You close or you hit the bricks. Decision. Have you made your decision for Christ?" To Moss, who asks Blake's name, the district sales manager responds, parodying the First Commandment delivered at Mount Sinai in which Yahweh introduces himself as "the Lord thy God, who brought you out of Egypt, out of the house of bondage" (Exod. 20: 2): "Fuck you, that's my name." Naming is similarly critical in the scene in Arthur Miller's *Death of a Salesman* that Mamet has acknowledged as the principal inspiration for his play: "*Glengarry* is an extrapolation of Willy's scene with Howard," he tells Mary Cantwell. In fact, to the playwright, "'Shelly the Machine' Levene and Willy Loman are the same guy, except my play deals with him at work" (Cantwell 281).[16] However, by setting the first act in a seedy Chinese restaurant, at once talismanic and culturally coded, Mamet immediately establishes a marginal ground.[17] Neither home nor work space, this "combat zone is so powerful," observes Nicholas de Jongh, "because it avoids Arthur Miller's breast-beating melodramatics" (1994, 794).

In each of three masterful "Mamet mosaics" that comprise act 1, and are "Written like obscene vaudeville riffs" (Brustein 1987, 70), the playwright portrays conversations between management and employee, friends of long standing, and a salesman and a mark, each rooted in betrayal, trust, and/or need. In each one a dominant character controls the conversation and concludes a deal, the act of listening contributes to the betrayal of trust, and the implication of fraud links past and present performance to a future event. Paralleling *Marranos, American Buffalo,* and *A Life in the Theatre, Glengarry Glen Ross* is driven by performance artists, salesmen Levene, Moss, Aaronow, and Roma—an outsider to the Jewish trio whose connection to his Jewish colleagues is his skill as a performance artist—who imaginatively and skillfully assume myriad roles and guises in their private dramas of survival. In scene 1, Williamson squeezes Levene for twenty percent plus "fifty bucks a lead" and a hundred dollars up front (24); in scene 2 Moss traps Aaronow as an "accessory before the fact" because he listened to the plan to steal the leads "In the abstract . . ." (45-46); and in scene 3 Roma shares a drink, "great fucks" that he has known, and a map of Glengarry Highlands with James Lingk, baiting and hooking his listener, and the audience, with his seductive "Listen to what I'm going to tell you now:" (48-51).

Comprised of echoic dialogue, the symphonic scenes reveal that success or failure is predicated on the power of the pitch and the confidence of the pitchmen. By showcasing the storyteller—a device he has used variously in *Sexual Perversity in Chicago, American Buffalo, A Life in the Theatre,* and *Prairie du Chien,* exploring the pervasiveness of betrayal and illuminating narrative as a means of enhancing self-image, escaping reality, and linking the past and present—Mamet discloses that his salesmen are empowered by the vitality of their imagination. Recalling his communication with the playwright, Mosher confirms this point. "'Look,'" Mamet informed the director, "'this is not a play about love. . . . This is a play about power. This is a play about guys, who when one guy is down, the other guy doesn't extend a hand to help him back up. . . . [and] where the one who's up then kicks the other guy in the balls to make sure that he stays down'" (Kane 1992, 239).

In the first scene, closely paralleling that of the aging Willy Loman in Howard's office, Levene pitches the office manager John Williamson on his worth and potential by drawing upon his numbers, much as Willy does, to remind him of his past success, to ensure his survival when tested, and to forecast future sales. Recounting his history with the firm and his reputation on the street, which notably predate Williamson's tenure, Levene tabulates and illustrates his accomplishments, as Willy Loman does for Howard in the earlier work. Citing chapter and verse on his watershed years in which his "Cold *calling*" (18) ostensibly generated sufficient income to support Moss, Jerry Graff, Mitch, and Murray, whose purchase of a Cadillac Seville the latter credits to Levene's sales, Levene endeavors to sell himself as a "*closer . . . a proven man*" (15). He does so not merely by facts and figures, but by projecting himself as the antithesis of Moss—whom he demeans as a mere "*order* taker"(17), that is, a man lacking entirely in sales ability—with the explicit intent of securing for himself premium leads and a bona fide opportunity to win the office sales contest. His willingness to negotiate "sits" recalls Willy Loman's efforts to engage Howard in contractual discussions that would permit the road man to work as a city drummer in order "to set his table" (Miller 80). Even Willy's rejection of charity, albeit repackaged, is echoed in Levene's appeal to an apparently impenetrable Williamson: "Do I want charity? Do I want *pity?* I want *sits.* . . . Give me a chance. That's all I want" (22). But Levene wants more than "sits"; he wants—and desperately needs—two premium leads. As Benedict Nightingale observed, the law of this "jungle-within-a-jungle . . . is starkly Darwinian. Sell and survive; fail and be fired. . . . a good lead brings the hope of a good placing on the board. A bad lead might as well be a one-way sign pointing over a cliff" (1984, 793).

Frequently analyzed, the value of content in this and other conversations in the play is typically overlooked. Anne Dean, for example, maintains that to analyze Levene's opening speech—which is also the play's—"is to learn almost everything about him and the life he leads." Indeed, characterizing Levene's rhetorical mode as a "tentative, although persistent, manner—the crafty, insidious approach of the professional salesman . . . [which] builds up a kind of rhythmic litany," Dean's exegesis of this opening speech approaches "his calculated ingenuousness" and "growing nervousness" (1990, 198-99) as Levene's counterpointed, controlled use of flattery and criticism, intended to emphasize his strength in a friendly but firm manner.[18] However, to gain a fuller picture of Levene's character and assess his discourse as a sales pitch intended to contain a terror so profound he will allow no chink in his linguistic armor, we must proceed further into scene 1; indeed, we must follow him on his journey throughout the play, cognizant that, as Mamet has noted, "There is always content in what's being said," even if "That content is not necessarily carried by the context of what's being said . . . [but] by the rhythm of the speech and the posture of the speaker" (Norman and Rezek 53).

From the beginning of the scene Levene sharply resembles the "none too heroic or learned" protagonist of the modern Yiddish story, whom David G. Roskies describes in *A Bridge of Longing* as "a typical down-and-out unsuccessful middleman" covering "failures as a man and as a breadwinner through verbal exuberance" (182). Paralleling biblical concerns with fallibility and temptation to the ways of the Other, the modern Yiddish story narrates "the intact world" of the Eastern Jew (Gilman 1991b, 34); what remains of that world is the fractured Yiddish, the proletarian speech of the secular Jew, a diminished hero. Levene's locution—for example, his indignation intensified by questions, sarcasm, ridicule, heartfelt invocation ("I pray it misses you" [16]), and phrasing, "Alright" (26), as in "you win, let's get on with it"—that Rosten identifies as Yinglish, or Yiddish-inflected English, immediately suggests his ethnicity and defines his identity. It is a marker of difference. Only progressively in his presentation to Williamson do we learn of his attachment to the past, faith in the future, familial responsibilities, and marginal status. A shell of the man he once was, whose given name in Hebrew literally means "dried up" (Kolatch 1984, 219), Shelly Levene is not merely down and out; he is desperate.[19] Recent deals have "kicked *out*" (16), his financial situation is precarious, and his anxiety so palpable that he seems to "sweat[s] out loud" (Corliss 84).

In preparation for his meeting with Williamson, Levene has conceived of a plan, albeit not very well thought out, to impress the office manager with a strong statement of his achievement. Yet as soon as Williamson states that the salesman "blew the last . . ." (15), Levene is instantly defensive. And although his repeated efforts to set the record straight threaten to derail his plan, Levene's insistence on the past signals its cultural importance. "To be a Jew is to be every moment in history, to keep history for breath and daily bread," observes Ozick (132). It is a motif articulated repeatedly by Levene, whose perception of the present is viewed through a historical lens. For Levene, like Willy Loman and Teach, "Jewish time is cyclical, and mythic" (Roskies 1995, 182); the past lives in the present. It is not ancient but "mythologized history" as Martin Buber puts it. Thus, when Levene draws upon statistical evidence, repeatedly echoing "look at the *sheets* . . . look at the *sheets*" (17), citing both ancient and recent history to prove his worth, he both realistically affirms what all salesmen know—that every day is a sales contest in which top dogs and bottom feeders alike must make their numbers to keep their jobs—and draws upon memory for confidence and strength to meet the biggest challenge of his career.

"A man acquires a reputation. On the street. What he does when he's *up*. What he does otherwise" (24), he tells Williamson, echoing Don's life lessons to Bob that " business is . . . common sense, experience, and talent" acquired "on the street" (Mamet 1977, 6). To deny memory and the power of history is for Levene a denial of himself and his skill. And if he pads his numbers— past or present—as we presume he does, to close the sale to Williamson, it may be his most valuable weapon in a rigged contest in which only those in the top fifty percent of the sales force get to compete; he and Aaronow get "toilet paper" (21). Fluctuating between the scatological and mannerly, Levene's speech provides further evidence of the linguistic cultural phenomenon that Mark Shechner terms "ghetto cosmopolitan," a quality of discourse comprised of the mundane and sacred that arrives from the "peculiar" condition of the Jew existing simultaneously in "two different, even radically opposed, worlds" of work and family, Jews and gentiles (1987, 33).

However, when Williamson defines and defends his own job as "marshal[ing] the leads," Levene's response to his dispassionate and dehumanized treatment of his sales force is explosive. "Marshal the leads . . . marshal the leads? What the fuck, what bus did *you* get off of, we're here to fucking *sell*. *Fuck* marshaling the leads. What the fuck talk is that? What the fuck talk is that? Where did you learn that? In school?" (19). Alternatively argumentative, defensive, aggressive, threatening, and apologetic, Levene, aware that his emotional outburst will impede his success in "closing" Williamson, reigns in his anger, adopts a more amicable tone, and personalizes his appeal. "That's 'talk,' my friend, that's 'talk,'" he continues, stressing that "Our job is to *sell*. I'm the *man* to sell. I'm getting garbage" (19).

Employing the new, unfamiliar discourse, and clearly no friend of Levene's, Williamson is disquieting in his defense of policy over people. Unlike Levene, he claims neither accomplishment nor skill; rather, he finds as a source of pride that "I do what I'm hired to do. . . . I'm *hired* to watch the leads. I'm given . . . I'm given a *policy. My* job is to *do that.* What I'm *told*" (19). Refusing to make exceptions to the rule—that is, until money enters the discussion— Williamson, coded as an extreme representation of the non-Jew, holds to a policy that is chillingly reminiscent of one described by Hannah Arendt as "the banality of evil" in which "terribly and terrifying normal" individuals contend that they are unable to affect or temper statutes established by superiors (1965, 276; 120-21). In formulating a original, disquieting definition of criminality, Arendt concluded that such individuals have "no motives at all" beyond following orders; in other words, their meticulousness and dedication to rules is manifested by an eerie indifference (215; 120-21). Hence, what Levene perceives—and we subsequently observe in the play—is a cold intractability to which he refers repeatedly. Therefore, in the penultimate confrontational scene in which Levene is shamed by his actions and remorseful within the world of the play, Williamson milks his role, needling Levene about his guilt and, it would seem to me, guilty of driving Levene toward the crime he has committed. Although certainly one may blame market factors, Levene's declining performance, and his own moral blindness for the position he ultimately finds himself in, the concluding scene reveals that Mamet's feelings for Williamson are not as sympathetic as they are for other characters about whom he tells Henry Schvey, "I always want everyone to be sympathetic to all the characters" (1998a, 92).

Although the burglary "is the action that finally defines and condemns" Levene, as Jon Tuttle asserts, that action is neither climactic nor dramatic: rather, it, like the interrogations that the police officer Baylen conducts, looms in our imagination (166). What looms larger on stage and commands our complete attention throughout *Glengarry* is the discomforting depiction of the Jew that is more characteristic of rhetorical anti-Semitism: a Jew who is ludicrous, mocking, unethical but with business acumen, both subordinate and aggressive, and pulling money out of his pockets to sweeten the deal. Mamet has taken on one of the strongest myths about "the polluted and polluting discourse of the Jew, the image of the lying Jew" (Gilman and Katz 321), unifying it with manifestations of the stereotypical Jew whose "criminal" nature, greed, and deceit have contributed to "the continuity and uniqueness of anti-Semitism in the United States" (10). As Robert Brustein noted in his review of the American premiere, "The powerful tensions he [Mamet] has uncovered between the ethnic underclass and the WASP functionaries who administer its employment opportunities pick the scabs off a lot of ancient half-healed wounds" (1987, 71). Repeatedly opposing Jew and non-Jew, the ethnic dialectic that characterizes *Glengarry Glen Ross* codes Williamson and Baylen as hostile to the Jew, and Roma, a more sympathetic non-Jew, as aligned with his Jewish colleagues' tenacity, wit, and performance artistry on the one hand and with Williamson's access and leads to affluence on the other.

For his part, Levene is uninterested in Williamson's work ethic or mindless loyalty. Rather, he rivets attention to how the aforementioned corporate policy is in aid of or impedes *"anybody"*—like him—who "falls below a certain mark" (19). To express his repugnance with an irrational, inhumane policy that destroys rather than motivates men, Levene reverts to typically Jewish rhetorical inquiry punctuated with Yiddish: "Then how do they come up above that mark? With *dreck...*?" His remarks are laced with ridicule, because the logic eludes him completely (20). One of only three Yiddish words in *Glengarry Glen Ross* (Roma's reference to himself as a *"schmuck"* and Aaronow's explosive *"meshugass"* in act 2), *dreck,* its inflection heightening and punctuating the stench of this dialogue, is positioned for maximum effect (26), revealing Yiddish as a powerful means of registering cynicism and sarcasm. Like the nuanced repetitions of "John: my *daughter. ..,"* that, as Mendes observes, "spread right through the play" (Kane 1996, 256-57), *dreck* associatively links the "toilet paper" (21) that he and Aaronow are getting to Levene's favorite epithet, "shit," a topic that Roma deconstructs with panache in his brilliant monologue in scene 3. Universally known as an emphatic term for excrement, *dreck* also means inferior merchandise and insincere talk (Kogos 29). All three interpretations, then, have validity in this context.

Almost as soon as Williamson rejects Levene's contention that he is "a *closer*," a dialectic ensues between the men on the meaning of terms: not only what one can say, but the validity of what is said. Despite the fact that Levene knows he must control his temper because "I got to *eat. Shit*, Williamson, shit" (17), he nonetheless tenaciously holds his ground, rejecting outright the office manager's inferred but intended umbrage: ". . . then what is this 'you *say*' shit, what is that? (*Pause*). What is that . . . ?" The oppositional "I" and "you" rivet attention to their differing perceptions of reality. A luftmensch reduced to begging for a break, Levene will brook no humiliation. Unwilling to let the affront to his reputation stand and the injustice prevail, he continues his harangue: "What is this 'you *say*' shit?" (17), employing ethnically coded accusatory and embittered intonations underscored by repetition and reiterated questions to force Williamson to retract the implication, although his confrontational tone threatens to derail his game plan further. The principal point in this typically Yiddish discourse, however, "lies in echoing the exact words" of the indignation, whose ironic intention is intensified by an apparently innocent question (Rosten 1989, 256).

Whereas Robert Vorlicky postulates that this exchange is gender coded "talk about talk" establishing the ground of their mutual understanding as specifically male speakers and listeners (1995a, 35), what he terms "social dialogue," I think that it underscores the impossibility of their understanding the Other's views given basic philosophic differences. Where Levene's rhythms are affirmative, insisting on his belief in himself, in his skill, in the future, and in life, Williamson's are negative, resistant, and pessimistic, reflecting an enmity toward Levene that he openly professes in the final moments. Granted that "the entire rabbinic tradition *is* argument (as opposed to credo)," as Ozick reminds us, Jews "are heirs to a mode of discourse wherein nothing is 'beyond argument,'" which in the context of this dyad with Williamson, may be translated as "nothing is beyond hope" (122). Therefore, when Levene attempts to override the manager's negativity with phrases like "That's defeatist. . . . Let's *do* something" (24), we learn as much from Levene's argumentative tone, his idiosyncratic questions, syntax and discourse, a Jewishness implicit in the nature of his questions and judgments, as we do from Williamson's laconism. For him, "talk" is wasted on Levene; "Either way," he tells him, "You're out" (21).

In his analysis of Levene's bargaining skills, Jonathan Cullick contends that "Levene's human side is just another aspect of his sales pitch," that he is forced to "argue in monetary, not humanistic, terms, for Williamson cannot be charmed, he can only be bought" (25). On the contrary, Levene confronts that reality when Williamson rejects his offer to prove himself:

"Just give me two of the premium leads. As a 'test,' alright? As a 'test' and I promise you . . ." The twice repeated word *test*—whose biblical connotation and implied rigor coupled with *promise* strongly intimate a covenant—signals Levene's contractual commitment to outpace his reputation, his implicit endorsement of and abiding belief in himself and in the future. However, Williamson's curt reply, "I can't do it, Shel" (23), signals something entirely different: he will not "give" Levene anything, a point underscored by his condescending use of Levene's first name. Reminiscent of Howard's rejection of Willy Loman's request for an opportunity to work in New York City—"But where am I going to put you, kid" (Miller 73)—this exchange closely parallels one in Abraham Cahan's *The Rise of David Levinsky* in which Levinsky, addressed as "Dave" by a gentile with whom he was conducting business, perceived the form of address as an implicit anti-Semitic affront: "It implied that . . . I was his inferior . . . a Jew, a social pariah" (501-2).[20] The fact that the moment passes without further comment does not mean our judgment of the situation is not encouraged. On the contrary, "Mamet's aesthetic," Hudgins proposes, "relies on the audience to ferret out 'conscious' structural connections and the meaning they point to" (1996, 22). Indeed, it is by indirection that we principally ascertain Mamet's thematic concerns.

Thus, "when muscle-flexing, bullying, and all the other, as it were, actions on his list have failed" (Mendes qtd. in Kane 1996, 251), and the approaches of human decency, charity, and compassion prove fruitless, Levene, now increasingly wise to the fact that Williamson will sell but not give him the leads, moves into the second phase of his panic-driven plan, opening negotiations at 10 percent. Williamson both ups the ante and clarifies the deal: "Of what?" he asks. "Of my end what I close" (23), replies Levene, and the inverted, ethnically coded syntax emphasizes the differing discourse separating the Jewish salesman from the dominant culture and belying his business savvy. As long as power resides with individuals whose compassion is measured by "what have you done for me lately" rather than "you're a good man"—with its double meaning of mensch and producer—you're only as good or as valuable as tomorrow's sales, and Levene's promises, however sincere, have little tangible worth to Williamson, who raises the stakes, exploiting the desperate salesman: "twenty percent, and fifty bucks a lead" (24). That Levene comes to Williamson prepared to offer a bribe when all else fails strongly implies not only that Levene "realize[s] that policy is not carved in stone, despite Williamson's assertion" (Vorlicky 1995a, 35), but that he is willing to make a moral compromise to support his family in order to survive in a world inhospitable to dignity and aspirations, and he has prior knowledge that Williamson can be bought. Indeed, we wonder if

Williamson hasn't emphasized his role as an unbiased guardian of the premium leads in order to escalate their value and Levene's bid.

As the scene draws to a close, Williamson demands advance payment for the leads: "Put up or shut up," he implies, a phrase whose equivalent Yiddish expression, *Tochis afn tish,* buttocks on the table (Rosten 1989, 524), would be well known to the salesman. The deal is a simple one: two premium leads, one hundred dollars, a chance for Levene to save his job. Like the broke "deadbeats" on "the B list" who cannot even afford to "buy a fucking *toaster*" (21), Levene's offer of a thirty-dollar token payment—so insignificant an offer that it may be construed as an insult—communicates by its insufficiency both his insolvency and the impossibility of a capital investment in his own future. Paradoxically, it also lends validity to Williamson's earlier contention that Levene is not a proven closer, confirming he "talks a good game" but can't afford to play. Yet, having concluded the deal, Levene is so close he will not be deterred by his lack of hard cash. Playing for time, he endeavors to keep the deal alive by persuading Williamson to bank on him, extending credit until "tomorrow." Enigmatically, he refers to having money "back at the hotel": "I get back the hotel, I'll bring it in tomorrow. . . . I've got it at the hotel. (*Pause.*) John? (*Pause.*) We do that, for chrissake? . . . I, you know, left my wallet back at the hotel" (25-27). We wonder how Levene can function throughout the business day without his wallet. Was there any money in the wallet he left at the hotel? How could he possibly have intended to execute his plan that included the eventuality of bribery—he clearly knows that Williamson is corrupt or corruptible—without bringing money to the meeting? Or did he never intend to have to buy with cash what his reputation on the street had previously earned? Although David Sauer contends that Levene may be an accomplished salesman but "a neophyte at bribery" (150), it is more likely that he hoped the only capital he would have to invest would be verbal—the "understanding" at which Vorlicky avers they, as men, can arrive, for "All throughout the play" the salesman "espous[es] the professional doctrine of technique" whose tacit message "is that I am therefore owed certain support because of what I've done, because of who I am" (Mamet qtd. in Roudané 1986a, 76).

And why, moreover, is this man, like Teach, living in a hotel? Mamet provides us with only the barest glimpse of how much Levene has lost since the real—or imaginary—"old days," the glory days when there was no need to beg or bribe to get hot leads. "None of us really knows what those old days were like," suggests Mamet, "but we long for order, and dream of that imaginary society which would make us feel secure" (1987d, 151). Conversely, Levene's residence in a hotel provides further evidence of his insecurity and marginal status, but without the benefit of back story—typically slim in any Mamet work—we are left to surmise a number of scenarios: that Levene's commission income barely covers his daughter's care, leaving an insufficient amount of money for a home or an apartment; that either of these magnify his instability, insecurity and isolation, that before being a city drummer, he was a traveling salesman who stayed in hotels and has some measure of familiarity with them, that he, like the biblical Levites, is in *galut* (exile) similarly lacking in home and financial resources. More likely we find the import of this allusive referent in perceiving Levene as the prototypical Jew who Leslie Fiedler contends is "eternally not at home . . . lost in the nightmare of goyish history . . ." (56-57) represented in *Glengarry* by Williamson, Baylen, and the downtown bosses.

Only after Levene has exhausted all other avenues of argument does he make a last-ditch, albeit hesitant, appeal to Williamson as a human being. Notably the broken line is framed by pauses that intimate what Levene cannot say or refuses to say: "I'm asking you. As a favor to me? (*Pause.*) John. (*Long Pause.*) John: my *daughter* . . . (26). Dorothy Jacobs, whose reading of the positioning of Levene's daughter is representative, has theorized that Levene's allusive personal reference to his daughter—both at the beginning and end of *Glengarry*—conveys little genuine caring for her. Rather, in Jacobs's view, it exposes the depth of his desperation to use any ploy to sway Williamson when charm clearly has failed, thus arousing further inquiry about Levene's motivation, approach, and credibility. Indeed, "At an extreme of skepticism," she notes, "we might even question the existence of a daughter at all" (108).[21] Similarly, Linda Dorff, though discerning that "the play's dialectic" concerns "the (past) valuation and (present) devaluation of money and people," misreads Levene's intended proffering of money at the beginning and conclusion of the play as evidence that he "is not the resourceful, individualistic pioneer he would have everyone believe" (200).

On the contrary, Levene epitomizes what Mamet characterizes as "individual pragmatism." "The way to survive as an individual," he has told Desmond Christy, "is not to look for an answer from an institution" but rather "to look around you as an individual to see what it is you want as an individual and what will get it for you. It's the good part of the Frontier philosophy" predicated on an individual's securing his own survival (Christy 5). As such, Levene is an "individualistic frontiersman, the tongue-slinging man of action who 'lives on his wits'" (Malkin 156), a man whose resourcefulness is seen in the energy and emotional capital expended to meet his familial responsibilities, even at the cost of personal integrity. Likewise, his Jewishness is articulated in the distinctive tone and strength of his family instincts, both in "his ability—and need—to care for others" (Alter 1969, 114). For much like Saul Bellow's heroes, Shelly Levene, whose given name also has "the connotation of protection" (Kolatch 1967, 129), suffers from what Robert Alter terms "humanitis," the difficult business of being human. Williamson's linguistic and emotional behavior is ethnically coded as well. Because he keeps his emotions under tight control, much as he does the leads, Williamson's response to Levene's request for benevolence is perceived by him and the audience as unequivocal and unsympathetic, and implicitly less troubled. Additionally, his position that he cannot—more likely that he does not want to—extend himself in any way for Levene suggests that his decisions to abide by or impose restrictive policy pose him neither moral choices nor consequences. "The power of a person to serve," Mamet avers, "is in direct proportion to the strength of his or her resistance to the urge to control." And while "status" and "power" may be granted to us by virtue of our position, he continues, "To choose whether or not to *act* on such an urge *is* within our power" (1989b, 97). That Levene's personal appeal is perfunctorily rejected signifies Williamson's exploitation of his power to control when, as Mamet submits, he might have perceived his power as an opportunity that would have served as an "*example . . .* [of] the power to make our lives easier and ourselves less fearful" (97).

Tellingly, when Levene changes the playing field from professional to personal, Williamson is prepared "to walk," permitting the salesman's protests to fall on deaf ears: "(*Pause.*) Is that it? Is that it? You want to do business that way . . . ?" (26).[22] Ironically, Levene's lament calls direct attention to the fact that they have not been "doing business" at all. In fact, that Williamson impedes and subsequently terminates negotiations reveals that, as the salesman stated earlier, "things get *set*" (15) with regard to the premium leads. Thus when Williamson claims that he can't split the two premium leads, only one of which Levene apparently has the money to secure with a down payment, the logic of the manager's position, like the logic of the sales contest that similarly perplexes the salesman, eludes Levene. In the absence of a response to his question, "Why?" (26), we are left to wonder if Williamson is deprived of the power to negotiate, like James Lingk, the hapless mark duped into the purchase of land. In his reiterated expressions of impotence—"It isn't me"; "I can't do it, Shel"; "I wish I could" (18-25)—Williamson leaves Levene and the audience to ponder whether he is unwilling to negotiate if the price is not right, just following orders, mean-spirited, indifferent, or merely intolerant.

Like the *Glengarry* salesmen, the men Mamet worked with in a real estate office (in a temporary position he held shortly after he graduated from college) "were a force of nature. . . . They were people who had spent their whole life in sales, always working for a commission, never worming for a salary, dependent for their living on their wits, on their ability to charm. So a man once started on the downward path," Mamet recalls, "had little hope of returning. This slide was exacerbated by the fact that the salesmen were primarily performers" whose act demanded "overweening self-confidence."[23] Similarly, evidence of Levene's backpedaling and weakening resolve is notable in his apology to Williamson that bespeaks his despair coupled with a humanity extended to the latter, despite Williamson's utter indifference to Levene and the deal. It is a moment that eerily foreshadows the poignancy and powerlessness of Lingk exposed in a conversation with Ricky Roma in act 2. Given the affirmative rhythm of Levene's speech throughout their exchange, fueled by braggadocio and pride as much as by crushing need, his acknowledgment of failure is indirectly conveyed in his off-hand remark, "I'd like something off the other list," refusing as a point of pride to articulate the phrase "the B list" (27). Bitterly and with no small measure of self-pity and sarcasm, in a tone and locution that reiterate the differing ethnicity of the two men, Levene adds, "Which, very least, that I'm entitled to. If I'm still *working* here, which for the moment I guess that I am. (*Pause.*)" (27). Quickly recovering and repairing the mask, Levene employs an apology as the bridge between the present moment and the previously concluded deal implicitly mocked by the sales manager's intransigence to Levene's most recent bargaining ploy. And of promises made across this table? They are as elusive as the paltry sum that Williamson ultimately leaves on the table.

Similarly ambiguous is whether Williamson was playing by his own rules all along: both laughing at and lying to Levene when he gave him the leads from "the B list." Among the many mysteries in the play is whether the lead to the Nyborgs—which Williamson knew would kick out, assuring Levene's loss of employment—was among the two that Williamson gave him. In fact, when Levene appears to be a magician turning dead leads into live deals—coal into gold—in the second act, he and we begin to realize late in act 2 that Williamson has given him "some stiff" (25). For the moment, despite Levene's bravura performance, his abject poverty and exhausted showmanship place him on a plane with the "fucking Polacks."

Echoing similarly derisive racist sentiments, scene 2, linked associatively, thematically, and linguistically to the first, opens on Dave Moss's attempts to comfort his friend George Aaronow, whose low placement on "the board," like Levene's, presages his imminent loss of employment. Engaging Aaronow in a diatribe against the "Polacks and deadbeats" and the tightfisted Indians, Moss immediately assumes the role of instructor, asking rhetorically, "How you goan'a get on the board sell'n a Polack?"

(29). While Moss's tirade about "the Patels" "conveys a simultaneous sense of 'knowing' the Patels well enough to be able to 'teach' Aaronow about them—and of feeling helpless about their apparent impenetrability," argues Deborah Geis (1996, 126), Moss's defamatory remarks, reminiscent of Lenny Bruce's scurrilous, profane epithets, remind us that as Whitfield has noticed, "there is special animus to Jewish humor" that functions "not only as a shell against the outside world, but also a weapon against the goyim." Wryly he adds, "It too is one of the needle trades" (1984, 124).[24] Thus, when Moss concludes of "the Patels," that "They like to feel *superior* . . . A supercilious race" (29), his deprecatory grousing is a wonderfully ironic transference of criticism—either overt or subliminal—presumably aimed at Aaronow and Moss that they have displaced on the Other rather than internalized as "Jewish self-hatred," what Gilman describes as the response of a group defined as different by society, as well as by itself, to stereotypical images of its discourse.[25] Yet, despite the offensiveness of their racist jokes, the opening moments of this scene, left intentionally ambiguous, have "clear theatrical purpose." In fact, the preponderance of pauses punctuating Moss's remarks reveals them to be "diversionary," suggests Mosher, for like Levene, Moss, too, has a plan.[26] Not only is he compelled to finalize the deal that night, but like Levene, he has only one opportunity. Cautious in divulging his proposition, "he's flanneling until the point he can find a way of getting into the conversation" (Mendes qtd. in Kane 1996, 253).[27] And while Moss's racist slurs may alienate members of the audience,[28] they catalytically spark the appearance of unity between associates whose shared experiences, knowledge, frustration, insecurity, and discontent provide fertile ground for Moss's potentially fruitful business plan. In fact, Moss's stroll down memory lane—"remember when we were at Platt . . . huh? Glen Ross Farms . . . *didn't* we sell a bunch of that . . . ?" (30)—and his appeal to Aaronow's vulnerability, integrity, and innate sense of humanity advance the impression of a united front by eliciting a more secure past. In the ensuing dialogue, the interplay of "I," "you," "we," and "they"—a typical Mametic antithetical technique—implicitly underscores the trope of inclusion and exclusion sounded as early as the first scene of the play. Moreover, it serves to set the stage for Moss's sales pitch that, framed in abstractions and fabrications, draws Aaronow into a web of truths and falsehoods, entrapping him in a crisis of conscience. Put simply, Moss's deal is: "In or out. You tell me" (46).

Initially, the pairing of opposites—Moss who sketches in broad strokes and Aaronow who fills in the details—parallels a stand-up comic routine with Aaronow playing straight man for Moss, reminiscent of comparable comic riffs between Teach and Don in *American Buffalo,* most notably when Teach is pontificating on the injustices of the world and the infringement of personal freedom punctuated by Don's yeas and nays. Mirroring and parodying the *pipul shel hevel,* the traditional Talmudic mode of argument based on analogy and approximation rather than logic, which we observed in the planning of the robbery in *American Buffalo,* the implicit Judaic and pedagogical framing of this speech, complete with "send-ups of Talmudic learning" (Whitfield 1988, 68), satirize an impositional rather than a dialogic manner of instruction in which the instructor's morality and methodology are tested and exposed as flawed. Thus, when Moss presents his persuasive object lesson on the criminality and injustice of a profane world defined by its abandonment of humanity, responsibility, and respect for others, echoing the biblical figure Moses, he initially presents a line of thinking that is principled and humanistic, demanding biblical vengeance in equal measure for the injustice perpetrated.

Characteristically, Aaronow attempts to clarify and delimit "the subject of our *evening* together" (73), to borrow Levene's phrase, through a series of questions. Moss's evasions and denials, like Don's with Teach, serve to confirm what Aaronow suspects:

Aaronow: We're not actually *talking* about it.
Moss: No.
Aaronow: Talking about it as a . . .
Moss: *No.*
Aaronow: As a *robbery.*
Moss: As a "robbery"?! No.
Aaronow: *Well.* Well . . .
Moss: *Hey.* (*Pause.*)
Aaronow: So all this, um, you didn't, actually, you didn't actually go talk to Graff.
Moss: Not actually, no. (*Pause.*) (39-40)

Although the comic banter appears to be the inane chatter of a couple of incompetent crooks (Moss's "What did I say?" echoed by Aaronow's "What did you say?" is a nod to the classic routine "Who's on First"), Moss's cleverness is seen in his indirect approach *and* his choice of Aaronow. Correctly intuiting Moss's intention to steal the leads, Aaronow cuts to the quick of his argument: "What could somebody get for them?" (38), he asks directly. Thus, whether they are "just *speaking* about it" or "actually talking about it" (39), Moss attempts to charm and then coerce Aaronow into doing the deed, an act that resembles Levene's plan to influence Williamson to "Get on my side" (24), although the method, motivation, and payoff differ sharply.

Aaronow, however, presses Moss for concrete information such as "Did you talk to Graff . . . What did he say? . . . What will he pay?" the latter clearly the wrong question from the point of view of morality and legality (41). "And the moment he says that," notes Mendes, "Dave [Moss] knows he's more than just 'talking'. . ." (251), evidenced by the fact that their discussion metamorphoses from the merely theoretical to the practical. But as Lerner observes in *Jewish Renewal*, "Jews, like anyone, who has ever contemplated becoming a . . . critic of the established order, ask whether the risk is worth taking, whether enough can be accomplished to make it worth the personal pain" (73). To those who would hesitate for fear that "we might bring upon ourselves the . . . ire of the powerful," he continues, "Judaism is trying to tell us that it's worth the risk!" (73). Put simply, the "correctness" of Moss's vision on the subjects of injustice and inhumane treatment, as Hudgins has also noticed, is clearly stated, if little else is: "It's *medieval* . . . it's wrong" (32), positioning his allusions to persecution historically, as Teach has done. However, Mamet intentionally complicates the dilemma of being "for oneself" and "only for oneself" by framing the positive values of justice, independence, and ethical behavior within an immoral choice, given that "the language of morality is not identifiable by the use of a specific discourse but by the context and the use to which the words are put" (Spero 3).

Hence, when Moss tempts Aaronow with a fifty-fifty split of five thousand dollars that on its surface has the appearance of fairness and the implication of full partnership, Aaronow is more enthused about Moss's taking him into the deal and the promise of a new job with Jerry Graff—the way out of a company that would "*enslave* them, treat them like *children, and fuck them up the ass*" (36)—than he is about the money. Yet, as he subsequently learns, Moss, delivering a lecture on the unfairness of their working conditions, plays him for a fool: Moss stands to gain double Aaronow's share. Having expounded on the virtues of fair play, fair stake, and fair share, Moss shows Aaronow a bit of fair tactics and fair promises; apparently, all's fair in a world where covenants and contracts are as illusory as the principles of decency and humanity about which Moss has spoken. Given that "the promised land [of America] was no Eden," as Allen Guttmann precisely puts it, "Jews converted to the Age of Enterprise" (28), and Moss's speech reveals he has adopted its discourse. Thus, while Roudané reads Aaronow as "simply baffled" (1986b, 41) and Tuttle as "naive to the point of being easily manipulated" (165), Aaronow is cannier than he lets on. To paraphrase a Yiddish witticism: "When a fool keeps quiet, you can't tell whether he is foolish or clever" (Galvin and Tamarkin 306). In an ingenious reversal of scene 1, where we observe that Williamson can be bought for a price, Aaronow tenaciously holds his ground, rejecting out of hand Moss's scheme, intimidation, and promise of a "big reward" (42). He, too, manages to "keep it simple": "you know," he says, "it's a *crime*" (46, 40).

In this classic opposition of simpleton and wiseman, whose wisdom is converted to evil, one that characterizes biblical and Yiddish narrative, the simpleton wisely differentiates wisdom from folly. "The world speaks of the right of might," suggests Benjamin Blech, "but [the] Jew recognizes the might of right," a central tenet of Judaism explicitly conveyed in the Hebrew word for wisdom, *khakhmah*, which poses and answers the crucial question: "What is power?" (123). However, what Moss employs to persuade Aaronow is *khukhmah*, the clever speech of a khukham, a wise guy, posing as a wise man. If Moss has sought to encourage Aaronow to commit the deed that he cannot execute himself, he has misjudged Aaronow and shown himself to be lacking in both confidence and character. For as Roskies reminds us, *khakhmah* can be "used for evil as well as for good," but the laconic man who feared God (Job 1:1), "always carried positive associations" (44).[29]

Paralleling the previous scene, their apparently circuitous conversation, like those of characters in Chekhov and Pinter, increasingly manifests itself as Moss's inane and inept attempt to seduce Aaronow into *doing* the deed. "Coveting the power and income of Mitch and Murray, who reap the profits of others' labor," Moss, argues Tuttle, "doles out the dirty work of breaking into the office to whoever is desperate enough to be his minion." And if "Swindling a colleague proves no cause for consternation," he continues, it is that having observed Williamson, "who knowingly doles out worthless leads to those salesmen whose livelihoods are in the most jeopardy," Moss concludes that "treachery is the surest path to success" (164). Yet, if treachery appears on the surface as the fast track to success, for Moss it is a function of his inability to act independently—or otherwise— and a conscious distribution of the moral and legal burden. It is a conscious strategy to hide his inadequacy rather than a primary cause of action. In contrast to Teach, who imagines himself in business, Moss knows that the "hard part" of "Going into business for yourself" is "the *act*" (35). In this regard he closely resembles Moses's failure to be "self-assertive," one manifested by his preference for sharing "the burden of authority" (Ackerman 84). Despite his skill as a strategist with Aaronow and (presumably) Graff, Moss's hesitation to act without counsel and cooperation, paralleling Moses's inclusion of Aaron in the incident of the water and the rock, an appropriation of divine power for which he was subsequently denied entry to the Promised Land, exposes him as a brilliant idea man but no more. Such an individual would surely fail Don's definition of a "stand-up guy," an individual with the "Skill and talent and the balls to arrive at your own *conclusions*" (Mamet 1977, 4).

Moss has made a sage decision in bringing Aaronow into the scheme as a partner in crime because the latter's low standing on the board implicitly suggests a high degree of interest and obvious motive for his receptivity and participation, he has also sought to complement his big mouth with Aaronow's taciturnity: what Don would appreciate as "depth on the team" (1977, 53). Similarly, it appears that he has sought in the amiable schlemiel, the archetypal wimp whose self-worth is negligible, someone to whom he can delegate his personal responsibility to deliver the promised leads to Graff. "I have to get those leads tonight. That's something I have to do" (44), Moss tells Aaronow, but because "It's not something for nothing. . . . you have to go" (43), ironically inverting what Mamet has characterized as the negative aspect of basic American "frontier ethic": "always something for nothing" (Bigsby 1985, 111). And although Aaronow doesn't quite follow the plan—"Why are you doing this at *all* . . . ?" (45), he asks quizzically—because Moss's sophistry impedes his stated intent to "keep it simple" (46), Moss's dissembling is a marvelous linguistic tool to impress Aaronow with great truths, with his punctilious planning, and with promises of a big payoff. It also serves to communicate in a manner that is neither dogmatic nor sentimental those values that the playwright shares, such as the virtues of independent, analytic thinking, the pursuit of justice, knowledge, and wisdom, and strength of character.

Moss's last attempt at coercion is a veiled threat of biblical retribution, not unlike the metaphorical punishment he imagined exacting on Mitch and Murray by the theft of the premium leads that he knew would "hurt them. . . . Where they live" (37). While admittedly a accomplished speaker, fine strategist, and fair teacher, Moss, however, has not followed his own plot/lecture/act to its logical or dramatic conclusion, neither anticipating nor preparing for the eventuality of Aaronow's opposition. Rather like Teach, unprepared for a quiz or a challenge to his plan, Moss, who apparently knows as little about law as Teach does about numismatics, extemporaneously and inventively coins new definitions for criminal actions, hoping that playing fast and lose with fixed terms of art such as "accomplice" and "an accessory. Before the fact" (45) will buy Aaronow's silence and assure Moss's protection from criminal liability. Unable to persuade Aaronow to commit the robbery through *khukhmah,* crafty speech, Moss, a *momzer*—an individual who is irreverent, clever, quick-witted, and offensive (Rosten 1989, 373)—if there ever was one, now attempts to preclude Aaronow from speaking out by intimidation, literally assigning to him the role of scapegoat. If "they *take* me," Moss warns, he will name his accomplice. And preposterous as it may first appear, Aaronow is buffaloed into thinking, "here I'm a *criminal*" (45).

Having had enough of double-speak, what he wants is a dose of straight talk, but in stark contrast to his former loquacity, Moss rejects outright Aaronow's plaintive request: "*talk* to me" (45). In this case straight talk would illumine what we, the audience, know: that as mastermind of the plan, Moss, according to the definitions and terms of American and English jurisprudence, would surely be guilty of being an accessory *before* the fact, defined as "One who orders, counsels, encourages, or otherwise aids and abets another to commit a felony," though absent at the commission of the crime.[30] In fact, taking this eventuality into account and believing he is providing himself with an airtight alibi that would limit his exposure to prosecution, Moss's scheme includes a plan for him to go to the movies and then appear at the Como Inn, where, no doubt, others would vouch for his presence at the time of the crime. However, from the perspective of Jewish law and ethical practice, it is Moss whose action would be considered morally and legally offensive. Guilty of the "stumbling block principle," the placing of a metaphorical obstacle before the weak, the ignorant, and the inexperienced, or tempting one to do evil, he would be viewed as a "moral accomplice" responsible for "deliberately offering misleading advice for selfish reasons of personal gain"; whereas the recipient of advice, having confidence in the sincerity of the advisor, is considered by law blinded to the trap laid before him (Lev. 19:14). But Mamet puts an ironic spin on a clear application of this ethical injunction given that Aaronow is not "blind" to Moss's purpose, despite his protestations, nor is he absolved from the responsibility of every individual to act in a moral and ethical manner as if he or she were forewarned, because, as Spero explains, from the Jewish perspective, moral judgment applies equally to motivations and intentions (137). What Mamet leaves deliberately vague is the extent of Aaronow's liability, that is, whether he would legally be considered an accomplice to the crime at all, given that this term of art describes "one who *knowingly,* voluntarily and with common intent unites with the principal offender in the commission of a crime." As an individual who neither reported nor impeded the commission of the crime, however, he may be liable as an accessory during the fact.[31] From a ethical perspective Aaronow's errors of omission evince moral lapse, yet it is clearly no accident that Mamet does not reveal the penalty—or the individual involved in the perpetration of the crime—until the end of act 2. As questions conclude this scene, much as they serve to advance it, the play implies that "Law and morals impinge upon human activity with different force and range" (B. Cohen 12).

That Moss's criminal scheme lacks fair play is obvious; less transparent is his motivation. Indeed, when pressed on the subject he not only refuses to respond to Aaronow's question, "You need money? Is that the . . ." (46), recalling the strapped Levene motivated by the security that money buys, in typically Jewish form Moss responds to Aaronow's question with a question, turning the focus from the financial to the psychological: "What I need is not the . . . what do *you* need . . .?" (46). Imposing unfair rules on the hapless sucker who reminds him he "didn't ask to be" a party to Moss's scheme, Moss coldly dismisses Aaronow's litany of anguished questions that fall under the heading of: "Why me?" with the stinging rejoinder, "Tough luck, George" (45), leading Bigsby to conclude that "Relationship . . . is a trap, communication a snare and friendship a means of facilitating betrayal" (1985, 118). However, to the schlemiel, which Aaronow surely is, "Tough luck" is the only kind of luck a luckless schlemiel knows. For his part, Moss is not the cold, calculating tough guy he pretends to be. Neither Williamson setting down policy as if it were law, nor Moses presenting the Decalogue to the Jewish people as an ethical way of life, *he* is the inheritor of the tough luck here. Misrepresenting himself to Aaronow and Graff, Moss reveals himself to be "a furious nobody" (Christiansen 1984, 2), who deceives himself as well as the others.

Like "Many Jewish American comedians and comic writers" Moss doesn't "drip with suffering." A wise guy rather than a "wisdom figure," he recalls Jewish comedians who, Anthony Lewis argues, "have traditionally posed as either predator or prey (the metaphor taken from Lenny Bruce), antagonistic or ingratiating." Lewis continues that these individuals "have found these postures not simply good performance attitudes, but two perfect vehicles through which they could comment, consciously or unconsciously, on their being Jews" (62). Like them, Moss is "not simply [an] angry social critic or born loser"; he is an "angry Jewish critic and Jewish loser" (62). We recall Levene's earlier remark to Williamson in scene 1 that in "the old days," a term that repeatedly animates the theme of the Jew for whom past and present are integral, Moss, Jerry Graff, Mitch, and Murray "*lived* on the business I brought in" (22). If Levene were not just exaggerating his earnings to inflate his status, then this Mametic clue, what the playwright terms a "tell," alludes to years of Moss's discontent with himself and his job—did he work *with* or *for* Jerry Graff, we wonder—and a discernible decline in standing and fortune, pointedly underscored by his being rebuffed by a schlemiel. Thus, as the scene concludes, Moss sees no alternative but to seek out Levene, an equally desperate salesman with a good line and bum leads.

Vorlicky contends that Levene is the "unsuspecting victim of Moss's plan" (1995a, 32), and while his premise has validity, I believe that although clearly exploited, Levene perceives collaboration with Moss as an opportunity and an investment in his own future (the chance about which he spoke with Williamson), closely paralleling the dream opportunity that he sells to the Nyborgs. In short, from his vantage point, Levene has little to lose. Having stooped to a scheme of bribery and learned a secular meaning for the word "Respect," Levene, who has bartered his pride and integrity, is humiliated by his inability to provide for his family. And faced with the loss of his job, it is either "Do the Dutch" (101) or do the heist. With the former, there is hope that suicide will put him out of misery, but without the least expectation that he is worth more dead than alive—as Willy Loman believes he is. The promise of a substantial cash bonus and a job offer from Jerry Graff is not only seductive, it is, more importantly, life-affirming. Driven to unethical behavior by the pressures of familial responsibilities, Levene finds himself trapped in a dilemma, a perspective from which he deceives himself into believing that his crime is justified. Thus in Mamet's dramatization of corruptibility, the Levene/Levite figure sacrifices righteousness for what he believes—or prays—is the right reason. While Levene's choice is clearly unethical, Mamet provides sufficient motivation for it to be understandable.[32] It is a compassionate position shared by Jewish tradition as well, namely that "a sin committed from good motives [such as stealing to provide for one's family] is more meritorious than a legal act performed with indifferent motivation" (B. Cohen 12).

"Robbery, the alternative method of escape Moss finally proposes," observes Steven Price, proves "no escape at all since it merely repeats the same course of action pursued by others" (1996, 7). In fact, seduced by temptation, the invocation of actors reenacting previously scripted roles "accounts in part for the atavistic quality of their language and actions: they re-enact crimes so ancient, so formative, so paradigmatic, that they have already passed into myth" (7). But is that not Mamet's intent? Rather than the arch-conspirator he appears to be, Moss has been cast as a parodic Jewish figure whose plan to commit theft exposes the most inflammatory of anti-Semitic canards: Jewish conspiracy. Those critics who view Moss as a diabolical principle and who see his disloyalty, rebellious behavior, and desire for vengeance, conquest, and personal power as manifestations of corruption overlook, as Walter H. Sokel elucidates in another context, "the importance of seeing that principle embodied in a Jew" (167). On this point Ruby Cohn recognizes that the three Jewish characters, Levene, Moss, and Aaronow, "speak similarly in an argot of questions, elisions, interruptions and pleonastic obscenities" (1991, 166). Yet their linkage to Judaism is discernible not merely in their patterns of speech. They are aligned in their disloyalty, desire for personal wealth, destructive assertion of will, and delineation as thieves and liars—all of which bespeaks the mythological portrait of the Jew that has contributed to their diabolization."[33] Importantly, Mamet refutes this odious stereotypical image and mind-set— implicitly addressed in *American Buffalo*—by humanizing his working men who, continually tested, tenaciously pursue some measure of economic independence and dignity in a world hostile to these goals through tactical and tensile strength of mind and character and by empowering their outspokenness on the subject of injustice, even when their lives, livelihood, and freedom are (con)tested. Put simply, Mamet's parodic Jewish characters "have found useless the virtues of compromise with our environment" (Mamet 1987d, 74).

As scene 3 opens, Roma linguistically closes the gap between James Lingk, the occupant of an adjacent booth in the Chinese restaurant, and himself by initiating a conversation in what amounts to the shortest scene and the longest-running sales pitch in the play. "[A]ll train compartments smell vaguely of shit" (47), Roma muses, recalling Levene's favorite profanity, his opening gambit, a vulgar, provocative, and irreverent monologue that immediately engages Lingk's attention—and the audience's. Evoking the world of the urban drummer commuting back and forth from the northern suburbs of Chicago on "the El," and its historical referent, the railroad, whose role in the history of business of America and its hub, Chicago, is inextricably linked to the traveling salesmen. Unifying the mundane and the profane, much like the older Glengarry salesmen, Roma strikes a balance between gentility and vulgarity that closely mirrors "a form of verbal capital" that Timothy B. Spears has recognized as common to the traveling salesman and urban drummer alike, just as the proffering of alcohol was as "customary component" of the salesman's performance as his seizing the psychological advantage to close the sale (107-08, 219). Neither greenhorn nor second-generation Jew, Roma and his "flashy clothes, dirty jokes, and habitual treating for drinks," nevertheless are aligned to "the most frequently criticized aspects of the old-time [Jewish] drummer's ways"(7).[34] In fact, in *Glengarry Glen Ross* those aspects of the traveling salesman and Jewish urban drummers are conspicuously associated with the character of Roma, a leading man whose "patent leather hair," silk suits, and paronomasia were noted by critics and audiences alike in Mosher's New York production (Brustein 1987, 71). In seizing upon the salesman—"a quixotic knight . . . a liminal trickster and performer"—as the focus of his play, Mamet masterfully merges ethnic history with that of the salesman to whom "special status in American cultural history" has accrued (Spears xiii, 10-17).

In scene 3 of act 1 when Roma consummates a deal with Lingk and in act 2 when he desperately tries to save it, echoing Levene's pitch to the

Nyborgs, "his patois, and his purpose in speaking the lines," Hudgins maintains, present "the most moving and emphatic statement of the central theme of choice" (1996, 33).[35] Nonetheless, critics swayed by their perception of Roma and his ostensibly offensive speech, which marginalizes and humiliates others, "reject both the validity and significance of Roma's speeches" (33), whose mimesis, unmistakable throughout Mamet's canon, is echoed in the similarly inspirational remarks of Bernie to his daughter in Mamet's two-person play, *Reunion* (1977): "You got to take your chance for happiness/You got to grab it" (23-24). Dorff's view of Roma is representative. For her, Roma is "The most skilled con man in the office [whose] protean duplicity leaves doubt about the veracity of everything he says" and whose narrative technique is little more than "an attempt to distract him [Lingk] from the sale" (204). Yet that narrative skill and performance art align Roma with the Jewish salesmen in the office from whom he has learned and perfected his artistry. Like them, he endeavors to empower his "leads" and himself in order to survive solely on his own performance—part *chutzpah,* part absurd genius, and part comic invention.

One reason for this generalized misreading of the character of Roma is that "scruffy surfaces," as Hudgins has it, impede our valuing Roma's stoical philosophy of life. Moreover, Roma's rejection of powerlessness, his demonstrated, if rarely expressed, *chasidut,* or kindliness, and his historical view of life link him to the other Jewish salesmen. Ten years younger than the others and lacking overt Jewish characteristics, most pointedly of name, locution, and overt complicity in criminal behavior, Roma nonetheless vigorously builds what the playwright terms a "line of affirmatives" (Allen 40) that bears striking similarity to Jewish tradition and law: he advocates self-reliance, the belief that principles of morality and conduct in periods of crisis must be at the discretion of the individual who, "guided by conscience, a sense of justice, experience, and wisdom" must determine conduct (B. Cohen 18). Further, he values "the pleasures of food and sex" that halakhic tradition accepts as a "legitimate . . . positive good" (Spero 47). Moreover, like the older Jewish salesmen, he confronts the world "through the force of the imagination," confident in language's "ability to negotiate, bargain, protect . . . and ensure survival" (Baumgarten 45, 87). And if the speed of Roma's delivery offers little opportunity to evaluate his affirmative rhythms and philosophy, when Roma finally comes up for air, sighing, "It's been a long day" (50) as a means of engaging the reticent Lingk in conversation and extending his customer's stay in the restaurant, we gain a clearer picture of his monologue's salient elements and of his reserve energy that derive from having "the strength . . . of *acting each day* without fear." Not only does he reject powerlessness—"no to *that.* I say" (49)—but he chooses to improve the lot of others through compassion, or what passes for compassion. A marked distinction, of course, is that whereas Levene and Aaronow make the moral decision to lie "as a means of survival . . . [and] the force of circumstance" (Gilman and Katz 321), Roma's lies ruin people's lives. Clearly, Roma is not Jewish, but in the ethnic coding of this play he is coded as such. In sharp contrast to the other non-Jews in the play, notably Williamson and Baylen, Roma is the more sympathetic figure. Independent and affirmative, his defiance of authority is nothing short of *chutzpah,* and his survival—indeed success—in the world of cutthroat sales is predicated on quick wit and dazzling linguistic dexterity. And as such, I believe that he "acts" Jewish in the broadest sense of the word. On this point, Joe Mantegna, who portrayed the role of Roma in both American premiere productions, recalls that "One of the great joys" of this role was "the constant affirmation" of power. Rejecting the easy interpretation that "This guy's really despicable," he cites among Roma's talents, temerity, and philosophy, his "confidence . . . respect . . . compassion, caring" (Kane 1992, 257, 256). However, to most readers and audiences, Roma's confidence betokens a confidence man who tailors his presentation to each situation and circumstance.[36] In fact, the playwright fosters this perception through his theatricalization of the sales pitch, whether delivered by Roma in the Chinese restaurant or subsequently by Levene in the Nyborgs' kitchen, implicitly fusing betrayals of confidence and conscience with the American cultural tradition of the confidence man. In *Postmodern Theatric[k]s,* Geis presents a cogent argument on the strong correlation that exists "between narrative (especially monologic) language and deception," one especially apparent in Mamet's "business plays"—*American Buffalo* (1977), *Water Engine* (1977), and *Glengarry Glen Ross* (1983)—wherein "monologic language enacts the consummate sales pitch" precluding interruption and permitting the player "to appear 'personal' and 'confessional' even when he or she is only acting" (1993, 99, 104). Hence, although the confessions that we overhear are intensified by the lateness of the hour and the crucible of the sales contest (paralleling a similar pattern in Chekhov's *Three Sisters* in which a fire creates a credible milieu for confessions), Roma's "confessions"—canned as they are—are coupled with "a line of affirmatives" that immediately inform the character and establish a credible linguistic and emotional link between two strangers.

Once again Mamet turns to ethnic and literary history to link his disconnected salesmen in the present to a recollected or illusory past that glorifies them. Of all the men in the real estate office, Roma in particular recalls confidence men with a sharper image for whom all ideas are facts; thereby he succeeds in gaining Lingk's confidence not once but twice. "In the national iconography shaped early by the historical uniqueness of experience open to the nation, by the Romantic faith in the self, and by the competitive energies of capitalism," claims Warwick Wadlington, "Americans are peddlers of assurance" (10). Hence the promise of America became synonymous with the Yankee Peddler, a benign figure who, like the Jewish peddler who replaced him (subsequently conducting business in the urban centers of the nation), was "the icon of self-confidence" whose slyness in trading took the form of "a game of merchant self-reliance versus customer self-reliance" (11). In fact, confidence men, as they were known, were so persuasive that their customers showed their confidence in them by a purchase of land (195). The analogues to *Glengarry Glen Ross* are clear. Yet Mamet's great admiration for such a figure may derive not merely from the "realm of appearances" (Klaver 179) but from the depth of character of the players, from the artistry and invention of their performance, and from the sheer skill of being able to provide a living solely on the ability to charm, the courage to face crushing daily challenges, and the power of positive thinking—what the playwright has termed "inspirational . . . classic Stoic philosophy" (Allen 41). Such a figure was well known to him. "The gift for cunning gab seems to gallop in my family," observes Mamet, whose grandfather, Naphthali, "sold ten-cent insurance policies" and could "charm the birds off the trees" (Lahr 1995, 33).

Roma, who also has "the gift for cunning gab," moves in to close the last sale that will put him "over the top" on the contest board and put a lock on his Cadillac and $6,000 bonus. The leading man, Roma literally and figuratively closes the gap between Lingk and himself by suggesting a drink, exchanging intimacies, the most private of which is identity, and moving to join Lingk in his booth.[37] No sooner has he suggested another round of the gimlets that Lingk is drinking to extend his presence in the restaurant than the salesman covers the table with a map of Florida, the sales pitch ongoing: "What is that? Florida. Glengarry Highlands. Florida. Florida. '*Bullshit*'. . . . This is a piece of land" (50-51). Voicing the question that has stumped both critics and audiences given that no land is ever visible, Elizabeth Klaver wonders if the Glengarry salesmen are "selling real land," noting that "land appears in the play only in the context of real estate contracts, leads, and the swirl of talk and theatricality of the salesmen—the written and spoken languages of a semiotic and performative universe" where opportunity supplants "referents or products" (177). For Roma, however, a man grounded in reality, profit and loss are measured in concrete terms: to eat or to starve, which aligns his con-artistry with that of his Jewish colleagues for whom the business of survival means earning a living solely on one's wits. Echoing Levene and Moss on the subject, Roma's link to Lingk parallels one articulated earlier in the evening by Moss to Aaronow: "You go in the door. I . . . 'I got to *close this fucker,* or I don't eat lunch'" (30). Yet, as the concluding scene of act 1 makes abundantly clear, Roma differs from the Jewish characters in his ability to dictate an alliance with Williamson—to "speak his language," as it were, to assure his own survival—and in his lack of understanding of the Jews' paranoia, sensibilities, loyalty, and shared experience.

Act 2 reveals innumerable reversals in tone, tension, speech, action and setting, a ransacked real estate office that clearly confirms a robbery and biblical retribution no longer "In the abstract . . ." (46). Worried about Mitch's and Murray's loss, Moss's and his own fate, and his impending interview with the officer investigating the break-in, Aaronow repeatedly asks anyone who will listen whether Mitch and Murray were insured.[38] Yet, voicing ethical and humane concerns, he reveals through his interminable questions a stereotypical portrait of the Jew obsessed with knowledge, crippled by worry, gripped by paranoia, and powerless. Thus, although his concern is genuine, typical of his personality, he clearly worries about "What kind of outfit are we running where . . . where anyone. . . .Where criminals"—himself included—"can come in" (58). Roma's question, "What do *you* care . . . ?" not only focuses attention on Aaronow's overwrought state of mind and preoccupation with the certain loss of his job—"I'm, I'm, I'm, I'm fucked on the board" (55-56)—but it lays bare both Roma's talent for sarcasm and limited understanding of Aaronow's coded speech. In short, in a business in which "Close makes the man," Aaronow believes he is "no fucking good" (57). Although Roma's "generous attribution of talent to his colleagues" underscores Aaronow's, and the other salesmen's, "tenacity and courage in an untenable situation" (Hudgins 1996, 40) where judgment of performance obviates judgment of character, Roma's philosophy ultimately leads to his success and their failure. "Fuck that shit, George," Roma says. "You're a, *hey,* you had a bad month. You're a good man, George" (57), an appellation whose truth will be revealed in Aaronow's humanness, decency, and outrage, though the top salesman "is really interested in what's gone from his drawers" (Mendes qtd. in Kane 1996, 260). However, Aaronow, for whom "worry is . . . a handy mask for a basic feeling of unattractiveness and unworthiness" (Mamet 1989b, 137), has nothing in his drawers to worry about. Rather, when he confesses that his mind is "in other places" (56), namely Williamson's office where Baylen is interrogating Moss, Aaronow implies that he has more to worry about than "the board."

As his anxiety about his own interview with Baylen escalates, Aaronow seeks Roma's advice. And just as he advised Lingk to act "*each day* without fear" (49), Roma dispenses words of wisdom: "Always tell the truth" (61).

The irony is rich coming from someone who rarely does. Moreover, Mamet satirizes the absurd situation by having Roma stage a mock interrogation of his own that in retrospect reveals the sharp division in sensibility, history, and experience of the Jew and gentile and foreshadows the anti-Semitic interrogation to which Aaronow will be subjected. "Were you the guy who broke in?" Roma inquires, and when Aaronow responds in the negative, Roma concludes—erroneously—that he has "nothing to hide" (61), whereas Aaronow knows that innocence of a crime provides no protection for him. In fact, as this schlemiel well understands, telling the truth may be "the easiest thing to remember" (61) but the hardest part to live with. In not telling the truth as he thinks he knows it, he undertakes the conscious moral decision to be dishonest. Or to phrase it differently, when the choice is between the betrayal of a friend—which the Talmud maintains is closer than a fraternal relationship—and the betrayal of the truth, which is the greater evil: having knowledge or using it against an individual for destructive ends, as Williamson subsequently does?

Holding a personal vigil during Moss's interrogation, Aaronow agonizes over his predicament in silence, while Roma's scathing indictment of Williamson is a collective expression of disgust and disdain for authority and individual assertion of power. That Williamson understands and responds to Roma underscores a critical fact: for all of his professional and personal similarities to his Jewish colleagues, Roma and Williamson "speak" the same language, one that sharply differentiates the gentiles from the Jews. Seeking to blame Williamson for the injustice wrought on them all, Roma habitually maligns him and marginalizes the minorities on whom they are all dependent for their living, scoring his point to the office manager with whom, as the conclusion reveals, he has the upper hand. "Fuck that, John. You know your business, I know mine. Your business is being an asshole." As he concludes with the warning, "I'm going to . . . figure out a way to have your *ass*" (63), Levene, whose "ass" is virtually on the line, bursts into the office. The transformation of Levene, whose hangdog demeanor, miserable prospects, and pitiable begging revealed a man at the end of his rope in scene 1, is striking; Levene is all moxie. "Get the *chalk*. Get the *chalk* . . . get the *chalk!*" (63), he shouts in his familiar triadic rhythm. Not only is "the Machine" back, he's back on top.[39] And he's buying lunch, immediately recalling his image of "the sport" (echoing Teach's alleged springing for "coffee . . . cigarettes . . . a *sweet roll*" [1977, 10]) evoked in scene 1. Confident that he's not merely passed the test, he's won the lottery, Levene is bursting with pride and satisfaction further enhanced by his having closed miserable "deadbeat magazine subscription leads" (63), a point he underscores with a significant gesture: slapping the contract on the Prophet of

Doom's desk. And lest John Williamson miss the scope, size, and significance of his sale, Levene frames his *tour de force* in figures, for which his
affection is well established: "Eighty-two fucking grand. And twelve in
commission. John . . ." (63), reminding Williamson and the audience that
the "Effective commercial traveler [and urban drummer] not only closed
sales but also kept their eye on the complex web of factors that went toward
the profitability of those sales" (Spears 63).

The first to congratulate Levene and denote the return of "the
Machine" is the ever humane and generous George Aaronow, who at the
moment is summoned to the office for his dreaded interview with Baylen.
Passing Moss on the way out of Williamson's office, he overhears and
correctly understands Moss's reiterated and ethnically coded admonition:
"Anyone talks to this guy's an *asshole* . . ." And although Roma typically
mocks Moss's fiery temper and oratorical hyperbole ("What, they beat you
with a rubber bat?"), Moss's explosive retort, "Fuckin' cop's got no right talk
to me that way, I didn't rob the place . . ." (65-66), is consistent with his
previously articulated distrust of oppressive authority, disgust with injustice,
and anger, paralleling that of the biblical Moses. More importantly, it
presages the comments of the apparently meek Aaronow whose ensuing
vocalized outrage is truly notable.

Shelly Levene's recounting of the tale of his sale is a wonderful piece of
theatre, its message of empowerment both entertaining and inspiring.
However, in contrast with Levene's story, in which presumably he held
Harriett and Bruce Nyborg in rapt attention in their kitchen by inspiring
them to believe in themselves, his performance in the office is continually
interrupted by the disgruntled Moss. Trying to regain center stage, Levene
begins anew, but he is caught in the crossfire between Roma and Moss, who
silences the effusive salesman with "Shut the fuck up." While it is indeed
possible to read Moss's demeanor as evidence of "a mean streak" (69), his
angry exchange with Roma serves to mask his intent to remain in the office,
when clearly there is no work to do, to ascertain whether Aaronow or Levene
is going to give him up to Baylen.

Counterpointing Roma's resonant ranting, generated by the loss of a
month's work and the fear of interruption of income, and the detail that
embellishes Levene's story, Moss's recapitulation of the interview with
Baylen is atypically cryptic, his reticence lending credence to the theory that
Moss really *did* commit the robbery or that more ensued in the inner office
than Moss cares to share in the public forum. Thus what remains unspoken
by the bombastic Moss is more potent by implication, serving as an
ethnically coded warning to Aaronow to prepare himself for a brutal
interrogation among strangers. Ironically, although we think we know that

Moss did not rob the office, essentially because he told us in scene 2 that he "has spoken on this too much" (43), Aaronow clearly thinks that he did and endeavors to protect his friend. Thus, although Aaronow is in a position to betray Moss, he chooses not to, Mamet tells Bigsby, "because it is more important to him to keep a promise" (1992, 215).

While Aaronow undergoes a trial by tirade in the inner office, Moss and Roma are locked in a verbal battle of wits and words in the outer office over personality, performance, and ranking on the board. What is increasingly apparent is that Moss, who repeatedly threatens to go home, has remained in the office to lend moral support to Aaronow—and to evaluate his friend's ability to withstand the interrogation. Beyond the sound and the fury, it becomes startlingly clear that if Levene has sold eight units, then Moss has slipped to third place in the sales contest, Aaronow to last. That is, of course, unless Aaronow gives Moss up and he goes to jail, which, given Aaronow's fragile state when he sticks his head out of the office asking for coffee, appears to be a distinct possibility. Given the hostility of the exchange between Moss and Roma, punctuated by the mightily frustrated Levene, whose story of the sale to the Nyborgs is continually interrupted by "Fuck *you,*" "fuck the leads," "fuckin' garbage," and "fuck is *that* supposed to mean?" Aaronow's meek request, "Can we get some coffee . . . ?" temporarily halts the torrent of verbal warfare long enough for Moss to inquire of Aaronow, "How ya doing? (Pause.)" (66-68), a phrase of encouragement that seems incompatible with his hostile behavior to Roma and goes relatively unnoticed by the others in the office. But as Worster remarks, "the power to remain silent under great pressure to speak" evidences Aaronow's notable "strength in silence . . . easily missed" in this scene and play dominated by speech (386). Moreover, in this situation, it confirms that Moss, having first-hand knowledge of the interrogation, has genuine compassion for his friend.

When Moss finally leaves the office, suggests Mendes, Levene "should walk out and go down the road with Moss and say, 'Hey, now what happened last night? What happened in the room?'" (Kane 1996, 249-50). Yet, at that moment Roma both picks up the dropped thread of Levene's narration, "You were saying?" and draws him back into the story of the sale to the Nyborgs by throwing him cues and shifting tenses that situate the act and action in the present moment: "Come on. Come on," he says, "you got them in the kitchen, you got the stats spread out . . . you can *smell* it. Huh? Snap out of it, you're eating her *crumb* cake" (71-72). Typically loquacious, Levene is here silent, distracted more by the unspoken communication between Moss and himself than by Moss's derogatory invective. However, animated by Roma's interest, he responds to and rewards the attentive listener by reiterating eidetic lines of his *spiel.* "'What we have to do is *admit* to ourself that we see that opportunity . . . and *take* it,'" he continues, his *carpe diem* message to the Nyborgs intended to motivate them as much as himself. Wrapping up both the sale and the story, Levene concludes, "'And that's it.' And we *sit* there" (72). Not unlike Sholem Aleichem's hero, Tevye, a peddler of cheese, who, as Roskies observes, is possessed of the "ability to reshape personal griefs and collective tragedies" through narrative (1995, 156), Levene is sustained by his own storytelling talents, or to be more precise, "his ability to alter the nature of experience by narrating it" (167). Not merely an escape from reality, which includes his complicity in the robbery of the leads, storytelling for Levene, like those Jewish storytellers who precede him, serves as "communal release . . . token[ing] an heroic past" (174). It is a communal activity that establishes a link between the past and the present, much as Mamet does.

Inspired by an audience, the irrepressible Levene cannot refrain from performing the rest of his shtick for Roma, relating how he "overpowered them [the Nyborgs] with rhetorical force" (Malkin 158). "I say, *fuck* it, we're going to go the whole route. I plat it out eight units. Eighty-two grand. I tell them: 'This is now. This is that *thing* that you've been dreaming of, you're going to find that suitcase on the train. . . . the bag that's full of money.'" Recounting how he handed them the pen and sat silently for twenty-two minutes, Levene concludes both sale and tale, triumphant, "Like in the *old* days" (72-73). Laying out the terms of his contractual arrangement with the Nyborgs, Levene expects Roma and the audience to believe that he is capable of remaining silent for twenty-two minutes, a feat of mythic significance almost as remarkable as his sale. While Jacobs and Almansi, for example, are among the critics who have read this scene as a seduction, presumably viewing the pen as a phallic image concomitant with the Nyborgs' "coital" slumping, Levene's story of this successful "double fuck," as Jacobs puts it (111), concludes not with the Nyborgs "*imperceptibly slumped*" (74), but with a solemn ritual that unites the couple and salesman physically and spiritually.

Bigsby has observed that Mamet's *Glengarry* salesmen, beyond the image of "hawking dreams for hard cash," are "story-tellers, actors of genuine skill who respond to the human need for reassurance . . . and belief" (1992, 214-15). However, the idea that certain people by their verbal intercession can inspire others is a fundamental tenet of Judaism. Notably, Levene's extended arm and the celebratory drink that consummates the sale have a distinctly ritualistic and biblical resonance. For the biblical referent, one turns naturally to the outstretched hand or arm as a sign of divine power typically associated with Moses (Gen. 31: 29; Mic. 2:

1). Similarly, American Jewish history and humor illumine this scene. Harry Roskolenko's recollections in *The Time That Was Then* casts light on the ritual dialectic and culminating gesture associated with commercial activity between Jews whose discourse was and is highly theatrical. The purchase of a suit on Orchard Street, he recalls, was "something of a Yiddish drama done in mock tragedy. It was inventive, if without known script—commedia dell'arte, totally . . . because it had a myth within its circumlocutions—the *landsman* myth." Characteristically a *schnapps,* or several, were consumed to consummate and sweeten the deal after typically emotional, argumentative exchanges, reminding us that Roma buys Lingk a gimlet to consummate his deal (94-96). But lest we forget that Levene has the Nyborgs in the kitchen, Jenna Joselit reminds us that "kitchen Judaism," that favorite phrase linking "cuisine and culture" (1994, 171), presupposed "the inviolability and sanctity of the Jewish kitchen" manifested in home cooking. This is hilariously mocked by Harriett Nyborg who reveals that she is no *baleboste,* a Jewish homemaker, when she serves Levene store-bought crumb cake (217). Even Roma, who subsequently does ten minutes on "Home Cooking" that would do Lenny Bruce proud, knows enough to add, "Fuck *her . . .*" (72).

Coming off the high of his sale and his story and blindly exuding confidence in the future unaware that his eight-unit sale is a Pyrrhic victory, Levene conveys his inspirational and characteristically Jewish message of resilience to Williamson, "What I'm *saying* to you: things can *change*" (76). Or, more particularly, they have changed with Levene's robbery of the office and betrayal of himself. And although profoundly unnerved by Williamson's implication "if the sale [to the Nyborgs] sticks, it will be a miracle" (75), Levene prefers to believe that his eighty-two-thousand-dollar sale has literally secured him the promised land, a fantasy vacation to Hawaii, and the Cadillac, the salesman's dream car. Moreover, that it has saved his job, enabling him to meet his familial obligations and survive another day, and figuratively won him a free ticket out of jail. Operating on the principle that the best defense is a good offense, Levene assumes the role of Bellovian reality instructor anxious to teach Williamson the facts of the marketplace. "You can't run an office. . . . You don't know what it *is,* you don't have the *sense,* you don't have the *balls,*" he tells the office manager, who typically "marshals" his sales force by terror tactics: "I were you, I'd calm down, Shelly" (76), he quietly threatens. Like Mickey Sabbath, the anti-hero of Philip Roth's *Sabbath's Theater,* who knows that "If Yahweh wanted me to be calm, he would have made me a goy" (1995, 334), Levene takes up the challenge with a dash of *chutzpah: "Would* you? . . . Or you're gonna *what,* fire me. . . . On an eighty-two thousand dollar *day?*" (76).

Seizing linguistic control, Levene freely dispenses his own didactic lessons and implicit threats: "You *see?*" he says, "This is where you fuck *up,* because this is something you don't *know.* You can't look down the *road.* And see what's *coming.* . . . Might be someone *else,* John. It might be someone *new,* eh?" (76). Perceiving Williamson's ignorance of history as his principal weakness, Levene lectures him on history's merits: "you can't look *back.*" Their dyad is deeply ironic given that Levene, blind in the context of the play, faults Williamson for his blindness, but if Williamson "can't look *back,*" Levene certainly doesn't want to "look down the *road.*" And if he is cognizant of the penalty for his actions—for he is too wise to believe that the magical transformation of the sale is anything more than transitory—Levene plays the moment, finding temporary refuge in history.

Culturally and ethnically coded, "history" is the catalytic agent that cues a repeat performance of Levene's record of professional achievement recited in scene 1, with the crucial addition of his greatest achievement, the education of his daughter. Not only does it link previous and subsequent pedagogical references, but in itself the statement is unique in the play, implicitly evoking central Jewish values of family and education: "And I put a kid through *school.* She . . . and . . . Cold *calling,* fella" (77).[40] Levene's allusive references in the first scene and final moments of the play call direct attention to her as if she were a dependent daughter. Mendes's insight here is perceptive: "[H]e has something none of the salesmen have because *there* is a man who has clearly coped . . . I think Mamet, it may be the sentimentalist in him, in a sense, . . . does want to portray an element to Levene which is a good man. There's an element to Shelly which is the emotional core of the play . . . whereas Ricky is its balls, you know" (Kane 1996, 255-56).

Significantly, we are given scant back story, permitting us only the barest glimpse of Levene's ordinary life that speaks to his struggle, familial loyalty, responsibility, Judaic values, and capacity for love of others. What is abundantly clear, however, is that in sharp contrast to his elaborately narrated story of the sale to the Nyborgs, the most important story of Levene's life goes unheard. It is a stunning moment in which his silence, striking in one so loquacious from the moment we first encounter him, enigmatically elicits a stirring narrative in which belief in oneself and an obligation to others motivate the striving and struggle that are a part of his story and evidence of its truth. In a reversal of scene 1, in which Levene worried that Williamson would "can my ass" (18), the salesman, empowered by the memory of his achievement, asserts, "Fuck you and kiss my ass" (77), voicing the belief that "a man who has a trade . . . can tell the rest of the world to go to hell!" (Mamet qtd. in Roudané 1986a, 80).

The performative genius of Roma and Levene is given full expression in the Roma/Lingk/Levene scene in which Roma struggles to save his sale to Lingk and retain his coveted position on the board. Casting Levene in the role as D. Ray Morton, "*the* senior vice-president American Express" (82), Roma provides the opportunity for the older Jewish salesman to show us first hand the mythic skill to which he repeatedly refers in speech and fiction. In fact, reminded of the Jew's narrative and linguistic skill, Roma takes full advantage of it to save *his* sale, reminding us that survival is the name of this game. In stark counterpoint to their charade, Aaronow, freed from Baylen's interrogation, which in retrospect sets Moss's intimidation of Aaronow in scene 2 in comic relief, is revealed to be a man who refuses to be cowed or silenced. Given his characteristic laconism, Aaronow's statements on injustice have great currency. Whereas act 1, scene 2 concludes with Aaronow's prototypical Jewish "martyrdom, and self-pity, and 'everything terrible happens to me'" (Whitfield 1984, 126), phrased as "Why are you talking this way to me?" (45), his response to Baylen's abusive speech is a furious rhetoric that communicates his full understanding of the abhorrent ethnic bias and focus of Baylen's investigation. In a play dominated by speech, that the typically laconic Aaronow, enraged by anti-Semitism, communicates his rage at a world inhospitable to the Jew is startling. Rather than reify ancient prejudice of the Jew as evil-doer, Aaronow stands as a positive image of the Jew. Thus, if he has withheld the truth as he knows it *from* the police, he exhibits no hesitation in telling the truth *about* the police.

Gaining strength with each nuanced repetition, Aaronow vocalizes his fury, "I'm *through,* with *this* fucking meshugaas. No one should talk to a man that way. How are you *talking* to me that . . . how can you *talk* to me that . . . that. . . . Where does he get off to talk that way to a working man?" Juxtaposed with Roma's fluid, flawless delivery and slick sales pitch brought to bear upon the increasingly elusive sale to Lingk in the brilliantly conceived D. Ray Morton scene, Aaronow's phrasing is disjunctive, revealing him caught up in his own personal drama. "I meet *gestapo* tac . . . I meet *gestapo* tactics . . . I meet *gestapo* tactics," he rants repeatedly, finding referents in history and choking on the rage generated by his interrogation, one that he clearly likens to the persecution and dehumanization of Jews (87-89). Traditionally, the schlemiel is an eternal innocent prone to "saying the inept word at the inappropriate moment" (Howe 1987, 23). For Mamet, however, he is not a source of colorfulness; he assumes a moral stance, his frustration and fury evident in "his anguished intellectual struggle against both his weakness and an indifferent world" (Alter 1969, 119-20).

To further magnify the sense of devastation and ruin, and the irony of his speaking out on this issues, the only one listening to Aaronow's diatribe on injustice and inhumanity is Williamson, a point that rivets our attention to the dichotomy between Aaronow's social responsibility and Williamson's fiscal concerns. The seriousness of Aaronow's criticism, moreover, is underscored and undercut by Williamson's hilarious "Go to *lunch*. . . . Just go to lunch. . . . Will you go to lunch?" (88-89), which under the guise of his promoting an atmosphere conducive to business further marginalizes Aaronow, reiterates the threshold imagery that unifies the play, and wryly calls attention to the Jew's cultural association with food. Tracing the archetypal figure of the schlemiel in her landmark study, *The Schlemiel as Modern Hero*, Ruth R. Wisse observes that the schlemiel, typically employed in Yiddish literature "as a cultural reaction to the prevailing Anglo-Saxon model of restraint in action, thought and speech," has particular appeal in American literature as a character whose humanity is evidenced "by loving and suffering in defiance of the forces of depersonalization and the ethic of enlightened stoicism" (82). Rather like Bob in *American Buffalo*, who is not above deceit, Aaronow finds the concepts of inhumanity and indecency entirely elude him. In this regard, Mamet tells Roudané that Aaronow comes "closest to being the character of a *raisonneur*":

> for throughout the whole play he's saying, "I don't understand what's going on." "I'm no good." "I can't fit in here." "I'm incapable of doing those things which I've grasped." . . . Aaronow has some degree of conscience. . . . Corruption troubles him (1986a, 75)

In short, posits Mamet, "he's troubled by whether his inability to succeed in the society . . . is a defect—that is, is he manly enough or sharp enough?— or if it's, in effect, a positive attribute" (75).

To Sauer, Aaronow's role fails to satisfy the criterion of a *raisonneur*. "Instead of the one with the (playwright's) answers," he argues, "he is the one with the questions, with doubts" (153 n.1). Yet Sauer, like other critics, has failed to grasp the elevated position held by the question in Jewish learning and in Mamet's plays. Rather than reveal the absence of knowledge, it is the most direct path *to* knowledge. Indeed, by raising the metaphysical questions "Why?" "How?" "To what end?" Aaronow focuses on the fundamental drama of man's inner drives and moral choices, the moral dilemma that is fundamental to Mamet's canon and American Jewish writing. Indeed, this ongoing inquiry informs Aaronow's series of open questions which crystallize in his penultimate, plaintive cry, "Oh, God . . ." (108), an outburst of unrequited grief *and* a plea for divine guidance.

Once Williamson thwarts Roma's sale to Lingk and Aaronow finally leaves the office in search of Moss, the office manager receives a rebuke from his top salesman: "You fucking *shit*. Where did you learn your *trade*. . . . You *idiot*" (96) he sneers, underscoring both the empowerment of skill and the pedagogical trope sounded in the first scene with Levene. Performing a bit of drama, Roma starts into the room where Baylen has interrogated the salesmen, half-hoping that Williamson is the thief, a convenient, comic way to rid him permanently from their lives, but his action also clears the stage for Levene's trenchant monologue. Alone with Williamson and emboldened by his sale and Roma's attack, Levene picks up the dropped thread of Roma's speech and lectures Williamson on the importance of thinking on one's feet, of acquiring knowledge through experience, and of extending loyalty to one's partner. Hudgins contends that Levene's intent in this speech is to "aggrandize his own power . . . to claim a moral superiority that he doesn't deserve" (1996, 33). However, echoing Aaronow's previous tirade on injustice, I think that the context of his words and their implicit ethnically coded referents convey that Levene, despite his desperate action, retains a moral stance. In fact, when Williamson breaks off the lecture by *"[b]rushing past him,"* Levene lays one more lesson on him: ". . . you be as cold as you want," he tells him, "but you just fucked a good man out of six thousand dollars and his goddamn bonus. . . . if you can do that and you aren't man enough that it gets you, then I don't know what, if you can't take *some thing* from that . . . (*Blocking his way.*) you're *scum,* you're fucking white-bread" (98).

Although he reiterates his opening, deprecatory remark, "you be as cold as you want," Levene's fury at Williamson's incomprehensible insensitivity and apparent lack of compassion is voiced in the acrimonious coupling of "scum" with "white-bread." For those less familiar with the phrase, "white bread" is indicative of a deep division between classes, namely "those who ate white bread"—which "symbolized an unattainable style of life"—(of gentiles) and those who didn't (Heinze 34-35). However, it is Lenny Bruce's famous comic routine that exposes the specifically ethnic reference—and implicit censure—of the term: "I'm Jewish. Count Basie's Jewish. Ray Charles is Jewish. . . . Kool Aid is goyish. . . . Evaporated milk is goyish even if the Jews invented it. Spam is goyish and rye bread is Jewish. . . . As you know white bread is very goyish" (Novak and Waldocks 60). For Bruce, humor provides an opportunity to shock the Jews and "*shpritz* the goyim," as Pinsker has it, to get at the serious issues of divisions in American society through the comic. In other words, *Glengarry Glen Ross* deliberately establishes and exposes the antipathy between Jew and gentile as a means of underscoring issues of anti-Semitism and its concomitant inhumanity, thus bringing to full light the continuity of these concerns in Mamet's writing.

Ironically in a world in which the watchword for survival is "Always Be Closing," Levene does not know when to close. In saying one thing too many—he, after all, has a bigger mouth than Moss—Levene reveals himself as the thief, giving Williamson the opportunity and evidence to (re)solve three problems in one shot: unraveling the mystery of the theft, securing his job, and ridding himself of the "know-it-all," self-righteous Jew. In fact, as the story of the Nyborgs and its promise fades into fable, magic turns to muck as Levene oversells Williamson. The ensuing conversation between them recalls and parodies the end of scene 1, but Levene has pushed the hot-button issue of anti-Semitism, and he reaps the rewards of having framed his criticism of the office manager within the boundaries of an ethnic dialectic that will inform much of Mamet's later work: the Jew as passionate, warm, fiery dogmatist; the gentile as cold, critical thinker. Thus, when Levene, understanding all too well that Williamson has traced the robbery to him, nonetheless presses him to articulate the extent of his knowledge—"Don't fuck with me, John. . . . what are you saying?"—Williamson responds, "Well, I'm saying this, Shel. . . .You want to talk to me, you want to talk to someone *else* . . ." (99). In doing so, Williamson underscores his superior position and power to enforce law by explicit threats coupled with the intent to humiliate that is unmistakably communicated in his demeaning use of Levene's first name.

Acting as the emissary, minion, true prophet, and judicial arm of an unseen trinity, the divine force of Mitch, Murray, and Lemkin (a natural extension of his earlier enforcement of their policy), Williamson threatens Levene with sure and swift punishment. A seasoned performance artist, however, Levene plays out the scene, frenetically adopting myriad roles: alternatively naive, confused, contentious, sarcastic, supplicatory. Prevaricating and protesting too much, however, he provides Williamson with the confirmation, if not the concrete information, that he seeks. To push the panic-stricken Levene to confess, he offers a deal: "If you tell me where the leads are, I won't turn you in" (100), the conditional tense connoting a choice when clearly he has none—itself a wry comment on Levene's "chosenness." On its surface, it appears to be an offer in good faith, one that Judaism views as a central moral principle crucial to interpersonal relations. The "good faith" (*hin zedek*) imperative presupposes that when an individual makes a commitment, it is his or her intention to carry it out (Levine 6-7). That Williamson has not intended to bargain in good faith is evident when he articulates the parameters of his one-time offer: truth or consequences. In contradistinction to Levene, who sold the Nyborgs on the idea of how much they had to gain, Williamson makes clear what Levene has to lose: "you have five seconds . . . or you are going to jail" (100). Like Baylen,

Williamson is empowered with an imperious rhetoric, and he "puts the screws" to Levene, to borrow Moss's medieval metaphor, subjecting him to an inquisition without benefit of counsel: he is judge, jury, and prosecutor. "Believe me" he warns, and Levene trusts that if he confesses to the crime, Williamson will not turn him in (100). "The tyrant strikes a silent bargain with the tyrannized," suggests Mamet: 'Identify with me, obey me unthinkingly, and I will provide for you with this wonderful service: I will tell no one how worthless you are'" (1989b, 98).

To ensure Williamson's silence, Levene does what Aaronow pledged that he would not: he talks, turns in Moss, exposes the plan, and implicates Jerry Graff. Williamson's question, "How much did you get for them?" (100) puts a wonderful ironic spin on one Aaronow posed to Moss, given that it is Levene who is revealed to be the criminal. Sensing that the truth will not set him free, Levene sees an opening in Williamson's unspoken interest in his (and Moss's) profit margin and seizes upon it to assure his own freedom. Playing to his audience, he delivers that speech that he believes will "covert the motherfucker" (72): a sympathetic rationale for his unlawful behavior, a statement of contrition; a proposal of partnership. Contrasting sharply with scene 1, Levene endeavors to sell Williamson on a high-yield investment scheme, but the office manager is not buying. Not easily deterred, Levene continues: "List . . . list . . . listen. . . . here's what we're going to do," his use of the inclusive "we" and future tense intentional (103). Inventing a plan as he speaks, much as Moss attempted to secure his freedom from the firm and Aaronow's silence in scene 2 by improvisation, Levene predicates his proposition on his belief in himself and his knowledge of Williamson's proven affinity for bonus dollars and long-term investments. Framing the entire speech in the future tense and building a "line of affirmatives," Levene again promotes himself as a proven man in a nuanced version of "I have closed," "I'm going to *close* for you . . ." With each repetition of "This is only the beginning" (102), Levene and the audience know the imagined transformation eludes him, that lying is an amplification of his performance artistry, the application of discourse a method of survival, much as Mamet reveals subterfuge to be in his novella *Passover* (1995).

Endeavoring to avoid incarceration for a crime he admits to committing so that he may continue to meet his responsibility to his daughter, Levene's proposal concedes that Williamson has "the *advantage* on me now" (102), underscoring the high price he will pay to survive. In so doing, he barters his skill for power that the gentile retains in the depersonalized business world. The irony is rich: Williamson has always enjoyed the security of his leveraged position, whether or not Levene has admitted this fact to himself. And were Williamson to chose to become Levene's partner, it would clearly be a losing proposition given Levene's past performance and potential for future sales; moreover, he would become an accomplice after the fact, aiding and abetting a criminal. Hence, although Levene beseeches Williamson to deal honorably with him in the present and invest in futures, as he does, the office manager prefers to rid himself and his office of this pushy Jew. A consummate con man, Williamson draws Levene to the bait and springs the trap: "No, I don't think so, Shel" (102).[41] So artful is Mamet's transition from tirade to denouement that we nearly miss the point that Levene's calling Williamson "fucking white-bread" leads him to lay one better on Levene: you're a criminal, a thief, a destructive force that has induced chaos.

If Willy Loman was correct in his assumption that a salesman has to be "well liked" to succeed, then the implication is clear: Williamson has never liked Levene. "[O]ur sympathy grows for Levene the Machine," Cohn maintains, "as he boasts of bilking an old couple, as he connives with Roma to defraud his client, as he tries to bribe Williamson." Indeed, "By the time Williamson explains his incrimination . . . we *do* like Levene, for his brazen stupid bravery against all odds" (1991, 167). While implicit, Mamet's intent is clear: Williamson has made it personal. In fact, his "ontological antisemit-ism"—what Sokel terms "hostility toward the Jew that concentrates on their being" (154)—is directly related to "the destructive aspect [that] connives in the Jew" (164). He confirms as much when he cites as his reasons for turning in Levene: "You have got a big mouth. . . . you fucked up my office . . . [and] I don't like you" (102-04). Tuttle maintains that in stealing the leads, "Levene performs the act which he believes will free him"; ironically it entraps him in "a singular and defining role" (166). That "single and defining role" of villainy has been ascribed to the Jew for centuries: a thief, a polluter, a liar, a disruptive, disloyal corrupting element. Mamet's take on this rhetoric is to uncover the mythical signifier for what it is: flagrant, abhorrent anti-Semitism.

In the play's final accounting, each of the characters locates himself spatially within or outside the office: Moss is in, or on his way, to Wisconsin, presumably safely across state lines; Aaronow is paralyzed at his desk; Williamson turns Levene into Baylen; Roma will be at the Chinese restaurant ostensibly conducting business as we first saw him. This ordering gives the impression of circularity, but the imperceptible change wrought by time is tacitly conveyed. Reiterating the ethical and pedagogical trope, "There's things that I could learn from you"(105), Roma indirectly provides further evidence of his kindliness, as he did earlier in the day (and the act) with Aaronow. In the face of Levene's impending arrest, which Roma has deduced based on the evidence that the robbery could not have been committed by Aaronow or himself and was most likely not committed by Moss, Roma compliments Levene's consummate skill as a wordsmith so recently manifested in "that shit you were slinging on my guy" (105). Unsentimentally, Roma attempts to minimize his colleague's terror by compliments, his proposal to apprentice himself to the master teacher, "Shelly, the Machine, Levene" (64) in what remains of a longer, concluding speech on education cut in production.[42] Articulating those emotions that Levene would express were he not struck dumb with fear, Roma pronounces: "it's a fucked up world" (105), an epigrammatic Mamet gem that indirectly provides an outlet for frustration and an indictment of the American business ethic. Moreover, his impassioned tribute to Levene both animates our sympathy for the older salesman, "crushed by those circumstances that we all fear," and celebrates the nobility and perseverance with which we and the *Glengarry* salesmen attempt to make choices to live dignified, compassionate lives (Hudgins 1996, 41-42).

If Mamet has struck a raw nerve and sparked controversy with *Glengarry Glen Ross,* exposing mendacity and moral bankruptcy in the marketplace, he has also generated sympathy in his unsentimental parabolic tale tempered by his admiration for the virtuosity, imagination, and temerity of men who, in Ricky Roma's words, "live on their *wits*" (96). Roma's tribute to "members of a dying breed" is wonderfully ironic, given that he, for all intents and purposes, bears no recognizable (yellow) badge of the members of a "Dying breed" of Jews whose diminishing numbers provide at least one way to interpret the top salesman's evocative proposal that strength is not a function of numbers but of community. "That's . . . that's . . . that's why we have to stick together" (105), he says, his artful ploy open to interpretation, either a classic case of thinking on your feet or a bravura performance cloaking a perfidious fraud, ironically and brutally undercut by his message to Williamson: "I GET HIS ACTION" (107). Recalling the admonition of the spies sent to investigate the Promised Land in the Book of Numbers who foresaw a land of opportunity ripe with the potential for corruption of values, Roma's deception imbues the past and the future with a clarity not yet realized. Ten years younger than the other salesmen, and learning from them all, he will inherit—or at least profitably sell—the Promised Land, quickly moving in on Levene's territory once the older man is silenced. Indeed, we are left to wonder whether Roma, whose affinity for power is well established, may have cut a deal with the obdurate Williamson from the outset.

And the members of the "Dying breed" to which Mamet alludes? "Dying they may be," observes Brustein, Mamet's "sleazy, smarmy race of losers still has a volatile energy, even an elegiac aura of heroism" (71). Thus, when Roma takes a commanding position with Williamson, tenaciously holding his ground in an indifferent world, he behaves in accordance with the inspirational philosophy he learned from Levene and conveyed to Lingk: "If security concerns me, I do that which *today* I think will make me secure" (49). Security, he has learned from Levene, is a function of strength.

"FUCK MONEY. . . . BUT DON'T FUCK 'PEOPLE'"

> "*We* are no fools. *We* know when someone is
> mouthing off in order to get into our pants, or in
> our pockets. *We* know that we will hold judg-
> ment of some one's character until we see *how*
> *they act.*"
>
> —David Mamet

IN THE EIGHT-CENTURY-OLD TRADITION OF DEPICTING THE STAGE JEW, observes Ellen Schiff in her encyclopedic study, *From Stereotype to Metaphor: The Jew in Contemporary Drama,* "The Jew is cast everywhere along the gamut of malevolence, from simple foil . . . to the wicked perpetrator of cruelty conceivable only by a mind possessed of the devil" (5). The Jewish usurer as a stock type—one who acquires and lends money—she continues, amply illustrates "the versatility and endurance of the nefarious stage Jew" (8). Although the stereotypical portrait of the deceiver and wrongdoer was vastly reduced in the eighteenth and nineteenth centuries and humanized in the twentieth, especially in the decades since the Holocaust in which the stage Jew is again conspicuous by his presence, playwrights have imagina-tively transformed the Jew "from object to subject" (Schiff 28).

Speed-the-Plow is just such a richly imagined play. In its hilarious opening scene, Bobby Gould and Charlie Fox, rhapsodizing about the "Great big jolly *shitloads*" of money they "stand to make . . ." (20) producing their hot new property, Gould pronounces, "Money is not the important thing. . . . I piss on money." Fox, punctuating his comment, draws a laugh line: "I know that you do. I'll help you" (21). Mamet's most overt depiction of the stage Jew lusting after bulging money bags inspires the profitable and

prescient question: Why are these characters Jewish? Equally pressing is
what Mamet's inspired reformation, what Schiff terms "updatings of time-
consecrated images" (35), reveals about the increasing visibility of the Jew
in his canon?

Toby Zinman maintains that "Mamet has raised Jewish allusions to
the level of universal shorthand that Roman Catholic allusions have always
enjoyed" (212), but in her fine study of *aporia,* the trope of doubt, in his
plays, she does little to advance our knowledge of Mamet's Jewish allusions
perceived by most critics (and audiences) as arcana. Notably, although she
perceptively illumines Fox's allusive Jewish reference to Gould's intention to
remain behind in the office "to Hide the Afikomen" (34), Zinman
undermines her exegesis as possibly "overreading the text considerably"
(212). In fact, the arcana of *Speed-the-Plow,* like the rich mother lode of
Jewish allusions in Mamet's early and late work, is considerably underread.

Setting *Speed-the-Plow* in Hollywood, a urban setting that is itself an
eidetic and ethnic referent, the playwright rivets immediate attention to the
ethnicity of characters whose cultural inheritance links them to "the city of
the modern gold rush" (Mamet 1989b, 139). With its implicit reference to
Jewish development and dominance of the film business, Hollywood allows
Mamet to endow his characters with history and historical depth. And in his
imaginative and provocative reshaping of the rich legacy of the stage Jew, he
grounds *Speed-the-Plow* in personal, historical, and cultural references
whose evocative allusions are everywhere present in this play.

As Michael Hinden notes in "Intimate Voices: *Lakeboat* and Mamet's
Quest for Community," Mamet "tends to see community as an idealized
nexus of human relationships" that when nourished by intimacy has the
potential to dignify "the enterprise of collective work" (38, 46). However, in
"Film Is a Collaborative Business," the playwright describes the film
business as anything but collective enterprise: "From a screenwriter's point
of view, the correct rendering should be, 'Film is a collaborative business:
bend over'" (1989b, 134),[1] or as Charlie Fox quaintly phrases it in *Speed-
the-Plow:* "Life in the movie business is like the, is like the beginning of a
new love affair: it's full of surprises and you're constantly getting fucked"
(29).[2] In numerous interviews and essays Mamet has characterized Hollywood as "a sinkhole of depraved venality"(1987d, 77),[3] inspiring critics like
Richard Stayton to read Mamet's caustic, corrosive, and comedic portrayal
of corruption in *Speed-the-Plow* as "a scathing indictment of the way that
Hollywood does business" (1988, 6). Fueling the fire, Mamet admits with
little effort to conceal his purpose, "I hope so. It's very dishy. A very, very
inside Hollywood play" (6). Wryly drawing out the inside joke, he
encourages the perception that *Speed-the-Plow* was inspired in general by the

scurrilous manner in which Hollywood conducts business and spurred in particular by antagonism, among Mamet, producer Art Linson, and director Brian De Palma during the months preceding the filming of his script for *The Untouchables* (1988, 136).[4]

We make a great mistake, however, in equating Mamet's essays, however much they provide a gloss for his work, with the work itself, and in delimiting *Speed-the-Plow* as a shallow, cynical hatchet job on Hollywood as innumerable critics have.[5] Frank Rich's review of the New York production of the play is representative. Observing that "Hell hath no fury like a screenwriter scorned," Rich sees Mamet engaging in "the same scorched-earth policy toward Hollywood that Nathanael West first apotheosized in *The Day of the Locust*," and characterizes *Speed-the-Plow* as possibly "the most cynical and exciting of six decades of literary reaction to Hollywood" (1988, C17). And whereas West, like F. Scott Fitzgerald in *The Last Tycoon*, used "Hollywood for his satire on an America in the process of moral implosion," *Speed-the-Plow*, "lack[ing] West's paranoia and anger, his apocalypticism, as it does Fitzgerald's sense of tragedy" nevertheless "is aestheticised," opines Christopher Bigsby; "it becomes a badly plotted script . . . shot through with irony" (1992, 228).

In the absence of apocalypticism, my understanding of *Speed-the-Plow*'s dominant tropes of revelation, transformation, wealth and wisdom, and its triadic structure is immeasurably enhanced by exploring the historical and cultural references that inform *Speed-the-Plow* and code it dramatically and ethnically as a "very, very inside Hollywood play" in ways that are implicit rather than explicit. In a plot rich in theology and practical lessons—inclusive of those that Mamet acknowledges that he has learned from Bob Rafelson, his first Hollywood sponsor, and Art Linson—that have improved his screenplays and have carried over into his crafting of plot for stage plays, one naturally presumes that a critical motif in *Speed-the-Plow* is learning.[6] Indeed, pedagogical relationships are integral to this play. However, the playwright's sardonic synopsis of his conversation with Linson regarding revisions for the opening scene of *We're No Angels* (1989) provides a critical and hitherto neglected point of departure for analysis of *Speed-the-Plow* as a comedy that discloses culture both overtly and covertly: "Linson tells me, 'You gotta start off with a bang.' So I say to him, 'You whore,' as I usually do, that's my Jewish salutation, 'you don't know what you're talking about, you swine. I was making my living as a playwright while you were still a tout at the racetrack'" (6).[7]

Like the interlinguistics, code-switching, scatological language, and argumentative tone that link Mamet's characters to their ethnic heritage, the playwright's humorous remarks serve to remind us of his connection to the continuum of the motion picture industry, which from its inception has been associated with Jewish movie moguls.[8] Why, we might ask, is a Jewish writer, particularly one who has returned to practicing Judaism, drawing attention to the venality of Hollywood, particularly when so many others precede him in their denunciation and vilification of Hollywood as a primarily Jewish business? And how does change as subject and context relate to Mamet's parody? Clearly the rise, profit, and conspicuousness of Jews in the entertainment business, especially their development of and prominence in the motion picture industry, concomitant with the Americanization of the Jew, situate Mamet's focus on duplicity, power, and loyalty in Hollywood firmly on ethnic ground, connecting this play to other Mamet works that similarly address ethical dilemmas posed by the temptation to affluence, the desire for acceptance, and the betrayal of self and Other.

Mamet provides several clues in *The Disappearance of the Jews* (1982, 1987), a one-act play that precedes *Speed-the-Plow* and chronologically parallels the playwright's experience in Hollywood as a journeyman screenwriter.[9] In scene 5, two characters of long-standing friendship, personal dissatisfaction, and tenuous connections to Jewish communal life set their experience against the background of history, placing the success of Jewish movie moguls in the forefront. As Joey romanticizes Jewish life in Eastern Europe in the *shtetl* and in New York City's Orchard Street at the turn of the century with more relish than his own life of disconnection, his friend, Bobby, posits a more inviting fantasy: "You know what I would, I'll tell you what I would have loved, to go, in the *twenties,* to be in *Holly*wood. . . . *Jesus,* I know they had a good time there. . . . I mean five smart Jew boys from Russia, this whole *industry* . . . " (18-19). Rejecting the poverty of the *shtetl* and communal immigrant life, Bobby imagines Hollywood in the 1920s as an unparalleled opportunity for enterprise and ingenuity, a paragon of power, an ethnic community of promise, and a place of unimaginable wealth. The history of the motion picture industry and its transformation by Jews—"like out of some damn fairytale" (1988, 10)—empowers and connects him to entrepreneurs who pioneered the motion picture industry and managed to "centralize production, distribution and exhibition" (May and May 7).[10]

Literate but ill-educated entrepreneurs, they had a great advantage as outsiders. Endowed with intuitiveness, vision, sensitivity to changing taste in an industry driven by consumer desires derived from their experience in the clothing industry, and an understanding of the desire for leisure entertainment in the urban community, they seized an opportunity "not already monopolized . . . by the host culture" (May and May, 11).[11]

However, as Arthur Hertzberg astutely perceives, the principal reason for pursuing dominance of the movie industry had little to do with a Jewish tradition of entertainment in Eastern Europe or an expressive heritage. Rather, excluded from white-collar jobs in banking, insurance, railroads, steel-making, and coal-mining, as well as institutions for higher learning, on the basis of their ethnicity, these Jews saw the movie industry as representing an opportunity for financial survival, demonstrating "how the Jews, when society was intent on excluding them from established businesses, found their way into the American economy" (209-10).

"From its origins," Stephen J. Whitfield argues, "Hollywood has been stamped with a Jewish personality, but nobody was supposed to know about it," a paradoxical fact given that the era of the 1930s through 1950s "marked the perihelion of the studio system, whose brilliance was due almost entirely to Jewish personalities" (1986, 324, 327).[12] However, what Leonard Dinnerstein characterizes as "The worst period of American antisemitism . . . sandwiched between the ends of World War I and World War II"—a period whose societal changes in the 1920s and Great Depression of the 1930s paralleled the development of the movie industry— revived "The Shylock image of [the Jew as] economic exploiter," generated in great part by a perceived domination by the Jew who "menaced" America by controlling the fields of communication (212-16).[13] Together with the archetypal Christian image of the Jew as rejecters of the truthfulness of Christian teachings, what the anti-Semite of the nineteenth and twentieth century viewed as the "embodiment of the power of darkness constantly conspiring against the principle of light" (Sokel 155), American Jewry came to be viewed principally as economic exploiters and degenerators of culture whose vulgarizing proclivity rendered them "incapable of producing authentic, ennobling spiritual products" (Katz 244).[14]

The principal Jewish response to virulent anti-Semitism, both in Hollywood and in American society in general, was an enhanced desire for invisibility, accomplished through cultural assimilation, exogamy, and Reform Judaism. Therefore, although the movie industry employed "a veritable army of talent both in front of and behind the camera, many of whom were Jewish" padding their payrolls with family members and serving matzo ball soup in their commissaries, the movie moguls, despite a close network of ethnic ties, were intent on being viewed as "American" and thus divorced from the taint of commerce and its attendant anti-Semitic criticism (Whitfield 1986, 328). To that end, Hollywood, disassociated from the urban Jewish centers of New York and Chicago, was established as a *secularized* environment, what Whitfield terms "the Hollywood version of the marrano"(327), whose Jewish producers invented and projected gentile fantasies upon a gentile nation.[15] This translated into a film industry in which Jews were neither mentioned by name nor represented on the screen. Ultimately, the horror of the Holocaust brought home the fact that assimilation offered no protection from anti-Semitism (2). Alain Fink- ielkraut frames the dilemma perfectly: "And then (for we must always come back to it) there was the Holocaust. It was an event that had the double effect of accelerating the process of assimilation and depriving it of its *raison d'être*" (108). Yet until that reality took hold in America "The attempt at almost total assimilation by the powerful men who ran the studios reflected itself in a de-Semitizing of the action that took place in front of the lens" (Desser and Friedman, 2), and a way of life considered "high" by some standards, pagan by others.[16]

It is against such a background of social success as fact and dilemma that Mamet situates *Speed-the-Plow*. Conflating myth and reality in the historical periods of the 1920s and the 1980s, Mamet sets personal experience against the background of cultural experience; focusing attention upon the ethnicity of his characters Fox and Gould, whose surname is an assimilated form of Gold and whose Jewishness and link to a tradition of commerce is as apparent as Levene's, Moss's, and Aaronow's in *Glengarry Glen Ross*. Fashioning a complex construct in which to examine ethnicity and cupidity, Mamet intensifies the ironic disparity between the 1920s when sagacious producers, energized by the knowledge that only the smartest survive—like Harry Cohn, well known for his obscenity, and Samuel Goldwyn, for entertaining the customer—were Hollywood *mach- ers,* big wheels, who commanded enormous authority and salaries, vigorous- ly pursued their objectives, and "settled their biggest deals over all-night poker games" (Haver 73). In the 1980s, Fox and Gould, their visibility and impact diminished and "their value system . . . impoverished" (Hudgins 1992, 218), flatter themselves with the illusion of their initiative and convince themselves and others of their importance in an industry in which omniscient conglomerates manage producers as effectively as owners Mitch, Murray, and Lemkin in *Glengarry Glen Ross* handle their employees. But if Goldwyn's motto was "A producer shouldn't get ulcers; he should give them" (Whitfield 1986, 328), at least in the Hollywood of the 1980s and 1990s producers maintain the mirage of power.[17] Seeing and seizing opportunity in the 1920s, Jewish movie moguls, by dint of their heritage, timing, and outsider status, came to dominate Hollywood (as they did the entertain- ment business), a fact that linked them inextricably then and now to the gold rush and the stigma of money-hungry Jews. Acknowledging the initiative and business acumen that drove Hollywood and confronting head-on both the lure and license of Tinseltown, of assimilation and the prevalence of anti-Semitism, Mamet in this pivotal play simultaneously reveals the disparity between Fox's dream of affluence and the reality of its corruptibility.

Reading *Speed-the-Plow* as a "Dark View of Hollywood As a Heaven for the Virtueless" in which Fox and Gould, long-time friends fantasizing about how much money they can make, "engage in a sub rosa power struggle—a warped, Pinteresque buddy movie of their own," (1988, 1), Rich observes that the basis of comparison between Pinter and Mamet may be found in the arena of power, and Ruby Cohn rightly specifies the source of that power as linguistic, noting that Pinter and Mamet "pitch telling phrases with deadly accuracy" (1995, 58).[18] Mamet acknowledges as much when he tells David Savran, "the point is not to speak the desire but to speak that which is most likely to bring about the desire" (137). And in Mamet's plays (like Pinter's), the "expression" of choice is consistently narrative.[19] A marvelously imaginative storyteller, Mamet characterizes his work (inclusive of his screenplays) by the pervasiveness of narrative. A plethora of unverifiable stories, erotic fantasies, unreliable narrators, disruptive chronology, and tales of domination and betrayal inform his drama. Indeed, for Mamet, "The *story* is all there is to the theater—the rest is just packaging . . . " (1987d, 14-15).

Narrative is so fundamental to his drama that Christopher Bigsby, devoting an entire chapter to it in his landmark study, *David Mamet*, argues that it is "not only a central strategy of the writer, struggling to give coherence to a chaotic experience, but also a basic tactic of characters for whom it becomes a resource, a retreat, and ultimately the only redemption, if only because it implies the minimal community of taleteller and listener" (1985, 22). However, in *Deception*, Philip Roth illuminates a significant reason for the predominance of stories in Mamet's plays (as in his own novels): "With the nigger it's his prick and with the Jew it's his questions. You are a treacherous bastard who cannot resist a narrative" (1990, 93). In familiar and lesser-known Mamet plays, episodic or classically structured, realistic or mythic, as varied as *Marranos, Lakeboat, The Water Engine, Sexual Perversity in Chicago, American Buffalo, Prairie du Chien, Reunion,* and *Glengarry Glen Ross,* compulsive fictionalizers attempt to contain and mitigate fear, enhance self-esteem, substitute stability and substance for chaos, recover and suppress memory, and achieve their objectives through narrative. Never merely a literary device in Mamet's work, storytelling is essentially aggadic, "teach[ing] the practical wisdom which is the hallmark of Judaism" (Kepnes 215). It mediates the past and the present, continues a tradition of moral ethic, and wields the sword of irony to illumine a process of preservation and transformation.

Paralleling the three revue sketches of the first act of *Glengarry Glen Ross* employed to enhance self-esteem, promote personal agenda, and contextualize past and present events, narrative is crucial in *Speed-the-Plow,* giving Fox the opportunity to recount his story about Douggie Brown coming to his house with the screenplay "like out of some damn fairytale" (10); Gould the opportunity to tell Karen how "To *make* something, to *do* something, to be a *part* of something. Money, art, a chance to Play at the Big Table . . . " (40); and Karen the opportunity to recite the story of the decay of civilization and the possibility of grace. The "other" story not directly related but subtly communicated is that everything has changed since Gould's title as Head of Production was put on his door. Opportunities for aesthetic, sexual, emotional, personal, and professional betrayals are as numerous as all "those fine folk" who keep calling, "Guys" who want him to make "remakes of films haven't been made yet" (6).

Since his early episodic plays, Mamet has emerged as an ingenious storyteller, and in *Speed-the-Plow* he spins a number of stories whose focus is the possibility of change as well as the process of transformation: as newly promoted Head of Production, Gould is empowered to make choices and effect change; Fox possesses the potential to alter his career, finances, and the way others think of him; Karen, herself a catalytic character right out of "the Temporary Pool," has the potential to promote change for the world and, we subsequently learn, for herself (78). Although "All plays are about decay," observes Mamet, and reveal to us "the necessity of change" (1987d, 111), significantly in *Speed-the-Plow* narrative depicting change defines structure and informs subject in richly imagined and varying forms: the novel *The Bridge: or, Radiation and the Half-Life of Society. A Study of Decay* on impending apocalypse, the fairy tale of a producer who strikes it rich, the saga of cupidity in Hollywood revealed in a roman à clef (replete with references to Mamet's experience during the making of the film *The Untouchables*), the chronicle of treachery, the story of seduction, the fable of redemption, the screenplay for the "Doug Brown, Buddy Film." And lest we forget, there is the classic Dr. Seuss fable of "Yertle the Turtle," in which Yertle, like Gould, who thinks he is king of the turtles, stands on the backs of all other turtles until he falls into the mud when a turtle, not unlike Fox, sneezes, bringing Yertle down to an earthly reality.[20] Two other literary works, in-jokes as it were, serve to gloss the play: Mamet's six-page prose piece, "The Bridge" (1985a), about a nameless protagonist haunted by nightmares of nuclear holocaust that bears some likeness to the novel of the same name; and *Edmond,* repackaged for another medium as the "Doug Brown, Buddy Film," complete with the degradation, prison imagery, rape, homosocial

relationship, "some girl. . . . Action, blood, a social theme . . ." (13).
Cumulatively, they illumine the subject of power: its promotion, perception, and abuse.

Equating the power relationship in "The Subject and Power," with
"agonism," Michel Foucault argues that all power relationships, whether
consensual or coerced, are inherently unstable (428). Expanding upon
Foucault's interpretation of agonism and his triadic pedagogical structure,
Pascale Hubert-Leibler maintains that the Mametic teacher-student dynamic is characterized by a juggling of roles (79-80). In *Speed-the-Plow,* however,
Mamet is a magician of sorts: he tricks us into seeing Gould as wise teacher
in his pedagogical relationships with students Fox and Karen, whose
motivation and method to advance their education in the movie industry
differs to the extent of each one's skill and profit, only to reveal that Gould
is the naïf, "educated" by one and enlightened by the other. This inversion
of our initial perception illustrates what Deborah Geis terms Mamet's
"increasing preoccupation" with trick-playing (1992, 65).[21] But, not only
does Mamet show us "the trick 'from the back'" (64), he shows it to us
backwards, revealing it first in practice and then in theory.

To illustrate the trickery of the "People Business" (22) in practice,
Mamet opens act 1 of *Speed-the-Plow* with a play-within-a-play (a device
he used with great success in *Glengarry*) entitled "Young America at
WORK and PLAY" (31) in which "the play's the thing," wherein we catch
the cunning and the craft—if not the conscience—of the king. Panto-
mime, pageantry, patronage, masquerade, and performance are all. Newly
anointed Head of Production, Gould easily assumes the role of king, while
Fox, his Harlequin (or rather *badken,* a Jewish jester afforded the privilege
of caustic humor and social criticism without reprisal), and Karen (his
courtesan?), assume supporting roles. Gould is a natural, commanding
that protocol be observed, that coffee be flowing, that appointments be
changed, and bank holidays declared. From his elevated position, he
opines, coaches, admonishes, persuades, stipulates policy, and teaches Fox,
who has crawled in his shadow and on whose back Gould has achieved the
power to bestow on him the name of producer of his own commodity.
Although they joke that their friendship since the mailroom offers Fox
entry, "somebody I could *come* to . . . " (15), what we observe is that the
property, not the person prevails; indeed, as Gould becomes more
enamored of the Doug Brown film, Fox, who has proffered the expected
obeisance and gratitude, finds Gould warming up to the reality of profits
and prestige for himself. As he has since *Marranos,* Mamet discloses the
shift in attitude subtly by replacing "I" with "we," as the following
exchange illustrates:

Fox: "I'm going to be rich and I can't believe it."
Gould: Rich, are you kidding me? We're going to have to hire
           someone just to figure out the *things* we want to buy . . . (19)

And as he did in *American Buffalo*, Mamet reveals through a now familiar theatrical prop, the telephone (one that in *Oleanna* will emerge as a third character), that Gould's power extends beyond his name on the door, but as his end of the conversation reveals, as did Donny's with the coin dealer, Gould, too, is in a supporting role to the head of the studio, Richard Ross. Despite his demonstrated dictatorial behavior, Gould's efforts to produce Ross in the flesh and within the hour fail miserably, tarnishing his self-aggrandizing image. Although he secures an appointment as promised, he is bumped until the following morning, creating a race to keep their option, their partnership, and their fairy tale viable. However, in the "People Business" and, by extension, all power relationships, Mamet reveals that power shifts in direct proportion to the individual who dominates speech. Even with the shadow of doubt that Ross will return from New York to greenlight their project within the prescribed time hanging over their deal, what is evident in this play is that a compact exists between Fox and Gould whose consummation now translates into a apparently easy, raunchy, banter between partners, from which Fox, protected by this masquerade, gets in more than one cutting remark that belies the equality of their partnership, exposing their friendship, like their deal, as inherently fragile and their discourse as a steady stream of vacuous, ethnically coded phrases that Cohn terms "monosyllables with shards of education" (1992, 116). And to celebrate their good and near great fortune, Fox, "The Master of the Revels" as he is dubbed by Gould, breaks into song.

Typical of Mamet's use of lyrics, the song not only underscores *Speed-the-Plow*'s central theme of loyalty but wonderfully renders ironic comment on it. Characteristically, the playwright inserts just the briefest suggestion of the lyric, ". . . singing a song, rolling along" (29), yet further and fuller examination of the song's title, "Side by Side," and lyrics renders the choice hilarious, as Fox has been in Gould's shadow for eleven years in a relationship he describes as "kissing your ass" (31). Counterpointing the sacks of gold that they have yet to make, the first stanza, "We ain't got a barrel of money/Maybe we're ragged and funny/ But we'll travel along, singing a song/ Side by side" is jubilant in the manner of the moment but clearly the wrong choice, as Fox, the only one without a barrel of money, is singing alone. And the second stanza foretells betrayal: "Through all kinds of weather/ What if the sky should fall?/ As long as we're together/ It won't matter at all." Yet, when Gould turns philosophical, undoubtedly in response to the incomplete, unsung lyric, it's time for a lesson.

It is in the role of educator and sagacious advisor that Gould dominates both speech and their relationship. Spoken from a position of wisdom and experience and an elevated stature of power, Gould's speech in the guise of a lesson linguistically reestablishes his dominance and Fox's supporting role. We intuit the irony of Gould's prudent advice to his friend literally and metaphorically "stepping up in class" and out into the line of fire (26). "They're going to plot against you, Charlie, like they plotted against me," Bob warns. "They're going to go back in their Tribal Caves and say 'Chuck Fox, that *hack*. . . . Let's go steal his job . . .'" (26).[22] Drawing upon his depth of knowledge gleaned from a quarter century in the entertainment business and from personal experience, Gould imparts words of wisdom and valuable survival skills about how to "Play at the Big Table" to Fox who is ignorant of its codes (40). The basic wisdom in such a situation, advises Mamet, is to keep one's "mouth shut and . . . eye on the action" (1987d, 95), but when Fox reveals his ignorance, Gould pounces on his error, turning it into an opportunity for a lecture:

> Gould: Char, Charlie: permit me to tell you: two things I've learned, twenty-five years in the entertainment industry.
> Fox: What?
> Gould: The two things which are always true.
> Fox: One:
> Gould: The first one is: there is no net.(33)

Gould apparently forgets the second "truth," because the only truth of any consequence in Hollywood is the operative concept: "gross."[23] Although the corollary to Gould's first principle remains an unspoken maxim, implicit in "there is no net" is the truism that Gould, balancing on a high wire without a net is a less "*secure* whore" (26) than he would have Fox, or us, believe, a point underscored by the fact that "Jews—even more than other moderns—generally work without a safety net of faith" (Whitfield 1986, 337). It is in the area of faith—or the glaring absence of it—that Gay Brewer finds Gould "a parodic, inverted Christ figure, savior son of the studio" whose "deific allusions" are heretical (52). Having come amazingly close to the archetypal depiction of the Jew as satanic figure, Brewer, not alone in missing both the ethnic coding of Mamet's character and the play's intended satire, argues that "the non-existence of net profits constitute[s] the extent of Gould's godly beneficence and wisdom" in one who "pander[s] to America's baseness" (53; 52).

And indeed, pandering is one of those things that Gould does best. Dismissing Fox ostensibly so that he can calculate what he stands to gross on the "Doug Brown, Buddy Film," inclusive of "the rentals, tie in, foreign, air, the . . . the sequels" (20), prior to their power lunch at the Coventry, Gould turns his attention to another figure worthy of delight: Karen. In Fox's view "she falls between two stools," neither a "'floozy,'" on the one hand, nor "so *ambitious* she would schtup you just to get ahead" (35). When Gould rephrases the characterization, Karen emerges as "neither, what, dumb, nor ambitious enough," a description clearly losing something in the translation, but not so much that either will pass up the opportunity to gamble on whether or not Gould can bed her for five hundred dollars (36).

Eric Partridge describes "floosie" as a "'good-time girl,' a tart, an 'enthusiastic amateur,' or even a prostitute"(164), and this range of skills and experience raises the issue of whether Karen is a student or professional, angel or whore. Indeed, much has been made of Madonna, the Material Girl playing the spiritual girl in the original production (Hall 150; Henry 1988).[24] However, of much greater interest is that for the second time this morning Gould has adopted the role of educator. Intent on squeezing the seduction in before lunch and winning his five-hundred-dollar bet with Fox, he engages in a theoretical discussion on the movie business as a mode of soliciting sex, reinforcing the connection between coitus and commerce explored in *Glengarry* (Jacobs 1995, 109-11; Zeifman 1992, 131).[25]

Contrasting sharply with a steady stream of advice delivered to Fox in an imperious manner earlier in the morning highlighting Gould's position and power as a man on whose "*coattails*" Fox has been "riding, several years" (63), Gould—his diction cleansed of vulgarity—adopts a more informal pedagogical attitude toward Karen, encouraging her to address him by his first name, patiently explaining the nature of her error in calling the Coventry to reserve a table for him without identifying him by name, and forgiving a clearly monumental mistake given that his name not only opens doors but (in his dreams) gets movies made—the highest accolade one can have in Hollywood. "Listen," he says, "there's nothing wrong with being naïve, with learning" (39), he instructs her, revealing himself as a patient, supportive teacher, encouraging a dialectic, asking rhetorical questions, and answering them in simple, often simplistic sentences. He explains terminology and identifies personalities, and commends her on her observations. To put it bluntly, "To get to the body," notes Jack Kroll in his review of the play, "Bobby has to deal with the head" (1988, 82). Finding what he believes to be an eager ingenue, Gould extends familiarity even further by encouraging Karen to sit down and by revealing a secret that in the telling is no longer one. Echoing Ricky Roma's line to Lingk, "Listen to what I'm going to tell you now:" (1984, 51), Mamet exposes the pitch packaged in the promise that seductively suckers Karen and us into listening to the elusive articulation of illusion.

As he conveys the mysteries of the movie business in a steady stream of abstractions that intimate community and creativity, Gould's words, "To *make* something, to *do* something, to be a *part* of something" (40), have the power of sharing some profound truth, when in reality both community and his contribution are elusive, if not illusory. However, when faced with Karen's question concerning the artistic quality of Fox's buddy film, Gould is momentarily silenced. Artfully turning the question to his advantage, Gould uses it as an opportunity to illustrate his point that the movie business is addictive and exciting, whereas it offers him an opportunity to strut his knowledge and his status in one area of his life in which excitement and connection appear attainable. As lecture, Gould's specious attempt to reduce complex information into comprehensible concepts is uproarious; lacking cogency and coherence, it reveals his *spiel* as just so much sanctimonious pretension, providing critical evidence of his mind wandering from the subject to the seduction:

> Gould: Well, it's a commodity. And I admire you for not being ashamed to ask the question. Yes, it's a good question, and I don't *know* if it is a good film. "What about Art?" I'm not an artist. Never said I was, and nobody who sits in this chair can be. I'm a businessman. "Can't we try to make good films?" Yes. We try. . . . The question: Is there such a thing as a good film which loses money? In general, of course. But really, not. For *me,* 'cause if the films I make lose money, then I'm back on the streets with a sweet and silly smile on my face, they lost money 'cause nobody saw them, it's my fault. . . . There is a way things are. Some people are elected, try to change the world, this job is not that job . . . (41)

Circumventing Karen's question on artistic quality that he cannot answer, Gould delivers a muddled defense, an apologia, a *pilpul* of sorts that exonerates, exculpates, and vindicates his deeds and decisions, shifting the focus to what enhances his commanding image of responsibility and delineates his job as one, "bullshit aside" (62), with sufficient status to charm the pants off her quite literally. Like Roma's speech to Lingk, it is a brilliant piece of artifice, mocking Fox's observation, "It's only words, unless they're true" (71), intended to mask meaning and intent. Seeking a sign of her comprehension by repeatedly inquiring, "You *see?*" "You follow me?"

"You get it?" (41-42), Gould simultaneously seeks approbation, acknowledgment, and affirmation reminiscent of Pozzo, who after his set-piece in *Waiting for Godot,* similarly seeks comments and compliments. Remarkably Karen, apparently hanging on every word, responds to his associative muddled peroration and questions with "Of course" (41), proving herself at the minimum an attentive student and more likely his equal at trading in equivocation and obfuscation.

Ostensibly having grasped the concept of Gould's lesson up until this point, Karen claims (or feigns) confusion when the concepts—what Carol in *Oleanna* terms "concepts" and "precepts"(Mamet 1993, 14)—become increasingly more complex, as in what defines depravity. As subtly as Gould attempted to seduce her smoothly with his wisdom, Karen, whose orgiastic repetition of "yes" with its echoes of Molly Bloom scores her increasingly more pointed, personal line of inquiry, exploits the allure of her innocence to stimulate Gould's introspection. Taking the lead in their discussion, Karen converts Gould's method of simplification into one of mystification, postulating a slippery correlation between judgment and principle. "Perhaps I'm naïve," she posits, "but I would think that if you could keep your values straight, if you had *principles* to *refer* to, then . . ." (44), but inexplicably she leaves the premise incomplete. Paralleling Karen's earlier response to unfamiliar concepts, Gould is perplexed by her use of "principles," which this seduction-as-sport and his subsequent treatment of Fox dramatically illustrate are a mystery to him, confusing them with a term of commerce he typically associates with the myriad *principals*—agents, "artsy" writers, and studio heads, to name a few—involved in making a film. Yet, unlike his previously successful attempt to sidestep a question, Gould's efforts to change the subject fail. Pressed to respond to her implied question, he not only concludes her premise, he concedes her point, punctuating it for the first time with his signature obscenity: "Okay. (*Pause.*) If you don't have *principles,* whatever they are . . . then each day is hell, you haven't got a compass. All you've got is 'good taste'; and you can shove good taste up your ass and fart 'The Carnival of Venice'" (44-45).

In this one brilliant Mametic moment, Gould, reminded of revelry on the one hand and his impending lunch date on the other takes a commanding step toward winning his bet by quickly cleaning up his diction and reverting to the courtly behavior that previously has played so well. However, the comment is not without its significance as an in-joke, as Mamet, the artsy writer of *Speed-the-Plow* renown, would subsequently write the screenplay for *Ace in the Hole* (1989), a remake of *The Big Carnival,* Billy Wilder's acclaimed 1951 film noir about exploitation. And as an "enthusiastic embrace of bad taste often incorporating scatological references and activities" (Desser and Friedman 115) that marks Mamet, like Mel Brooks and Lenny Bruce, as direct descendants of a tradition of American Jewish comedy, the playwright, echoing Brooks's infamous "As long as I am on the soapbox farts will be heard!" similarly nods to Brooks, for whom "Good taste is meaningless. . . . It's not a factor in art" (Desser and Friedman 117, 115).[26]

On the face of it, then, Gould's vulgarity appears to be merely a slip of the tongue. Nevertheless, tracing the link between anti-Semitism and the discourse of the Jew, Gilman argues that historically the language of the Jew, viewed as corrupt and corrupting, has served a marker of identity, merging representation of the Jew as impure whoremongers and liars—"the verbal equivalent of usury and poisoning" (1986, 47)—with those of the confidence trickster, liar, defiler, and dissembler established in the Middle Ages. Reflecting a shifting anti-Semitic rhetoric in the nineteenth and twentieth centuries, the image was redefined: "The Jew is either the dogmatic, illogical Eastern Jew "whose language is that of commerce," or the *Luftmensch,* the wheeler-dealer, rootless, without morals or goals" (9). And Gould, in his thousand-dollar suits, reflects them all. Thus, avers Gilman, "When those who are labeled as marginal are forced to function within the same discourse as that which labels them as different. . . . they are forced to speak using the polluted languages that designates them as Other" (14), whereas post-Holocaust writers and creative artists "must claim their right to speech" in a discourse that for Mamet sparkles with obscenities (323).[27]

In this scene, however, Karen's speech and logic are baffling though ironically persuasive, confounding Gould into thinking that she has the answer to the truths implied by her apparently logical structure. Yet both her logic and Gould's acceptance of her statement are fallacious. As Douglas Watson explains in *Begging the Question,* the failure to meet the burden of proof may be best defined as a fault of logic, "begging the question," because the prover in practice must "assume or (ask to be assumed) what is required to be proved" (1991, 10). Paradoxically, notes Watson, broad usage of the term "to beg the question" in the modern period has rendered it vacuous to the extent that is applicable to any failure to respond or reply satisfactorily to a question (10-12). From this perspective of common, contemporary inverse usage broadly taken to mean failure to raise a question, Gould's tacit acceptance of Karen's initial premise is implicit in his response—"If you don't have *principles,* whatever they are" (44)—and may be (mis)construed as "begging the question" because Gould's failure to question Karen's premise may be perceived as conceding her point *as* proof. More likely, rather than conceding her point, his mind is focused on another: engaging her in bed rather than in debate.

However much their ensuing dialogue is advanced by a series of inane if amusing platitudes of appreciation and admiration, echoing those exchanged between Fox and Gould earlier in the morning, we are drawn backward into the circular reasoning and gaping hole of Karen's ethical hypothesis. Indeed, her presumptive conditional, what Watson denotes in *Slippery Slope Arguments* as "the appropriate linking relation" when "the issue concerns a discussion of a best course of action in a particular situation," it appears to have true premises—"if you had *principles* to *refer* to"(44)—but no conclusion (1992, 216-17). Where logic fails, then, is its "defeasible (rebuttable) nature" (218). The fallacious structure, or the *incompleteness* of Karen's presumably logical premise, is critical—not merely foreshadowing its conclusion but casting doubt on Karen's wisdom— because at the very least it establishes the presumption that further premises that she promulgates on the condition of the world and the correct course of action in it are at best questionable. Like her promotion of *The Bridge*, Karen's argument is flawed. Implicit, then, as act 1, twice as long as acts 2 and 3 combined, draws to a close is a presumptive conditional posed by Mamet: If Karen's reasoning is specious (or self-refuting) sophistry, then by extension so is her philosophy-cum-theology that with Christian canon those who are lost will be found.

On the surface, however, mirroring the conclusion of Fox's earlier lesson, all is jest and merriment. With Karen's promise secured to complete a book report assignment on *The Bridge*—a screenplay that subsequently competes for his attention and allegiance with the "buddy film" proffered by Fox—to be delivered to his home later that evening with the clear implication of assignation, Gould, having scored twice on his first day as Head of Production, is heady with glee. In fact, with "a sweet and silly smile on my face" (41), Gould can barely contain his delight, insisting that Karen call Fox's secretary so that Fox gets the message that Gould won the five hundred dollar bet in advance of their lunch, "confirming," as Ann Hall notes, "that he has neither principles nor good taste " (154). "It's the old Jewish joy of the deal," jokes Mamet. "Besides, the people in Hollywood are so funny. It's a place full of gamblers, hucksters, and con artists, including me. We're all rug merchants" (qtd. in Christiansen 1989, 18).

Blinded by ego, Gould believes that he has beguiled the ingenue with a slick solicitation of sex in the guise of a lesson; what he has failed to see is that Karen's act has been all "smoke and mirrors." Duped by a sharper image than his own on a mission for initiates, Karen has transposed the lesson into a solicitation for souls. In the background we can almost hear the strains of the lavish musical number, what Desser and Friedman describe as a "sumptuous Busby Berkeley parody" that Mel Brooks wrote (with Ronny

Graham) for *History of the World, Part I,* a film about religious fanatics—in this case Torquemada—whose persecution of Jews masquerades as education intended to purify their souls:

> We have a mission to convert the Jews.
> We're gonna teach them wrong from right.
> We're gonna help them see the light
> And make them an offer they can't refuse.
> (qtd. in Desser and Friedman 156)[28]

While David Radavich contends that Karen promotes "'the moral high ground'" (56), inspired no doubt by Mamet's comment "that he believed that he was writing a latter-day Joan of Arc" (Jones and Dykes 68), Mel Gussow identifies her as possessing "an other-worldliness" like Miss A in *The Shawl* and Dr. Ford in *House of Games* (1988, 55). Hall reads her as a woman, "neither saint nor whore," capable of seeing and responding to Gould's insecurity (157), and Rich characterizes her as a "catalytic character" at once "so unused to thinking in a 'business fashion' that she can hardly fetch coffee" and "the axis on which the play turns—an enigma within an enigma" (1988, C 17). Charlie Fox, a rug merchant himself similarly seeking approbation, comes closest by cutting to the chase: "What is she, a witch?" (69). A wise reader of character and conduct, Fox is not far off the mark, for Karen may be profitably viewed as a mythical trickster figure. Tricksters and con artists are abundantly familiar inhabitants of Mamet territory; but as early as *Marranos,* in which the children's governess is uncovered as a collaborator of the Inquisition who has kidnapped a child for the purposes of conversion, Mamet's women have been a mystery to men.

Notably, in *Speed-the-Plow* the mythical trickster figure serves to bridge the mythic and the metaphysical in ways critics have not noticed. The trickster figure, observes William J. Hynes, is capable of engaging and bridging "unceasing sets of counterpoised sectors, such as sacred and profane, life and death, culture and nature, order and chaos, fertility and impotence" (34). Alternately a "messenger and an imitator of the gods," a "deceiver and a dissembler," a sacred/lewd *bricoleur* and "notorious border breaker" empowered with "the ability to overturn any person, place, or belief, no matter how prestigious," the trickster figure is a cultural transformer who demonstrates one or more of these cluster characteristics (35-42). Typically appearing in art and literature as a mythic, metaphoric figure with links "to crafts and commerce," whose identity remains cloaked in mystery, who assumes the form of male or female, old or young, and whose lewd action and artful cunning achieve his or her full powers at night, the complex trickster in all its manifestations leads to the erotic as a means of human connection (Doty 49, 62-64). It is the *bricoleur* aspect of the trickster that Hynes defines as capable of causing lewd acts "to be transformed into occasions of insight" that I find the most intriguing, given that sex serves to illuminate in more ways than Karen intends. For this "tinker and fix-it person . . . [who] traffics with the transcendent" (42) is a consummate trick-player ultimately "trickster-tricked" (35).

Possessing many of the trickster figure's more prominent talents and traits, Karen does her best work at night, coupling eroticism and social catharsis in a didactic methodology that is as orgiastic, ecstatic, and frenzied as Gould has fantasized. But, bridging lust, arousal, and copulation with stirring passion and spiritual elucidation, Karen guides Gould into an intercourse characterized by sacred rather than carnal knowledge. Transposing the teacher/student dynamic dramatized earlier in Gould's office, Karen dominates their discussion in act 2 in what Brewer terms "Gould's mock temptation" (54)—although I would argue more mockery than mock—by quoting at length from *The Bridge*, which it appears she has not so much read as digested. In her role as educator Karen parallels Gould in her commanding control of the lecture whose focus is the *prima facie* statement that "things as we know them" are over (55).

Interested in neither the book's content nor its conclusions, Gould attempts to redirect the line of thought to her accomplishment in reading it as a means of furthering the expected seduction. However, as she did earlier in the day by questioning his principles, Karen now confounds and silences Gould by questioning his judgment. "Are you ever wrong?" (54), she asks, manipulating the discussion back toward her interpretation and focusing its thrust on the principles of right and wrong. And whereas Karen formerly understood his lesson, or gave the impression of doing so, Gould's confusion is reflected in a litany of queries providing explicit evidence that he is not only utterly mystified by her lesson but incapable of refuting her statements. Repeatedly asking, "You see?" (58), Karen seeks signs of affirmation and comprehension, as Gould did in his lecture, but in contrast to her experience in which the book "spoke to" her, Karen elicits Gould's outburst: "No, I don't understand. . . . No. . . . I don't understand you" (59). Just as Gould's slip of the tongue earlier in the day may be read as ethnically coded, given that we, or at least she can "find the answers. In the book " (58), Karen's ability "to see" in contrast to Gould's blindness implicitly conveys, as Gilman has noted, proof of the Jew's refusal to accept the word of Christ. And, as Gilman adds, "it is also clear that if one of the roles of the Church is to propagate the faith, then the Jews must hear the truth" (1986, 25). And hear it Gould does.

As the following scene opening act 2 reveals, much of the comic energy derives from the humor of Gould having bet his friend five hundred bucks to boff "the broad" (69), only to find himself in the grip of Karen's passionate embrace: of "The Book" and its message. Karen tells Gould: "when I *read* it . . . I almost, I wanted to sit, I saw, I almost couldn't come to you, the *weight* of it. . . . He says that the radiation. . . . all of it *is to the one end*. To *change* us—to, to *bring about a change*"(48). Whereas Cohn views this scene as "lacking the comic energy of his [Mamet's] business scenes" and concludes that the "satire falls flat" (1992, 117), the satire falls flat only if we misread Mamet's point—that Karen's turgid tone is deliberately "flat," devoid of the humor that inspires the dyad between Fox and Gould. My reading of the linguistics of *The Bridge* and Karen's conversion of Gould is further enhanced by William Novak's and Moshe Waldoks's twin criteria for the Jewish joke: "one that no *goy* can understand and every Jew has already heard" (1981, xx). Their tracing Jewish humor to religious sources and "the minority condition from which such a sensibility could so naturally emerge" (Whitfield 1988, 68) provide ample support that by definition Jewish humor is conspicuous by its absence in *The Bridge*.

Moreover, in its inverted syntax and grammatical chaos, there is not only "method," to borrow Cohn's phrase, but meaning (1992, 111). In its trinity of titles, apocalyptic allusions, reiterated catchphrases ("grace" and "peace"), and its itinerant priest, *The Bridge* is not merely "quasi-mystic." Its characters, motifs, opaque imagery, linguistic rhythms, and "threshold quality" of text and title reflect what Frank Kermode, in his analysis of the Book of John, identifies as the new form of eschatology that centered on a divine revelation in the centuries immediately before Christ. Common in these oracular texts was "a sense that contemporary events, if correctly understood, could be seen as 'signs of the times' that would reveal the imminence of the appointed end" (McGinn 526). Contrasting with the Revelation at Sinai, which a classic Jewish joke describes as deal between Moses and God—"The good news is that I got them down to ten; the bad news is that adultery is still in" (Telushkin 97)—Jewish apocalypses are typically revealed to believers and concealed from the unworthy. One such revelatory experience occurs in the Book of Daniel. Well-known, well-placed, and much-loved, Daniel is at first glance a likely gloss for Bobby Gould (Wiesel 1991, 100). The analogue collapses, however, when he also shows himself to be a man devoted to Jewish worship and to his friends, a Jew who can "make it" among gentiles without giving up his faith. Experiencing an apocalyptic vision and instructed by the heavenly messenger, Gabriel, not to disclose the vision, Daniel is confused—not unlike Gould who twice refers to himself as "lost." As such, says Wiesel, "Daniel is defined by contradiction: not entirely man, not entirely prophet, not entirely emissary, not entirely guide. A genuine Diaspora Jew, he is always torn by two forces at once" (113).

In contrast, the Book of Revelation is read by "Millions of Christian fundamentalists . . . in a highly literal way as a blueprint for coming crisis . . ." (McGinn 523), their missionary zeal inspired by Matthew 2: 8: "Go therefore and make disciples of all nations." As Jewish and Christian revelatory texts are characterized by the intervention of a heavenly messenger (526), Karen, whose name in Hebrew is derived from *shomer,* 'to watch over' (Kolatch 1984, 351), would seem to fit the bill as divine angel, while other interpretations of her name, 'horn,' 'power,' and 'capital' (419) similarly if ironically announce her mission, and that of *The Bridge:* to witness and convert. And from this perspective, the "work" and the "word" that Karen is peddling in Hollywood as the stories that "people need to see" and the ones, she contends (59), that Gould was put on earth to make, are oracular: His stories about His love. Radiating hope, communion, and courage out of "the planes, the televisions, clocks" (48), *The Bridge*'s spokesperson, Karen, sounds like religious broadcaster Pat Robertson, whose Christian Coalition, financed by what Gould might call "Great big jolly *shitloads*" of money (20), flooded the airwaves with a messianic message of morality.[29] A prophet for profit, Karen weasels herself into Gould's consciousness with her promise of "Perfect Love" (78), and he, desperate for meaning and security in his life, succumbs—as Lingk does in *Glengarry*—to the sales pitch whatever its source, mirroring a familiar pattern in American Jewish literature that repeatedly depicts the central dilemma as a conflict between meaning and money (Shechner 1979, 203). In this context, then, we better understand the irony of the novel's title and its mythic as well as metaphysical evocation. As metaphor and eidetic image eliciting myriad literal and literary bridges between tradition and modernity that lead immigrant Jews to abundance and away from identity, I understand the bridge to be what Roskies characterizes as "a bridge of longing."

Yet Bernard Weiner, in his review of the play, admits to being "confused and disturbed" by the dichotomy that pits the stereotypical Jewish producers as money-hungry manipulators against Karen, an "angel of salvation," observing that the "hope and change" (1989, 77) that she offers is not your garden variety" but religious fundamentalism.[30] The dichotomy, he correctly suggests, is no coincidence. Aware of Mamet's public affirmation of Jewish pride ("Plain Brown Wrapper" was published first in *Tikkun* in 1988), he concludes unresolved: "Is Mamet, the former Reform Jew yearning for total assimilation, showing us what happens when Jews, who should know better and have a moral tradition that calls on them to pursue higher things, mirror the worst traits of yuppie goyim? Or could he possibly be suggesting that Jewish souls are lost to God unless they open their hearts to Jesus?"(77). Rejecting the latter premise, Weiner might have done well to reject part of the former premise as well, for he takes literally the stereotypical portrait of the producers rather than perceiving that Mamet's rapier wit slashes the portrait of whoring depravity.

Hersh Zeifman would have us read "The homosocial world of American business" as it is portrayed in Mamet's plays as "a topsy-turvy world in which all values are inverted by characters who think with their crotch" (1992, 125-26). And Radavich contends in "David Mamet's Homosocial Order" that *Speed-the-Plow*'s "homosexual imagery is noticeably positive and comic, accepted without reservation by the two main characters" (1991, 55), given that Fox and Gould casually refer to themselves as "Two Old Whores" and "*Fair*-haired boys" (26, 19), "trade gay references" such as "'Just let me turn One More Trick'"(26), and apparently share—with Mamet, the essay implies—"the perception of women as sexual 'weakeners' or 'corrupters' of men" (57). While it is tempting to see *Speed-the-Plow* as a logical progression of this paradigm—supported by Gould's proposal that they "go swishing by Laura Ashley" to purchase "some cunning prints" (32) to decorate Gould's office as a "bordello" (26), by Fox's expression of love for Gould, by his jealous explosion of anger, "you squat to pee. You old *woman*" (70)—coupled with their apparent love of money, lack of ethical and moral principles, and perverse behavior, it is also erroneous. Mamet's portrait of the homosocial Jew is neither "noticeably positive" nor essentially comic.

As Gilman illustrates in *The Jew's Body*, "The association of the venality of the Jew with capital," namely the perception that perversion of the Jew is integral to his sexualized relationship to money, commonplace throughout Europe in the nineteenth century and persistent in the twentieth, not only contributed to the Holocaust but "echoes the oldest and most basic calumny against the Jew, his avarice . . . for the possession of 'things,' of 'money,' which signals his inability to understand (and produce) anything of transcendent aesthetic value" (1991b, 123-24). Further, "in taking money," notes Gilman, the Jew, like the prostitute to whom he is likened—substitutes money "for higher values, for love and beauty" (124). However, the linkage between sex, commerce and greed dates to the Middle Ages, where in John Chrysostom's *Adversus Judaeos* (Homily I), the vilification of the Jews etched anti-Jewish imagery for posterity, delineating Jews as "'gathering choruses of effeminates and a great rubbish heap of harlots'" and "the synagogue" a "brothel and a theater'" (Lazar 1991, 48). Hence, Leslie Fiedler suggests, "gender ambiguity is perhaps already implicit in ethnic [identity]" since "like all Jews" a "man"—

the connotation is of a circumcised male—is viewed as a "woman," or "androgynous at least" (1991, 56). The inspired satire of this act, beyond the fact that Karen is as accomplished in masquerading as Fox and Gould, is Mamet's depiction of the saint as a seeker of profits and power challenging the stigmatized portrait of the Jew as power broker and whoremonger incapable of producing or participating in anything but depravity.

Paralleling Jenny Lingk in *Glengarry Glen Ross*, Karen does her best work offstage and out of sight, encouraging Gould to confront his fears, forgiving his iniquities, converting him to see the light of her prophecy, promoting boldness and community, and convincing him that she is the answer to his dreams and his prayers. Her amazing ability to quickly curry Gould's favor inspires one to inquire whether she is a truly a wise person, a *khakham*, rich in learning, or wise to Gould's weakness, in other words a *khukham*, a masterful trickster of duplicity, anxious to get something for nothing. Jewish humor places an inordinate amount of emphasis on business jokes (Telushkin 68-72), and surely a theory is viable that Karen is more—or less—than meets the eye.[31] Thus, if Fox and Gould had wondered earlier in the day if she would schtup Gould for money *or* ambition, both have misread the signs: A saint abroad and a devil at home, "she shtupps to conquer."[32] As he has done in *Glengarry* and *House of Games*, Mamet cuts to act 3 without depicting Gould's conversion but evidencing it linguistically. Thus, in stark contrast to his demeanor and discourse in act 1, Gould is strangely silent; and when he does of speak of "alien" concepts like "respect" and caring, his discourse is notably devoid of the bawdy humor that has historically been viewed as a marker of the Jew, "an atavistic sign" of his or her "sexuality" (Gilman 1991b, 136).

Citing the subject of whores and robbers in his review of the play, Rich opines that it is entirely feasible that in *Speed-the-Plow* "God Himself [is] just another exploitable concept—or con—in the greedy machinations of American commerce" (1988, C 17). Yet, when Karen convinces Gould that he was "put here to make the stories people need to see. To make them less afraid" (59), Fox, spotting a scam, is prepared to lay one more story on Gould:

> Fox: Why did she come to see you? Cause you're the Baal Shem Tov? You stupid shit, I'm talking to you . . . Why does she come to you? 'Cause you're so good looking? She *wants* something from you. You're nothing to her but what you can *do* for her. (72)[33]

Mamet's resonant, ironic reference to the Baal Shem Tov, the revered and respected Hasidic teacher to whom disciples flocked, cohesively connects

Fox's suspicion that neither sex nor scholarship attracted Karen to Gould and underscores what we have witnessed: that Gould is a far better student than teacher. Implicitly conveying its own cultural (hi)story, the rich allusion to the Baal Shem, moreover, wonderfully links the tropes of ethnicity, education, and enlightenment dramatized in *Speed-the Plow,* for the founder of Hasidism, possessed of outstanding personal spiritual attainment, projected the finest example of Jewish teaching: a unity of doctrine and Judaism as a way of life, an intertwining of the profane and the holy, sexual fantasies and business affairs (Breslauer 53-55). In his Nobel acceptance speech, Wiesel tells a wonderful story about the Baal Shem and his faithful friend that has relevance to *Speed-the-Plow*'s paradigms, parody, and celebration of power, friendship, and spiritual illumination. In this Hasidic legend, the Baal Shem "undertook an urgent and perilous mission" to hasten the arrival of the Messiah because the world was "beset by too many evils." For interfering with history, he was banished to a distant island where he lost both his mystical powers and memory. Aided by his friend, he regained his memory and, with it, his identity and power (1990, 237-238). [34]

Similarly, Gould has lost his memory, his focus, and apparently his judgment. Not only has he been persuaded to greenlight the radiation film and thereby bring a message of grace to the world—a book that he knows "Won't Make A Good Movie" and "won't Get The Asses In The Seats"(53)—but he has betrayed his friend in favor of Karen. The abrogation of his oral promise that he would promote Fox's buddy film and further his career by naming him co-producer is conduct that Jewish ethical law would denote as morally objectionable, namely the violation of trust (Levine 124). Thus, when Karen subsequently says, "I think I'm being punished for my wickedness" (80), she is not far off the mark, because apparently empowered by the apocalyptic novel, Karen attempts to induce change in a done deal, conduct that would similarly be viewed as unethical. As an interfering third party who profits by "Snatching away another's anticipated gain" just prior to the consummation of that deal, Karen, according to Jewish law, would be termed a *rasha,* one who is wicked, whose crime is not the interference in the deal but the perversion of the truth (Levine 124).

Each character in *Speed-the-Plow* is on the verge of change at the end of this play, just as he or she is at the beginning, and Fox's transformation in this act is most notably communicated in his commanding speech and actions. In fact, "change" rather than "currency" or "commerce" is the play's operative concept, and Gould's metamorphosis serves as its arc. On the verge of what he presumes to be profound change in his life, career, and financial status, Fox is confronted with an age-old dilemma—one that parallels and sharply contrasts with Gould's dark night of the soul. He engages in a Talmudic argument with himself whether, on the one hand, he is worthy of being rich and, on the other, whether he can live with the guilt of being greedy—what Sanford Pinsker characterizes as archetypal "Jewish conflict" and Mamet implies is Jewish guilt. Having resolved that it would not be a sign of *chutzpah* to remind Gould to promote Ross both on the commodity and the dynamic team of limitless potential that brought it to him, Gould presents Fox with a dilemma that he did not even include in his deliberations: namely, that Gould would renege on his promise to option the Doug Brown film.

Stunned at the betrayal, the immorality of his friend breaking an oral contract, Fox is furious with Gould and with himself for failing to heed Gould's advice to watch his back. Seeing his fairy tale devolve into a horror story, he is deeply shaken, but adopts the pose of deference and confidence that barely masks his unmitigated rage—a mockery of his behavior in act 1 in which a "crescendo of demented gratitude" barely masked his combative desperation (Kroll 1988, 65). Fox attempts to assure Gould that his concern is for Gould's welfare and that he bears him no anger. But his words, "I'm not upset with you" (reflecting the propensity of Yiddish to invert and so emphasize the intended meaning) belie both his emotional state—"I have to siddown"—and the truth that in the course of a single day he has seen his greatest dreams and worst fears realized (65). Sharply contrasting with act 1, energized by a giddy Fox crowing, "I'm gonna be rich" (21), act 3 confronts him with a grim reality implied in Gould's promotion of *The Bridge*: not only is he going to be poor, but his name may not even be "a *punchline* in this town" (69). Suddenly he understands that Gould's former assurance that "Ross, Ross, Ross isn't going to fuck" him out of this deal in no way protected him from Gould, who *is* "going to fuck" him out of it (22).

Endeavoring to (re)gain Gould's attention and so save the deal, Fox says, thrice repeating the phrase, "Now, listen to *me*. . . . now, listen to *me* now. . . . listen to *me* now" (65, emphasis added), as if the mesmerizing power of his voice, of the phrase, and of their friendship will serve as the "*wake*-up call" (69) Gould seems to have missed this morning. Fox attempts to swing the pendulum in his direction, reestablishing the prominence of his influence and his project before time runs out on his deal. And the difference in his demeanor and discourse is most apparent in the substitution of arrogance for deference. Thus, instead of complimenting Gould to curry favor as he formerly did, he insults him. "I'm talking to you like some Eastern Fruit," Fox rants, exploding when Gould attempts to interrupt him; "Shut up," he says imperiously, "I'm not done speaking" (66), recalling the now classic distinction between "*speaking*. . . . As an idea" and "*talking*" that culminates the dyad between Aaronow and Moss in *Glengarry Glen Ross* (39) and reemerges between Carol and John in *Oleanna*. Armed with reason, ridicule, threats, and humor, Charlie Fox, whose name implicitly conveys his sensory acuity and heightened survival skills, springs into action, barbs flying, attacking Gould where he lives: "*your* contract's shit" (66, emphasis added), he yells, threatening him with the worst evils that can befall him:

> . . . you're going to become a laughingstock, and no one will *hire* you. Bob . . . You'll be "off the Sports List." *Why?* Because they will not understand why you did what you did. You follow me. . . ? That is the *worst* pariah. Your best *friend* won't hire you. *I* won't hire you. . . . Are you *insane?* (66)

Punctuating his diatribe with interrogatories and ethnically coded reference to the "worst pariah," who is evidently a pariah's pariah, Fox projects a future of disaster for Gould and acclaim for himself, alternating his vision with the present moment, which from his perspective spells disaster for them both. As the switchbacks in Fox's speech reveal, he is keenly aware of time, both in the literal sense that time is running out on his package, and the metaphysical as it pertains to his "historical self" (28).

Fox's peroration is peppered throughout with questions, the majority of which are not intended to elicit information, but rather as culturally encoded speech that underscores both the absence of *shtick* in act 2 and the linguistic rhythms of act 1, where each anticipated or completed the other's lines, and the unity that those rapid-fire, quick-witted dyads—resembling well-rehearsed stand-up comic routines—implied. Expressing his rage and crushing disappointment verbally and physically for Gould "going toidy all over my whole life" (68), Fox seeks a rational explanation for Gould's irrational behavior and consequent betrayal: "Have, Bob, have you always hated me?"; "Some secret . . ."; "Doubted my loyalty, my . . ."; "Then, why are you doing this?" (68). While his inverted speech, unfinished sentences, and seemingly incessant interrogatories may be written off to his heightened emotional state, mocking the anxiety and mania that typified his discourse in act 1, Fox's audible emotion, like that of Teach in *American Buffalo* and Levene in *Glengarry Glen Ross,* similarly bespeaks his ethnicity. Among the myriad questions is the unasked but implicit archetypal Jewish question: Why me?

One may cynically presume that deference and arrogance having failed, Fox employs concern as yet another ploy to win over Gould, for he increasingly demonstrates a mounting anxiety about Gould's aberrant behavior. Indeed, Fox's litany of interrogatories—"What the fuck's *wrong* with you . . . ?"; "what's happened to you . . . ?"; "What's the matter?" (66-

70)—firmly and not insignificantly situate the locus of Fox's obsessive behavior outside of himself where, according to Jewish thought, it should be. Clearly, it seems, there is more at stake than either his career or Gould's: his friend since the mailroom, his mentor, and his ticket to ride, Gould is either breaking under the strain of his new job or has been converted by Karen, a presumption strengthened by the intimacy of their relationship and merely intimated by Fox's earlier comment in act 1, "I know you, Bob. I know you from the *back*" (34). And when Gould addresses his friend of eleven years in a rhetorical pattern and word choice that is totally alien, Fox, convinced that personal disaster transcends professional, concludes, "You've proved yourself insane" (69). "In a good play," Mamet reminds us, "the [important] information is delivered almost as an aside." In fact, when two characters are "screaming at each other, really out of control. . . . You have not only been given information, you've been told to please look the other way," prompting you, he suggests, "to put your mind on afterburner" (Norman and Rezek 56). Thus, within the context of venting his rage, Fox's choice of words is credible, but as ethnic coding, "insane" speaks volumes. "Is there anyone who doesn't know that *meshugge* means crazy? Crazy, nuts, wildly extravagant, absurd," asks Rosten? (1989, 353). Indeed, the word *crazy* in this context, as opposed to Fox's insane antics in act 1, conveys an idea "so silly or unreal it defines explanation" (359). However, in the 1950s, notes Gilman, the term "insane" came to be associated with "Jews [who] have no center": self-hating, they internalize and identify with the anti-Semitism projected against the Jew (1986, 306-07). Given that Gould seems to have lost his "voice," he has, by the loss of this clear ethnic marker, "proved" Fox's initial presumption as fact.

Fox brings about a change in Gould, thereby saving his own life and career and that of his friend, by identifying Karen as "Some broad from the Temporary Pool. A Tight Pussy wrapped around Ambition" (78). His action ironically gives new meaning to Gould's earlier approval of Fox's loyalty: ". . . you stuck with the Old Firm, Charl, you stuck with your friends" (15). However, Fox wins his point when he coaxes Karen into admitting "We decided" [to make *The Bridge*]; "there are no 'we' decisions in Mamet's Hollywood," Cohn wisely observes (1995, 68). Rather more importantly, Fox wins Gould's attention by his depiction of Karen as a power-hungry broad who has used her body and whatever brains she possesses to win Gould's confidence and sucker him into buying an artsy novel "On The End of the World" (53), whose story Gould is hard-pressed to tell Fox. While his vulgar job description is one that has engendered criticism of Mamet's presumed misogynistic portrait, Fox's rhetoric touches a familiar and familial cord in Gould, its overt obscenity a shofar call intended to awaken his friend by implicitly reminding him that *we* are different from her. Having been forsaken for the Other, Fox turns the trick, I believe, by playing the memory card, by calling upon Gould directly: "I need you to remember me" (79). The biblical allusion, coupled with Fox's code-switching, his scatological language, and the shorthand between friends of long standing, brings the play to a rapid conclusion that underscores their unification.

In fact, Gould's subtle shift toward unity with Fox is once again communicated linguistically as he assumes a commanding diction and expels Karen from their space by cutting off her speech: "We're rather busy now. . . . Mr. Fox will show you out," he says, reordering the trinity of relationships and leaving Fox to wonder aloud, "That was a close one. Don't you think?" (80), and the audience to ponder how many times Gould has been so tempted before. Karen's confession that she was motivated by ambition and personal gain, critical to the shaping of Mamet's well-made play, equates all three as whores while judging some actions more or less moral than others. Ironically, in this world obviously devoid of personal conscience, Karen's admission of cupidity opposes Gould's insistent demand for honesty: "Without the bullshit. Just tell me. You're living in a World of Truth. Would you of gone to bed with me, I didn't do your book. (*Pause.*)" (77). Although she speaks the truth, her negative response confirms that in the "World of Truth"—better known to audiences as the world of illusion—where conscience, courtesy, and kindness are conspicuous by their absence, and in the "People Business," people betray people (22).

Torn between the dream that she held out to him and her forced confession, Gould is in despair: "Oh, God, now I'm lost. . . . I'm *lost,* do you hear me, I'm *lost*" (78-79), confirming what Whitfield has observed regarding the Jews' relationship with God: "Jews are not the only people to have talked to God but are . . . the only people to have talked *back* to God, to have attempted to bargain and negotiate" (1978, 56). Not unlike the plaintive cry of Aaronow (and by implication his biblical counterpart, Aaron) that concludes *Glengarry Glen Ross,* Gould's *cri de coeur* acknowledges what David Damrosch identifies as "the shock of the Exile" (72). Indeed, beginning in act 1 of *Speed-the-Plow,* Gould has referred to the wilderness. Lost in reading *The Bridge* when Fox walks into his new office, also in a untamed state of chaos, Gould quips, "I'm in the midst of the wilderness" (3). A marginal state, the prototypical wilderness, invariably implies in its numerous biblical references a paradigmatic sacred world, sanctified and separated (Leach 586-88).

Thus Mamet brings the play full circle, linking exilic imagery to earlier allusions to hiding the Afikomen, the unleavened bread of affliction associated with the Jews' expulsion from Egypt. The exilic reference in *Speed-the-Plow*, inextricably united to the trope of transformation and illumination made manifest through education, becomes progressively clearer, moreover, when we recall that the Book of Exodus, "probably the quintessential book of culture formation in exile," records the historical period in which "the cult is forged, the laws . . . are given, the covenant is renewed . . . their history of being chosen, backsliding, being chastised, and renewing commitment" are enacted (Fredericksen 37-38). Exile, in other words, is a transforming experience, what Damrosch terms "the necessary lacuna, between cultures and between past and future history" that structures "alienation [as] the basis for a renewed ethical closeness" (76, 74).

What has all of this to do with Bobby Gould in whose world there is little sacred in content or conduct and whose knowledge of law extends only to the provisions of a contract measured in millions? I would argue everything. Exilic imagery and the motif of lost identity in American Jewish literature were first articulated by Abraham Cahan—to whom Mamet refers in the preface to *Writing in Restaurants* when he describes recognizing himself as a "lapsed Talmudist" (1987d, viii). Cahan, whose collection— *Yekl and The Imported Bridegroom and Other Stories of the New York Ghetto* (1896) and subsequent acclaimed novel *The Rise of David Levinsky* (1917) depicted uncouth, sordid, and ambitious immigrants striving for acceptance and affluence, defined the American Jewish experience as a "modern exodus" that brought Jews to "their Promised Land" where "good people [read observant Jews, moral individuals] are morally degraded in the struggle for success" and ethical values are exchanged for money (1896, 15). Not only is Gould in that lacuna between cultures, but his secular visions of sacks of gold and unbridled sex pale before the loss of connectedness brought about by disregarding his ethnic identity. If like other Americans Jews Gould thought that forsaking Judaism would gain him acceptance, implies Mamet, his reasoning has been terribly flawed: assimilated, he is connected nowhere. Thus, we may fruitfully read, and reread, *Speed-the-Plow* as a parable of the wilderness: of being chosen, backsliding, being chastised, and renewing commitment.

When Fox finally queers Karen's deal and reestablishes his own, he not only threatens Karen's life—"You ever come on the lot again, I'm going to have you killed" (80)—but for good measure throws *The Bridge* out after her. While Fox's saber-rattling is consistent with his apparent goals, his motivation may be viewed as having a deeper Judaic justification, seeing the threat of the stranger as a manifestation of Amalek, the hated biblical figure linked to the Jews' backsliding in the wilderness. Hence, Fox's actions gain new meaning when we observe him as a friend, one who sharpens Gould's thinking, questions his insights, and helps clarify his dilemma (as the Hebrew word for friend, *haver* connotes). Even if these actions also serve his own interests, he is empowered to save Gould's professional and spiritual life. And saving a single individual, the Talmud reminds us, is tantamount to saving the world.

Echoing the book's refrain, "'How are things made round . . .'" (81), Fox signals the circular conclusion of *Speed-the-Plow*, one that conveys the illusion that little has changed. Indeed, the subtlety of *Speed-the-Plow's* conclusion, in which all fairy tales of promotion, promiscuity, and profit are inverted and Gould returns from changing his shirt as easily as he previously shifted allegiances, has led many critics to misread signs (Stafford 45; Hall 157; Rainer 1988, 7), to presume that the play circles back to Hollywood "business as usual," what Cohn terms "lethally circular" (1992, 120). The view that *Speed-the-Plow* is an "unrivaled celebration of darkness" (Brewer 61) echoes the conclusion at which Carla McDonough arrives regarding Fox and Gould: "like so many of Mamet's other characters," they are "right back where they started having learned or grown little" (205). On the contrary, as Fox implies through the technique of indirection, religion—or at least ethnic identity—may provide a source of connectedness, of renewed awareness and redemptive possibility, and ultimately of change.

Assuming the role of educator, as Gould and Karen have before him, Fox delivers a lesson that is more important for what it does not say directly than for what it does. Historically, Judaism has advocated the pursuit of education as a worthy goal in its own right and criticized those who would abuse pedagogy for material gain. Buber reasons that education exists for the formation of character; "The real choice," he contends, "does not lie between a teacher's having values and not having them, but between his imposing those values on the student" (Friedman 181). Notably, Fox's methodology and message differ markedly from that of Gould and Karen, both of whom are didactic rather than dialogic in the pursuit of their goals. Implicitly addressing the issues of anti-Semitism and the assimilation of American Jews into Christian America who foolishly sought and seek acceptance and affluence through secularization in an ethnically coded "lesson," Fox's speech in the concluding moments of the play bears a striking similarity to those subjects raised by the playwright in his essay, "A Plain Brown Wrapper":

Fox: Well, Bob, you're human. You think I don't know? I know. We wish people would like us, huh? To Share Our Burdens. But it's not to be.

Gould: . . . I suppose not.

Fox: You're goddamn right, not. And what *if* this fucken' "grace"
          exists? It's not for you. You know that, Bob. You know that.
          You have a different thing.
Gould: She told me I was a good man.
Fox: How would *she* know? You *are* a good man. Fuck *her.* (81,
          emphasis added) [35]

Motivated by fear and his desire "to do Good" (81), which unifies
him with other Mamet characters "trying to do good in a bad world"
(Mosher qtd. in Kane 1992, 242), Gould became, in his own words,
"foolish"(81), fooled into thinking that a "different thing" was a better
thing. On this subject Mamet is even more direct in his essay, "The
Decoration of Jewish Houses," in which he recounts that in his youth
"someone who obviously *was* Jewish and sought to deny it, primarily
through the adoption of a Christian religion, was in our homes an object
of wonder and scorn," not only "despised as a weakling" but pitied as a
fool. "Or to distill: What would induce you to renounce the only people
who love you?" (1989b, 12). Echoing the same idea in *Speed-the-Plow,* Fox
turns Gould's confession of error in judgment as it pertains to theology
and human relationships, as well as business, into a pedagogical opportunity. In place of his former heated censure and furiously funny condemnation of Gould—"you *wimp,* you *coward . . .* now you got the job, and
now you're going to *run* all over everything, like something broke in the
shopping bag, you *fool . . .*" (70)—Fox responds with compassion and
camaraderie, complying with Jewish ethical law, which rejects reminding
a repentant person of his misdeeds (Levine 203). "Well," he says, "so we
learn a lesson" (82), reaffirming their unity in business, friendship, and
Jewishness. Contrasting sharply with his former loquaciousness, Fox's few
words connote what Lawrence Kushner has characterized as "the most
powerful moments of teaching [that] occur, when the teacher has enough
self-control to remain silent" (1991, 33) or, in Fox's case, nearly silent.
And picking up directly from the dropped thread of his previous thought,
Fox adds, "Because we joke about it, Bob, we joke about it, but it *is* a
'People Business,' what else is there . . . ?" (81). Fox's rhetorical question
and twice repeated phrase, "we joke about it," following directly upon his
previous discussion, both celebrates humor as a mode of survival and satire
in American Jewish literature and life and parodies the "depraved venality"
that passes for business in Hollywood and by extension in America.

From a Jewish perspective, however, where cultural identity is
configured as a "people" rather than a nation, the business of living *is* a
"People Business" reflected in acts of selflessness and the primacy of moral

choice. On this point Fox reflects Mamet's perspective on "the admixture of the desire to hope and the desire to accept" that two friends find through each other (Stayton 1988, 7), what Brustein has recognized in *Speed-the-Plow* as "a further development of Mamet's belief in personal loyalty as the only cement in an unstuck public world" (1988, 30). Seeking neither grace nor salvation—both concepts alien to Judaism—nor requiring angel or advocate, Gould and Fox know that their place and their work is in this world. We better understand the complexity of Fox's connotative concluding question, "What are we here to do (*Pause*) Bob?" (82), if we see it as the culmination of his lesson whose thesis bears strong semblance to Judaic teaching, namely that "Judaism sees only one world, which is material and spiritual at the same time" (L. Kushner 1991, 28). Thus, when Gould says, and subsequently recants, that he "prayed to be pure" (59), his self-doubt may be perceived as the beginning of self-knowledge, heightened moral sensitivity, and spirituality, what Kushner characterizes as the beginning awareness of God (26).[36]

"Perhaps more than any other Mamet play," Hall correctly observes, "*Speed-the-Plow* is filled with religious imagery and syntax" (151).[37] In fact, religious allusions do not merely "fill" the play, they flood it from Gould's opening words, "When the gods would make us mad, they answer our prayers" (3), until the play's closing beat. Linking title, text, and theme, each conversation renders ironic statement on the stereotypical portrait of the Jew as profligate and serves as a code encrypting and simultaneously revealing through parody the temptation to affluence that informs American culture. Paralleling portions of *The Bridge* that resonate throughout the play, religious references (both explicit and elusive, Judaic and Christian) enhance the clarification of concepts, ironize conduct, and reveal both sacred and secular tenets. And while several critics have puzzled over the play's curious title, the director of the play's American premiere, Gregory Mosher, posited that the phrase "has to do with turning fresh earth—and of course there is a sexual pun'" (Henry 1988; 98). Notably, the "fresh earth" and "sexual pun" plays on the double-entendre of Karen's "freshness" and implied "naïveté" (67), the bet between Fox and Gould, and Fox's allegation that Gould remains in the office "to Hide the Afikomen" (34). The sexual allusion has roots in theatrical and religious history, as well as movie history, notes Whitfield, where the appearance of the *shiksa,* a young, non-Jewish woman, was a familiar concept in Hollywood by 1927, "the visible, romantic reward for 'making it,' the certification that all barriers had been scaled" by "a once-despised people" (1986, 326). And Zinman adds that the term *afikomon,* denoting "after-dinner revelry," is associated with the festival of Passover; thus the allusion serves as "the perfect halakic indictment of

Hollywood movies," parodying the subsequent illicit behavior and "infidel carryings-on" between Gould and Karen (212). However, Joe Mantegna's anecdotal recollection of the Passover seder held at Ron Silver's parents' home for the cast of *Speed-the-Plow* during the run of the New York production grounds the line in cultural and ethnic experience: "Well, we were just kind of joking around having a good time at the Seder. Ron Silver started to explain to all the non-Jews who were there what each of the aspects of the evening were, and when he got to the part of 'hide the Afikomen,' somebody said something, and I think David [Mamet] then made the comment, 'Yeah, Joe, in your neighborhood you used to play that too, didn't you, but you called it something else!'" (Kane 1992, 264-65).[38]

Advancing inquiry into the "fresh earth" imagery and furthering the link between Thomas Morton's play (1800) and Mamet's in "*Speed-the-Plow* and *Speed the Plough:* The Work of the Earth," Stafford finds that ploughing and earth imagery, as well as contest and disdain for and acceptance of work, contribute to our perceiving the importance of Fox's connection to the ground as a "suspicious, cunning, and devious" animal, Karen's aloof position above what she terms the "depravity" of Hollywood, and Gould's place in the middle (41). Indeed, his close reading of *Speed-the-Plow* confirms and extends Hudgins's (1992, 216-17) and Hall's (150-51) explication of the passage from Thackeray's *Pendennis* that serves as the play's epigraph and poses the question as to who "does his duty best: he who stands aloof from the struggle of life, calmly contemplating it, or he who descends to the ground, and takes his part in the contest?" Stafford thus concludes that this quotation serves as "the basis for the dialectic poles in Mamet's play," grounding Gould in the middle, as it were, as "the Everyman of the medieval morality play" obsessed with the meaning and purpose of his life upon the earth (41).

However, the characterization of Fox as a "suspicious, cunning and devious" animal, concomitant with the analogue of medieval drama, engenders the stereotypical image of the Jew that Mamet is parodying. As Harold Fisch reminds us, the Jew was "ubiquitous" in medieval drama, his popularity in mystery and morality plays attributed to the medieval taste for the depiction of the Jew as "devils," "bawdy flouts," and cringing outcasts who were contrasted with "saints and the pious" (20). In the morality play, in particular, he continues, "the good Jew," typified by his constancy, covenant, privilege, and patience, "lurks in the background," while "the bad Jew," the figure of the villain and the clown, assumes a position in the foreground (16-20).[39] Moreover, Gould, rather than Fox, is "a person of the soil," in Hebrew an *am ha-aretz,* one who is unlettered, uncultured, and ethically insensitive: a Jew without Jewish spirituality.

Arguably, the agricultural topology, the literary and liturgical allusions, the play's dialectical opposition of the oracular and opaque, mystical and secular, pure and corrupt, material and spiritual leads us to see these various structures and signs within the context of the play's principal tropes—education and transformation—and the playwright's work in the 1980s. Plays such as *The Disappearance of the Jews* and *Goldberg Street,* coupled with Mamet's intensifying focus on the process and value of education (explored overtly in *Homicide* and *Oleanna),* and his growing cultural and religious identification, clear the field for further inquiry in literature, liturgy, and enlightenment, whose answers, Karen avers, may be found "In the book" (58). Further study of biblical narrative, invaluable in analysis of *Marranos* and *Glengarry,* repays our efforts.

Whereas the prevailing concept in the Hebrew Bible is an insistent message "to remember," one specifically employed by Fox to awaken Gould to covenant and community, that of the New Testament is "see, know, [and] understand" derived from its focus on the transformation of the world and a belief that all is understandable (Jospovici 520-21). Hence, Karen's contention that "we find the answers. In the book" (58) promulgates this lesson clearly articulated in 1 John 2: 8: "the darkness is past, and the true light now shineth." Likewise, evidence of transformation and growth imagery is everywhere evident, suggests Michael Goulder, in the Pauline Epistles in the New Testament where recurring "images of sowing and harvest" are complemented repetitions of "grace" and "secular examples of plowman . . . farmer, and shepherd" (483-86). And had we doubt about the link between the antithetical structure of *Speed-the-Plow* and the import of religious imagery, we note in 1 Corinthians (9:10 and 9:11 respectively), that carnal imagery alludes to the unconverted Jew: "If we have sown unto you spiritual things, [is it] a great thing if we shall reap your carnal things?"

Significantly, the quotation from *Pendennis,* with its reference to the teacher who cries out that the ways and "works of the world are evil" and the mystic who flees from the world leaving us with our feet and work firmly planted upon the ground may be fruitfully read as a coded reference to the *Zohar,* "the guide book of guide books" to Jewish mystical thought that is intimated in Fox's coded reference to the Baal Shem Tov (Epstein 55). A compendium of numerous commentaries and midrashic fictions concealed beneath the apparent text of biblical narrative, the *Zohar,* "like all great works of mysticism . . . draws freely from the mother lode of spirituality: the congruence of God and innermost self" (Kushner 1991, 131). Although a detailed discussion of Jewish mysticism, the Zohar, and Kabbalah lead us away from *Speed-the-Plow,* suffice it is to say that Mamet's fascination with mystical study—its codes, cabals, journey imagery, elevation of watchfulness, emphasis on humaneness and *earthy* humor—suffuses this play. And typical of Mamet's minimalism, Fox's instruction to Gould at the end of *Speed-the-Plow*—"But we aren't here to 'pine,' Bob, we aren't put here to *mope*" (82)—reinforces the Baal Shem Tov's "life-asserting" teachings that emphasize purpose and work in daily life upon the earth.

Bridging revelry and revelation imagery, announced early and reinforced frequently, the question of "How are things made round?" in *Speed-the-Plow* may be answered by examining more closely the Jewish holidays of Purim and Passover, allusions to which Mamet drops as sparingly as he does Levene's reference to his daughter in *Glengarry*. Certainly the carnivalesque atmosphere at the beginning of the play, Gould's allusion to Fox as "The Master of Revels" (28), one customarily responsible for dramatic masques at court, and his subsequent obscene joke on the remake of *The Carnival of Venice* appear entirely consistent with the mood of frivolity and the farce of desperation played out by Fox and Gould. And, the wearing of masks, the acting out of masquerades, the yoking of revelry and revelation, the outwitting of an oppressor, the retelling of the story of survival of the Jewish people faced with extinction, and the death of a hated enemy—Haman, mastermind of the plot [a direct descendent of Amalek][40]—that typify the celebration of Purim is no mere coincidence in this play with its inextricable connection to Jewish survival in the face of threatened extermination. Nor, is its connection to the history of parody in Jewish literature that has repeatedly employed Purim as an opportunity to satirize contemporary life.[41] Moreover, Passover compels Jews to remember and retell a threat to survival in every generation, a lesson that, if Gould remembers, will provide him with a compass out of the wilderness.

The celebration of life and friendship that concludes *Speed-the-Plow* does not begin to suggest that the play concludes on a bed of ease; rather, it ends on an ongoing moral injunction to choose wisely. This focus on what Mamet has called the only "fit subject of drama" (1987d, 58), puts Gould's burden and responsibility to "Decide, decide, decide" (24) in the proper light, because as the playwright observes, "[A] lot of times corruption doesn't come from evil, just from a lack of watchfulness" (Stayton 1988, 6). And that watchfulness, at least in part, is necessitated by "deeply divided impulses in American-Jewish life—to swallow the popular culture which surrounds it, to, in a word, assimilate *everything;* at the same time, to remain separate . . . culturally intact" (Pinsker 1992, 249). Consistent with his increasing use of humor to blunt the impact of bigotry and ethnic hatred and expose the serious dilemma of the modern Jew, who in Shechner's phrase is "neither wholly or comfortably Jewish nor cozily American" (1987, 155), Mamet raises parody to paroxysm in *Speed-the-Plow*. His unappealing money-hungry Jewish producers, however offensive, follow in the great film tradition of Mel Brooks's characters who, despite their sacrificing "morality on the altar of immediate riches," as Desser and Friedman would have it, "are far more attractive and lovable than the people they exploit" (149).[42]

Both articulated and appreciated, Jewish humor "is central to the subculture of American Jewry," the principal medium for memory and affirmation of community that is more concerned with lack of identity than of faith (Whitfield 1978, 48). Tapping a shared background and identity through ethnically coded language, Mamet employs comedy to undercut moral vision, promote a sense of commonalty, and provide a mechanism for referencing common motifs. Thus, when Gould tells Fox in act 3 that "We have different ideas, Charlie," Fox responds to the statement with a characteristic and parodic Jewish response: a question. Offering his friend collective identity as a source of meaning, if not precisely strength or security, Fox attempts to dismiss Gould's comment out of hand: "We do? Since when . . . ?" (67). Presented as an in-joke, namely that if you put two Jews together you get three views—four, if one is schizophrenic—the playwright would also seem to be alluding to the sharply different ways in which Jews define their Jewishness.

Although I differ with Hudgins on his conclusion that Karen is a positive force of love, I would concur that "The title [*Speed-the-Plow*] is typical of Mamet's comedy and humor in general. It reverberates; it's thematic, entertaining, and funny. In this instance, finally, it's both a prayer and an indirect statement of faith in both the divine and the human" (1992, 225). It should be of little surprise, then, that Mamet, for whom comedy discloses culture, would not fail to refer in his title both to the Torah, which cautions "Make not make the Torah a crown with which to aggrandize thyself, nor a spade with which to dig" (*Pirke Avot* 4: 7), and to Wallace Markfield's classic novel, *You Could Live If They'd Let You,* a book in praise of stand-up comedy. In it Markfield's narrator, Jules Farber, jokes: "Sure they'll beat their swords into plowshares—and then, then first they'll give it to you with those plowshares" (73), a familiar concept to a people who know that "anything, even a plowshare, can become a sword" (Shechner 1987, 147-48).

Speed-the-Plow is not, as some critics have misconstrued, a revenge comedy of "no holds barred, no quarter given, and no expletives deleted" (Beaufort, 276), or a cynical portrayal of "the evil men do unto each other in the name of buddyhood" (Henry 1988, 279). Neither is it merely a satire of Hollywood's cupidity, an apologia from one who admittedly loves making movies, nor "On its deepest level" in the tradition of what Kroll terms "darker disclosures" of the movie business such as West's *Day of the Locust,* Fitzgerald's *The Last Tycoon,* Schulberg's *What Makes Sammy Run?* (1988, 273). Nor is it, as Rainer contends, "a plague-on-both-your-houses" (7), or "*advice* to Hollywood" on the "opportunities for salvation," as Colin Stinton believes (Jones and Dykes 71). Mamet's condemnation is not reserved for the Hollywood, that he knows we know is "a sinkhole of depraved venality" (1987d, 77), or directed against Charlie Fox, habitually viewed as emblematic of venal behavior and social and moral decay. In fact, Mamet maintains that the reemergence of "The human urge to celebrate, which is to say the reemergence of religion . . . and that which tends toward release and reaffirmation, will be seen to reassert itself in the profane, commonplace, and pagan aspects of our lives . . ." (1987d, 37). And within the context of the playwright's complex comic irony, "comically evoking a religious vision," *Speed-the-Plow* does criticize "'wrong beliefs' and follies and sins" and engender sympathy for Mamet's characters whose "sins and follies" we recognize are "much like our own . . ." (Hundgins 1992, 225; 199). But whereas Hudgins would have us believe that at the conclusion of *Speed-the-Plow* the playwright intends us to see Gould as failing, that both "his 'reconversion' to *Fox's* gospel . . ., and the system [is] being indicted for its destruction of love and art" (1992, 223-24), and Dean posits that Karen's "idealism and fecund creativity leave their mark on an otherwise barren and arid play" (1992, 66), both astute readers of Mamet's work fail to take into consideration the nature of the vision of change that Karen presents and the purpose of Gould's rejection of the messenger and the message whose condemnation of degradation and depravity in Hollywood ultimately educates him about his own worth. Mamet's play is neither arid nor barren but a fertile ploughing of new territory—daring in its focus, inherently Jewish, and comic in its treatment.

Speaking in 1989 to an audience—of which I was a member—in Cambridge, Massachusetts, who had gathered for a reading of *Some Freaks,* Mamet's second collection of essays, several months after *Speed-the-Plow* had opened in New York, Mamet characterized "the two big fears in Hollywood [as] fear of being poor and fear of being Jewish." Echoing the connection that the playwright drew in a conversation with John Lahr when *Glengarry Glen Ross* premiered in London that his family's rejection of Judaism was largely motivated by poverty (1983, 476-77), Mamet's comments illumine and contextualize Fox's satiric summary of *The Bridge:* "'A Story of Love, a Story of Hope'" and "[A] talky piece of puke" by "An Eastern Sissy Writer"(62; 23),[43] "a euphemism for 'Jew' when it doesn't mean 'Jew-bastard'" (Fiedler 133). And it is not without some irony that Mamet had in the late 1980s been unsuccessful in attracting financial

backing from major Hollywood studios for *Homicide,* a buddy film that extends his dramatization of ethnicity and education. Indeed, his comments enhance our understanding of Mamet's higher purpose in *Speed-the-Plow.* Tropologically and thematically linked to his body of work, this play is also a turning point in the playwright's career, exposing corruption and corruptibility, espousing the possibility of self-awareness and self-knowledge, and overtly sounding both the potential for ethnic pride and the dilemma of conflicting loyalties. More specifically it examines Gould's choice to reject what Karen, in her wisdom, characterizes as "degrading to the human spirit" (55) and, in the best sense of the word, to reject what Karen offers: the temptation to achieve acceptance and love in American society by denying ethnicity.

Responding to a persistent, indeed growing, charge of dual loyalty, many American Jews, argues Alan Dershowitz in *Chutzpah,* avoid rather than affirm their identity.[44] Thus, although Mamet has observed that there a number of things that one cannot say in this country, without their being construed as *chutzpah,* such as "You cannot say you are a Jew first and then an American. And you cannot say that the movie business is a Jewish business" (Norman and Rezek, 149), in *Speed-the-Plow* he has said both. Ironically, Mamet's most overt dramatization of Jewish sensibility has been largely overlooked, as has the richness of his complex comic terrain, by those who have seen little new in his Hollywood schlockmeisters and have failed to discern in its crudeness and lewdness *Speed-the-Plow's* commonalty to a rich tradition in American Jewish humor that takes aim against the merchandising of redemptive love. Nor has it been recognized that for Mamet beyond the tallying of profits and sequels humane acts of kindness validate a spark of human divinity.

Defining his job as a dramatist, Mamet recently noted, "The drama is not a prescriptive medium. Part of what the drama can offer—because it should work on the subconscious level—is the relief that comes with addressing a subject previously thought unaddressable" (Norman and Rezek, 60). It is thus of little surprise that within a year of writing *Speed-the-Plow* Mamet had written the first draft of *Homicide* (1989/1990), a film that similarly confronts Jewish identity, deracination, and self-hatred but takes aim against a Hollywood that rendered the Jew invisible and rethinks the legacy of the Holocaust that rendered all measured distinctions of the Jew impossible.

FOUR

THE HUMANIST FALLACY

"Jewry is losing its ethnic identity, [and as such
has] the potential to fulfill Hitler's utopia, a
world that is *Judenrein*"
                                    —Leslie Fiedler

"[W]e are too dazzled by power and prestige as
to forget . . . [that] close by the train is waiting."
                                    —Primo Levi

AN INCENDIARY, UNNERVING EXAMINATION of the power dynamic,
Oleanna opened with perfect timing, about six months after the Clarence
Thomas–Anita Hill hearings on sexual harassment.[1] At the time many
believed that Mamet had ventured into the fray of sexual warfare with a
time-released grenade that explodes in our faces and implodes in our minds.
No stranger to controversy or criticism of his own misogyny, Mamet has
likened its premiere, at which the play occasioned strident student accusations of the playwright as "politically irresponsible," to staging " *The Diary
of Anne Frank* at Dachau" (Stayton 1992, 20, 66).[2] Mirroring the heated
exchange between playwright and student, audiences and critics alike have
been divided in their sympathy and antipathy for the play's characters,
taking their lead from the play's promotional materials that announced to
ticket buyers that they could be among the first to "take a seat—and take a
side"—at *Oleanna*. So intense and incensed was the reaction to the play that
Mamet told Benedict Nightingale, "I thought they were going to burn
crosses on the grounds of the theatre" (1993, 37). Kevin Kelly's representa-

tive review, "*Oleanna* Enrages—and Engages," perfectly captured the emotions of audiences, many of whom believed that the controversial play fed the firestorm of controversy already aroused by the national debate on sexual harassment.[3]

Subsequent audiences in New York City, where a production of the play opened with a revised third act and scorching, violent ending—its *Playbill* published with two covers, a bespectacled man seated on a chair with a bull's-eye emblazoned on his chest and a female in exactly the same position on a different cover[4]—were audibly vicious and violent, shouting such epithets as "Kill the bitch," in their support of the professor against Carol, the student accuser whose charges of sexual harassment destroy her teacher, John.[5] Demonstrative behavior did not abate when *Oleanna* was staged at the Court Theatre in London the following year, leading Christine MacLeod to conclude in her recent, insightful essay, "The Politics of Gender, Language and Hierarchy in Mamet's *Oleanna*," that "Ever since it was first staged in May 1992, Mamet's *Oleanna* seems . . . to have been perceived, publicised and reviewed almost exclusively as a manifestation of backlash sexual politics—that is, as a work characterised by outrage and hostility toward the agenda of contemporary feminism" (199).

Whereas critics and audiences, typically engaged or enraged by sexual harassment, have perceived it to be the controlling trope of *Oleanna*, this hot-button cultural issue is a "flag of convenience" for the playwright, to whom the power play is "about failed Utopia . . . the failed Utopia of Academia" (1993a, 10).[6] Indeed, Camille Paglia has correctly postulated in "The Real Lesson of *Oleanna*," that "Mamet is using sex war to explore a much larger subject," that of education (6).[7] Although pedagogy is central to his vision in this play, as it is the body of Mamet's work, *Oleanna* is not principally concerned with the nature or usefulness of higher education in America. Rather, Mamet is concerned here with the broader issue of education of character, as Martin Buber would have it, that focuses upon teachings as a way of human life.[8] Situating the dialectic in the university at the highest level of intellectual inquiry, where communication between teacher and student ideally takes the form of dialogue, Mamet explores the promise of what Buber terms "dialogic communication"—language as a link between human beings, the ideal of the I-Thou relationship—and the consequences of the breakdown of dialogue into mono-logos, the I-It relationship, with its potential for propaganda and dehumanization.

Unifying the playwright's interest in higher education—issues of entitlement, usefulness, pedagogy, and personal responsibility—with power relationships,[9] the conflicts and pressures of professional and personal responsibility and identity that he began to explore in *Glengarry Glen Ross* and *Homicide,* and the issues of legacy and home(land) that inform his plays and screenplays in the 1980s, *Oleanna* reflects Mamet's profound apprehension about the resurgence and "the absolutely virulent eruption of a new puritanism" (Mamet qtd. in Nightingale 1993, 37). Moreover, it stages his heightened concern with issues of intolerance and assimilation, specifically the contemporary practice of intellectual Judaism closely paralleling the model of denial of ethic identity in the 1920s, behavior that afforded no protection from the Holocaust.[10]

Structurally dialectic (a distinctive feature of American Jewish literature and Mamet's canon), the play seemingly "sucker[s] [us] into thinking it says one thing" only to discover it is "saying the exact opposite" (Feingold 1992, 357). However, its opposition of truths and Truth, intellectual inquiry of conflicting ideas (the stance upon which John's liberalism rests on human dignity, human happiness, and moral equality), and the simplification of ideas—the prophet who offers the keys to Utopia—gives the play its tensile strength and substantive pedagogical, ethical, and ethnic subtext. And, what begins with an exploration of knowledge ends with Nazi book-burnings where "Politically Correct language . . . has become the new "Nazi-speak of today" (Tinker 7). Put simply, in *Oleanna,* in which Jewish identity is inextricably linked to the twin poles of language and learning that undergird the play, Mamet stages the ethical, aesthetic, philosophical, and personal experience of the Jew as scholar and scapegoat in historical and present time.

Expanding his inquiry of the Jew's role and place in a Christian society explored in *Glengarry Glen Ross,* Mamet extends and intensifies his dramatization of an ethnic dialectic in *Oleanna,* riveting attention to the opposition between the Jew and gentile with stunning clarity. Situating the drama within academia, the playwright focuses on discourse in a politically and culturally charged atmosphere in which speech is not valued for its content or intelligence but rather judged on its (political) correctness. The play's implicit reference to language as cultural signifier and racial marker and nexus between human beings is crystallized in a particularly startling moment near the conclusion, when the student Carol presents her professor with "a list of books" that her group "find[s] questionable" (73). The moment is dramatically effective, establishing a salient link between the banning of John's book, whose concepts and precepts bedevil her, and the language in which it is written.[11] In Carol's challenging John to clarify his ideas and change her grade, the opposition between student and teacher puts in a clear light those who are comfortably receptive to intellectual inquiry of conflicting ideas and those for whom one idea is superior to all others.

For in charged historical periods during which "the articulation of perception" shifts, contend Sander L. Gilman and Steven T. Katz in their introduction to *Anti-Semitism in Times of Crisis,* especially "whenever there is a need for a 'true devil,' a 'real, palpable enemy,' such as we observe in the contemporary period, that search typically "result[s] in the use of the Jews as the essential Other through which to define the integrity of the self" (1991, 5).[12] As he has in *Speed-the-Plow,* Mamet conflates several historical periods, working with and against mythical imagery. Juxtaposing the thirteen century, known to Jews as the Talmudic era, when universities were the site of the highest levels of learning, particularly the study of Judaica, and the repression of the Jews and their books were the most virulent, the book banned was the Talmud, a compendium of commentaries on the Hebrew Bible. Contrasting this period and European racism of the nineteenth and twentieth centuries with contemporary political correctness, one finds unusually rich analogues. Drawing a substantive linkage between "the intellectual awakening of the twelfth and thirteenth centuries, on the one hand, and simultaneous changes in Christian anti-Judaism, on the other," Jeremy Cohen postulates that "the increasingly hostile ideological stance of the church toward the European Jewish community" and its focus on Jewish books underlies the Christian anti-Jewish polemic that was crystallized in the thirteenth century (1986, 593). Propelled by an unquenchable thirst for discovery, scholasticism, which reached its zenith in the universities, continues Cohen "contributed to the flowering of an applied or missionary theology"; and while not confined to the ivory tower, preachers, inquisitors, and missionaries supported "the same ideological premise: intellectual activities were appropriately governed by Christian principles and directed toward Christian ends" (605). Concurrent with its efforts to understand biblical teachings and Talmudic and midrashic texts (commentaries on the Hebrew Bible), "Anti-Jewish polemic assumed a much more direct and aggressive character" in "undermin[ing] the presence and security of the Jew in a properly ordered Christian society" (606-07). Ultimately it led to the convening of a legatine commission whose express purpose was judgment of questionable texts, specifically the Talmud, subsequently banned and burned in 1242.

Similarly, the increasing hostility against European Jewry after the Enlightenment, the civil emancipation of the Jews, is informed by what Gilman terms, "a linguistics of race." Tracing "the shift of rhetoric" applied to the Jews from "religious to scientific" (1986, 212) and its coupling with "the idea of a special language of the Jews . . . as salient marker of race" (18), Gilman convincingly concludes that this emphasis on language anticipated and laid the foundation for the Holocaust. Hence, in an atmosphere politicized by issues of "correctness," where judgment of behavior is based on perception rather than worth, right or wrong, "good" as opposed to "bad," one is prompted to look for the mythological stage Jew or his or her parodic prototype, such as we find in *Glengarry Glen Ross, Speed-the-Plow,* and *The Disappearance of the Jews.* However, upon initial inspection we find in *Oleanna* neither money bags nor characters lusting after women, and none conniving to steal. No profane language, no cunning, no crafty characters, no sensuality, and no wit.

On the contrary, in their stead are the higher aesthetic senses of sight and intellect. A self-assured, confident professor, John is concerned with issues of judgment, responsibility, legacy, identity, and status. His discourse is the language of reason, the mode of discourse that distinguishes the Enlightenment's positive image of the Jew.[13] In replacing the Jew identifiable by Yiddish locution or name, Mamet has undertaken discussion of a broad range of Jewish tropes, among them pedagogical, ethical, and cultural, through the portrayal of "the new Jew," as Ellen Schiff puts it, neither parvenu nor pariah. As Hannah Arendt observes in her important essay, "The Jew as Pariah: A Hidden Tradition," the Jew can neither "stand aloof in society, whether as a schlemihl or as a lord of dreams" nor can humanity desist in coming "to terms with a world in which the Jew cannot be a human being either as a *parvenu* using his elbows or as a *pariah* voluntarily spurning its gifts. Both the realism of the one and the idealism of the other are today utopian" (1978, 90). Posing a "third alternative," she argues, Kafka portrayed "the real drama of assimilation" in which a "man of goodwill"—his euphemism for Jew—pursued a career, desiring only "his rights as a human being: home, work, family, and citizenship" (85-90).

Paralleling Kafka's encoded portrait of the assimilated Jew, Mamet's complex portrayal of the assimilated American Jew in *Oleanna* is inferred, its allusion to the conspicuous position of Jews in the learned professions implicit.[14] Although he identifies the professor only by career and the extent of his caring for family and student, much like Kafka's "K.," he is "involved in situations and perplexities distinctive of Jewish life" that signify more than any "typically Jewish trait" (Arendt 87). And while neither his profession nor his diction, cleansed as they are of Yiddishisms and Yiddish locution, specifically reveal his identity, "Learning, which had been a Jewish value when applied in a traditional manner to religious texts" prior to the Enlightenment, emerged after the civic emancipation of the Jew, notes Michael Meyer in *Jewish Identity in the Modern World,* as "an independent characteristic of Jewish identity." In fact, "serious study of any worthy subject became a way of being Jewish" (20). Anchoring his exploration of "the rights of a human being" in the assimilated Jewish professional, the "new Jew," Mamet employs a wide range of mythic and contemporary markers that privilege language and foreground questions of status and security. Indeed, Mamet recalls that in his home Judaism was eschewed, equated with powerlessness and poverty, whereas "a Jew [who] could rise to prominence . . . *without* being overtly Jewish, without playing Jewish parts, without being stereotyped," was cause for great joy (1989b, 12).

A quintessential precursor to assimilation, "Status became the single most important quality that Jewish self-definition claimed for itself" (Gilman 1986, 113). Emerging in modern European and American society, the Jew was nonetheless confronted with new markers supplanting or extending mythical ones. Coded a "social climber" (Stern 298), a "New York" intellectual, the paradigmatic "elitist Jew" (Fiedler xiv), and maverick destabilizing "established order and its values" (Katz 235), this individual identifiable by his or her spirit of dissidence and liberalism was a perceived threat to society. Moreover, as the "bearer of subversive modernity," as Walter Sokel puts it, the "new Jew" came to be identified as one in whom "the hunger for material riches and earthly power" predominates and "the destructive aspect connives" (164); in other words, individuals whose blindness derives from the limited "reading and comprehension of the divine text," and badness "tied to their materialistic nature" (Gilman 1986, 30). Hence, the Jew who did not want to be seen *only* as a Jew frequently sought refuge in a profession, and life in the ivory tower of academia, in particular, offered the Jew not merely vocational escape; for the professor with publications, academia offered status and the promise of a secure future in tenure with its implicit utopian dream of acceptance and home(land).[15]

John's Jewishness, then, is progressively apparent in his rhetorical brilliance, virtuosity of dialectic reasoning, passionate commitment to ideas, inquiry and predilection for discussion. It is notable, as well, in his appreciation for and ideals of education, flair for narrative, distinctive tone and strength of his family instincts, and compassion—particularly for the underprivi-leged—as well as his insistence on sensory evidence, literalism, spirit of dissidence, preoccupation with justice and judgment, and the impact of past striving that colors his present endeavors. Even his name is theophanic (Kaganoff 40).

Maintaining his objectivity and ironic detachment, as James Joyce does not in his depiction of Leopold Bloom, the modern, assimilated Jewish father-figure in *Ulysses,* Mamet presents John as fallible.[16] Sharing much in common with the self-serving charlatans we meet in the novels of Saul Bellow and Philip Roth, John is not only capable of noxious, racist, elitist, and sexist remarks, he is contemptuous of colleagues with whom he works and arrogant with individuals with whom he negotiates. Continuing in the fine tradition of Sholem Aleichem's outcast, Gimpel the Fool, and Bellow's intellectual, Herzog, one that has repeatedly cast Jews in literature and film as educators who teach the world "the value of being a fully rounded and human being" (Bernstein 42), John establishes his performative role from the outset by both answering questions posed to him by his student, Carol, and provoking her to find her own answers.[17] The role of an intellectual proves problematic for the professor, after all, inasmuch as the term "intellectual" is itself a double helix betokening status *and* stigma; whereas it provides "deep cover" for the essential Jew (Shechner 1990, 32), to Hitler the coded word *intellectual* (especially the psychoanalyst), was synonymous with Jew (Gilman 1986, 13), a label that immediately marked such an individual as both deviant and imperiled.

Thus when Carol judges John a patriarchal, privileged nonconformist, one who perceives himself "entitled. . . . To *buy,* to *spend,* to *mock,* to *summon*" (1993b, 64-65), she draws upon a wealth of stereotypical and mythical images of the Jew as a power-hungry, "self–aggrandizing" (47) literalist, a storyteller with a penchant for the theatrical, a materialistic *"maverick"* (67) who "doubts all and any truths" (Gilman 1991, 136), a "little yapping fool" (71) who is racist, imperialistic, and "elitist" (47). Depicting him as *"vile* and *classicist,* and *manipulative* and *pornographic. . . . and exploitative"* (51-52), she essentially views John as the world has viewed the Jew for centuries: perverted and perverting.

> . . . You love the Power. To *deviate.* To *invent,* to transgress . . . to *transgress* whatever norms have been established for us. And you think its charming to "question" in yourself this taste to mock and destroy. . . . But I tell you. I tell you. That you are vile. And that you are exploitative. (52)

To this litany of charges Carol adds that John has presumed to show her "'some light.' . . . *Outside of tradition*" (emphasis added); that he has employed "Polite *skepticism*"; that he "BELIEVE[S] IN NOTHING"; that he is a perverter of youth who exploits his "paternal prerogative"; that he is a rapist (67). Attacking an individual concerned, in her view, with power and stature, Carol's calumny mirrors the depiction of the mythic Jew, one who deceives, corrupts, and lusts after women (Lazar 55), concomitant with "The Jews' supposed predilection for mockery . . . a leitmotif in the fin de siècle" (Gilman 1991, 135). In sum, viewed through the prism of Carol's zealotry, "John's skepticism," observes John Lahr, "marks him as a heretic" (1992, 124). And, with a stunning clarity we understand that in *Oleanna* not only does the Other stand accused, Jewishness itself stands accused.

Consistent with the Talmudic perspective that anti-Semitism "reflects ontological *givens,*" namely archetypal animosity evident in "conflicting worldviews" (Gilman and Katz 8), survival presupposes "learning to live with the conflict" through power (which Jews were long denied) or discourse (Peli 110). John Peter surely recognizes this in his review of *Oleanna,* characterizing it a savage two-handler which is "a confrontation between people and between values" (20). Although "human beings' never-ending battle to dominate one another" is, as Steven Ryan notices, "one of Mamet's most basic themes" (393), obtaining and retaining power is a basic tool of survival (or the illusion of it, signified by Teach's gun or the knife in *Passover*), one that illumines Mamet's characterization of *Oleanna* as "a tragedy of power."[18] Neither of *Oleanna*'s protagonists, however, is very likable, and both behave in ways that are "dishonourable" (Mamet qtd. in Nightingale 1993, 37). Whereas John is a smug, pompous, frequently insufferable man whose power over academic lives he unconsciously abuses and whose "surface generosity and concern" fail to "mask an underlying unctuousness and condescension that were deeply disturbing" (Zeifman 1994, 3), Carol, a fully realized female character, initially appears a mousy, confused cipher whose failure to understand "the concepts" and "the precepts" presented in John's class and book has motivated her apparent appeal for instruction and the pressure that she has brought to bear on him to change her grade. As their Socratic exchange metamorphoses into a battle of wits and ideologies, Carol's shyness, fear, and vulnerability discernible "in her initial helplessness," metamorphose into a smugness and arrogance inflamed by her group "as she inch[es] her way toward" what Hersh Zeifman characterizes as "a painful, exultant, and decidedly Pyrrhic 'victory'" (3), John appealing to her humanity, she endeavoring to convert her antagonist.[19]

By setting his play in a university faculty office, Mamet immediately establishes his idiosyncratic not-home work space that is distinctive in linking John's professional and personal responsibility, principally through the telephone, a ubiquitous Mamet prop. Both literal and metaphoric, the office is congruous with the playwright's dramatic and cinematic world in which the discussion we overhear is credible, engaging, and seemingly realistic, and it privileges the professor as an authoritative figure whose "name," he subsequently tells Carol, is "on the door" (76), recalling a similar comment made by Gould to Fox in *Speed-the-Plow* to signify and validate his own commanding position. With its potential for entrapment and vulnerability to both realistic and ephemeral intrusions, John's office is simultaneously familiar and defamiliarized, the site of a philosophical (and, upon closer inspection, Talmudic) tutorial and the "alleged" scene of the crime where sexual harassment does or does not occur. Not only does a university setting situate *Oleanna* in a position to examine credibly "the struggle between the privileged professor (who criticises education while lapping up its benefits) and the under-privileged student (whose desire to learn is hamstrung by anger)" (Sierz 740), it stages, as Robert Skloot remarks, a competition to maintain and attain "certain kinds of privilege: academic, economic, and sexual" (2). Additionally, the university is brilliantly conceived as signifier, questioning the nature and value of education, reflecting the radical change from liberal community to battlefield where zealot dominates scholar, riveting attention squarely on "the issue of *teaching*," and implicitly heightening Mamet's preoccupation with education, the process by which "facts, customs and feelings are transmitted among inhabitants of the same social and cultural space" (2).

In fact, within moments a portrait of John emerges as an educator who loves what he does, whose tenure announcement is public knowledge, whose interests, goals, and priorities encompass family responsibilities, security (of home and position), the trappings of privilege, tradition, and inheritance manifested in "The yard for the boy" (2). His elitist attitudes and desire for acceptance extend to his advocacy of private school for his son, and his self-absorption and social irresponsibility are revealed in his reluctance to pay his fair share of taxes to assure educational opportunities for others. Apparently rapacious, miserly, and self-serving, he is a man determined to achieve and enjoy material goals pursuant to his new status and equally preoccupied with rights, privileges, and contractual agreements. This struggle between opposing poles proves an important "pointer" (24) to the man and his subsequent dilemma.[20]

From the first moments, John's character is established through a commanding voice and diction. Focusing attention on "The land. . . . The land" or rather the house he is on the verge of acquiring (1-2), John is alternately assured and assertive, rattled and decisive, in his attempt to calm his wife. "We *aren't* going to lose the deposit" (2), he tells her confidently, concerned about his rights and protections on the one hand and their loss on the other. The subject of a long opening monologue with Grace, the land, both promised and presumably protected by contract, ignites an animated telephone conversation peppered with terms of endearment and juridical jargon, legalisms such as "term of art," "easement," lawyers, and contracts, which reveals in its interrogatories, elliptical phrases, and incomplete sentences a shorthand between intimates in which each understands what the other says despite the cryptic nature of the communication. Ultimately frustrated in his attempt to allay his wife's and his own fears concerning their purchase of a new home, John's dialogue is not only expository, it lays bare subtle shifts in confidence, providing a minimalist foreshadowing of the entire play. John's opening position is commanding, authoritative, and firmly confident in battle: "Look: Look. Did you call Jerry? Will you call Jerry?" That pose is tempered to "Look: Look, I'm not minimizing," and finally John communicates an ersatz hopefulness, a false bravado: "We *aren't* going to lose the deposit. All right? I'm sure it's going to be . . . (*Pause*) I hope so" (2), all of which ironically augurs that not only is the professor going to lose the desired protection and security of tenure, he is going to lose the house, the land (homeland), and his deposit on the future. In fact, "From the opening words of *Oleanna*," Sandra Tomc notices, John's vocabulary "sides thematically with notions of stability and order" (165). Communicated as much through the play's "various social stabilizers, from his home and family to his active pursuit of tenure, the ultimate in career security," as the vocabulary that he both uses and defines for Carol, such as "term of art" (2), "index" (24), and "paradigm" (45), John centers and anchors the play just as Carol's "reliance on rules and strictures is what fuels her allegations of misconduct" (Tomc 166). In other words, "John is all orders and authority; Carol is subservience in a schmatte" (Lahr 1992, 121).

Thus, although neither speaks about power in act 1, power relations, implicit in the teacher-student dynamic, communicate metaphorically, compelling attention to their uneven hierarchical relationship glimpsed spatially and linguistically in the selection of topic and discourse coherence. Carol, after all, must wait for John to conclude his conversation before she can initiate a discussion and advance an argument on the issue of her failing grade, and initially it is she who is on the defensive. As Hubert-Liebler reminds us, "the teacher-student paradigm in Mamet's plays is especially susceptible to disruption." Moreover, "In the event that the student hopes to learn from the teacher, he is mainly interested in getting fast answers, recipes, magic formulas." And as Mamet's is "a closed world," an impression the claustrophobic office setting precisely conveys, teacher and student "are often trapped as it were together" providing a situation ripe for "a struggle for the empowering position . . . of the teacher" (Hubert-Leibler 79). Therefore, in act 1 what initially appears to be a lesson about education bearing upon the politics of passing or failing a course—the latter an option that Carol deems untenable—ultimately is revealed to be a competition to the death, a subtle minuet comprised of poses, precepts, positions, and principles in which student and teacher jostle for power to determine who is empowered to "set" the course (material), which, of course, as John points out, is the essence of (academic) freedom.

Oleanna's triadic structure, paralleling that employed in *American Buffalo* and *Speed-the-Plow*, is similar to stories of discipleship (*hitkarvut*) that are central in Judaism in which the tripartite story typically takes a surprising turn (Roskies 1995, 41). That Mamet's play turns on a series of escalating, increasingly aggressive surprises is immediately notable in the first unscheduled appearance of John's student, Carol. Appearing without warning or appointment, she surprises the professor who is about to leave his office, but once there she finds herself unable to broach the subject, either because she is intimidated by the professor "whose position and . . . knowledge makes the gap between them almost unbridgeable" (Lahr 1992, 121), or lacks the language to articulate the problem. Keeping to form Mamet observes his own dictum by "withholding *all* information except that information the absence of which would make the progress of the story incomprehensible" (1991b, 20), a technique that "forces us to chart our path through the play with only our speculations and prejudices to guide us" (Richards 1993, 5). All that we know initially is that the objectives of the characters are diametrically opposed: Carol wants to resolve a problem; John is anxious to dispatch the student and terminate the unscheduled appointment in order to meet his wife. To expedite closure of the meeting, he solicits succinctness about the purpose of Carol's visit and the nature of her problem, paralleling the aggressive technique predicated on logical cogitation we overheard in John's prior conversation with Grace. "Let's take the mysticism out of it, shall we?" he urges. "I'll tell you: when you have some 'thing.' Which must be broached? (*Pause*) Don't you think . . . ? (*Pause*)" (3). Evidencing a pedagogical methodology intended to promote Carol's thought processes, "The line," Lahr notes astutely, "haunts the evening. Mysticism of power is precisely the point on which John will be shafted" (1992, 121).

However, Carol's subsequent stuttering and bewilderment, "Did . . . did I . . . did I say something wr. . ." (3), occasion John's repeated apologies and awaken him to the fact that his distraction has exacerbated the discomfort and anxiety of his student, who appears to be as intimidated by him as by the material in his book. Admonished by her confusion and chastened by her embarrassment, John initiates the dialogue anew. Attempting to create an atmosphere that is conducive to discussion about her failure in his class by an apology for his preoccupation, a clear statement of fact ("I find that I'm at a *standstill),*" and an empathic if enigmatic expression of compassion for her obvious humiliation ("I know how . . . *believe* me. I know how . . . potentially *humiliating* these . . . I have no desire other than to help you" [5]), John admits that he not only understands her pain, he has a shared experience of failure. On the surface it appears that as one who came late to learning and teaching, John identifies another parvenu who may benefit from his example and positiveness; nevertheless, given his personality, it is not difficult to imagine that the professor may also be "reach[ing] out to her because her inabilities challenge his confidence in his power to work educational miracles" (Ryan 396). Indeed, glossing Buber, John evidently believes that curriculum should be designed to meet the needs of the individual pupil and that the only access to the student is through confidence, which the educator must earn "by direct and ingenuous participation in the life" of the pupil (1959, 107). In either case, rather than discuss hypotheses germane to his course, John and Carol engage in a dialogue that both reveals their conflicting views and presages Carol's susceptibility to a group that will tell her, as John will not, what to think.

Notably, Buber's theories on the two principal techniques through which individuals can influence others and communicate their values (discussed earlier in relation to *American Buffalo*)—either as propagandist or educator—have particular relevance in this context. A propagandist, Buber maintains, is one who "tries to impose himself, his opinion and his attitude on the other in such a way that the latter feels the psychical result of the action to be his own insight." The educator, on the other hand, "is always concerned with the person as a whole," and moreover "not by teaching but by meeting, by existential communication," can the student reach his or her potential (1959, 180). Whereas this "meeting" of minds is an interactional, humane, and humanistic exchange of ideas fostering "the mutual awareness of actual feelings and thought and intimacy on the highest plane" (the finest example of the I-Thou relationship), "propaganda," as L. S. Dembo points out, "is based on a form of dehumanization, of its recipient no less than its subject" (143). It best identifies the I-It situation. In fact, education is one aspect of the I-Thou relationship in which human beings encounter one another, not as the self encounters the Other in a competitive, exploitive I-It relation. In propaganda, on the other hand, there is no interplay, no exchange; "rather, the recipient . . . [is] duped into believing that the ideas are his own" (143).

In this vein, as a way of extending "intimacy on the highest plane," John recounts a story of a traumatic childhood experience to assure Carol that she can master crippling self-abnegation and to reassure her of her ability to succeed. Capturing her attention by narration, John succeeds in establishing a common ground for communication that bridges his past and her present experience, although, as the play reveals, his knowledge of her experience as viewed through the lens of his sensibilities proves decidedly limited. In the story John recalls that his "most persistent memories are of being told that I was stupid"(16).[21] Speaking from the perspective of a child, the professor remembers believing that there were two distinct groups of people, those like himself who were, by implication, the bad people who could not learn, and "the people other than myself.

The *good* people. The *capable* people. The people who could do the things, *I* could not do: learn, study, retain . . ." (16). Drawing upon his own experience as illustrative model, John extrapolates a story, and continuing the long, colorful tradition of Mamet raconteurs, he seduces his audience with the familiar come-on: "Listen to this. If the young child is told he cannot understand. Then he takes it as a *description* of himself. What am I? I am *that which can not understand*" (16). A similar pattern of the adult narrator speaking about himself as a child, suggests Shlomith Rimmon-Kenan in *Narrative Poetics*, reveals that the adult's "language is sometimes 'colored' by his perceptions at the time of narration (external focalization), sometimes by those of his younger self (internal focalization) and sometimes remains ambiguous between the two" (28). Likewise, although the voices of his youth have ceased, John tells Carol, when "tested," as he is during the tenure procedure, the judgmental voices of his youth that judged him both unworthy and ill-prepared resurface, continuing, as it were, "to speak" to him, despite the fact that he has learned that the educational process is neither a "mystery" nor "Magic" (16, 19).

Surprised and offended that John likens the teacher-student relationship to a parental one and that the absence of intimacy in his youth sanctions his apparent desire to advance intimacy with her, Carol is skittish that he favors a "personal" (sexual) relationship. However, as Adam Newton postulates, "the *binding* quality of storytelling" encompasses "the binding nature of obligatory response. . . . undergird[ing] even ordinary narrative give-and-take" (112), none more so than the parental relation, which aligns parental responsibility and education, given its common root in Hebrew: parent, *horeh,* and teacher, *moreh* (Telushkin 46). For John, who sees himself first as a parent and then as an educator, his remark equating student and child, though unintended offense, is a sincere expression of his intention to help Carol to achieve her personal goals, one reflecting his commitment and obligation. Rather than teach her "certain definite things," he seemingly concurs with Buber, for whom the continuity of life depends wholly on generational interaction, "a human link" between teacher and student (1963, 140, 145).

Frustrated by the fact that "Nobody *tells* me anything" (14), what Carol desires is "a concrete body of information" rather than stories drawn from her professor's personal experience, or his ramblings on hazing and the "'Virtual warehousing of the young'" (11). In fact, "[D]esperate not to fail, Carol frantically searches for the objective information that will assure her of that most concrete of realities, a passing grade" (Ryan 396-97), but she might just settle for the answer to her conundrum: "Who should I *listen* to . . ." (36). Whereas John expresses an abiding interest in "How people learn"

(16) and accepts responsibility for his student not learning—"And that is not verbiage" (17)—it might as well be verbiage, for his words don't advance her comprehension of content so much as they seem to enhance his grandiloquence. If John's lectures are perceived by Carol as sound and fury signifying nothing, it may well be, suggests Todd London, that "the first section of *Oleanna* makes language" an "inadequate conveyor of meaning" one trapping professor and pupil in "mutually exclusive languages" (19) comprised of cultural and ethnic codes.

To the degree that the fault rests with the teacher, however, Mamet provides ample example of John's repeated attempts to teach Carol coupled with his fallibility, self-aggrandizement, posturing, and absorption in personal goals and achievement. For Mamet, although the professor is "to a large extent a raisonneur character," sharing the playwright's view that higher education is "prolonged 'hazing,' or ritual bullying," victimizing those in pursuit of "greater status and economic power" (Nightingale 1993, 37), John patronizes his student and perplexes her intellectually with abstruse academic jargon. Hence, from the professor's perspective, quips Peter, "education is teacher-centered"; the professor "has the power, the pupil has the responsibility: the definition of an intellectual whore" (1993, 20). Still, we are encouraged to judge John not merely on his pedagogical skills but on interpersonal skills, on compassion for others. And in this regard, too, he is flawed. Although John exhibits interest in Carol's learning, he displays behavior that borders on self-satisfaction. Defining ego as "arrogance," Lawrence Kushner postulates that to the degree to which we judge ourselves more significant than another, and extoll ourselves "in the presence of and at the expense, of someone else" we are guilty of "idol-worship": worship of self (1991, 46-47). Examples of John's aggrandizement of his own worth are numerous, the most obvious, of course, his preoccupation with house and tenure hearing, both of which privilege his image and position as the rationale for the meeting that, in essence, Carol called for her own advancement.

On the subject of advancement and personal worth the professor assures his student that "tests" that one "encounter[s] in school, in college, in life" are not an index "of your worth," but "a test of your ability to retain and spout back misinformation" (23), thereby employing the process of judgment that he is undergoing currently by the Tenure Committee as an illustration on point. Once again, what emerges from this lesson is that it misses its mark with Carol, who fails to see both its finer points and its applicability to her. As in his previous illustration, this reference to John's personal and professional experience, stripped bare of "the Artificial *Stricture,* of 'Teacher' and 'Student'"

(21), is a pointer to John's arrogance, egotism, and ethnicity, with the significant addition of paranoia, its biblical echoes of testing and judgment reminiscent of *American Buffalo, Glengarry Glen Ross,* and *Speed-the-Plow.* "Look at me. Look at me," he tells her, typically employing his favorite word, "Look," ironic for one who sees so little:

> . . . The Tenure Committee. The Tenure Committee.
> Come to judge *me.* The Bad Tenure Committee.
>
> The "Test." Do you see? They put me to the test. Why, they had people voting on me I wouldn't employ to wax my car. And yet, I have to go before the Great Tenure Committee . . . (23, emphasis added)

Anxious for their stamp of approval, John nonetheless admits the "urge . . . to puke my *badness* on the table, to show them," in effect, "'I'm no good. Why would you pick *me?*'" (23). Although the committee has announced John's tenure, he is gripped by nagging doubt coupled with fear—a bone-deep, pervasive paranoia—that "*they*" will yet uncover John's "'dark secret,'" which is "an index of my badness," in effect rendering evidence of his lack of merit (24). Foiling Carol's effort to focus the meeting on her fears, John reveals profound anxiety that rather than ratify and endorse his future security, the committee will judge him "wanting" (64), cast him out of his home at the university, and deny him his house. In so doing he once again links his deepest fears to Carol's fear of failure: "You see? Do you see? . . . I Know. That. Feeling." (24). Is this a rear-guard defense against assumed and expected rejection? Indeed. Maybe it is also the stronger sense of self that comes with ancient, recondite wisdom. Given the context of judgment, it seems hardly insignificant that John reiterates the term "pointer" and its variant "index" (24). Itself an emblem of the mythical depiction of the Jew—an extended "index" either on the stage or in art served as a further extension of "the questions put in the mouth of the Jew" to signify understanding only of the letter and not the spirit of Scripture (Lazar 61-62, 79)—John's use of the terminology serves as a pointer to the meagerness of his self-scrutiny.

Desperately seeking success as much as John does security, Carol diverts John's attention from his musings on his own self-worth and "badness" to hers by posing the vexing problem of her grade, the "pointer" to her self-worth or, rather, despised self. As he can in no way effect the judgment being rendered on him or negotiate on his own behalf, John sets about negotiating a deal with Carol that directly opposes the unyielding attitude and hard bargaining we overhear in two earlier telephone conversations concerning his real estate purchase in which he positively bristles at the idea of being "*bound*" (2) by an easement that would, by definition of this term of art, compel him to cede his rights. Ignoring the intrusive, ringing telephone and its binding connection to home, John proposes in the best tradition of Mamet's salesmen, producers, and con men to negotiate with Carol: "I'll make you a deal. . . . Forget about the paper," the grade, and attendance at lectures (25). Clearly a "boundary smasher" willing to go "beyond the 'is'" in favor of "the 'ought'" (Lerner 43), John not only sanctions breaking the rules but enters into a contract with Carol that guarantees her what she most desires, an "A" for the course, which even if she does not deserve it, will ensure others' enhanced perception of her worth, if not raise her own self-esteem. A rebel in the best tradition of Judaism, John exhibits in his discourse, as well as his decisions, a leap of faith in freedom from oppressive rules. Thus his justification, "What is The Class but you and me? (*Pause*)" (26), is both profoundly accurate, if we grant the Buberian premise that relationships that are dialogic strive to achieve the quintessential I-Thou relation of freedom and openness, and fallacious, given that it rests on the faulty presumption that no one is harmed by or profits from their arrangement other than John and Carol—he by enhanced power and she supposedly by the grade and superior tutorial instruction. As presented by the professor, echoing Levene's offer to the Nyborgs and Roma's to Lingk, it's a "win/win" situation: Carol take all.

Hence, although his opening gambit is they "are two people . . . Both of whom have subscribed," in John's phrase, to "Certain institutional . . . [codes?]" (10), he endeavors to quell Carol's concern about the "rules" governing their teacher-student relationship. "We'll break them," he tells her. "We won't tell anybody" (26), the result of which is a "negotiated" contract having the appearance of authority on the one hand and conspiracy, subversion, and exploitation of power on the other. Although Carol initially worries about the legality (and the ethics?) of such a decision, John's assurances clear the path for learning, encouraging her inquiry. Both parties in the negotiation are clearly served. Recalling other forceful Mamet personalities whose power is reflected linguistically, John circumscribes the hierarchical relationship implicit in the teacher-student paradigm: "Say this is the beginning. . . . Of the class," he postulates. Over her objections that they "can't start over," an imperious John dictates academic policy: "I say we can. (*Pause*) I say we can" (26), evidencing the "danger" that "the will to educate, may degenerate into arbitrariness" (Buber 1959, 100). As MacLeod avers, "The salience of the verb 'to say' in this passage provides a textbook illustration of discourse power not lost on Carol," who subsequently assumes "the power of definition" and masters the mechanics of power, disclosing that "she is a far better student than either her teacher or her detractors care to admit" (208). For when Carol asserts the power of definition, it is *she* who lectures John, "You think, you think you can deny that these things happened; or that if they *did,* if they *did,* that they meant what you *said* they meant" (48-49). Facing failure, Carol sets about acquiring her goal—"To be *helped.* . . . To *know* something. . . . 'To get on in the world'" (12)—with an urgency and resolve that veritably illustrate Mamet's premise that the will to power and success unifies them even if their ethics, expression, and methodology drive them apart.

Neither purely reminiscence nor self-promotion, John's speech repeatedly turns to narrative as a pedagogical methodology, one that codes him culturally and links him with such storytellers as Teach and Levene, who similarly found fiction a method of inspiration, communication, and eidetic memory. Employing a story that is as problematic as the problem it problematizes, the anecdote that John narrates about the copulation patterns of the rich and poor to illustrate his thesis that despite class, culture, and intellectual disparity, we retain information and value it "as an article of faith" without subjecting it to inquiry (32) offends Carol and is perceived by her (or it is judged subsequently by her group) as vulgar, thus providing fodder for her notebook, itself a storehouse of valued but unexamined information on John's comportment.[22] In both the choice of the story and its discourse, Mamet provides yet another linguistic clue to discerning John's identity as a "ghetto cosmopolitan." That John's discourse reflects what Irving Howe termed "demotic upsurge," a unity of gutter vividness with university refinement, does not diminish its perceived response as boorish and sexually insensitive. Neither is it inconsistent with intellectual and aesthetic endeavor, suggests Mark Shechner, who contends a character of this type may pose "a puzzle" to those "for whom education implies refinement, decorum, *breeding,*" yet would be considered "a standard intellectual type" among Jews (1990, 46).

Although John's professed love of teaching and concern for students sporadically allay her anxiety, his defining his role as an educator who tries to "provoke" his students perplexes Carol, for whom obscure concepts, such as "'prolonged and systemic hazing'" (32, 35), and "'Virtual warehousing of the young'"(11), and iconoclastic ideas on higher learning glossing those of Thorstein Veblen are confounding and confusing. Her frustration overflows in an emotional outburst: "I DON'T UNDERSTAND. DO YOU SEE??? I DON'T *UNDERSTAND.* . . . *Any* of it. *Any* of it. . . . What are you *talking* about? What is everyone *talking* about?"(36). "For Carol," suggests Ryan, "John's class, and probably most of academia as well, is a 'Tower of Babel,' where each professor hawks his—or her—own peculiar, contradictory doctrine" (396), but since teaching in her view is commensurate with "telling" rather than thought-provoking analysis, she is equally baffled by the content of John's lesson and the methodology that not only turns a fact or predicament on its head, it presupposes that the student actively engage in the process of inquiry. Seizing upon a concrete example, the professor illustrates the importance of employing an inverse perspective in the contemplation and analysis of the dictums or "article[s] of faith" that we as a society hold as "an unassailable good"(32-33), which, in his view, is the most efficacious method of distinguishing fact from myth. Indeed, "the mythology of America," suggests Mamet, "is that we've always been susceptible to exhortations to do what is right, but we've never been susceptible to exhortations to *think* what is right and arrive at our own conclusions" (Zweigler 43).

One of those things about which we should think, John posits, is higher education. "Somebody told *you*," he theorizes, "and you hold it as an article of faith, that higher education is an unassailable good. This notion is so dear to you," he continues, "that when I question it you become angry. Good. Good, I say. Are not those the very things which we should question?" Proposing the notion that "college education, since the war, has become so a matter of course . . . a fashionable necessity, for those either of or aspiring *to* the new vast middle class, " John contends that "we *espouse* it, as a matter of right, and have ceased to ask, 'What is it good for?' (*Pause*)" (32-33). Enumerating several reasons for the "pursuit of higher education?" among them, "love of learning . . . mastery of a skill . . . economic betterment" (33), he ceases speaking to write a note, ostensibly for a future publication.[23]

Writing about economic betterment and entitlement in *The Good Life and Its Discontents: The American Dream in the Age of Entitlement 1945-1995*, Robert J. Samuelson maintains that entitlement as we know it expresses a "modern conviction" that "certain things are (or ought to be) guaranteed to us" (6), though this claim, he argues, is a mirage. Its essence lies in "the quest for control" (49). Although early in the century it was generally recognized that "hard work, thrift, and competitive struggle" assured success, today, he continues, we presume that those who "play by the rules," as John perceives his bid for tenure, should prosper. Further, Samuelson sees a direct correlation between "The rise of entitlement [and] a decline of the sense of responsibility" the corollary being that if entitlements are denied, as Carol perceives her threatened position, we assign responsibility (or blame) elsewhere (15). Within the context of the play, then, entitlement, framed in academia, calls attention to student and teacher aligned in their self-hatred and common view of themselves as entitled. And whereas John's illustrative example generates ideas that the professor believes will be of future value, Carol's speech reveals the impact of his provocative technique and inferred lesson, particularly his focus on economic advancement—a subject of primary interest to Carol, evidenced by her enhanced control of language. Thus, when John spontaneously interrupts her to encourage her analysis—"Good. Good. *Good.* That's right! Speak up!"—he is summarily silenced by the now assertive student with the wonderfully Mametic injunction, "I'M SPEAKING . . . (*Pause*)" (30). Somewhat embarrassed but undaunted, Carol confidently challenges John to explicate his ideas, demonstrating, in effect, that John's interrogatories have, in fact, propelled the dialogical event, the ideal I-Thou relation that draws individuals into closer unity. Nonetheless, although dialogue may be the "ideal" mode of address and relation, as this play of missed communication and miscommunication powerfully dramatizes, we typically fall short of the mark, given "the simple truth that none of us ever hears exactly what someone else means to say" (Feingold 1992, 357).

Rather than clarify her confusion, John continually deepens it, crystallizing Carol's feelings of failure and her inability to understand "*Any* of it": be it concepts, precepts, statistics, or graphs. Indeed, once John interrupts the dyad to record his deftly crafted ideas on education, he both slights his student and disturbs the delicate balance of their exchange. Sensing that the moment is lost, Carol apologizes for detaining John, calls attention to the passage of time, just as numerous phone calls throughout the act have insistently done, because engaged in a spirited, if abbreviated, discussion with his pupil on such issues as prejudice, justice, and fairness that in retrospect lend greater import to this seemingly aimless conversation, John, and we, have lost track of time. Nonetheless, pleased that his time, effort, and encouragement have resulted in Carol's apparent enhanced self-worth, John endeavors to extend the lively exchange of ideas and the (assumed) success of this tutorial meeting by engaging Carol in closer scrutiny of the "demographics, wage-earning capacity, college and non-college educated men and women, [between] 1855-1980" hoping to "wring some worth from the statistics" and the lesson (35). Balking at his codification of concepts and precepts, the resistant student refuses outright. "No," she says, stopping the flow of conversation in its tracks, distracting the audience from examining what John *is* saying, and commanding our complete attention with her outburst: "I DON'T *UNDERSTAND* . . ." (36). Stumbling into the many audience traps that

Mamet springs in this play and throughout his canon, we get so caught up in the moment and in her outburst that we fail to see its relevance to structure, theme, and character, paralleling a similar technique in *Glengarry Glen Ross* in which Levene's cryptic allusions to his daughter compound the mystery and reveal the man.

Framed as a lesson, John's speech, with its telling juxtaposition of history and contemporary events, rivets attention to the trend of upward mobility among lower classes "aspiring *to* the new vast middle class" (33) most of whom view higher education as the principal path to personal and economic progress. Taken together with his previous references to the trappings of privilege, we see that like the producers, salesmen, and wannabes that populate earlier Mamet plays, John has bought into the success myth: he is in thrall to the power of his profession, a classicist on a power trip much like Bobby Gould, commanding this, ordaining that, or formulating a new school policy. One of those Mametic "tells" or clues to the action, this speech is a mother lode, a cornucopia of information about John that serves as a pointer to character implicitly conveying ethnic identity and cultural history. Like Levene speaking with Williamson, John puts his foot in his mouth, but neither Carol nor we know it. Upon closer inspection of this speech, we wonder what John is talking about. Has he gotten so caught up in his lecture that he has made an error in referring to educational trends from 1855 to 1980 that goes undetected by his student?[24] More likely it is a Freudian slip, for how many men and women attended college before the twentieth century in sufficient numbers to make review of these statistics valuable? While the reference to lower classes aspiring to the vast new middle class betokens parvenus like himself and Carol, what do the demographics and statistics tell us? More importantly, how does John's slip cast light on the present moment, the play's action, and the impending tragedy?

In a trenchant history of American Jewry, Arthur Hertzberg characterizes the second half of the nineteenth century in American history as that period in which Jews in America were obsessed with acceptance as Americans and "Getting Rich Quick" in a country that offered Jews unparalleled economic opportunity. To accommodate both these goals, Reform Judaism emerged as "the religion of the successful middle class," that eschewed all trappings of tradition, and became "the most radically untraditional sect in all of world Jewry" (1989, 144). Eighteen fifty-five, the date at which John suggests we "look" at the demographics, is a pivotal moment in the American Jewish experience when a pitched battle between Orthodox and Reform movements reached a defining moment at a national conference of rabbis intended to reconcile opposing factions. A challenge posed by the

Reform movement resulted in a split between those who would henceforth define themselves as "a new American Judaism" and those who defined themselves as a centuries-old people (128-30), paralleling the analogous split between European Enlightenment Jewry, for whom acceptance, security, and comfort became the watchwords for survival, and Orthodox Jews (Ashkenazi Jews), who privileged centuries-old tradition and learning. If John's allusive references and historical approach to knowledge suggest that he has given more than passing thought to the events and the history of those who bartered identity and spirituality for affluence, his materialism and predilection for the trappings of privilege strongly imply that success for him is measured by materialism rather than substance. Yet the very mention of a concrete manifestation of concepts and precepts intimidates Carol, proves the proverbial straw for this student, providing her with a position— absolute confusion—from which she can oppose John's interrogatories with some of her own, effectively terminating any discourse on the demographics to which John referred. "[W]ear[ing] her lack of intellectual finesse like a badge of beleaguerment" (Hassell 59), Carol demands: "[W]hat do you *want* with me? What does it *mean?* Who should I *listen* to?" (36), a line of inquiry that speaks volumes in subsequent scenes.

Eager to soothe Carol's anxiety and console her with a sympathetic word, John invites comparison to a concerned parent or individual in his ready identification with the plight of others more vulnerable than himself, a role consistently recognized as integral to the Jewish experience (Lerner; Dershowitz). "Sshhhhh. . . . Just let it go," he repeatedly tells her, and she complies, confessing intimate secrets. Though embarrassed by her revelation, "I feel bad. . . . I am bad," Carol provides further avenues of correspondence between John's feelings of self-hatred and fallibility and her own. Reassuring her three times, "It's all right" (36-38), John believes he is on the verge of establishing a rapport, just as he previously initiated revelatory dialogue by his persistently provocative interrogatories framed within an atmosphere of trust. For although John knows that "Compassion is not always easy," he is cognizant of the fact that to "listen to the stories of those whom you might be tempted to demean" (Lerner 116-17) encourages the development of this skill. Always one to limit back story and capture our attention through "the juxtaposition of [uninflected] images" (Mamet 1991b, 7), Mamet cuts off Carol's confession, shattering the ephemeral intimacy by the ringing of the telephone, captivating John's complete attention within seconds, and reminding us that throughout the scene he has felt compelled to choose between two responsibilities about which he feels strongly, either by ignoring telephone phone calls or verbalizing his choice to remain with his student in response to his wife's insistence that he keep his promise to appear "As soon as . . . [possible]"(2). "This is important, too" (20), he tells her.[25]

In the final moments of the act, John is overheard on the telephone yelling about those issues that absorbed him in the opening monologue. The house, the easement, the contract, his rights are the very distractions that contribute to the loss of John's tenure and have themselves been diversionary. He and we are shocked to learn that Grace and Jerry have attempted to lure him into coming to a surprise party at the new house in honor of his tenure announcement by perpetrating a ruse, the pretext of which is threatened legal action, which leads John to conclude prophetically, "there are those who would say" that a surprise is "a form of aggression" (41). Carol's puerile and eerily portentous question, "Is it your birthday?" (40) illustrates yet again that we misread Mamet's text—and subtext—at our own peril, for this query proves the perfect opportunity for the playwright's sly allusion to similar modern texts of exile, both Harold Pinter's *The Birthday Party* and Franz Kafka's *The Trial,* in which the male protagonists, Stanley and Josef K. respectively, surprised on their birthdays (presumed and veritable), are charged, judged, shattered, and subsequently expelled from their communities.

Paralleling the break-in of the real estate office in *Glengarry Glen Ross* that occurs between acts 1 and 2, and the betrayal that occurs between acts in *Speed-the-Plow,* the second act of *Oleanna* opens with the revelation that more has transpired between acts than John's surprise party. In fact, while John is attending a party to laud his achievement surrounded by friends, family, and legal advisor, Jerry, Carol has benefited from time spent in the company of advisors, her "group," whose lessons in self-worth and pupil power seem to have been "drip-fed" into her brain (Morley 792). And while Mamet does not adhere strictly to the Aristotelian twenty-four hour period he observes in his tragedy *American Buffalo,* stretching the elapsed time between acts 1 and 2 to the Beckettian "one day," the playwright, apparently concluding that a reasonable amount of time must logically transpire for Carol's indoctrination to appear plausible, is nonetheless aware that no amount of time would be sufficient for those who view Carol's metamorphosis from "dimwit" to "New Woman" as less than credible. For not only is Carol now enlightened, she is linguistically empowered. Catching John off guard, she fires off a surprise that tops one perpetrated by his family and friends: a formal complaint recounting John's offensive deeds proffered to the Tenure Committee, whose final judgment on John's tenure is still pending. Recounting his offensive deeds and character, a coded reference to the "character issue," a term loaded with anti-Semitic baggage that has long served as ample excuse for the exclusion of the Jew from places of employment,[26] Carol's complaint evidences her intention "to damn the antagonist out of his own mouth," suggests MacLeod, "deploying to best advantage the best available weapons" (206-07): rhetorical strategies, sexual politics, her gender, and the element of surprise.

The scene opens as before in John's office, but rather than his shouting into the phone, John addresses Carol in a long, modulated monologue already in progress. It differs markedly from the opening monologue of act 1 in which John was engaged in an agitated conversation about a purchase of land with his wife. Here the stakes are decidedly higher and intangible. We immediately notice a transformed John, who "in the spirit of *investigation*" and self-preservation invited Carol to his office to ascertain the nature of the malfeasance he has committed against her, to "make amends" (46), present a reasonable defense on his own behalf, and negotiate a deal. Not unlike Teach, Roma, Levene, Gould, and Fox, who adapt their demeanor and discourse to win the hearts and minds of their respective audiences, John adopts a pose at once assured and self-reproachful, delivering a carefully crafted opening argument, a defense, an apologia, a *pilpul* of sorts, intended in the best-case scenario to refute, rebut, and repudiate the charges that impugn his good name and threaten his career and, in the worst, to diminish or blunt their impact. Neither muddled like Gould nor arrogant like Fox, John, as befits his profession, persuasive power, and previously displayed obfuscation, is polished, masterfully shifting the focus to what enhances his commanding professorial image, professionalism, superior intellect, compassion, and decency and humanizes him as individual committed to students and family, torn between aspirations and humility. In short, he presents himself as a man who is capable of misdeed.

Thus, if Carol, interrupted by the telephone at the end of act 1, did not have an opportunity to confess her deepest secrets, John takes full advantage of the confessional mode, not to confess or vomit his "badness" but to acknowledge his human weakness, what he defines as "*covetous*" behavior (43), with its obvious ethical implications. Hence, while giving scant mention to Carol's charges of professional impropriety, what her report characterizes as "heterodoxy . . . 'to the detriment of, of my students'" (43) John's speech reflects both rumination and rationalization. Apparently John, paralleling Fox, who similarly found himself threatened with the imminent loss of a dream deal, has been confronted and conflicted by an age old dilemma of worthiness. And like Fox, John has engaged in a Talmudic argument with himself in which he "asked and *ask*" whether he is worthy to be rich and richly rewarded for his accomplishments, and whether the goal he coveted and covets is itself a worthy one. For indeed, he has identified what is important to him: "A home. A Good Home. To raise my family" (43-44).

> That I *would* pursue it. That I *desired* it, that I was not pure of longing for security, and that that, perhaps, was not reprehensible in me. That I had duties *beyond* the school, and that my duty to my home, for instance, was, or should be, if it were not, of equal weight. That tenure, and security, and yes, and *comfort,* were not, of themselves, to be scorned; and were even worthy of honorable pursuit. And that it was given me. Here, in this place, which I enjoy, and in which I find comfort, to assure myself of—as far as it rests in The Material—a continuation of that joy and comfort. In exchange for what? Teaching. Which I love. (44)

Although John's affirmation of home and family clearly underscores his prioritizing what he most values in life, his conflating and confusing the worthiness of "honorable pursuit" with "comfort" discloses that John now regularly worships himself in what Lerner aptly terms the "Glorification of materialism and the cult of individualism" (xxii). Differing from Fox's soul-searching, John's attempts to sell Carol on his worthiness seem desperate; he has long since bought into the sophistry, the ideal, of entitlement-as-worth, as has she.

Employing his consummate oratory skills as his first and best line of defense, both to convince others and assure himself, John's stunning set-piece is a stratagem to cover nakedness and ebbing confidence. Put simply, John is aware that he is in a "struggle for survival in a climate . . . [read academic community] that wants you gone" (Mamet 1996a, 89). However, like Roma, John, a smooth-talking salesman who must rely on his wits, is a man who Joe Mantegna well understands, is not "this kind of bad person" but rather an individual among whose attributes were confidence, intellect, ambition, compassion, and caring, in other words a *mensch* blinded by comfort who has obviously concluded, "'Fuck it, I'm not apologizing'" (Kane 1992, 256). Empowered to play the professor for all it's worth—"To strut. To *posture.* To 'perform'" (51), as Carol puts it—and to grab the advantage, to establish his superior status, to swing the pendulum in his direction, John, in short, must control "the whirlwind of . . . passion," and "must acquire and beget a temperance that may give it smoothness."[27] Indeed, for one who prides himself on his skilled performance, *this* is the part: to confront Carol's rage with reasonableness and the force of logical argument, to present a convincing portrait that is at odds with the aberrant individual of questionable decency and merit portrayed in Carol's report to the Tenure Committee, to take home the Tony. And in Carol's view, he is a flop, a dismal fiasco.

Whereas Karen in *Speed-the-Plow* neither claims nor feigns confusion when Bobby Gould, after a puzzling peroration whose similar intent is to polish his image, questions her: "You see? . . . You follow me? . . . You get it" (1985, 41-42), ostensibly having grasped the gist of Gould's lesson, Carol, who cannot tell a precept from a paradigm, cuts to the quick of John's argument with a clarity that stuns us in its percipience. Disaffected by his appeal, she asks, "What do you want of me" (45); the subtle revision from her earlier question in act 1, "what do you *want* with me?" (36), is striking. His tentativeness and rage evident in pauses and elliptical phrases, John, playing on her sympathy, admits to bruised feelings, wounded pride, and perplexity at the allegations she has brought against him, but determined to maintain the flow of communication and control over his emotions, he begins a recitation of the charges. "All right. You find me pedantic. Yes. I am. By nature, by *birth,* by profession" (45), he admits, alluding to the stereotypical image of the Jew as literalist, not unlike Mamet, who similarly told Michael Billington, "I am by nature a pedant. It think it comes from my people having studied the Talmud for 6,000 years" (1989, 21). Knowing that pedantry could not possibly be the crux of her complaint, John opts for a different approach, which emphasizes his role as a learned educator (recalling Mamet's beloved Stoics) and provides an opening for dialogic communication: "The Stoical Philosophers say if you remove the phrase 'I have been injured,' you have removed the injury. . . . Just tell me. Literally. Literally: what wrong have I done you?"(47).

Carol's "J'accuse," however, remains notably unanswered. For either there is no exact word for John's offense or its breadth cannot be contained in one word she either knows or will recite, or as Winston Churchill aptly phrased it, "We are in the presence of a crime without a name."[28] Indeed, rather than delineate John's specific crime Carol abstracts it so that "*Whatever*" John has done will appear in "my report" (47), a bill of particulars that outlines his "badness" as Carol perceives it. Thus, if John is "always looking for a *paradigm*" (45), Carol has found it in his behavior, which she has meticulously recorded during two semesters, compiling a ledger of his deeds, a catalogue of his calumny. Hearing his words stripped of context, John judges this gospel according to Carol "*ludicrous*" (48), recalling a story of the Baal Shem Tov who likewise rejected a student's handwritten book as inaccurately reflecting his words (Kushner 1991, 42-43).[29] But unwilling to lose sight either of his goal or his previously stated responsibility to his students, John presses on in search of truth and justice, despite the fact that Carol increasingly challenges him: "Do you deny it? Can you deny it . . .? Do you see? (*Pause*) Don't you see? You don't see, do you?"(48). And John does not see, any more than she acknowledges what, or that, she feels. Determined to regain Carol's attention and his power position—and so save his life, his tenure, real estate deal, and all that it implies—and elevate their discourse to a higher level of "concepts and precepts," ethics and values to live by, to impress upon her the significance and consequence that her allegations have in "the *real* world," John brings the conversation around to the subject of rights. "[Y]ou talk of *rights*," he insists. "Don't you see? *I* have rights too. . . . This is my *life*. I am not a *bogeyman*" (50), his allusion to Moloch, the god of the Phoenicians to whom children were sacrificed, implicit. The simplicity of his statement is stunning, as is her revelation that she agreed to the meeting both "as a *favor*" to him and to advance her group's agenda (50).

Her recitation of the litany of charges against John, intended to give the lie to the fact that he is "not a *bogeyman*" paints another portrait, however, of a monster of iniquity, indecency, and impropriety who is power-seeking, exploitative, and destructive. Contemptuous of his pleas that his accomplishments and aspirations have value and should be valued while he devalues those of aspiring "*hardworking students*" (52), Carol hammers the final nail into his coffin by rendering her judgment on him: "I tell you. That you are vile. And that you are exploitative. . . . you can look in yourself and see those things that I see. And you can find revulsion equal to my own" (52). That Carol's condemnation is odious, offensive, and hostile goes without question, that it exceeds out of all proportion John's transgressions, most would also concur, and that it is politically biased is unequivocal. That it is encoded, the playwright leaves little doubt.

In opposition to his opening monologue in act 2, a dialectic on ego and selflessness, Carol's discloses that she seeks to empower herself by disempowering John as representative, privileged individual. Clearly, he is not blameless of all these charges, for he has given ample evidence of self-aggrandizing, patriarchal, and inappropriate behavior. Nor is he blameless of the charge of heterodoxy. However much her monologue seeks to narrate the personal struggle of students, like her, who "*slave*"(52) in order to attend university, and "Overcame prejudices," both economic and sexual (69), what it does do is validate John's previous allegation that she is "*angry*" and has sufficient cause (7) and confirms that she wants to unseat him from his "so-protected, so elitist seat" (52) so that she can claim it.[30] In objectifying, labeling, and dehumanizing John as a misogynist, she oppresses another individual as surely as she has "endured" oppression herself, her behavior as wrongheaded, abusive, and disrespectful of another human being as his. For although Marc Silverstein finds that the play's "demonization and terroristic exclusion" of Carol as spokesperson for "those who identify themselves in terms of difference" compels our attention to the equation of "difference with distortion and divisiveness" (118) the demonization and terroristic exclusion is perpetrated by Carol rather than the other way around.

For what are we to think of such an individual whose "acts" are characterized as "deviat[ing]," "transgress[ing]," "mock[ing]," and "destroy[ing]," who covets power, and who is "vile," "self-serving," "exploitative" (47, 51-52)—in short, one who is an object of revulsion? Accused of poisoning humanity, Jews have long been perceived as a menace to the social and religious well-being of Christians. The most notable expression of this attitude, Luther's *On the Jews and Their Lies,* added scatological insult and biting sarcasm to an ever-growing paradigm and advocated stripping Jews of their books and forbidding their teaching henceforth. Given that overt Jewish connection to the Jewish language or culture after the Enlightenment, especially among Western Jews, was largely diminished, particularly by assimilation, fin de siècle scientists and philosophers, such as self-hating Jews Otto Weininger and Peter Altenberg, theorized that "the ability to 'see' the Jew encompassed both "the observable [qualities]" and "the *hidden*" invisible, internal ones (Gilman 1991, 201, emphasis added). This shift from external to internal traits evolved into what Altenberg determined to see as a "morphological definition of race rather than a genetic one," which evolved into "the genotype of the Jew" (Gilman 1991b, 201).[31] It was and is, therefore, not too far a stretch to "see" the Jew's diseased moral state and to perceive him or her as the disease of the body politic (208). Dragging out the tired epithet "dirty Jew" and expanding on the model of the Jew as conspiratorial, aggressive, exploitive, power-seeking, and disloyal, nations in the late nineteenth and early twentieth century closed ranks against the "Alien Menace," an untrustworthy, deviant wolf in sheep's clothing cynically fooling a good-natured, gentile society for whom the Jew was perceived as devoid of social morality and possessing every kind of threat to conservative values (Stevens 244-45; 175-76). In short, when the world looked at the Jew, he or she saw a superior calculating intellect, a domination of finance, a materialist. Ironically, claims Finkielkraut, "The postfascist age no longer thinks in terms of evil races or natural subversives, only of vile rhetoric and bad behavior" (151-52). Indeed, "without the least allusion to racism," he adds, "all Jews find themselves guilty" (153).

Hence, however loathsome Carol's ignominious indictment, what she does not say directly speaks equally loudly, her chiding of John ironic: " *We* don't say what *we* mean. Don't *we? Don't we? We do* say what *we* mean" (49, emphasis original and added). Upon closer inspection Carol's speech is punctuated throughout with the word "you," which in effect assigns specific meaning and hammers home the point: "you" (people) are different from "us"; "you" are to blame for these ills. Like fascists who initially drove Jewish professors out of Western European universities (and disproportionate numbers of middle-class Jews from their places of employment as lawyers,

doctors, small-businessmen, journalists and teachers) into exile, camps, or
the ovens, surprising individuals like John who believed they were protected
by their elevated economic status (Lerner 192), "American Judeophobes
blamed"—and some continue to blame—"all the ills of modern American
life on 'the Jews'" (Gilman and Katz 10).[32]

In an essay, Mamet exhorts us to be intolerant of anti-Semitism which
he characterizes as "insanity—human rage directed against a target deemed
both allowed and unprotected" (1996a, 206-07). Differing from Aaronow's
vocalized fury in response to Baylen's verbalized attack in *Glengarry* ("No
one should talk to a man that way" [1984, 87]), John, as befits his profession
and discourse, notably opposes Carol's monologue, a withering defamation
of character, with a bold attempt at communication. "Nice day today" (52),
he says, refusing as a point of principle to validate her rage by addressing her
comments directly. Providing neither "explanation, reason, tolerance," nor
silence, responses Mamet rejects as "disastrous" (206-07), John attempts, as
he has throughout the play, to establish a linguistic link—dialogue and
inquiry instead of tirade and the imposition of a single idea—that directly
addresses the absence of mutual respect in a society torn apart as much by
objectifying the Other as by ignorance.

As we hear, John is resolved to fulfill his responsibility as an educator,
endeavoring to combat hateful propaganda "funneled" into her head, as
Buber phrases the mode of propagandists, presumably by her group, who
has answered her complaint, "Nobody *tells* me anything" (14). Employing
an opposing pedagogical technique, the authentic communication of
dialogue, he engages the mind of the pupil in a proactive process of learning
informed by compassion that has much in common with the Jewish concept
of *chesed,* which recognizes constraints in opposing positions, neither
diminishing nor conceding moral obligation. In place of "acceptance [of
others' complexities]," posits Lerner, "one may move effectively toward what
ought to be" (113). In fact, Carol is so startled that John is talking to her
after she has had her say, as are we, that she responds to the common
courtesy with surprise. But the ploy is a masterstroke. Before she realizes it,
she is drawn back into the room and into the humanizing act of communication, which in essence, explains John, is a tacit agreement that "we are
both human (*Pause)*" (53). From this point alone exists the potential for an
"I-Thou" relation whose origin may be traced to the Torah, which instructs
us not to oppress the stranger or repeat the ways of the stranger (Lev. 17-26).

And it is from this vantage point that John diminishes the intensity of
her hateful rhetoric and its criticism of him by a simple, effective equation:
"I'm not a . . . 'exploiter,' and you're not a . . . 'deranged,' what?
Revolutionary?" (53), or more likely its inverse, reactionary, though lost on

her is the irony that they are both "border smashers." By equating their respective "labels" John progresses logically toward neutralizing both labels by identifying each as fallacious—that is, if one is fallacious, so is the other—while engaging in a mediation that acknowledges their differing positions, the worthiness of their desires, the validity of her complaints, his errors of omission or commission, and their imperfections as human beings—as in "we are just human" (53). Indeed, Mamet told Hank Nuwer: "It's not our job to change the world. It is our job to act according to precepts we perceive to be right" (1985, 12).

Avowing that both his and her actions are self-serving, John moves to the crux of his argument, relying on reasonableness and responsibility that were the trademark form and focus of his earlier monologue. Apparently the teacher has remembered that "teachings live in the life of a responsible human being" (Buber 1963, 140). He has also remembered that learning cannot take place without comprehension and mutual respect and that neither can living. In stark contrast to his obfuscation that, at the least, further alienated and confused his student, John takes great pains to formulate his argument in lucid vocabulary and short sentences, pausing frequently to choose his words carefully and confirm that Carol is following his line of thinking, aware that teachings do not exist for themselves but as a model for ethical deed. Therefore, when he opines that their talking "is the gist of education" (56), John, in effect, foreshortens Buber's philosophy of pedagogy, a paradigmatic example of Mamet's minimalism.

Broaching her complaint and her inflammatory condemnation as a piece, John proceeds resolutely:

> . . . And where I'm *wrong* . . . perhaps it's not your job to "fix" me. I don't want to fix *you.* I would like to tell you what I *think,* because that *is* my job, conventional as it is, and flawed as I may be. . . . But just like "nice day, isn't it . . . ?" I don't think we can proceed until we accept that each of us is human. (*Pause*) And we still can have difficulties. We *will* have them . . . that's all right too. (*Pause*) Now: (53-54)

Mamet is as masterful with the monosyllable as he is with the aria, and as this tiny word "now" reveals, John's con artistry has almost slipped our attention, for even as he has called attention to their mutual survival in the university and the greater community of society, he has not lost sight of the fact that his current "difficulties" threaten *his* survival, just as in the first scene Carol was concerned with her failing grade, a "pointer" to her survival. Establishing what he believes is the basis for a significant dialogue with the potential for an "I-Thou" relation rather than "I-It" competitiveness, John is on the verge of initiating a discussion of her complaint, both because conflict with a student poses "the supreme test for the educator" (Buber 1959, 107), and because, as the switchbacks in the opening monologue of act 2 revealed, he is keenly attuned to the passage of time and impending events. In posing that "we're just human" (53), John ostensibly echoes Don in *American Buffalo,* who draws on his common humanity with Bob to broach his breach of trust. Yet, as I read this scene, John's attempt to talk with his student—"nice day, isn't it?"— is along the lines of what Emmanuel Levinas proposes as a means of effecting communication between people on the most basic level. As Levinas puts it, "even the smallest and most commonplace gestures . . . bear witness to the ethical. . . . This concern for the other remains utopian in the sense that it is always 'out of place'" (Kearney 32).

Interrupting John just as he is about to make his pitch for a deal advantageous to them both, Carol makes the point that the exigency for discussion of the complaint is obviated by the fact that "we're talking about it at the Tenure Committee Hearing. (*Pause*)" (56). Insistent on observing the norms of "the 'conventional' process" of the tenure deliberations, as he did not the protocol of the classroom, Carol, essentially in control of the speech act, limits further conversation of the complaint despite pressure exerted by John: "Yes, but I'm saying: we can talk about it *now,* as easily as . . ." (56).

Recalling Aaronow's and Moss's classic exchange in *Glengarry,* we remember that "actually *talking*" differs from "just '*talking*'" and substantively differs from "just *speaking*" (1984, 39), for as David Worster correctly recognizes "just 'speaking' about a subject keeps it in the comfortable range of abstract 'idea'; actually 'talking' about a subject crystallizes it as an action—a robbery, or a business deal, or a sale" (377). Paralleling *Glengarry, American Buffalo,* and numerous other Mamet works in which "talking" concretizes speech as action, John's proposal is presented as a viable, logical, prudent, and profitable option available *now* that would therefore obviate the need for future "talking" and "acting." Even if Carol does not catch the disingenuousness of John's phrase "we can talk about it *now*" as we do, or if she does and has decided to shore this tag-line against the ruins of his Tenure Committee hearing as she has previous gems in her notebook, in either case her decision to "take our differences" to the committee signals in her one-word response—"No" (56)—that she retains the advantage and he's all but lost his appeal. Recalling and mocking the intrusion of the telephone call at just that moment at the end of act 1 in which John had convinced Carol of his sincerity and encouraged her to speak from her heart, John similarly has begun to speak "frankly" (54). Therefore, it is with alacrity that he terminates the call from Grace, "Babe, baby, will you just call Jerry. . . . Just *trust* me. . . . I can't talk now" (55), a remark we take at its literal and figurative level.

In retrospect we see that John's desire for resolution between pupil and student was at best evanescent, even illusory. One reason for this, claims Silverstein, is that Mamet portrays him as "failing the values he invokes" (117). On the contrary, in support of those values John encourages Carol to supplant animosity with civility, mono-logos with dialogue. Each successive act and word of courtesy reinforces his premise that each individual has the potential to conduct himself or herself "with worth and dignity" (Kogos 55), an idea that undergirds the play. The slippage, therefore, from civility to animosity is jarring when John, grasping at straws, "impinge[s]" on her, as Carol phrases it (56), attempting one verbal ploy after another to constrain conversation and restrain Carol from leaving his office. "Believ[ing] there was no problem . . . which he couldn't surmount . . . [by] thinking harder, and by being more inventive,"[33] John casts about for the best way to approach Carol, intimidating her with fear tactics (his own fear displaced on her), "You're going to make a . . ."; appealing to her sense of protocol and process, "There are *norms,* here"; and assuming an ethical responsibility for his student, "Look: I'm trying to *save* you . . ." (56-57).

The irony of the sage professor playing savior is not lost on Carol: "you're trying to save *me?*" she asks, incredulous, initially offended at his patriarchy, his "'paternal prerogative'" (57, 67), for if he is attempting to save anything at this point, it is his own chance at the brass ring, she believes, and in this she is not entirely mistaken. But the wonderful ambiguity of the word "save" deepens the irony of the term in this context, given John's recent explication on the value of mutual respect between those holding opposing positions and desires and the inevitability of ongoing conflicts between people who inhabit this place, be it the classroom, university, or society. To her John evidences arrogance, what she perceives as patriarchal protection that is unwarranted, offensive, and presumptuous. "Save it," she might as well have said. Further, as Carol subsequently reminds him, and their linguistic exchange progressively reveals, power has shifted to her. The beauty of this multivalent phrase, however, is that it returns us to Carol's tirade, where deeply entrenched in her coded speech of "transgress" and "confess" is the lesson that John's "'freedom of thought'"—his elitist humanism, liberalism, and skepticism—are the root causes of his being "found *wanting,* and in error." Astounded, she chides him, "You think you're going to show me some 'light'?" (64, 67). Lacking insight and knowledge of "The True Word," he remains "unseeing"—blind to revelation and beyond salvation.

Certainly, Carol is correct in understanding that John's house and private school for his son are "all about *privilege*" (65), but they are also about fear of poverty, responsibility to family, and need of permanence. And while she does not catch the irony of her statement, John has indeed "*worked*" to achieve power (64-65), finding little value and much threat in powerlessness. Her inability to understand the difference between the need to have power over one's life and power for its own sake reveals the yawning gulf between them, from which misunderstanding of his speech and actions follows naturally. From his vantage point, a clearly Jewish perspective, the word "save" connotes liberating an individual from oppression, or its equivalent, protecting him or her or relieving humiliation. To John, "saving" is a *mitzvah*, what he comprehends as his ethical responsibility. Saving a single human being from oppression and its consequent degradation, John thus acts in accordance with Talmudic wisdom.

Observing that "Humility" and "Aggression" are two ways to play the Game of Life, Mamet recalls what "Kipling (and my father)" and poker sages about whom he writes "understood as 'the Great Game:'" Aggression (1996a, 14). Poker sages, he continues, "inform us that the game is legitimate prosecution of one's own interest." Hence, "we should, therefore, shun the questionable position" and pursue "any and all real advantages, . . . and that pursuit and employment of such advantages must eventually prevail, where reliance on chance or arrogance will invariably come to grief" (14-15). Deprived of his superior advantage, dialogue, and presented with a challenge to his knowledge, position, and education, John, relying on chance and arrogance, ultimately fails in a crucial attempt to win the play. Thus, when Carol refuses him the courtesy of continuing their discussion, he oversteps the bounds of civility, in her view, by restraining her physically against her will.

Despite his protestation that he has "no desire" to constrain her (57), his act belies his words. As Adam Newton observes, the "act" of coercion is twofold: linguistic and physical. Consistently John has employed terms that have sought to influence others' perception: "Look"; "Listen"; "Tell." However, when he compels Carol to speak, that is, to sit down and continue the conversation, John is in essence coercing her compliance "such that supplication and demands are acts of coercion" (114). Deepening the irony, John's act fixes our attention on the conflicting senses of vision and touch, the latter, as Gilman notes in "Goethe's Touch: Touching, Seeing, and Sexuality," a figure firmly "eroticized" (1991a, 33). From this perspective then, John's misunderstood act of frustration inflates into a charge of battery and attempted rape, with its distinct cultural baggage, foreshadowing in this moment his penultimate threat and act of violence in the last scene, "I wouldn't touch you with a ten-foot pole. You little *cunt . . .*" (79). Ironically, though, as the scene concludes we see that John brings the tragedy upon himself by acting in a manner that he has advocated against. Neither trusting nor perceiving John as a source of salvation, Carol looks for help to that source, the group, that the professor correctly intuited represented a threat to them both. Mamet's point, I believe, is that John is well-intentioned, if self-absorbed, and, genuinely perceiving her to be in need of help, acts out of magnanimous sensibilities. Prophetically Carol, who perceives herself threatened by the professor, has the last word, a monologue heard far beyond these walls. As Dembo warns us, "Monologism . . . becomes the voice of tyranny; anti-Semitism, which begins with the slur, ends in persecution. . . . the single-minded obsessive speech that destroys the humanity of the speaker just as he, literally and verbally, destroys the Jew" (9).

The last scene of the play presents yet another view of the teacher-student dynamic, but subtle and substantive changes in discourse and subject reveal a New World Order in which student instructs professor.[34] This shifting of power actualized linguistically in Mamet works such as *Squirrels* and *A Life in the Theatre* is starkly executed in *Oleanna*. Now it is John who has requested a meeting, Carol who acquiesces to hear his explanation and apology and demands a response, "What is it that you wish to tell me?" (61), implicitly conveying that she is not only aware of the time, but she is allotting him just so much time to make his point. Shifting the focus from matters that human beings resolve among themselves to those matters on which the courts or mob power rules, John and Carol are again portrayed as holding opposing views, he preferring the flexibility and accuracy of "accusations" and she insisting on the certitude of "*proved . . .* facts" (61-62). One point, however, is not debatable: John has been accused and judged. And it is from those facts that Carol "wrings some worth" (35), finding her power validated by the Tenure Committee's decision not to grant him tenure. In the absence of disclosure of those factors that influenced the tribunal "To whom *evidence* has been presented . . . [and] have *ruled*," Carol freely draws her own Truth from their judgment, namely that John is "*negligent*" and "*guilty*," that he is "found *wanting*, and in *error*" (64). While these are to her incontrovertible facts, a viable contradictory premise may be postulated that judgment has been influenced by the university's fear of the specter of scandal or avoidance of litigation rather than issues of John's worth or "crimes." In any case, John will be "disciplined," as Carol quaintly phrases it; he will be dismissed, discharged, and expelled from the academic community, deprived of professional credibility and future employment "As full well," she avers, "they should" (64), the undefined, faceless "they" that fed his paranoia. If his actions are not "Sufficient" to have ruined his reputation and career, speaking for herself and her group, Carol is satisfied that justice has been served, and self-satisfied that John's "*own actions*"—for what he "did in class. . . . [and] *in this office*" justify her own (51, 64).

Significantly, Mamet illustrates the shift in power linguistically: Carol dominates speech, controls the agenda of the meeting, and dictates both permitted areas of discussion and the signification of terms. Whereas in act 1, John sought to "awake" her "interest"(26), here Carol's intent is to achieve the group's interests. Thus, if John derived pleasure from "play[ing] the Patriarch" (51), as Carol puts it, it is now Carol's turn to play the tyrant, to abuse authority, to extort, and to rule by Draconian measures. Even before we know the specifics of her agenda, we understand that she will achieve tolerance, empathy, and respect for herself and the aspirations of her group at the price of intolerance of the Other, that is, by imposition of oppressive orders that diminish them both as human beings, given that "Every oppressive order is based on forcing or convincing human beings to be less than they can be," what Lerner defines as the central insight of Judaism (66).

Notably in this scene their discussion of responsibility and feelings lays bare John's alignment with personal responsibility to family, students, and ethical positions, and Carol declares her loyalty to the "group," and by extension the institution. We intuit a direct link between John's earlier discussion about responsibility—namely that it was not Carol's "job to 'fix'" him—and evidence he provides of having engaged in self-flagellation and meditation. The result of John's soul-searching is a heightened awareness, a confession of sorts that "there is much good" in what Carol refers to; that he is "not too old to *learn* and . . . *can* learn" (70-71); that he "cannot help but feel" that his student is "owed an apology" (61). John's transformed demeanor and discourse is indicative of *teshuva*, known in Judaism as a moment of elemental reversal. As L. Kushner observes, this experience encompasses neither "self-rejection" nor "remorse." Rather than simply a "repudiat[ion] of evil" both intended and committed, it signifies "epiphanic, transforming experience," resulting in heightened sensitivity, the acknowledgment of motive, error, recognition, and "real apologies" (1991, 78-80).

Carol, too, is transformed. She has metamorphosed into the Voice of Enlightenment, mocking books and methods "Outside of tradition" that advocate "that fine tradition of *inquiry*. . . . [and] *skepticism*" (67). In her new capacity as Arbiter of Interpretation and Definition, Carol demonstrates that not only is she in control of language, she can bend it, like John, to her will by imposing censorship, or employing misanthropy, orthodoxy, persecution, and xenophobia.[35] Hence, Carol's (mis)perception of John's touch as sexist is hammered home: ". . . I SAY IT WAS NOT. Don't you begin to *see* . . . ? Don't you begin to understand? IT IS NOT FOR YOU TO SAY." (70). Thus, as Lahr notes in his review, "Mamet exposes the central paradox of 'political correctness,' which demands diversity in everything but thought" (1992, 124). As a spokesperson "for those who suffer" and on whose behalf it would be unjust to "forgive" or "forget," Carol summarily rejects John's numerous attempts to engage her in dialogue about what it would cost her to "forgive" him, if she "were inclined" (65-66). What is the value of this line of questioning now that the professor has lost his bid for tenure? And why is the subject of forgiveness important to him personally and to the progress of the play? The exchange is revealing for several reasons. First, the figure of the "tightheart," whether Jew or Gentile, male or female, is a familiar one in Jewish fiction and drama, typically counterpointed to one possessed of *menschlekeit* (ethical responsibility, social justice, and decency for others expressed in kindness) that is a principal foundation of Jewish life. As this moment tacitly underscores, the "tightheart" is condemned, or condemns him or herself, for limited understanding and humanity. A classic example is that of Sergeant Nathan Marx in Roth's short story, "Defender of the Faith," who, encountering one who was stingy with kindness is inclined to act in kind. Although his chastened *rachmones* is revealed as mere gullibility, his kindliness mocked by Grossbart's cynical exploitation, Marx, nonetheless, chastises himself as "a penny pincher with kindness" (1966, 138).

Yet, as we see, Carol is just such "a penny pincher"; not only does she stand apart from John's frustration, pain and rage, she mocks it: "It is not that I don't feel it," she tells him; "But I do not see that it is deserved" (73), a stance that Stern recognizes as silent "literary anti-Semitism" implicit in the omission of sympathy. Second, as offenses of one individual against another according to the Jewish faith require overt and direct apology to the offended individual, John must, like Don in *American Buffalo,* seek forgiveness directly from the aggrieved party, just as Teach in his fashion apologized to Don. Yet on this point Carol denies the appropriateness of accepting John's apology, implying that he cannot be forgiven "his trespasses." From one who craves understanding, Carol's dearth of understanding of John's vocabulary, gestures, sensibilities, and the ethics that sustain his life carries a stronger message than her hollow words. For as Finkielkraut reminds us, history provides us with a chilling precedent of behavior devoid of mercy (147).

Analysis of Carol's canned speech brings to light a chilling portrait of the power of propaganda and its consequent effect on mind control. Apparently, no amount of apology is sufficient: John has no power to ask Carol to consider subjects not on her agenda. And in the New World Order humanizing concepts and precepts like mercy, forgiveness, and compassion, *chesed*, are not only outside her purview; they have been redefined or obliterated, her radical reduction of vocabulary and drastic redefinition of words intended to disorient the victim, evoking what Lawrence Langer terms "the linguistics of the Holocaust." For hers is not a mission of charity but one of conversion and indoctrination. "I came here to instruct" you (67), she tells him. In other words, beneath the doublespeak John hears that she is neither empowered nor programmed to "hear" his apology or grant forgiveness. "YOU BELIEVE IN NOTHING. YOU BELIEVE IN NOTHING AT ALL," she reproaches him: "You believe in what *you call* freedom-of-thought. . . . *You* believe in freedom-of-thought *and* a home, and, *and* prerogatives for your kid, *and* tenure. And I'm going to tell you," she adds, firmly in control, that "you believe *not* in 'freedom in thought,' but in an elitist, in, in a protected hierarchy which rewards you. And for whom you are the clown. And you mock and exploit the system which pays your rent. You're wrong. I'm not wrong." (67-68). In one compelling moment, the Portia-like Carol delivers judgment on the Jew in the name of her group. Echoing and parodying Gold's confession of self-hatred in *Homicide*, "All my goddamned life. . . . I was the donkey . . . I was the 'clown'" (1992b,103), Carol and her group want "their pound of flesh." Proclaiming him an infidel in error, Carol signifies his exclusion from the community by the subtle interplay of "I" and "you," the distancing of mono-logos supplanting the linking of words and people in dialogue. In response to this chilling propaganda William H. Macy, playing the professor to Rebecca Pidgeon's Carol in Mamet's productions at the Hasty Pudding Theatre and in New York, remarked to me, "When I look in Rebecca's eyes every night, there's no doubt that the stage has left, and she doesn't know how to stop it."[36] For although Carol claims she has not come "to gloat" (68), that is exactly what she does when she tells John, "I came to explain something to you. You Are Not God" (67).[37] In the presumed absence of "a protective deity"—what Mamet terms the "depriv[ation] of a pharaoh (parent) to worship or fear"—Carol and company, like the Israelites, reject "Freedom (adulthood)." Desperate "to return to their preadolescent state" (1996a, 165-66), they, in essence, demand "make us gods" (Exod. 32).

Contrasting with Carol's jargon is the legalistic discourse that comprises the controlling jargon of the play drawing our attention to a specialized knowledge, a code, in which John has demonstrated proficiency. Ostensibly fluent in terms of art pursuant to his purchase of a home, in this scene John, struggling to retain his dignity and possibly his job, gets a refresher course as terms of art are redefined. When applied to personal life rather than real estate deals, the terms "offer," "easement," "personal jurisdiction," "indictment," "allegation," and "rape" have fixed meanings that once established by law are immutable. Yet the pseudo-legalism, "act of friendship," surely smacks of an act of enmity rather than friendship, unless, of course, one considers the malleability of the term "friend" in works such as Pinter's *No Man's Land* and Mamet's *Things Change,* both of which explore issues of inclusion and threatened identity. As disingenuous as John's earlier offer to negotiate Carol's complaint in his office "as easily as . . . [the tenure hearing]" (56), "act of friendship" epitomizes the kind of doublespeak that repackages "firing" as "downsizing" and "extermination" as "special treatment."

Therefore, when Carol, in her own version of the confidence game, presents John with a beguiling proposition, "What if it were possible that my Group withdraws its complaint. (*Pause*)" (71-72), an act from which it can ostensibly "derive nothing," he, thinking he is nobody's fool when it comes to deal-making, is prompted to wonder if she is empowered to negotiate and inquires, "In exchange for what." "But I don't think, 'exchange,'" Carol replies, because in this negotiation there is no "exchange": no avenue for barter or trade (as he has teaching for material comforts) and no terms of negotiation but the ever-so-slight deference to his spineless plea that yes, they "might speak to the committee" (72-73). In other words, this is *not* a negotiation that to be successful must serve *both* parties. Seduced by Carol's offer of salvation, John forgets what Mamet terms a "good first principle": "When something looks too good to be true, it is not true," because "When you play in the other man's game, you're most likely going to have to pay the other man off" (1996a, 12).

By any stretch of the imagination and intellect, the perquisites, the spoils of war, are Carol's. Her group derives everything; his option is no option: Hobson's choice. Give up your profession or give up your identity. Recounting Herbert Yardley's poker wisdom in three irreducible adages, Mamet reminds us: "If you've got nothing, get out. If you're beat, get out. If you've got the Best Hand, make 'em pay" (15), and to the cheers and horror of both men and woman alike in America and in numerous venues throughout the world where *Oleanna* has been staged, Carol does exactly that. At this moment, the playwright puts a new spin on John's earlier conversation with Grace at the end of act 1. We recall John in a commanding voice fully confident in his rights guaranteed by the contract he holds in his hand, shouting into the telephone just before Grace and Jerry spill the beans about their surprise: "I have the *paper*. . . . the paper. . . . List, *Listen, screw* her. . . . you tell her the next time I *see* her is in court" (39). Now the paper isn't worth the ink it's written in. "I have the paper" meant "I have the power." Now it is the disciple, having supplanted "dogma for thought, mission for mastery" (Lahr 1992, 124) whose metamorphosis is as notable as his, and who is transformed from lost soul to true believer.

That "We are learning to believe that we do not require wisdom, community, provocation, suggestion, chastening, enlightenment," observes the playwright, "that all things are known and that we need not even know them," is to Mamet "terrifying demagoguery. . ." Not only does "the demagogue endorse the individual's greed and hatred," but history's chronicles reveal that "in times of uncertainty" it is the demagogue "who allays the uncertainty with a lie" (1996a, 159-60). It is not without significance, therefore, that Benjamin Blech understands that in the lie rests the "awesome power" of the presumably holy group, given that the word "group" and "falsehood" are comprised in Hebrew of the same letters (*kesher* and *sheker*), for "If enough people repeat something untrue, the world will believe it" (68-71). Mamet has similarly noted that "a group can be transformed into a jury, which organism can potentially dispense justice. . . . [and] a group can be transformed into a mob" (159-160).

Now, Carol holds the only paper that counts. Proffering "a list of books," which she and her group "find questionable," the student, in the guise of an offer, sets down conditions gussied up as a deal: "If you would like me to speak to the Tenure Committee, here is my list. You are a Free Person, you decide (*Pause*)" (73-74). Carol's remark, "You are a Free Person" is deeply ironic. Free in what respect? That he is "free" person, as opposed to an "oppressed" group? That he signifies, aspires to, and defends free thought, free speech, academic freedom, rights, privilege, prerogative? That he is a libertine? That his choice is without moral and ethical price, or that given his declared responsibilities he could act "freely," unfettered? That any decision undertaken with a gun to one's head could be construed as "free"? That one is free of one's fate and one's character? The presumptive conditional, Douglas Watson reminds us (1992, 216-17), presupposes that if the first part of the bridging conditional is reasonable—"If you would like me to speak . . ." (74), as Carol proposes, then, one presumes the outcome or consequence—"you decide"—is also possible or plausible. And once John has been suckered into reading the list, he reveals both his blinding need to grasp at straws and his absolute vulnerability.

If he had harbored either doubt or hope that the terms of Carol's offer were negotiable, his student springs yet another surprise foreseen in act 1 as "an act of aggression" (41) in the form of a "statement" of public confession of offenses against the student body, and by extension the institution, which John would also be required to sign or preferably to read aloud, which when employed as Mamet's original Cambridge, Massachusetts, ending proved disturbingly effective.[38] Thus, inverting her previous concern that John would force her into recantation, Carol finds that she is empowered by John's weakness to persuade him to do just that. Gambling on his willingness to admit his guilt to retain his job, Carol offers a plea bargain: a statement of recantation that comprises a list of banned books, including his own, reminding us that her announcement that she would drop the charges of harassment against John was a classic Mamet con, one that leads him incorrectly to presume that he is safe. Culminating "the trajectory of Carol's rise" and implicating his utter failure, this final scene leaves John "in his last known activity on stage, a mere shuffler of paper" (Skloot 2). Perusing the list's salient points concurrently with Carol's running commentary, the enraged professor finally explodes, "LOOK. I'm reading your demands. All right?! (*He reads*) (*Pause*) You want to ban my book? . . . to ban my *book* . . . ?" (75).

Singularly unprepared for this precondition, John balks at the notion that this emblem of heritage will be denied to his progeny. But of course, within the context of this play, John's book is much more than his legacy to his son. Throughout centuries of persecution, as Gilman capaciously illustrates, not only was "the individual as teacher linked to the books he taught" (1986, 28), but for centuries "The Jews' books became the embodiment of the blindness and dangerousness of the Jews." Hence "identification of the Jews with their books and the attempt to purge the Jews through the destruction of their books" (31-32) is inextricably linked in the modern period to Holocaust bonfires in which Torah scrolls were incinerated along with books of philosophy and literature in a process undertaken by university students in university towns throughout Germany working from prescribed lists—an abhorrent precursor to the incineration of a race. In other words, to remove the book is to remove from the Jews "the source of their intransigency," the consequence of which is to reduce the individual to "the status of a dead man" (35, 50).

Finding his voice, John finally asserts, "No, no. . . . I'm sorry. I don't know what I was thinking of":

> I'm a teacher. I am a teacher. . . . And I have a respon . . . No, I'm sorry I have a *responsibility* . . . to *myself*, to my *son*, to my *profession*. . . .

> . . . .

And, and, I owe you a debt, I see that now. (*Pause*) You're
dangerous, you're *wrong* and it's my *job* . . . to say no to you. . . .
You want to ban my book? Go to *hell,* and they can do whatever
they want to me. (76)

John's rejection of Carol's proposal, however tempting and however much
he covets tenure, is definitive. But lest we see John's behavior as merely an
illustration that "Mamet's people are often at their best when standing on
their dignity" (Case 72), the intensity of John's ardor and ethical principle
concomitant with his position as an educator gains deeper significance
when illumined by Wiesel's injunction that "whoever lives through a trial,
or takes part in an event that weighs on man's destiny or frees him"—as
John surely has—"is duty bound to transmit what he has seen, felt and
feared" (1965, 174).

Believing that he has survived and resolved his professional and
personal crises, saved by the clarity of his ethical decision, a relieved John,
betraying a pliant optimism that is the victory of the human spirit over
intolerance, is reminiscent of Levene and Teach who convince themselves
that they are capable of pulling together their lives from the wreckage
around them and the wreckage of their own lives. Speaking with his close
friend Jerry, John assures him: "I am all right, now, Jerry. . . . I got a little
turned *around,* but. . . . I've got it figured out. . . . I got a little bit mixed
up. But I am not sure that it's not a blessing. It cost me my job? Fine. Then
the job was not worth having. Tell Grace that I'm coming home and
everything is fff . . . " (77). The quest for home, a recurrent trope in
Mamet's work, foregrounded in the opening speech, "And what about the
land? . . . the house. . . . The yard for the boy," has proven to be the arc
for this character. On this point Mamet is clear: "At the end of the day we
want someone to hold our hand. . . . to share our *idea* of home" (1996a,
114-15, emphasis added).

If God dwells in the details, then the blessings, the mitzvot, to which
John refers, pack a hell of a curse. For Carol has come with more than her
papers for this meeting. As John learns from Jerry, the deliberateness of this
speech revealed in all its careful Mametic minimalism, Carol's got a fistful
of surprises, not the least of which is that she has charged him with "battery"
and "rape." "You tried to rape me" (77) she informs John, reminding him
of his restraining her when she attempted to leave his office; "I am told. It
was battery" (the passive tense revealing that she has all but given up
independent thought) (77-78). While "The rhetoric may be denounced as
unscrupulous," as MacLeod correctly recognizes, it nonetheless is "a gut-
grabbing metaphor with no literal referent" and without parallel in the play

(210).[39] It matters little to John that only the battery charge is "plausible," as Alan Dershowitz, who advised Mamet on the legalisms of this play, terms it;[40] nothing is further from John's mind. In a world in which words are stripped of their meaning, how could he possibly have believed he was home, as in "home free," with its "thematic associations of a place of shelter or refuge." For this Diaspora Jew, "Home is thus a goal both desired and deferred" when the world is turned into a funhouse (Leitch 25).

In an ironic reversal of John's initial concerns, the professor has shifted his priorities with shifting ground and shifting meaning. Endeavoring in the climactic conversation with his attorney to acquire a grasp of the events, his reiterated questions, "[W]hat can they do . . .?" "What do you mean? . . . What does it mean? (77)—recall the vacuity of ideas in Carol's paper and accentuate the point that he may not yet understand the legal ramifications and consequences of Carol's charges, but he does know that betrayal rules the day. Failing to privilege ethical values, John, like Don Dubrow and Shelly Levene, has bought into a false position, his "power-trip" come to a shocking, devastating end. Hence, Carol's earlier question and answers, "What has led you to this place? Not your sex. Not your race. Not your class. YOUR OWN ACTIONS" (64), remind us that John, like Don, has disregarded the value of being mindful. Moreover, he has learned that "Not only does learning *not* protect a person from sin; the hubris born of learning is the hardest sin to extirpate," because, suggests David Roskies, "the acquisition of knowledge—both John's and Carol's—becomes . . . a license . . . to fancy oneself a god" (1995, 291). That John's betrayal of himself is not the key issue in *Oleanna* speaks to the fearlessness, the disturbing power of this play, what Jack Kroll correctly notes is its "cunning logic" (65). In addressing the potential for the abuse of power, Mamet envisions a Kafkaesque world in which the accusations against John drive him to rage and to question himself.

As his penultimate phone conversation with Jerry implicitly conveys, John's hope for the triumph and resiliency of decency over decadence is short-lived, the price of security exorbitant: he has lost the home, the tenure, the golden dream, the desired permanence, and the one thing that he thought he still possessed, his innocence. Stripping John of this last illusion and ratcheting the stakes higher, Carol's charges have thrust John into a higher court of appeal than "the Great Tenure Committee" (23) and its counterpart, "The Tenure Committee, Good Men and True" (50) where, presumably, he will similarly fight and fail to clear his name. Moreover, in this tragedy, John's hard-won knowledge implies harsh judgment of his worthiness and morality. With Carol's parting shot—or what we think is her parting shot—Mamet shifts sympathy toward John in a conclusion that is both surprising and inevitable, arousing our empathy for his profound personal loss and fear that we, too, are as vulnerable and blind as he. One last telephone call bifurcates John's attention between the love of his life and his adversary, as Carol, impinging herself *into* John's conversation and offstage life adjudicates the appropriateness of his calling his wife "Baby" (79), reminding us that in the New World Order the mob that worships power knows no bounds.

Recalling *American Buffalo* in pace and structure, *Oleanna* intensifies toward an explosive moment, effecting some kind of reconciliation or rapprochement at the conclusion. Beautifully prepared by the breakdown of language and reason, John's outcry, "You vicious little bitch. . . . You little *cunt*" (79), and violent attack on Carol in the last ninety seconds nonetheless shocks us—and him—by its ferocity and inhumanity. It is a stunning theatrical moment—a moment of truth for both. That John's three physical gestures escalate into "an epiphanic coherence of gesture and meaning" reflects upon the play's opposition of order and ambiguity (Tomc 166). "Misunderstood the first time when he touches Carol's shoulder in regret and sympathy, partially misunderstood the second time when out of frustration he bodily tries to stop Carol from leaving the office, John, Tome continues, "is finally unequivocal in the last moments of the play," when, in a fit of rage and violence, he beats Carol to the ground" (166). Taking his cue from his filming of *Homicide,* Mamet admits that "I learned the traditional bang-bang-bang way is wrong. It's too fast. Do it like a slow dance. Let the audience take it in. Be gentle with the violence. Then it terrifies. Then drive, drive, drive to the end" (Holmberg 1992, 95).

Few would suggest that Mamet sends his audience out of the theatre whistling or comforted with answers. Indeed, there is little consensus about the violence, the case or the conclusion of the play.[41] Elaine Showalter, for example, argues that "The disturbing questions about power, gender, and paranoia" raised in this play "cannot be resolved with an irrational act of violence" (17); and Silverstein, faulting the playwright for finding resolution in misogyny, much as students at the play's early performances in Cambridge confronted him with charges of "political" and artistic irresponsibility, finds that *Oleanna* "perpetuate[s] the very crisis of cultural fragmentation it seeks to address"(119). Admittedly, John's violence resolves nothing. Nor, I suggest, was it meant to. Coupled with his knocking Carol to the floor and threatening her with a raised chair is the terrifying knowledge that though he draws no blood, as Nick does in *The Woods* when he strikes Ruth, John possesses the power and, in that moment, the will. Unlike Nick he does not dissolve into a stream of shamed apologies. Rather, in *Oleanna,* a war of words turns on sharp exchanges: Mamet's minimalism packs the punch. Where is one to go and how is one to find a way back to human communication, he ponders, when two civilized, intelligent, and well-intentioned individuals (and, by extension, opposing factions of any stripe) lose their focus and their way? Possibly one way to view *Oleanna* is as a "text of exile," containing as Newton explains, both "rupture" and "the way back," and in so doing providing a space in which to coexist and communicate with one another. Tentatively, John posits a verbal course, as he did earlier in the play, whose intent is humanizing exchange: ". . . well . . . ," he begins. Carol's response, too, is measured, in words Mamet continually rewrote, frequently in my presence, during both the play's premiere run in Cambridge, Massachusetts, and prior to the New York opening. "Yes," Carol cryptically continues, "That's right . . . yes. That's right" (80).

Recently Robert Vorlicky has argued that *American Buffalo* "ends neither in violence nor in business, but in sparse dialogue" opening up a space of "self-awareness" (1995a, 227). Not only is Vorlicky's astute observation absolutely applicable to *Oleanna,* but like *The Woods,* this play ends neither in reconciliation nor in violence, despite the reverberant metaphor of the raised chair. Riveting our attention to the expressions of rage and need in relationships of varying degrees of intimacy, whether political or personal, *Oleanna* stages our efforts, however tentative, to acquire knowledge and protect what nourishes our humanity. Mamet's minimalist dialogue opens up a space of awareness that perceptibly widens to accommodate comprehension—however tentative—of the Other. That a moment of significant understanding and agreement is achieved is a direct consequence of the breakdown of humanizing speech. Shocked by their capacity for violence and destruction of the Other, teacher and student commence a dialectic that engages both characters and audience in an examination of the provocative stimuli that have energized and inflamed violent speech and acts. Their attempt at civilizing communication, halting first steps, affirms that words are links not merely between other words but between human beings.

Although *Oleanna* lacks the subtle, profane genius and wit of his other major plays, Mamet has fearlessly written an important work about ethical lapse, ethnic hatred, and endangered humanity, fused its subject and structure, and taken it to its logical, horrifying conclusion. Situating the polemic in a place of learning, Mamet personalizes and politicizes contemporary cultural battles. Opposing ethical deed and ethnic hatred, the present seen through the prism of the past, the playwright leaves us, much as he does John and Carol, to ponder a world devoid of freedom of thought and ethical deed, one ravaged by what Albert Halper terms "the pogrom against human decency." If *Oleanna* enrages and engages—and it most certainly does (Pidgeon was hissed at several performances I attended)—it is largely because Mamet lays bare the pernicious, pervasive evil of thought control. It is simply too easy to dismiss the play as antifeminist, even misogynist. Male and female alike, we understand that Carol's interpretation of the Truth—however much it cost her—has little to do with the abolition of elitism and sexism. What we are speaking about here is fascism. "In this play," admits Mamet, "the unthinkable, the unbelievable becomes real" (Holmberg 1992, 95). In asking "How did we get here?" Mamet is squarely on target.

COMING HOME

"Each seeking out of a moral, philosophic, posi-
tive verity . . . is an *aliyah,* a homecoming of
Judaism to itself and to its keeping of the books."
—George Steiner

"The Past is a Foreign Country. They do things
differently there."
—L. P. Hartley

"[N]OTHING IS MORE DEEPLY INGRAINED in the Jewish experience than
the idea of the past, the claim of memory," writes Irving Howe (1977, 4),
and this claim is to be found everywhere in David Mamet's landscape. In his
plays and screenplays alike lie scattered keepsakes, collector's items, mementos, photos, reminiscences, and memories. *American Buffalo*'s junk shop is
awash in history, a buffalo nickel, a compact from the World's Fair, an
outdated book. Similarly, history shapes *The Woods*'s narratives of Ruth's
grandmother threatened by Cossacks and Nick's father trapped in the woods
during World War II; history evokes tales of Levene's salad years in
Glengarry Glen Ross; and in *Oleanna,* John recalls a childhood marred by
failure. Likewise *Reunion*'s keepsake bracelet, a gift from a father to his
daughter engraved with the date (though incorrect) of her birthday, and
Things Change's mandolin, coins, and codes trigger recent or repressed
memory. Precious and ersatz remembrances of times past and photographs
turn up in *Marranos, The Shawl, Things Change,* and *Homicide,* each
resonant with meaning and history, for "most of us," suggests Mamet, "tend
to surround ourselves with tchotchkes, so we can actually be sure we have a
past. . . . Or a life" (Lahr 1997b, 82).

From the opening moments of *The Cryptogram,* the pull of memory is so strong that Donny, Mamet's most complexly drawn woman (who inspired the original title for the play, *Donny's March),* the mother in this domestic drama set in Chicago in 1959, can hardly contain her glee at discovering a memento of her youth.[1] Surprising Del, a close family friend, with her discovery— "Look what I found up in the attic" (16)—a cache of memorabilia, historical relics, tokens, and tackle boxes, Donny rivets his attention on the photograph, one that will occupy them for much of the first scene of Mamet's cryptic play as they seek to piece together personal and shared history. However, what Donny uncovers in her own living room aligns this incandescent play with such Mamet works as *American Buffalo* and *Glengarry Glen Ross,* in which unethical behavior is relentlessly brought to light by Mamet's now familiar dramaturgy of revelation. In fact, Donny's accidental sighting of the photograph proves the catalyst for a fervent search for truth in the places of the heart.

Family photos are ordinary objects that tell us the story of how we tell the story of our family. Like the memories that we store (or repress) in our minds, photographs trap the flux of life into fixed, retrievable images that recover the life of an individual or lost culture, much as the figurative snapshots that Bobby and Joey share in *The Old Neighborhood* recapture the Chicago of their youth, or shtetl life, of which nothing remains save photos. As timeless icons, photographs are "mementos from another time and another place" inextricably bound to "notions of continuity and discontinuity" (Kugelmass 34, 41). Accordingly, Del remarks, they are "very seductive" (23). Yet, as Donny's prized find reveals, photographs are also "icons of identity," evocative of a distant time and "a distance bridgeable by the individual's spiritual journey" (Kugelmass 42). Indeed, they recover and uncover a world from which individuals, and especially Jews, seek to open a dialogue with the distant past. Hence, "more than any other object in the home," Mihaly Csikszentmihalyi and Eugene Rochberg-Halton suggest, "photos serve the purpose of preserving memory of personal ties," of shaping, as it were, "a context of belongingness" (60). And as such they prove "the ideal figure" for "unraveling . . . the old discourse of home and family. . . . enter[ing the play] as carriers of an undeniable dissemination, of which the first causality is the mythic family of [cultural/ethnic] tradition" (Chaudhuri 108).

Fittingly, Mamet anchors the place of this play in the family home,[2] at once recognizable and strange, a place as marginalized in Mamet's canon as the three marginalized Others who take center stage in *The Cryptogram,* a mother, a child, and a gay man, none of whom have previously made an appearance in a Mamet work.[3] The device of the family home coupled with the dramatization of marginalized Others affords the playwright an opportunity to fictionalize biography and, as he has done in *Oleanna,* to dramatize alienation within the primal family and from cultural history. Stripped of overt, identifying emblems of Judaism, particularly Yiddish, which Mamet employed in *Speed-the-Plow* and to which he returns in *The Old Neighborhood,* the family home in *The Cryptogram* portrays in its obvious poverty and tenuousness that for acculturated American Jews, "Sometimes the family was about all there was left of Jewishness; or, more accurately, "all that was left of Jewishness had come to rest in the family" (Howe qtd. in Joselit 1994, 5-6). And in Mamet's home, as he has written in "The Rake" and elsewhere, even the semblance of family was missing in action.

In coming home, *The Cryptogram,* Mamet's most personal work—one in gestation for fifteen years—[4]merges personal history with cultural history, for the family in Jewish culture has long been viewed as "the secret of cultural transmission, the Jewish double helix that codifies and replicates the historic destiny of an ancient people" (Whitfield 1984, 257). For centuries, this destiny has been defined by rupture and endurance. By portraying marginalized individuals—those who are Others to Others—the playwright not only achieves distancing from a wrenching personal history through an extended family, he dramatizes the marginalization of those linked by the primal relationship *and* driven asunder by inimical, unethical behavior. In sharp contrast to the terrain of hard-boiled con-artists, the family's living room becomes the setting for personal treacheries in an encoded drama that transpires on three evenings, the last one separated by a month's interval. Linking the nighttime scene and the evocative power of three—the heavenly number of the soul; the family; the triads of truth, courage, and compassion; and past, present, and future—*The Cryptogram* signals a night journey inherently dangerous, harrowing, and ultimately enlightening. As Una Chaudhuri observes, "The dramatic discourse of home is articulated through two main principles, which structure the plot as well as the play's accounts of subjectivity and identity: a *victimage of location* and a heroism of departure. The former principle defines place as the protagonist's fundamental problem, leading him or her to a recognition of the need for (if not the actual enactment of) the latter" (xii).

With characteristic Mametic minimalism and seeming simplicity, the home from the outset of this tragedy houses a family in extremis in which a father's abandonment of his wife and child immediately invokes questions of mendacity, legacy, and exile from home. The site of border crossings and confidence games as fierce as we have ever seen in a Mamet play, Donny and Del's interaction in the home which brings the "picture" of the present into sharp focus, parades "the whole fucking progression" (88) of abrogated promises, obligations, and covenanted relationships of marriage, friendship, and parenthood, and locates the action not in any observable locus but in the elusive place that we call memory. "Time is truth's transport and its native ground," writes George Steiner. "What better lodging for the Jew?" (1996, 327). As if it were possible to recall with accuracy the people and places of one's youth and through reminiscence recover them, Donny initiates a sentimental journey, a figurative stroll down memory lane that in the absence of back story sketches the contours of her long friendship with Del through points of reference—a photograph, a blanket, a book, a knife—and exposes the nature of their relationship, placing Robert, Donny's absent husband, more firmly in the past than in the present. Pressuring Del to look at the snapshot that she has recovered in the attic, Donny explicitly enjoins him to "remember"—the powerful motif that derives from Judaism: the injunction to remember.[5] Unable to remember or make sense of the photograph, Del muses, "Mn? When you were up there?" (17).

Bounding down the "staircase [that] links the two worlds of the play— the 'reality' bound living room space, and the elevated world of the unseen attic and bedrooms, upstairs spaces that . . . are meant to exist *beyond* the house/theatre, *beyond* the sight of one's opened eyes" (Vorlicky 1995b, 3), John, Donny's precocious ten-year-old son, engages in conversation with family friend Del prior to her appearance and alerts us that he, too, is about to embark on a journey. Unable to sleep, he cannot contain his excitement about a journey into the woods with his father scheduled for the next day: "A trip. Yes. Oh, yes . . . that I'm excited . . . to go in the *Woods* . . .?" (4), he tells Del. "A natural teacher [who] uses any opportunity for a lesson," [6] Del amuses the insomniac boy by teaching him a game to hone his skills of observation, evaluation, and retention, an exchange that privileges the play's central pedagogical trope and alerts the audience to the implicit trust— subsequently tested and negated—between "teacher" and "student." Not only is the competitive game "To see who has observed the best" (33) an enjoyable diversion with options for discovery and testing one's knowledge, it is also a versatile survival tool. As Del puts it: "If you were lost it could assist you to orient yourself" (34), peculiar advice, we learn, from an individual who is not only an armchair traveler but rudderless himself, especially when John sights the disorienting "Dear Donny" letter later in act 1 and finds himself utterly lost in the once unequivocal milieu.

The two journeys thus evoked—John's anticipated trip into the woods and Donny and Del's excursion into the past—thrust *The Cryptogram*'s unsettling temporal shaping into sharp relief, its backward and forward motion of linear and psychological time-frames linking past and present worlds, the seen and unseen. Fixing our focus on time travel, as it were, references to mapping, beacons, signposts, guides, and compass signal the individuated spiritual search for connections in the present and with one's past that undergird the play and the boy's journey. Puzzling over the photograph, Del can't make sense of it. "(*Pause.*) When was this taken?" (17), he asks, setting the course of inquiry that pervades the play. "Who?" "Why?" "Where?" "When" disclose from the first a charged atmosphere brimming with questions, bristling with tension, cloaked in secrets, and heavy with mysticism, totemic images, keepsakes, and transformation symbols. Through indirection, whose subtlety and effectiveness in this work are assured by the fluctuating rhythm of "reverie and association," Mamet progressively reveals "a world of secrets . . . beneath its occluded surface" (Newton 273). Thus, even as Donny, Del, and John locate their lives in varied places—"at the lake" (29), "at the Office" (11), "In England" (45), "Outside my room" (48) "at Jimmy's" (55), and "In this *shithole* (*Pause.*)" (62)—they principally "fix" their lives *in* time: the reverberant "When" echoed in "soon" (11), "every night" (11), "When I was packing" (17) "years ago (26), "before the War" (38) "*Tomorrow*" (48); "*now*" (56). Despite their efforts to fix time and place, they are ensnared in a quagmire of questions. "[T]rying to decipher and make sense of . . . [a] world that stubbornly refuses to yield up its secrets," they find themselves, opines Hersh Zeifman, "lost in cipherspace" (1997, 1).

Yet, as Lawrence Kushner suggests, "Meaning comes from what something is connected to" (1993, 87). Hence, one animates (forgotten) memory and devines meaning "By joining pieces of our lives together" and recalling what precedes an event in order "to set it in a larger context" (87-88). Mamet illustrates this point when Del recognizes the photograph that Donny has located among the items in the attic by the sole remembrance that he was wearing Robert's shirt,[7] his memory ostensibly triggered by what Saul Friedlander terms "the curious preciseness of memory" (52). But why does it matter that—or if—Del was wearing Robert's shirt in the photograph? Attuned to the fact that meaning in Mamet may be mined from the most minimal of Mametic tells, of course we presume meaning and are subsequently rewarded with verification of our conjecture. By implication, at least, Del has traded places or identities with Robert, his presence in Robert's home, his appropriation of Robert's place as *paterfamilias*. His assumption of a whole array of responsibilities and roles—teaching John life skills, fetching medicine for the feverish boy, consoling the distraught Donny devastated by Robert's impersonal (and cowardly) announcement of his intent to dissolve their marriage of more than a decade, and abandon her and the boy—reveals that Del is Robert's *doppelgänger*, wearing the pants in Robert's house as well as his shirt. And as his penultimate confession reveals,

Robert and Del have made a trade of significant, far-reaching consequence: Robert's pilot's knife for his use of Del's hotel for a tryst.

Repeatedly self-deprecating in acts 1 and 2, Del's performing self portrays the role of an individual of limited knowledge of the macho world of camping and warfare. Whether in his initial remarks about John's anticipated adventure— ". . . a Trip to the Woods. . . . with his Dad? It's an *event*. I think. What do I know? . . ." (15), or in his subsequent references to matters of warfare, both of which introduce the subject of pedagogy and wisdom, Del reveals himself to be a neurotic urbanite, a (Jewish) intellectual more comfortable in his familiar niche in the library than in the unknown wilds of the backwoods, a homosexual who lacks combat experience, and a man who lacks a home and family of his own. He is a reflective, contemplative, and frequently witty individual, a bit of a bookworm who recites children's rhymes and retains arcane trivia.[8] However, in a play whose secrets are as tantalizing as the recovered past, that Del is both witness to and willing participant in treachery possessing the key to knowledge of Robert's absence, extramarital relations, and future intentions is one of the play's great ironies and most devastating discoveries.

In the early twentieth century, "the feminization of the Jewish male . . . was so frequent a theme" that "Jewish males'" supposed effeminacy became one of the essential signposts of Jewish . . . racial difference" (Pelligrini 108; Gilman 1991). Hence, homosexuality offers a critical opening for an exploration of "historically contested" and closeted identity. Looking at the other features of Del's life and conduct—the transience of his housing, his scholarship, ignorance of activities aligned with machismo—it appears obvious that Mamet's configuring of the Jewish male as homosexual offers a plethora of interpretations consistent with the alterity and secrecy intrinsic in this play. "Far from being the symbol of Americanness," Daniel Itzkovitz maintains, Jewishness has long been thought "to hover along the outskirts of an unstable border of normativity. In particular, Jewish male identity was represented as both a disruption and . . . an inauthentic participant in heterosexuality." In short, the Jewish male was a "a secret perversion of the genuine article" (178-79). And as such, Del's performing self and inferred homosexuality provide a firmly established foundation from which Mamet explores "the most prominent of these commonalties . . . the trope of secrecy, or hiddenness." In this equation, the Jew, like the homosexual, is traditionally viewed "as having a hidden identity"; both apparently perform secret acts that substantiate [their] elusive identities" (179). Evidence that the correlation between homosexuality and Jewish male identity continues to function strategically is notable in prevailing questions of the Jewish male's ability to fight or in a perceived weakness of the male articulated in Del's self-portrait of limited knowledge of activities aligned with men—parenting, fishing, warfare. This stereotypic equation of "thinkers" versus "fighters" is one that the playwright takes up again in *The Old Neighborhood.*

It is in the area of anti-Semitic rhetoric of the Jew as weak, criminal, and secretive—the allusion to "fantasies of dangerous secrets behind the eyes of the suspect Jew" (Itzkovitz 185)—that Mamet's foregrounding of the homosexual in *The Cryptogram* is so intriguing. Clearly the dramatization of marginalized figures typically closeted, concealed, or denied voice in social and cultural settings is pivotal in a play whose principal focus is uncovering concealed secrets, and it illuminates one criterion for Mamet's use of the homosexual, the mother, and the child figures, all of whom, Zeifman also notices, are aligned in their marginalization, vilification, and powerlessness (1997, 4). However, for much of the first half of this century, "The Jewish male was . . . always suspect, always on the verge of the criminal . . ." (Itzkovitz 191; Garb), a trope that has been of particular interest to Mamet since *American Buffalo* and will be more fully considered in *Homicide.* In *The Cryptogram,* however, Mamet plays with *and* against the stereotypical equation of homosexuality, criminality, and secrecy, revealing that the language of anti-Semitism "utilizes and is bound up with the discourse of homophobia in particularly resonant ways" (193; Gilman 1991b), notably the coefficiency of weakness and criminality that have been absorbed into the language of the Jew as self-hatred. In "outing" what Itzkovitz terms "closet identities," Mamet stages an ancestral story that incorporates and refutes "the popular imagination that conflates dangerous sexual, racial, economic, and national secrets" (195). Conversely, in *The Cryptogram* the Jew "comes out" as a human being whose "dangerous secrets" deceive him and destroy those whom he loves. Hence, secrecy, self-hatred, and the perversion of ethical values are revealed as agents of this individual's "criminal" behavior.

Juxtaposing the Old World and the New, the old idea of belonging, affiliation, and "the qualities of rootedness," as Chaudhuri has it, with images of displacement and discontinuity, Mamet progressively discloses the defamiliarization of the home space (with its primal associations of familiarity and secure haven), its intimations of rupture, sounded early in the shattered tea kettle, and its uprooting—the paradigmatic Jewish exilic experience[9]—manifestly depicted in packing boxes at play's end. As John Lahr notes in his review of the premiere production, "Mamet works his way back to childhood—specifically, to that irrevocable, buried moment in a child's life when the safety net of parental embrace collapses, and the world . . . is suddenly full of danger" (1994, 70).

On this subject, Naomi B. Sokoloff's *Fictive Voices: The Discourses of Childhood,*[10] an illuminating study that analyzes the Otherness of the child as marginalized figure through which a writer explores such themes as transition, (ethnic) identity, growth, assimilation, and the developing voice of the adolescence, has broad application to *The Cryptogram*. As Sokoloff observes, "the young make highly mutable Others," for their "accelerated process of growth and change" reveal them constantly in transition. Living at once in the highly imaginative inner world of the child and poised "to usurp adult power, [the child] lives on extremely dynamic and shifting margins," which the writer employs to envision "confusing demarcations between self and other, identity and difference" (4-5). Drawing upon a broad range of modern Jewish secular literary works, Sokoloff postulates, moreover, that "the child's consciousness serves as a congenial instrument for capturing instabilities of meaning. . . . [and] the elusiveness of [Jewish] identity," for as "both insider and outsider to the sphere of adult [Jewish] activity," the child is positioned as an inquisitive "Other of the Other" (39, 8). Problematic affiliation, assimilation, and generational links resonate throughout Mamet's body of work, but in the character of John, a figure literally and figuratively marginalized within his home, his predicament "particularly poignant because of his youth and vulnerability" (Zeifman 1997, 1), Mamet has located an apt figure for rendering the twin topics of personal/cultural alterity and the chasm between generations, confronting in his most intimate play familial and cultural history, the mystery of ethnic heritage, and the rich bond, bounty, and burden of the past.

Modern secular Jewish literature, particularly the Bildungsroman, the educational novel favored by Jewish writers that typically delineates the adolescent's journey out of the home into the wider world from the familiar Jewish environment to the wider (assimilated, alien, and potentially hostile) social milieu, privileges the depiction of children (Baumgarten, Sokoloff, Desser, Friedman). In works such as Henry Roth's *Call It Sleep*, Sholem Aleichem's *Mottel*, Jerzy Kosinski's *The Painted Bird*, and Mike Gold's *Jews Without Money*, the prevalent portrayal is that of a boy or adolescent "treated as a little adult and grievously denied a genuine childhood"(Sokoloff 9).[11] Similarly, *The Cryptogram*, which might be accurately entitled "Call It Sleeplessness"—its "Issues of sleep" (3) foregrounded from the opening beat until the play's end—positions John in the family and on the margins of the wider world, a young male abruptly stripped of childhood, forced into manhood, betrayed by his mother, and misunderstood by those around him. His planned trip to the woods and excursions up the stairs metaphorically convey the Unknown within his once-familiar home, offering both adventure in the attic and terror in the bedroom. And recalling the boy in *Call It Sleep*, John similarly "appropriates symbols of power [i.e., the knife] and insight," deciphering signs "in order to find the codes of conduct, value, and belief crucial for his physical and psychological survival" (Lesser 159).

Like those examples of the Bildungsroman previously mentioned, *The Cryptogram* is dominated by a child with an agile mind, fertile imagination, inquisitive nature, developing independence, and wrenching maturation. A preadolescent approximately ten years old (shy of thirteen that is the traditional Jewish definition of manhood), whose age mythically implies initiation into adulthood, John is an animated, articulate, astute boy, whose fiercely intelligent mind and quick grasp of facts are quickly borne out by his precise questions and keen responses in the opening moments of the play that depict John and Del engaged in a lively lesson. His premonitions and misgivings, reflected in his desire to stay in the living room, are similarly articulated in pointed, reiterated questions that rarely receive direct responses, confirming for him and the audience that more is concealed than revealed.

Like *Call It Sleep*, the classic Jewish novel of revelation and familial abuse, *The Cryptogram* may be read as a "semiotic Bildungsroman," to borrow Naomi Diamant's phrase, its world comprised of potent signifiers that acquire meaning and are subsequently "burned into the awareness" (Feingold 1995). And as Mamet's methodology of indirection imperceptibly discloses, its twin narratives of a boy's bewilderment at the mysteries of his parents' marriage and assumed infidelity, and of the (once) beloved mother frame this coming-of-age memoir, its penultimate note of exile a correlative of illumination.

John's insomnia, the source of nightly conflict between the boy and his mother, proves a propitious device through which Mamet dramatizes the boy's anxiety, a credible excuse for redundant questions concerning his father's late arrival and a convenient source for interrupting conversations between Donny and Del so that the revelation of truth and consequences is repeatedly postponed. As the playwright told Lahr, "it finally occurred to me, about the billionth draft [of the play], well, it's about why the kid can't sleep? . . . So the kid can't sleep because he knows, subconsciously, that something's unbalanced in the household" (Lahr 1997a, 66). However, John's insomnia has significant purpose for Mamet in *The Cryptogram*, introducing from the first Emmanuel Levinas's philosophy of "ethical responsibility as *insomnia* or *wakefulness* precisely because it is a perpetual duty of vigilance and effort that can never slumber" (Kearney 30). Alert and watchful, John is not only responsible, in his view, for protecting the home from misfortunes, he literally guards love within the home, his "wakefulness," concomitant with ethical responsibility and love as expressed in "the incessant watching over the other" (Levinas qtd. in Kearney 30). The telling line, "Where did you get the knife, though?" (28), repeatedly asked by John (and his mother) is a case in point. For Mamet the line and its resonant references keep the knife in the forefront of our minds—like those that keep the absent father "alive" as a performer in the play and real or imagined anxiety a player. Hence, the stage prop displayed frequently as tool and potentially dangerous weapon—that ultimately cuts the covenant of friendship and marriage and the cords of childhood—functionally focuses attention on "the real story."

Expanding upon the presence and rhythmic role of the knife in "Three Uses of the Knife," Mamet explains, "the knife becomes, in effect, congruent to the baseline in music" which we understand as "the driving inevitability . . ." Thus, "the irony of the recurring knife is affecting," writes the playwright, given that "The appearance of the knife [is] the attempt of the orderly, affronted mind, to confront the awesome" within the realm of "Theatre and Religion" (1998, 67).[12] In *The Cryptogram,* like Mamet's "beloved novels, there is no question of waiting till the final act to see the knife used—the knife is used in every scene. The aura of foreboding is not an effect designed to manipulate the reader's [audience's] interest. . . . it is the narrative." And, like "the true novel . . ., specifically [of] the Immigrant Experience, it must be largely an attempt to describe the unsettling" (1996a, 90-91).

From the opening beat, John's skills of observation are tested: his matter-of-fact "I couldn't find 'em"(1), relating to a pair of slippers he has packed for his camping trip in the woods, announces the significance of mindfulness and anticipates John's vigilance to sounds, sights, and most importantly, the knife. "What John really can't find in the environment of subterfuge and coded speech which engulfs him," remarks Lahr, "is the reality of his parents and of his own emotional life" (1994, 71), though progressively with maturation and enlightenment the focus of John's scrutiny shifts from the mundane to the mystical and metaphysical. Although encounters with such varied responses as "wonder, awe, terror, love . . . and death are the very stuff of any childhood," as Sokoloff reminds us, what lends John's prophecies and preoccupation with definition and clarification particular weight is their similarity to "the abiding concerns of twentieth century Jewish writing: readjustments and reappraisals of faith, redefinitions of community, and responses to catastrophe" (38-39). Comprising paradigmatic "instability of setting, periods of transition, and interpretations of language [that] have been staple features of Jewish literary circumstance and subject matter in the modern period" (36), *The Cryptogram* bears witness to traumatic personal and cultural loss. It is the testimony of the survivor overlaying and informing unimaginable estrangement, enmity, and dislocation.

Earlier Mamet plays explore many of these issues less directly, but the earliest Mametic depictions of persecution and imperiled survival find form in *Marranos*. Initially begun two years after *Marranos* and *American Buffalo*, *The Cryptogram* most closely parallels the latter play, a family play, which discloses the destruction wrought by betrayal and the lack of mindfulness and responsibility within a familial unit of three individuals. Yet, it shares much in common with the decidedly less complex *Marranos*. Although the figure of the mother remains offstage and out of sight, spoken about and awaited throughout the play, a figure much like Robert, the grandfather, a figure resembling Del but incorporating dual roles of Don/Del, teaches the young boy, Joao, about his Jewish identity, narrates stories (both biblical and fairy tales), demonstrates survival skills to enhance the youngster's powers of observation, and assigns him life-affirming responsibilities to preoccupy and divert the boy. Like *The Cryptogram*, *Marranos* comprises issues of loyalty, love, deceit, truth-seeking, deception, and performance, staging the uncovering of family secrets, of a cache of photographs, actually seriographic images rich in associations, and the family's betrayal by a trusted (extended) member of the family. Depicting an evening of exposure, with disaster hovering just on the edge of their consciousness, family members in *Marranos* respond to explicit and implicit threats to their safety, and at play's end the prepubertal boy escapes camouflaged in his father's cloak after the presumed (and symbolic) death of the family, his ethnic identity assured, his legacy bestowed, his chance of survival, though imperiled, empowered by a clear vision of ethical behavior.

Paralleling *Marranos*, the enigmatic, complex *Cryptogram* portrays John as having an active imagination, inquisitive nature, and authentic response to the upheaval that he perceives in his home. Like Joao, who finds diversion from fear and stability in fairy tales, John is susceptible to the power of magic. His fixation on the Wizard's tale—one of *The Cryptogram's* several embedded narratives—whose Three Misfortunes, portentous omens that he correctly prophesies, discloses this story to be a variant of the classic fairy tale of three caskets, the third typically releasing disaster. Because "The fairy tale proceeds in a manner which conforms to the way a child thinks and experiences the world [that is, "polarization" dominates both the fairy tale and the child's mind]," suggests Bruno Bettelheim, the child can often derive a consolation from the fiction denied him or her in "adult reasoning" (45).[13] Given that the precipitating event for many fairy tales is the actual or mythical death of a parent and that fairy tales are by design the uncomplicated, concise articulation of an existential dilemma, John's obsessive retelling of a familiar tale yields the illusion of stability of a recognizable story and it offers him a mythical means of articulating fear provoked by his father's unexplained absence. Moreover, the tale that John recalls is not only prophetic but revelatory, for its empowered witch and juxtaposition of good and evil pose a moral dilemma. Paralleling the texts of Kosinski, for example, in which the child's imagination is molded by the language of fairy tales, John's heightened imagination encompasses both the probable and the improbable. Hence, we notice from the play's inception—typically in Mamet an interrupted or continuing conversation analogous to Sholem Alecheim's stories (and Yiddish diction)—the defamiliarization of the familiar environment is reflected in a discourse that is multivalent, disjunctive, rhythmic, and ritualistic, its reverbant references to the story of the Wizard intruding upon and obstructing adult conversation. Coupled with repetitive encoded phrases, the cryptic exchanges between intimate members of a family—John and his mother and longtime friend Del—leave unspoken the exposition one typically acquires through dialogue, effectively distancing the audience, and frequently John, from much of early discussion. Thus as John repeatedly endeavors "to decipher and make sense of the opaque adult world. . . . The answers he receives . . . are always maddeningly cryptic . . ." (Zeifman 1997, 1-2), at once heightening his anxiety and exacerbating his sense of dislocation.

Similarly, apprehension is reflected in Donny's discourse and behavior. One first encounters her anticipating the return of her husband, alternately concerned about the welfare of her son and irritated with him—emotions attenuated by Robert's customary late arrival from the office and the ritual of John's insomnia. At play's end, as Richard Christiansen recognizes, she is a "tortured, torturing wife and mother. . . . Pathetically wailing in despair and lashing out in rage," behavior boldly illustrating "both the injustice and the just cause of her plight" (1995, 14). Initially, however, Donny appears unflappable when the shattered tea kettle foretells a shattered marriage and insecure future. "I'm alright" (7), she tells Del, her voice carrying from the unseen kitchen, her reiterated phrase echoing throughout the play, which retrospectively proves painfully ironic and an accurate reflection of her life-affirming tenacity. Preparing tea for two—a nightly ritual we wonder?[14]—as constant as the young boy's insomnia and Robert's absence, ostensibly necessitated by his working late (that is, until we subsequently learn of his extramarital relationship), Donny provides no information about Robert's profession, which, like that of Del, is not pertinent, pressing, or revealed. The only work about which we glean first-hand knowledge is Donny's. Motherhood in Robert's absence is a full-time profession, one that inspires the exhausted mother to long for "A fantasy of rest . . . (*Pause*)" (24).

Though Del teases out the outlines of Donny's "Oriental Fantasy" (23) of rest, meditation, contemplation, and isolation, it is apparent that she is more animated when speaking about the past than when thinking about the present, a diversion like the photo, affording her the opportunity to figuratively slip out of her dual roles of mother/wife and the present moment into another time. "[C]onsumed with guilt"(40) about her desire to be separated from John, she is nonetheless anticipating his weekend trip to the woods with his father almost as much as, or more than, he. Obviously his maturation, implicit in her musing—"(*Pause.*) It goes so quickly . . ." (22)—combined with all this talk of "old times" has made her reflective, even melancholic, but only the barest intimations of her veiled fictional (and personal) story are disclosed, otherwise remaining encrypted for much of the play. Certainly John's chronic insomnia and repeated, insistent questions exacerbate her emotional state, presenting a viable explanation for her desire for rest. However, the striking contrast between Donny's animated speech as she recounts her life as a new bride and mother and manifest exasperation and distraction (that is, forgetting her son's favorite fairy tale, dropping the tea kettle) suggests that the source of her exhaustion is mental rather than physical, that Robert's stern behavior toward his son and lack of availability to him has thrust Donny into the roles of father and mother and further marginalized her in her own home and marriage. In short, intimacy and warmth are lacking between husband and wife as well as between father and son.

Mamet, as Michael Billington rightly observes, "is here tapping a new vein of direct emotion: both in the anguished wife who yearns to know why all the men of her life betray her and even more in the boy who is simultaneously the play's moral touchstone and tragic victim" (1994, 799); yet Donny is not a maternal mother figure, if maternal means being affectionate. Rather, like Ruth in *American Buffalo*, Ruth in *The Woods*, and the offstage Grace in *Oleanna* (an anxious, caring mother of a young boy), Donny sets a high standard of (moral) behavior. Although space does not permit a detailed comparison among these characters, each figure, soothing or prodding the men in her life, functions to some degree as the link to familial, cultural, or historical memory. Whereas these other maternal figures are largely offstage or, in the case of Ruth in *The Woods*, in a dramatized abusive relationship, Donny is at the center of the conceptual power of the drama. Although no direct clue to her ethnicity is revealed, Donny's concerns and behavior, particularly with her son, align her with other Jewish maternal figures of similar conduct in the 1940s and 1950s whom Zena Smith Blau confirms were especially volatile, expressive women—"naggers" and "screamers"—who typically placed great intellectual and moral demands on their children. Blau maintains, moreover, they were more likely to "control[ling] their children *mit guten*, that is by explanation, reasoning, distraction, and admonishment," and to communicate their expectations through "verbal expressions of approval or disapproval," which were "likely to take the form of a sudden outburst" (172, 184).[15] Alternately indulgent and demanding, Jewish mothers rarely resorted to corporeal punishment, the domain of the father or father-figure, as was the transmission of cultural values and scholarship. Mothers, who had strong bonds with children, were typically inclined to induce the child's compliance through silence and to foster their independence. Evidence of this behavioral pattern is notable in Donny's relationship with John, with whom she is irritated; with little coaxing she accedes to his going up to the attic, permits him to use his father's survival knife and assume responsibility for packing for the camping trip. Likewise, her discourse with John is of an adult nature, exemplified in her responding to his precocious questions, "Were you frightened for him [when Robert was in battle]" (46); addressing the source of his anxiety, "Alright, what are the three misfortunes?" (30); negotiating bedtime, "Johnnie. . . . I think. . . . you have to . . . [go to bed]" (54), or expecting a mature response to the father's abandonment, "I'm speaking to you as an adult" (82).

Analogous to the Jewish mothers one finds in Clifford Odets's plays, such as *Awake and Sing,* Donny, doubling as mother and father, is a shrewd judge of character and a shrill, hypercritical woman, what Michelene Wandor terms a "double outsider." Concerned with history as well as endurance, she is not merely the repository of the family's chronicle, she is the individual most concerned with the family's economic and physical survival, attending to all facets of their relocation and responsibilities of child care.[16] Unlike the stereotypical, overbearing Jewish mother "who smothers her son with guilt-inducing love," a constant in Jewish humor, such as one finds in Philip Roth's *Portnoy's Complaint,* "Annoyance and dismay" characterize Donny much as they do the mother in Woody Allen's *Radio Days* (Desser and Friedman 86). Though *The Cryptogram*'s subtle, recurrent allusion to the (absent) patriarch's responsibility for disciplining the child has both biographical and broad cultural reference (and finds fuller evidence in "The Rake" and *Jolly*), it nonetheless provides a viable explanation for Donny's conduct with her son. As one unaccustomed to discipline, she either pleads or shrieks. Yet, in her a frank emotionality, she manifestly illustrates Mamet's view "that women are better, stronger, more truthful, than [the] men" she trusts and loves (1989b, 24), that is until she "eviscerates John," as Felicity Huffman phrases it, with the knife of her betrayal.

In the first act of *The Cryptogram,* the playwright presents ample evidence of Donny's responsiveness to her boy's unease, especially when she sends John to the attic to participate in preparations for the anticipated trip to the woods. Her instructions to "Find the [fishing] box, open it, and check it out" (21) and to straighten the attic seem harmless enough, and do after all occupy the hyperactive, insomniac child, for whom the attic provides both playground and occasion for an industrious boy to demonstrate that he is mother's little helper. And it affords her the space and privacy to speak with Del as she had earlier intended. However, "the attic, being a performance, a mimetic space, is no match for reality" (Chaudhuri 79).[17] It, too, serves up its secrets. Not only does the attic suffice in lieu of the boy's aborted trip to the wilderness, it functions as the repository of the past, the site where John discovers the primal blanket and Donny sees the photo and knife—signifiers with long associations casting light on the discovery of truth. Ironically, John's rummaging in the fishing box he locates in the attic proves a self-fulfilling prophecy of devastation, just as he had feared.

Descending the stairs from the attic seeking information about what coat to pack for his trip to the cabin, for permission to cut the twine on the tackle box, and to apologize for tearing the blanket—the "primal tear," as Lawrence Kushner has it, releasing the child from the childhood home to maturity which Mamet ultimately dramatizes at play's end—John is especially attentive to unspoken words and snatches of conversation whereby he recognizes danger reflected in his mother's growing anxiety. Attuned to subtle changes in his environment, John, an astute, alert boy, intuits faint variations in speech. For "in an unhappy family relationship/political situation/trial," states Mamet, "you are dealing with a much more attenuated decimal point of meaning to gauge the other's intent" (Lahr 1995, 34). Mamet's language is typically allusive, disjunctive, and cryptic, and the coded language in *The Cryptogram* (words and cluster images) has inspired several critics to address the subject. Markland Taylor's reading of the play's feigned normality and miscommunication comes closest to the mark in understanding that John's "dogged . . . search for meaning in words and life, suggest[s] the possibility that to children, adults speak in codes or ciphers" (1995, 59), a fact literally validated in Jewish homes of the 1950s, where the use of Yiddish was specifically employed to prevent—and ostensibly to protect—children from understanding what was being said. Despite "that old 'don't let the *kinder*' [children] know, attitude," a common practice among second generation Ashkenazi Jewish families, in which Yiddish was relegated to diminished use, "things got through."[18]

In John's home, too, "things" get through. Reiterated questions regarding his father's whereabouts and anticipated time of arrival call attention to the temporal framing of the play, as do the disturbing intimations he culls from the adult's hermetic speech. Repeatedly, John receives Donny's evasive responses, confirming her doubts about his father's whereabouts, whatever she tells the child; and as such, the unsaid further enhances his as yet unvoiced fears. Conversely, Donny can readily "place" Robert in the past by riveting attention to his position in the group photo taken some seventeen years before at the lake, the war looming, and through allusions to Del wearing Robert's shirt in the photograph, her narration of a story that places Robert and Donny in London during the war where the blanket (subsequently used for John) was purchased—as was the knife, whose associations deepen throughout the play. Moreover, her recollection of making love with Robert under that blanket focuses her reminiscences on a happier past, where she recalls Del, at a distance, aware but not intrusive. Hence, Robert emerges as a phantom figure with stronger associations to the past than connections to the present. In fact, the intrusion of "remembrances of times past," which in the "telling" become the contemporaneous present, becomes so pervasive that one loses sight of the present moment and the progression of time in act 1 so that the appearance of the "Dear Donny" letter, as well as its contents, comes as a shock, and proves a turning point, henceforth anchoring attention on a vanishing present and uncertain future.

Opening act 2, John's speech attests to a disordered world and psyche. Central to our understanding of the dissolving world is the manner in which Mamet employs the precocious child's speech. Formerly extraordinary in its articulateness, John's discourse reflected a mind acutely attuned to the "awareness that words are instrumental . . . in clarifying experience" (Sokoloff 136). But traumatized, his speech lacks order and meaning. When faced with an unspeakable, terrifying reality, language proves "at once crucial and ineffective" (139). Put simply, words fail to order the chaos that is John's mind. Confessing his fears to his mother, an anguished John admits:

> I thought that maybe there was nothing there. (*Pause.*) I thought that nothing was *there.* Then I was looking at my *book.* I thought "Maybe there's nothing *in* my book". . . . or on my *globe.* You know my globe? You know my globe?. . .
>
> . . . .
>
> Maybe there's nothing on the thing that it is of. . . . Or in *history.* In the *history* of things. Or *thought.* . . . maybe there is no such thing as *thought.* . . . or that things go on forever. (*Pause.*) Or that we're *born.* Or that dead people moan. Or that, or that there's *hell.* And maybe we are there . . . (53-54)

Tormented by the unreliability of previously accepted truths—history, thought, human life—John's atlas imagery perfectly positions him in a world no longer recognizable, no longer peopled. Suffering "the terrors of placelessness," as Chaudhuri has it, his "globe," like Hamlet's, is a wretched place.

Certainly the lateness of the hour, John's sleep deprivation and fever, and the disquietude and suspicion rooted in his father's failure to appear on the previous night or since heighten the credibility of his confused speech—the collapse of language linguistically exposing the separation of the child from the adult world, the recognizable from the strange. However, it is the boy's startling disjunctive discourse in one previously articulate beyond his years that lends impact to the shattered, shared codes of understanding now conspicuously absent. In place of cluster images of warmth—slippers, a coat, a cap, a blanket, a cup of hot tea, the passion of youth, and the comfort of "strangers"—John's febrile disease reveals something terribly awry in a scene of heightened domestic realism, resembling the "supra-realism," to use Lahr's term, of Pinter.[19] In fact, "John is starting to fragment before our eyes . . . [the] voices and spectres that accompany his fear of abandonment and his sense of annihilation . . ." (Lahr 1994, 72) are laid before us in a dizzying spray of speech that will not hold. Exhibiting evidence of trauma anxiety and the futile search for the familiar in the defamiliarized, the Otherness of the child, then, serves a performative role, like that of the homosexual. When linguistically played out, it excruciatingly discloses a child no longer "at home" in speech or setting, an outsider locating himself in an alien world, just as the child was formerly shown to be Other in the discourse of adults. That the "discourse" is contained "*on the site of a catastrophe*," as Cathy Caruth explains, points the way to knowledge that is "discovered and not fully comprehensible" (34).[20]

Poignantly aware that John is held captive by his thoughts, Donny endeavors to calm his agitated mind by first coaxing him back into her sphere of influence, and then engaging him in rational conversation whose intention it is to lessen terror's irrational hold on her distraught child. When that tactic fails to satisfy and pacify, she tries to coax the frightened child back to bed, addressing him as "Johnnie," a soothingly affectionate, if juvenile, diminutive, guiding him in that direction but without duress. "Please, please do [go to bed], though" (54), she pleads, this mother's fatigue unmistakable, her outward composure on the verge of shattering. Yet, when Del enters the room, presumably having been sent to retrieve medicine for the boy, Donny, though directly addressed by John's appeal, "Mother . . .," ignores his call and grills Del, her cryptic question, "Did you . . .," a shorthand he comprehends immediately and to which he responds with the similarly succinct "No" (54). Believing or hoping that he has failed to understand her correctly, she rephrases, amplifies, and repeats her question. "Did you find him?" (55), she demands, proving to herself that she has been heard and affording us the clarity critical to her subsequent inquiry. Twice asked and twice answered, the response is irrefutable. Apparently, Del was not merely sent in search of medicine for the sick boy; he has been dispatched to hunt down lost husbands, balm for broken wives' hearts, much as John had been sent to the attic in scene 1 to participate and bring order to chaos.

Firing off a volley of questions—"Where did you look? . . . Did you try The Eagle? . . . Why *not?* Why *not?*" (54-55)—Donny, in her twin roles of wife/mother and crack detective, is not a woman to be trifled with. Quizzing Del, much as Donny has earlier in the play about the photograph or the weather at the cabin on the previous weekend and whether Del recalls seeing John's beloved gray hat, Donny pursues a line of questioning more pressing and pertinent than the former. At both interrogations, Del fails to provide the desired information or perform as expected. However, Donny's interrogatories reveal far more about her frantic, chaotic state of mind, which, like John's, is cluttered with more questions than answers. Echoing her son's agitated speech rhythms, she urgently needs to track down clues and chase down truths that might cast light on an unfamiliar, nightmarish landscape that she cannot wrap her mind around. And like her son, she is wracked by grief, guilt and fear. "The master Mametian idea here," Donald Lyons writes, "is that the breakdown of family can be expressed in the breakdown of language . . . Words . . . as dysfunctional as people . . ." (7).

While John's linguistic rhythms mirror the fragments of unspeakable thoughts, Del's and Donny's failure to communicate with one another appears, on its surface, to be a breakdown of the lines of communication rather than what it is revealed to be—an avoidance of or failure to articulate the truth. Del may very good at giving instructions, as he did when he taught John how to perfect his skills of observation, but apparently he is neither mindful of nor particularly adept at applying the skills he taught, or as we learn later in the scene when Donny's skills of detection and observation outsmart his at obfuscation, he is "a human *being*. . . . [who] cannot conceal himself" (8). At the heart of their dispute is that Del assumed that she would telephone The Eagle, and other locales we presume to be late-night spots or bars that Robert might frequent. Donny, wisely reasoning, "Why should I call them, if they'll say he wasn't *there?* Even if he *is* there . . .?" (55), breaks with the Mametic tradition of relying on the ubiquitous telephone to link individuals to offstage partners, producers, family, friends, upper management, middlemen, wisemen, and women, whose connection to leads, legal advice, money, censure, and comfort offers a stunning counterpoint to visible relationships in varying states of disconnectedness. That he has failed in his mission is obvious. Accordingly, then, Del offers a glib apology to pacify her—"Well, then, I made a mistake" (55)—which Donny presumably accepts on face value and with good faith. However, Del's concentrating his attention on pouring the medicine into a spoon for John, the rare stage direction in a Mamet play, implicitly undercuts an apology that we subsequently learn falls far short of the mistake he has made and has to this point successfully concealed, his not spilling the medicine metaphorically communicating his not spilling the real story behind the cover.

In contrast, Donny is capable of juggling both her needs and John's. Placing the demands of her child before her own, she is revealed to be a woman possessed of the myriad, magical powers of Motherhood—a tensile strength by which she wills back her tears and tends to John's fears. Thus, while she controls the terror that grips her, she directs her full attention to calming her troubled son. But when John refuses the medicine that Del has purchased and spurns her attempts to treat him kindly, which, given her strain and sleeplessness, has sapped her energy, Donny's frustration and exhaustion break through in her exasperated speech. "Take the medicine. . . . and you're going to *bed* (56)," she instructs him, adding a coercive threat for good measure, that if he fails to comply he will be taken to the hospital, a place of mystery and terror all its own. However, that the child is more afraid of going to bed than he is of his mother's anger alerts her to the depth of his terror and to his need for her to address the terror directly,[21] that is, to make it recognizable, and hence less fearful, by naming it. "I . . . I . . . I know it *frightens* you . . ." (57), she tells John, but in leaving the "it" that drives his fears ominously undefined, Donny confirms that the source of John's fears—and her own—*is* the Unknown, and her speech, like Del's apology, falls miserably short of the mark.

In her attempt to give her overwrought son what he needs, Donny attempts again to soothe his troubled heart by promising what she, and the medicine, clearly cannot deliver given that the trauma of abandonment from which he suffers is not a "healable event," to borrow Freud's phrase, but an open wound. "Alright, alright, I'm going to *promise* you," she tells him, "I'm going to *promise* you if you take this and . . . you take this and then go upstairs, then you won't be afraid . . ." (57), but her quartet of "promises" (the latter two punctuated by pauses) assures neither John nor us that she is capable of keeping her promises, any more than is his father. Nevertheless, to counter his fear that his night sweats will soak the sheets, Donny proffers both the protection of her bed and unwavering acceptance.

"That's alright. Do you hear what I'm telling you . . . ?" (58), her direct question demanding confirmation of her message. Exhausted, John acquiesces to Donny's request that he go to bed, take the medicine, and accept his mother's offer of nurturing implied in his sleeping in her bed. Yet, Del's maladroit attempt at normality in the form of the ritualistic, "'My blessings on this house . . .,' the Wizard said" (58), threatens to undo Donny's and his efforts to mollify John's agitation, because the recurrent phrase rings false, expressing a mood and a time irrevocably distanced by the trauma of the father's infidelity and abandonment. Answering Del's refrain with one of his own—"When is my father coming for me . . . ?"(58)—the echoic query, "Will he be home *soon?*" (11, emphasis added), markedly altered to reflect the changed reality of Robert's confirmed and presumably permanent absence, followed in short order by John's wrenching question, "What's happening to me . . .?" (59), the child gives proof positive that divorce is not merely a condition but a severing, a catastrophic, shattering event that impacts each member of the family, one earlier signaled and signified by the shattered family tea kettle (a source of comfort in its own right), and torn blanket, a signifier of the family's frayed tapestry.[22]

Endeavoring to offer solace and succor in the face of the enormity of his loss, Donny embraces her son physically and caresses him linguistically. "Hush. . . . Shh. You've only got a fever. Shhh . . .," she soothes him, misguided in the belief that lies in the form of her assurances that "You've only got a fever"—a curable condition—and that "It's alright," and that John is "fine" (59) serve the best interests of the child. "Those of us who have held authority know how great the temptation is to supersede our limits, to act 'in the best interests of those under us,' to, in effect, betray them for their own good," observes Mamet. And those of us "on the receiving end . . . know there is no good, no boon to be gained, no lesson to be learned from someone who treats us with contempt" (1989b, 94, 96). Accordingly, then, as Donny will illustrate, "blind obedience" affords a controlling individual the opportunity to elude "the onerous duty of examining his preconceptions, his *own* wisdom, and finally *his own worth*" (1987d, 32).

Although John admits to being fatigued and ascends the stairs to the dreaded upper level and his mother's room, the overwrought, insomniac child remains awake, awaiting the long-delayed and presumably illusory arrival of his father, alone with thoughts and fears. Yet, unaware that Del and Donny's voices are overheard by the restive child, her "good intentions" (21) to protect the boy by deception from the truth of his father's abandonment of her and the family unexpectedly miscarry. "It's a fierce and ironic moment: an act of violence couched in the language of love"

(Lahr 1994, 72), which reveals how much more harm, however unintentional, is done by her concealing what the boy has already surmised. The moment, in retrospect, is a turning point, John having made the devastating discovery that "it was possible to swear falsely, and that there was, finally, *no* magic force of words capable of assuring the truth in oneself or in others, and so became adult and very serious and monotheistic in one hard moment" (Mamet 1987d, 6).

Act 1, in which Donny's decision to send John to the attic to participate in the preparations for his upcoming journey into the woods with his father freed her to play the parlor game of "Twenty Questions" with Del, recounting "old times" and uncovering buried secrets, is paralleled in act 2. Donny's successful efforts to dispatch John upstairs and out of earshot, releases her to find her some peace of mind and moral support for herself. The world having grown darker and more treacherous for her, as it has for John, and the stakes higher than on the previous evening, Donny's taste does not run to playing games. For his part, Del offers a plethora of comforts, clichés, distractions, games of chance, maxims on marriage, and fictions to soften the blow of Donny's rejection and deflect his guilt, but clearly absent from his grab-bag is a proposal of adult party games, "sex" being, after all, in Mamet's view, "the true nature of the world, as between men and women" (1989b, 90). If there is a latent attraction, *The Cryptogram*, true to its name, keeps its counsel.

Instead of proposing sex between friends, Del offers oft-repeated, ostensibly heartfelt (but hollow) apologies for his failure to locate Robert, makes an overture to resume the pursuit, suggests an offer of a drink and a game of Casino or Gin rummy (the cultural allusion sounded in Woody Allen's *Radio Days*),[23] all of which are capped off with a characteristic, self-deprecating joke. "Well. I know I know I'm limited," he admits, providing one of the play's rare lighter moments (60). Drawing direct attention to Del's homosexuality, Mamet confirms that this (presumed) close friend of the family may offer emotional support and diversion from the marital crisis but no viable alternative for the spurned wife. Donny decides on liquor to buoy her spirits, "In *trial*... in *adversity*... (*Pause*) and you can't, you can't go always look[ing]. ... for *answers*," muses Del, "the answer comes. In reaching out. Or, ... In getting drunk" (62). Donny's despondency, fatigue, and giddiness mix in equal parts with the lateness of the hour, the affiliation of old friends, and Del's penchant for specifying, producing a heady, jarring moment of ceremonial toasts to their close friendship.

Alone with Donny, however, his duplicity begins to wear thin, lending credence to the premise that he has stopped to have a few drinks in all those bars in which he did—or did not—look for Robert in, for cracking through the shell of the best friend's lively patter is a moroseness we have not noted before, which, it becomes quickly apparent, is not brought about by his sharing Donny's anguish— "[W]hat am I going to do? You tell me?" (66)—but rather by his immersion in his own despair. Burbling to the surface, punctuated by the pauses Mamet uses so well to reveal Del's rambling thoughts and deceit (one echoing a technique employed by the playwright in Moss's speech at the beginning of scene 2 of *Glengarry*), is evidence of his flawed attempt to repress memory and responsibility for the betrayal of Donny's trust, a momentary lapse he attempts to salvage by turning to humor to cover his guilt. Stripped of reference, though, most of the speech, a classic Mamet tell, goes largely unheard by Donny, who is meditating on her loss.

What she does hear of Del's presumed maudlin speech—"I don't *give* a damn. (*Pause.*) In this *shithole. (Pause.)* Well. I'm not going to *dwell* upon it. (*Pause.*) You drink, and then, when you *remember* again—this is the good part—when you *remember* again . . . (*Pause.*) It's later on." (62)—she ironically (mis)interprets as the musings of a lonely man. Thus her (misplaced) compassion inspires a joke between friends hardened long ago into cliché: "'You should get married'. . . . 'We'll find them for you'" (63). The moment and misunderstanding, worthy of Chekhov, are certainly worthy of our attention, for in situating two characters in close quarters but light years apart, each lost in his or her thoughts, Mamet underscores their separateness (rather than their closeness to which they drink), the isolation of which Donny speaks to John when she says, "*Finally, each* of us. . . . Is alone" (90). Though fleeting, the moment, like Levene's laconic reference to his daughter in *Glengarry*, has a ripple effect in the play, its emphasis on repressed recollection protected but dulled by time, first sounded by Donny when she produces a photograph in act 1 that Del cannot place and reframed in the concluding tableau which positions John, ascending the stairs, distanced from Donny and Del.

Attempting to ingratiate himself to Donny and assure his (secure) position in her home by offering to look in on the boy, Del's reiterated apology for his failure to locate Robert, "I Didn't find him. . . . But I *looked* for him. (*Pause.*) (63)—a variant of John's opening line "I couldn't find 'em" (1)—is intended to put him a good light, position him as a trustworthy friend, and extend the bluff, in effect concealing the high stakes game. Even Del's slip of the tongue, "I suppose I thought . . . that it wasn't a good *idea* to have him come here" (63), is packaged as caring, echoing Donny's unilateral control of the information she believes in is the boy's best interest, what Lahr aptly notes equates con and parent, mark and child (1997b, 79). While authentic to the 1950s, a chronological period "built on lies" much as Del's homosexuality was "closeted" (Siegel 1995, 50), Del's patronizing of Donny is nonetheless deeply disturbing. What it confirms, among other things, is the hegemony of the male in this period and cultural group, a subject that Mamet will take up again in *The Old Neighborhood*. Concurrently, Del's show of concern serves his ends. His continuing effort to weave a fabric of lies to protect himself from discovery of his complicity in Robert's betrayal thus postpones his inevitable, deserved expulsion from Donny's home. For as Steiner emphatically states, "[a] true thinker, a truth-thinker, a scholar, must know that . . . no moral ideal and necessity . . . is worth a falsehood" (1996, 321).

While Del attempts to rivet Donny's attention to the suddenness of Robert's absence, what becomes obvious is that Donny, temporarily freed from the burden of caring for John (his having finally been sent off to bed), having both the opportunity and the intellect to piece together the puzzle of the events that have transpired within the last twenty-four hours, has come to the realization that "However much we . . ." fail to or refuse to see the signs, Robert's departure is neither "a shock" (64), as Del puts it, nor an entirely mysterious event. The warning signs were there, she concedes, her memory triggered by seeing Del use Robert's knife to open the liquor bottle. Indeed, had she and Del been perceptive, she correctly conjectures, they "could have anticipated it" (64).

Although he has been anticipating and dreading this moment of revelation, Del's pose of naiveté, shocking in one who has positioned himself as a trusting friend and teacher of small boys, leaves one speechless. In fact, his reiterated comment, "I don't understand" (64), is an artful ploy, a typical Mametic con to deflect suspicion away from himself and create the illusion that he lacks (and lacked) knowledge of Robert's actions and motives. As such, he is a mystery to Donny, who assumes the role of instructor and interpreter of signs, illuminating and clarifying the meaning of Robert's "going away present" to Del of his "Big German [pilot's] knife, "The Odd Gesture," as she puts it, whose symbolism is to be found in its practical purpose, "to cut the *cords*" (64-65) and release the flyer should he become trapped. "He tried to tell you" (64), she explains to Del, leaving unsaid any mention of the signs by which Robert presumably tried to tell *her* of his departure, signs that she has clearly missed or misread. Though she finds comfort in the illusion that the conundrum of Robert's rejection of her is a cryptogram that in time will be rendered intelligible, Del comes closer to the truth in defining the rupture in the family structure as "a shock" (64). As Caruth observes, trauma is a "double failure of seeing," which one cannot foresee or perceive; it is best understood as a "shocking and unexpected occurrence" whose impact is detectable as a "breach in the mind's experience of time, self and the world," one "marked not by a simple knowledge, but by the ways it simultaneously defies and demands our witness" (4-5).

Paralleling a number of Mamet works in which embedded narrative figures importantly, Donny's explanation of the knife's purpose and the gift's significance in *The Cryptogram* presents Del with an opportunity to "rewrite" history by crafting an clever fiction that ironically celebrates Robert's generosity and provides a credible pretext justifying Del's possession of it: "[H]e was opening a can. With it. And I said . . . actually, he saw me looking at the knife. And he wiped it. And he gave it to me. (*Pause.*)" (66). However, unbeknownst to Del, and at this point to the audience, Donny's astute memory, of which we have been given ample evidence in act 1, is triggered by the sight of the knife. Given her acute perception of and familiarity with the sound and shape of Del's speech, which now is notably punctuated by pauses and at odds with the fluidity and deliberation to which she is accustomed (and of which the audience can find ample proof earlier in the play when Del was better able to maintain the role of friend without perceiving his every word judged and challenged), his words aid her to disentangle two conflicting narratives. Juxtaposed with her earlier reverie of rest and Del's pipe dream of forgetfulness, Donny's relentless search for the truth exposes the friendship with Del to be as false as the bogus story and war memento.

At issue are her recent memory of packing for the camping trip, recounted in act 1, and more distant memory of unpacking from the previous camping trip a week before recounted in act 2, both of which are at odds with Del's narrative situating him at the campsite in the previous week. Donny's efforts to piece together clues and confirm the facts—or the fallacies of Del's story—by pointed, reiterated interrogatories provide him with ample opportunity to reveal the truth and disprove her growing suspicions. Yet, as she moves steadily and unwaveringly toward decoding the embedded narrative, Del's rebuttals provide further evidence to support Donny's theory of his perjuring himself. Picking up the interrogation begun on the previous evening by John, who repeatedly challenged Del's story concerning his possession of Robert's knife, Donny twice asks Del, "Did you *say* he gave that knife to you when you went camping?" And when Del hesitantly responds, "Yes. (*Pause.*) . . . That's right. (*Pause*)" falling back on his spurious story, Donny traps him in his own words and telling pauses, revealing that she has proof to dispute his lie. The disparity between Del's avoidance of the truth and Donny's search for it gives her an unquestioned moral authority. Rather than shrinking from the potentially devastating disclosure, Donny brings to her pursuit of the truth the same attention to detail, precision, intellect, concentration, and passion that she previously

brought to clarifying the photograph, locating its meaning in an amalgam
of time, place, and persons, and anchoring it to memory. In fact, when the
illusion of the truth proves more comforting than the revealed truth, Donny
does not waver in the face of treachery. And neither does she suffer fools.

Stunned at being caught in the act of betrayal, Del holds tight to the
unraveling tapestry of lies, and though digging himself a deeper grave, he
goes on the offensive, attempting to stave off confession by introducing the
element of doubt into Donny's recollection. Quickly recapping the facts
already established, however, Donny separates fact from fiction, her clear
memory of the knife in the attic sufficient proof refute Del's narrative:

> Donny: You said he gave it to you when you were camping. *(Pause.)*
> How could he give it to you when you were *camping*, when
> it was here in the trunk when you both came back? *(Pause.)*
> Del: There must be two knives. *(Pause.)*
> Donny: I . . . I don't understand.
> Del: There must be two knives.
> Donny: What?
> Del: I bet if you went to the trunk to look right now you'd see.
> There was another knife. (70)

What she, and eventually he, does see, is that the game's up. [24] Backing away
from the lie—what the playwright observes is "the subject of drama," given
our inclination "to lie to others, to lie to ourselves, and to lie about whether
we lie" (1998, 79, 78)—Del now permits an opening for doubt to creep into
his recollection: "I . . . I don't know," he responds. "It's a mystery to me"
(71), a phrase that speaks volumes. Indeed, it is a mystery that Del thought
he would successfully and indefinitely deceive Donny; a mystery that Del
was unprepared with a credible rear-guard cover story if questioned; a
mystery that he thought he would save himself by doubling the betrayal, a
mystery that he did not see that choosing deception was the unethical
position, a mystery that someone who had everything to lose—the perfect
love of a child, the loyalty and friendship of a woman, and a safe haven—
would gamble what he had for so little.

When Del is backed into a corner by Donny's directness in the
question regarding Robert, "Did he do that?" (71), his fallback position is
to use plausibility and reasonableness as a defense: "It's possible. . . . I think
that's. Um, that's *exactly* what he did. I *think*. *(Pause.)*" (72). And then, of
course Donny knows indubitably that he has been lying to her, her
rhetorical question so important that she repeats it, reminding us that the
act of betrayal that has been perpetrated against her is no mere "slip of

memory" (72) but the conscious, craven act of a coward caught in a lie. Coloring his act of deception as an act of kindness designed to protect his friend from the truth, recalling the manner in which Donny earlier in the scene circumvented the truth of John's father's abandonment in an effort to deceive the child, presumably for his own good, Del finally relents, decoding the convoluted tale of the bogus camping trip (which explains his inability to recall any information about the cabin), of his collusion, complicity, and prior knowledge of Robert's adultery and abandonment of his wife and child, of the exchange of the knife, "a War Memento"(87) for Robert's use of Del's hotel room for a tryst, and implicitly of his delivery of the "Dear Donny" letter. Hence, Del's confessional narrative, for good or for ill, reminds us that fictions have the capacity to "forge ties"; hence, the binding nature of narrative is discernible, suggests Newton, in "the *telling* or the *hoarding* of secrets [that] serves as the glue which binds person to person" (123, 247).[25]

Calling direct attention to the play's central motifs of memory, legacy, accountability, and transition, Del, cornered by Donny, channels his anger at himself into verbal violence directed at her: "We didn't *go!* Do I have to *shout* it for you . . .? We stayed *home*. What do you *think?* He'd traipse off in the *wilds* . . . with *me?*. . . . Some poor geek . . ." (74). Although Donny and the audience may be thinking of more suitable epithets for Del just now, his calling himself a "geek" is a befitting choice, whose varying interpretations, including the effeminate, the nerd, dupe, fall guy, pawn, wimp, and schlemiel, appropriately cover the gamut of fact and self-deprecation implicit in this appellation. Eric Partridge's reading of the term, moreover, adds much to our understanding of the word's brutality in this context. Since World War I, Partridge notes, *geek* has also been used to describe "the lowest kind of carnival performer, perhaps one who is merely stared at" (179), a definition that seems particularly apropos at this moment as Donny metaphorically pins Del to the wall, his performing self stripped of any shred of recognition or moral justification. In short, he is as defenseless as Don in *American Buffalo* who initially excuses his culpability for lying and exacting punishment on Bob—"we [he and Teach] didn't want to do this to you" (1977, 95)—and is then forced to beg for forgiveness.

Del's defense, then—"This is the only bad thing I have ever done to you" (74)—encourages Donny and the audience to ponder: What bad thing? Telling the story? Lying to cover Robert's betrayal? Lying to cover his own? Lying to the boy? Lying to himself? Clearly his banter with the boy, his tale of searching for Robert, "the toast to Donny and friendship—all are flimflam" (Lahr 1994, 72). And we are left to wonder if Del's intentions were "good" intentions gone awry, like Donny's with John.[26]

Writing about the Bible's prohibition of the spreading of gossip, Kushner explains, "our sages have warned, there are three who are involved in every act of gossip: the one spoken about, the one who speaks, and the one who hears. But they startle us with their insight that the one who hears is injured the most." Although the information may be henceforth "disproven," he adds, the harm is the result of "The suspicion [that] persists" (1993, 51). Ironically, positioned as "truth-teller"—a Wandering Jew or *maggid* (an itinerant teacher), who lives in a hotel, much like Levene in *Glengarry Glen Ross*—Del is dependent on those who is are willing to take him in (and have generously done so) and listen to his story. Yet he reveals "a worthless secret," one that inflicts great pain upon the recipients of the "gossip." Although the purpose of confession "is to reify (if possible) unethical action through ethical language," that is, "confession, as in confession of a secret, produces reckoning of both facts and persons" (Newton 250) having unburdened himself on his host and longtime friend, his warning thrice repeated of the destructive power of his tale, Del offers little in the way of "reckoning" and much in personal humiliation through his narrative. It is an admission of fact, not a confession of deed. Hence Robert's and Del's motives remain an enigma, confirming that the only truth worth having is one that Donny arrives at herself. The moment clearly illustrates Mamet's conviction that "to discover a truth is to have it come out of your own mind. It is not an objective reality. . . . It's a matter of perception" (Nuwer 1985, 12). Indeed, from the first moments of *The Cryptogram* (like *Oleanna*), attention has been paid to perception: shattered teapots, long-lost photos, torn blankets, issues of sleep and sleeplessness, husbands long delayed, anxiety barely hidden. Thus, significantly, as the narratives unfold, as they do throughout Mamet's body of work, the injunction repeatedly is: "Look," "See," "Hear," "Remember." Preeminent among these senses in this play is vision, which implicitly and explicitly draws attention to "seeing, seen, and . . . seeing unseen" (Newton 262).

What Donny hears in Del's truncated apology for his role in the deception reveals that he has learned little from his mendacity, and if he is at all contrite, he has yet to find the words to express his repentance. Rather, Del continues to hide under the shawl of language, advocating the position of weakness, namely that "we can't always choose the, um . . . (*Pause.*) [what we do?]" (74). However, absolving oneself from accountability for words or actions is clearly the unethical position, one at issue in every Mamet work. As Mosher, who has staged numerous plays by Mamet, observes, "You start with the whole idea that life is made up of choices, that man's fate must be balanced by a very active use of the will" (Jones and Dykes 48). Del, however, not only shuns "the active use of the will," he "seeks refuge without responsibility" (Peter 1994), forgiveness without confession. Culminating an evening of metadrama in which Del has played both the hero and the heel, his remark, "we can't always choose . . ." rather than his scathing characterization of Donny as "stupid," "blind," and "nuts" (74) thus earns him her contempt and unequivocal banishment from her home.

Paralleling Chekhov or Pinter (Ranevsky's response to her spurned daughter Varya in *The Cherry Orchard* or Ruth's comment to her departing husband Teddy in *The Homecoming* come immediately to mind), Mamet typically opts for minimalism when outrage strikes us as a more fitting retort to Del's scurrilous behavior. In place of vocalized pain, however, the plausible, requisite response to unspeakable experience that defies comprehension and articulation is Donny's. As the playwright told Terry Gross, "We've all had the experience . . . of being in extraordinary dramatic-like situations like birth, death, loss, betrayal, enlightenment, danger, humiliation. . . . We and those around us tend to act in an undramatic manner because the task and our difficulty is so vast that we have no energy left over to describe them to ourselves or to communicate them to others." In sum, "We have only enough energy to do them as simply as possible because our life depends on it."[27]

Waking to voices, real or imagined in nightmare, John believes that he hears his mother calling, and indeed she is, crying for herself and for what her husband Bobby has wrought. Confounding his own anguished cries with hers, and channeling thoughts and fear of death into Donny's "death," John relives the trauma of his father's abandonment—a symbolic death of the father figure—by imagining the death of his mother, such that he experiences both the nightmare and "*the experience of waking from it*" (Caruth 64).[28] "Trauma theory often divides itself into two basic trends," Caruth contends: "the focus on trauma as the 'shattering' of previously whole self and the focus on the survival function of trauma as allowing one to get through an overwhelming experience by numbing oneself to it," both of which Mamet stages in *The Cryptogram*.[29] Reworking Freud's classic interpretation of the narrative of a burning child who has died of fever and whose body is consumed by an overturned candle unnoticed by the father sleeping in another room and who, when visited in a dream by the dead child, is unable to recognize "the child in its potential death" (103), Mamet creates the circumstances whereby in the father's absence, John, attentive to voices and his mother's cries, is responsive to their call. "Are you dead?" John asks her (75), and "In a sense," Michael Feingold rightly notices, "he's not wrong. The house is full of dead things: love, marriage, friendship, affection between mother and son" (1994).

Answering Donny's cries for her husband Bobby—notably the son answers to the father's name just as he subsequently receives the wrath intended for the absent father and feckless friend—the young boy recounts a night vision of visual images and audible sounds in a narrative format. "I heard you calling. . . . I heard voices . . .," he says, "And so I said, '. . . there's someone troubled'" (75-76). His narrative, in which he imagines himself walking around on the upper level where he spies a candle illuminated in his room, is illustrative of what Caruth characterizes a "kind of double telling," both "impossible and necessary," offering testimony that oscillates "between a *crisis of death* and the correlative *crisis of life:* between the story of the unbearable nature of an event and the story of the unbearable nature of its survival" (7). Awakening in a panic, the sense of his abandonment "pass[ing] through the protective wall of sleep," as Friedlander would have it,[30] John sees with utter clarity that it is he who is "troubled," the dream a brilliant device for rendering the chasm between illusion and reality, between the desired comfort of home and the mental anguish of isolation, between the innocence of youth and the knowledge of maturity.

When John looks for validation and confirmation from his troubled mother that he has acted properly in responding to the voices—in essence, his own verbalized plea to his mother to be seen, heard, and acknowledged—Donny is at a loss for words. Mirroring the beginning of the act in which John was burning up with fever and delirium, Donny *"cradles"* (76) her son. Though alert to his call—"Mother. . . . do you think that I was right" (76)—she has no answer for John other than her embrace, for like the boy, Donny desperately lacks and needs assurances herself. In fairness to Donny, the twin betrayals, the burden of the distraught child, and an uncertain future have savaged her security, rendering her reverie for rest a distant memory. Hence, John's confusion functions as a filter through which we perceive the madness that surrounds him, giving us just cause to believe that overhearing Del's decrypting of the cover-up, coupled with his own earlier perceptions wherein he could not locate himself in familiar surroundings, have led him to newly acquired wisdom; as Morley succinctly states it, "adults deal in bad faith, children will listen" (1994). Contrary to his earlier notion that "We are just *dreaming*" (54), John has learned that not only does hell exist, it is not "Other people," as Sartre averred. Rather, as John fears, it is the absence of truthful, caring, ethically responsible people.

Paralleling the circularity of *American Buffalo,* act 3, *The Cryptogram*'s finest and briefest, opens to reveal Donny's home literally as well as emotionally "barren." It is a scene of homecoming and departure, of connection and rupture, of condemnation and forgiveness, of discord and concord. Packing boxes in evidence confirm that physical and emotional comfort is in short supply; yet, amid the boxes that bespeak an impending transition, Donny retrieves personal items to give John some semblance of home and safety in his new environment, her gesture of maternal concern, typical of Mamet's minimalism, nearly overlooked by the audience. A deeply disturbing conversation between a mother and her severely depressed son is already in progress. Despite Donny's assurances, the devastating effect on John of deception and disjunction are notable in the issues that trouble him—disembodied voices, visions, and thoughts of suicide, "Issues of sleep" having been long abandoned as a source of conflict or discussion.

Now, when it is clear that the "upheaval" he spoke of with Del in act 1, prior to the planned trip to the woods, has proved to be anything but "a minor one" (8), John's mind is again "full of thoughts . . . [of] *leaving*" and of what he is "going *toward*" (6). "Do you think things. . . . Do you ever wish that you could die? (*Pause*.)"(78), the disheartened youth asks his mother. Evading his questions for her own self-protection, Donny, a pedagogue in her own right, teaches him some axioms to live by that reflect her (limited) understanding of the world, namely that all things cannot be known: "John: Things occur. In our lives. And the meaning of them . . . the *meaning* of them . . . is not clear. . . . At the time. But we assume," as she must, that "they have a meaning. . . . And we don't know what it is" (79). Evocation of the unknown and its place in our lives scores Mamet's work, especially in *The Woods, The Shawl,* and *Edmond,* but receives its clearest statement in *The Cryptogram,* where we come to see "that texts, like persons, cannot entirely be known" (Newton 284-85) and more importantly, that the ephemeral, whether secrecy or ceremony, that haunts our memories also shapes our lives. Such wisdom from a woman who draws her strength from history, as well as harsh reality, is lost on her child who desperately clings to the hope that the questions plaguing him will have unambiguous answers. When she begins again, Donny's succinct lesson, "One has to go on" (82), a pithy statement of the central ethic of Jewish survival, explains in good part her tenacious affirmation of life. Though her lessons are less accessible (or attractive) to the boy than Robert's that the green fishing line is the strongest or Del's that anxiety associated with upheaval is common to adults and children alike, Donny's crash course in perseverance may be the most prized.

Delivered from the other room, however, where she has gone to make tea, the technique undercuts sentiment as well as effectiveness, given that John, unbeknownst to Donny, has left the room. Thus, although ironically unheard by John, "One has to go on" is not merely advice for her son; it is Donny's mantra. And if she is far better at commanding than comforting—Donny's "How can I *help* you . . ." (79) falls far short of the embrace he requires—this mother communicates wordlessly by her presence that while the men of John's life abandon him, she remains, though "the disease of grief," as Mamet puts it, predictably turns "lamblike self-sacrifice to wrath" (Mamet 1996b, 242). Concluding her life lessons with the profoundly unsatisfactory but honest appraisal of what they are both experiencing— "It's an unsettling time" (79)—Donny, in effect, echoes her earlier attempt to put the boy at ease by assuring him that his feverish mind was a healable condition that would improve with time. Similarly, this statement expresses her fervent wish that the despair that John and she are experiencing is of limited duration. In the interim, she proffers the ubiquitous cup of tea. Offstage preparing tea, it is to John, rather than to Del, as in act 1, that she calls out: "What sort of tea *do* you want?" (81), the play's subtle reference to choice in our lives that is secular and spiritual, trivial and profound.

Appearing at Donny's home after a lapse of one month, Del has returned bearing gifts and a long-delayed confession. Tellingly, Mamet situates Del outside the house rather than comfortably "at home" within it. Literally marginalized by his deed, Del is an outsider excluded from the family where he previously enjoyed the comforts of home and close relationships with Donny and her son. Now he hardly makes it through the door before he encounters John's outright rejection and Donny's chilly reception. But with Del's sudden appearance, John has lost interest in tea. In fact, he attempts to escape upstairs to avoid even speaking to Del other than to inquire ritualistically in words that have lost their meaning, "When is my father coming?" (81), his having wisely intuited that Del, rather than Donny, is wise to his father's whereabouts, no doubt having overheard the adults' conversation and confrontation. Acknowledging his presence, Del's apology is immediately prompted by the perceptive woman who recognizes it for what is: satisfaction of Del's need for forgiveness. "What do you need to say?" (82), she asks, echoing Carol's demand of John in *Oleanna*. Whereas Carol conveyed her lack of interest in what John had to say and categorically expressed that she was granting him just so much time to "have his say," here Donny conveys by her terseness that she has neither the time nor the interest in engaging in a dialogue, her energy sapped by her son's deepening depression and her attention directed toward the needs of herself and her son, implicitly informing Del and reminding us where her loyalties lie. Presumably, Donny's carefully wrought phrase, "What do you need to say," alludes to Levinas's definition of "*saying*," as that which "makes the self-exposure of sincerity possible; it is a way of giving everything, of not keeping anything for oneself." In other words, "Man can give himself in saying," Levinas contends, "or he can withdraw into the nonsaying of lies. Language as *saying* is an ethical openness to the other . . ." (Kearney 28-29). Hence, although Donny's perturbation with Del, perceptible in speech and manner, differs starkly from act 1, and her immersion in issues of separation from her home and relocation is implied by the bare room and packing boxes, she does not fail to notice that fearful of rejection, Del holds back, not through an effort to defraud, as he has done previously, but because the act of admission of responsibility and the plea for forgiveness are daunting.

Del, however, has much to say, and the manner in which he has "his say" is as striking as what he says. His "saying," in other words, is a performance that meets the twin criteria, as Newton defines them, of "a proposing and exposing of the self" (3). Although he has a prepared, if clumsy, confession, its shorthand notably lacking the connective between confession and conduct, Del's discomfort is reflected in an attempt at humor to deflect attention away from his error, mirroring his behavior in act 2, when he awkwardly sought to soothe the rattled woman while maintaining his own composure and cover. At first attempt his words minimize and generalize his lack of judgment as humanity's flaws, such that "I am sorry [for] what I did" is metamorphosed into "The things *we* do. . . . [and] Swine that we are" (82-83, emphasis added), coupled with an admission that he has "wronged" (84) the boy. Though bearing gifts for Donny and John, her book of the Wizard's tale that he has discovered in his room, and the knife for John, Del is nonetheless defensive; in Donny's view, only the gift of himself would atone for Del's contemptible behavior. Wisely abandoning the notion of bringing Donny flowers, signifiers of love and fertility, Del feels compelled nevertheless to bring the boy the knife as "a propitiation" (83), his gift intended "to put the supplicant in the properly humbled frame of mind to receive any information which might be forthcoming" (Mamet 1989b, 173).

"Del's will is driving this act," Mamet told Ed Begley, Jr. when directing the American premiere. "Everything you're doing is an offering: here's a book, here's the knife," each item projecting perseverance in the face of rejection that "I'm going to succeed in some way . . . to gain control."[31] Both the book and knife, however, are devalued as gifts and as symbols. For as soon as Donny examines the book, she concludes that it is not her possession but Del's, a souvenir of *her* friendship to him, a fact immediately confirmed by its inscription, "May you always be as . . ." (88), a variant, we note, of "And May we Always be as . . . Close to each other . . . As we happen to be right now (*Pause.*)" (61), their ironic toast to a friendship of which little or nothing remains. And by the looks of things, so is the Wizard's blessing—"'My blessings on your [this] house'" (14)—stripped of its former significance. If in her prior encounter with Del Donny sought to decode the mystery of Robert's abandonment and in the process learned the painful truth that the men she has loved have betrayed her, it is now she who possesses and reveals knowledge that has the potential to inflict injury on Del—to wit, that Robert's flyer's knife is as worthless as his gesture of giving it to Del.

Donny, we recall from act 1, is blessed with a long memory, as evidenced by her ability to recall places, people, and events nearly twenty years old. Therefore, although Donny's sparring with Del is stripped of reference, much as his morose murmurs were in act 2, implicit in her acerbic answers to his questions about the pilot's knife is the grudge that she bears him for his treatment of her and her boy. "According to the Torah and later rabbinic tradition," writes Kushner, the only way to avoid bearing a grudge, which the Bible strictly forbids ("you must not bear a grudge against one another" [Lev 19:17-18]), is to "'tell someone when they have hurt you,'" but even this "telling" has strict covenants to minimize injury and reduce embarrassment to the offender, strictly forbidding "a twist to the knife so as to cause pain . . ." (1993, 79). If any such frank exchange of views has ever taken place between Donny and Del in which the "telling" of her injury occurred—and their stiff behavior with one another argues against it—we are unaware of it and therefore presume that in one whose sharp memory has been clearly established in previous acts, Del's treachery is neither forgotten nor forgiven.

Hence, if it were not her express intention to harm him, as she claims, Donny's irascibility with Del reflects the cumulative effects of Robert's desertion, the burden of the distraught child, financial misgivings about their uncertain future, the stresses associated with relocation, the torment of the treachery perpetrated by Del. Responding to his questions about the knife, Donny devalues the very artifact, plunges it into Del's heart, and "twist[s] so as to cause pain": "Could he capture it in the Air? . . . Could he get it in the Air? You 'fairy'? . . . You fool"(86), her lashing out at him a pale harbinger of her ensuing verbal abuse of John. Undeterred in his endeavor to win her forgiveness, and repeating his apology three times—"I'm sorry I betrayed you" (93)—Del fails to achieve the desired goal, though his dogged perseverance provides proof of his craving Donny's forgiveness and the security of her home, much as Teach's penitence was inspired by his need of Don's affection.

What Del has learned in his month-long isolation surpasses the advice that Ruth in *The Woods* (Mamet's first dramatization of an intimate relationship between a man and woman) gives her abusive boyfriend, Nick: "So little counts, Nick. Just the things we do. (*Pause.*) To each other. The right things" (1985c, 24). Conversely, Del, ostensibly through introspection, has acquired the wisdom that we are all capable of doing "the wrong things." In short, he has come to understand that with the best of intentions human beings make bad choices. His confession that "it is not the sins we commit that destroy us, but how we act after we've committed them" (83), confirms the efficacy of "the cleansing mechanism of confession," through which, suggests Mamet, "we lay our burden down—or are offered that choice" (1998, 78-79). Implicitly, then, while the play postulates that like Donny, we condemn in others what we are willing to tolerate in ourselves, it also implicitly conveys that her calling him a "faggot"—light years away from the "geek" he called himself—is a moment of such brute force that it renders ironic Donny's earlier quip, "Isn't it funny? Though? The things you find? (*Pause.*)" (17). Mournful rather than "funny," what she finds is that she can go for the jugular, the men in her life having found her trusting nature a too easy target.

On this basis, Janet Haedicke correctly surmises that in "Refusing the sentimental equation of womanhood and sacrifice, this (M)other realiz[es] that not only the dominant male and but also this othered male have defined themselves against her and betrayed her," and she "struggles for an identity through 'Othering' the 'faggot' . . ." (1997a, 19). Yet, in treating him with the same inhumanity for which she has previously held him accountable, Donny acts out her pain, rather than learn from it. It is nevertheless a telling moment that takes the curse of sentimentality off this scene, renders Donny human, and redirects our sympathy to the play's victim, the young boy John. Thus, when Del presses for her forgiveness, she rejects out of hand his expressions of repentance and affection:

Del: No—I need you to forgive me.
Donny: Why would I do that?
Del: You should do that if it would make you happy.
Donny: No, look here: don't tell me I'm going to make a sacrifice for
              you, and it's for my own good. Do you see? Because every
              man in this shithole . . . Don't you dare come in my house
              and do that. You faggot. Every man I ever met in my life . . .
Del: *Well, why does it happen?* (94)

The question hanging in the air, ripe with speculation, Mamet typically cuts beyond the back story, reminding us that "The language of love is, finally, fairly limited. . . . Love expresses itself, so it doesn't need a lot of words. On the other hand, aggression has an unlimited vocabulary," to which this exchange brilliantly attests (Lahr 1995, 33).

Though Del fires off his share of barbs, his opportunities to match wits with Donny are repeatedly interrupted. His patriarchal judgment of her—

"for quite a long time I've watched you" (95)—is ironic in one who seems to have lost any moral standing in this house, and it manifests a rear-guard defense against what he rightly perceives as an attack and rejection of him.[32] As he has done in *American Buffalo*, *Glengarry Glen Ross,* and *Oleanna,* Mamet repeatedly employs unsympathetic characters to deliver insightful judgment of others of whom we have a more favorable impression (Hudgins 1996; Schvey 1988). Yet Del has come to Donny's home with conciliation and reparation on his mind. "But I would like to talk to you. (*Pause.*) If I might. (*Pause.*)," he says, "In spite of . . ." (88), his understatement as stunning as Donny's earlier comment to John that "It's an unsettling time" (79), his vulnerability as salient as her son's with whom he competes for recognition and response.

While the pauses in Del's speech reflect anew his hesitancy, unease, and the desperate urgency of his need for the family, safe haven, and friend he has betrayed, the opportunity to continue his appeal never presents itself, for John, appearing on the stairs, commands his mother's full attention and subsequently the full force of her rage. John is again cold, distraught, and distressed by voices, a defenseless child searching for the confirmation and comfort he had hoped to obtain in an earlier conversation with Donny, which was interrupted by Del's (re)appearance.

Though Donny acts more or less appropriately with Del—that is, out of a deep reservoir of hurt, pain, disillusionment, and distrust—she displaces her anger onto John, depriving him of his needs and reacting with unprecedented ferocity, behavior at odds with the thoughtfulness and maternal instinct we noted earlier in the scene in her gathering John's "things" for their new home, the activity interrupted by Del's unexpected intrusion. Despite John's repeated, insistent supplication that "grows in effect into an incantatory wail," it fails to "penetrate Donny's own hurt" (Gerard 95). Echoing Carol in *Oleanna*, Donny lashes out at her boy: "John? I'm *speaking* to you. What must I do? . . . What must I do that you treat me like an animal? . . . Do you want me to go mad?" (98-99). Her questions confirm Mamet's view that "all rhetorical questions are accusations" (Lahr 1997a, 54). In fact, Donny's piercing outburst not only "demonstrates how thin the line can be between emotional and physical child abuse" (Austin 1995, 13), it amply exposes an emotionally exhausted woman whose anguished rebuttal to inhumane treatment by the (adult) men in her life she punitively channels into bestial rage against her son, the most maligned of the three marginalized Others. Horrified we recognize her plight as our own, or as Huffman succinctly phrases it, "She is us."[33]

Withstanding her withering attack, John knows his only link to the (secure) past is the stadium blanket, a poor substitute for his parents' protective warmth but one he insists on obtaining, his discourse "suffused with the knowledge that there has already been an end to innocence" (Sokoloff 152). In pinpointing the turning point between childhood and adult life, Mamet, for whom "No child is free from care" (1996a, 189), depicts the boy as emotionally, if not physically, transformed into a young adult. Whereas John formerly anticipated the need for warmth, a task he easily masters by wearing socks in lieu of the slippers packed for the trip to the woods, the boy is now faced with the staggering task of locating warmth in a hostile world that rejects his very presence, with attending to his own protection from real or imagined terrors. And as such the knife, bequeathed to him by Del, his having insisted that he requires it to "open" the box in which the blanket is packed, empowers him to defend himself.

Of course, the knife with complex associations, is, as Del correctly presumed, the boy's legacy in all its varied permutations—"a symbol of the father's phallic betrayal" (Feingold 1995), an emblem of the empowerment of the child against the demons that threaten him, potentially a method of suicide, a linkage to the tradition from which he has been abruptly severed. Whereas the knife was given to the boy for limited use in act 1 and then returned to Del in whose possession it had remained, Del's gift of the knife as propitiation at this moment dramatizes his recognition that John is no longer a child, for "How could a knife be a suitable gift for a child. . . . we know it can't" (88). Although the knife plays a prominent role in *The Cryptogram*— and literally evoked a gasp of shock from the audience in the closing moments of both Mosher's and Mamet's productions—[34] knives (and guns) appear in numerous Mamet plays and films (i.e., *Lone Canoe, Edmond, Prairie du Chien*, and *The Edge*), as offensive weapon *and* defensive tool. Paralleling the language that, in the playwright's words, "Everybody uses to get what he or she wants" (Norman and Rezek 53), blanket and knife, signifiers with long associations, are vital to John's survival. Like the matriarch in Mamet's novella, *Passover*, who believes her family is endangered and wisely uses a knife to ensure their survival, John has learned that one survives by "[one's] wit . . . on margin" (1987c, 74), a key ethical First Principle in Mamet's canon. And his survival, as the concluding moments imply, is inextricably bound to one's ability to sever the literal and figurative cords.

From the outset of the play Mamet has been "playing with distances," as Newton has it: in Othering characters who are marginalized; in threshold imagery (for example, John ascending and descending the stairs, Del at entry foyer to Donny's home), in postures of observation, in the traumatized John "distanced" from his physical and emotional context; in the distance between trust and broken promises; in Robert's extramarital affair; and in the widening gulf between mother and son. The most obvious of these distancing contexts, one that specifically and literally "points up the distance John has traveled" (Newton 261), is the boy's ascending position on the staircase that is the focal point of the play.[35]

Trying to effect calm in a tense family situation and achieve his desired refuge, Del, a proven go-between in the best—and worst—sense of the word, assists the overwrought mother as she endeavors to settle John off to bed, negotiating a peaceful settlement on the issue of the blanket already "packed" for the movers. With her tacit permission, Del (re)assumes his proxy paternal role, the implication being that she has historically deferred to him (and to men) the responsibility of disciplining John, a role Del has played in Robert's absence on two earlier evenings. "But might he have it?" (91) Del reasons, his words echoing his mediation on behalf of John in scene 1 when John requested the knife to cut the cord on the tackle box. "In the unconscious and conscious," Bettelheim reminds us, "numbers stand for people: family situations and relations." Whereas one represents a single individual, two when perceived as "'Two against one'" traditionally represents either unfair treatment of the individual or one "hopelessly outclassed in a competition" (106). Although Donny and Del's unified front is not overtly threatening, it confirms for the boy, at least, that he is Other to the betrayers, absent Robert, Del, and Donny.

Whereas Donny formerly queried her son, "What would your father say?" and reluctantly accepted his fib, "It's alright. . . . yes. Oh, yes" (27), here she disregards all thought of what Robert would think, her unspoken words implying not only how much is no longer "alright," but that she is the master of her own domain (ironic as that may seem on moving day), a point she makes abundantly clear to Del: "Don't you *dare* to dispute me in my own home" (99). Learning that the knives are packed, Del advises the boy, "you'll have to do without. But you'll be fine, I promise you" (98). His message, a Beckettian concision of Donny's earlier Stoic apothegm, goes unheeded: the speaker distrusted, the pledge worthless, the text implicitly reminding us that rabbinic scholars enjoined parents not to make promises to their children that they could not keep, because they would thereby teach their children to lie.[36] Hence, although Donny and Del "think they can pacify him by being reasonable," as Peter observes, "this never really works. The child, who as we all know is the father of the man, quietly registers that these adults are useless" (1994, 796). From this perspective, then, trauma may be understood as both "the very incomprehensibility of one's own survival" and "the experience of waking into consciousness"(Caruth 64), signaling the end of the world as John has known it.

Despite all that is incomprehensible to John, what is entirely comprehensible to the boy is adult culpability, complicity, cowardice, and weakness.

Prescient from the outset, when he feared the Third Misfortune, and astutely perceptive to the unsaid, John at least has a firm grip on the truth of what he has heard, perceived, and intuited. Having learned well Del's harsh lesson to observe closely the moments of upheaval in his life, the boy ascends the darkening stairs. Indeed, as Sokoloff has noticed in numerous examples of the Bildungsroman in which the Jewish child is abandoned or threatened by an alien, hostile world (or as in *Call It Sleep* when the father, enraged by the mother's presumed infidelity, threatens the life of his own child), "childish resistance"—as we have seen in John's insistence and resilience—"comes to signify power, while adults, beset with new beginnings or uncertainties, are cast as childlike in their unpreparedness and vulnerability" (13). In fact, recalling the minefield of his own youth, Mamet wryly notes, "It was succeed or die" (Lahr 1997b, 73).

Although Del, a master of appearances, creates the impression that he is principally concerned with the boy's needs (paralleling Donny in act 1, who sought to dispatch the boy to the attic or bed to speak with Del privately), he serves his own interests forthwith in successfully concluding the negotiation between mother and son on the issue of the blanket. Having coerced John's promise and numerous repetitions thereof of the coded password, "I promise," Del expedites John's access to the blanket. As the boy ascends the staircase, Del spontaneously gives him another gift, the lost and recovered text. "John: Here. . . . Take the book," he tells him. "This is the book, John. . . . It's yours now. . . . F'you can't sleep, *you read it.* It's alright now. . . . Off you go . . ." (97, emphasis added). Why, one wonders, does Del bequeath his copy of the book to the child? In retrospect, of course, we understand John's inheritance is twofold. No mere tokens or totemic images, knife and book—which the Jew has carried "on his back, [his] antennae toward menace"(Steiner 1996, 309)—double-bind the boy to Jewish history, empowering him physically and spiritually. "You read it," Del says, that ancient and timeless call to the text that, as Steiner claims, is "the central motion of personal and national homecoming." When "A Jew enters on manhood, he is admitted to the history of Judaism, on the day on which he is, for the first time, called, literally, to the text, on the day on which he is asked and allowed to read correctly . . . from the Torah. This summons entails, to a greater or lesser degree of self-awareness, a commitment to the clerisy of truth, of truth-seeking" (Steiner 1996, 322).[37] In its literal application, this "calling up" is a rite of passage. Indeed, one way to read John's position on the stairs is to perceive it as a literal, physical, and spiritual rite of maturation, which, in Jewish tradition, is comprised of three *steps:* removal from the past, liminal or threshold ascent, and postliminal, the incorporation of "ritual recognition" into the new position, or rather as "a portent and a promise" (Seidman 88-89). Hence, John's call to commandment may be seen as both a symbolic bar mitzvah and the ascent to manhood.

As the boy ascends the stairs, his desperate appeal for his mother's confirmation unanswered, "her silence leav[es] him and the audience on the border . . . between stability desperately sought and instability vainly denied" (Haedicke 1997a, 22). Coupled with her rejection, which cuts to the quick, John's drawn dagger, so potent an image, has prompted numerous critics to presume that this dark drama closes on the child's suicide. Lahr's review is representative in its contention that John's possession of the knife signifies "the promise . . . of murderous fury directed at John or at the world" (1994, 73).[38] Yet this moment of isolation and indoctrination into manhood, which positions John on the stairs, begs for further analysis, for the knife and the book with varied associations metaphorically communicate that John's options and Mamet's intentions have deeper repercussions and biblical resonances. As Kushner explains, in writings on the search for self and spirituality, "the pain of being a human being (and thus for many, the resultant evil that people do) originates in two primal, psycho-spiritual 'tearings.'" Whereas "In the first tearing, a part of ourselves is rejected and identified as 'enemy'"—the Othering of John, for example, by his mother—"The second tearing involves every human being's separation from his or parents, the process of individuation" (1991, 66-67).

I believe that John's distancing from Donny and Del is as a primal tearing necessary to his survival. In fact, the Jews' act of leaving captivity and their being bound up in history has bearing upon John's cutting of the cords and symbolic departure at the end of *The Cryptogram*, for his act may be seen to cut the cords and "bind" him to his father's deed, its double-edged blessing of bequest and betrayal combined with biblical judgment. In like manner, consistent with the ethical, educational, and ethnic framing of the play, and its privileging of history, memory, and accountability, the Voices that John hears and to which he responds in the last moments of the play suggest that the Voices are of a piece with the cluster imagery of the inherited knife, book, and staircase which the boy ascends in the closing moments. Notably, John's perception of voices pervade the play. Excited on the evening before his anticipated trip to the woods, he cannot sleep. Del provides a reasonable explanation for his insomnia, namely, the boy's "full thoughts" (6). Later that evening, agitated and still unable to sleep, John asks Donny, "Do you ever think you hear singing? . . . or think you hear a *radio*. . . . Playing music. . . . Or *voices?* (47). While the boy's allusion to the radio is credible given the chronological period in which the play is set, his repeated, enigmatic reference to "the radio" from which mysterious voices are emitted recalls Desser and Friedman's reading of the figure in Woody Allen's film *Radio Days* as "the realm of fantasy" (78). Listening to radio drama as a boy, such as "Suspense," and "Yours Truly, Johnny Dollar," and "The Shadow" while "rolling through the prairies outside of Chicago" on family car trips, Mamet fondly recalls "listening to the intimate voices" (1987d, 12). The Voices to which John alludes in *The Cryptogram,* however, are neither familiar nor reassuring. One way to decrypt them is to perceive them as the "objectify[ing]"—what Mamet defines as our "insecurity and self-loathing in the form of outside forces endeavoring to punish us" (65). Conversely in act 2, which stages the events of the subsequent evening when a feverish John reports "*see*[ing] things"(56) and hearing "calling" (75), both can be discounted as the delirium or nightmare of a precocious child confusing the sounds in the living room with imagined terrors, behavior not unusual in the healthiest of children and most secure homes and certainly credible in the most imaginative of minds, which, like John's, would hold themselves accountable for a father's rejection or death.

However, in act 3 the Voices clustered with the knife, book, and stairs gain prominence and signification. Surrounded by the breach of faith and the abrogation of promises, the young boy on the threshold of manhood hears "Voices" that grow increasingly more defined from their initial, diffuse form into a personalized summons. Insistent that he hears "calling," John tells Donny in words that are unwavering, solemn, ritualistic, "They're calling me. They're calling my name. (*Pause.*) Mother. They're calling my name" (100-101). Hence, as John ascends the staircase, with its associations to Jacob's ladder, the affiliation here with Jacob, though implicit, is very persuasive. Like Jacob, John is starved for sleep, has a terrifying dream from which he awakens in a fright, fears being cast into hell, ascends a ladder connecting the secular and sacred worlds (Ginzberg 352), hears a powerful, insistent voice at night, is privy to revelation, and sees a fire in the form of an individuated light (Gen 46: 1-4), lending the play's concluding moments a mystical, metaphysical interpretation. Such "calling" may be seen to replicate a summons to commandment, what Newton terms "the name/ answerability formula" in the books of Exodus, Isiaih and Deuteronomy, when the patriarchs Abraham, Jacob, and Moses were awakened to obligation by a Voice calling their name. Indeed, that "the communicated word . . . possesses such power has . . . always been Judaism's first implicit principle of faith after the belief in God" (Alter 1969, 60). Linguistically marking the boundary between the innocent and the initiate and further distancing him from the deaf-and-blind Del and Donny, whose "cryptic codes of evasion, half-truths and outright lies . . . constitute the source of their own oppression" (Zeifman 1997, 6), the boy's earlier innumerable, unanswered questions are quelled by answerability and apparent awareness that bespeak a response of personal obligation. And as such, Steiner maintains, to "hear and accept a summons" is commensurate with "answerability of the most rigorous intellectual and ethical sense . . . of communal identification for the Jew" (Steiner 1996, 304).

In a final, riveting, evocative snapshot, the play's shattering conclusion wordlessly summons the past, captures the burden and blessing of history, and bridges personal and cultural heritage. Merging memory and fantasy, personal nightmare and cultural experience, *The Cryptogram* is possibly one of Mamet's finest and surely one of his most resonant works. A microcosm of his canon, *The Cryptogram* is about the business of living attentive to the higher call of ethical behavior. It is, above all, about accountability. As John Peter astutely recognized in his review of the play's premiere, "Here is the finest American playwright of his generation at full stretch" (1994).

GATHERING SPARKS

"Spawned in America, pogroms a rumor, *ma-maloshen* a stranger, history a vacuum . . ."
—Cynthia Ozick

THE PERIOD BETWEEN 1982 AND 1987 was an especially prolific one for David Mamet during which time *Edmond; Glengarry Glen Ross; Goldberg Street*, a collection of short dramatic works; *Writing in Restaurants*, the playwright's first collection of essays; and three minimalist works on the subject of Jewish identity, cultural identity, and bonds of memory, *The Disappearance of the Jews, Goldberg Street*, and *The Luftmensch*, were produced, published, or aired as radio dramas. These works articulate the ambivalence of confused cultural identity expressed in the attempt to recover the past, reestablish the bonds of memory, reclaim personal dignity, and confront anti-Semitism. Yet they have been largely ignored and dismissed by scholars as unimportant and/or unintelligible.

In 1989, during his writing and filming of *Homicide*, a work that also raises issues of Jewish assimilation and affiliation, which will be discussed in the following chapter, Mamet was inspired to revisit *The Disappearance of the Jews* in light of his growing interest in these subjects. *The Old Neighborhood*, comprised of *Disappearance of the Jews, Jolly*, and *Deeny* (formerly called "D")—the latter two works written in 1989[1]—unites three works in a single bill, through which Mamet explores "the personal terrain of memory" (Holmberg 1997b, 7) in three interrelated plays that complement one another in a subtle but compelling manner. Completed in 1989 and revised in 1997, *The Old Neighborhood* is central to the study of Judaism, ethics, and pedagogy in Mamet's work in the late 1980s and early 1990s and is a precursor to *Oleanna* and *The Cryptogram*, both informed by memory and the quest for and loss of home. Hence the trilogy serves as a pivotal link between the motifs developed in Mamet's earlier work, especially *Glengarry Glen Ross* and *Speed-the-Plow*, and that of the 1990s, which increasingly reveals his further exploration of identity, family, memory, and ethnicity.

In Mamet's view the structure of *The Old Neighborhood* is "an unusual form. It would be too grand to call it a trilogy," he suggests, "but it's something trilological. Three explorations of the same theme which make the evening partake of the dramatic, I hope, and also of the epic" (Holmberg 1997a, 9). Although he acknowledges that the term "epic" is somewhat surprising for these seemingly slight works, given its sweeping temporal and historical panorama and the journey that the character Bobby Gould makes to his boyhood home to visit family and friends after an interval of many years, *The Old Neighborhood*'s triple bill "generate[s] a unique synergism," as Richard Christiansen points out in his review of the world premiere, in which the plays "speak to each other and resonate, making up a whole that is greater than its parts" (1997). Tropologically and linguistically linked by Bobby's return to Chicago and unified by a trio of reunions through which he confronts his past—personal, familial, ethnic—or, as Mamet puts it "to close out some unfinished business" (Holmberg 1997a, 8), the play raises unsettling questions about "how to deal with a legacy that, as it slips through our fingers, shapes our lives" (1997b, 7). Searing the mind with stunning images and radiant poetry, the trilogy speaks of the loss of illusion and of faith, of the healing power of memory, of the redemptive power of love.

This chapter will also open a dialogue on the formerly neglected elegiac *Goldberg Street* in concert with a close reading of *The Old Neighborhood*.[2] Both are breakthrough plays whose tropes, emblems, and unmistakably Jewish characters provide stark evidence of the playwright's staging of conflicted Jewish identity in a luminous symphonic structure that particularizes and humanizes experience. The dyads and triads of this trilogy not only traverse the old neighborhood, they provide critical avenues to explore the sites of heightened conflict between professional and familial demands that inform Mamet's most recent and highly personal plays, screenplays, and memoirs. Anchored in place and deeply personal experience, this work may be among Mamet's most intimate in subject and structure, inspired as much by his maturity as a dramatist as his commitment as a Jew.

Visiting three individuals who have shared and shaped his life—Joey, his oldest, closest friend "since grade school" (1997a, DJ 28); Jolly, his sister with whom he is bound in pain; and Deeny, his first love—and who have remained *in* the Old Neighborhood as he, marrying outside the religion and venturing into the wider world, has moved away from place and whatever gave a sense of rootedness to his life, Bobby makes a journey that is educational, one disclosing familiar and forgotten truths. In each of these plays he engages a close friend or family member in dialogue, or, more accurately, they engage him in conversation and the binding relationship of listener and storyteller providing a fitting venue for his airing confessions and questions about his prior decisions and future endeavors. As he reminisces with each of these individuals closely aligned with his youth, a structure perfectly suited to the "kitchen play, a reflective family oriented play" typical of the 1950s that Mamet has previously eschewed (Weber 1997, 12), Bobby's reunions serve as clustered border-crossings in which the dialogue straddles timelines and spans emotional terrain typically unexplored by this playwright, with the exception of his heart-piercing *Cryptogram*.

Whereas *The Disappearance of the Jews* dramatizes a conversation between two old friends who chew over old times, lost opportunities, and faded dreams, their longing for connection to their Jewish heritage and feelings of disappointment in themselves and in their marriages revealed or implied in the rich subtext, *Deeny* is an acknowledgment of lost love and a recipe for renewal. *Jolly*, the longer middle play, is the centerpiece of this trilogy, its remunerative questions into the nature of mothering, memory, guilt, atrocity, love, and legacy deeply affecting and unsettling. A poignant work, *The Old Neighborhood* is immediately recognizable as Mamet country by its idiosyncratic invective, comic irony, and raunchy profanity that make a unique backdrop against which "times past," the controlling figure of this play—and to lesser or greater degree all of Mamet's canon—are repeatedly projected. From the outset Mamet portrays Bobby Gould as grappling with regret, learning to face his past and value its lessons, the most notable that "his problems are rooted in rootlessness" (Feingold 1997). However, Mamet doesn't so much plot Bobby's story linearly as map it out on coordinates of character and place. Swirling around these points of reference the play-wright coils Bobby's moody, ruminative, obsessive inquiries into the nature of memory, guilt, atrocity, love, and restoration, so that we perceive the trilogy's structure essential to Bobby's talmudic investigations into memory's inevitably incomplete record.

Analogous to Chekhovian scenarios that similarly evoke the vacillating, prismatic, confounding emotion of love tempered by joy, hope, disillusion-ment, and the searing pain of loss, and a seemingly quiescent surface that belies fluidity, Mamet's plays share a stasis more noticeable than in recent works.[3] And like Chekhov's plays, these works rely on the unspoken to reveal the distance between thought and meaning, between illusion and reality, between a person's conception of him or herself and the conceptions of companions, and between the speaker and the listener. But therein lies their intimacy, poignancy, and poetry. "[L]aced with a yearning to return to friends, and family, and a past . . . and, perhaps, most of all to his neglected Jewishness" (Cummings 103), *The Old Neighborhood* reveals that in going back to native ground, Bobby, a landsman among landsmen, frees himself to move forward, for "'It is only through the great truth of returning to oneself,'" observes Lawrence Kushner, that one locates "'the light of life'" (1993, 32).

In a now familiar structure of playing with distances, Mamet positions Bobby Gould in transit as a marginal man on the brink of change who returns home for much the same reason that Lyubov Ranevesky returns home to Russia from Paris in Chekhov's *The Cherry Orchard*. As Mamet has observed, Ranevsky does not return "to *save*" the orchard and estate, but rather "To lick her wounds, to play for time, to figure out a new course for her life" (1987d, 122). "None of these is a theatrically compelling action," he reminds us, for the latter could be satisfied "in seclusion" rather than in the company of old friends and family. What is to be gleaned from "returning," is a universal sentiment that Bobby's sister Jolly ratifies: we all need comfort. Likening *The Cherry Orchard's* structure to "the revue play . . . the *theme* play," in which "a series of review sketches" are linked by "a common theme" (124), Mamet presages a structure he has adopted for *The Old Neighborhood,* with the distinct difference that this trio of plays, the first two episodic and the latter a single scene, has a through-line and a protagonist who, in the process of confronting his past and himself, undergoes a journey of self-discovery, a search for truth.

Bobby Gould, who reappears with varying surnames and dilemmas in *Speed-the-Plow, Bobby Gould in Hell, The Disappearance of the Jews,* and *Homicide,* his name inspired by what Mamet views as the most common American first name and recognizably Jewish surname, and admittedly the playwright's alter ego in this work,[4] is a man on the margin—a man on the brink of divorce, an outsider to tradition, a weekend traveler visiting the old neighborhood, a stranger to himself, an acculturated Jew. In each of these circumstances he bears the traces of biography. Speaking recently with Bruce Weber, Mamet affirms in a comment he then deflects by humor "that he, like other writers tend[s] to write about their [his] youth" (1994 C10). Hence although the playwright cautions us that dramatic biography ends and must end "by reverting to fiction" or rather, "the dramatic elements must and finally will take place over any 'real' biographical facts," which are, finally, only a supervention in what we viewers can understand as a fictional drama" (1998, 29-30), this work is suffused with personal and cultural memory—Mamet's hometown, the neighborhood in which he grew up, a childhood scarred by rejection and violence.

Although *The Old Neighborhood* explores the motifs of love-hate bonds, of evanescence, of learning in the absence of reliable mentors or ethical elders, of the devastation wrought by unethical parental behavior that was so riveting in *The Cryptogram*, this play, which also depicts an unsettled character—whose mind is "full of thoughts" about what he "is *leaving*. . . . and what they're [he is] going *toward*" (1995b)—is similarly a memory play, but it is more clearly focused on history, as seen through the eyes of a disillusioned, deeply pained man disappointed in love and in life who returns home rather than escape from it. Principally concerned with the very uniqueness of American Jewish life—who or what defines a Jew, the responsibilities of Jewish men and women, the effects of deracination, the pitfalls of intermarriage, the illusion of assimilation, and the difficulty of maintaining ritual—*The Old Neighborhood* raises questions about the difficulty of being Jewish in America confronting both the issues of self-hatred and anti-Semitism in ways not previously addressed by Mamet. Drawing us into the vortex of swirling emotion that only occasionally breaks through the veneer of stability that Bobby struggles to maintain, the play announces its return to home ground from the outset by counterpointing past and present realities. That Mamet also returns linguistically to the "old neighborhood" is reflected in diction and discourse, the musical Yiddish rhythms, inverted word order, intimate vulgarities, dropped phrases, and the absence of verbs, whereby authentic sounds of home underscore Bobby's outsider status. For although he displays knowledge of this discourse, he is cut off from it, neither using it nor finding refuge in the past that is so vital an element in Joey's and Jolly's lives.

Characteristically, Mamet depicts his characters engaged in fiction-alizing, novelizing, mythicizing, and embellishing their lives in vintage Mamet stories—"The Plaid Raincoat," "The Fucking Skis," and "The Rogers Park Broads"—but as Ben Brantley recognizes, their "fantasies of an alternative world, in which religion, family and erotic love have a formal, enduring substance" stand in opposition to lives lived in quest of these (1997, B12). Moreover, *The Old Neighborhood,* like *Oleanna* and *The Cryptogram,* manifestly illustrates Mamet's increasing interest in personal narratives that afford greater visibility to ethnicity. And his methodology here is especially impressive, where concision belies immense cumulative power. Employing a paradigm that Walter Benjamin illumines in his famous essay, "The Storyteller," Mamet draws upon reminiscence *and* remembrance. "Memory is the epic faculty *par excellence,*" Benjamin writes, and "by virtue of a comprehensive memory can epic writing absorb the course of events on the one hand and . . . the passing of these . . ." (97) on the other. As "Memory creates the chain of tradition which passes a happening on from one generation to another," he adds, narrative assumes the form of "perpetuating remembrance" complemented by "the short-lived reminiscences of the storyteller" (98). Recalling a technique perfected by Saul Bellow in which "The fragmentary nature of flashbacks" precludes the work from "bogging down in the past" (Alter 1969, 108), *The Old Neighborhood* acquires a broad sweep. Set once again in an urban setting, the elegiac and eidetic play not only taps into the yearning for safety and connection, but the very uniqueness of American Jewish life, expressed in such issues as intermarriage, deracination, and what Alan Dershowitz terms the "Vanishing American Jew."[5]

Prior to its world premiere in 1997, only *The Disappearance of the Jews*, staged in 1983, has received critical attention.[6] For Dennis Carroll it is "one of the playwright's bleakest" (146); for Jeanne-Andrée Nelson, Joey and Bobby, the play's protagonists, whom she likens to Didi and Gogo in Beckett's *Waiting for Godot*, "seemed to have missed their appointment with meaning and identity" (464); and for Christopher Bigsby, "The play's title seems to suggest not simply loss of identity through assimilation," but the "erosion of the self which stems from the denial of history and of the power of the individual to intervene in his own life" (1985, 41). What none of these critics addresses, I believe, is that the act of reminiscence and remembrance that informs these works is a powerful act of will, however subtle. "To forget is, for a Jew, to deny his people—and all that symbolizes," Elie Wiesel argues; "[it is] also to deny himself" (1990, 9), whereas remembering, with its resonance for the Jew, is by implication a return toward self.[7]

Joey Lewis and Bobby Gould, childhood friends in their late thirties and Jewish archetypal "stoop philosophers" in Mamet's *The Disappearance of the Jews*, are two such culturally and ethnically detached American Jews. Longing for a life of connection, value, and tradition but finding themselves detached from Jewish identity, family, and each other, Joey and Bobby fabricate their own connection—however temporary—through memories and myths in which they functioned, or imagined functioning, as a dynamic duo. Rich in Jewish tradition, humor, irony, and discourse, the comedy of *The Disappearance of the Jews*, releases by "the superimposition of the tragic upon the trivial" (Shechner 1979, 234) and the sensual upon the serious, portraying assimilated American Jewry in transition, whose portrait is colored as much by persecution to which the Jew has been historically—and recently—subjected as the habit of self-irony.

Mamet situates his obviously Jewish characters in a hotel room in Chicago where together they recreate a panorama of the largely Ashkenazi Jewish community of their youth—Chicago's South Side from Seventy-first Street to Jackson Park, and Rogers Park, the site of major Jewish migration from the West Side in the early 1950s.[8] Mamet employs the Chicago landmarks of the Conservative synagogue, Temple Zion, Rodfei Zedek, the delicatessen Frankels, the Jewish cemetery Waldheim, and the Ravenswood line of the "El" train to stake out authentically "the corner(s) of their world" (Mamet 1992a, 125-26).[9] And although he signals his return to the home turf that has served as setting for numerous works through recognizable Chicago iconic emblems, such as the Cubs and Marshall Fields Department Store, allusions to Jewish historical landmarks, such as the shtetl, the Lower East Side of New York City and Maxwell Street in Chicago—better known as the "New" Old World—and Hollywood, the site of development of the motion picture industry, and Europe under the Nazis evoking the Holocaust and the death of six million Jews, provide a cultural backdrop for the fixed and fluid continuum of Jewish experience anchored not in place but in time. Their visiting these "monuments" of their common past has, as Pierre Bourdieu observes in another context, "all the clarity of a faithfully visited grave" (31)—a ritual that we learn Joey and his wife Judy regularly perform—binding the men's time travel to the past to the grave of parents and grandparents, an excursion that bears little likeness to the promiscuity and propinquity of their youth. But as much as Bobby's and Joey's recollections of their youth reveal a kind of "anthropologically focused tour to ancient sites," it exposes "an underlying insecurity in contemporary Jewish life" that bears directly on their collective identity and unease (Kugelmass 44).

Employing an episodic structure of seven scenes, Mamet conveys the passage of time that has made these men older, if not wiser. Mood, method and motifs are immediately signaled by reminiscence, narrative, and controversy, such that they communicate Bobby's and Joey's disquietude through "Their macho posings and posturings, what's said, what's held back" (Siegel 1997, 4). "What I remember . . . what I remember was that time we were at Ka-Ga-Wak we took Howie Greenberg outside," Joey begins, but in trying to identify Howie Greenberg, "Red hair. Braces," (1997a, DJ 3-4), Bobby and Joey immediately widen their frame of reference and establish sharply opposing memories in an ethnically coded dialectic marked by their argumentative tradition. Bobby's rejoiners are representative: "I got to tell you something, Joey, it was not Howie Greenberg. Howie never went to Winter Camp. (*Pause*) Am I right? (*Pause*) Am I right? Jeff went to Winter Camp. Tell me I'm wrong. (*Pause*) You fuckin' asshole . . ." (DJ 5)

Inspired by a prank that they played on Howie Greenberg—or was it Jeff?—at Camp Ka-Ga-Wak, they recall an even better time with two Jewish girls, Debbie Rubovitz and Debbie Rosen, whom they met in Rogers Park. Reminiscent of Bobby Gould and Charlie Fox in *Speed-the-Plow,* the two friends engage in a "high stakes" bet to determine which of "The Rogers Park Broads. . . . Some Jew broad . . . Some folk dancer" slept with Bobby. "For five bucks, which was mine. . . . For ten bucks?" (DJ 11, 16), Bobby dares his friend in a line that reveals that neither remembers these finer points of their youth, although both have the larger picture in focus. Such an erotic memory triggers Joey's questions about Bobby's wife, and the seemingly casual way in which the playwright juxtaposes the profane and mundane and the present against the backdrop of the past—or from a Jewish perspective, views past and present as synchronous—is distinctively Mametic. In contrast to the easy banter of two guys sharing war stories of the women they have bedded, in other words, safe territory and topics, Bobby is noticeably reticent. Although his parsed responses yield little about the source of his distress, suddenly piqued at Joey's questions, he explodes, exposing a man both vulnerable and seething with "rage . . . simmer[ing] below the surface" (Shalhoub qtd. in Marx 108). "You been reading 'Redbook' . . .? What is this all of a sudden . . . (*Pause*) You want to know how she is? She's fine," thus cutting off further inquiry, but whether or not Bobby is "fine" remains to be seen (DJ 17).

   In an even more outrageous fantasy of masculine prowess, Joey imagines himself "a great man in Europe . . . Reb Lewis, he's the strongest man in Lódz" who "'once picked up an ox.' (*Pause*) Or some fucking thing" (DJ 28-29).[10] Rewriting history, Joey believes he was built to be "hauling stones," "Building things," or working the land instead of "schlepping all the time with heart attacks, with fat, look at this goddamn food I sell . . . that stuff will kill you . . ." (DJ 29). And how he would have worked in Lódz. An urban center of Polish Jewish life in the late 1800s, to which many shtetl Jews gravitated, often just prior to their migration to America, Lódz figures importantly in Jewish history as a barbed-wire-enclosed labor camp where between the years 1940-1944 two hundred thousand men, women, and children died of starvation and exhaustion, and the men quite literary worked like oxen dragging dead bodies to open pits before all perished in liquidation camps (Howe 10; Adelson and Lapides 197-98). But Joey's image of greatness and imagined physical strength in the shtetls (the Jewish villages in the Pale of Settlement that have been "painted with a fresh coat of romanticized nostalgia" since the end of World War II [Desser and Friedman 25]), gives rise to an even more fantastic theological image of Bobby elevated to the status of a learned man, a rebbe: "I'll tell you where I would of loved it: in the shtetl. . . . You, too. You would of been Reb Gould. You would have told them what Rabbi Akiba said . . . (34).[11]

Implicitly referring to the aggadic narrative tradition that has long been the method of choice employed by Jewish theologians from biblical times to the present to communicate halakah—the set of rules for the way in which Jews are "to walk" in life, to behave in business, in family life, and in the synagogue—Joey remembers (or imagines) that biblical narrative is and was interpreted "not by a clear presentation of its theme or meaning, but by the telling of a new tale about an aspect of an old one," which in turn, "discloses by answering one question and conceals by raising new questions" (Kepnes 213). With the mention of Rabbi Akiba, a learned, beloved rabbi martyred in death by flaying at the hands of the Romans, Joey implicitly suggests that a learned man, one wiser than he, like Bobby—"Mr. Wisdom," as he teasingly terms his laconic friend—would metaphorically extract the meaning of Jewish historical existence and his own, thus connecting him personally to a cultural and ethnic history. In such an idealized world, instead of "the doctors, teachers, everybody, in the law, the writers all the time *geschraiying*, all those assholes, how they're lost," suggests Joey, "They should be studying talmud . . . we should come to them and to say, "What is the truth . . .? And they should tell us. . . . what this one said, what Hillel said, and I, I should be working on a forge all day" (DJ 29). Reb Gould, he imagines, would be studying Talmud and conveying "the truth." Sprinkling his speech with Yiddish phrases, some of which are not entirely understood by the audience, Joey employs an idiolect, like that of *Glengarry, Speed-the-Plow,* or *Oleanna,* that confirms the authenticity of the world evoked.

Whatever deprivations the shtetl entailed, it encompassed a world of values, order, and meaning that gave members of the community a sense of belonging and purpose. Thus, Joey's lyric romanticism of the shtetl reflects the manner in which American Jews typically hold East European Jewry at a spatial, spiritual, and temporal distance that, as Jack Kugelmass notes, is "a representation of the essential Jewish self uncorrupted by the compromises of the many" (41). Therefore, in a world of disconnection and disappointment, such as Joey's, his repeatedly distancing himself from his present reality, responsibility, and perceived entrapment in business and marriage and glorification of the past signal a longing for community and connection barely satisfied in fantasy. Further, as Joey's musings on marriage underscore, the gulf between Bobby's and his middle-class marriages and a lost world known only to assimilated American Jews through fantasy and photos is vast. In this context, the world of the shtetl represents an intact world of ritual, spirituality, and community[12]—a world apart from the dominant culture—that by definition sharply contrasts with contemporary American life, adding yet "another layer of complexity to a never ending discussion on what it means to be a Jew" (Kugelmass 50).

Bobby, who has an overabundance of complexity in his own life, imagines shtetl life in far more profane, pragmatic, and erotic terms, ponders the feasibility of sex in the shtetl or outside it with Polish whores:

Bobby: You think they fooled around?
Joey: Who? In the shtetl?
Bobby: Yeah.
Joey: The guys in the shtetl?
Bobby: Yeah.
Joey: I think it was too small. (DJ 34)

Hence, however tempting Bobby's dream of adultery, Joey's sense of history tells him that sex with "some young Jewish thing" has more merit than with Polish whores, his shocked remark—"Inside the shtetl?"—questioning what kind of a Jew would even think of defiling his own home. Their conversation darkens when Joey admits reluctantly and, in effect, shattering the sexual fantasy, that if a Jew "wanted to go out and fuck around who'd have you? If you stayed home [in the shtetl] you would be found out. I think. (*Pause*) But on the other hand who's to say what could go on. At night. In Europe" (DJ 36). It is a question that surely suggests infinite possibilities of nocturnal pleasure and plunder. Inspired by Bobby's reverie, Joey scripts a scenario in which he imagines his wife Judy stricken with an incurable disease, his grief and libido assuaged by "Some young, the daughter of one of my customers, the orphaned daughter . . . is this what you're saying?" (DJ 37), the elliptical rhythm, the absence of verbs, and observational nuance of Yiddish calling attention to the fact that as a "culture" that "exalts reasoning, no less than faith . . . Jewish wit hinges on logic to celebrate illogic" (Rosten 1989, xviii).

Although the phrases, "Who's to *say* what could go on. At night. In Europe," promise adventure, illicit pleasure, and freedom implicitly un-available to the unhappily married Bobby and Joey struggling with monog-amy and the reality of disconnection within their own homes,[13] Joey's delight at imagining a liaison with a sweet young thing is a vespertine vision more menacing than pleasurable. Setting us up with a bawdy, long-running joke, whose echoes may be found in dyads of men sharing stories about propositioning or bedding women in *Lakeboat, Sexual Perversity in Chicago* or *Speed-the-Plow,* Mamet strips the reminiscence of shtetl life of even a hint of romantic nostalgia with a "laugh" line that hits us broadside with its implicit reference to anti-Semitism in its myriad, mundane, and horrific permutations. Countering the illusion of illicit pleasure with the reality of plunder and pillage in the shtetl, Joey's comment—"Is this what you're saying"—and its pregnant pause permits us to enjoy the fantasy, on the one hand, only to find ourselves walloped by the recoil. For the veiled reference to nighttime raids connotes night terrors far removed from a night of pleasure, given the recollection that pogroms took place under cover of night to plunder, pillage, and prey upon unsuspecting Jews long before the SS "night-knock" rousted them from their homes during the Holocaust.

Conversely, Bobby's fantasies of power and potency are inspired neither by intellectual esteem traditionally accorded a rebbe, a teacher of ethics and moral behavior, nor by carnal knowledge. Nor is he particularly interested in reliving the American Jewish immigrant experience on Orchard Street in New York City, or Maxwell Street in Chicago, the "folk past" of pushcarts idealized in Joey's postnostalgic vision of an intact community, a romanticized portrait at odds with that depicted in Abraham Cahan's *Yekl,* Mike Gold's *Jews Without Money* and Henry Roth's *Call It Sleep,* classic novels of the urbanized immigrant experience. In fact, like Maxwell Street, Orchard Street lacked stability and cohesion precisely because it was the place where "old country Jewish ideals" battled a "powerful disinheriting America" (Klein 189, 222).

In his fictionalized account of American Jewish history, Bobby echews nostalgia for glamour and power. He would have "loved" to have been a maven and mogul in "Hollywood" in "the twenties" in an industry run solely by "five smart Jew boys from Russia," convinced that "they had a good time there" (DJ 38-39). As I discussed in my analysis of *Speed-the-Plow,* Jews utilized their commercial savvy to create a world apart in Hollywood. Far from the urban Jewish life of New York City, it lacked all semblance of religious ritual. Thus, in retrospect, we note the irony of Mamet's depicting Joey searching for cultural anchorage in the shtetl and Bobby, an assimilated Jew, finding his historical place in a de-Semitized Hollywood. However, that both seek refuge in a distant past strongly intimates that they are both "undergoing crises of faith and family" (Christiansen 1997, CN1).

As in previous dyads, Joey's and Bobby's banter quickly turns to quibbling, and once again Joey's interrogatory rhythms, which are themselves reflective of his Yiddish inflected speech, characterize his discourse. In fact, Joey speaks English laced with Yiddish, or what remains of the language, punctuating his points with such juicy phrases as "this shit is dilute, this is schveck this shit" (DJ 29). But when Bobby rattles off the names of the Hollywood moguls "Mayer. Warner. Fox." from memory, Joey is at a loss. Mulling over the name "Fox," Joey admits to thinking it "a goyish name" (DJ 40), which sets in motion a game of ethnic "Trivial Pursuit": "you know who else was Jewish?" (DJ 41). "'You know who's Jewish . . .,'" writes Mamet, "was a recurring phrase at my house," one that ratified that a person, "*particularly* in the entertainment industry . . . had 'passed' . . . into the greater world from the lesser" (1989b, 12). By association, then, Joey tries to top "Mr. Wisdom" by besting him with his knowledge that "Charlie Chaplin was Jewish" (DJ 40-41). Linking a story that brings them both back to their youth, the traditional visits to buy shoes at the neighborhood shoe store, Miller-White Shoes, and the Charlie Chaplin reference, Joey reveals that Mr. White was not only Jewish, a fact he had long doubted, but that he was "the shamus [a sexton] at Temple Zion thirty years" (44). His point is that "People fool you" (41), a resonant remark whose intent is both humorous and ironic, as the conclusion of the trilogy amply reveals. Chaplin, who both Joey and Bobby (and apparently Mamet) concur was Jewish—in fact, it is one of the points on which they do agree without argument—was generally believed to be Jewish. Mamet cites him among the cultural icons to which Jews refer in framing a Jewish identity: "We have our rare ballplayers, we have our tales of Charlie Chaplin and Cary Grant. . . . we have our Jewish food. . . . and we have our self-deprecating humor" (1989b, 12-13). Indeed, Chaplin was blacklisted by the House Un-American Affairs Committee, was concerned about Jewish issues, as his films from *The Immigrant* to *The Great Dictator* attest, and was "influenced by Jewish humor," but in the case of Chaplin, like Bobby's wife Laurie, about whom we learn much more, "people fool you": the mythos surrounding that individual—Chaplin was not Jewish—is more convincing, or in Laurie's case more worthy, than the truth (Desser and Friedman 9-11; Robinson).[14]

However, Bobby's fantasy, so unrelated to his life and a marriage ripe for divorce court, returns them both to the present and the nightmare reality that plagues each in differing ways. Joey's lament, "Life is too short" elicits a story that has in fact fueled his fantasies and memory, that he has not only dreamed of changing his life by murdering his family, he believes he has. "I can't tell you, Bobby . . . I have a pistol, I can end it any time" (DJ 48). Like Teach, a man with a gun, Joey is just a Jew stuck in a store living on dreams. Trapped in his delicatessen selling "heart attack" food, Joey seeks the power and freedom that he lacks through a criminal act—murder, mayhem, and adultery—and alternatively prays that ritual will enrich his tedious existence. Worst of all, he fears that he is going to die like this—a disconnected "schmuck" powerless to realize his potential. For "Men get together under three circumstances," observes Mamet: "to do business," "to bitch," and to have "*fun* with each other" in the company of other men in which "one is understood . . . not judged . . . [and] not expected to perform" (1989b, 87-88). These men have clearly come together "to bitch," comforted by the fact that in an atmosphere devoid of shame, each "at some point [will] reveal that, yes, *they* are weaklings, too." If men "are *not* sensitive to women," acknowledges the playwright, "we are sensitive to our own pain and can recognize it in our fellows" (87). Hence, recalling the rationale for the choice of setting for this work, Mamet states, that "the scenic element essential to the dramatic thrust of the play . . . is that this is a place [a hotel room] where these two guys can be alone and be intimate with each other" (Savran 143).

Sympathetic to Joey's pain and increasingly honest about the depth of his own, Bobby echoes Joey's desire to radically change his life by obliterating his marriage. "I should never have married a *shiksa*," he confesses (DJ 18). Initially, Joey makes a joke at Bobby's expense, teasing him about his dating non-Jewish women. "Yeah. I know," he says. "Cause that all you used to say, 'let's find some Jew Broads and discuss the Midrash . . .'" (DJ 18). However, Bobby's cryptic remark acquires broader significance when, in answer to Joey's provocative "Mr. Wisdom . . . speak to me" (DJ 18), Bobby gives him an earful. Prior to his leaving for a visit to Chicago, a touchstone of identity, Bobby and Laurie have discussed and obviously disagreed about their son's ethnicity, a subject that initiates a discussion on the "law" from the maven, Joey, who knows. To Bobby, on the other hand, the issue is simple and settled: "The kid is a Jew" (DJ 20), regardless of Conservative and Orthodox Jewish law that recognizes the boy as Jewish only if his mother is Jewish. As their banter reveals, Joey and Bobby may be close in age but light years apart in religious philosophy. Yet they are quibbling over a matter of far more importance than which of the Debbies each slept with or whether it was Howie Greenberg or Jeff they threw in the snow, an illustration, suggests Allen Guttmann, that "The anxiety accompanying the discussions of Jewish identity is greatest among secular Jews and least among Orthodox." Whereas the former have no idea who they are, "the latter have no doubt" (11).

Enraged by Joey's point of law, the typically terse Bobby is suddenly loquacious: "They start knocking heads in the schoolyard looking for Jews, you fuckin' think they aren't going to take my kid because of, uh. . . . 'Cause he's so blond and all. 'Let's go beat up some kikes . . . Oh, not that kid . . .'" (DJ 21-22). Beyond the painful realization that his fair-haired son, who is not even considered a Jew by Conservative or Orthodox law, will nonetheless be the victim of anti-Semitism in the schoolyard is the harsh lesson that Bobby has learned, that anti-Semitism begins at home—*his* home. Like Joey, Bobby has a harrowing tale to tell, but it is no fantasy. "Well, listen to this Joe, because I want to tell you what she says to me one night. 'If you've been persecuted so long, eh you must have brought it on yourself'" (DJ 22).[15] That Bobby's ethnic dislocation has come full circle is manifest when he appears to intellectualize, even condone, his wife's anti-Semitism. "Self-hatred arises," writes Sander Gilman, "when the mirages of stereotypes are confused with realities within the world, when the desire for acceptance forces the acknowledgment of one's difference" (1986, 4). Revealing the discourse of the majority, "saturated with the imagined projection of the Other" (13)—in this case the fallacious myth that Jews are responsible for the hatred directed against them—Bobby's self-hatred is reflected in his conceding, even for a moment, that Laurie's premise has merit, that "it got me thinking," and that he remained silent in the face of her challenge (24).

If we've missed that point in Bobby's silence, Joey, who has been pondering Laurie's statement and his friend's reaction, brings it to the forefront of our consciousness. Mamet uses the opportunity to highlight subtly that each friend assumes the role of mentor to the other, dispensing lessons to live by and asserting Jewish values, privileging compassion and respect, on the one hand, and assertion of pride in one's heritage and identity, on the other. Notable, as well, is that Bobby and Joey dispense these lessons in a manner consistent with their characters, which simultaneously rivets attention to the studious intellect and the performance artist. Hence, although both Joey and Bobby live lives of quiet desperation, devoid of the power, potency, and confidence that colors their fantasies and characterized their youth, an empowered Joey, still mulling over Bobby's wife's remark and finding not a kernel of logic in Laurie's statement, rejects the sophistical reasoning for what it is. "Wait a second. If we've been oppressed so long *we* must be doing it" (DJ 22, emphasis added). Typically at his best in crafting imaginary scenarios, Joey sets forth his sage wisdom in a mind-numbing monologue with classic Mamet flair, counseling Bobby to jettison such a premise from his mind (much as Roma advised Lingk in *Glengarry* to ignore his wife's advice), challenging him to reject his guilt, self-flagellation, and self-hatred, and encouraging him to question a relationship disrespectful of his identity as a Jew. In doing so Joey draws upon the history, tenacity, eloquence, and wit of his ancestors, both in the literal and figurative sense, to convince his friend of 30 years of the wrongheadedness of his thought, and in so doing manifests what Wiesel has defined as "the importance of friendship to man's ability to transcend his condition" (1990, 238). Illustrating that "the stoic ideal is goyish, having a tantrum is Jewish" (Whitfield 1984, 127), Joey is in rare form:

> Ho, ho, ho, ho, hold on a minute, here, ho, Bobby. Lemme tell you something. Let me tell you what she feels: she feels left out, Jim. Don't let that white shit get into your head. . . . they got, what have they got, you talk about community, six drole cock-suckers at a lawn party somewhere: "How is your boat . . ." Fuck that shit, fuck that shit, she's got a point in my ass, what the fuck

did they ever do? They can't make a joke for chrissake, I'll tell you something, you are sitting down, the reason that the goyim hate us the whole time, in addition they were envious is; we don't descend to their level.

Pause

because we wouldn't fight. . . . Because we have our mind on higher things.

Pause

. . . .

My dad would puke to hear you talk that way. . . . your father, too, to hear you go that way. What are they doing to you out there? (DJ 24)

Tucked away in Joey's tirade is the key phrase, "white shit," which in his hysterical vitriol is easily missed. However, as Itzkovitz observes, the ongoing debate of the early twentieth century in America and of late has swirled around the issue of the "white" Jew, raising the question inferred in Joey's offhand, ostensibly insignificant remark: "Does a Jew who *is* able to appear white . . . remain a Jew?" (182). Itzkovitz puts the question regarding the Jew's whiteness to the test, wondering whether "the Jew's performance of whiteness—the self-erasure of the Jew's Jewishness"—not only "enables his or her smooth assimilation" but is a reflection of the border-crossing, one that illustrates that assimilation is concomitant with "passing as white" (184).[16] And as that clearly is what Bobby has attempted to do, he suddenly finds himself listening not merely to Joey's tales but to his wise counsel.

In like matter and on the related subject of race, Mamet reverses course, and it is Bobby who challenges Joey's brazen braggadocio that one could prove his manhood in Europe during the reign of the Nazis by "standing up," presumably in the Chicago definition of the phrase as one who is faithful in the broadest interpretation of the term[17]—"the stand-up guy" sanctioned by Don in *American Buffalo*. Joey is not wrong that the posture of the Jew is one of conscientious objector, that is, having the courage to recognize inhumanity and speak out on it. And the Holocaust is the one subject, as Dershowitz has noted, that typically aligns Jews (1991), if for no other reason that it taught the harsh lesson that, like the boys who would pick out Bobby's son in schoolyard because they thought he was a

Jew, the Nazis incinerated "cosmopolitan," assimilated Jews along with shtetl Jews. It was and is race, not Jewish law, that determines how the Jew was or is seen by others, as Bobby's wife Laurie has made abundantly clear. In vehemently objecting to Joey's glib "Fuck the Nazis . . . I'm saying, give a guy a chance to stand up," Bobby matches fact with Joey's fiction, proving how he has earned his moniker. "That's romantic shit," he tells him (DJ 31), reflecting at once Mamet's proneness to unequivocal statement and Bobby's impatience with Joey's bold front.

One of the lessons to be learned from the study of the Holocaust, Bobby explains with his characteristic conciseness, is that "You don't know"—nor can we know—what went on in Europe "with the Nazis" (DJ 32, 30). In lieu of the nexus of guilt that typically aligns the comfortable American to European victims of Nazism, Joey's preposterous claim that he would have had the courage and strength to endure the concentration camps, though unintended offense, is nonetheless pernicious, defaming the memory of Holocaust victims and survivors of Nazism, and Bobby calls him on it, just as Joey similarly rejected Bobby's self-hatred. Joey's impropriety so disturbs Bobby, a man of few words, that he reiterates his objection several times; in short, "it's profaning what they went through" (DJ 31).[18] And because the character has little to say, that which he does say gains greater impact, both in this play and in *Jolly*, the second of the trilogy, in which his loquacious sister threatens to drown out his thoughts and speech. An empathic figure, Bobby imparts a cautionary comment to his friend, affirming that his is a recondite wisdom, a heightened sensitivity to persecution, which in *Jolly* Mamet reveals is in part the result of a protracted exposure to brutality and oppression where he learned first hand the price of sacrifice that does not occur on behalf of anything. Moreover, Bobby's insistence on respect owed the dead and the survivor illustrate that although he is an acculturated Jew who has ceased to observe practice and prayer, he is attuned to what David Roskies terms the catastrophe of "memory of past destruction" (1984, 14).

That they are changing and have changed is the *other* narrative implicitly conveyed in this play. When Bobby is particularly withdrawn, Joey observes, "you never fuckin' changed you know that, Bob. 'Fuck you, I don't need anyone, fuck you . . .'" (DJ 17), by which we assume he refers to Bobby's stoic silence, but both have grown older and wiser, learning, among other things, that there is no statute of limitation on anti-Semitism. In reflecting upon their youth, expectations, and identity, Bobby and Joey, disconnected from wives, families and those whose "questions are answered with ritual" (DJ 52), have in speaking about their spiritual alienation, rekindled personal memory, (re)established cultural bonds, and reflected the desire for enhanced spirituality. Joey's complaint that "Everything, everything, everything . . . it's . . . I'll tell you; it's a mystery . . . (*Pause*) Everything is a mystery, Bob . . . *everything*. . . . And we have no connection" (DJ 51-52), echoing the guilt, confusion, and alienation experienced by assimilated American Jews, is belied by *his* connection—brief in time and long in memory—to Bobby. Deeper still are the bonds of ethnicity, education (spiritual as well as sexual), tradition, and Jewish history.

Although critics are quick to dismiss these characters as accepting of the emotional and ethnic malaise in their lives, Beckettian pals who "refus[e] to take action while they wait for something to validate their lives" (Holmberg 1997b, 8), *The Disappearance of the Jews* amply illustrates that their contemplative mood comprised of both reminiscence and remembrance does not signify acceptance, nor does it acknowledge the "disappearance" of the Jews, as the playwright told me.[19] Conversely, given the context of their talking about the difficulty of maintaining connections (to Judaism and Judaic practice), in other words, of finding ways to foster (ethnic) identity and pride, their discussions explore the literal and metaphysical aspects of "returning home." In this manner they not only visit the past, they participate in rewriting the present, commencing a process of healing. Thus, although Bobby is an acculturated Jew *outside* tradition, the potential exists for him to find his way back *into* a body of collective history "through his very consciousness of being outside it" (Alter 1969, 29). Or as Thorstein Veblen precisely puts it, "by loss of allegiance, or at the best by force of a divided allegiance to the people of his origin" the marginalized Jew "finds himself in the vanguard of modern inquiry. . . . [Yet] it does not follow that he [who goes away] . . . will swear by all the strange gods whom he meets along the road" (1948, 474, 478), an observation that has broad application to Mamet's experience. As numerous critics, theologians and sociologists have noted, the disappearance of American Jews through acculturation, assimilation, and intermarriage has been a prediction solemnly intoned for the past several decades. As Robert Alter observes in "The Jew Who Didn't Get Away," with or without demographic data—the method by which the John in *Oleanna* sought to illustrate trends—one finds, instead, "the stubborn insistence" of a surprising numbers of American Jews gravitating back to religious practice, a trend that might be termed "a glimmering of an American Jewish culture" (1986, 281).

In *Jolly*, the second play, and the most devastating of the three, Mamet dramatizes Bobby's reunion with his younger sister Jolly. Here the playwright revisits the territory he charted in an autobiographical reminiscence, "The Rake," the lead article in *The Cabin*, a collection of reminiscences dedicated to Mamet's sister Lynn. She has written a play about a dysfunctional family entitled *The Lost Years* (1995) in which the character of the sister characterizes their family as "the reigning champions" in the

"'Dysfunctional Family Olympics'" (15).[20] In *Jolly* Mamet forges a link between Bobby's and Jolly's familial experience of disjunction, dysfunction, and cruelty and the emotional events that currently overwhelm him. And he has never come closer to revealing the dysfunctional family or dramatizing the rationale for Bobby's self-imposed exile from the old neighborhood. In a rare use of invective, scatology, and irony, Jolly, we soon learn, has never been jolly by any stretch of the imagination, for her life—"A rich 'full' life" as she puts it (J 52)—has long been denied any whiff of the mirthful or the joyous. And while she is jocular after a fashion, Jolly is true to her name only in her ability to "jolly along"—to gladden, encourage, and uplift—Bobby's flagging spirits and self-worth.

Set in Jolly's home, the three-person, three-scene play takes place over the course of less than one day. It opens on an evening discussion among Bobby, his sister Jolly, and her husband Carl that is already in progress. Bobby has returned to Jolly's house, where he is staying for a brief visit after an absence of many years, and the initial scene finds him engaged in dialogue, or rather responding to Jolly's expository stories and diatribes in the informal, seemingly comfortable surroundings of her home. Like the conversation between Bobby and Joey in *The Disappearance of the Jews,* the dyad between sister and brother initially appears "deceptively casual and meandering" (Holmberg 1997b, 8). In fact, when the play opens, Jolly is recounting a telephone conversation with her stepfather to her brother, whose planned visit to Waldheim Cemetery with Joey, though neither confirmed nor denied, suggests a credible explanation for Bobby's somber mood obviously exacerbated by his sister's tale of the stepfather's brutal conversation with her.

As Jolly describes their stepfather's disapproval of the way in which she is raising her daughters, establishing the parameters for a trenchant discussion of parenting, both in the present and in the past, Bobby, who has been mostly restrained in his conversation with Joey, quickly builds to a wrathful rage. Advising her that she must cease all communication and connection, "all *meetings, dialogue. . . .* You should take an oath never to talk to, meet with" (J 4-5), he taps a reserve of repressed bitterness. But when she protests, ". . . but the children . . ." Bob's response is instantaneous and even more adamantly obsessed with the protection of Jolly's children: "And the children most especially. . . . are we going to expose another generation to this . . . this" (J 5), his disjunctive speech breaking under the weight of his anger, the words "another generation" providing minimal Mametic back story. Subtly framing the play as an exploration of their linked past and troubled lives, Mamet signals that like *The Disappearance of the Jews, Jolly* is a memory play; however, here the memories evoke little laughter and immense pain. With the barest brushstrokes Mamet paints a picture of divorced parents, stepparents, and siblings, of resentments, jealousy, preferential treatment, and mostly the cold reality that the memories and experiences of siblings sharply differ. As they rake up the past and reopen old wounds, or confront ulcerated ones, announcing, as in *The Cryptogram,* the journey in time, the play further reveals that Bobby's transient status naturally accelerates and condenses the revelation of family stories and personal dilemmas so that the unfolding of these appears in the natural flow of a compressed visit dredging up in a mere twenty-four-hour visit and within the safety of their relationship a seemingly endless ocean of pain. As Mamet tells Terry Gross, Jolly and Bobby "go back through the 'attic,' as it were, of their childhood, which was apparently not a very—not a very diverting time" (1997).

Bobby's anger, so well controlled—or hidden—for much of the time that he spends with Joey, even eerily suppressed as he related dispassionately his wife's heinous accusation that Jews deserve the persecution brought against them, here he is almost uncontrollable at times, his vacillating between despair about what effect his leaving his failed marriage will have on his own children, and his recollections of the rejection and confusion he felt as a boy, "the psychological sleight of mind" by which his parents "project[ed] their inadequacy onto their children" (Lahr 1997b, 73-74). Hence, Bobby's outburst to Jolly, "That's their swinish, selfish, *goddam* them. What *treachery* they have not done, in the name of . . ." (1997, 7) breaks off, as many of his comments do, evoking her support, their common memory, and the impossibility of his finishing his sentence:

> Jolly: . . . I know . . .
> Bob: . . . of 'honesty.' God *damn* them. And always 'telling' us we . . .
> Jolly: . . . yes.
> Bob: . . . we were the bad ones . . .
> Jolly: . . . Well, we were. (J7)

Thus even as the text elicits through reminiscence the presence of strangers—the *sheigetz,*[21] the gentile man that their mother married, stepbrothers and sisters—and the absence of mentors, Mamet simultaneously evokes through fragmentary flashbacks that Bobby's and Jolly's lives are still held hostage to the past, their resentments and repressed feelings as much a part of their marriages as they were a part of their parents'. As Jolly justifies furthering the communication with their stepfather to herself, her husband Carl, and her brother, reminding Bobby and implicitly informing us that he was not living at home during her most painful and unprotected years, and neither did he care for their dying mother, nor visit Jolly during a period that has again been a trying one, Mamet leaves open the question of whether Bobby, like the maligned Carol, even returned to Chicago for his mother's funeral. Thus, while she sketches in the details of the most recent telephone conversations with her father, sharing with Bobby the current example of her father's parsimoniousness (emotional and well as financial), Jolly illustrates that this latest exchange is consistent with her father's longstanding criticism of her, revealing a woman "almost gnawed away by unappeased anger over her childhood, her mother's death, her stepfather's maneuvers over the estate and at Bobby" (Feingold 1997), the most loved and least available of the two children.

Sharing a gem that they both relish, Jolly ignites another round of vituperative rage directed at the offstage stepfather who, it seems, is undergoing therapy, which Jolly ridicules as so much "psychobabble." Continuing her story, she adds, "Oh, oh, he said, he's learning—you're going to love this: "learning to live 'facing his past'" (J 14). Indeed, learning to confront the past and move on to face the future emboldened or saddened by its lessons is the larger subject of *The Old Neighborhood,* for as the playwright amply illustrates, release does not come from the mundane but from matters of the soul. "The theater," he writes, "exists to deal with problems of the soul, with the mysteries of human life, not with its quotidian calamities" (1998, 27). Overarching the mundane details of family, business, and the activities of a family weekend—popcorn, pancakes, Monopoly, and movies—is Jolly's running narrative, a circuitous and often hilarious tale that progressively closes in on anguish tearing at the soul. In typical Mametic fashion, however, spare speech cuts to the quick, exposing profound sadness, anxiety, disappointment, and despair, and "conflicting layers of past and present selves," as Brantley has it (1997, B3).

Unique in *Jolly,* however, is that Mamet has afforded this character a distinctive dignity and discourse rare in Mamet's depiction of women. A raconteur of unique talent with a flair for the dramatic, Jolly peppers her stories with profanities not heard since *Glengarry Glen Ross* through which we feel the full thrust of her fury, frustration, and anguish. Much of this early scene is a running monologue occasionally interrupted by Bobby's interjections—"Fucking leeches" (J15) or "What in the hell *possesses* a man. To *treat* you like that" (J 29)—and interrogatories, and Jolly's husband Carl's reverberant instruction, "Tell him," compelling Jolly to speak and constrain the listener in the binding role of narrator. Mamet's paradigmatic counterpointing of a taciturn figure and a voluble one, which indicates the conscious suppression of information or evasion of speech and moves the fiction forward toward the revelation of facts repeatedly engulfed by the flood of emotion that overtakes Jolly and listener alike, is especially effective in this scene. One telephone call leads by association into another in a continuing saga that reflects in Jolly's inimitable vernacular and fictive style facts about which Bobby has little or no knowledge, namely that all her requests for financial assistance during a period of dire fiscal exigency, the result of her husband's unemployment, have been roundly rejected by the stepfather who is kept dramatically alive as a pivotal figure, as is the dead mother, through lively and frequent allusion to these offstage personae. Framed in equivocations and legal jargon such that despite Jolly's urgent need for funding her stepfather not only refuses to "*invade* the trust. . . .," but, as she explains, continuing her story, "it gets worse" (J 21, 25). Or more accurately, the picture comes into greater focus as Jolly sketches in the sordid details of her petition for assistance and recognition of her claim to her mother's estate. Her stepfather's outright rejection deems both petitioner and petition unworthy. Similarly, Jolly's solicitation of iconic emblems of her mother's life and legacy—an armoire, an old mink coat, antiques with all the resonance of history and heritage—is disregarded and denied by the patriarchal figure empowered to facilitate her repeated appeals: "And so I *told* him," Jolly continues her dramatic narration of her telephone call to the stepfather with appropriate mimesis:

> He'd say, "waaaaalll . . .: that's a very special *piece* . . . uh. Huh huh." What do I get? NOTHING. NOTHING. Nothing. Some cheap . . . and it doesn't *matter*. . . . But she was my mother. And I was there when she was dying. *I* was there. *I* was there. He'd drop her off, and I was left, an infirm woman. . . . And that sonofabitch that *cunt* that *cunt* that Carol. DIDN'T EVEN COME TO THE . . . the *funeral*. And who gets the armoire? (J 17)

Indeed, as Arthur Holmberg notices, "Among the many surprises lying in wait in *The Old Neighborhood*," is "that David Mamet, bulldog of male invective, attacks . . . patriarchy," as he has done in *The Cryptogram*, "for the psychological damage it inflicts on women through contempt" (1997b, 9). Furthermore, in choosing Jolly as that character who has both the voice and the vocabulary to win our attention, Mamet emphatically illustrates the high cost of disrespectful discourse to men and women alike.

Fusing *mamaloshen*, the Yiddish that comes easily to her lips with its bawdy vulgarity, Jolly, clearly without benefit of the counseling she mocks, channels her substantial rage into narrative. Contrasted with this discourse is a language of affection also rare in Mamet's canon; Jolly not only deciphers the coded phrases that intimate with few words the depth of her brother's pain, she communicates her profound love for him. Repeatedly using that wonderful Yiddish phrase (of varying spellings) "Bubeleh"—or the shorthand, "Buub" for which there is no apt English equivalent other than that it bespeaks unconditional love, and when used by his now-deceased mother cloaked judgment. For Jolly, however, the word is not only a natural expression of affection but a marker of the dual worlds in which she functions as an angry, hurt adult badly scarred by horrific memories and recent history—a woman who labels any uncaring action, whether in the past or the present, as an unethical exchange—and conversely a caring mother, wife, and sister who is one of Mamet's most fascinating women and dedicated teachers.

Counterbalancing to some degree the painful heritage of abuse dredged to the surface of the play, Jolly is a figure of reconciliation whose life-affirming and sustaining family activities nurture Carl and her daughters in an effort to initiate a new legacy, notably through giving the gift of herself—in playing games with her children, home cooking (its echoic allusion to Roma's and Levene's shtick that glorified home cooking in *Glengarry Glen Ross*), and inventing weekend ceremonies that have the full force of ritual. Additionally, Jolly implicitly conveys that despite—or because of—the burden that she carries, she at least sets an ethical example for her daughters, lessons to which they may refer after her death. Simply put, as Jolly tells Bobby, linking her past experience and current choices, she creates in a different model: "If they [their parents] had loved us. Mightn't they have *known* what we might want. I know what *my* kids want" (J 36). Thus it is with delight that she playfully makes Bobby admit that he slept well in her home because it is "Safer than Anyplace in the World" (J 57). "You see, Bob? Do you see? This is a *family*" (J 39), though in a surprise ending Mamet reveals how tenuous the concept of "safe haven" is for them or any of us, no matter how appearances and reiterated code words may shore up the illusion.

As a child Jolly felt her home was anything but safe. Her recollections of rejection—of literally being kicked out of bed by a stepsister, an iconic sign that signals her exilic, unprotected condition within the home—are linked to her mother's rejection of Jolly's plea to recognize the validity of her claim and her place in the primal family. Although Bobby readily acknowledges that the family treated Jolly "like filth," Jolly's disturbing childhood recollection is a case in point that implies her lingering resentment of her beloved brother who left her to face her oppressors alone:

> . . . Do you know, you don't know, cause you weren't there—
> when they first came. *Mother* told me, I was ten. So she was eight;
> she was going to sleep in my bed. She took up the bed, as she was

a "creeper," you know. I'm a rock. You put me in a bed. And unmoving. Morning. She was all over the place. And I went and told Mom that I couldn't sleep. She said, "she is his daughter, and this is the case. . . . If you can't sleep, sleep on the floor." (J 10)

In retrospect, it is an event that opened the floodgates for all manner of verbal and physical abuse inextricably bound to this test of a mother's love, or rather the failure of the mother to protect Jolly from the intruder in her bed and, by extension, in her home. That the support was nonexistent, in fact, that the event was marked by the withdrawal of support, solace, or expression of affection—the ripping away of the proverbial blanket, that emblematic token with associations that we recall from *The Cryptogram*—is the most graphic indication of childhood abuse that finds form or phrase in *Jolly*. Like the "white shit" in Joey's monologue, Jolly's three-word phrase— "you don't know"—nearly missed in the narration of her horrific experience, represents the gulf of experience between a sister and the brother she adores who is physically, emotionally, and psychologically out of touch with her life. In sharp contrast to the brutalization of Mamet's sister portrayed in "The Rake," Jolly's psychological trauma is the only one at issue, for even as they differ, as Brantley also notices, Jolly's and Bobby's past is "their central defining reality, its particulars recited and repeated like a litany" (1997, B3).

Awakened in the middle of the night by uneasy dreams and disquieting thoughts, Bobby and Jolly continue their conversation in scene 2, their intimacy attenuated by the lateness of the hour. From the outset their conversation turns to a distant time when as Jewish children they celebrated Christmas. "One thousand generations we've been Jews and she marries a *sheigetz* and we're celebrating Christmas" (J 44), Jolly notes with little humor, as brother and sister recollect their mother's marriage to a gentile that stripped life of all familiar traditions and customs and supplanted them with a loveless life, a despised, violent stepfather, the trial of coping with the spectacle of Christmas, and the ritual of unwanted gifts that came with disclaimers but dared not be returned. Yet, in contrast to scene 1, Bobby and Jolly assist one another is recovering the past, each scripting forgotten details of the other's story in a scene that is alternately bathed in pathos and brightened with humor, although undergirding the scene, and occasionally rising to the surface of the dialogue, are the sadness, haunting memories, and troubling thoughts that have awakened both siblings. Bobby recalls "A plaid . . . a . . . a plaid something" and with the aid of his sister weaves a hilarious, touching story of his being given an unwanted plaid reversible raincoat from Marshall Fields that he so detested that he returned it, trading it in, and "Oh my God. Jol. For, what, then, a year . . .? . . . . For a *year*," he remembers being hounded, 'Where is that raincoat, Bubby . . .?'"(J 33-34). Desperate to stop the questions, he went to Marshall Fields "TO SEE COULD I BUY BACK THAT COAT. . . . And that woman at Fields. Sent to fucking *Germany* to see, could they replace that raincoat" (J 35).

The conversation goes "round and round," picking up the threads of subjects picked up and dropped earlier in the evening or in the scene, one that merges immediate past and ancient history. Jolly is apparently obsessed with convincing her brother that Carl, the man her family rejected as unsuitable for her, their despised daughter, is a prince and she a nurturing mother. As she speaks incessantly, however, her words are reminiscent of the two ways in which Pinter has described silence, as the absence of speech and a torrent of speech.[22] Implicitly, the play suggests that neither her marriage nor her life is a fairy tale but rather a daily struggle, a point underscored by Carl's irritation with Bobby when he queried Carl earlier in the evening about how Carl—an outsider who inherited their miserable misfortune by marriage—can endure the saga that is their family's history.

Like the protoganists in *The Disappearance of the Jews,* Jolly and Bobby are storytellers with vivid memories, pained lives, terrifying nightmares, and fantasies of an alternative world. That these two adults dwell on their deprivation "with such virulence after so many years dramatizes its lasting psychological significance" suggests Holmberg, wisely noticing their seem-ingly insatiable need to pick the scabs off the scars (1997b, 9). Jolly, for her part, has two stories to share with her brother that concern their mother. The first is a memory of her mother's continuance of the gift-giving rituals to which she and her brother were subjected as children. Disregarding either the wants or the needs of the recipient for the "Big Present," her mother ignored Jolly's specific appeal for money for shoes for the girls, no doubt a link to a similar, earlier request, though on a vastly different scale, to her stepfather for assistance to cover basic needs. This allusion also serves as a narrative transition to Bobby's and Joey's conversation in the first play of *The Old Neighborhood* about Miller-White Shoes and Joey's recent visit to the shoe store they had frequented as children.

The second story is a recurring nightmare that since her mother's death continues to savage Jolly's dreams. Whereas she embellishes the shoe story, Jolly demurs on the subject of the nightmare until the following morning just prior to Bobby's departure when juxtaposed to the figure of security, her childhood recollections of an intact world—of grandparents, of fathers who returned at the end of the day, of holidays spent as a family, of favorite foods, of Jewish ritual—flood the conversation and bring her fear and pleasure as a child into sharp focus. The technique not only builds anticipation, it arouses curiosity, intimating that in one who is rarely silent on any subject, her choice to defer discussion belies a nightmare so troubling that she prefers postponing rather than uncovering it. Further, it intimates that Jolly so cherishes the time with her brother that she delays until a future time a tale that will undoubtedly mar her visit with him. Setting the scene, Jolly picks up the dropped threads of the shoe story sharply paralleling that of the unwanted raincoat. "I'd say Shoes. They need shoes," she goes on, but at "The end of her stay, she would give them, God Bless her, these, two *incredibly* expensive, what are they, 'vanity' sets" (J 42-43). Jolly's best tales are of the "fucking *skis*" and the red bookbag that, unlike Bobby, she did not have the courage to return to Marshall Fields and resentfully carried for three years, much as she still shoulders the burden of that memory. In this case, it is Bobby who prompts Jolly in her performance of the story of "The Christmas Skis," cueing her with the line "What Is That Behind The Door" (J 44), that in scene 3 takes on new meaning as we come to understand how much is hiding behind the facade of stability and security that Jolly works so hard to maintain.

The late-evening encounter, however, proves an opportune moment for a more intimate line of questioning and confessions that finally draws brother and sister into a discussion of the marital problems that have sent Bobby to Chicago in search of the safety and comfort of Jolly's love. Maintaining a respectful distance from her brother's personal life Jolly nevertheless uses this opportunity to question her brother's future intentions, and he appears to surprise himself by revealing a previously unacknowledged decision that he has no intention of returning to his destructive marriage and anti-Semitic wife. Whether that decision is the result of discussions with Joey or Jolly or both Mamet characteristically leaves open to our interpretation. Conversely, Jolly's expression of unequivocal support, regardless of Bobby's decision, illustrates the lessons she has learned from manipulative, exploitative, sadistic relationships that rewarded her with love or gifts as they served others' needs and disposition. Yet, the stability of her love for him is bested by the chaos of her life which receives substantial clarity as she relates a story of going the wrong way on a one-way street, one which validates the fragility of *her* state of mind and her entrapment in the past. This provides the perfect transition to Bobby's fragile emotional state tacitly conveyed in his long silences and sudden rages. Through intimation rather than explanation, Mamet reveals the depth of Bobby's anguish in a single, disjunctive statement that, like Levene's allusion to his daughter in *Glengarry,* implies how much more pain remains unspoken. Coming from him, Bobby's expression of grief—"Oh, God, I get so *sad* sometimes, Jol. I can't, it seems, getting up from the *table . . .*"—yields one of the play's most poignant moments and anguished revelations (J 53).

Scene 3, which takes place on the following morning, sets up the scenario for Carl's departure for work and Bobby's for places unknown. Yet brother and sister cannot say goodbye. The play's briefest scene, it packs a powerful punch as Jolly's long-delayed narration of her nightmare has yet to be aired. Juxtaposing her memories of the intact world of her childhood before the divorce that has deeply scarred her with that of the nightmare, Mamet achieves a stunning contrast in images of exterior and interior space, of a protected world and an appalling one, of a life of connection and deception, of affection and enmity through which we make "the discovery," as Lawrence Langer writes, "that memory is not only a spring, flowing from the well of the past, but also a tomb, whose contents cling like withered ivy to the mind" (1991, 69). Whereas the two earlier scenes counterbalance Jolly's expressions of anger and outrageous invective, this scene is unrelentingly painful as we witness a woman for whom no amount of fictionalizing and romanticizing can render this picture anything but bleak. Like the world of values and cultural history to which Bobby and Joey retreat in their fantasies, Jolly, too, locates pleasure in the distant past, retrieving at will the world of her early childhood enriched by connection, ritual, observance, and love. When Jolly tempts Bobby, "We could go back" (J 61), the emblems associated with safety are to be found *way back* in a home imbued with love and tradition, both familial and cultural, an intactness that preceded a family fractured by divorce and de-Semitization and a childhood savaged by cruelty. In that idealized time "Dad would come home every night, and we would light candles on Friday, and we would do all those things, and all those things would be true and that's how we would grow up" (J 62). In short, in the ceremonies and rituals, the sights and the smells of the old neighborhood, Jolly finds a prescription for happiness and the pain of loss. While the pull of the past, especially cultural memory, is a source of strength in Mamet's domestic plays, it may well be that the remembered past is illusory, even trustworthy, and that Jolly's idealized home precludes her full engagement in her present reality.

In contrast, her recurring nightmare strips away the fantasy and thrusts her into the swirling world of disempowerment that she has struggled to escape. Revealing betrayal and the language of lie that gives life to it, Jolly's riveting narrative binds listener and audience to the nightmare vision: "I'm having this dream. How's *this* for dreams . . .?" she asks, drawing Bobby into the tale.

They're knocking at my door. . . . "Let me in," and I know that they want to kill me. . . . *Mother's* voice from just beyond the door: "Julia, Let Me In." "I will not let them hurt you. . . ." the

sweetest voice. "You are my child . . ." and it goes on. . . . "You
are my child. I *adore* you." . . . I open the door, this sweetest
voice, and there is *Mom*. . . . (*Pause)* And she wants to kill me.
(*Pause*). (64)

A stunningly dramatic moment, Jolly's matter-of-fact narration is a shocking conclusion to this play, which reminds us, "as Freud suggests," writes
Mamet, that "there is the *manifest* dream, the dream we remember, and . . .
the *latent* dream—the dream the manifest dream is intended to obscure, the
dream we would rather forget . . . which is too unsettling" (Mamet 1996f,
59). As emotionally wrenching as anything that Mamet has written, *Jolly* is
a deeply moving, complex work, which reveals that memory is a double-
edged legacy that both binds us to the past and shapes our lives.

In *Deeny*, the briefest, most circuitous, and subtlest segment of *The
Old Neighborhood*, Mamet dramatizes Bobby visiting his first great love
Deeny about whom he queried Joey in *The Disappearance of the Jews*.
Learning that she lives in Chicago, has been recently divorced, has inquired
about Bobby, and works in a local department store selling cosmetics,
Bobby apparently hopes to find something in this reunion. *Deeny* is in
essence a monologue, whose impression of a single voice is supported by the
laconism to which Bobby has retreated. Indeed, Bobby's responses are
principally monosyllabic and few in number in contrast to Deeny's stream
of consciousness. She speaks about her professional success, about a garden
she intends to grow but never plants, about early frosts, predictions, the
unhealthy aspects of cigarettes and coffee, smudge pots, and "the folly of
passion and the function of rituals" (Holmberg 1997a, 9). Buried under
layers of metaphor and understatement, Mamet has created, as it were, a
scene reminiscent of that between Dr. Astrov and Yelena in *Uncle Vanya* (a
play Mamet has translated), in which apparently nothing and everything is
communicated between two people.

"D," an affectionate term for Deeny, whose name comes up in myriad
contexts in *The Disappearance of the Jews* yet is never acknowledged in this
play, is a shorthand of former lovers. Having learned from Joey the Marshall
Fields department in which she works, Bobby, reunited by design or by
chance with those with whom he had close relationships before marrying,
decides to see Deeny. Whereas the depth of their relationship, in contrast to
that of Joey and Jolly, remains unspoken, its tangible impression of loss is
nonetheless felt. Typically, Mamet cuts directly to the scene of Bobby and
his former girlfriend sharing a cup of coffee (which, ironically she disparages
even as they drink it, making a joke of which she, too, is aware), leaving the
audience to draw its own conclusions about his and her motivation, the

seriousness of their former relationship, the wisdom of his seeing her in his emotional state, the price of an encounter that may further exacerbate his emotional distress, if only by setting him up for further disillusionment. Unlike the two earlier plays, however, Bobby and Deeny do not dredge up the history of their relationship or bicker about the facts of their separation. Neither do they reminisce. Yet, "the more she talks, the more we realize that nothing she's saying is tangential" (Siegel 1997, F4).

Juxtaposing the spiritual and the mundane, the "higher" things of ritual integral to the maturation of a young man with planting—both of which "force," as she puts it, new life—*Deeny* contains some of Mamet's most moving lyrical poetry. This representative exchange reveals the impact of Bobby's visit to the world of his youth, implicitly suggesting how distanced he and Deeny are from that time. But unlike his other reunions, Bobby listens attentively to her without apparent anger or angst. As she speaks about Oriental faiths, ritual, and change,[23] Deeny, like Joey, alludes to the subject of "spiritual practice." Finding her references to faith enigmatic, Bobby becomes lost in the maze of her ideas, which makes his attentiveness to her telling remark on loss, bereft of nuanced sentimentality, all the more remarkable: "It's just something somebody says is true. And you say, 'Yes. I'll believe that that's true.'. . . But having lost the feeling that things will right themselves. (*Pause.*) What? It becomes harder . . . " (D 10). Attuned to the fact that in his exceedingly vulnerable state he may not want to hear her clear-eyed vision of loss she hesitates but after she queries him three different times, she segues into a discussion of planting a garden that has more to do with why we act or fail to act, even on those decisions that we feel will bring pleasure and benefit. It is a beautiful interior monologue, but Bobby is lost in thought, or rather stuck on the one thought (as Joey was earlier on Laurie's statement) he has been pondering as she continues speaking: " . . . that things will not come right" (D 11).

In a different key he had expressed a similar view to his sister when Jolly inquired about whether he intended to return to his wife Laurie, revealing his distress that the impact of his decision to leave the marriage would be hardest on his children, just as he and Jolly have themselves endured the scarring experience of divorce. Despite its ostensible indirection, the power of Deeny's rambling speech is cumulatively effective, for at play's end it becomes apparent that her monologue is "futility spill[ing] out a stream of small talk for larger purpose: to awaken the affair, to reestablish a connection, to inspire new love" (Christiansen 1997). She, too, is needy, bitter, hopeful, resigned. And although it does not appear so at first glance, the seemingly nondirectional speech is both a protective stratagem against his anticipated rejection of her and a loosely constructed narrative that for a time holds his attention even if it does not rekindle love. Yet, "When the final goodbye comes," her "Goodbye, then, love," quite startling in its contrast to the meandering conversation, confirms a deep, first love that "tolls like a death knell. But with the parting, one feels not only sorrow, but also release, the release that comes with the possibility of rebirth" (Holmberg 1997b, 9) implied in those gardens waiting to be planted.

Hence, as Bobby leaves the woman he once loved and the old neighborhood, his time expired and quest concluded, one is left to wonder whether the lessons he has acquired from Deeny, a message of faith in the possibilities of life, together with those he acquired in his reunion with Joey and his sister, will cultivate healing and renew the ethnic ties sought in his return home. At play's end we are left to ponder the ethical exchange and the recognition that Bobby has achieved. To the playwright that exchange is "something very gentle. Perhaps it's on the order of one can't go home again, or perhaps not" (Holmberg 1997a, 8-9). In either case, Mamet does not send us out of the play uplifted by this reunion; rather, with a glimmering of hope we intuit that in returning home Bobby has found, as Michael Lerner has it, "a path to healing and transformation." For as the playwright has written in another context, "When something shines through . . . when you are *done* with it. . . . you see the sadness less" (1991a, 292).

Inspired by a story of the persecution and extermination of his mother's relatives in a forest during World War II, David Mamet's *Goldberg Street* is a minimalist gem—no longer than one scene of *The Disappearance of the Jews*—in which a father teaches his daughter about her ethnic identity, her history, and her responsibility as a Jew. In dismissing the play as "nearly cryptic," "utterly aporetic (*what* are they talking about?)," and "heartbreakingly moving," Tony Zinman reflects a common response to Mamet's minimalism (213). Conversely, while the stories themselves may be cryptic, the play is not.

"To be Jewish," Wiesel reminds us, "is to remember—to claim our right to memory as well as our duty to keep it alive. . . . For memory is a blessing. . . . creating bonds between present and past, between individuals and groups" (1990, 10). Analogous to the plays in *The Old Neighborhood*, this is principally a memory play, animated and informed, as are the others, by biography. What they are speaking about is education and ethical behavior, namely the responsibility of the older generation to teach the younger about a history of persecution, the moral imperative of religion founded on ethical principles, and the importance of each Jew's believing in and contributing to what Mamet describes as "the *excellence* [of] Jewish

Culture" (1989b, 9). And dominated by interrelated experiences that reveal the binding relationship of story, *Goldberg Street* manifestly illustrates Benjamin's premise that "*Memory* creates the train of tradition which passes from one generation to another" (98).

We overhear a seemingly aimless conversation between a Jewish man and his daughter in which he recounts through the medium of two complementary midrashic stories (resonant with cultural connotations) memories of two incidents of his youth, each of which occurred in the woods, that continue to haunt him in old age. One event apparently took place in Bregny, France, where he fought in World War II and where he remembers soldiers armed with semiautomatic weapons hunting "deer"; the other, when he and his unit were lost in the woods during training maneuvers in Arkansas. The former is an implicit reference to the brutality of "the hunters" whose persecution of Jews is tellingly chronicled in Martin Gilbert's *The Holocaust*.[24] Lynn Mamet recalls that she and her brother both have a distinct memory of a family remembrance of "a brace of trees into which the men [of her mother's family who remained in Poland] went and from which they did not return."[25]

The latter story is an overt example of anti-Semitic behavior directed against American Jewry. The father relates an incident that occurred when he was a young soldier. When his platoon became lost in the woods, he volunteered to use a compass to lead the group back to their base

> I said, well, I'd never *held* one. . . . but I supposed I . . . took it. Read it. Followed the map. Led us back to camp. . . . It was a joke. For anti-Semitism in the army. Then. Even now. . . . They scorned me, as I assume they did, for those skills they desired to possess. (33)

Because he had the survival skills, he was ridiculed; because he was wiser— or fool enough to volunteer in the army—he was awarded a Unit Citation.[26] "Reading a compass was easy enough," recalls the father, "if you just take away the thought of someone coming to help you (*Pause*)" (33). However, confronting the unit's anti-Semitic behavior exceeded his ability. Even with the passage of time, a period left intentionally vague by Mamet, the man is pained by the knowledge that he could read both the compass *and* their minds; and knowing they thought him "ludicrous," the soldier was nevertheless willing and "glad to go" (34), not unlike the children in *Jolly*, drawn into the games of the grownups.

While fertile, the metaphor of the compass as a navigational tool pointing toward magnetic north is a paradoxical one whose meaning becomes increasingly apparent throughout the play as the father points his daughter in the direction of ethnic pride. The term "north" in Jewish tradition, observes David Fass, is a richly symbolic one whose myriad interpretations depict it as the locus of the powers of the universe, the source of evil and destruction, the source of justice tempered by mercy, and "redemptive transformation" for the exiled Jew of the Diaspora (473). Therefore, although the father's thought is never verbalized in its entirety, his obsession with fixing his priorities and behavior, as if they were in disrepair, assumes the double meaning of fixing a point on a compass to find the way to the "pride *in myself*—for the alternative is to say that I am not a man, or that I am impotent or *stupid*" (32), in other words, the schlemiel (or "*schmuck,*" as Joey describes his impotence) who allowed himself to be mocked by other American soldiers in Arkansas. The lesson that the man wishes to teach his daughter is that one must have pride in oneself, belief in one's ability to influence the direction and actions that one takes, and responsibility for "those things where one *cannot* refer to someone" (32). Echoing the same idea in "The Decoration of Jewish Houses," Mamet exhorts Jews: "We are a beautiful people and a good people, and a magnificent and ancient history of thought and action lives in our literature *and lives in our blood*" (1989b, 13).

Creating a broader field of focus and thereby uniting recent journeys and events distanced by decades, the daughter encourages her father to relate the story of his returning to Europe sometime after the war. Lacking in precise details, his enigmatic narrative sketches a story of reunion and remembrance, which by all implications took place at or near the American Cemetery in Normandy, "right by the cliff" (34). "They remembered you. (*Pause*) They remembered what you'd done" (34), she immediately recognizes, but this memory, too, strikes a chord for the father, for it triggers a mythos that all this talk of old times has not altered: "Patton slapped that Jewish boy. They said . . . (*Pause*)" (34). Differing from several fictions in this short piece, for which the man has ample personal experience, this tale is drawn from common knowledge, though incomplete. In the absence of back story what is striking about the father's clipped phrase is that when he fought the majority of the "men" *were* all boys, as, presumably, was he. Even with the passage of time this anecdotal story triggers his memory; in the remembrance of things past, certain events and facts remain crystalline, "I knew they thought me ludicrous" (34) as vivid a humiliation as the Plaid Jacket or the fucking skis.

In fact, as the father correctly remembered, while touring military hospitals in Sicily in August 1943, General George S. Patton slapped and verbally abused two soldiers suffering from combat exhaustion, charging them with being cowardly shirkers, a coded term that had long attached itself to the Jew (Gilman 1991b, Hertzberg, Dinnerstein). Whereas the first incident may have gone unnoticed, in the latter incident, which occurred five days after the first, the soldier, responding to Patton's query about the nature of his ailment, said that he believed he was suffering from nerves. Patton slapped the soldier with his gloves, called him a "yellow bastard," and kicked him in the behind. Emerging from the tent, he was heard by correspondent Noel Monks to shout, "There's no such thing as shell shock. It's an invention of the Jews" (Knightley 320).[27] According to Martin Blumenson, the first reports of the incident in the American press failed to note that the soldier was of Jewish descent and that Patton had called him yellow-bellied or yellow-streaked Jew. Two weeks after the incident, the published story about the soldier being Jewish was retracted—he was, in fact, a member of the Nazarene Church—and Patton apologized publicly for his derogatory comments about Jews (791). Subsequently he claimed that his intention was merely to shock the soldiers out of their battle fatigue, but the event incurred the wrath of his superiors and nearly ended his career. The event has been mythologized among Jews as illustrative of the kind of anti-Semitic smear campaign to which Jewish soldiers were submitted which maligned their character and presumed cowardice under fire. Thus, long after the retraction, Jews maintained the belief that Patton's behavior was motivated by anti-Semitism. Hence the man's remark, "Patton slapped that Jewish boy. *They said* . . . *(Pause)*" (34, emphasis added), retains that element of doubt and renders proof that the event has evolved, like Chaplin's identity, into an intact mythos. The father double-backs to his purpose to impart some worthy lessons, instructing his daughter to remember her identity and to acknowledge it with pride. With the benefit of age and lucidity the father acknowledges, "They sent me for a joke. . . . Our shame is that we feel they're right *(Pause)*" (34).

Not unlike those of second-generation American Jews, Mamet's childhood was "expunged of any tradition. . . . The virtues expounded were not creative but remedial: let's stop being Jewish, let's stop being poor" (Lahr 1983, 476). In *Goldberg Street,* however, the virtues expounded are creative, namely the "fixing" of priorities alluded to by the father, such as the criticizing of Jewish self-hatred and the denouncing of anti-Semitic behavior. Thematically linked to *The Disappearance of the Jews, Goldberg Street* picks up the subjects of impotence, spiritual malaise, and anti-Semitism raised and dropped by Bobby and Joey in the first play of *The Old Neighborhood* and focuses attention on assuming the central responsibilities of the Jewish parent sounded in *Jolly:* teaching ethical conduct and performing timeless, sustaining ceremonies. Although the father may have received his citation many years ago for reading the compass correctly, it is only now that he has begun the journey toward redemptive transformation. Indeed, observes the father wisely, "But sometimes . . . (*Pause*) And sometimes, also—you must stand up for yourself. . . . At some point (1985, 31).

Although *The Disappearance of the Jews, Jolly,* and *Deeny* are self-contained works, *The Old Neighborhood,* is aggadic as well as elegiac. Comprising the rich tapestry that is American Jewish history, its threads link past to evolving present, a point signified by generations of grandparents, parents, and children situated on and offstage. By recasting *The Disappearance of the Jews* in a larger frame, Mamet's dramatization of Bobby Gould's return to his home in *The Old Neighborhood* acquires immediacy and the weight of history. Thus the trilogy, Mamet's first, merges the minimalism of *Goldberg Street* and the dazzling language that we identify as Mametic, its clear articulation of culture encompassing the double-bind of legacy as blessing and burden in a teaching moment that envisions an ethical contract between individuals within or outside the margins of family, both seminal and communal.

A WORLD APART

"The movies stand between the past and the future, between human history and human extinction."
— David Mamet, "Encased by Technology"

"We Jews are not painters. We cannot depict things statistically. We see them always in transition, as change. We are storytellers."
— Franz Kafka

AN AVID FAN OF THE MOVIES FOR MUCH OF HIS LIFE,[1] David Mamet was offered the opportunity to write his first screenplay, *The Postman Always Rings Twice* (1981), for Bob Rafelson, a fortuitous relationship that Mamet credits for his education in filmmaking and the opportunity that has launched a "second" career as screenwriter and director.[2] Since then Mamet has written more than a dozen screenplays including *The Verdict* (1982), for which he was nominated for an Academy Award; *House of Games* (1987); *The Untouchables* (1987); *Things Change* (1988) *We're No Angels* (1989); *Homicide* (1991); *The Edge* (formerly entitled *Bookworm*) (1997); and *The Spanish Prisoner* (1997); as well as filmscripts for his own plays such as *Glengarry Glen Ross* (1992), *Oleanna* (1994), and *American Buffalo* (1996).[3] The attraction to writing film, suggests Mamet, lies in the commonality between film and dream, from which we seek answers that "our conscious mind is [in]capable of supplying" (Billington 1989, 21).

Although these diverse films reveal the range of Mamet's work for the screen, I have selected three—*Things Change, Homicide,* and *The Edge*—as illustrative examples of screenplays whose tropological consistency with the body of his writing for the stage illustrates his multifaceted treatment of transformation myths in which he explores what he terms "the obsessive search for success. . . . [and] the abandonment of a sense of community and collective social goals" (Ranvaud 231). Exploring diverse genres, such as the fable and melodramatic thriller, these screenplays probe the mystery of legacy, friendship, and the paternal relationship, the pull of family and history, the seduction of power, prestige, and affiliation. Each entails a quest—an odyssey of discovery of self and Other—in which plot twists, false leads, feints, or a series of surprises—the very stuff of Mametic con artistry—are coupled with survival skills, high adventure, and the threat of exposure or death, disorienting characters and audience alike. Each pairs a couple, typically friends, partners, or competitors, within a larger family of associates (Mafia, police department, film crew) engaged in work, play, or a struggle to survive in which issues of loyalty are examined, the betrayal of self or Other dramatized, and ethical behavior compromised or affirmed. And each film foregrounds pedagogy, notable in myriad lessons, lectures, sages, guides, reference books, and the acquisition and untrustworthiness of knowledge. Similarly issues of identity—mistaken, ethnic, or assumed— reveal implicit or explicit ethnic tensions and loom large in these films in which embedded narrative not only calls attention to itself through the overt or implicit use of fairy tale (as in the case of "Cinderella" or Aesop's "Ant and the Grasshopper" in *Things Change* or Ojibway lore in *The Edge*), biblical story, or fable as structure and/or reverberant reference, it functions as a means of evoking cultural and personal history. In short, narrative creates frames of reference that anchor and destabilize meaning. Brimming with multivalent, mythical symbols, such as totemic objects, books, and compasses, or items imbued with long associations, like the ubiquitous photographs found in Mamet plays, each film is notable for its use of hermeneutic languages, be it kabbalistic, numerical, esoteric, or merely unfamiliar (Yiddish, Hebrew, Italian), and insider codes appropriate to a profession or organization.

Likewise, game-playing as structure and element of plot is a controlling figure in these films, much as it is in Mamet's stage plays and critically acclaimed film noir, *House of Games.* Writing specifically about game-playing in Alfred Hitchcock's films, Thomas M. Leitch's insights have broad relevance to Mamet's films.[4] "[G]ames," suggests Leitch, "provide a frame which contains, defines, or sharpens the suspense evoked by a genuinely threatening situation" or may serve as the controlling metaphor of the work relative to game-playing impulses, including solving the game, and games screenwriters play (8-10). Expanding upon Roger Caillois's theories of game-playing that comprise *agon*, competitive games; *alea*, games of chance; *mimicry*, role-playing and masquerade; and *ilinx*, games intended to disorient, Leitch contends that rather than function independently, these categories cohere in varying combinations in Hitchcock's cinema. Similarly central to Mamet's plays and films, where we note allusions to gin rummy, poker, casino, roulette, charades, and cryptograms, game-playing evokes complex concordances from which the audience derives pleasure "from having followed the director's lead" (18). Mamet's films, like Hitchcock's, "beguile audiences" enticing them to follow the action as "a move in the game" that surprises or disorients them, "encourag[ing] them to fall into misidentifications and misinterpretations which have specific moral and thematic force" (19). Leitch's argument that "Games are important because they help the audience to confront fears and desires" (31) closely parallels one that Mamet has proposed in "Radio Drama," namely that "The essential task of the drama (as of the fairy tale) is to offer a solution to a problem which is nonsusceptible to reason" (1987d, 13).

Viewed as a succession of moves in a game, Mamet's use of game-playing in film, like his use of the con in other genres, plays upon a premise that Pauline Kael has noted typifies Mamet's films, namely that "Mamet piles on improbabilities in a matter-of-fact style. . . . bring[ing] [the audience] into hip complicity with him. He gives people the impression that in making them wise to the actors' games he's making them wise to how the world works—that he's letting them in on life's dirty secrets" (128). That impression, however, is illusory. Aware that plot structure is pivotal to screenwriting—film being "a narrative medium"—Mamet is firmly against "putting narration into the movie" (Yakir 22). Rather, he "tell[s] the story in the cuts. . . . through a juxtaposition of images that are basically uninflected" (1991b, 2).[5] By put[ing] the audience in the same position as the protagonists: led forth by events, by the inevitability of the previous actions," Mamet "makes" them "wonder what's going on " (Yakir, 22; Mamet 1991b, 14). Or, as Arthur Magida succinctly puts it, "A Mamet film requires faith: Things are rarely what they seem. His works are exercises in metamorphosis. Or in illusions. Take your pick" (64).

Written with cartoonist and children's book author Shel Silverstein, *Things Change* (1988),[6] Mamet's second directing effort, filmed one year after *House of Games*, is a starkly different film that like much of his canon is "a tale of quiet personal revelations and bizarre shifts of fortune" (Strauss 25). "Essentially a heart warmer" (Kael 128),[7] in which a dignified Sicilian-born shoeshine man tempted by mobsters offering a sweetheart deal emerges unscathed through his integrity and strong ethical code, *Things Change* has been described by Mamet as "a fable . . . [whose] setting is mythic" (Strauss 25). As he told Ben Brantley, "I always loved gangster films because they were very virile. . . . They're about a guy who wants something and would do anything to get it" (38). However, denying that the film was intended "as any kind of comment on the Mafia," Mamet explains that he and Silverstein share a common heritage as Jewish Chicagoans, for whom "the idea of organised crime is part of the Chicago myth. . . . to which we [they] are entitled" (Billington 1989, 21).

Consistently he has explored issues of personal ethics, ethnicity and education in his plays and films, and *Things Change,* a deceptively slight film, is no exception. Here Mamet has struck upon a story that unifies these controlling tropes with techniques such as mistaken or assumed identity, mock criminality, secret codes, cons and cabals, subjects that he especially favors, spiced with a dash of the comic irony that typifies his work. His fondness for "codes"—such as "jargon, the secret symbols, the fraternal hailing signs" (1996a, 4),[8] and penchant for twisting a story and springing surprises on his characters and audience alike, in short, for perpetrating the con in his work and on his audience, is well known. In *Things Change,* however, Mamet plays with and against the double meaning of code as ethical behavior and insider language, uniting mythological elements and emblems of the fable with the American Jewish story, which as Nancy Haggard-Gilson observes, typically concerns itself with "impart[ing] a lesson . . . through a historical narrative," linking "generations otherwise separated by a gulf of experience," the construction of identity, particularly the use of secularized events to portray "Americanized" Jewish identity, and "the testing of morality and character under the weight of capitalism" (23-25).

Thematically linked to such Mamet works as *American Buffalo, Glengarry Glen Ross, A Life in the Theatre,* and *Speed-the Plow, Things Change* reveals a commonality between Mamet's theatre and film in which storytelling functions structurally; tradition, skill, and knowledge are highly valued; an object inspires myriad associations; a central metaphor, be it performance or gambling, shapes the action; and characters are tested in myriad ways. Moreover, the prominence of the mentor-protégé dynamic whereby "the older generation instructs the younger from the 'quality of its actions,'" as Dennis Carroll has it (80), is conspicuous in the film, reminding us that legacy, one of Mamet's persistent themes, is sharply opposed to the desire to belong at any cost, what Irving Howe characterized as typical American Jewish "urge to push in and to find one's place" (Desser and Friedman 65). As in the work of Jewish filmmakers such as Woody Allen and Mel Brooks,

Mamet's films rarely feature overtly Jewish characters, with the obvious exception of such films as *Homicide* and *The Edge*. Yet *Things Change* reflects a Jewish sensibility evidenced in its dramatization of marginality, focus on close familial relationships, treatment of history and memory, the foregrounding of show business—a key trope of American Jewish literature and cinema—and what David Desser and Lester D. Friedman term "Issues of social justice, personal freedom, and the right to express oneself" (32).[9] Unmistakable in Mamet's film is the figure of the outsider defined and distinguished by accented speech who repeatedly disguises himself to achieve status, acceptance or wealth. Likewise we recognize the schlemiel or bumbler who proves incompetent as criminal and philosopher, the rags-to-riches journey from alienation to acceptance, "be it geographic, personal, social, cultural, or psychic" (Baumgarten 8), and the motif of memory yoking cinema and culture.

Recalling Mamet's early and late stage work, issues of identity, loyalty, and acquisition of knowledge are central to this film. Hence, when Silver, a spokesperson for the Mafia don, Mr. Green, differentiates "public knowledge" from "insider knowledge" (1988b, 5), we are put on notice that only a select few "made men," or Chosen Ones, possess this knowledge, a fact that ironizes the "call" that Gino receives to play a role based solely on his appearance. Further, the premise that the proper application of knowledge and coded speech enable the outsider to enter the group is inextricably linked to the idea of recognition operative throughout the film—the term "friend" literally the coin of the realm—whether that recognition is of a person, idea, or code, be it cultural or ritualistic, just as "landsmen" are literally people from the same country.[10] Thus, in foregrounding the performative dimension in *Things Change,* Mamet humorously juggles the antithetic "summons" from a higher power to perform ethically and the Jew's exchange of identity for acceptance.

Like much of his later work for the stage and the screen, this film is an odyssey of self-discovery shaped by memory in which issues of legacy, family, and ethical behavior are questioned, challenged, and threatened. As in much of American Jewish narrative, particularly that of second generation Jews, *Things Change* is flooded with memory. Fittingly, the opening shot merges memory with talisman. A coin sitting on a worn leather photo album is removed by an unseen hand, and the book is opened to reveal its secrets. A melodic tune evokes the contemplative mood, establishes a contrast between New and Old World, and strikes the right cord of duality—of dream and reality, country and urban setting. In fact, the mandolin's tune, "gives way to the train's metallic screech" (Brewer 69), clearly situating *Things Change* within the urban environment of Chicago, the paradigmatic setting for Mamet urbanals. Just as abruptly, memory cedes to the intrusive presence of Silver and Frankie, a pair of mafiosi—spokesperson and muscle—who have followed Gino, a shoemaker, into his place of business. Silver delivers a cryptic, compelling and canned message: "A friend of ours would like to speak with you this evening" (4), the subtleties of which turn on the phrase "a friend of ours," Mafia code for a "made man" as opposed to a friend (of mine), an individual for whom one vouches, though the message, like the messengers, are a mystery to the shoemaker. Together with a calling card and the inducement of a hundred-dollar bill, Silver leaves the shoeshine man perplexed but convinced of a summons by an unseen authority, a pattern replayed by emissaries of Don Vincent, who subsequently but similarly visit Gino in his suite at the Galaxy Hotel in Lake Tahoe with the intent to inspire compliance with authority.

When Gino appears later that night at Green's mansion toting his shoeshine box, Mamet provides us with a bit of insider knowledge: Green, whose name may be read as an ironic Americanization of "greenhorn," Silver, to whom Mamet has given his own maternal name,[11] their dead friend Aaronberg, and the Mafia don's "friend" Plesetska, a well-placed and implicitly corrupt judge in the Twenty-eighth District, share a common Russian-Polish ethnicity. Yet Green is neither poor, Yiddish-speaking, unsophisticated, or apparently Jewish. He has "passed" into mainstream America, finding opportunity in a world of crime.[12] As Green's representative, Silver opens negotiations with Gino by outlining in a narrative frame the facts of a case in which "a friend of ours has been mistakenly identified" as a murderer (5). Sketching out the details of a contract, Silver maintains that to the individual who would trade his identity for another for whom he would "pass," Green is prepared to pay for each year of incarceration. Speaking for Green "with a practiced monologue easily mistaken for earnestness, he displays," suggests Brewer, "no knowledge of the corrupt ironies his clichés rest upon," namely "that justice is served by purchasing a murderer" (70). However, when Silver presents the offer as a business proposition—"scapegoat assumption of guilt for the price of Gino's dream"(71)—rather than a humane dilemma to which he can relate, Gino's face is uncomprehending. Rich in legalisms—murder, sentence, crime, and injustice—Silver's speech establishes one of the film's recurring themes, the pursuit of justice, whose subsequent references, such as "getting off probation" (13), "slapped your wrist (17), and "We're in some very. deep. shit" (52) when spoken by members of a crime family and their underlings or "criminals" Jerry and Gino contribute to the delicious ironic tone of the film.

Sensing that a psychological approach, akin to one used by Ricky Roma with James Lingk in *Glengarry Glen Ross,* may be more efficacious,

Green assumes control of the negotiations, attempting to tap into the shoeshine man's hidden desires and henceforth conclude the deal: "You must have a dream . . . do you have a dream?" Gino concedes, "A boat" (6). However, when the "son of a bitch immigrant" neither respects him by agreeing to the terms of the deal,[13] nor fears him, Green, perturbed by Gino's independence, for which he is singularly unprepared, accustomed as he is to boot-licking underlings, and annoyed by the need to secure a replacement for Gino, unleashes a tirade of bigotry, hatred, and disdain that insults the outsider by speaking about him as if he were not present:

> A man comes into my house. What does he want? I tell him, whatever you want. Says buy me a boat. Fine. I'll buy him a pushcart. I'll buy him an organ and a monkey and he can put a bandanna on his head. Son of a bitch immigrant said he wants a boat. I'll give him a boat.[14]

Drawing direct attention to the ethnicity of the ungrateful outsider, Green's reference to the Jew as a peddler and showman is unmistakable, one that Mamet has used to describe himself: "I am a showman. . . . I'm a peddler too . . ." (Lovell 7D). Framing marginality as a key motif in the film, Mamet shapes this fable about assumed identity in counterpoint, much as Woody Allen does in *Sleeper*, juxtaposing "self-image and self-deception . . . aspirations and actualities" (Desser and Friedman 50), revealing that Gino's chosen independence, like his decision not to trade his identity or ethics, has its rewards and its price.

Once Gino fails to play the victim in Green's drama, the latter drops the congenial tone he has adapted to con him into accepting the deal. He starts barking orders, "let's go, boy" (8), but the shoeshine man, distracted by the presence of Miss Bates, whose name is a play on the confidence man's code, "Mister Bates" (Mamet 1996a, 5), is seduced by her sexuality and aloofness. Grabbing the opportunity to "play" the gentleman rather than the immigrant, Gino literally rises to light her cigarette, but she, noting his dirty hands and nails, rebuffs him. Pained by her "withering look" Gino blurts out, "I do it" (8). Seizing the moment and trading the future on his own terms, ostensibly for the intangible pleasures that money can buy, he reveals he is seduced by the "dream" of wealth, akin to what Desser and Friedman, writing about Mel Brooks's *Young Frankenstein*—another film of alienation-assimilation—characterize as "something of a Jewish fantasy, even wish fulfillment, to exchange some mental power for sexual enhancement" (136).

From the outset the outsider or little man in *Things Change* is excluded from established, acceptable modes of behavior by coded language and gestures that deny his reality and identity. Once Gino agrees to the deal, he undergoes an initiation process that assures his future compliance and celebrates his indoctrination into the conspiracy. The scene evokes a ceremony of manhood during which Gino is elevated from his marginal status as a "boy" to an associate in the club. Conducting the ritual, Green first extends a Sicilian coin to Gino, which he places in the latter's hand saying, "'A big man knows the value of a small coin'" (9), an aphorism that is not merely a secret code used among Mafia members but, given Green's recent reference to Gino, an enigmatic one. To complete the ceremony, informed by an amalgam of codes, crime, and coins, Gino is told to sign the confession and to pick up the gun in order to place his fingerprints on it, orders with which he complies, after which Green drinks with Gino, the consummation of their transaction reminiscent of Levene's dream deal in *Glengarry*.

With variations, the same scene is replayed in the kitchen of Green's mansion, where Jerry, one of Green's gangsters who has fallen out of favor, has been banished, the butt of the other mafiosi's jokes that mock his demotion, marginal status, and impending expulsion. Denied his identity, salary, and masculinity, Jerry is seen washing dishes outfitted in a woman's apron, the emasculated male barely recognizable to the others for whom he is an individual with "No pay, no pals, no prospects" (11), his superior's deprecatory reference recalling Green's to Gino. However, when Silver requests an individual to prepare Gino for his court performance, providing a credible link between the two outsiders, one an alien and the other a bumbler banished to the kitchen, Frankie appropriately assigns Jerry to the task of watching Gino, thus uniting the wiseman and the wiseguy. Jerry views the assignment as his ticket out of the kitchen and onto the "home" team, but unwittingly, Frankie's reverberant reference to him as Cinderella anticipates Jerry's and Gino's ensuing conversion, announces the film's fabulous enactment of the classic transformational rags to riches tale, and engages us in their odyssey of discovery and assertion of independence. Once the two are literally and figuratively driven out of Green's compound and deposited at a shabby hotel, we understand that Gino and Jerry are locked out "without contacts and connection, in rootless isolation" (Brewer 73)—the quintessential pose of the Diaspora Jew—an image that is subsequently mocked once they trade the squalor and imprisonment imposed on them for their fantastic journey to Lake Tahoe and the Galaxy Hotel's Criterion Floor. There Gino, like the protagonist of Woody Allen's *Zelig*, who "evolves into a celebrity solely due to his ability to emulate" (Desser and Friedman 62), is smothered by individuals seeking to effect connections.

After a brief time spent in rehearsal, Gino proves to be "a quick, adroit study of his role as criminal [and] Jerry . . . an efficient line coach" (Brewer 73); however, the latter is far more skilled at playwriting—scripting the scenes that permit each to achieve his dream, if only temporarily. Echoing *Waiting for Godot,* Jerry offers Gino a number of things to do "while waiting," but his range is clearly limited by previous assignments as hustler or panderer. Although he offers Gino "a couple of *broads. . . . tickets* to something," which he thinks is surely preferable entertainment for someone "going to jail for ten years" (14-15), Gino hesitantly requests "Could we maybe. . . . take a walk by the beach?" (15). Instead of the "walk by the beach," Jerry offers Gino a deal he cannot refuse: a walk on the wild side, a magic ride to Lake Tahoe where they experience the true meaning of power, pleasure, and performance, echoing gambler Mike Mancuso's travel plans to Las Vegas to enjoy gaming, gambling, and women in Mamet's film noir, *House of Games.* "In any really intense friendship," Mamet has told Dennis Carroll, "one looks for the precipitating event" (81), "those moments—those images—[that] can make a film go" (Goldstein 27). And Jerry's harebrained idea, which bonds them in adventure, danger, and friendship, leaves little doubt that their loyalty to one another is forged here. Or as Gino aptly puts it when he plays a game of chance, "We partners, whatever happen . . ." (31).

Casting off their former selves, buddies Jerry and Gino travel to Lake Tahoe for a weekend of fun and frolic, and in so doing offer Mamet and Silverstein a panoply of situations, principally through the device of a play within the film (the embedded narrative with which Mamet is particularly enamored) to stage the dilemma and hilarity of assumed identity introduced earlier at Green's mansion. As outsider and bumbler step off the plane into a fantasy world of private jets and pristine forests, a conflation of pleasure and potential peril await them. Although Jerry, "playing the moment" in the role of boss, reminds Gino that he alone is in control while they are under cover—"And when I say it, out here, *do* it" (16)—he has apparently given little thought to masking their identities other than adopting a low profile, but when challenged by Billy, a gangster in the employ of the local don whom he knows from previous gambling junkets, about his having "had to Stay After School"(17)—a prime example of Mamet characters, about whom Jeanette Malkin has observed, "speak only in clichés"[15]—Jerry literally creates identities for Gino and himself out of thin air, cloaking Gino in mystery to enhance his own status: "Babe, this is the guy, *behind* the guy, *behind* the guy . . ." (19).

Since Jerry has failed to anticipate the practical aspects of his plan, Billy takes charge, delivers the two to the "company" hotel, and arranges for premier accommodations on the Criterion Floor, where Randy—pun intended—extends to the two impostors every conceivable service of the hotel—financial, legal, secretarial, gastronomic, and sybaritic. Assuring Jerry that he "completely understand[s]" their position (23), Randy's prepared speech is a marvel of understatement, given that they are just beginning to comprehend the breadth of their artifice themselves, as evidenced by Gino's "voyage of discovery" (24) around the magnificent duplex suite complete with Roman sauna.

Pampered, coiffed, and dressed to kill, Gino, distinguished in a dark suit and white shirt, his nails now buffed clean and giving no hint of his social class, and Jerry in the parodic mafioso ensemble of a gray suit, black shirt, and tie,[16] having acquired the costumes, and in Gino's case, the stage name Mr. Johnson, to go with his new role—with its intended sexual innuendo and allusion to Brooks's myriad "Johnsons" in his *Blazing Saddles* (1974), similarly set in the mythical West—enter the Galaxy's casino for a night of gaming.[17] This scene gives Jerry the occasion to act the part of instructor, teaching Gino the finer points of playing roulette—"you got *black*, you got *red*, you got *numbers* . . ." (31), and the opportunity to play godfather by staging a deception in which "Mr. Johnson" would "win 'a little'" at the tables (30). Entering into a "contract" with the assistant manager to return Gino's winnings to the house, Jerry quickly loses control of his scheme, not unlike his idea to gamble on their lives by going to Lake Tahoe for the weekend, when Gino, momentarily unsupervised by Jerry, wins $35,000. To avert disaster, Jerry strikes just the right tone in appealing to Gino's sense of honor; the scene is a marvel of minimalism as Gino, enjoying his fifteen seconds of fame, gambles and loses his "winnings" on the Wheel of Fortune. Taking in a revue, featuring Jewish comic Jackie Shore, whose routine, a hodgepodge of overworked witticisms, stale one-liners and "wife" jokes in the tradition of Jewish comics Shecky Greene, Alan King, Buddy Hackett, and Henny Youngman, foregrounds the place of performance and show business in American Jewish life and film and plausibly creates the circumstances by which the little man and the schlemiel win at love. A master of ceremonies and local outsider, Jackie serves as go-between, agent, and procurer in his own right, introducing showgirls Cherry and Grace to Gino and Jerry.

The pivotal scene is staged in the Roman tub of Gino and Jerry's suite, complete with togas, champagne, and the nymphs Cherry and Grace. It is at once a parody of the sexual fantasy of Jewish men replete with the sexually alluring *shiksas* that typify American Jewish films and literature, a nod to Brooks's classic scene at Caesar's Palace in his *History of the World, Part One,* complete with Vestal Virgins, and a realistic opportunity for the laconic Gino to reveal both the power of narrative and his recondite wisdom.[18] In a scene that marvelously opposes the profound and the profane in song, story and image, foreshadows Gino's future, and wordlessly evokes the film's central theme, the rewards and price of trading one's identity, the wise storyteller recounts an abbreviated Mametic version of Aesop's tale, "The Ant and the Grasshopper," in which the grasshopper "beholden to the pleasure principle," as Bruno Bettelheim puts it, and having failed to provide for his own survival, "he eat-a the ant" (44). Hence the embedded narrative at once entertains and anticipates that "nothing but doom awaits" (43).[19]

The duality of the material and spiritual at play in *Things Change,* elegantly enhanced by overlaying realistic events, places, objects with deeper associations (like the knife, photograph, and blanket in *The Cryptogram*), and cluster images of water, nymphs, gaming, mythical symbols, and highly charged numbers culminate in Mamet's variant of the Aesop fable, presenting an auspicious opportunity to consider the mythical and archetypal structure characteristic of legends and folk tales.[20] One way to approach the film is to read it as a navigational myth in which the journey, alternately depicted as flying, dreaming, and traveling (by boat, plane, or limousine), an activity emphasized by the allusion to tickets lost and found, a pass, and a furlough, is "never merely a passage through space, but, an urgent desire for discovery and change" (Cirlot 164-65), or as Gino puts it, "Hey, if everyone knew everything, there wouldn't be no school, eh?" (48). From this perspective, suggests J. E. Cirlot, studying, inquiring, and "seek[ing] . . . to live with intensity through new and profound experiences are all modes of travelling," given that "the true Journey is neither acquiescence nor escape— it is evolution" (164-65), as *The Cryptogram* movingly illustrated.

In this context, the phrase "things change," whether used by Gino or Frankie, each of whom adheres to sharply different codes of behavior, bespeaks an altered state, whether a figure of confidence or consequence. Both the film and the embedded fantasy turn on a series of dualities—old man and youth, tradition and boldness, justice and intuition—that are themselves archetypal. Although the screenplay is rich in symbolic allusions, those that cohere around the figure of Gino are revelatory, especially images of water and the activity of fishing, notably Jerry's spin on their predicament that Gino will be the bait, and Gino's hilarious and fortuitous "fishing" for the key to the getaway car and the coin that save their lives. Aligned to the activity of fishing is the literal and mythic evocation of bodies of water— Lake Michigan, Lake Tahoe, the Roman bath, a walk on the beach—that propel the plot given the mythic coupling of water and intuitive wisdom (Cirlot 365-66), which may be understood as "extracting the unconscious

elements from deep-lying sources" (108). Likewise star, symbolic of the
spirit, "nearly always alludes to multiplicity [as Mamet will make abundantly clear in *Homicide*], and the forces of the spirit struggling against the forces
of darkness" (309), are evidenced in the name of the Galaxy, the fairy-tale
hotel in which Gino's fantasy is realized.

With the appearance of two mafiosi who summon Gino and Jerry to
appear for lunch at the hunting lodge of Don Vincent, proving once again
that both are responsive to orders issued by representatives of a higher
authority, it appears that the fairy tale has come to a screeching end.
Paralleling the earlier scenes at Don Green's, the action is split between the
public spaces and the kitchen, where Jerry and the audience overhear
preparations for the evening's festivities—a gathering of national dons
complete with a gift-bearing ceremony as propitiation to Don Vincent—
and observe the action between Don Vincent and Gino. Characteristically
Mamet undermines our presumptions and Jerry's fears of gloom and doom
through a classic Mametic trick employed in such works as *Prairie du Chien*
(1985b), where brutal violence is played out in narrative. Similarly, in the
kitchen of Don Vincent's hunting lodge, Harry Hardware's story of "the
swing-shift broad. . . . Used to go out with whatsisname . . . the big guy . .
." (55) holds Billy Drake, whom we have previously seen at the Galaxy
arranging for Gino and Jerry's luxurious accommodations acting on his
instincts and Jerry's cues that Gino was a Sicilician don, in rapt attention.
What makes the snippet of a story so intriguing is its subject of betrayal and
the lurid facts of two-timing—"She's hiding the sausage with both of
them"—and graphically depicted violent death.[21]

However, at this moment in the film when we anticipate the
exposure and fear the death of Gino, the story of betrayal and brutal
stabbing, (Chekhovian in its juxtaposition of intimate narrative and
public setting), coupled with the typically Jewish paradigm of the fusion
of the profane and mundane prominent in Mamet's plays, lend it power,
as does the fictive form that permits the free range of imagined violence,
both enacted and foreshadowed. Related among dirty dishes and dinner
preparations, the profane tale stands out among the mundane events,
framing the ensuing discussion between Don Vincent and Gino. As the
former attempts to ascertain both the intent (presumably malevolent) and
the identity of his guest, "whatisname," Kenny, his second, glides behind
Gino, dagger drawn, ready to deal with the anticipated betrayal forthwith.
Threatened with exposure, expulsion, or death, Gino, perceptive but
laconic, offers a series of responses to Don Vincent's progressively pointed
questions about his identity and purpose: "Do you see what I mean? What
brings you here. . . . What brings you to this occasion? (57). His questions

underscore the pursuit of knowledge that plays a key role in Mamet's work. Sensing danger but having no idea how to protect himself, Gino *"fiddles nervously"* with the Sicilian coin, and *"as if throwing him a cue,"* Don Vincent turns his attention from Gino to the coin. And his guest, a consummate performer, does not fail to perform his line, the memorized, coded expression, "'A Big Man Knows the Value of a Small Coin'" (57), which suffices to save his life. Welcoming him to the inner circle, Don Vincent, echoing the phrase used by Don Green, "It's always good to make a new friend . . ." (57), wordlessly triggers our memory of the earlier scene at Green's mansion, where Gino sold his freedom for acceptance—here extended to a higher level of affiliation. Yet the Mametic screenplay (and film) not only inverts our expectations in the scene enacted at Don Vincent's hunting lodge through its portrayal of a Mafia don with a heart, it ironically gives truth to Jerry's earlier observation that "everybody likes you when you're somebody else" (51).

Although Gino wins acceptance by playing a role to perfection, that is, by displaying his possession of coins and knowledge of codes (an act that the don matches by revealing his tattoo, affirming he is a marked member of the tribe), he endears himself to Don Vincent by remaining true to the individual that he is. Gino's lack of pretense coupled with his wisdom and sensitivity to the burdens of responsibility and their physical effects on the don's health inspire Don Vincent to extend the hospitality of his home, to let down his guard, and to give Gino a gift of a "lucky quarter" whose value will be divulged when Gino's life is once again threatened. Mirroring and mocking the toast at Don Green's house earlier in the film in which Green and Gino sealed their contract, Gino knowingly toasts Don Vincent in Sicilian, the power of a traditional phrase opening the don's heart to the stranger. "I haven't heard that in thirty-five years," replies the Don *"feelingly"* (58), a wry reminder that whereas Gino bet thirty-five thousand dollars at the Wheel of Fortune and lost the gamble, here the payoff, the recognition of Gino as a landsman, is an unexpected, delicious windfall.

Friends from the Old Country in spirit if not in actuality, and ostensibly of common ethnicity and tradition, a fact punctuated by their smashing their grappa glasses into the fireplace, the two leave others to question, "What are they? Friends from the *Old* country?" (63).[22] Typically the screenplay tells the story in the cuts, keeping its own secrets. Hence when the two are relaxing on the beach, skipping stones together like young boys, Gino, seduced by the allure of affiliation, appears sufficiently secure in the don's acceptance of him that he playfully sets a wager, challenges the don, wins the point with his goodness and sagacity, and gives Mamet ample liege to extend the gaming trope humorously within the context of Gino's gambling on his life.

That the pressures of office are understood by Gino, and that he intuits Don Vincent's failing strength, even depression, occasions the wonderful attempt at humor, a change of subject, a subtle expression of caring expressed by the gesture of his splitting a cigarette between the two men, and his spare speech: "You tired, Don Giuseppe. . . .You alright. (*Beat*). You trust an old man . . ." (59). "Gino's uniform," observes David Denby, "is silence, which is perceived by the hoods as the reticence of power"(102). Yet the don's knowing smile and the little man's lighting a cigarette to be shared between the don and himself in a coded expression of their friendship, has broader significance in underscoring the dichotomy between the earlier scene at Don Green's when Miss Bates's repulsion inspired Gino to sell his future. Typically, Mamet sets the two incidents in counterpoint, expecting the audience will draw its own conclusion in the cut to Gino's reaction to the fulfillment of his fantasy.

As the dons gather at Don Vincent's, Jerry, aware that Don Green's imminent arrival poses a direct threat to their lives given that he can expose Jerry's and Gino's actual identities, searches frantically throughout the don's mansion for Gino, his action furthering the prevailing trope of pursuit set in motion from the opening beats of the film when Silver and Frankie sought out Gino. His attempt to save them both is nearly foiled when Gino, patting his pockets, discovers that he has left his lucky coin in the room, a gesture and discovery that parallels Jerry's on the previous day when he remembers that the airline tickets were in the pocket of his old clothes. Both symbols of passport, one a ticket home, the other a ticket to safety, are essential to the resolution of the story. When Gino returns to the room, his identity is nearly revealed by Miss Bates. Ever the pragmatist and survivor, Gino grabs the Smokey the Bear hat sitting on one of the mounted antlers on the wall, in effect pulling off a "hat trick" that permits him, despite imminent threat, to avoid detection and escape unscathed. But his sense of honor and knowledge of the codes of hospitality forbid him from stealing away like a thief, although his "sense of sadness, of longing, of wishing that the myth was indeed true" (Desser and Friedman 132-33) is so strong that he exposes himself to danger in the process. However great the temptation "to assimilate to the culture," Gino, the figure of the outsider, possesses the "outsider's intellect [that] recognizes the hollowness" at the center of this fantasy (132-33).

Once Jerry and Gino effect a miraculous escape from the hunting lodge and heavily guarded compound, Gino, who must now confront the inescapable reality of his impending imprisonment, attempts to induce Jerry, who he wisely perceives has intimate knowledge of the experience, to prepare him for the role of convict as he mentally prepares himself for his impending incarceration. Mamet chooses the quintessential Beckettian locale in which to explore the depth and complexity of their friendship. It is evening, a country road, a night full of stars, two men. "Tell me about it," Gino asks, and Jerry, clearly uncomfortable in the role of educator, quickly summarizes the information in a nutshell, and, in his inimitable manner concludes, "the time passes by very quickly"(81). When Gino repeats his words, ". . . It goes by quickly . . ." (81), Jerry, struck by his own disingenuousness and the hollowness of his falsehood and platitudes, begins to prevaricate. His hesitations coupled with fabrications reveal an increasingly difficult effort to put a positive spin on prison life, which he fears Gino will not survive.

Thus, as Gino and Jerry respond to the reality, to their separation, and the depth of their friendship, each in his own way attempts to color the facts to assure the other, in short, creating a fantasy to eclipse the harsh truth. Sensing Jerry's discomfort, as he previously intuited Don Vincent's poor health, Gino's version of the story, which skips incarceration altogether, is even shorter and more sanguine than Jerry's, the pedagogical moment underscoring the value that Gino places on learning, friendship, and shared memory. Progressively, as the beats or pauses in their speech expose, even the striving to sustain their connection through dialogue, inspired by allusions to the past or future, proves arduous:[23] Thus, although both play along with the game, shoring up memory, speech itself becomes too difficult, undercutting Gino's fantasy and revealing it as such.

Returning to the shabby hotel to enter the final phase prior to Gino's court appearance, Jerry blurts out, "We got almost five hours. (*Beat.*) Whaddaya want to do . . .? Naaaaa . . ." (83), reminding us that the last time Jerry starting thinking about what to do while waiting he hatched a getaway plan. And we can almost hear the wheels turning as Jerry, without the inspiration he formerly had in the way of a photo advertisement of a Lake Tahoe revue, begins to devise and implement his plan. While it lacks the panache and pleasure of their Roman holiday, it grows more and more justifiable and feasible, to Jerry at least, the more he works himself up to it: "DON'T GO! . . . . You walk. . . . Who's going to find you? . . . Who's going to *look* for you? Go on. Go on! . . . " (83-85). Attempting unsuccessfully to employ logic to challenge Gino's sense of honor, he rails at the deal: "This is not a *deal*," with its implied meaning of fairness. "It's a *hustle* . . . they *hustled* you" (84), he concludes, reactivating the gaming idiom employed throughout the film.

As escape plans go, this one, like his former escapades, lacks prescience, creativity, and credibility but nonetheless reveals that though he is no great thinker, Jerry's heart is in the right place. Frustrated by Gino's tenacity, he physically ejects him from the room, in effect locking him out of compliance with the deal. In a wonderful treatment of the classic Beckettian line "Let's go" (*They do not move*), Gino's knock at the door demanding entrance effectively communicates by his presence that he's "tied" to this place, to his contract, and to an ethical code of behavior. For him, past pleasure and present obligation are mutually exclusive, and as if speaking to a student, Gino distinguishes the finer points of difference between the world of fantasy and reality, between the behavior to which we hold others and that to which we must hold ourselves. Notably, Gino begins his "lesson" by drawing upon memory and those emblems of class, conviviality, and personal recognition that he especially values: "*Jerry,* we had a good time in Lake Tahoe, eh? We drink the champagne, with the *girls,* Guy on the Stage, says 'Mr. Johnson, take a bow'" (85). Whereas Jerry is troubled by the injustice of Gino's deal with Green, given his fear—or foreknowledge—of the Mafia's notorious abrogation of contracts, to Gino whether "they" keep or break their word has no bearing on his own actions: "What they do no matter. I give *my* word," a point so important that he reiterates it (85).

Slipping into the aforementioned bathroom, Gino emerges a changed man dressed for another part, having trimmed his mustache and donned a costume (the gray coat that has hung in the hotel room for three days). Thus he appears to be the man in the photograph that Silver showed him at Green's mansion whose identity he has contracted to assume. With the surprise arrival of Frankie, however, the crime family's intent is obvious, Green having seen fit to send only the muscle. Flanked by Jerry and Frankie, as if going to an execution rather than to court (the sly allusion to the concluding scene of *The Trial* inescapable), Gino and the mafisosi walk through the streets of Chicago, Gino slightly out in front, where he has metaphorically and ethically always been. More talkative than the older man, who has stoically resigned himself to prison, Jerry's interrogative rhythms, "Where we goin?. . . what's going on?" challenge Frankie, speak to his unease,[24] and underscore the purpose of interrogatories throughout this film—and Mamet's body of work—to test knowledge, ethics, and identity. Ironically, it falls to Jerry to defend Gino and the contract that he has so recently deplored. "He knows his stuff. He's going to keep his word . . ." (90).

Now as they approach the beach, Frankie spins out *his* tale, a variant of the events that reveals that the deal was a confidence game from the first to justify Gino's "suicide." Bluffing, Jerry first protests and then resorts to screaming, "You sonofabitch! What the . . . who *are* you, all of you. . . . You set the guy up, *promise* him this. . . . The guy does it, he stands *up.* . . . You're going to turn around and *kill* him?" (91). With his inimitable talent for simplifying complexities—the crucial equation in Mamet being "you promised/you lied"—Jerry both grasps the facts of the case and misses his participation in it. Ethical behavior from the Jewish perspective, as Mamet has dramatized in previous stage and screenplays, is predicated on one's responsibility to *and* for another. Thus it is of less surprise to the audience than to Jerry, who clearly has more to learn, that the issue of where his loyalties lie falls to him, Gino's choice having long been made. The typifying Mametic technique of linguistic counterpoint, one that differentiates between the inclusiveness of "us" and the exclusion of "them" illustrated through the subtle but pervasive use of "they" and "you" and "us," draws us sharply back to the central issues of marginality and personal responsibility. Reanimating the pedagogical focus of the film, Frankie's specific instructions to Jerry, "*You're* gonna kill him. . . . You shoot him right above the eye. You put the gun in his hand, let it fall. . . . You got two minutes," brook no objection, question, aversion, or scruples.

For Jerry, it is time to perform, to assume the responsibilities and actions of a man, to follow commandments to the letter of the law. Reluctant to play the role of villain—the man with the gun—he is literally shoved onstage by Frankie, who watches his act to grade his performance under pressure, standing ready to perform his role if Jerry flounders. However, when Jerry approaches Gino, words and courage fail him. The shoeshine man, recognizing the scarf-wrapped gun and Jerry's dilemma, as he formerly recognized both danger and opportunity, holds firm to his ethical position, in effect, making Jerry's choice an impossible one. And it is on Gino that Jerry displaces his fear and frustration with an unjust world, as he had earlier in the morning when Gino had failed to "follow orders" to flee. Angrily he explodes, "Didn't I tell you to *run?* I *told* you to run" (92). His meaning is transparent: if Gino had acted according to the lines and stage directions Jerry had written, the latter would be absolved of playing the part of the Chosen One and committing the dishonorable act against one whom he has characterized as a "stand-up guy."

Jerry's two minutes having elapsed, Frankie approaches him, and though torn by conflicting loyalties, Jerry chooses life, however temporary, aligning himself with Gino's exemplary example of ethical behavior. Lacking the keys to the car, the means to escape violence in the urban jungle as they formerly did when hotly pursued in the forest, Gino goes "fishing" in his pockets and comes up with the fly-fishing box, the lucky quarter, and Don Vincent's phone number: "I only got, all I got . . ." (93), he begins, but his resourcefulness and goodness speaks for itself. Having knowledge and the wisdom to use it, an intact moral code, the talismanic coin, and the don's phone number, Gino is empowered.[25] The film thus validates his morality and tenacity, ironically recalling Teach's protestations when tested by Don on his preparedness for the heist that something always turns up, or in his inimitable phrase, "We're seeing when we get there" (1976, 50).

The film's final scenes in a courtroom and the shoeshine shop present twists and turns in the narrative that are both surprising and credible, requiring the audience to supply the back story that Mamet and Silverstein omit, content to tell the story in the cuts. In both scenes we observe a reversal of fortune and a change of clothes or coats that complete the tale through typical Mametic sleight of hand. In the former, Frankie is punished to the full extent of the law for having botched Gino's murder, "functioning," as Brewer notes, as "scapegoat *for* the scapegoat" (89), the quintessential role of the Jew, though I doubt Brewer perceives Mamet and Silverstein's irreverence as such. Announced early and affirmed late, justice, a key trope of American Jewish literature that typifies Mamet's body of work, is implicit in the film's final shot opening on what appears to be Sicily: "*The sea. White houses. A fishing boat.* However, when "[*a] hand reaches through the picture and comes back with a shoeshine rag*" (95), *Things Change* comes full circle, exposing the hand that opened the photo album in the opening shot of the film. Now this rendering of Gino's dream life is in full view in the shop, an overt reminder of who he was and is, an emblem of pride in himself and his heritage. One last twist of the story surprises: the presence of Jerry, whose shoes Gino polishes, and who, hidden behind a newspaper, wears the apron of a shoeshine man he has traded for one worn in Green's kitchen. Together they present a vital picture of connectedness, confirming that in fable, if not reality, the act of sharing skill, pride, knowledge, and love unifies the figurative father and son.

Despite appearances, *Things Change* is no mere confection but a wry and avowedly wicked treatment of Chosenness. From the initial call to Gino to trade his identity for that of a murderer, his uniqueness for the allure of belonging, and to Jerry, tempted by the call's implicit message of position and privilege, "Hey Cinderella . . . comeere" (12) both have heeded the call to perform myriad roles, only to discover that the call to responsibility and commandment supersedes all others. Back in the shoeshine shop, the proverbial flip of the coin, both are a long way from the Roman baths. But Jerry who is "too stupid, and finally too decent, to be a criminal" (Denby 102), and was never cut out for a life of crime,[26] finding a place in a family where all that is required to prove oneself is a strong code of ethical behavior, and the wisdom to know that "The shine comes from underneath" (48), a conclusion that reminds us that the transformation myth, Cinderella, "isn't a simple progression from rags to riches, as we often presume . . . but to greater riches" (Gould 23).

• • •

Homicide, David Mamet's third movie as writer and director, is possibly his most transparent, depicting a self-hating, self-deluding, and self-destructive American Jew, a stranger to other Jews and to the Jew in himself. Set in the shadowy world of crime, conspiracy and cabals, *Homicide,*[27] inspired by Mamet's cousin Edward Mamet, a captain in the New York City Police Department, is a police melodrama that portrays a contentious world of ethnic hatred, cultural ignorance, and confused loyalties. Taking up the complicated questions of ethnicity, identity, and integrity, treated in a lighter vein in *Things Change,* Mamet is unflinching in *Homicide* in investigating what it means to belong to race and place. Through a circuitous journey that opposes the search for a wanted criminal with the desire for home, Mamet heightens awareness of the powerful association and discourse that conjoin "place and personal identity" with "the figures of belonging and exile" (Chaudhuri xii, 12). The film explores this powerful association in ways that illumine the idea of home, depicted in its various, contradictory permutations, as a marker of identity and the site of tension between the self and other. In other words, observes Una Chaudhuri, "The home as house (and, behind it, the home as homeland) is the site of a claim to affiliation" (12).

Hence Elie Wiesel's provocative essay, "The Stranger in the Bible," which casts light on the mystifying questions "WHO IS A STRANGER?" and "What is a stranger?" as perceived by the Jew, is especially valuable. For the Jew, suggests Wiesel, questions of identity and locality are persistent and profound, "pertinent and poignant. No elaborations are necessary. Since our beginnings, with rare exceptions, we have been considered strangers" (1990, 55). The Bible, he observes, employs three terms for stranger: *ger, nochri,* and *zar.* Connoting legal and geographical relationships to the Jew, the *ger* is indicative of movement toward the Jew, the *nochri,* alienation from the Jew; *zar,* the least respected category of stranger, is reserved only for the Jew, "the Jew who remains a stranger to other Jews—and to the Jew in himself" (67). Perceived as the eternal stranger, Amalek, the *zar* engenders hostility because he "knows our weakness and—perhaps—is our weakness" (70).

The protagonist of *Homicide,* Detective Robert Gold, a Jew in name only—a *zar*—is a highly decorated homicide detective on a big city police force. He has repressed his Jewishness but remains defenseless in the face of anti-Semitism from non-Jews and reverse anti-Semitism—rejection of Gold by Jews—because he isn't sufficiently Jewish. If he were a "real" Jew instead of an assimilated one, we are led to believe, he would be cognizant of Jewish history and would understand that the threat against Jews never ends. In short, "To the non-cops he's a cop, but to the cops he's a Jew" (Mamet qtd. in Brunette 21). Thus, as Vincent Canby observes, the vicious verbal exchange with a black superior officer who calls Gold a "kike" early in the film is notable not only because "These sorts of outbursts have probably happened before but . . . for what happens later" (1991, 56).

Originally adapted from William Caunitz's novel, *Suspects,* as a police action thriller (Brunette 21)—"a buddy film. . . . Action, blood, a social theme" comparable to Charlie Fox's dream project in *Speed-the-Plow*—the final screenplay, rejected by Orion largely because it was "too Jewish,"[28] bears little resemblance to the novel but much to Mamet's plays and two earlier films. The language is quintessential Mamet, the setting a generic Mamet city, the plot—a nexus of two racially charged cases—characteristically clever and compellingly crafted, the story disturbing and unsettling, the comedy wicked and satiric. A mesmerizing thriller, "a fast-paced, nitty gritty police action and . . . [a] deeper psychological drama about ethnicity," *Homicide* "plays like a house afire, consuming Bobby Gold in a desperate search for his Jewish soul" (VerMeulen 1; Ansen 70). But lest one think that Mamet is dabbling with the Jewish aspect of this script, Joe Mantegna, longtime Mamet collaborator who portrays Detective Gold, whose efforts to be both a good cop and what he thinks is a good Jew entrap him in a tragic moral bind, likens the playwright's treatment of Jewishness to his use of obscenity:[29] "He's made the central character a Jew, and he really deals with it, not the way Hollywood would normally do it, you know, let's make this guy a Jew and have him put on a yarmulke halfway through and go to Passover dinner" (Brunette 13, 21).[30] No yarmulke-wearing, seder-attending Jew for Mamet, whose essays, such as "The Decoration of Jewish Houses"(1989b), "A Plain Brown Wrapper"(1989b), and "Minority Rights" (1996a), address his own Jewishness with growing pride, anger, and a profound sense of loss. For Mamet authenticity may be summed up in one telling sentence: "I don't know what a Jewish home looks like" (1989b, 14).

Dislocation or homelessness is not a new theme in Mamet's work. It pervades his entire canon. Eschewing "the home as the *loci* of spectacle," Mamet's theatre spaces, in stark contrast to those of American playwrights such as Arthur Miller, Eugene O'Neill, Edward Albee, and Tennessee Williams, are repeatedly urban places of work—parodic or proxy homes.[31]Aside from the obvious exceptions of *Reunion, The Cryptogram,* and *The Old Neighborhood* (in *Jolly*), Mamet situates his characters (i.e., in *Lakeboat, The Woods, A Life in the Theatre,* or *Bobby Gould in Hell*) outside the home. However, the absence of and search for home in *Homicide* is unique in Mamet's work where marginality, specifically the homelessness and exile of the American Jew, informs both the subject and structure, mirroring the experience of the deracinated playwright and that of his friends "who grew up in reformed Judaism . . . [and] didn't feel sufficiently either Jewish or American which is much the position that Gold in this movie finds himself" (Mamet qtd. in Brunette 21). Having traded his identity for an "assumed" one, that of an assimilated, whitewashed Jew, Gold has deluded himself into believing that his denial of self and heritage has bought him greater acceptance in the police family. As a hostage negotiator, a go-between aptly poised between two worlds—"The Orator" as partner Tim Sullivan calls him—Gold is a figure of alterity whom L. S. Dembo describes in another context as a "Monological Jew," one, who though severed from monotheism, "still feels himself to a be a Jew—and not yet a Jew," having literally "replace[d] a lost ethical reality . . . a theological order with a linguistic one" (4). Moreover, his "gift of gab" and paradigmatic Jewish capacity for empathy, "two of the most indelible of all the traditional Jewish markers" underscore that Gold has "not 'passed' entirely into that 'greater world' of the cops" (Horn 20).

The opening scenes of this film firmly situate Gold "at home," however imperfect, in the workplace of a police station, the locus of his primary loyalty. A victim of unseemly questions about his loyalty by a black assistant to the Deputy Assistant Mayor, unwarranted anti-Semitic verbal abuse by a superior officer, and unexpected and unprovoked attack by a violent prisoner named Grounder who has murdered his family, Gold believes—or maintains the illusion—that fellow officers are his family and he theirs. Characterized as a professional, courageous, ethical, intelligent, and highly regarded team player, Gold not only enjoys the camaraderie of fellow officers, he benefits from their instinctive defense of him, his Jewish identity "largely a reaction to the antisemitic (and homophobic) stereotype of Jewish men's effeminacy that his colleagues brandish" (Streicker 49) counterposed by his boldness in the face of danger evinced in his always opting to be "the first one through the door" (1992b, 45).

"Homes," as Leitch postulates, have numerous "thematic associations" that the director of a suspense thriller "routinely trades on: the safety of a place of shelter or refuge, the stability and security of longstanding assumptions, the basis for self-definition through family relations and a genetic sense of identity." Concurrently, "home is a ludic topos . . . a place like home in games of baseball and Parcheesi, a final goal the pleasurable lack of which makes play possible" (25). Paralleling Hitchcock's uses of home, Mamet's protagonist has devised a plan from the "git go" to bring "home" Randolph, the murderer of two cops, who has eluded the FBI for two years and continues to threaten the safety of the city. "It's a fucken walk," he tells Sullivan. "You want this Randolph, we go down ta the gym, he's not there, we get Sims, we tail him, we nail him, we turn him over, we shake him, he gives us Randolph" (14). However, on the verge of persuading

Sims to reveal the whereabouts of Randolph, Sullivan and Gold are separated by an order from "downtown" (recalling the downtown bosses in *Glengarry*), reassigning Gold to the homicide investigation of Mrs. Klein, an old Jewish shopkeeper, on the basis of his ethnicity and his having stopped at the site of the crime to assist an officer in distress on his way to Beal's Gym to question Sims. Despite his protests ("What am I, a fucken Jumping Bean?"), he is informed that Dr. Klein, the son of the murdered woman and a man of considerable influence, has specifically requested him because "you were there, you're his 'people'" (41, 40). Hence, although the detective "catches" the candy-store case, Gold maintains contact with the "home team." And, if Mamet's plot, like Hitchcock's, "subverts" the idea of home by pulling the hero/protagonist out of a safe haven, "even undermining the notion that a secure identity can be based on one's ties to one's home" (Leitch 25), the confluence of past and present reality communicated through his character's compulsive inquiry engages our interest as a potent figure of unsettled and unsettling conflicts.

Through just such a plot device Mamet deftly juxtaposes Gold's figurative and literal home on the police force with the home of a rich Jewish family grieving the death of Mrs. Klein. Contrasted with the profanity and cacophony of the police station, the Klein household, shrouded in mourning, is strangely quiet. It is a home rich in tradition, signified by a magnificent menorah and Sabbath candlesticks in full view;[32] in material wealth, evidenced by the expensive furnishings; in love witnessed by the outpouring of affection at the death of Mrs. Klein; and in memories substantiated by the *shiva* call of friend and fellow freedom-fighter, Benjamin, and photographs of a youthful Mrs. Klein taken decades before in Israel and America. Gold, though Jewish, is "odd man out," linguistically excluded by their use of Yiddish, which he does not understand, and emotionally removed from these people by his self-hatred. The detective's anti-Jewish sentiment is further aroused by the doctor's questioning of his professional performance coupled with the threat of repercussions (recalling the impact of the slur "kike," which burned in his consciousness long after it was expressed by a mayoral assistant), further alienating a Gold still bitter at being cut out of the big bust.

His vicious and virulent anti-Semitism is apparent in a one-sided telephone conversation with Sullivan, with whom he attempts to solidify his familial relationship with the "home base," to keep abreast of the "flash" case, and to separate himself from these Jews: ". . . You should see this fucken room (*Pause*) . . . . Not . . . 'my' people, baby . . . *Fuck* 'em, there's so much anti-Semitism, last four thousand years, they must be doin *something* bring it about. I'll see you at the house half hour" (60-61),[33] his remarks reminiscent of the race hatred voiced by Bobby Gould's gentile wife in *The Old Neighborhood*.[34] Thus Mamet continuously weaves both plots through Sullivan's unheard news that Randolph's "old lady" agreed to give up her son, the plan that Gold set in motion before he was derailed by this "candy store pop" (79),[35] and the detective's derogatory comments, ostensibly blaming the wealthy Jewish family for the old Jewish lady's death. In fact, as in *American Buffalo* and *Glengarry,* the audience "confirms" the content of their conversation by the detective's enthusiastic and contemptuous responses to Sullivan's remarks: "Fanfuckin*tastic*. . . . Some bullshit, somebody's taking 'shots' at them. . . . *Fuck* 'em" (61).

Gold's Judeopathy (anti-Jewish resentment of success) does not go unheard by Miss Klein,[36] the dead woman's granddaughter, crying quietly on the couch in her father's study, who rivets attention back to the quintessential figure of home: "Do you belong nowhere . . . ? (*Beat*)" (63). Prismatic, the question of what it means to belong to race and place hangs in the air. Chastened by Miss Klein's criticism and cognizant that no words will compensate for his shameful lack of respect in the house of the dead, Gold promises as propitiation to find Mrs. Klein's killer. The stunningly effective moment is ironic, given that Gold has distinguished himself as a cop by "his (crypto-Jewish) linguistic skill" that, as J. Hoberman rightly observes, is "only a trick for the goyim" (15). In fact, the blacks and Irish cops with whom Gold works, the criminals who he tracks, and the victims he encounters are more conscious of his ethnicity than he. In unifying the racially charged plots through recurrent ethnic slurs like Sullivan's remarks, the ghetto boy's remark that he intended to get "that *fortune*. . . . in the old Jew Lady['s]" basement (1990, 142), and the patrolmen's presumption that Mrs. Klein's presence in the ghetto fosters violence, *Homicide,* as numerous critics notice, is "flamingly current . . . its incendiary collision between blacks and ethnic whites on an urban battleground" (Carr 33), a veritable "cauldron of contempt" pitting "black against white, Jew against non-Jew, Jew against Jew" (Magida 64).

The quest for Randolph and the search for Mrs. Klein's murderer thus set in motion entails a modern-day quest for information that leads logically to the question one is encouraged to ask of the screenwriter and director: Why now? Mamet's *On Directing Film* offers an illuminating, provocative response: "Why does the story start now? Why does Oedipus have to find out who his parents are? This is a trick question." Rather, as Mamet notes, "His simple quest for external information led him on a journey which resulted in his discovery. . . . that he's the guy" (1991b, 79, 95). Similarly, Gold's search for the elusive Randolph and murderer of Mrs. Klein entails a modern-day quest that takes him on a literal and metaphoric journey resulting in his discovery of his identity, his family, and his home. But Gold is not nearly as committed or as focused as Oedipus. Mamet presents him with a characteristic dilemma of divided loyalty between professional obligation and Jewish identity illustrated by his division of time and attention between the gripping police chase and the case imposed on him by rich, influential Jews, a "doubleness of vision. . . . between assimilationist impulses and ancestral allegiances" crucial to our understanding of American Jewry (Whitfield 1984, 2). To tell the story of divided loyalty and self-discovery, Mamet's complex screenplay brilliantly synthesizes and deliberately obscures two paradigmatic spiritual quests: that of Sophocles' *Oedipus*, "intelligible," Francis Fergusson reminds us, "as a murder mystery," and Kabbalah, Jewish mysticism, whose secretive nature is no less mysterious. The "peculiar virtue of Sophocles' presentation of the myth," suggests Fergusson, "is that it preserves the ultimate mystery," arranging plot so that "we see the action as if it were illumined from many sides at once" (17), or what a talmudic scholar would term "three sides to every question." By starting the screenplay near the end of the story, as does Sophocles Oedipus's quest, Mamet reveals Gold's past and present, to use Fergusson's term, "in each other's light," so that the quest for the murderer of Mrs. Klein becomes a quest for the hidden reality of his own past. In a demythification of Oedipus, whom Fergusson views as a district attorney who "convicts himself" (16), Mamet demotes Gold to a detective who accumulates clues but is his himself part of the riddle, at once trapped by the cabal and his own fear. To this end, Mamet portrays him as progressing in his investigation of a conspiracy perpetrated against the Jews at whom shots *are* fired, while simultaneously depicting him as duped by yet another conspiracy.

Significantly, both Oedipus and Gold seek answers to the mystery that elude them from a seer—or in the case of Gold, the Judaic equivalent, a chasidic scholar, underscoring the ethical and pedagogical focus of the screenplay. Whereas Tiresias shrinks from the vision that he sees, informing Oedipus, "I will tell you nothing" (24), a Jewish librarian and a chasid studying in the library, appear far more cooperative in assisting Gold to piece together clues—the enigmatic term GROFAZ, a list of names found in Mrs. Klein's basement, and an anti-Zionist poster taped to the storekeeper's door—into a coherent, composite picture. Linking the historical past and current events (a Judaic motif conspicuous in Mamet's work) the librarian tells Gold that GROFAZ was a little known acronym for Hilter used at the end of World War II by the *Sonderkommando* assigned to the extermination of the Jews. Yet, when pressed by the detective for information on this term in connection with contemporary anti-Semitic acts, she blocks the inquiry.[37] Similarly, mystery is evoked and enhanced by the chasid, who draws Gold deeper into Kabbalah, a mystical journey toward the divine characterized by symbolic descriptions of creation and revelation, numerical permutation, and the belief that "true" truth is concealed.[38] While seemingly unconnected to Gold's quest the scholar's exegesis on the differences between the pentagram, the five-pointed badge that Gold wears, and the hexagram, the six-pointed Mogen David symbolizing Judaism, is essential to Gold's quest but eludes the detective. The reasons are many and critically important.

Set in a library, rich in its metaphoric and religious allusions and the promise of knowledge, the film's central scene, uniting ethical, ethnic, and pedagogical tropes, reveals a side of Gold seen neither at the police station nor at Klein's household. Like other Mamet teachers (Bobby Gould and Karen in *Speed-the-Plow* come immediately to mind), the chasid painstakingly guides the student and audience through unfamiliar territory, repeatedly asking Gold, "You see?" to ascertain his level of comprehension (90). Through explication of myriad symbols and stories that define Judaism, the scholar illumines their concealed meaning, and as we progressively come to understand them, so we better judge the extent of Gold's profound ignorance and puzzlement. Initially, the chasid links the secular and the spiritual quests for knowledge through an exegesis of the five-pointed and six-pointed stars. During the period of Emancipation of the Jews in the nineteenth century, the hexagram, "already hallowed by tradition," came to be a "kind of holy symbol for the Jews that the Cross and the Crescent are for other faiths" (Scholem 1971, 279). The chasid's interpretation of the symbolic significance of the Mogen David, moreover, links kabbalist symbolism with that of the brilliant twentieth-century philosopher Franz Rosenzweig, who aligned its interlocking stars with the Jew's relationship to God.[39] Thus when the chasid's explanation eludes Detective Gold, the scholar illustrates Rosenzweig's theory graphically by separating and intersecting two paper triangles, at once reminding both Gold and the audience of Gold's previous—and immediate—identification of Mrs. Klein as a Jew by just such a six-pointed star worn around her neck.

Explanation of the symbolic significance of stars leads associatively to the story of Esther, whose name we are told is derived from star, and to which the scholar refers Gold, having established the detective's ethnicity by direct inquiry: "You're Jewish . . . ? Are you Jewish?" (90). Unable to read Hebrew, however, absolutely basic to the study of Torah—which may be read for its simplest meaning, allusion, inference, and secrets—and Kabbalah, from which it derives, Gold cannot know that "When [the Torah] enters the soul, light comes with it. . . . Even more it is truly firelike" (Epstein 26). Lacking this illumination, Gold remains in the dark: he can neither decipher the story of Esther (also known as the *Purimspiel)*, and its inherent numerology nor understand its pertinence and parallels to his professional and personal quests. What remains hidden in the passage, then, is that Esther had two names, one that was Hebrew, Hadassah, and the other Persian, adopted to hide her Jewishness when she married Ahasuerus, King of Persia. Later, when Haman, a direct descendent of Amalek and prime minister to the King, becomes convinced that the large, flourishing Diaspora Jewish population is disloyal and plotting to take over the world—the paradigmatic conspiracy theory of Jewish world domination—he persuades Ahasuerus to issue an edict for the extermination of all the Jews of the empire. Esther, on the advice of her cousin Mordecai, who proudly affirmed his Jewishness, endangers her own life to intercede for her people. The Book of Esther, then, is an "awe-inspiring fairytale," a parable of ethnic hatred and redemption (Wiesel 1991, 133).[40] "Instead of soothing our fears . . . with its seeming simplicity" it serves as a wake-up call (135). But since Gold, a "historical cretin," to borrow Cynthia Ozick's phrase, knows nothing of his Jewish history, he cannot apply its lessons to his investigation and his life.

Ignorant of Kabbalah as well, Gold would not know that the Hebrew language has two alphabets: one revealed, one hidden. Nor would he know that the secrets of Hebrew words may be deciphered from the cumulative sum of the numerical value of each letter known as Gematryia. Nor would he know that specific numbers, such as two, five, seven (the numbers that comprise Gold's name), thirteen, thirty-six, twenty-two, and eighteen, for instance, have profound significance (Blech 159). Taking his cue from the mystics, Mamet compounds the mystery that surrounds Gold's quest for information about Mrs. Klein's murder—and by extension his quest to belong at any cost—by continually employing coded languages, among them a numerical one, throughout the screenplay to bridge Gold's secular and spiritual search. Hence Gold's duality is mirrored in the number two appearing in the margin of the sheaf of paper that the chasid offers to Gold containing the Book of Esther that suggests Esther's hidden and revealed identities.

Notably, the number two reverberates throughout this film, mirrored in two families, two cases, two stars, two meanings of the term badge (a symbol that Gold wears and a six-pointed badge that Jews were forced to wear), two languages, two cops killed by Randolph, two shots fired on the Klein's apartment. We notice two photographs of a youthful Mrs. Klein (one concealed), two meanings for the term 212 (a police code and the name of a clandestine Jewish organization), two explanations for the term GROFAZ, two times that Chava serves as a translator for Gold, the partnership of Gold and Sullivan, and Gold's dual loyalties. Moreover, two is repeatedly emblazoned on the walls of the basement in the climactic scene between Gold and Randolph as Gold, hunting for the man who murdered his partner, shadowboxes with his double. Two is also the number of perspectives that Mamet provides of key scenes: two views of Gold's relationship to his police family at the beginning and end of the film; two meetings with Benjamin, two with Chava in the diner, two inspections of Klein's variety store, two searches of two basements, two cops pinned down, and two explosions. Linking the secular and spiritual worlds, two is the numerical value of the second letter of the Hebrew alphabet, *bet*, which signifies house and home. Ignorant of all the secrets of Hebrew words, of the mystical connotation of numbers, of Torah, of Kabbalah, and of his history, Gold is a mystery to the chasid, who wonders: "You say you're a Jew and you can't read Hebrew? What *are* you then . . . ?" (91). His question hangs in the silence, underscoring once again Gold's cultural and linguistic exclusion.

Literally left holding the book whose passages and numerology he cannot decipher, Gold follows the only clues he knows how to follow, the address of 212 Humboldt Street left intentionally in full view to lead him to the cabal. Although he goes of his own volition and is received as an unexpected, unwelcome intruder, the setup at the library leads Gold to 212 as surely as if he had received a calling card like that left by Silver and Frankie in *Things Change*. In fact, the ensuing scene bears remarkable similarity to an early scene in that film in which Gino, an immigrant summoned to appear at Green's heavily guarded compound, is offered a deal intended to protect one of the clan that would require that Gino accept responsibility for a crime he did not commit in exchange for something he desires. When he declines, he is maliciously maligned but then impetuously accepts. "I do it," he says, buying into the fantasy world signified by a young woman, at which point the elaborate con/contract is certified by intricate ceremonies and explicit responsibilities to which this ethical individual adheres. Similarly, Detective Gold is also lured to 212, a gated schoolhouse heavily guarded with armed bodyguards and attack dogs. This scene is also delimited by the presence of a stranger, a persuasive stratagem exerted by a powerful man intent on protecting one of their tribe, and a deal offered and then sweetened by a bribe intended to appeal to Gold's desires and vulnerabilities. However, *Homicide* opposes two individuals who signify the power of higher authority: Gold as that of a police officer, and Benjamin's as the apparent leader of a cell of militant Israelis, who locates his authority in the State of Israel and, by extension, God. That the edifice is an abandoned schoolhouse is not without ambiguity and significance, given that Benjamin adopts a tutelary position, an artifice that fosters his scheme. The negotiation, moreover, posits a sweetheart deal with all the trappings of a one-time offer: the exchange of one valuable item for an intangible benefit—logged evidence for the promise of affiliation for the crypto-Jew.

Initially, Gold is silenced and excluded as he was at the Klein household and the library by a language barrier, spoken Hebrew, the language of Israel, of Torah, and of men. Not only is the use of Hebrew authentic, but as Streicker observes, in eschewing Yiddish (*mamaloshen,* the language of the home and women), these militants insinuate that they are a force to be reckoned with, "tough Jews" empowered "to defend home and people" (53 n. 10).[41] However, the silver-tongued Benjamin, who ironically mirrors Gold's role on the police force as a "pacifying, arbitrating influence," negotiating and effecting betrayal (Brewer 148), switches to English in an effort to have Gold's search for Mrs. Klein's murderer serve his ends—that is, by encouraging Gold to turn over the list of names found in her basement. Inviting Gold to sit down—in other words, to make himself "at home"—Benjamin advances the intimacy by proffering food. Paralleling Miss Klein, Dr. Klein, and the chasid, the negotiator finds the right key in appealing to Gold's sense of pride and loyalty. Extolling Mrs. Klein as a hero, not a gunrunner, he further suggests that other friends of Israel, "Good Americans. Good Jews"—no doubt Gold himself—may work for the good of Israel. "You . . . you are such a *man,*" he tells him; "You'd like . . . to fight. For your home" (98-99).

Home now takes on a strikingly different perspective in Mamet's film. Neither the imperfect, marginal home of the police force nor the alien home of his "Yids," the home to which Benjamin refers is a literal and spiritual home: Zion, the homeland of Israel. Caught in the horns of a dilemma in which so many Mamet characters find themselves stranded, Gold is told he will be figuratively welcomed "home" if he surrenders an original, logged piece of evidence—the list of names found in Mrs. Klein's basement—and literally thrown out if he does not. Motivated by a burning passion to prove his worth as a Jew while maintaining his oath as a police officer, Gold is forced to choose between his loyalty to the police force that has been his home, and Judaism, which has not. Benjamin hopes to inspire or coerce the irresolute, spineless officer by spelling out his name in Hebrew, a pedagogical technique employed formerly by Mamet in *Marranos* when the grandfather sought to influence his crypto-Jewish grandson to forswear his allegiance to Catholicism in favor of his ethnic heritage.

Unsuccessful, he switches tactics, resorting to lecturing and shaming Gold into action with the clear lesson that the adult Jew in name must also be a Jew in deed. While this is of course a first principle of ethical behavior and of Jewish belief that Mamet has dramatized throughout his canon,

Benjamin here engages in sharp practice to serve his own ends. Echoing and twisting Miss Klein's challenge to the detective in an earlier scene, he challenges Gold: "Are you a Jew, Mr. Gold?. . . Then be a Jew! (100-101), in effect reminding him that to be called by one's (Hebrew) name is to be called to (covenanted) obligation. As he previously disgusted the chasid by his ignorance, Gold infuriates Benjamin by his lack of commitment. "WHERE ARE YOUR LOYALTIES?" the Israeli demands. "You want the Glory, you want the *Home,* you are willing to do nothing . . . " (101). Despite his previous assertion, "I would do anything" (99), Gold, a sworn officer of the court, is unwilling to do the *only* thing requested of him. His refusal to provide the list prompts Benjamin to question Gold's Jewishness; in short, "being a Jew becomes coterminous with obeying an authority that claims to speak in the name of Jewish interests" (Streicker 54). Speaking for his group (what Streiker characterizes a "deified identity"), he exploits Gold's need, guilt, and shame. Benjamin, in fact, manifests the power of mind-control organizations who abuse their position as the voice of higher authority (as Mamet stages in *Speed-the-Plow* and *Oleanna*), demand allegiance as the price of entry, and "offer a great boon: They allay anxiety, the sickness of the age" (Mamet 1996a, 164).

Gold's hesitation is sufficient cause to arouse Benjamin's disgust, his return to speaking in Hebrew thus effectively rejecting Gold linguistically even as he instructs others to eject him physically. Benjamin's question, "WHERE ARE YOUR LOYALTIES," primary in every Mamet play, is paramount in this screenplay, reminding one of Ozick's succinct definition of a Jew: "Being a Jew is something more than being an alienated marginal sensibility with kinky hair. Simply: to be Jew is to be covenanted; or, if not committed so far, to be at least aware of the possibility of becoming covenanted; or, at the very minimum, to be aware of the Covenant itself" (123). Yet in the parting threat to Gold, "don't bother to return" (101), Mamet takes full advantage of the double meaning of the phrase, as in returning to place and *teshuva,* to return, which in Jewish belief signifies a Jew's enlightenment to error, and manifestly altered behavior.

Expelled from 212 and motivated by Benjamin's lessons, which triggered raw need, Gold chases after Chava, whom he has previously met at the Klein's home, in an attempt to "be Chava," a committed and courageous defender of Israel. Chava, whose Hebrew name reflects the growing tendency by Israelis to adopt Hebrew names, the revival of the Hebrew language, and the establishment of the state of Israel, is in fact the oldest of Hebrew names (Gen. 3:20). Also spelled Hava or Hadassah, as in the portion of Esther that Gold could not understand, is the name of Eve, "the mother of all living" (Kaganoff 57; 77-90). Doubly suggestive of the potential for Gold's new spiritual life and Eve's biblical role in advancing intellectual and spiritual awareness, Chava, whose name means life and may be viewed as the feminine principle of deity, ignites a redemptive illumination in Gold. Although he does not know the ancient history of the Jewish people symbolized by the story of Esther, with its concomitant elements of Hamanism, persecution, courage, survival, and retribution, or the modern history of Israeli freedom-fighters like Mrs. Klein whose courage assured and assure the survival of modern-day Israel, Gold nonetheless is consumed by a desire to be part of history in the making. Simply put, Benjamin's question burns in his consciousness, just as the defamatory slur "little kike" infuriated him earlier in the film. Approaching Chava as she exists 212, hard upon Benjamin's rejection, Gold offers his help in "What you're doing tonight" (102), a variant of Gino's "I do it," with the distinct difference that he does not accept blame for another's crime but commits himself to initiate his own deed. In his delayed acceptance of Benjamin's "bribe," Gold has effectively bought into the faulty premise that his shot at Jewishness is a one-time offer available only on the terms set forth by the militant leader, one that draws him deeper into the con and brings destruction in its wake.

The detective is evasive where Benjamin was direct, but the audience correctly concludes that a conversation between Chava and Gold ensues out of earshot (a recurrent pattern in Mamet's stage and screenplays in which the story is told in the cuts), continuing in the diner with Gold's response to Chava's (unheard) query regarding the motivation for his terrorist activity:

> Gold: What can I tell you about it. They said . . . I was a *pussy*. .
>   . . a pussy, because I was a Jew. Onna' cops, they'd say,
>   send a Jew, mizewell send a *broad* on the job, send a *broad*
>   through the door . . . All my goddamned life, and I
>   listened to it. . . . I was the donkey. I was the "clown". . .
> Chava: you were the Outsider.
> Gold: . . . yes . . . (103)[42]

In a moment sparked by emotional release and spiritual quest, Gold shows signs of repentance, a turning toward covenant. His is the ecstasy, the rapture of Return. In what is possibly the most intimate and moving moment in the screenplay, Mamet simultaneously builds upon Gold's growing knowledge of himself as an Outsider as he reinforces the film's central, mystical image of home. Juxtaposed with the reality of the "fucken Donkey" that plagues Gold is the dream of what it must be like "To have your own country." "I'm gone so much of the time," replies Chava wistfully.

"But I think about it" (104). Gold's response, a wordless nod of comprehension, speaks volumes.

Unbeknownst to him, Chava is the critical linchpin in both Gold's search for knowledge about the "conspiracy" and the cabal's plot to manipulate Gold by trust or by guilt to relinquish the list of names. In a classic Mamet con she dissuades Gold from participating in the destruction of Andersen's Model Train Store, whose back room serves as a print shop generating neo-Nazi hate propaganda. Wrestling the explosives from her, Gold declares his intent to do the deed. Though stunned and nauseated by what he sees—a Nazi flag, a picture of a soldier firing on a mother and child (a classic photo of the Holocaust), and boxes of hate literature—we do not miss Mamet's touch of genius in this scene: literally hundreds of miniature toy trains symbolizing real cattle cars for which Gold's is an act of redemption and (re)dedication. As a reflection of his identification and rage, and to underscore this moment, Gold seizes a train and smashes a miniature train station, a microcosmic remembrance of Nazi death camps, soldiers, and boxcars, just prior to placing the explosive device on the printing press.[43] In one symbolic act, Gold torches the toy shop and ignites the divine spark within him. Concealed in his action, however, is the fact that the militant Israelis, believing that their goals justify their violent means and manipulation of the detective's need, guilt, and shame, have sacrificed Gold for the larger good.

At the diner, Gold is exhilarated by his act, but the moment is evanescent. With the arrival of members of 212, the detective finally comprehends that he has been set up and self-deluded; his new-found sense of identity "leads not to the hoped for catharsis, but to destruction and betrayal" (Louvish 20). Naked in the glare of the camera, Gold has been caught on film coming out of the toy shop. What for Gold had been an act of commitment was in fact an elaborate sting to coerce Gold to release the logged evidence. Tucking the mementos of the evening into his pocket and punching him in the stomach, the hit men deliver the harsh message that Gold's symbolic act is essentially flawed, for while others have fought and died for a homeland, he continues to straddle two lives. The more important lesson, however, is that Gold has permitted his judgment to be clouded by his burning need to belong at any cost, reminding us of Sullivan's advice to his partner: "When you start coming with customers, it's time to quit" (84). Mamet subtly links Gold's secular and spiritual identities by the souvenir photos courtesy of 212 and a passport on which is scribbled "'Third and Racine, 5:00 A.M.'" (112), the time and place of the police stakeout to bring in Randolph, about which Gold has completely forgotten. Having been "persuaded to join the conspiracy against this conspiracy [the reactivated GROFAZ]," Gold learns it is "impossible to belong both to these militant People of the Book and the forces of law and order" (Combs 16).

In *On Directing Film,* however, Mamet reminds us that "'The end of the quest'" is not "the end of the story. . . . Any good drama takes us deeper and deeper to a resolution that is both surprising and inevitable. . . . the two essential elements we learned of from Aristotle, *surprise* and *inevitability*" (1991, 95-96). Therefore it is both surprising and inevitable that although Gold races to the meet, the building is in flames, the bust has gone sour, and Sullivan dies in his arms. We are prepared earlier in the film when Sullivan rhapsodizes about the bust and the sweet taste of success ("We'll play some cops and robbers, we'll bust this *Big Criminal,* we'll swagger around . . ." [80]) as Teach does in *American Buffalo* about the heist, for the possibility that it will not come down that way. Typically, the price of Gold's neglecting his responsibility to his partner—his family, as Sullivan is quick to remind him—is terrible. Coming upon a firefight at 5:03 A.M, Gold hears the lieutenant's warning to Sullivan to clear the building, but the order comes too late and the officer, pinned down on the second floor, lays severely injured and bleeding. As Gold, overcome by guilt for failing to provide backup for his partner, charges into the building amid shots fired, Sullivan is conscious but slipping. In a rare sentimental moment, Mamet reunites the partners, intimating Sullivan's imminent death by his reminiscing with Gold. In a line equally at home in *Sexual Perversity in Chicago* or *The Old Neighborhood,* Sullivan's memory—"You remember that girl that time . . .?" (117)—anchors the two in the "old days," which Sullivan only recently evoked in images that were rakish and virile. Noticeably missing from his speech, however, are reproach and recrimination, which, augmenting his own self-censure, Gold receives aplenty from a chorus of officers.

Gold's chasing the fugitive through a maze of tunnels and descending levels in the building's basement underscores that "*Homicide* is a symbolic exploration of the unconscious. . . . It's the myth of the Minotaur" (Mamet qtd. in VerMeulen 1). When Gold loses his gun in a fall, he instinctively grabs a piece of chain as a weapon, [44] but is clearly at a disadvantage against the desperate, hunted criminal. However, we remember that Gold has won twenty-two citations for valor and anticipate that with the added incentive of revenge, he will outsmart Randolph. What we are not prepared for is that Gold, the respected hostage negotiator, able to convince Randolph's mother to give up her son, to challenge a superior, and overpower a Rottweiler while armed only with a piece of meat and a towel, simply folds in front of the criminal because he no longer values his own life. When he refuses to beg for his life, Randolph mocks him, "Ain't that a shame, then. After all your

trials. It come to nothing." Besting the murderer's mockery with truthfulness, Gold, in a variant of Miss Klein's question, exposes the scheme he
hatched with Randolph's mother: "[Y]ou weren't going nowhere" (120).

As he prepares to flee out the window grate, Randolph responds with
scathing sarcasm to what he perceives as Gold's wiseguy, superior attitude,
"Oh, you know, huh? One Smart Kike. Ain'tcha Mr. Gold?" (121),[45] his use
of "Mr. Gold" echoing the contemptuousness that Benjamin employed
earlier in the evening. Entirely misreading Gold's acquired knowledge as the
mark of a smart-aleck Jew, Randolph fails to appreciate that Gold's hard-
won wisdom is the consequence of his betrayal of Sullivan, of his code of
ethics and of himself, what Mamet characterizes as "derangement [which]
results in him abrogating his duties, or at least his happiness" (VerMeulen
1). In sharp contrast to the opening scene when a black superior's use of the
term "kike" ignited his rage, Gold allows the remark to roll off his back,
apparently giving truth to the statement, "I'm a piece of shit" (122). In
seeking to ascribe a meaning to his worthless self, which, as Richard Combs
notes, is "bereft of confidence, compensation, friends, allies, purpose and
self respect"(17), Gold's quip appears a trenchant, definitive representation
of the self-hating Jew; yet, typically in *Homicide,* as in Mamet's body of
work, the slipperiness of the language coaxes the reader and viewer to
decode "rigged" appearances.

In fact, Gold's actions belie his words. Cradling the head of the fleeing
murderer seriously injured by a SWAT team, Gold lies on the floor of the
basement crying out to the approaching policemen, "Don't hurt him . . .
don't hurt him" (124). While Diane Borden maintains that Gold's cradling
of Randolph forms an "ironic pieta parallel to the earlier pieta of the dying
Sullivan in Gold's arms" (24), I think, on the contrary, that Gold's concern
for Randolph, as for Sullivan, demonstrates an inherent decency in the man.
Further, it reveals him to be a Jew whose acts manifest a compassion for
others and the belief that all life is sacred, key Judaic premises. In fact, that
Gold does not die but gropes his way tentatively toward a new life from this
nadir of shame, having acknowledged his conflicted, divided soul and the
pull of legacy, is an ending concomitant with the life-affirming conclusions
of *American Buffalo* and *Speed-the Plow,* and of Judaism itself.

Several critics have commented on *Homicide's* disturbing, dark conclusion, which portrays its protagonist as an emotional and physical cripple,
alienated by both families: the cops and the Jews.[46] Though lacking the
tragic grandeur of Oedipus, Gold nonetheless fulfills the classical require-
ments of scapegoat: he is broken, crippled, outcast, and ultimately enlightened. He is the historical figure of the Jew as Other, whose "faulty gait" has
long been viewed as a racial marker that distinguishes the Jew (Gilman

1991b, 39).[47] Like Oedipus, Gold has found his people; he is no longer a stranger to himself.

Consistent with *Homicide's* focus on the enigmatic, Mamet aims for what Ozick terms "the deepest point: concerning Jews, the deepest point is always most implicated when it is most omitted" (123). Through indirection Mamet has led us to what is "most implicated": the circuitous journey in search of the wanted criminal has brought Gold face to face with himself, a "wanted" criminal for acts of defamation of heritage and denial of self. That moment of self-doubt is also, as Lawrence Kushner explains, the first step in the journey of self-knowledge, for "Jewish spirituality is about. . . . seeing, feeling, hearing things that only a few moments ago were inaccessible" (1991, 28). Rather than providing an unrelentingly bleak conclusion, this scene portrays Gold as just beginning a search for clues to his Jewish identity, a man in transit for whom "displacement . . . personal, historical and cultural . . ." is unexpectedly aligned with homecoming (Chaudhuri 93).

Admittedly, Mamet's final shot of Gold standing in front of the doorway numbered 203 (with its intended glimpse of Grounder who earlier promised to tell Gold the meaning of evil) illustrates the price of Gold's betrayal of his partner and the police force; he is excluded and demoted from *Homicide.*[48] However, to the kabbalist, the doorway or gate is the primary figure of transition, of access to knowledge, the scene more important for what it merely intimates rather than what it portrays, that the fifth gate on the way to mystical knowledge signifies hypocrisy, one side of which lies doubt, anger and nihilism; the other, faith and humility (Epstein 7). It is entirely fitting, then, that in the last frame of the movie, Gold is handed the results of the police department's search for the meaning of GROFAZ. Like "Rosebud" in *Citizen Kane,* this term has eluded the homicide investigator. "In a melodrama," suggests Mamet, citing Hitchcock's melodramatic thrillers as illustrative example, "a MacGuffin is *that thing which the hero is chasing.* The secret documents . . . the great seal of the republic of blah-blah-blah. . . . The MacGuffin is *that thing which is important to us*—that most essential thing. The audience will supply it, each member for himself" (1991b, 38-39). Hence, only in the last moments does Gold learn that whatever its meaning—bird seed (GROFAZT) or a masterplot against the Jews—GROFAZ is only one piece in a jigsaw puzzle and remains a mystery, the film's ambiguity and double vision intended to obstruct any "this for that meaning" in its unfolding of the human mystery (Borden 27). Those who search for a moral in *Homicide* will find none, suggests Mamet: "It has no moral. It is not a cautionary tale. . . . It's a myth" (VerMeulen 1).

Perhaps, Robert Alter's "The Jew Who Didn't Get Away" sheds some light on Mamet's apparently dark and depressing conclusion. "The central fact about American Jewish fiction," argues Alter—and I suggest Mamet's *Homicide* as well—is that "it is an expression of Jews in transition," an attempt "by American Jewish writers . . . to articulate the ambivalences of a confused cultural identity, or the reflex of guilt in the transition from one identity to another." One finds "in the fiction [or film] a potent image of their own unsettled and unsettling conflicts" (1986, 272-73). In this context Streiker's contention that American Jews who lack "religious or communal commitment" are "likely to base their sense of Jewishness on support for Israel and . . . on the Holocaust" and formulate "a reactive Jewish identity" inspired by "fear of persecution and the desire to use force" (61) offers a valuable way of reading *Homicide's* seemingly negative portraits of Jewry—a self-hating cop, a rich, pushy doctor, and the exploitative, disingenuous Jewish self-defense group. While nothing in the characterization of the zealots excuses their moral turpitude or logically invites Gold's solidarity with them, abdication of his ethical and legal responsibility, and good common sense, encountering Jews who know who they are and who are willing to fight for their Jewishness at once tempts him, victimizes him, and frees—or forces—him to question himself. If at the end he is repelled by some Jews' betrayal of him and his betrayal of Sullivan, his refusal to advocate silence and invisibility reflects his enhanced awareness of ethnic identity. Mamet, however, admits "I am neither expecting people to call it *[Homicide]* anti-Semitic, nor will I be surprised if they do." The movie "is not about what Jews are or are not. It's about a guy trying to belong. . . . torn between several allegiances" (VerMeulen).

Employing the story of Esther, the *Purimspiel*—historically the earliest form of Jewish drama[49]—which bears no connection to the bastardized Hollywood version of a yarmulke-wearing seder-attending Jew, Mamet conflates historical and contemporary events into a master-plot of conspiracy, deception, and retribution. He thus raises our consciousness about pressing concerns of the American Jewish community: an increasing secularized Jewish culture; charges of dual loyalty; pervasive, pernicious, and increasing evidence of anti-Semitism; the legacy of the Holocaust in which too many assimilated Jews find their affiliation to Jewishness; the need to reclaim a heritage of pride, courage, and ethical conduct. To Mamet the Book of Esther, though unfamiliar to most movie audiences, is "the *essential* story of the movie. To me," Mamet adds, "the essential aspect is that if Jews are going to be killed, they are going to be killed in the palace as well as anywhere. . . . you can be a Jew or not. You're kidding yourself if you think you're going to be protected. On the other hand, great benefits can acquit you from being afraid in the face of danger with your people."[50]

   More than a mere projection of the intermittently guilty conscience of the assimilated Jew, *Homicide* conveys Mamet's deeply personal quest for spirituality and community, a trope that closely aligns the conclusion of this film with *Things Change*. Whereas Gino manifests integrity in the face of temptation and when trapped is magically rewarded as befits the fable, Bobby Gold, on the other hand, blindly stumbles, succumbing to a hitherto hidden desire for Jewish identity at any price by aligning himself with a group of Jews who he believes and expects are possessed of the power to validate his standing as a good American Jew. Bereft of friend, like Charlie Fox in *Speed-the-Plow* and the pseudo-son Jerry in *Things Change*, the enlightened hero must discover a way of being Jewish that fosters an ethnic identity informed by integrity and meaningful affiliation. That Mamet offers "blunt questions instead of glib answers and challenges instead of reassurances" is surely not an occasion to curse the messenger for the bleakness of his vision but rather an occasion, Peter Travers rightly suggests, "to bless him"(99).

An original screenplay, *The Edge* (earlier called *Bookworm*), written in 1995, is one of Mamet's most recent. It is an action-packed, hair-raising suspense thriller of mythic proportions.[51] Set in the far North, fraught with danger and abundant in wealth, its harrowing manhunt and arduous journey portend a ghastly murder in the woods, a thrilling gold rush, and a great tale of survival. However, upon closer inspection, *The Edge* is an intrinsically Jewish story. Its forced peregrination, persecution, loss of faith, threatened extinction, and "contract with survival," as Steiner would have it, suggest the quintessential Jewish experience. In the years since *Homicide,* Mamet has become a student and sometime interpreter of Torah.[52] And as he has done in *Glengarry Glen Ross,* he finds inspiration in biblical narrative, sublimated as subtext, which he has fashioned into a richly textured thriller. Whereas the Book of Numbers provides a multifarious, fertile frame for *Glengarry,* the writings of three prophets, Isaiah, Jeremiah, Eziekial, as well as talmudic midrash (biblical commentary) find form in *The Edge*. The powerful, far-reaching symbol of north (variously interpreted in ancient Jewish texts), and the cornerstone tropes of his work—ethical behavior, learning, and legacy—have been melded into one of Mamet's most creative and disturbing depictions of a individual threatened with destruction by the timeless and ongoing struggle between higher instincts and the forces of corruption, signified by the idolatrous lust for wealth and the distrust of the Other.

"The term 'north,'" writes David E. Fass, has acquired meaning in Jewish tradition as a multivalent symbol of incredibly powerful range. "[O]wing to the ancient and widespread belief" that "the powers of the universe" were located in the north, it attained mythic significance as a powerful symbol of evil, a force of retribution, and the term for the locus of redemptive forces (465-67). Thereafter, the symbol-formation process is enhanced in Jeremiah, whose usage of north presents three basic themes: north as the source of great evil, the termination of exile, and the destruction of Israel's enemies. And in the Talmudic era, north takes on provocative new meanings as the source of material wealth, as the site of "challenge," and that direction of "unfinished business," as in the individual's defeating the sources of darkness within him in concert with the divine (Fass 471). Tapping into this rich vein, *The Edge* plumbs them all. Intertwining biblical narrative with Indian lore of the Ojibways, self-sufficient nomads who survived by outsmarting their enemy,[53] the screenplay is structured "almost along classical lines of suspense . . . [in] which no question is really answered in any single sequence" (Mamet qtd. in Yakir 22). Leitch maintains that "thrillers entertain audiences by making them apprehensive, uncertain, or frightened . . . who [then] willing[ly] . . . defer the principals' desired arrival home for the sake of their entertaining adventures along the way" (25-26). Mamet's thrillers, in particular, like Hitchcock's, engage his audiences in an ever-changing game in which the rules "are always in danger of being broken," and where pleasure "is complicated by their [audiences'] having taken the wrong side," conned into the game-playing in which "every interpretation is suspect" (27-29).

Like *Homicide*, *The Edge* is a powerful racial drama that deals squarely with hatred, both of the Other and of the self. However, it is far more subtle in probing race hatred, ethical responsibility, and repression of ethnic identity than is the earlier film. Lacking the overt mechanism of the chasid, the Israeli militant, the biblical story, and contemporary Jewish history, *The Edge* shifts responsibility for the pertinent, puzzling questions about ethnicity and ethical imperative to the protagonist. In lieu of the many characters of clear-cut Jewish affiliation and overt participation in ritual depicted in *Homicide*, *The Edge* is stripped bare to two principal characters, one of whom is identified as a Jew. As this screenplay reveals, "truths" are harder to come by when dealing specifically with fantasies and fictions associated with the Jew in a modern, secular culture. Through a complex, contradictory construction of Jewish identity and candid, even bold, depiction of racial fears, *The Edge* pulls its protagonist out of a protected environment, both literal and lettered, and puts him to the test, giving Mamet an open field in which to challenge what he terms "The heresy of the Information Age" which diverts us "from our knowledge of our worthlessness" (1998, 70, 53). Counterpointing ignorance and knowledge, loss and gain, delusion and truth, the Jew and the gentile, *The Edge* draws us into a gripping tale of lust and death set in the mythic Yukon. Rarely does this urban writer situate his work in a non-urban environment, although *The Woods* is a fine example of a departure from Mamet's paradigmatic urbanals. However, as Stanley Kaufman's review of the film recognizes, "the impulse to test sophisticated characters in primitive conditions reaches its extreme in *The Edge* (26).

The Edge opens in a small Alaskan airport where Charles Morse, a casually dressed man in his mid-to-late thirties, toting a bookbag, is seen observing the off-loading of equipment from a Gulfstream jet to an ancient Dehavilland 'Beaver' amphibian plane. In his party are James, a male model; Mickey, his supermodel wife; Robert Green, a fashion photographer; and Green's assistant, Stephen. Although conversations in these early scenes with the shopkeeper, a lumberjack, a pilot, and the others are cryptic, Mamet typically uses these opening moments to establish key information: Morse's reluctance to reveal his identity to a lumberjack who admires the Gulfstream; the concern of the jet pilot for Morse's well-being and his advice to avoid flying in the amphibian in "any low ceiling, any possibility of ice, or birdstrike," a very real danger during bird migration in the fall months (4);[54] the pervasive threat in the North of man-eating Kodiak bears; Morse's unease with the party with whom he is traveling as revealed by his opting to remain on the margins of the group where his wealth and nonprofessional status (and his birthday) credibly set him apart from the others—an outsider with a penchant for observation. As the party packs into the small amphibian plane, the pilot jokingly advises his passengers that up North, "housepests . . . are six feet tall and weigh eight hundred pounds" (8),[55] which presents Green, a wag, with an opportunity for a joke indirectly anticipating the plot of the film, and exposes Morse as a pedagogue (not unlike Del in *The Cryptogram*) and quibbler for whom any linguistic exchange, even a joke, presents an opportunity to examine the finer points of meaning. Green has the audience eating out of his hand: "Two guys in the woods. . . . Guy says, 'I don't *have* to run faster than the *bear*, I just have to run faster than *you* . . .'" (8). Laughing along with the others, however, Morse is quick to point out "hidden *hostility* on the part of the man who brought the shoes. (*Pause*). It indicates," he says, "that he *brought* the other man into the woods to kill him." Intrigued by Morse's theory, Green questions him, "How do you see hostility?" (9), but before Morse can answer him, the sound of the amphibian's engines drowns out their conversation. In a device common to Mamet's plays and screenplays in

which a provocative, unanswered question triggers the action, such as Miss Klein's questioning of Bobby Gold in *Homicide,* "Do you belong nowhere . . . ?" (1992b, 63), Mamet similarly propels the film's pivotal question—"How do you see hostility?"—to the forefront of our minds and leaves it hanging, a conundrum fundamental to the film's action.

Just as the amphibian is about to take off for Tamarack Lodge, the site of their lodging and proposed shoot, the pilot of the jet runs up to the plane with documents for Morse to sign—and that we are afforded an opportunity to read—reiterating the reference to his birthday and revealing that in his signing, Morse accepts a valuable inheritance and fiduciary responsibility for family "holdings, directorships, stocks, securities . . ." (10). Absentmindedly he places the paper clip, which held the papers, onto his lapel, behavior consistent with the pedant's constant acquisition of facts, such that he possess a repository of knowledge so impressive it is common knowledge. The paper clip, like other items introduced early in the film— the rifle and the pocket knife; the watches, both contemporary and classic; planes, both state of the art and antiquated; a global positioning device and a rudimentary compass—serve as they do in Mamet's plays and other screenplays (*The Cryptogram, Goldberg Street, House of Games,* and *Homicide* come immediately to mind) as practical implements that acquire widening associations throughout the film. Similarly, the prominently displayed photograph of John Hawk, a Native American friend and hunting buddy of lodge owner Jack Styles,[56] evokes a cultural cohesiveness and authenticity associated with an earlier historical period analogous to that of the *shtetl* in *The Disappearance of the Jews,* the war years in *The Cryptogram,* the Old Country (Sicily) and Israeli pioneers glimpsed in *Things Change* and *Homicide.* The picture of Hawk motivates Green and Morse to relinquish the relative safety of the lodge for high adventure in the backwoods of the North country, what Mamet has described in "The Northern Novel" as a story "about survival" (1996a).[57]

At the Tamarack Lodge the group is welcomed by Jack Styles, "a robust man in his sixties with a terribly scarred face" (11), evidence of a battle with a bear who got away, who reiterates the pervasive presence and danger of bears. Morse gravitates to the lodge library, a place whose artifacts—deer heads, quivers, spears, and old canoe paddle—literally evoke history and put him immediately at home. Noting that he and Styles are in possession of the same wilderness reference guide,[58] Morse strikes up a conversation, the normally taciturn observer loquacious when engaged in a discussion of arcane knowledge. Whereas Green formally won the group's approval with his joke, Morse now dazzles them and impresses Styles with his knowledge of the Ojibways who used an oar with a panther on one side of the blade, and a rabbit on the other. Typically self-effacing Morse prefers to identify himself as ". . . just a Student" of the North, proof that he is not only rich in material wealth but in humility. Stephen, who has missed the discussion about panther and rabbit, spies Morse staring at a calendar but he barely has time to express congratulations on Morse's birthday before he is brusquely summoned by Green, one of those arrogant, outspoken, pushy Jews always ready with a smart line, obsessed with setting up tomorrow's photo shot.[59] Returning to his room, Morse undresses and settles into his book but his wife cajoles him into going back downstairs to find her something to eat. As Morse putters in the kitchen, he is attacked by a bear, or what appears to be a bear. In fact, members of his own group have conspired with Styles to set a trap for him, a surprise birthday party on the order of that described by John in *Oleanna* as "a form of aggression" (Mamet 1993b, 41).

Assuming the role of *badken*, the Jewish jokester, and master of ceremonies, a performance anticipated by his readiness with a joke earlier in the day, Green is verbose, even effusive, in an attempt both to put a positive spin on the brutish trick played on Morse and to cover the awkwardness of their having so terrified him that he is still shaking. Enjoying the limelight, Green takes a circuitous route around his subject much as the "bear" encircled the trapped man in pajama bottoms, attempting to contrast the superficiality of the world in which they work and the solid character of this man. In words that are especially ironic, given that he is always obsessed with visual appearances and clever answers, Green's remark, "Let's face it: it's a superficial world. We don't often say what we mean. . . . But I'm going to take it upon myself to speak 'for the group,' and say, what I think we all mean" (26) reminds us of Mamet's premise that "No one really says what they mean, but they always mean what they mean" (Savran 137). Ever the showman, Green ultimately winds up his windy birthday toast—which is initially awkward, for reasons we subsequently confirm when Morse does, then ruminative, and finally celebratory—with words that laud the celebrant as "A good companion, a good friend, and a good Sport," praise to which Mickey adds, "and a *very brave* man . . ." (26-27), seemingly oblivious to the fact that Morse's actions belie her words. Not only does the toast call further attention to the role of ritual in this screenplay, to Morse's position as outsider, and to Green's duplicity, Mickey's acclamation, an attempt to take the sting out of the joke at her husband's expense, will come back to haunt Green when these two men engage in a fight to the death in ensuing scenes. Indirectly advancing the element of suspense in the film, Styles interrupts them to warn that "in the true *event*," Morse's panic and backward movement "s'a textbook case what *not* to do . . ." (27). Retaining such facts, Morse files Styles's lesson while the others, debunking his admonition, enjoy the festivities at hand.

From his wife Morse receives a gold pocket watch in a classic Hunter case,[60] whose affectionate engraved sentiment we glimpse, its small white gift box noticeably embossed, "Stearns and Harrington—Fine Jewelers and Engravers Since 1867."[61] Like Mickey's gift, Stephen's suggestive French postcard from the 1920s and Green's gift of an engraved pocketknife have historical significance or timeless craftsmanship. Notably, Morse's expression of appreciation reveals that like Teach in *American Buffalo* and Levene in *Glengarry Glen Ross*, he finds his referents in history, though his are decidedly more literate. Citing Mamet's beloved Victorians, he quips, "The Victorians said: the two questions one gentleman never should ask another: 'Do you have the Time? and: May I borrow your Knife'" (29). As he did formerly, Styles undercuts sentiment with fact, or in this case superstition, that if someone gives another a knife, a coin must be exchanged, or, as Morse explains, "it 'cuts the friendship'" (29). Casting light on that tradition, the billionaire bookworm tells Styles, the group having dispersed for bed, that it probably dates to medieval times, and more likely Roman, again finding referents in the past. Providing ample evidence of his erudition, Morse explains that "To give a coin for the knife" confirms that the gift of a knife is not the "transaction" of "wellborn man, condemned to die" whose close friend would deliver a knife to the incarcerated man to offer him the option of suicide (33). Although both the coin and the five dollar bet are the subject of much discussion, only the bet Morse won when he answered Styles's question about the Ojibway paddle is paid, leaving the question of the nature of the transaction between Green and Morse a problematic one which, if superstition or tradition holds, has the potential to "cut the friendship" of which we have little evidence other than an expensive gift and hyperbolic speech. The scene not only confirms the commonality among Mamet's late plays and numerous films in its revisiting of three tokens relevant to the acquisition of knowledge about self, legacy, and ethnic culture—a photo, book and timepiece—it confirms the dialectic shaping of the film.

Morse awakens early to a pristine scene; his gifts—the pocket watch, the knife, and a global positioning device from his staff—a portentous cluster of signifiers. Green, Mickey and Stephen are already on location at the log gazebo. As Morse walks out toward the shoot, he slows to observe Mickey and Green, whose casual intimacy and sexually explicit banter enrage him. Frustrated and helpless, he returns to the lodge, betraying nothing of what has apparently stirred his blood. Rather, he and Styles engage in a lively discussion about the diverse ways "to find north," among them the fact that a magnetized needle floating on a body of water functions as a compass, the very method that he will utilize in subsequent scenes when he is literally lost in the woods. What appears casual, however, is a staged performance with hidden agenda, Styles's cordial banter little more than chicanery to put his guest at ease while diverting Morse's attention from the hunter's baited trap.

Styles and Morse are interrupted when an agitated Green returns to the lodge. Frantic to find a substitute for James, who is ill, Green notices the photograph of Hawk. Recalling Jerry in *Things Change,* similarly inspired by a picture, he sets his sights on shooting Styles's American Indian friend: "*This* is the guy we should be shooting, the *first* place, you want to sell a Plaid *Jacket* . . ."(40). The plan born of necessity is brilliant in theory confronting the twin problems of James's unavailability and Green's impending failure to deliver the film as promised, while having the potential to achieve a rare authenticity in a spread of backwoods clothing. Despite Styles's warning that Green's expectation of finding Hawk, an avid hunter, at home in hunting season is fallacious, the fashion photographer endeavors to draft Morse into joining him for an afternoon flight to Hawk's home.

Opting for security and further discussion with Styles, Morse initiates a new line of inquiry about the bearskin mounted on the wall, one inspiring the latter's discourse on the Kodiak bear, a "man-killing machine. (Pause). . . . You don't want to put the smell of *your* blood in the air . . ." As Styles expounds on the bear's partiality for berries, cautioning his guest "That's where the *bear* is" (42-43), his speech drifts associatively into the story of his own mauling by a bear in a berry patch. In an performance reminiscent of Ricky Roma's interaction with James Lingk in *Glengarry Glen Ross,* Styles smoothly segues from a seemingly sincere observation on the beauty of the environment—"Such a perfect spot. Such a privilege. (*Pause*) A shame everyone can't enjoy it" (44)—to a blatant proposition to merchandise that beauty to this billionaire. Since their arrival Styles has repeatedly referred to the group's intrusion on hunting season. Although Morse does not suspect that he is the big game that Styles has been stalking, the apparently unsophisticated backwoodsman broaches a scheme to develop the property, believing Morse either idly rich or a starry-eyed patsy so enamored of the North that Styles could induce him to part with his fortune. Affronted by the lodge owner's spurious pretense, which offers ample evidence of the film's epigraph—"There isn't a law of God or Man Goes North of Ten Thousand Bucks"[62]—and insulted, as well, by his intrusive inquiry about his wife on the previous evening (reinforcing our notice of Morse's sensitivity on this subject sighted previously at the airport and the dock with Green), Morse reverses his decision, deciding to escape

Styles's clutches by joining Green, the lesser of two evils, on what will be an ill-fated adventure to locate Hawk.

At Hawk's cabin, Green, Morse, and Stephen discover a note confirming that Green's "model" has indeed gone hunting some sixty miles northwest and Green entices Morse to track him. However, if Morse does not have reason to fear, the audience, familiar with Green's glibness, certainly does. Establishing the suspenseful scenario by which the group does not make it back "safe 'n'sound"—storm looming, change of itinerary, removal of the note from Hawk's cabin, threat of bird strike—Mamet undercuts it by Green indelicately bringing up the issue of Morse's money: "I was watching you, back at the airport. When you couldn't even tell that guy your name. . . . How difficult that must be. Never know who your friends are, n'what they value you for. (*Pause*)" (52). His speech punctuated with pauses that expose his unease in an attempt to strike just the right tone of sincerity and sympathy, like that of Moss in *Glengarry*, Green literally gives himself away when he muses on the high price of fame and material wealth, recalling Mamet's comment that one's envy of "talent" or "genius" resembles "one's envy of the rich" (1996b, 242). But Green is unprepared for Morse's perspicacity. Quick on the draw, he retorts: "What do *you* value me for?" Green typically recovers by camouflaging his duplicitous strategy in a joke, "I like your style. (*Pause*) And I think your wife's kind of cute, too." Humor, as he has previously demonstrated, serves as a handy scrim to hide his emotions and a rear-guard attack. Yet he is singularly unprepared for Morse's tenacious persistence in gaining ground and holding the advantage over his opponent, a personality trait that will be increasingly clear as Green and Stephen come to rely on Morse's skill, scholarship, and character. Continuing his relentless interrogation, Morse figuratively traps Green: "How are you planning to kill me?" (52), both shocking and completely logical given the signs that Morse has read, judged, and turned to advantage.

At that moment, before Green or we can grasp the billionaire's intent or anticipate the outcome of the heightened tension of his double-barreled pursuit of the seducer of his wife and fortune, the plane, felled by a bird strike, rapidly descends into the water and begins to break up, threatening to kill them all. During the terrifyingly anxious moments in which their lives are suddenly endangered by exposure to natural elements rather than man's bestial nature, the pilot succumbs, Green struggles to the surface, and Morse heroically saves Stephen. With Green's pernicious scheme exposed, the unlikely trio of Easterners—bookworm, photographer, and (homosexual?) assistant—whose photo shoot has suddenly turned lethal, find themselves lost in the wilds in hunting season unarmed except for Morse's knife. Relying on logic, optimism, and kindling for a signal fire, Morse expectantly envisions rescue, weather permitting, but faith soon turns to despair when Morse discovers that the "hunting" party will not even know where to search for them, Green having recklessly but predictably taken Hawk's note "as a prop for the shoot" (62). His moment of impetuousness thus threatens the survival of the three men who, lacking food, warm clothing, and an adequate supply of flares, must rely on their ability to "see" clearly, to utilize their individual and collective emotional, physical, and intellectual resources to find their way out of the woods—or die trying.

Blending carefully plotted elements of power, sex, money, murder, guilt, and accountability with equal parts ethnic tension, envy, and the power of ritual, Mamet thus rivets our attention to the trio's co-dependence as stripped bare of civilized life, protection, and hope of discovery, they are tested on their ability to survive a high stakes game solely on their wisdom, wits, generosity, faith, and courage. Recalling earlier Mamet plays and screenplays, characterized by his idiosyncratic treatment of questions of ethical behavior, judgment, justice, moral authority, and the power of memory, *The Edge* not only provides capacious evidence of Mamet's expanding interest in such issues as temptation, corruption, guilt, forgiveness, spirituality, and myth, which have during the course of his career occupied his attention to a lesser or greater degree, it takes full advantage of the dramatic elements of a life and death struggle at once magnified and clarified in the austere North country whose beauty betrays, as does Morse's wife, danger lurking everywhere.

Juxtaposing the lure of profit with the quest for the atavistic exemplified by Green's folly to turn the authentic—that quality that Hawk represents—into artifice and commercial advantage, Mamet has written a splendid plot rife with hazards, perils, deadfalls, suspenseful tricks, even a deadly ravine, in which men in the company of men are beset by all manner of threats. Green, whose ill-conceived, impulsive venture is responsible in great part for their being lost in the remote North country, repeatedly puts their lives at risk by his rash, consistently negligent behavior. But the story thus set in motion is neither simple nor transparent. Indeed, Mamet, whose portrait of ethnic identity and race hatred has rarely been more provocative, portrays men challenged as much by unpredictable elements as their distrust of the Other. Ratcheting the high stakes even higher, Mamet's con artistry is everywhere apparent in *The Edge,* trapping the men and the audience off-guard. Counterpointing Morse's attempts to guide them to safety, which are repeatedly hamstrung by Green's reckless, swinish conduct and Morse's own overly confident reliance on book learning, with their cooperative efforts to survive and save the overtly fragile Stephen, Mamet creates a drama within a drama in which we witness a spectacular big-game hunt played out on realistic and mythological planes of experience in which the men hunting one another are big game hunted by a man-eating bear that is the projection of their envy for one another. For as Lawrence Kushner points out, "Most of the terrible things human beings do to one another, they do by telling themselves they are actually fighting against some external evil. But in truth more often than not they have only taken the evil into themselves, and become its agents" (1993, 128). The struggle for power, which has long been a trope of particular interest to Mamet, receiving fascinating treatment in recent plays such as *Oleanna* and *The Cryptogram,* is here mined by the writer intrigued by the power of the mind, idolatry, hatred, and the cleansing power of ritual.

In top form in this suspenseful screenplay, Mamet takes full advantage of the element of fear to pit the idolatrous Jew against a character whose identity is defined by his wisdom and wealth—financial, intellectual, and generosity of spirit—rather than delimited ethnicity. Not since *Glengarry Glen Ross* has Mamet depicted a Jew of such apparent villainy. A predatory, aggressive artist-for-hire, Robert Green is a seducer, deceiver, and arch-exploiter whose plot to murder the billionaire whose money he covets even more than he does his wife, stands as testimony of the corruption wrought by the lure of the babe and "boodle" (72). An individual who inspires boundless contempt and a paucity of compassion, Green is enamored of iconic idols—money, beauty, power. He is quick to anger and harbor suspicions. Although quick-witted, alert to his environment, and emotional, traits that could "figure as positive 'Jewish traits,'" suggests Tamar Garb, these characteristics "easily feed into a mythology of the Jew as excessive, dangerous, and suspect" (26), an apt characterization for this charming performance artist who fashions his conduct and speech to fit the times. Moreover, as a dealer in art, Green appears to be the "archetypal modern Jewish male diminishing Art, subsuming it into the vulgar world of Capital and commerce" (Garb 26); in other words, he is the stereotypic signifier of Jewish identity, a point underscored by an injury that renders Green lame, "Judaism and the lame foot . . . always metaphors for one another" (Gilman 1986, 145), as we saw in *Homicide.*

Expanding upon the model of the marginal Jew-as-thief dramatized in *Glengarry Glen Ross* (and implicit in *American Buffalo*), the Jew-as-merchandiser of second-rate art in *Speed-the-Plow,*[64] and the Jew-as-liar in innumerable works, Mamet depicts Green, a city dweller lost in the woods, as an individual seemingly devoid of ethical responsibility, personal integrity, and loyalty; his acts and artifice are driven, as is he, by profit. In Mamet's stage Jews of questionable morality, whether Gould in *Speed-the-Plow* or Levene in *Glengarry,* the writer inspires us to inquire why such individuals are delineated as Jewish, and more importantly, why a writer like Mamet, who has recently turned to practicing Judaism, has depicted a Jew in this way? I suggest that in *The Edge* he daringly invites us to "read" the conflict not as one between clearly delimited opponents or opposing races (whose history is burdened by centuries of hatred and misunderstanding) but rather as an ongoing battle between our "lower" and "higher" nature. Playing with and against our weakness to stereotype and scapegoat the Other, whether Jew or gentile, he rejects a white/black or good/evil dynamic, befitting the suspense thriller and the best of Mamet's work. Planting abundant clues to create reasonable doubt about the character, motivation, and weakness of both Green and Morse, he destabilizes a facile reading of either character. For example, decried by Green, Morse fits the profile of the stereotypic gentile who in his view is one of those anti-Semitic white-bread WASPs—"Drinks and Golf. Screwing the Maid"(104)—cool-headed in a crisis, laconic, intellectual. In identifying the gentile as the cause of his distress, much as "Christian Europe [and America] elected the Jews as the cause of its distress," Green reveals that "once elected that race suffer[s] not because it was the cause of . . . unrest, but because it was *not*" (Mamet 1998, 52). In fact, in demonizing Morse as a Jew-hating gentile, Green's hatred, as Mamet reveals, like race hatred of any stripe, is profane.

Whereas Green's "lower nature," opposes the portrait of the uninspired, seemingly level-headed bookworm, Morse emerges, in my view, as more than the sum of his distrust or Green's jealousy. Rather, Mamet has drawn him as a flawed individual whose suspicion is destructive. Yet rather than read him as the gentile of Green's imagination, I would suggest that Morse may be viewed as a mythic Jew whose ethnicity is implicit rather than explicit. Upon closer inspection and without benefit of delineated ethnicity, we are invited to draw our own conclusions that Morse is an individual whose birthday celebration occasions the transfer of a valuable inheritance, maturity and responsibility. He craves rootedness, is a person at home with books, a student of history, and a collector of memorabilia, a quibbler of words in the tradition of the *pipul,* a man who can see beyond surface realities to deeper meanings, an individual who feels an ethical responsibility for others, as Levinas would have it, and who is a sharp observer of his environment. He values learning and readily applies its lessons. As a marginal man in possession of the knife, that mythic signifier long associated with the Jew (Fiedler 20-21; Lazar 50, 54), Morse speaks to the "higher nature" of intellect, moral imperative, affirmation of life. Moreover, called to responsibility, Morse is "chosen" to perform; he "cannot unwill his destiny," or flee as "exile is his mythic-ethnic condition" (Fiedler, 55-56).

As in *Homicide,* Mamet rejects an easy "this for that" signification, the men's forced peregrination continually putting into question the validity of all presumptions that will not take root in the slippery ground of murder for money or revenge. When Green acknowledges his error of judgment in an understatement that belies the gravity of their situation, Morse manifests his famously generous good nature, turning Green's potentially paralyzing shame into an opportunity for a lesson, thus establishing a thematic link to earlier scenes in the library and other Mamet works in which learning and the mentor/student relationship loom large. "I read an interesting book one time," Morse recalls; "It *said* that most people lost in the woods. . . . die of shame. (*Pause*). . . . And that prohibits them. From doing the one thing which would save their lives. . . . *Thinking*" (63). Putting his money where his mouth is, Morse draws a diagram (one reminiscent of the chasid's pedagogical technique in *Homicide* in which a complex theological concept is clarified by a simple model), laying out their position with respect to the Tamarack Lodge, the "home" base, and Hawk's cabin, where the search party will expect to locate them.

Plotting a path to the lodge, Morse gives the others much needed hope and encouragement that the goal is literally and figuratively in sight. Recalling with Morse that a snowstorm is moving from the North, we intuit what he leaves unsaid but that Green picks up, even if Stephen does not— that their survival is dependent on their getting South of the pass before it obscures their vision, cuts off their path, grounds a search party, and traps them in the woods at night. As neither Green's nor Morse's watch is working after the crash obviating a handy device to locate South, Morse fabricates a rudimentary compass by floating the paper clip still on his lapel pocket in a body of water in the manner he previously described to Styles. Convinced of the efficacy of his compass, Morse stores his treasured directional device in the small white gift box, where we spy but cannot read a receipt. Subsequently we learn both are tokens of betrayal.

Green picks up the threads of a long delayed conversation, the follow-up to Morse's accusations leveled against Green before the plane crashed. As Morse struggles to keep up with Green and Steven, Green seizes the moment to flog him with vexing questions intended to refute Morse's deduction that Green has murder in his heart: "Why would I want to kill you, Charles? . . . For *Mickey?*"(69-70). When Morse reveals that something Green said about his inheritance was "private knowledge," a confidence between Mickey and Morse (a reference that recalls the coded language of *Things Change* and the secret codes and foreign languages used in *Homicide*), the billionaire inadvertently reveals that his suspicions are a projection of his own inadequacies, a classic Mametic tell that a man reveals himself.

Green picks up the idea and twists it into what appears to be a perfectly plausible rebuttal of Morse's theory, his bluff all but convincing Morse, and the audience, that the billionaire has wrongly accused him: "And I said 'inheritance,' n' that means I want to kill you. (*Pause*) Well. Baby, you know what, the rich *are* different. (*Rising*) You're a sick chappie, Charles" (71).

Backpedaling, Green, a masterful manipulator whose quick humor, one-liners, slick delivery, and salacious speech align him with a long line of sleazy Mamet salesmen, makes a pitch whose intent it is to deflect attention away from him, to inspire Morse's trust, and to profit from the bookworm's superior knowledge of the woods, which he admittedly requires to lead him to safety. "I don't mean to Blow my own Horn, but I'm a *Fashion* Photographer, I got more ass than a proctoscope, Love. I don't got to take somebody *else's* wife" (71-72). While Green absentmindedly munches berries, his humorous quip—"nothing is safe"—acquires a chilling new meaning when Morse spies the gigantic footprint of the Kodiak just at the moment that he recalls Styles's admonition that the bears are attracted to berry bushes. As the three men retreat, running for their lives, only momentarily slowing down to catch their breaths, take another reading on the compass, and don their jackets, the chill, both physical and psychological, apparently settling in, the frightened Stephen raises the question "What if we're not *headed* South?" an anxious query that receives Morse's confirmation that the compass, unlike men is the implication, is unerring, having "no choice" (75).

With the reappearance of the bear, Stephen, now terrified, takes off in a mad dash chased by Green and Morse who find themselves staring at a ravine whose portent of disaster does not presage their survival, "the bear cresting the rise" (78). Mamet has crafted a masterful scene rich in mystery and the real possibility of a dead fall, which intensifies the suspense, tests their mettle, strips them bare to reveal each man's frailty and surprising strength, and ironically mocks Green's former admission that his safe arrival home depends on Morse's skill. "We," on the other hand, suggests Mamet, "exercise our survival skills, racing ahead of the protagonist, feeling vicarious fear, while knowing ourselves safe" (1998, 31). Typically undercutting *our* expectations by luring us into believing that this setting presents a perfect spot for Morse's murder, the writer puts us in the horrifying position of helpless witness only to set us up with astonishing evidence of Stephen's pluck and Green's courage as each "walks the plank" to safety. Hence, Green's sarcastic "[a]in't that a bitch . . . 'needing' people . . .?" (76) acquires an unforeseen interpretation when the photographer, his superior physical condition previously established, literally pulls Morse, dangling over the ravine, to safety, thereby reminding us that Mamet's characters, like

Hitchcock's, do not fit neatly into simple categories of innocent and guilty in any technical sense. Rather, "two-dimensional moral labels of good guys and bad guys" are deceptive (Leitch 29), and his characters' complexity affirms the ambiguity that typifies Mamet's work, inhibiting our ability to "solve" the mystery at hand.

Paralyzed as much by his near-death experience as the newly acquired knowledge of Green's saving him, which puts into question his previous suspicions of Green, now apparently groundless, the billionaire is gripped by guilt that he has wrongly accused the photographer, who dismisses his act of heroism with humor. On the face of it, at least, despite Morse's accusations, Green, who has saved the man at personal risk to himself, appears to have more decency than Morse gave him credit for—in fact, more decency than Morse. In other words, when he could have used the opportunity to serve his own presumably nefarious ends, the photographer has seemingly revealed himself to be a principled, decent human being, a man of true grit despite his caustic tongue and carelessness with regard to the feelings or safety of others. And when Morse remains crippled by shame because of the loss of the flares as he dangled over the ravine, he is humbled, revealing that the trap of jealousy, suspicion, and projection inspired by inadequacy that undergirds the screenplay works both ways.

Importantly, Morse's disgust in himself not only prompts questions about his identity—Who am I? How have I chosen to live my life?—but contrasts "the 'gentleman' idea with its code of honor, heroism, valor" previously alluded to at the birthday party and "the Jewish code of moral decorum—*mitzvah*" (Ozick 215). However, as Green and Morse press on, confirming by their laughter that they are "home free" and homeward bound, their confessional speech distracts attention from what we notice: a flight of geese flying in a direction opposite to the one in which they are traveling. As Stephen looks down and spies their abandoned fire, much as Morse previously spotted the bear track, they discover to their horror that they have been traveling in a circle, Morse's "compass" apparently deceived by the metal buckle of Morse's belt that interfered with its magnetic field. Reminiscent of a moment of epiphany in William Faulkner's "The Bear," in which the boy learns that only when he abandons man-made devices is he free to face the challenge of the bear, Morse takes the first steps toward self-knowledge and survival in the woods when he relinquishes confidence in the "compass," and acquires confidence in his instinct and integrity, finding hope not in the expectation of their discovery, but in himself, the expectation—however tenuous—that "we can walk out of here" (87). "The true way for the man to . . . [survive] his wilderness experience," suggests Stewart Edward White, "is to go as light as possible. . . . To go light is to play the

game fairly. . . . It is a test, a proving of his essential pluck . . . and manhood"
(5). Like the Ojibways, Morse proves a skilled improviser and superior
guide, his highly developed flair for survival evident in his "always sniff-
ing—testing the impression of the other" (White 209).

In a tailspin, Green demands Morse's assurance that they will be saved,
a reversal of his assurance to Morse on the previous day that he would get
Morse home safely. And, no sooner has Morse calmed Green than Stephen's
screams fill the air, Mamet's bag of cinematic dirty tricks a veritable plethora
of ways to incite terror. Attempting to fashion a spear, Stephen has gashed
his leg with Morse's knife. Seeing the blood spurting, Morse springs into
action, tying off the bleeder while consulting his wilderness guide on "field
dressing . . . wounds"(90). Attempting to return the favor, Stephen begins
to betray a confidence about Green, but his mauling by the bear, hot on
their trail, prevents Morse and the audience from ever learning the
information, underscoring the billionaire's survival or death to be a function
of his ability to acquire and decipher the signs about Green—and all that
he, like the North, symbolizes—with the same proficiency he demonstrates
in reading signs in the wilderness.

Just as we feel confident that further danger has been averted for the
day, Mamet stages one of his most harrowing scenes. Though beautifully
prepared by Styles's lessons about the Kodiak and Green's paradigmatic
disregard for others, we are, nonetheless, horrified to see lightening illumine
the injured, screaming Stephen chased by the roaring bear, his bloodcur-
dling scream and whimpering reminiscent of the birthday charade. Unable
to do anything but save themselves, Morse and Green take off running, a
wicked parody of Green's joke about two men in the woods chased by a bear
who need only run faster than the other man in order to survive. Having
almost given up hope of a search party locating them, the sound of an
approaching aircraft brings them excitely to their feet. Celebrating their
discovery too soon, they are miserably dejected. Green turns on Morse,
unleashing a vicious diatribe, whose earlier signals we read in Green's
vilification of Stephen when the frustrations of the shoot, Morse's interference, and James's illness motivate him to find a scapegoat. The photographer, unable to keep his head in the crisis, now turns on the billionaire,
revealing that more than envy of Morse's wealth, Green's resentment is a
deep-seated enmity for the Other. Projecting his insufficiency, the photographer turns his wrath on Morse—"Maybe we're right to've let you people
run the country" (105)—which it appears, as Stephen may have known, not
to be merely a function of ethnicity but of his lusting for what Morse has.

Despite ample evidence of Morse's knowledge of survival tactics, the
effects of their long, cold trek in the snow and several days' exposure to the

elements are manifested in their drawn faces and shredded shoes. Green, limping badly from a fall, is supported by the exhausted billionaire. His sighting of the bear stalking them, as Styles had forewarned, finally drives Green, customarily competent under fire to crack under the pressure and babble incoherently at his impending death: "What are we going to do, Charles?" (111-12). Studying the wilderness guide, Morse plans to wreak revenge on the bear and effect deliverance, confirming Mamet's position on "the true revelation of character: how people react under pressure" (1987d, 142). Mulling his options—to choose to die without a fight, to submit to persecution (annihilation), or to stand and fight—Morse overcomes terror by repudiating any thought of failure and, animated by faith in himself, sets about crafting a plan predicated on transposing hunter and hunted. Illustrating the efficacy of his game plan to lure the bear into a deadfall, that is, by having the bear's enormous weight work to their advantage, Morse outlines the logistics of his plan to lure the bear by his own blood, to ensnare him, and to "kill the motherfucker" (115) with a spear, which we observe him honing with the ubiquitous knife, in the manner depicted in the photograph that Morse shows to Green—the image glimpsed as recently as Morse's sighting of Hawk's note depicting an Indian killing a cougar as the bookworm was about to burn it in his bonfire. As John Lahr notes, " In *The Edge* Mamet quite literally shows the triumph of thought over terror" (1997b, 82).

Morse's methodical scheme does not prepare them or us for a full-scale battle with a bear. Recalling the frightful sounds of Morse menaced by the "bear" at the lodge, and Stephen eaten by the bear, the two men trapped and terrorized by the bear whose sound and size augers a blood bath, seem easy victims until Morse pits brains against brawn. Hence Morse's indomitable courage under fire, so easily mocked by Green, is revealed to be cause for celebration, a harbinger of his commitment to take control of his life. His plan is a brilliant success, and the two gorge themselves on a celebratory meal, fashion a remembrance of their near sacrifice in the form of a bear necklace (which they hang around their necks in the manner of Mickey's bandanna in an early scene), and with Morse wearing the cured hide, the "boodle" with ritual associations, they recommence their journey home.[63] Subsequently, in a man-to-man talk later exposed as an elaborate confidence trick to bait and trap Green, Morse takes up the long-abandoned subjects of love, trust, marriage, inheritance, and murder, exposing his doubts and fears that his wife married him for his money, that she did not love him, that she has been lying in ambush awaiting his death, and that Green was somehow implicated in the plot to kill him. Supplanting thoughts of death with the promise of life, Green spots their (or rather his) ticket home—a cabin, a canoe that floats, a bottle of whiskey, and a map—but Morse's simultaneous discovery, quite as unexpected, pays a higher dividend. Relieved of the need to fight the bear, Morse notices, we presume for the first time (or addresses fully the clues of which he has been cognizant, possibly since the lodge), the similarity of the engraving style of his watch, the gift from Mickey, and the knife from Green. Having squirreled away the torn receipt that he had earlier saved from the fire, listing engraving for three items, the watch, the knife, and Green's watch, Morse has the verification of the treachery that he has long suspected. Never betraying his hand, Morse coaxes Green to show him his watch to match its inscription to the receipt: "TO BOB FROM MICKEY: FOR ALL THE NIGHTS" (130). "The chance discovery of the old love letter, the personal erotic code, three words or symbols on a florist's card . . ."—or in this case, a receipt not intended for his eyes—Morse taps into "the anger, the self-loathing, the embarrassment, [which] are confusingly sharp . . . at such moments," writes Mamet, when "Relics of decision and . . . folly are both proved by time to've been operating in service not of our personal dreams but of the mating instinct" (1996a, 112-13). Morse's discovery about himself and the betrayal, then, spur a plan to bring Green and Mickey's affair and his marriage to a timely conclusion.

"The major stumbling block for the screenwriter," Mamet told Dan Yakir, is "how to put a people in a trick bag, so that to commit murder will be inevitable, that it's not really a choice" (22).[64] Thus, just when we thought that danger and death were averted, Mamet springs the trap, drawing us into the role of witnessing the slaughter we only recently imagined. Believing that he has all he needs to get out of the woods alive, Green, under attack from Morse, goes on the defensive: "Well, you had no business with that broad, *anyway. (Pause).* . . . Everyone in the *World* knew that (*Pause*)" (130). If indeed Morse, the man who knew everything, didn't know the key thing, suggests Mamet, he, like "the husband who is 'always the last to know'. . . . chooses to be [unaware]." In other words, "He colludes in his own degradation, and this is not a *side* effect of his ignorance, but the *object* of his actions. He *contrives* to be deluded, because he needs to live in a bizarre and unaccountable world."[65] Now, in an unrelenting pursuit of the truth about the length of the affair, Morse is taunted and teased by Green who will not ruin the enigma—or film—by irrefutable fact, or give Morse the one thing he lacks. Wresting power from Morse, Green orders him outside at gunpoint intent on committing the grisly murder we have been anticipating throughout the film when we first spotted Morse sniveling in fear for his life.

As Green lifts the rifle to fire at him, Morse, who now knows that one survives by turning knowledge, factual and spiritual, to advantage—the linguistic equivalent of "running faster"—proves that Green is no match for him. He has cleverly lured Green into firing at him from a position that requires Green to back up into a deadfall—that trick foretold in Morse's plot to trap the bear. However, unbeknownst to Green and to us, Morse, anticipating Green would make his move, much as he knew that Styles was setting him up for the kill, is prepared. He has put the matchbook in the rifle to "'plug up the breach'" (133), having retained Styles's lesson on the best way to prevent a rifle from firing. Hence Green's parting farewell, ". . . you know, life is a short thing, Charles. . . . full of betrayal" (134) is richly ironic, reminding us that the game of "Hide and Seek" has switched to "The Last Man Standing." With Green impaled in the pit, his moaning discernible, his pleas the classic double-talk of the betrayer, the opportunity seems ripe to finish him off, but Mamet reveals that unlike an act of defense against the bear or the revenge murder he may have contemplated, the changed Morse, refusing to give in to baser instincts, has no stomach for revenge or the cold-blooded murder of which Green is plainly capable. With Morse's emptying the rifle and attempting and then aborting a plan to perform a traumatic amputation on Green's shattered leg, Mamet implies that the wise man knows the limitations of his skill and the values of virtue.

Burying Green and all traces of his past and exilic experience—his pocket watch, his knife, Green's watch, his wedding ring, the matchbook, and the insecurity and self-loathing that took the form of distrust of the Other—Morse is spotted by a helicopter as the sun glints off that belt buckle that has bedeviled and saved him. Returned to civilization a changed man, still wearing his bear-claw souvenir, he acknowledges that his survival is inextricably linked to the others who died saving his life. "The true drama . . . calls for the hero to exercise will," writes Mamet, " to *create* in front of us . . . , his or her own character, the strength to continue." And, "It is her striving to understand, to correctly assess, to face her own character (in her choice of battles) that inspires us" (1998, 43).

SEEING CLEARLY

"[I]F YOU'RE LOOKING FOR SIGNIFICANT DATES in the history of Chicago—and American—theater," wrote Richard Christiansen, referring to the opening of *American Buffalo* at the Goodman Theatre on 23 October 1975; "there's one to remember" (1982, 12). What Mamet had described to Mosher as a "play about three characters set in a junk shop" was, in fact, a raw drama of three men planning a robbery whose brutal language and stunning power captured the futility of the lives of three outcasts and the attention of critics. Twenty-five years later, the Mamet play is still distinctively robust and electrifyingly vital, rhythmic and ribald, elliptical and illusory, comic and corrosive. Its central metaphor is resonant, its iconic emblems with cumulative associations clarified, its subtext of history firmly established. But in his recent plays, deeply personal family plays, the scenario staged in the home is more brutal than the dialogue. Memory plays a significant role, deepening the already compelling body of work. As Mamet told Esther Harriott, "The things which one is drawn to write about don't stem from intellectual prejudice or even affection, but rather from something much deeper" (78).

It has been my intention in *Weasels and Wisemen* to initiate a dialogue on the ethical core and values inherent in Mamet's work, and to illustrate that the moral imperative, linguistic resonance, narrative rhythms, and tropes of loyalty, legacy, and learning that we recognize as Mametic—and that undergird his diverse body of work—are fundamentally informed by Judaism and the American Jewish experience. Although he has been more vocal of late on the issue of his renewed Jewish faith, Mamet is "a conscientious objector," as Michael Lerner puts it, in the broadest sense of the term. For Mamet the play is "a strict lesson in ethics" (1987d, 25); in fact, "the theater affords an opportunity uniquely suited for communicating and inspiring ethical behavior" (26).

His idiosyncratic take on the world and his dramatic reflection of it, as I have discussed variously in his stage plays and screenplays, reveal a subtle, inextricable link between moral vision and ethical choice where humane acts of kindness validate a spark of human dignity. For Mamet, like Levinas, goodness and the true are aligned in "a peculiar ethical exacerbation of language which bends true to good" (R. Cohen 2), and founded on the responsibility of the knower to do good, to assert responsibility for the other, the central ethos of Judaism. As the playwright has observed, "My premise is that things do mean things; that there is a way that things *are* irrespective of the way we *say* things are, and if there isn't, we might as well act as if there were" (1987d, 68). Employing thematic and metaphoric cons and confidence games and elaborate narratives that enhance, recover, and protect self-image, Mamet conveys an ethical design for living whose subtextual recourse to Jewish cultural experience is integral to his artistic vision and which, in recent work such as *The Old Neighborhood* and *The Old Religion,* he has foregrounded. Through complex ironies, paradigmatic teachers, and parodic characters, he continues to explore familiar terrain in new and provocative ways in work that is continually energized by the particularities of Jewish ethical vision and cultural experience.

Mamet's strength lies in his ability to raise social questions on the nature of community and communication, to critique business as sacrament, to examine personal and professional betrayals, to heighten awareness of alienation and anxieties of the individual, to stimulate discourse on the interplay of public issues and private desires, to criticize our proclivity to barter morality as commodity, to portray gaps between word and deed, act and action. Exposing mendacity and moral bankruptcy, Mamet's works generate sympathy in his unsentimental parabolic tales tempered by his admiration for the virtuosity, imagination, and temerity of men and women.

To critics, and presumably, audiences, who find Mamet's work "unclear," however, the playwright suggests, "It occurs to me that what they mean is 'provocative.' That rather than sending the audience out whistling over the tidy moral of the play, it leaves them unsettled. I've noticed over the past 30 years that a lot of what passes in the theater is not drama but rather a morality tale. 'Go thou now and do likewise.' That's very comforting," he adds, "but then you're likely to forget it" (Norman and Rezek 53). No danger of that with Mamet, who, rather than sending us out of the theatre "whistling," sends us reeling from the curves he has thrown, the dilemmas he has posed, the betrayals he has exposed, the empathic depiction of lost love, friendship, illusions, or self-respect. Of course, as Christopher Hudgins has also noticed, Mamet also sends us out laughing—"with him, at his characters, and at ourselves"—his moralism pointing toward the affirmative rhythm that is "at the core of Mamet's work" (Bigsby 1992, 225), which, like its ethical underpinning, is fundamental to Jewish tenacity and endurance. In parodic characterization and dazzling parabolas that could have been written only by the "wordsmith," as Sam Mendes precisely puts it, Mamet delights and disturbs. And true to form, he refuses to tell us whom to trust and what to think.

Yet in 1978, the headline of the Arts and Entertainment section of the *Boston Phoenix* boldly questioned: "Will Mamet Make It?" (1). Despite his then soaring reputation, Carolyn Clay expressed concern that early success and a "premature canonization" by critics, similar to that of the young Edward Albee, whose career, the young Albee had claimed, was "nearly derailed by the trumpeting of the press" (12), had the potential to corrupt or destroy Mamet. "With all that's been written recently about this playwright," she mused, "it's hard to believe that two years ago, we'd hardly heard of him. Let's hope that journalists don't do such a job that two years from now we're wondering what happened to him" (12).

Now, more than twenty years later, with all that's been written about and by him, there is little chance of that. Mamet's growing stature as one of American's most important and influential playwrights invites our respect for a prescient Ross Wetzsteon, who in 1976 was "confident of the riches he'll bring to the American theatre" (101). Only Mamet could have foreseen the depth, breadth, and diversity of a body of work that encompasses screenplays, novels, memoirs, and essays of stunning perspicacity. Yet in 1976, seeing clearly into his own future, Mamet told Wetzsteon: "To always write 'my kind of dialogue' would be the kiss of death. I believe you should always tell the truth in a way that taxes your ability to tell the truth" (101). Dredged from memory and deeply personal betrayals, Mamet's latest works, *The Old Neighborhood* and *The Old Religion,* are a case in point, revealing even more clearly than *American Buffalo* the spring that animates his art and the aesthetic vision that informs it.

NOTES

INTRODUCTION

1. "I hope that what I'm arguing for, if I'm arguing for anything," the playwrighted has stated, is, "finally and lately . . . [an] *a priori* spirituality, saying 'let's look at the things that finally matter: we need to be loved, we need to be secure, we need to help each other, we need work.' What we're left with at the end of the play or the end of the day is, I hope, the courage to look at the world." Cognizant that though he lacks the answer to life's mysteries, Mamet is committed "to try to reduce all my perceptions of the terror around me to the proper place" (Bigsby 1992, 229).

2. In this regard see Bigsby's "All True Stories" (1992, 195-229); on the role of narrative in Jewish tradition see David Roskies's *A Bridge of Longing* (1995), a outstanding study of Jewish narrative tradition.

3. William H. Macy, interview by author, Cambridge, Mass., 20 May 1992.

4. Mamet addresses Jewish education, culture and assimilation in the revealing essays "Decoration of Jewish Houses" and "A Plain Brown Wrapper" (1989, 7-14; 15-20).

5. See Mamet's remarks in "Mamet on Playwriting" (1993a), and recent interviews with John Lahr, "The Art of the Theatre" (1997a), and Geoffrey Norman and John Rezek.

6. Richard Christiansen's prescient remarks appear in "The Young Lion of Chicago," including valuable information on *American Buffalo* and incisive commentary (1982). Ross Wetzsteon lauds the young playwright in "David Mamet: Remember That Name" (1976). For responses of other critics, see chapter 1, "The Comfort of Strangers."

7. Much has been written about the scatological language for which Mamet is famous. Especially worthwhile are Ruby Cohn's "How Are Things Made Round"(1992), and Guido Almansi's "David Mamet, A Virtuoso of Invective," among the most candid to address this issue.

8. See "Public Issues, Private Tensions: David Mamet's *Glengarry Glen Ross*" (1986b). Bigsby's scholarship includes his important study *David Mamet* (1985) and exegesis of plays (1992).

9. Speaking with his friend Charlie Fox in Mamet's *Speed-the-Plow,* Gould announces that he is "in the midst of the wilderness" (1988a, 3), a prototypical marginal setting, consistent with other border sites, that will receive further study in the body of this book: a lakeboat, a subway station, a prison, interrogation rooms, whorehouses.

10. Sander Gilman's landmark study, *Jewish Self-Hatred,* is without peer in advancing our understanding of Jewish tropes, identity, and discourse. See in particular (60-69).

11. Gilman's discussion of the "blind" Jew and the "seeing" Jew pervades his work, principally because it repeatedly calls attention to the Jew's ostensible blindness to the divine word. The "seeing" Jew who acknowledges Christ's divinity is transformed into the "good" Jew. See *Jewish Self-Hatred* (esp. 1-5; 22-50).

12. Gilman's recounts the experience of several Jewish converts who threw themselves with vigor into declaring Jews blind and intractable. Especially illuminating is his consideration of what he terms Luther's "Judeophobia," resulting in a series of pamphlets, among them his influential *Book of Thieves* (1528). On the pervasive influence of Luther and his contemporaries see Carl Cohen, "Martin Luther and His Contemporaries" (195-204); Jeremy Cohen, "Traditional Prejudice and Religious Reform: The Theological and Historical Foundations of Luther's Anti-Judaism" (81-102, esp. 88-91).

13. Harold Fisch's *The Dual Image: The Figure of the Jew in English and American Literature;* Edgar Rosenberg's *From Shylock to Svengali: Jewish Stereotypes in English Fiction;* and M. J. Landa's *The Jew in Drama* provide a wealth of information on stereotypical portraits. Ellen Schiff's *From Stereotype to Metaphor: The Jew in Contemporary Drama* offers a fresh look at the depiction of the archetypal Jew and its recast models in the twentieth century.

14. See, in particular, Gilman's important chapter, "The Language of Thieves" (1986, 68-86), on Luther's *Book of Thieves* depicting the Jew as liar and thief. He argues, moreover, that the language employed by thieves was a cant laced with Hebrew words, that their maps revealed the use of Hebrew letters, and that Yiddish predates Luther's texts by at least two hundred years and may have been erroneously identified at the time. See also Paul Wexler's "Jewish Interlinguistics: Fact and Conceptual Framework" (99-149).

CHAPTER ONE

1. *Marranos,* which ran for ten performances, premiered at the Bernard Horwich Jewish Community Center in November 1975. Mrs. Stanley (Bea) Owens provided the generous commission. Douglas L. Lieberman, director of *Marranos* and The Other Theatre Company of the Bernard Horwich Community Center, was interviewed by the author in his home in Skokie, Ill., 10 October 1991.

    A letter to the author from Lieberman, 22 May 1995, confirms that although Nestor Jones and Steven Dykes claim that *Marranos* was a St. Nicholas Theatre Company production staged at the Bernard Horwich, the St. Nicholas had no involvement in the production.

2. Haim Beinhart's *Conversos on Trial* offers a detailed discussion of the social and religious life and prosecution of crypto-Jews. On the brutality employed to encourage conversions, see Cecil Roth, *A History of Marranos.*

3. See the playwright's interview with Henry Schvey (1988a, 90); Mamet confirms the influence of *Waiting for Godot* and Pinter's early sketches on his early work in David Savran's interview (135).

4. Lieberman recalls that in discussions with Mamet about *Marranos* the playwright related his "wonderful work" on the other play (*American Buffalo*) that was writing. In his letter to the author, 22 May 1995, Lieberman specifically remembers Mamet telling him "he was working on another play about a nickel." In the fall of 1975, recalls Lieberman, the playwright "disappeared" for several weeks, leaving the director to complete revisions to *Marranos* (draft no. 3), a corrupted production version. This time period is critical, as William H. Macy similarly remembers that after an absence of several weeks in the fall of 1975, Mamet reappeared with *American Buffalo*, "which blew him away." Interview with the author, Cambridge, Mass., 22 May 1992.

   On the subject of *American Buffalo*'s key themes see, for example, Schvey's interview with the playwright (99); and Kane's interview with Mosher (1992, 239).

5. Lieberman remembers Mamet saying that he was looking forward to audience reaction to the Jewish Community Theatre's production that opened with a nun.

6. Mamet, unpublished manuscript (c. 1975). All references are to draft no. 2. I would like to thank the playwright for his permission to quote from this unpublished play and Lieberman for providing me with copies of drafts no. 1, 2, and 3.

   Regarding subterfuge(s), a key technique in subsequent Mamet plays, employed by *conversos*, see Beinhart (243-43).

7. See Herman Wouk, *This Is My God*, on the practice of bris and its connection to bar mitzvah (123-25); and Rosten on terminology (1989, 88-89, 378).

8. On Moses, see George Arthur Buttrick's *The Interpreter's Bible* (861), and Benzion C. Kaganoff's *A Dictionary of Jewish Names and their History* (47). Kaganoff observes that among Sephardic Jews (inhabitants of the Iberian peninsula) during the Middle Ages, belief in the Messiah was very strong and Jews gave their children biblical names, such as Moses and Abraham, for the first time in eight hundred years. Notably, Mamet employs a technique in *Homicide* that parallels the grandfather's actions in this scene, about which, he told me in 1992, he completely forgot.

9. For further discussion, see J. P. Fokkelman's "Exodus" and the second book of the Pentateuch. On the appropriateness of Joao's Hebrew name, see Wiesel, "Moses: Portrait of a Leader" (1976, 174-205). An assimilated Jew who concealed his identity, Moses was also the most solitary and powerful hero in biblical history. Known for his virtue and struggle for national liberation, he was ultimately entrusted with the Law (the Torah) that bears his name.

10. Interestingly, Pilpay's story describes "great intimacy" and "such ties of friendship" between the scorpion and the tortoise that one could not exist without the other. The conclusion of the original story, however, suits

Mamet's version of the story and trope of betrayal and loss: "I have it in my power," said the tortoise, "both to save myself and reward thee as thou deservest." But rather than doing so, he sank down in the water and allowed the scorpion to pay with his life as just forfeit for his monstrous ingratitude.

For further discussion of Mamet's interest in the fairy tale, see "Radio Drama" (1987d, 13-14). Mosher confirms the influence of Bruno Bettelheim's *The Uses of Enchantment* on Mamet's dramatic use of fairy tale and fable (1992, 235).

11. Myron Cohen, a Jewish comedian who regularly appeared on television in the 1950s, immortalized this joke: "*Q*: Are you comfortable? *A*: I make a living." See Esther Harriott's interview with Mamet in which he discusses the great Jewish comedians whom he watched on television and admired (87). Their impact on his early and late work is frequently implicit, though pervasive.

12. Lieberman, interview.

13. Directed by Gregory Mosher, *American Buffalo* premiered on 23 October 1975 at the Ruth Page Auditorium, Goodman Stage Two, Chicago, a joint production of the St. Nicholas Theatre Company and the Goodman Theatre. The play's cast included J. J. Johnston as Donny, William H. Macy as Bobby, and Bernard Erhard as Teach. It transferred to the St. Nicholas's new theatre space on North Halstead Street, opening 21 December 1975 with Mike Nussbaum replacing Erhard. Mamet won the New York Drama Critics Award for *American Buffalo*. Mosher discussed his fortuitous collaboration with the young playwright and the original and subsequent productions of *American Buffalo* in interview (Kane 1992, 232-35), and in "How to Talk Buffalo."

American Buffalo, directed by Ulu Grosbard, opened at the Ethel Barrymore Theatre, New York, 16 February 1977, with John Savage, Kenneth McMillan, and Robert Duvall in the role of Teach. Harris's research on the revision process, Mamet's collaboration with Grosbard, and the play's critical reception recounted in *Broadway Theatre* is very informative (102-10). The play's first London production—the first American play to be produced at the National—was staged at the Cottesloe Theatre, Royal National Theatre, 28 June 1978, and directed by Bill Bryden (who later directed the British premiere of *Glengarry Glen Ross*).

A notable 1980 revival of *American Buffalo*, directed by Arvin Brown and staged at the Long Wharf Theatre in New Haven, Conn., with Al Pacino as Teach, transferred to New York and the Duke of York Theatre, London. Although Pacino hoped to appear in the film version of *American Buffalo* (1995), as he did *Glengarry Glen Ross* (1992), Dustin Hoffman assumed this role in the movie directed by Michael Corrente, also featuring Dennis Franz. Produced by Mosher, to whom Mamet gave the rights, the film marks twenty years since its premiere at the Goodman Theatre. See my review, *David Mamet Review* (1996).

14. Mamet, interview by author, Boston, Mass., 12 March 1992.

15. Mamet, interview by Terry Gross.

16. Mamet's references to urban locales, especially those that are ethnically relevant, predominantly evoke Chicago but are not limited to his hometown. Although the locus of *Edmond* is New York, plays like *Duck Variations* and *Sexual Perversity in Chicago* are set in Chicago, as is *American Buffalo, Glengarry Glen Ross, The Cryptogram,* and *The Old Neighborhood.* See also "Memories of Chelsea" (1992a, 13-23); "Pool Halls" (1987d, 87-92).

17. I met with Macy in 1992, during the run of *Oleanna* at the Hasty Pudding Theatre, Cambridge, Mass. Our discussion covered a wide range of subjects, including his interpretation of his role in *Oleanna,* long-standing collaboration with the playwright, and recollection of the Chicago productions of *American Buffalo.*

18. See Rosten's *The Joys of Yinglish* for a compendium of Yiddish terms and their spellings and interpretations.

19. Breslauer's *Chrysalis of Religion: Buber's "I and Thou"* is an informative study of Buberr's theories on decision-making and deed performance within the context of Judaic thought defined by Buber. Friedman's *Martin Buber: The Life of Dialogue* considers Buber's philosophy of the dialogic event and education.

20. For a discussion of the *schlemiel, luftmensch* (Bermant favors the spelling *luftmenstch*), and *schnorrer* in Jewish literature and humor see Chaim Bermant, *What's the Joke?* (82-99). Ruth R. Wisse's *The Schlemiel as Modern Hero* is the definitive work on the subject.

21. Rosten's cites nineteen ways in which this expression may be used (1989, 391-92).

22. Macy, interview. Recounting the event in detail, Macy averred that Mamet's refusal to change the line was a measure of his attempt to retain aesthetic control.

23. Rosten's *The Joys of Yiddish* is an invaluable study of Yiddish linguistic devices and discourse. Galvin's and Tamarkin's *Yiddish Dictionary Sourcebook* is a compendium of popular expressions—advice, lamentation, toasts and wishes, contempt, put-downs, retorts, and curses.

24. See Gilman's incisive and illuminating analysis of the *pipul* in *Jewish Self-Hatred* and its link to the stereotypical depiction of the "bad" Jew as disputatious, aggressive and superficial—one that largely contributed to the racial anti-Semitism of the twentieth century. Moreover, Tamar Garb argues that the stereotypical image of the Jew counting coins or scrutinizing the value of property dates to E. Belman's now forgotten painting *Un Juif,* and serves as a signifier of difference (27-28).

25. Zeifman also perceives the religious implication of this scene, characterizing it as one in which Bob is bought off "with the Judas equivalent of thirty pieces of silver" (128). The expression "to jew someone down"—an anti-Semitic slur that relates to trading at the lowest price—is what Teach is engaged in doing. Having become "animals," the opposite of the *menschen,* Don and Teach behave in the way that they contend Fletch, a "thief," presumably behaved.

26. See *Encyclopedia Judaica* 5 (412-14); 15 (1306).

27. Joselit's *Our Gang* investigates the nature of Jewish crime, uncovering a cache of Yiddish monikers used by Jewish criminals (1983, 25-43); see also Arthur Hertzberg's *The Jews of America* for a discussion of the pervasiveness of gambling in Jewish immigrant communities (1989, 205-06).

28. Dean reads Teach's reference to God as his invocation of "*God*" to protect him (95). More likely, the typically Yiddish phrase "God forbid" is a pattern of discourse that comes naturally to him in such situations. See Rosten's exegesis in *The Joys of Yinglish*.

29. Mamet, *American Buffalo*, TS, 1975. The copy is held in the St. Nicholas Theater Special Collection, Harold Washington Library Center, Chicago, Ill. On the subject of the ending in the original production of *American Buffalo*, see my interview with Joe Mantegna (Kane 1992, 252); Mike Nussbaum recalls that the play's concluding lines changed frequently in the early weeks (1995).

30. Harris's study of the Chicago production and subsequent revisions is valuable and includes a range of critics' responses to numerous productions (98-101).

31. Other mitzvot are: hospitality to wayfarers, attending to the dead, comforting mourners, deference to the aged, and leaving the corners of the field for the less fortunate (generosity to the poor).

32. In a discussion during a break in rehearsals for *The Cryptogram* at the C. Walsh Theater, Boston, Mass., 1 February 1995, Mamet told the author that he believed that "all portrayals of Teach are wonderful, but [Mike] Nussbaum's was genius."

33. Much of the early critical response to *American Buffalo* considered Mamet's use of scatological language and Teach's character: John Simon saw Teach as "probably a psychopathic petty criminal" and "Mamet's games with language, semiotics and sociolinguistics" infused with "a large dose of scatology and obscenity to lend contemporary relevance" (1981); Clive Barnes read the character as "The roughest guy on the block" who is "nervily nervous," and found *American Buffalo* a "meaningful" play (1976); in his view the Arvin Brown production with Pacino was a "triumph" that rejected the "abject desperation" of Robert Duvall (1983, 143-45). Similarly, the British press saw "the brilliance of the play in Teach's great vocal parabolas of self-righteousness" (Cushman 1984). See also Dean (1990); Cohn (1992, 109-21); Almansi, (esp. 196-99).

34. Bobby Mamet told the author, "We were never brought up to think of ourselves as *victims*." The interview, conducted in Cambridge, Mass., 21 September 1991, included Mamet's brother Tony, and the family patriarch, Harold Palast.

35. For sleuthing this reference and furthering my interpretation of it, I thank Ingrid and Prof. Lawrence Eisman.

36. See my essay, "Time Passages" (1992, 30-49).

37. Mike Nussbaum, interview by author. Chicago, Ill., 27 December 1995.

CHAPTER TWO

1. The world (British) premiere of *Glengarry Glen Ross,* under the direction of
    Bill Bryden, took place in September 1983 at the Cottesloe Theatre at the
    Royal National Theatre, London, and featured Karl Johnson, Derek Newark,
    and Jack Sheperd as Ricky Roma. This production won Mamet the coveted
    Olivier Award, England's prestigious theatre honor.

    The American premiere, directed by Gregory Mosher, opened at the
    Goodman Theatre, Chicago, in February 1984, featuring J. T. Walsh, Mike
    Nussbaum, Robert Prosky as Levene, and Joe Mantegna as Roma. In March
    1984 the production moved intact to New York, opening at the John Golden
    Theatre, where Lane Smith replaced William L. Petersen in the role of Lingk.
    Mamet earned the 1984 Pulitzer Prize for *Glengarry Glen Ross,* the Drama
    Critics' Award for the Best American Play 1984, and the Joseph Dintenfass
    Award.

    Returning to Chicago in 1969, having completed the first drafts of
    Sexual Perversity in Chicago, Duck Variations, and *Reunion,* Mamet supported
    himself between acting jobs in a real estate office where salesmen peddled tracts
    of scorched earth in Arizona and swampland in Florida to gullible Chicagoans.
    What he intended to be a temporary job evolved into a year-long position that
    provided the playwright with the moral issues, human relationships, power
    plays, and scathing wit he would ultimately develop in *Glengarry.* "Written in
    five days or five seconds," director Gregory Mosher recently recalled, *Glengarry*
    fulfills the playwright's fifteen-year intention to write about that experience.
    Mamet's recollections of his experience working in a Chicago real estate office
    are recounted in the National Theatre *Study Notes for "Glengarry Glen Ross"*
    (6-7). See also his interview with Lehrer. My discussions with Mosher on
    Glengarry took place in an extended telephone interview on 2 August 1995.

2. The majority of theatre critics have addressed Mamet's idiosyncratic use of
    language; only a few, mostly British, have commented on the play's ethnic
    rhythms and referents. Among them, Robert Cushman noted, "American
    actors would find richer Jewish and Italian rhythms [than British actors]"
    (1983); David Nathan wrote, "When the pogrom starts, Lazar the Butcher
    goes to Chicago, where he could have known—or—been a grandparent of
    Shelly Levene. . . . As a result, Levene escaped a society where he would have
    been persecuted, to inhabit one where he is both victim and oppressor" (1994);
    Christopher Edwards observed that checks bounce that "the notorious, mad
    Jewish couple [the Nyborgs]" use as down payment for purchased property
    (1986); Jack Kroll noted that Mamet "makes the filthiest male-to-male
    dialogue pop with the comic timing of Jack Benny" (1984). Reviewing the
    1992 film, Walter Goodman mused, "Can Mamet be saying that America's
    Romas and Levenes talk a zestier English than those to the language born,
    hence are better people?" (1992).

3. Observing that "most immigrant peddlers came from the German-speaking
    parts of Europe, where the word *Judentum* was virtually synonymous with

Handel (commerce)," Whitfield, tracing Jewish commercial activity in America to the period prior to the late 1770s, argues that a vast network of merchandisers throughout the country testifies "to the rags-to-riches ideal." Moreover, he continues, the idea of "family business" was and is "pervasive" among the Jews, and the attraction of commercial freedom "unmistakable"; success in commerce perceived "an index of the economic and social opportunities" and a reflection of "the tenacity and virtuosity of the Jews" (1984, 232-33, 239). See also Howe and Libo, *How We Lived: 1880-1930.*

4.   In "Comedy and Humor in the Plays of David Mamet," Christopher C. Hudgins arrived at a similar conclusion that Mamet "has always felt himself to be an outsider," and that "His sympathies lie with the outsiders in his plays in their attempts to live *against* the world of the insider" (1992, 194-95).

5.   In interview with the author, Lieberman discussed *Mackinac,* Mamet's little known, unpublished play (1975) that dramatizes the life of Ezekiel Solomon, a Jewish trader who supplied traveling salesmen to the western territories with product and supplies. This revue skit, drawn from Great Lakes history, featured the character of Solomon, a narrator not unlike Tom Wingfield, playing the role of a "Master of Ceremonies," and Native Americans and French voyagers. *Mackinac* is a likely predecessor to Mamet's *Lone Canoe* (1979), and its tropes find form in the film, *The Edge. Mackinac* premiered at the Bernard Horwich Jewish Community Center, 4 July 1975, under the direction of Lieberman; an additional ten to fifteen performances in a "bus-truck tour" took place in numerous suburban Chicago communities during the summer of 1975.

6.   Spears reports that late nineteenth century Chicago came to be known as the nation's metropolis, central to "the developing ecosystem" in which "the commercial traveler's role proved vital." In fact, the salesman was the pivotal link: "At bottom, economic expansion owed as much to human capital as it did to the inanimate forces—financial, manufacturing and ecological"(57). Mamet has discussed the tremendous impact of Veblen's theories on him in numerous interviews. See also Jack Barbera and Roudané (1986b), who examines ethical perversity and "business-as-sacrament."

7.   Gayle Tuchman's and Harry Gene Levine's "New York Jews and Chinese Food" examines the phenomenon of abandoning traditional Jewish foods—gefilte fish and delicatessen—for "chop suey," an implicit indication of growing assimilation in the Jewish community, whose connection with food is an integral element of community identity. Jackie Mason's shticks on Jews and Chinese continue a long line of comic routines on the subject, such as Philip Roth's hilarious "safe *treyf*" in *Portnoy's Complaint,* in which urban Jews were viewed by Chinese as "some big-nosed variety of WASP" rather than greenhorns (1969, 90).

8.   Skirting the subject, Bigsby posits, "Perhaps there is something Jewish . . . [in] a rhythm of moral ebb and flow" inextricably linked to "Laughter and judgment" and "affirmation of values" in Mamet's work. Comparing Mamet with Miller, who has similarly drawn the universal theme of social

responsibility from the Hebrew Bible, he contends that "outside of fellow Jewish playwright, Arthur Miller, it is hard to find anyone in the American theatre, or indeed, American literature," who has "such an acute awareness of the threat to individual identity implicit in the compromise of language and the denial of community" (1992, 219). Yet Bigsby does not confirm or develop his suppositions. While Tony Stafford goes somewhat further in suggesting that "Mamet goes a step beyond mere social criticism [in *Glengarry*] by enlisting the aid of his own religion to depict the omnipotent power of greed" (1996, 193), he, too, fails, in my view, to support this premise. Though Stafford's study of the Promised Land, or promised lands, is imaginative and has a broad sweep, it adds little depth to an inquiry of the central issues of Jewish sensibility, values, humor, and biblical archetypes. Noting that reiterated place names evolve into "a sacred litany" of places and cluster images, however, Stafford focuses upon the correlation of places, names, and invocations of land and place-as-concept, and pursues historical paradigms and biblical—both Hebrew Bible and New Testament—aligned to the idea of "promised land," or rather the perversion of this sign (191-93).

While I concur that biblical reference to the Promised Land finds resonance in *Glengarry,* I found little evidence to support Stafford's argument that properties in Mamet's play have linguistic connection to Scottish glens. Rather, in a telephone interview with Mosher about whether these places were variations on "New South Hell," the term Mamet uses to describe the detested tract of suburbia in northwest Chicago, where he resided as teenager, or had personal resonances, Mosher concurred that he, too, assumed place names had "some personal connection for Mamet." *Streetwise in Chicago* (1988) confirms that many real estate developers in the Chicago area, who migrated from the East, named numerous north Chicago communities for towns, resorts, lakes, and other points of interest in New York, such as Glenview, Glen Ellyn, Oak Park, Forest Park, and Westmount. These are reflected in Glengarry's River Oaks, Brook Farms, Glen Ross Farms, Glengarry Highlands, and Mountain View.

Linda Dorff hypothesizes that *Glengarry's* properties recall in name and theme Charles W. Gordon's novels—*The Man from Glengarry* (1901), *Glengarry School Days* (1902), and *The Girl from Glengarry* (1933)—although the names are presented ironically by Mamet. In Gordon's novels, she explains, Scottish immigrants settled in an idyllic community in Ontario, Canada, where "not wealth, not enterprise, not energy but fear of God" was believed to be vital to nation building (203).

9.   Cullick argues that the names Mitch and Murray are merely "metonymic" (2). Conversely, the names Mitch, Murray, and Lemkin may be traced to the Hebrew Bible, where they share divine linkage. See Kolatch, for example, for the biblical origin of names: "Mitch" a variant of Michael, in Hebrew is one "who is like God." His first appearance in the Bible is in the Book of Numbers as a member of the tribe of Asher, and in the Book of David, Michael is the

prince of angels, closest to God, carrying out God's judgments. Similarly, Lemkin is likely derived from Lemuel, 'belonging to God' (101, 139).

10.   *Encyclopedia Judaica*, v. 2, s.v. "Aaron."

11.   *Encyclopedia Judaica*, v. 11, s.v., "Levi."

12.   Dembo insightfully reads the incident of the Golden Calf in the context of Buber's understanding of man's confrontation with things: "only God in his singularity can appeal to the totality of a person in his or her singularity." In supplanting God with idols, the people, seeking idols whose appeal is "to the senses alone" have lost an I-Thou relationship with God for the "hopelessly limited I-It relationship" (104).

13.   Worster's useful essay convincingly argues that *Glengarry* is "a 'speech-act' play because it is *about* language in a particular context," and "composed of language in a particular context" (387, n. 1). Tracing the play's speech acts, he illumines Mamet's treatment of key components of the sales speech act: as *speaker* or *listener*. Noting that close scrutiny of the salesmen's talk reveals much about "the significance" that each scene attaches to distinctive types of speech, he approaches linguistic exchanges as exchanges of power, in which speech is "a claim to power . . . the most brutal [being] *forcing* another person to speak" (385).

14.   A perceptive reader of Mamet's works, Hudgins offers a compelling analysis of Mamet's film adaptation of *Glengarry*. He maintains that audiences pay insufficient attention to what is intentionally marginalized by Mamet, namely "indicators pointing toward gentleness, a kind of love and a need for love, beneath often violent scenarios" (1996, 19). Taking as a point of departure Mamet's summary of Eisenstein's theory of montage presented in *On Directing*, Hudgins contends that Mamet encourages "the audience to do much of the work of discovery and interpretation" (22), a point with equal validity for Mamet's films and plays. Hudgins pays particular attention to the film's new scene, which, he argues, "evokes our sympathy for the abused salesmen," provides additional motivation for Levene and Moss's robbery of the premium leads, and "structurally serves as the central image for the economic system entrapping and belittling these men . . . [as] slaves, pawns," one that illumines "the resentment underlying these men's actions more emphatically than Mamet's infamous gutter language that is its reflection" (1996, 28-32).

15.   Director of the acclaimed 1994 revival of *Glengarry Glen Ross* at the Donmar Warehouse, London, Mendes spoke with me at length in a recorded interview, "A Conversation with Sam Mendes and Leslie Kane" (Kane 1996, 245-62). His incisive comments on the play in performance are enlightening (and often quite humorous), given that his highly regarded, bleak production was the first postfilm revival.

16.   Richard Brucher's "Pernicious Nostalgia in *Glengarry Glen Ross*" maintains that "Mamet subverts the inherited line of nostalgia operating in [Arthur] Miller's play"(213), substantively advancing our knowledge of Mamet's place and distinction in the continuum of American drama, specifically with respect

to the role of nostalgia and the salesman, notable in Willy Loman's and Shelley Levene's investment in children. Also useful is Marcia Blumberg's "Eloquent Stammering in the Fog: O'Neill's Heritage in Mamet," addressing spiritual bankruptcy and dissolving social contracts.

17. In her interview with the author, Nan Cibula, set designer for the Goodman and New York stage productions, said that she was driven to Jimmy Wong's in northwest Chicago, which Mamet had frequented in the 1970s and which he had imagined as the setting for scene 1.

18. Dean's most recent study of Mamet's use of language in *Glengarry Glen Ross* is an exegesis of the three dyads that comprise act 1 and commentary on what she terms "the language of anxiety"(1996).

19. Credit goes to Stu Kane for noting the link between "a shell of a man" and Shelly. Presumably this moniker echoes Willy Loman's comment to Howard, "You can't eat the orange and throw the peel [shell?] away" (Miller 75).

20. I am indebted to Dembo for reminding me of this incident in his "Levinsky and the Language of Acquisition" in *The Monological Jew* (84-92), a persuasive, perceptive study of discourse and the modern Jew. Posing the question, "What does the rise in *The Rise of David Levinsky* actually mean," Dembo argues that Cahan's attitude is "more complex and fraught with ambiguity" than at first glance (84), a statement equally valid for Mamet. The novel's "preoccupation with language—with the perpetual confrontation, encounter, or meeting expressed in and by dialogue" (85) and Levinsky's encounter with anti-Semitism find structural, ethnic, and linguistic echoes in *Glengarry*.

21. Jacobs offers the first substantive study of women in Mamet's work, but her unsympathetic reading of Levene's daughter has the support of numerous critics, like Dennis Carroll, who suggests that the daughter is Levene's "last card" in his play for sympathy (49). In the minority, Hudgins, attuned to the familial rhythms, perceives his love for her beneath "the narrative's violent exterior," as "ethical behavior as it should be" (1996, 24, 40).

22. Mosher, telephone interview. I asked Mosher and Mendes whether Williamson would have taken the money if Levene had it. Each answered without hesitation and their opposing views point to the complexity and ambiguity of *Glengarry*. Mosher responded, "Yes, *absolutely!*" More magnanimous, Mendes saw Williamson entering into the bargaining with Levene, but "he regrets it the moment he does it. And then he jumps at any opportunity . . . to withdraw. . . . He's lucky that Levene doesn't have the money on him for the bribe. In fact, he may *suspect* that" (Kane 1996, 250).

23. Mamet quoted in *Background Study Notes* (6-7).

24. See Anthony Lewis's "The Jew in Stand-up Comedy" regarding the impact of monologist Lenny Bruce on American Jewish comedy: "No comedian had a profounder impact on the course of stand-up comedy in the last quarter century," he argues, "who, in some respects, epitomizes the ways in which Jewish comedians reacted antagonistically to American society and to their own background. If Woody Allen conforms to the Christian notion of what a Jew should be, Lenny Bruce embodies that community's worst fears of what

a Jew could become. He was intelligent, but no intellectual, physical if not indeed violent, radical in his politics, utterly free-thinking in his approach to sex and language, and often purposely contrary" (65). Sanford Pinsker suggests moreover, that Bruce did not invent the expression "shpritzing the goyim"— "Words, showers of them, unleashed, sprayed, machine-gunned at the audience until they couldn't *stand* it anymore"—but it was his signature comic routine, and he was "its most important popularizer" (1987, 90); see also Mamet's interviews with Norman and Rezek and with Esther Harriott, in which he discusses Bruce's comic genius.

25.   Gilman's classic study, *Jewish Self-Hatred,* examines this phenomenon throughout six centuries of Jewish history, focusing upon events, individuals, and mythical tropes that have contributed to a discourse that marginalizes and demonizes the Jew.

26.   Mosher, telephone interview. Colin Stinton, who has appeared in numerous Mamet productions, told Billington that "sexist and racist language" in Mamet's plays is "a way of dealing safely with our fears" (1993); on the subject of the pause, Pinter has stated that the pause is an inevitable aspect of speech: "The pause is a pause because of what has just happened in the mind and guts of the characters" (Gussow 1971, 132). In the pause characters hide, judge, redefine, rearm, or receive needed confirmation; they contribute to the developing tension and forestall saying something. Space does not permit me to discuss Mamet's use of this technique at great length, or the cunning of a disjunctive discourse whose intent is negotiation. For a fuller discussion of the pause and its multivalent use in the drama of Chekhov, Beckett, and Pinter, whose influence on Mamet is notable, see my *Language of Silence: On the Unspoken and the Unspeakable in Modern Drama,* and "Time Passages."

27.   It is generally well known that Mosher and Mamet invited IBM salesmen and Fuller Brush ladies to demonstrate to the cast how to "'sell the sizzle, not the steak'" (Kane 1992, 257); the point, suggests Mamet, is "not to speak the desire but to speak that which is most likely going to bring about the desire" (Savran, 137). On the psychology of sales, see Spears, who suggests that as face-to-face salesmanship evolved, pamphlets published in 1913-15 (*Hints on Salesmanship* and *Business Psychology,* in particular), emphasized the importance of the salesman "'adjust[ing] himself to the wishes, reactions, and replies of the buyer'" and ascertaining whether the individual with whom he was dealing appeared susceptible to suggestion (215).

28.   For example, see Geis's "You're Exploiting My Space: Ethnicity, Spectatorship, and the (Post)colonial Condition of Mukherjee's 'A Wife's Story' and Mamet's *Glengarry Glen Ross.*" Geis's analysis of these two works in light of each other is incisive, inducing us to take a second look at the "othering" of ethnic groups in America, and at the issues of ethnicity, gender, and sexuality that play powerful roles in Glengarry.

29.   In *A Bridge of Longing: The Lost Art of Storytelling,* Roskies writes of Rabbi (Reb) Nahman of Bratslav who judged storytelling to be so crucial he placed it at the center of his creative life. "Closing the chasm between myth and mere

story," Jewish and European fairy tales, he "discovered the language of pure myth" (1995, 29); and, in "bridging Hebrew and Yiddish, the scholars and the folk, the mythic past and the historic present," Reb Nahman not only "invented a new form of Jewish self-expression" (55), he altered the way future generations of Jewish writers view the art of storytelling. In one of his most memorable tales, "The Wise Man and the Simpleton," Nahman resorts to "Scatology as eschatology" (51), a kind of "shock treatment," suggests Roskies, counterpointing pagan and sacred worlds and underscoring the iconic human passion for money. Notably, in this tale each character has an allegorical exemplar and is possessed of both debased and higher virtues. As the Wise Man, Moses, is possessed of both wisdom and cleverness; Aaron, blessing and wealth. Fluent in Yiddish, Mamet may be acquainted with Nahman's classic Yiddish story; indeed, the paradigm and purpose of storytelling, a world of crisis and souls who have strayed, of opposing natures and characters, and the use of scatology, find ample form in his work.

30. *Black's Law Dictionary*, 6th ed., s.v. "Accessory."
31. Ibid., s.v. "Accomplice."
32. Mamet's film version of *Glengarry* predisposes us to be more sympathetic to Levene's decision to rob the office.
33. See in particular Gelber and Gilman (1986, esp. 47; 68-86). Moreover, Schiff's "Myths and Stock Types" in *From Stereotype to Metaphor* (68-94) and Fisch's *The Dual Image* provide a good basis for enhanced understanding of stereotypical models and figures (16-20).
34. See photos in *The Jew's Body* (14-15).
35. The range of critical responses to Roma, whom Stinton has characterized as the "flash intruder who talks big" (Billington 1993), is vast. Whereas Hudgins's argument promotes Roma's stoical philosophy of life (1996), Vorlicky concludes that "Roma seduces the unsuspecting, but emotionally and psychologically vulnerable, Lingk, with what in fact is a strategically calculated speech and performance. . . . initially masked as pseudo-philosophical musings intended to lure Lingk into the web of what could be called 'Roma Reasoning,'" whose ostensible goal is "to empower Lingk" (1996, 91). And Geis argues that Roma, paralleling other "storytellers who inhabit the shady side of the business world derive much of their power to deceive others (and sometimes themselves) from monologic speech" whose inherent "ability to control time, space, and attention, gives them the capacity for manipulation and distortion of the truth" (1995, 99-100). Her "Theater as 'House of Games': David Mamet's (Con)Artistry and the Monologic Voice" in *Postmodern Theatric[k]s* offers a worthy discussion of the discourse and performance art of the con man (89-115).
36. Joseph G. Baldwin's *Flush Times of Alabama and Mississippi: A Series of Sketches* (1853) portrays a paradigmatic literary figure closely resembling Roma. Developed in the "flush times," an era when credit replaced capital, "prudence yielded to "profligacy," and "'all the departments of the *crimen falsi,* held riotous carnival'" (Lenz 97-98)—the metaphor that Roma uses as a metaphor

for life: Baldwin's Ovid Bolus was a swindler who derived pleasure from the transformation of an abstract idea into concrete cash, and differed in discourse and methodology from the earlier Suggsian model of the con man (based on Simon Suggs), a figure much like Levene, who stole in order to eat (100-01).

In her provocative essay Klaver maintains that Mamet and Jean Baurillard have "gone in search of America." Reading *Glengarry* against Baurillard's *America,* Klaver asserts that they reach their "purest point of intersection" in the "post-commodity culture," a dystopia that enacts America's "fatal attraction for the conman," a figure that she reads as "the archetypal postmodernist figure" (176-79). Contrary to general perception of Roma as conman par excellence, she argues that "In *Glengarry Glen Ross,* reversibility and seduction redefine the American trait of individualism, making Levene, who engages in both, the exemplary figure of the play" (178). Thus, although he is caught, Levene, in her view, "can play the game," evoking "a landscape inhabited by Levenes" (178).

37. In Mendes's production the use of a revolve and a blazing red wall in act 1 rivets attention to characters engaged in a series of duets, duels, and deals, but precludes the possibility of Roma "moving" from his booth in the Chinese restaurant to Lingk's. To Mendes the revolve asks for "dead-pan audience involvement" (249). I can attest that the revolve heightens the present moment, enhances anticipation about the future, and intensifies our awareness of a series of irrevocable personal and professional decisions. Mendes recalls Pinter's remarking, "'What's fascinating about the revolve is that it's so threatening. . . . because what is being said is in many ways very petty'" (257).

38. In the aftermath of the Polish pogroms of 1908, Mamet's family on his mother's side settled in Chicago and "made a lot of money out of real estate and insurance" (Mamet qtd. in Clinch 48). Aaronow's preoccupation with insurance links a thematic statement about personal and financial insecurity and "insurance" against loss sounded earlier in Roma's monologue, slipping in an inside joke that in the early days of the insurance industry, Jews in particular were predisposed to insuring valuables.

39. Striking a haunting echo in *Glengarry,* Morris Rosenfeld's poem "In the Factory" evokes the dehumanization of men who toiled in sweatshops. Driven by the clock, a tailor hears "'Machine'—and it cries to me. 'Sew!'" (151-53), lending a further ironic twist to Levene's nickname and the dehumanizing world in which the Glengarry salesmen toil for strangers.

40. Abraham J. Karp's *Golden Door to America,* especially "Education, Religion, Culture" (178-85), and Howe's *World of Our Fathers* recount the fervent desire of immigrants and first-generation American Jews to advance and secure their children's future by providing them with an education, a key Jewish value (184). Reflecting on the emotion and power of Levene's speech to Williamson, Mendes notes, "I think . . . the most eloquent line, almost, in the play, is the two-word split-line about his daughter. . . . I don't know if he's too emotional, or he doesn't want to bring it up, or it's too difficult and he can't express it. I tend to favor the latter" (256).

41. In interviews Mamet frequently compares *Glengarry* to *Men in White* or *The Front Page,* observing that "in these plays the protagonist is split into a number of different aspects, just as it happens in dream." Discussing *Glengarry* with Harriott, the playwright suggested that from "a psychoanalytic point of view. . . . Williamson stands for the superego. . . . for the character the protagonist has elected for itself to control its own actions, and therefore to instill in itself the possibility of shame, guilt, remorse, rather than living in a world where one's actions are controlled by others" (94).

42. Mosher, telephone interview (August 1995).

43. See Hudgins's discussion of the screenplay's "vision of friendship" between Levene and Roma, which is structurally prepared by the three earlier scenes in which Levene and Roma are seen sharing a drink. The closing moments of the film are thus "less dark" than the play's conclusion (41).

CHAPTER THREE

1. Mamet's essay aroused a great deal of commentary for its candor on backlot politics in Hollywood, but its value lies in his analysis of the dissimilar experience of the "screenwriter-for-hire" and the first-time director of *House of Games.* Moreover, it establishes an important timeframe and his expertise in film.

2. The world premiere of *Speed-the-Plow,* under the direction of Gregory Mosher, opened in May 1988 at the Royale Theater in New York, with Joe Mantegna as Gould, Ron Silver as Fox, and Madonna as Karen. The London premiere, also directed by Mosher, opened in January 1989 at the Lyttelton Theatre at the National, featuring Colin Stinton, Alfred Molina, and Rebecca Pidgeon.

3. See *On Directing Film* (1991), based on a series of lectures delivered at Columbia University in the fall of 1987, and "A First-Time Film Director" (1989, 117-33). Significantly, in this essay and speeches and interviews of the mid-1980s, Mamet demonstrates a propensity to employ Yiddish phrases and overt Jewish allusions in his prose.

4. Among those spreading the rumors was an apparently flattered Linson, who informed journalist Henry (1988, 279) that "Mamet has to get his material somewhere." Henry maintains that Ned Tannen, head of production for Paramount Studios, is the other model.

Research on the lives, behavior, and discourse of Harry Cohn, Samuel Goldwyn, and Adolf Zukor reveals striking parallels with the producers in *Speed-the-Plow.* In particular, Stephen J. Whitfield's "Our American Jewish Heritage: The Hollywood Version" presents a worthy historical perspective and richly detailed portraits of Hollywood moguls (1986, 322-40). While the principal thrust of Lary L. May and Elaine Tyler May's article, "Why Jewish Movie Moguls: An Exploration in American Culture," is the outsider status of Jews who emerged in the 1920s to form "The Big Eight" major movie companies (6-25), the essay offers a wealth of information on the men, methods, motivation, and success of the "Big Eight" who "virtually monopolized" the movie industry (7). Notably, May and May observe that those who laid the foundation for powerful movie enterprises entered the industry from jobs in the junk and grocery business, vaudeville and sales, paralleling the upward mobility evidenced in the immigrant Jewish community in the late nineteenth and early twentieth century.

5. For example, see Gussow, for whom *Speed-the-Plow,* like *American Buffalo* and *Glengarry,* is "a dog-eat-dog world . . . always superseded by self-interest and the survival instinct" (1988, 2: 5); Henry, for whom its "moral ambiguity . . . verges on cynicism" (1988, 280); and Peter Ranier, who finds nothing new in its "paper-thin" cynicism and "whore-master's morals" (1988, 7). To Mamet "it's not cheap thrills. It's writing about Hollywood. . . . it could've been 50 hours long" (Goldstein, 27).

6. Mamet's "A Playwright in Hollywood" (1987d, 75-79), discloses lessons he learned (and recalled from his early garage theatre experience) working with Rafelson on *The Postman Always Rings Twice:* a focus on plot, financial necessity, and "abiding concern for the audience," which are satirized in *Speed-the-Plow* (78). This essay serves as an interesting gloss to "Film is a Collaborative Business" (1989b), establishing Mamet's knowledge of the people and parlance. Mamet admitted to Stayton that "Movies are all structures of incidents, which is teaching me God's-all about how to write a play" (1985, 7).

7. Mamet's use of scatological language is consistent with a long tradition in Jewish humor. For numerous interpretations on the nature and function of Jewish wit see, in particular, Altman, Telushkin, Novak and Waldoks, Gilman (1986), and Shechner (1990). Woody Allen's joke, "My parents were very old world people. Their values were God and carpeting" is a classic example of the opposition between the sacred and profane that typifies Jewish humor.

8. The scholarship on Jewish movie moguls and the prevalence and prominence of Jews in the American film industry is prodigious. Consider David Desser and Lester D. Friedman's *American Jewish Filmmakers,* Budd Schulberg's *Movie Pictures: Memories of a Hollywood Prince,* Lester D. Friedman's *Hollywood's Image of the Jew,* Patricia Erens's *The Jew in American Cinema,* and Ronald Haver's *David O. Selznick's Hollywood.*

9. Although most critics and scholars assume that the conflict among Mamet, director Brian De Palma, and producer Art Linson during the filming of *The Untouchables* was the principal inspiration for *Speed-the-Plow,* it is more likely that the rejection of Mamet's screenplay for *About Last Night* based on *Sexual Perversity in Chicago* (another portrayal of depravity, disloyalty, and cruelty in which the characters are presumably Jewish) was the springboard. Mamet's growing ethnic awareness, evidenced in "On Paul Ickovic's Photographs" (1987d, 73-74), and *The Disappearance of the Jews* (earliest copyright date is 1983) strongly supports the premise that inspiration for *Speed-the-Plow* precedes *The Untouchables.* Jones and Dykes reached a similar conclusion,

linking Mamet's "disenchantment with Hollywood" to RCA's rejection of his film script for *About Last Night* (1986) and the studio's "perversion of the intention of the original play" apparent in subsequent rewrites of Mamet's screenplay, prompting him to disassociate himself from the film (86-87).

10. In *Adapting to Abundance,* a study of the evolving Jewish middle class in New York, Heinze offers rich insights on the "promise of abundance" and the "democracy of luxury." Arguing that time and capital were increasingly available to Jewish immigrants for leisure entertainment, he theorizes in an valuable chapter, "A Jewish Monument to the Masses: Marketing the American Film" (203-18), that entrepreneurs took advantage of this largesse by distinguishing both their product and their environment from a "network of theaters, arcades, dance halls, cafés, and vaudeville houses" well established in Eastern European immigrant communities. Cognizant of enthusiastic response to the new medium, these Jewish businessmen redefined movies "as a self-sufficient entertainment within the setting of an elegant theater" (204).

11. During the 1910s, Jewish movie moguls promoted new images of prosperity, capitalizing on the desire for upscale entertainment in an emerging Jewish class. For example, Zukor's recognition that the presence of stars in movies enhanced their attractiveness and profitability led to his importing long-playing, high-quality films from Europe and introducing the star system. Merging with Jesse Lasky and Goldwyn in 1916, Zukor assembled a "dazzling 'stable' of film stars" whose promotional use "partly resembled that of brand names," notes Heinze, attracting to the movie industry the consumer loyalty among the Jewish community similarly evoked by consumer products (207-10).

12. To illustrate the close ethnic bonds in Hollywood, Whitfield recounts a timeless Hollywood anecdote that so many of Louis B. Mayer's relatives were on the payroll at MGM that its initials stood for "Mayer's *ganze mishpoche* (whole family)" (1986, 328). Of far greater importance was a veritable ethnic network that united studios, establishing a tradition of transference of power within and between families.

13. In the 1930s, ethnic hatred was targeted at Hollywood. Evidence of this demagoguery is found in the remarks of William Dudley Pelley, the leader of the fascist Silver Shirts, who viewed Jews in Hollywood as "Oriental custodians of adolescent entertainment" who ravished "Gentile maidens" (Whitfield 1986, 322-23); see also Charles Lindbergh's comments on Jews as "the greatest danger to this country," and his opposition to "their ownership and influence in our motion pictures, our press, our radio, and our government" (Ribufo, 43-63).

14. See, in particular, *Anti-Semitism in Times of Crisis,* edited by Sander Gilman and Steven T. Katz (who also contributed fine essays to this collection), for a fascinating examination of "how the nature of representation of the Jew reflects and shapes (or is reflected and shaped by) the political reality of the Jew of the Diaspora" (2). Far-reaching in its hypotheses and conclusions, this fine collection traces the origins, manifestations, and ramifications of anti-

Semitism, from medieval anti-Judaism and the creation of stereotypical imagery to scientific anti-Semitism and Jewish self-hatred.

15. Paralleling the development of the Hollywood film industry, Yiddish film, which began in Vienna in 1921, sought inspiration in Jewish religious celebrations, like Purim, and cultural experience, such as the migration to America and experience of Jews prior to the onset of World War II. The work of Joseph Green is traced in *Yiddish Cinema* (1991), a documentary of Yiddish film history available at the National Center for Jewish Film Library, Brandeis University. Mamet narrates the documentary, a project that he was particularly enthused about when I first met with him in 1992.

16. The "whitewashing" of American film encompassed the changing of names, the rewriting of plots, and the reshaping of faces. Anecdotal support of what Whitfield terms a "universalist ethos" may be found in Desser and Friedman who recount a conversation alleged to have taken place between Louis Mayer (MGM) and Danny Kaye in which the producer told Kaye, "I would put you under contract right now but you look too Jewish. Have some surgery to straighten your nose and then we'll talk" (1). Similarly, the producer Sam Spiegel was asked, ostensibly for screen credits, to desemitize his name to S. P. Eagle or E. A. Gull (Zierold 198); likewise in *The Life of Emile Zola,* winner of an Oscar for Best Picture in 1937, Captain Dreyfus does not confront anti-Semitism, thus stripping Dreyfus's life story of both credibility and ethnic identity (Erens 1985, 162-63). See Mamet's essay, "The Jew for Export," on "closet" Jews in the film industry (1996a, 137-43).

Desser wrote me in 1995 that "when 20th Century-Fox produced and distributed *Gentleman's Agreement,* the most overtly Jewish-themed film made in two decades in the U. S., all recognized that it was the only studio which could have made the film since its studio head and the film's director [Elia Kazan] were not Jewish." Moreover, it is likely that the characterization of 20th Century-Fox as "the Goy Studio" stemmed from the fact that after the ouster of William Fox and during the Golden Age of Hollywood, it was the only studio headed by a non-Jew.

17. Macy, recalling personal experience in Hollywood, remarked, "They would sell their mothers." Interview by author, May 1992.

18. Of particular value is Cohn's often luminous comparative study of linguistic strategies, "Phrasal Energies" (1995, 58-93).

19. Taking as its point of departure Mamet's acknowledgment that Pinter's Revue sketches influenced his early work, see my "Time Passages" for an analysis of narrative in the work of Pinter and Mamet and of Pinter's impact on Mamet's plays, early and late (1990, 30-49). Consider also Bigsby's discussion of narrative function in *Lakeboat, The Disappearance of the Jews, Reunion* (1985, 22-45); Dean's (1990), particularly with respect to *American Buffalo, A Life in the Theatre,* and *Glengarry Glen Ross;* and Hinden's on recitative strategies and motivation (1992, 33-48).

20. The use of fable to inject moral instruction by indirection repeatedly informs Mamet's work. For overt examples see *The Old Neighborhood* and *Things Change.*

21. In "David Mamet and the Metadramatic Tradition: Seeing the 'Trick from the Back,'" Geis argues convincingly that "Mamet's works do not demand the breaking of the fourth wall to call attention to 'the trick from the back'. . . . Rather, Mamet foregrounds the existence of *devices* in his works." Notably, *House of Games* and *Speed-the-Plow* were written in the same year.

22. Mamet calls direct attention here to ethnicity through biblical allusion to the twelve tribes of Israel and to the pejorative labeling of Jews as "clannish."

23. However much Gould jokes about it, *Forrest Gump*, one of the highest grossing pictures, took years to pay out "net" profits, observes Bernard Weintraub in "'Gump' Still Isn't Raking In Huge Profits? Hmn?" (B1, 4).

24. Critics were divided about whether the enigma derived from the character or from Madonna's performance of seductive ambiguity: Brustein (1988) found her weak; Oliver (1988) thought that she struck a perfect balance, offsetting the cynicism of the producers; Gussow (1988) and Beaufort (1988) thought her overshadowed by design.

25. Speaking to the original London cast of *Glengarry* during the rehearsal process in 1982, the playwright, recalls Jack Shepard (as Roma), "pointed out that the process of salesmanship has much more in common with the act of 'getting laid' than it had to do with hustle and fast-talking and so on" ("*Glengarry Glen Ross*—Performance," in National Theatre's Education Department's *Background notes for teachers and pupils* 9).

26. For further study of Mel Brooks's films and aesthetic philosophy, see "Farts Will Be Heard" (Desser and Friedman 105-59), which has broad reference to Mamet's canon.

27. Gilman's *Jewish Self-Hatred*, an exhaustive study of language, discourse, and marginality, is invaluable to an understanding of the link between language and the stigma attached to its usage. Arguing that language is integral to our perception of the Jew, he observes that discourse is the key to identifying the often subtle shift from "unacceptable discourse" to the more "acceptable discourse" of the majority (1986, 145). On this point, he contends that "The Holocaust did not result from the Germans' perception of the Jews as speaking a different tongue [Yiddish], but this perception contributed to the overall impression of the Jews as essentially different" (315). See, also, *The Jew's Body* (Gilman 1991b)—especially "The Jewish Voice"—for further analysis of how the shifting anti-Semitic rhetoric and "the corrupt and corrupting nature of the Jew" are presumably communicated through a "hidden language" (10-39).

28. Desser and Friedman's wonderful analysis of Mel Brooks's *History of the World Part I* is illuminating. Noting its epic format, a "burlesque jaunt through time" from the prehistoric ages to the French Revolution counterpointed with Orson Welles's "sonorous narration," they illustrate that Brooks sets his "parodic sights" on "the destructive nature of religious excess as well as the brutal consequences of intolerance" (154-57). Erens discusses this scene in "You

Could Die Laughing: Jewish Humor and Film" but arrives at a sharply different interpretation—that conversion is "not forsaking Judaism" but rather "an awakening," a response to death she contends links the films of Brooks and Woody Allen (58).

29. Drawing upon Luce Irigaray's theory that women escape exploitation by subjecting theory, thought, and language to inquiry, Hall posits that Karen overturns "phallic power" by employing "subtle subversive strategies," among them linguistic, to disarm Gould (158); Robertson built the Christian Coalition with the help of financial support from his failed bid for the White House.

30. R. Cohn arrived at a similar conclusion, noting that Karen's discourse "imitates its maudlin, mawkish, quasi-mystic tone" (1992, 117).

31. Even if Gould is "blind," Mamet can, as Gussow puts it, "sniff out a fishmonger no matter what his profession" (1988, 55).

32. Desser and Friedman note that Brooks intended to call *Blazing Saddles* (1974) *She Shtupps to Conquer* "playing off his love of Oliver Goldsmith's [1773] drama" (159).

33. Regarding the Baal Shem Tov and Hasidism see Schwartz (99-101), Breslauer (53-55), and Hertzberg's, *The French Enlightenment and the Jews*.

34. Recounted in "The Nobel Lecture" in *From the Kingdom of Memory*, Wiesel emphasizes that the only thing that the two friends can remember is the "Aleph bet gimmel" (the ABCs), which they repeat until memory floods back. On this point Benjamin Blech explains that in Hebrew the word *truth* is comprised of the first word of the alphabet (aleph), the last (tav) and the exact middle of the 22 letter alphabet, (mem). Truth demands "accuracy from start to finish and at every point in between" (61). In other words, obfuscation is defeated by accuracy and clarity.

35. "Plain Brown Wrapper" is the first of Mamet's essays to address openly the issues of self-hatred, deracination, and ethnic pride (1989b, 15-20).

36. Lawrence Kushner is the mystically inclined rabbi of Temple Beth El in Sudbury, Mass. Kushner writes that "to be awake" and present "in this place" is to experience spirituality in the "dimension of living" (1991, 28). Mamet is an active member of his congregation.

37. See Hall's "Playing to Win" for an interesting comparison between the dialogue of *Speed-the-Plow* and that of Baptist preachers, a technique highlighting Gould's and Fox's use of traditional religious preaching style to "reverentially place themselves, their morals and their mission above mere money" (152).

38. On the subject of the Afikomen/hide the salami, Mantegna recalls that a conversation ensued: "And then it just became like a little joke on that and sure enough the next day here was this line [in the play] . . . that actually incorporated both those things, because now he [Mamet] was taking this phrase, and in a way using it as a reference to the sexual joke we had made about hide the salami" (Kane 1992, 264-65).

39. M. J. Landa's landmark study, *The Jew in Drama,* convincingly argues that "in every possible way the representation of medieval drama vilified the Jew," frequently costumed in hideous clothes, forced to speak doggerel, and portrayed as the Prince of Darkness (36-39). Landa cites as an example an intermezzo in the Coventry Mysteries in which the Jew is made to dance around the cross, a connection that suggests further significance to the arcane allusion to the Coventry early in *Speed-the-Plow* as the site of Gould and Fox's celebratory lunch. For further study of medieval drama see Fisch, *The Dual Image: The Figure of the Jew in English and American Literature* (esp. 11-37); Schiff, *From Stereotype to Metaphor: The Jew in Contemporary Drama,* esp. "The Tradition of the Stage Jew" (1-35). Edgar Rosenberg's study, *From Shylock to Svengali: Jewish Stereotypes in English Fiction* reveals that the Jew was typically depicted as the fox, vulture, weasel or rat (5-35).

40. Pinchas Peli's "Responses to Anti-Semitism in Midrashic Literature," traces the origin of anti-Semitism to the "primal biblical event" involving Jacob and Esau, establishing Esau as the progenitor of Amalek (107-08). On the correlation between Amalek, the wilderness and Passover, Edmund Leach argues in "Fishing for Men on the Edge of the Wilderness," that "the geographic wanderings in the Book of Exodus" are directly connected to the festival of Passover (586-88). Likewise, Fokkelman illustrates that the Book of Exodus encompasses both "the physical and spiritual birth of the people of Israel" (56).

41. For a comprehensive analysis of satirical *Purimspiels* (Purim plays) that parodied Christianity from the fifteenth to the twentieth century (when American Jewish life in New York and the career of peddlers were its favorite subjects), see Israel Davidson's *Parody in Jewish Literature.*

42. Citing a compendium of anti-Semitic clichés of "the Jew who," such as "the sexually insecure Jew who exploits women" or "the parasitic Jew who lives off the talent of others" (147-49), Desser and Friedman remind us that Brooks's film about the entertainment business, *The Producers,* is not only *about* bad taste, it is *in* bad taste. And Mamet, taking a cue from Brooks, holds the mirror up to life; only, like Brooks, he holds it "'a little behind and below'" (Desser and Friedman 116).

43. On the "Eastern novel" and the immigrant novel, see Mamet's "The Northern Novel" (1996a, 85-91).

44. Tracing the transformation of customs and beliefs of American Jews, particularly within the last generation, Dershowitz argues that "The core of our common heritage may be difficult to define, but it is easy to recognize, especially during times of danger." For some, he suggests, compassion for others, love for Israel and custom, rather than belief, defines ethnic identity. However, "For all of us, the shared historical memories of the Holocaust and the pogroms that preceded it over millennia form an unbreakable bond—and common fear of recurrence, albeit in different form." Indeed, Dershowitz astutely observes that the experience of American Jewry may be observed both in diversity and commonalty (1991, 34), a point taken up in Joselit's valuable

scholarship, *The Wonders of America,* which offers a fine analysis of traditional paradigms within the framework of the "'freedom to observe,'" now metamorphosed into "'the freedom to neglect.'" See in particular "Kitchen Judaism" (1994, 4-7; 171-218).

CHAPTER FOUR

1. The world premiere production of *Oleanna,* under the direction of David Mamet, opened 1 May 1992 at the Hasty Pudding Theatre, Cambridge, Mass., featuring William H. Macy in the role of John and Rebecca Pidgeon as Carol. The first theatrical production of The Back Bay Theater Company, *Oleanna* was co-produced by the American Repertory Theatre in its "New Stages" series. With a revised conclusion, the play reopened in October at the Orpheum Theater, New York, with its cast intact. Directed by Harold Pinter, a British production reprising the Cambridge, Mass., ending of the play, with Lia Williams as Carol and David Suchet as John, was staged at the Royal Court Theatre, London, in June 1993, transferring to the Duke of York's Theatre in September.

    Mamet began writing *Oleanna* in 1990. Then a resident of Cambridge, Massachusetts, a politicized academic environment that his friend Alan Dershowitz, a professor at the Harvard Law School, has characterized as "a witch hunt," the playwright was privy to numerous stories about sexual harassment. One, in fact, involved a close friend, a university professor whose position was threatened when charges were brought against him by a student encouraged by her advisor to pursue legal action (Stayton 1992, 20). Mamet has stated in numerous interviews, however, that innumerable drafts of *Oleanna* were already in progress.

2. This incident and the playwright's response are recounted in Stayton's "Enter Scowling." Both Stayton and I were among the playwright's invited guests at the dress rehearsal for *Oleanna* on 30 April 1992, witnesses to a hostile exchange between Mamet and several female students from Brown University. In a telephone call the following morning to friend Harold Pinter, Mamet admitted: "I almost lost it; I regressed. . . . I felt like the professor in my play" (Stayton 1992, 66). Writing about the charged environment at Harvard and similar institutions, such as Brown, Arthur Holmberg avers that *Oleanna* is "an urgent, upsetting examination of sexual harassment" that accurately reflects the climate at universities (like Harvard, where he taught) in which "The halls of ivy are now patrolled, on the one hand, by the guardians of political correctness, and on the other, by semi-literate students who can't read Charles Dickens's long sentences, but who deploy a brilliant array of blackmail tactics" (94, 95).

3. In "'Oleanna' Enrages—and Engages," Kelly argues that Mamet "has raised outrage to an art form" (1992). A representative sampling of American and British reviews parallels audience reaction, reflecting a focus on misogyny and

backlash sexual politics: Bill Hagerty views the play as a "chilling tale of political correctness run riot" (1993); Clive Hirshorn notes, "Mamet's play is a deeply misogynistic piece that is as manipulative as the actions of his vengeful heroine" (1993), a view shared by Alisa Solomon ("Mametic Phallacy") who finds *Oleanna* a "twisted little play" in which audiences are expected to believe that "she [Carol] is marching in step, and in uniform, with the p.c. brigades" (355). Jan Stuart describes her as "a quintessential Mamet minx" who "mysteriously blossom[s] into a semantic Godzilla" (1992). And Betty Caplan's "The Gender Benders" (1993) concludes that "Mamet pays women an appalling underhand compliment. He finds the Gorgon too daunting to contemplate." See also Daniel Mufson's "Sexuality Perversity in Viragos," which surveys response to the play.

4.   Publicity announcements for *Oleanna's* Cambridge production invited audiences to "hear the truth." The epigraph from which the play takes its title and its inspiration is a camp song about a desired Utopia that perfectly captures "Mamet's imperiled dystopia" (Wolf 1993, 77). The song was subsequently employed by Pinter in his 1993 London production. The publicity text states: "Inspired but in no way influenced by this perhaps folk song, this new play does or does not expose either the issues, itself, or the author's misconceptions about sex, education, love, and politics" (1992, n.p.); the announcement's graphic art rivets attention to an off-center pane of glass or spire—possibly a church or university building. *Oleanna's* second epigraph, from Samuel Butler's *The Way of All Flesh,* and included only in the printed version with the camp song, directs our attention to issues of freedom of thought, pedagogy, and survival.

The graphic art for the New York production, on the other hand, bears some likeness to Robert Delaunay's painting *Political Drama* (1914), depicting a bull's-eye, man, and woman. Mamet has been increasingly interested in enhancing the quality of and controlling production of graphic art (see his joint interview with artist Donald Sultan, who did the art for *Edmond*). Hence, the unusual decision to use two playbills for the New York production is an intriguing one, receiving fuller explication in Louis Botto's and Steven Ryan's articles.

5.   At several performances in Cambridge and New York that I attended, women staged protests outside the theatre, and men, in particular, shouted inside. Early in the play's run in Cambridge, Harvard professors stood up and booed the play, actors were accosted when they left the theatre, screaming arguments erupted between men and women exiting the theatre, and "people literally used to get into fist fights with each other" (Mamet qtd. in Rose). On the press night for the New York production, some individuals were so agitated that they approached the stage, shouted obscenities at Rebecca Pidgeon, and elicited outbursts among audience members, an oft-repeated paradigm confirmed by Macy. In an attempt to gauge audience response statistically to *Oleanna,* the Eisenhower Theater in Washington, D. C., erected a chalkboard in the lobby to which three signs were taped: "Is he right?"; "Could it really

happen?"; "Was she wronged?" "This being Washington," Megan Rosenfeld observed, "[audiences] mull their choices seriously"; most telling, she reports, was a question put to the usher: "Can I vote for both [him and her]?" (B1, 4).

6. In a rare question-and-answer session, "Mamet on Playwriting" (1993a, 10), Mamet described *Oleanna* as a play "about failed Utopia, in this case the failed Utopia of Academia." Notably, the taciturn playwright has discussed this play more openly and frequently than he has most of his work. See his interviews with Norman and Rezek, Nightingale, Charlie Rose, and Leonard Lopate, to whom he said that *Oleanna* "is not about sexual harassment. It's about power." And defending the even-handedness of the dialectic, Mamet told Bruce Weber, "The fact that the fellow was a professor is not proof against him becoming a brute. . . . The fact that this other person is a woman is not proof against her making a false accusation" (1994, C10).

7. Issues of power, communication, and the hierarchical aspects of the teacher-student relationship are the focus of several British reviews and scholarly essays. See, for example, Charles Spencer: "Mamet has always been in a class of his own when it comes to edgy, sawn-off dialogue in which characters desperately try (and usually fail) to make themselves understood amid a welter of interruptions" (1993); Graham Hassell notes, "If people can't agree upon the fundamentals of language and its meaning. . . . [and] teachers can't extemporize without treading on pupils' ideological toes . . . education becomes impossible (1993). On this point the playwright concurs, telling interviewer Rose, "I'm being the student saying to the professor, 'You can be clearer. You have a responsibility to me. I'm lost. I need your help. Paternalism's not going to help. Charisma is not going to help. Telling me to go do my homework is not going to help" (Rose).

    Several scholarly essays weigh in on the subjects of pedagogy and power. Robert Skloot's "*Oleanna,* or, The Play of Pedagogy" views *Oleanna* as "a meta-play" about education. Skloot, for example, opposes bell hooks's definition of teaching as "'performative act,' one 'offer[ing] a space for change" with the professor's, which he finds, "a pedagogy . . . *doubly* flawed, for he is *using* performative acts *not* to enlarge space for reflection and engagement but rather to beguile and enthrall his tuition-paying audiences" (5); Ryan's "*Oleanna:* David Mamet's Power Play" argues *Oleanna,* like *Glengarry* and *House of Games,* pivots on manipulation and intimidation. Verna Foster's "Sex, Power and Pedagogy" and Anna-Lis Rousu's "Closeness and Unequal Power: Some Aspects of the Teacher-Student Relationship in Shaw's *Pygmalion* and Mamet's *Oleanna*" find interesting parallels with other plays of pedagogy.

8. Buber's essays "Education of Character" and "Education," in particular, posit pedagogy as a medium of communion that enhances humanism and potentially releases pupil power. Situating the responsibility with the educator, Buber, who views knowledge as a fundamental link between generations, advocates adapting instruction to the student's needs. See Maurice S. Friedman's trenchant analysis of Buber's philosophy, *Martin Buber: The Life*

of Dialogue (esp. "Education" 176-82). Dembo's *The Monological Jew* offers incisive insights on the "I-Thou" relationship, in particular, in his "Introduction" and "Buber and the Dialogical Jew" (3-12; 26-31), wherein he discusses Buber's articulation of the role of education and the dialogic event in human relationships.

9.   See Mamet's "Sex Camp," in which he discusses his academic experience at Goddard College, where he was an undergraduate in the late 1960s. An "unstructured laissez-faire institution," it measurably contributed to his "develop[ing] a contempt for institutions of Higher Learning," and a longing for the "utopia of Stoic, self-directed scholars" (1996a, 24, 27-28). Mamet tells Rose and Stayton, "'So many of us suffered under bad teachers as young actors. It makes a big impression to have people humiliating you all the time'" (Stayton 1992, 24).

10. Mamet confronts Jewish self-hatred and identity in interviews with Norman and Rezek (1995) and Nightingale (1993), and in recent essays.

11. For further and fuller understanding of language as Jewish cultural signifier and salient marker of racial Judaism, see Gilman's landmark scholarship on self-hatred, especially the chapter in *Jewish Self-Hatred,* "The Linguistics of Anti-Semitism" (1986, 209-70), an astute argument on the Jew's language as "hallmark of the social outsider as social critic" (164). Also see Stern's enlightening work on literary anti-Semitism.

12. Lazar contends that the significance of "the millennium phenomenon, and the related First Crusade can hardly be overstated," constituting "a prototypical case of a society in spiritual, social, political and economic crisis, deeply steeped in utopic and dystopic exaltation" (50). His work also illumines distinctive characteristics of the polemical dialogue between Ecclesia and Synagogia, the old/veiled versus the new/unveiled.

13. The Enlightenment image of the Jew receives incisive study in Gilman's *Jewish Self-Hatred,* particularly his analysis of Lessing's *The Jews* (1749) and *Nathan the Wise* (1779) (82-85). See also Michael Meyer's "Enlightenment: The Powerful Enticements of Reason and Universalism" (10-32), a concise study of Enlightenment, the civil emancipation of the Jew, as "a utopia of acceptance" in which Jews traded identity for Hellenism and entrée to the greater society from the lesser, an exchange that exceeded all expectations, resulting in "Jewish identity [that] became vestigial" (26-27).

14. Once Jews were less recognizable by outward markers—diction, discourse, and dress—"new" markers fixated on archetypal motifs of exploitation, charges of usury, and materialism. Gilman recounts the events of the "Hep-Hep" riots in which the mythological anti-Semitic epithet "exploiter" gained new currency as a signifier of the Jews (1984, 163). Stern observes further that cultural signifiers for "the Jew in contemporary American society" (the American Jew) are ethnically coded expressions grafted on to mythological ones, which typify the Jew's (immigrant) status as an interloper, defiler, or "intruder in this game of socio-cultural anti-Semitism" (298). And tracing the history of the term "intellectual," Whitfield notes that this modern ethnic

coding for an individual of learned, liberal, and/or independent mind and "passionate commitment to ideas, . . . volubility and tenacity," was also utilized as a cultural signifier for the Jews, stemming from their vocal support of Dreyfus (1984, 30).

15. Regarding the conspicuous place of Jews in the learned professions, principally because other avenues of employment were denied them and professions of law, education, and medicine offered both status and financial security, see Charles Liebman's *The Ambivalent American Jew* and Herzberg's *Jews in America,* which relates that whereas Jewish academics attained intellectual status in the 1940s, they represented nearly twenty percent of all faculty appointments in the 1960s (309). However, in *Chutzpah,* Dershowitz, an outspoken, liberal attorney and law professor, recounts a personal narrative of recurrent encounters with pervasive anti-Semitism (1991, 35-85).

16. In "Joyce and Jewish Consciousness," Fiedler posits that "if James Joyce can be faulted for his treatment of Leopold Bloom" whom Fiedler characterizes as "the first archetypal modern Jew" (discernible in Bloom's recollections of deceased family and voluble rejection of persecution), Joyce errs on the side of sentimentality, losing both "objectivity . . . and detachment" (48, 51).

17. Several British reviewers acknowledge the professor's power over academic lives. To John Peter, "John is a familiar academic type: the man who knows that education derives from the Latin *ducere,* to lead, but for whom it simply means that he's out in front . . . relish[ing] the opportunity to lay down the law" (1993); Aleks Sierz comments, "the play examines the struggle between the privileged professor (who criticises education while lapping up its benefits) and the under-privileged student (whose desire to learn is hamstrung by anger)" (1993); and Bill Hagerty, who observes, Carol "resent[s] . . . the elitism which, as a teacher, gives John the right to exercise power over his class" (1993). On the issue of the professor as provocateur, see Dershowitz's *The Advocate's Devil.* Although Mamet, a friend and admirer of Dershowitz, may have been influenced by—or influenced—it, the following exchange in Dershowitz's novel between a student and professor casts light on John's and Carol's dyad and further illumes John's pedagogy and demeanor. Notably, in *The Advocate's Devil,* the student, Abe, an astute attorney, speaks with his revered teacher, Haskell, a man who holds skepticism in the highest regard. Whereas Mamet condenses this precept to one line, Dershowitz's prose explicates "[Haskell's] method of teaching [which] confused many of the students looking for answers. . . . Haskell didn't give answers, only more questions. 'My job,' he said, "is to deepen your level of confusion. Your job is to find answers that work for you. Only you can do that. I can help by questioning your answers'" (47). Sounding much like the professor John (and Mamet), Dershowitz recently commented in "An Ivory Cower," an article on speech codes, "In the massage parlor you're supposed to make the customers feel good. In the classroom you're supposed to make them twist and sweat and get angry" (12).

18. Mamet discusses this issue with Rose.

19. On 9 September 1992, I was invited to observe a day of rehearsals prior to the New York opening of *Oleanna;* the day was spent rehearsing act 2, scene 2 (with numerous rewrites of the closing exchange). The playwright/director reiterated the actors' objectives and opposing perspectives, framing their contrasting roles of dehumanizing and humanizing sensibility, reminding Carol (Pidgeon) that she should "convert John," and John (Macy) that he should "appeal to her humanity."

20. Given the context of judgment, it seems hardly insignificant that the professor reiterates the term "pointer" and its variant "index." Itself an signifier of the mythical depiction of the Jew, an extended "index" depicted on stage and in art was understood as a further extension of "the questions put in the mouth of the Jew" (Lazar 24).

21. That John's "story" encompasses elements of the playwright's "story" is confirmed by Mamet in his interview with Rose: "When I was a child I was told I was stupid."

22. Foster dismisses John's story as "an illustrative but irrelevant anecdote" (46). Yet, given that Carol subsequently employs it to support her claim of John's sexism, it is not only integral to the play but revelatory. Illustrative of Mamet's minimalism, it seduces the listener, riveting attention to the crucial issues of the play: the use and abuse of censorship and the nexus of narrative and pedagogy (on this point both Rosten's and Roskies's scholarship is valuable). John's use of a (profane) story told for pedagogical purpose is analogous to a talmudic anecdote related by Professor Graydon Snyder in his class at the Chicago Theological Seminary, for which he, too, was accused of sexual harassment. The gist of the anecdote is that one day a man at work on a roof falls off, accidentally coupling with the woman on whom he falls, an illustrative story that Snyder reportedly had used for thirty-four years to teach the "ethical and spiritual differences between the Jewish and Christian concepts of conscience." A female student in his class filed charges, citing Snyder's narration of the tale constituted "a literal exoneration of rape." Accused of "offensive" behavior, like John, he was placed on probation and ordered to receive therapy for teaching this talmudic tale (1994).

23. Dershowitz argues that although American Jews, comprise barely 2.5 percent of the population, "have earned power—economic, educational, political, informational, charitable, moral—disproportionate to their numbers"; for that success no apology is warranted. "No one gave us this power," he asserts. Rather, Jews have seen and seized opportunities; their success, often despite quotas in the fields of law, medicine, academia, has been aided by the advantages of "education and family stability" (1991, 128).

24. The correctness of this text has been confirmed by Harriet Voyt, the playwright's executive assistant.

25. Price's recent scholarship on telecommunications in Mamet's work has relevance to *Oleanna*. Although telephones are employed in *American Buffalo, Glengarry,* and *Speed-the-Plow,* as I have previously discussed, Price evaluates their role as instruments of intrusion in several works.

26. Regarding the use of the character issue see, in particular, Hertzberg (1989), Dershowitz (1991), and Lieberson.

27. *Hamlet*, 3. 2. 6-8.

28. "We are in the presence of a crime without a name," is the memorable phrase used by Winston Churchill in a broadcast to Great Britain, 24 August 1941 (qtd. in Gilbert, *Winston S. Churchill* (1173-74), one Gilbert subsequently uses in his landmark study, *The Holocaust,* to denote the contagious fever of Fascism.

29. In act 2 it becomes apparent that Carol's notes have not recorded the professor's ideas. Rather, her notebook contains a chronological account of his questionable discourse and demeanor, amassed into a report presented to the Tenure Committee critical of John's professionalism and contesting the granting of his tenure. I am reminded of a story about the learned rabbi, the Baal Shem Tov, in which a student came to the teacher "with a handwritten book and said, 'These are your words, which I have written down. This is the Torah of Rabbi Baal Shem Tov.' The Master read what was written and said, 'Not one word is my Torah'" (L. Kushner 1991, 42). Mamet also told this story to Rose, probably quoting Kushner, whom he praises in this interview.

30. Mamet, interview by Rose.

31. See Gilman for a further explication of the immense influence of Weininger's *Sex and Character.* Tracing the development of a racial politics inextricably bound to the shift in rhetoric, Gilman's "Linguistics of Anti-Semitism" is invaluable in this context (1986, 209-19).

32. As early as 1938, Jews were hunted in Austria. Although moving accounts have been written about attacks on professional Jews in the early years of the Third Reich, one of the most valuable is Gilbert's chronicle of a reign of terror preceding round-ups and exterminations wherein he quotes British journalist, G. E. R. Geyde, "who observed doctors, lawyers or merchants selected for public abuse," principally because "victims" belonged to the upper class (59). On a related subject, a representative letter cited in Dershowitz's *Chutzpah* illustrates that hate is not only alive and well in America in the 1990s, it has a face, a name, and a coded vocabulary: ". . . you people are asking for another pogrom, for you are increasingly behaving as the Jews of Germany did. You are all vile and will deserve whatever pogrom overtakes you" (1991, 96).

33. Mamet told Rose that his father would exhaust every possibility to serve his client.

34. Indeed, as David Suchet, who portrayed the professor in Pinter's London production (1993) has noted, "Carol advances into *his* language, and John reduces into *her* language." Suchet, interviewed by Dean (1993).

35. Alain Piette notices that "The result[ing] . . . sanitized language, a sterile code of euphemism. . . . [is] a form of intellectual inquisition" (184).

36. Macy, interview by author.

37. Ryan has also arrived at this interpretation.

38. See Zeifman's review (1994).

39. *Oleanna* rehearsal, September 1992.

40. Stayton quotes a conversation between Dershowitz and Mamet during rehearsals for the premiere production of *Oleanna* in: "David Mamet Meets Alan Dershowitz" (1995, 2).

41. Michael Quinn postulates that Mamet's "problematizing [of the student's accusation]" suggests that in the absence of "material evidence or convincing corroboration" the "real truth in *Oleanna,* like the idea of utopia itself, is ultimately deferred" (247-48).

CHAPTER FIVE

1. The world premiere of *The Cryptogram,* directed by Gregory Mosher, opened on 29 June 1994 at the Ambassadors Theatre, London. Lindsay Duncan appeared in the role of Donny, Eddie Izzard portrayed Del, and Danny Worters and Richard Claxton alternated in the role of John.

   The Cryptogram's first American production, directed by David Mamet, opened on 2 February 1995 at the C. Walsh Theatre, Boston. Produced by the American Repertory Theatre in its "New Stages" series (by special arrangement with Fred Zollo, Nick Paleologos, and Gregory Mosher), *The Cryptogram* featured Felicity Huffman as Donny, Ed Begley, Jr. as Del, and Shelton Dane as John. The New York production, with cast intact, reopened on 13 April 1995 at the Westside Theatre/Upstairs, earning Mamet an Obie for Best New American Play (1995) and Ms. Huffman an Obie for her performance.

2. Homes rarely appear in Mamet's work, although in retrospect the playwright has acknowledged that the junk shop in *American Buffalo* symbolically serves as a familial home (Schvey, Gross, Bragg); yet, recognizable familial homes do appear in *Homicide, Reunion,* and *Jolly,* for example. Typically in Mamet's dramatic world, homes are places to escape from (for example, *Duck Variations, Lakeboat,* and *Edmond.* See Matthew Roudané's discussion of sceneography, "Mamet's Mimetics."

   As *The Cryptogram* makes abundantly clear (as did *American Buffalo*), devaluation and compromised relationships and values can and do occur in ersatz homes or domestic space, the consequence of unethical conduct. Alternately, Michael Hinden posits that Mamet's quest for community is an "idealized nexus of human relationships" not be confused with specific geographic locations—Chicago, for example—or cultural places. As *The Cryptogram, Homicide* and *The Old Neighborhood* illustrate, however, the familial home not only triggers the search for cultural relationships but sustains the order, even the peace, that one ideally associates with youth, community, and the familial home. Clearly Mamet intended this home space to signify the primal family; during the play's final rehearsals of his production the playwright told the cast that John's entry and the question "Are you packed?" effect a "nice family moment" (31 January 1995).

3. In his dramatization of the extended family, Mamet literally depicts its Othering. Janet Haedicke's "Decoding (M)other's Cipher Space: David Mamet's *The Cryptogram* and America's Dramatic Legacy" is a perceptive discussion of this scenario (1997a). Although several scholars have argued that homosexuality informs *American Buffalo, Lakeboat,* and *Speed-the-Plow,* (for example Radavich, Zeifman, McDonough), a position I refute in my discussion of *Speed-the-Plow,* Mamet has not scripted a gay character prior to *The Cryptogram.* When the play was first written in the late 1970s, the character was merely identified as "a close friend" (telephone interview with Mosher 1997), although as I discuss further in this chapter, Del performs a number of roles, among them the Jewish male configured as homosexual. In this regard see Gilman's *The Jew's Body* and Fiedler's *Fiedler on the Roof.* Feingold characterizes Del as "one of those spinterish, sexually wavering 'friends of the family'" (1995, 37). In answer to my question as to why Begley wore white socks in his production, the playwright responded, "they were known as 'white socks' in my neighborhood" (rehearsal notes, 1 February 1995).

4. In *The Cryptogram* the playwright barely veils biography. Though critics have pondered the question, when asked directly by Susan Stamberg, "Is this an autobiographical play?" Mamet maintained the mystery (and cryptic nature) of the drama and his privacy by answering Stamberg's question in a typically talmudic response: "To be an artist, is to deal with the amalgam of something that either happened or something that might of happened, or some mish-mosh [a wonderful Yiddish phrase that captures chaos far better than "amalgam"] of the above. And, I—I've never felt it particularly important to separate those strands in—in my work. I mean, it's sufficient to have an idea—whether that's prompted by fantasy or memory is really irrelevant" (Stamberg). On this point, Mosher's "Director's Note," printed in the program for the premiere (British) production states, "The pleasure of the play lies not, of course, in whether the young boy's journey was Mamet's, but in whether it is ours." However, despite Mamet's laconism and Mosher's statement to the contrary, critics both in England and America have noted the striking comparisons between Mamet's wretched story of childhood, related in "The Rake" (1992a, 3-11), and *The Cryptogram.* See, for example, Christiansen 1995; Lahr 1994; Canby 1995; Peter 1995.

    Mosher first read *Donny's March,* an earlier version of *The Cryptogram* in the late 1970s, a time he places after *A Life in the Theatre* and before *Glengarry Glen Ross.* A collaborator and longtime friend who had by then directed several Mamet plays, Mosher thought the three-scene, three-character play depicting a mother, child, and close family friend "ready-to-go" into production, but the playwright repeatedly declined to pursue staging a production of *The Cryptogram.* For nearly fifteen years "off and on" Mamet worked on the play. Then, "as mysteriously as it had appeared" nearly 20 years before, Mosher received the revised play, Mamet apparently prepared to have it come to light at long last (conversation with Mosher, February 1997).

5. Wiesel, whose work is everywhere illumined by remembrance, repeatedly illustrates the link binding ethnic identity, commandment, and memory. Likewise, in his essay "Memory," L. Kushner recalls that Freud, like the Baal Shem Tov—to whom the aphorism "Exile comes from forgetting. Memory is the source of redemption" (inscribed into the stone over the entrance of Yad VaShem, Israel's memorial to those who perished in the Holocaust) is attributed—understood that in remembering, "we transform our lives into a 'seder,' an order of remembering" (1993, 89).

    Regarding the role of photography in recapturing personal and ethnic identity and history, see Kugelmass's valuable essay, esp. 33-38; 43-48. Susan Sontag has suggested that "A family's photograph album is generally about the extended family—and often, is all that remains of it" (1977, 9). Her observation offers another rationale for Mamet's use of the extended family in this play.

6. Rehearsal notes, *The Cryptogram*, C. Walsh Theatre, 1 January 1995.

7. L. Kushner suggests that memory is triggered by sights, sounds, and smells (1993, 89).

8. One of the bits of trivia that the erudite Del retains is that "there's a Fraternal Group called the Catholic Order of Foresters" (1995b, 68), possibly an "inside" joke as Shomrim, the fraternal organization of Jewish police officers is called the Jewish Order of Policemen, a subject Mamet and I discussed (interview, 1992) relevant to the response of its members to *Homicide*.

9. The *galut* experience, linked to expulsion and consequent loss of culture, possessions, position, and relationships, shapes many of Mamet's works, but it plays a prominent role in *The Cryptogram, The Old Neighborhood,* and *Homicide.* The scholarship on the subject of the American Jewish experience and the Diaspora is vast; see in particular Hertzberg's *The Jews in America* and Joselit's *The Wonders of America.*

10. Sokoloff's scholarship on the presence and prominence of children in literature, especially male characters, is without peer; and her treatments of childhood in Jewish secular literature comprising recollections of the immigrant and Holocaust experience are especially noteworthy, as is her introduction to the subject, 1-21.

11. Writing about *Call It Sleep* in *World of Our Fathers,* Howe observed that the novel "scrutinizes norms and aberrations of behavior with almost unnerving intensity," narrating the experience through "the phobic and dangerously overwrought little boy" whose vision is shaped by "the purity of discovery and terror" (1976, 589-90), a description applicable to Mamet's ostensibly cryptic work. Studying the novel from a different angle, Wayne Lesser recognizes that *Call It Sleep* is a story of a child who endeavors to understand his world by recognizing, interpreting, and manipulating its signs. Among the most notable signifiers are "The Cellar," "The Picture," "The Coal," and "The Rail," which find their parallel in *The Cryptogram's:* "The Attic," "The Picture/Letter," "The Knife," "The Candle." The boy is cognizant, suggests Lesser, that "his identity and self-preservation literally depend upon his ability to bring forth

the light in these moments of increasing darkness" (164). Lesser posits, correctly, I believe, that "The word 'sleep' designates . . . the paradoxical nature of human experience. . . . the paradox of one's escape from the bondage of space by the literalization of time into history" (175).

In fact, Sokoloff avers that in *Mottel, Aftergrowth,* and *Call It Sleep,* three of the most acclaimed and sustained literary explorations of Jewish childhood, "Constructed out of their authors' hindsights and insights," the child figures embody both optimism and despair, intuitiveness—verbal and nonverbal—and confusion, their powerful need for exploration and connection the perfect vehicle for addressing marginality and the acquisition of knowledge about self and the world one inhabits. Clearly such an argument is equally valid in *The Cryptogram,* where "The notion of Jewish history as a history of return . . . to origins of memory" (Caruth 12-13) similarly traces the passage of the prepubertal boy from home.

12. See Mamet's "Three Uses of the Knife" (1998, 64-70).

13. "Separation anxiety—the fear of being deserted" Bettelheim writes in *The Uses of Enchantment,* is not bound to a specific period of a child's development (15); rather, it may be perceived at any age as the emotion of "Being 'cast out.'" A prepubertal child understands this: "'If I am not a good, obedient child . . . , they will no longer take good care of me. Fairy tales convey to the child "in manifold form that "a struggle against severe difficulties in life is unavoidable," but one is capable of "master[ing] all obstacles" and "emerg[ing] victorious" (8). Resonant in Mamet's work in numerous plays and films, including his children's plays, Bettelheim's reading of fairy tales and fables is one of many threads in *The Cryptogram*'s complex tapestry of initiation.

14. Linkage between Jewish cultural life and personal memory, namely the Eastern European/Russian habit of drinking of tea—particularly in a glass of tea with a sugar cube or jam (which, as Lynn Mamet told me, the playwright associates with his Russian-Polish grandfather [interview 1991]) is implicit in *The Cryptogram;* other overt illustrations of this paradigm are apparent in "Jews. March 1989" (1990a, 5); "A Life with No Joy in It"(1991a).

15. As Blau observes in her article on strategies of the Jewish mother, Jewish mothers permitted their children a considerable leeway "to express negative as well as positive feelings" and were often granted wide latitude in conduct, behavior illustrated by the nature of John's dialogue with his mother (171). For a biographical perspective see Mamet's frank discussion with Lahr in "Fortress Mamet" (1997b).

16. In *Patrimony* Philip Roth recalls that his mother "was the repository of our family's past, the historian of our childhood and, as I now realized, it was she whose quietly efficient presence the family had continued to adhere" (1991, 36). The role of family historian was most likely played by the playwright's grandmother Clara (Mamet, interview with author, 1992), although the playwright alludes to stories his mother told him in "When I was Young—A Note to Zosia and Willa" (1989b, 154-57).

Joselit's "Yidishe Nachas" (1994, 55-88) is a wonderful resource on the mother's principal responsibility for cultural education in the traditionally child-centered Jewish family. Citing numerous sources culled from Yivo, an archival collection of immigrant and second generation Jewish life, Joselit observes that children (especially boys) have long held a privileged role in Jewish families.

17. Chaudhuri's discussion of the loft as "indoor wilderness" in *The Wild Duck* has particular relevance in this context (73-76).

18. Lynn Mamet recalled her family alternated between Yiddish, Pig Latin, and a smattering of French (interview with Lynn Mamet, 20 September 1991). Newton understands the methodology of narrative coding as complementary components: "the proairetic (the code of actions), the hermeneutic (the code of truth), semic (the code of thematic context), symbolic code, and ethical code" (300 n. 43).

19. See my chapter on Pinter's drama in *The Language of Silence* (1984, 132-57). When asked by poet, friend, and former teacher Barry Goldensohn (unpublished interview, 26 February 1996) about the role of realism in his work, Mamet replied, "I never understood what realism was or wasn't." And to his query, "Does anyone call you a realist?" the playwright replied, "Not to my face."

20. In addition to "the moving and sorrowful voice that cries out from traumatic narrative," Caruth cites as recurring motifs the figures of "'departure,' 'falling,' 'burning,' or 'awakening'" (5).

21. A boy's fear of the mother figure is the subject of two recent Mamet works: "The Room"(1995d) and "Soul Murder" (1996c).

22. Mamet told Rose: "I didn't know anybody in the 50s who knew anybody who'd been divorced, you know, let alone have it happen *to* my own family" (emphasis added).

23. Desser and Friedman notice the frequency with which the cultural signifiers gin rummy and casino appear in Allen's films.

24. See Mamet's essay, "Simultaneity" (1997b, 47-52).

25. In this regard Newton's "Telling Others: On Secrecy and Recognition in Dickens, Barnes, Ishiguro" (241-85), offers penetrating insights.

26. In his "Director's Notes," Mosher offers a perspective worth citing: "*The Cryptogram* isn't a gang comedy, like *Glengarry Glen Ross*. It isn't a Shavian, (that's to say, argumentative) play, like *Oleanna*. . . . Like *American Buffalo* this new piece is about a parent, a friend, and a child." And whereas "The *Glengarry* characters live in a vicious territory, where you kick the other guy when he is down. . . . the monstrous acts of *Buffalo* (or of *Cryptogram*) are motivated by the best of intentions. These characters, connected by the most basic family ties, act out of profound love. The secrecy (and consequent betrayal) in *The Cryptogram* is mostly unintentional. It is mysterious even to the perpetrators. And this is why it is puzzling to the child" (1994, n.p.)

27. Mamet, interview by Gross.

28. Caruth argues that Freud confronts the topic of "understanding history as the history of trauma" (60). Her work on trauma and its shaping influence on narrative, particularly as it relates to Freud's *Moses and Monotheism* and *Beyond the Pleasure Principle,* casts light on *The Cryptogram* (and is likewise useful in rethinking *Homicide* and *The Old Neighborhood*),

29. Caruth 131, n. 2.

30. In his recollection of the disorienting experience encountered as a child in the early years of World War II, Friedlander writes that "[M]emory's strange reconstructions" encompass "The perfect clarity of . . . a pervasive fear" (72). On the correlation of dream, nightmare and children, see Lawrence Langer's "Suffer the Little Children," in *The Holocaust and the Literary Imagination* (1975, esp. 135-65). Although Langer's subject differs markedly from Mamet's, his observations on the responses of children encountering a terrifying, alien world are illuminating. "Like so much of the literature of atrocity," he writes, the setting is "a dream" followed by "an awakening"; "the dream is a projection" of the anxieties of "'children without a passport or visa, . . . for whom nobody would vouch, now'" (136).

31. Rehearsal notes, 1 February 1995. On the subject of gift-giving (and Lévi-Strauss's theories as they pertain to women, in particular), see Gayle Rubin's "The Traffic in Women: Notes on the 'Political Economy' of Sex," in which Rubin maintains that "To enter into a gift exchange as a partner, one must have something to give. If women are for men to dispose of, they are in no position to give themselves away" (174-75). On gift-giving as propitiation, Mamet writes in "Black as the Ace of Spades," that money in a game of cards is "a propitiatory gift to the Gods. . . . the equivalent of Fasting and Prayer . . . to gain the God's attention" (1989b, 172-73), an insight of particular value in this context.

32. Interestingly, this exchange echoes with notable variation the emotions of Edmond's wife in scene 1 of Mamet's urban parable *Edmond* (1983), who, when rejected by her husband, unleashes a furious tirade, her rejection by him deflected in a barrage of speech spurred by his revelation that "for years" he has been "passing judgment" on her (224).

33. As Scott Zigler, director of several American productions of *The Cryptogram* told the author, "Donny is looking for understanding, but she is looking to be understood by a child. . . . There is no way the child could make intellectual leap to understand his mother—and he is in such great need himself."

34. Mosher told me that "dark pools of light" created by Dennis Parichy's lighting (of his production) created the Rothko-like impression that reinforced (or inspired) the response of critics and audiences alike that the hunting knife in John's hand was a tool of death (telephone conversation, February 1997), an impression augmented by the dark set and frighteningly steep staircase that disappeared into the flies in this production. Lahr, for example, suggested, "At the threshold of adolescence, John may use his knife on himself, finishing the job his father began or on the box, retrieving the torn blanket" (1994, Haedicke sees the knife as "the father's instrument of castration" (1997a, 21-

22). Rather than a means of castration typically associated with the stereotypical image of the Jew, it suggests a plethora of ritual/biblical interpretations. Prefigured in stereotypical figures of the Jew armed with the knife as instrument of death or the "pound of flesh," this knife is more likely to be a *zelbshuts,* to borrow the shtetl term for weaponry hidden "against the fear [of pogroms]" (Ozick 1984, 111). See Sheldon Dane's interview with Ellen O'Brien in which the young actor who portrays John offered the view that he was not at all sure that John kills himself. "It could be . . . that he takes the knife to bed to protect himself" (1995, 53), an interesting insight from a young boy to whom Mamet taught myriad survival skills, including Morse code.

35. Roudané has suggested that "Mamet's characters . . . are in the Emersonian sense 'Men Seeing' but with "shrunken insight'" (1992, 21). One way to interpret the distance that John has traveled, I believe, is to read this text against the intertext of Emerson's "Experience." "Experience" begins with the question "Where do we find ourselves?" The answer forthcoming is that in the midst of this life, "We wake and find ourselves on a stair . . . stairs below . . . we seem to have ascended . . . stairs above . . . which go upward and out of sight" (W. Gilman 327). To see each work in the other's light is to observe that both are centrally concerned with perception—or rather the ability to see imperfectly—and willing oneself toward understanding, speculations that ordinarily would seem to exceed the skill of a child of John's age. I am indebted to Richard Brucher for a profitable and instructive dialogue on Emerson and on the vision of "Experience," in particular. See Joselit's chapter, "Red-Letter Days" (1994, 89-133) on bar mitzvah practice in America and the Reform Jewish Movement's introduction of confirmation which supplanted the ritual of bar mitzvah, deemed by Reform Jews as "unduly 'oriental'" (105).

36. In "Images of Childhood and Adolescence in Talmudic Literature," David Kraemer acknowledges considerable attention to the education of children recounted in rabbinical literature. Midrash from *Kohelet Rabba,* in particular, he observes, stipulated the seven stages of human development from birth to death and specified informal education taught in the home emphasizing "the pedagogical necessities of the education of children." These include the need "to educate children with patience and sensitivity . . ." and tie "the child's education to the developmental period" (69). Notably, the period between ten and twelve years, when the child, described as "energetic . . . in his grown-up play" ["he skips like a kid"] was expected to experience significant cognitive development, commencing preparation for bar mitzvah, though it was oft-recounted in the rabbinical literature, notes Kraemer, that children were "'reciting their verses'" from an early age (68).

37. See in particular his brilliant essay, "Our Homeland, the Text" (1996, 304-327).

38. Among representative American reviews, Matt Wolf found *The Cryptogram* an amplification of Mamet's deepening nihilism (1994); Richard Zoglin saw it as "an assured, carefully crafted work, but also something of a

disappointment. The ricocheting dialogue verges on self-parody . . ." (1995, 76); and Kroll viewed *The Cryptogram* as "Mamet's fiercely unsentimental triptych of a self-cannibalizing family" (1995, 72), echoing Canby, who characterized it as "a horror story" (1995). For Ansen, "Everyone has betrayed everyone. John is the ultimate victim and the mini-oracle who sees into the darkness that surrounds this ordinary family committing their lethally ordinary treacheries" (1995, 72). Among British reviewers, Smith notes *twin* motifs: "There is a sense of a journey, of building a new life" as much as there is "a sense of reckoning, of personalities permanently altered and relationships irreparably altered" (1994, 800).

CHAPTER SIX

1. Lynn Mamet told the author that *Jolly* was inspired by a lengthy telephone call that she had with her brother during the filming of *Homicide,* interview 10 October 1990.

2. The world premiere of *The Old Neighborhood,* under the direction of Scott Zigler was 11 April 1997, at the Hasty Pudding Theatre, Cambridge, Mass. This production, featuring Tony Shalhoub as Bobby, Vincent Guastaferro as Joey, Brooke Adams as Jolly, Jack Willis as Carl, and Rebecca Pidgeon in the role of Deeny, was produced by the American Repertory Theatre, Cambridge, Massachusetts, in its "New Stages" series. *The Old Neighborhood* transferred to the Booth Theater, New York, opening 19 November, with Patti Lupone as Jolly and Peter Riegert assuming the role of Bobby Gould. Other cast members reprised their roles in a production directed by Zigler.

    Although the play was written in 1989, Mamet made numerous changes to the manuscript before and during the rehearsal process for the world premiere. Therefore, the unpublished version cited serves as the principal reference for this chapter; alphabetical lettering in parenthetic references denotes non-continuous pagination in this manuscript.

3. The trilogy's notable reliance on the unsaid is dramatized in sentences that abruptly stop or drift off, the avoidance of subjects, and the counterpointing of quiescent and loquacious characters. Its seeming stasis recalls the plays of Chekhov in its coalescence of phenomenal and psychological experience, particularly apt for these small, seemingly slight works. On the use of the unspoken and the unspeakable in Chekhov's plays, see my chapter in *The Language of Silence* (1984, 50-75).

4. Interview with Mamet, 12 March 1992; this subject was also taken up in our discussion, 30 September 1996.

5. The literature on this subject is vast. See in particular Alan Dershowitz, who addresses the issue of intermarriage in *The Vanishing Jew.*

6. Most interpretations of *The Disappearance of the Jews* read this reunion and the subjects discussed as aimless discussion about that which is lost. Roskies's

explication of the paradigmatic narrative of "rebellion, loss, negotiated return" in the Jewish experience is especially valuable in this context (1995).

7. The Talmud suggests that "Returning home" is, as Lawrence Kushner writes, "the easiest thing to do, for it only has to occur to you to return and you have already begun." See his "Coming Home" (1993, 31-33).

8. I am indebted to Bonnie Meltzer and the collaborative efforts of the Boston and Chicago offices of Facing History and Ourselves for their assistance in identifying numerous landmarks alluded to in *The Old Neighborhood*. See also Mamet's essay, "71st and Jeffery" (1992a, 125-28).

9. Referring to Mamet's *Duck Variations*, Steven H. Gale observes that the familiarity of the characters attests to their "stable relationship" achieved over time (208), a point whose validity is similarly demonstrated in the disjunctive speech of two men in *The Disappearance of the Jews* whose friendship spans 30 years, a recurrent paradigm in the discourse of siblings and lovers.

10. Joey's fantasies of physical strength are ironic in that he imagines himself in the image of a famous American heavy-weight champion, Joe Louis. Neither is he as comic as his namesake Joe E. Lewis, a Borscht Belt comedian of the 1950s and 1960s. Implied is Michael Gold's 1930 novel, *Jews Without Money*, set in the Lower East Side of Orchard Street about which Joey rhapsodizes, a place of yearning and evanescence that is literally the "World of Our Fathers," the immigrant experience that Howe records in his encyclopedic study.

    Given its context, Joey may have unknowingly confused "Lodz" with "Luz" in its varied biblical meanings. In this regard Schwartz's' "The Aggadic Tradition" is valuable (esp. 86-87).

11. Rosten maintains that the term *rebbe* is applied to one who is a spiritual leader—"rebbe, a rabbi, spiritual leader, or teacher" (1989, 429); "Reb," on the other hand, is a term of address similar to sir or mister. Unlike rebbe, it is never used alone, but must be followed by the *first* name of the individual, as in Reb Yankel. That Joey does not know this serves to deepen the irony and confirm his paltry knowledge of *shtetl* life, namely that his Yiddish/Yinglish is disconnected from history. Mamet has developed a strong interest in *shtetl* life and the Holocaust.

12. The huge undertaking to preserve, compile, and identify photographic images of a lost shtetl world as a way of recovering what can be recovered of shtetl life is addressed in Kugelmass's essay.

13. Holmberg contends, on the other hand, that monogamy is a subject of significant importance to Joey, who wants to commit adultery (1997b, 8)).

14. See in this regard David Robinson's well researched biography of Chaplin. I am indebted to David Desser for suggesting that I follow my instinct here.

15. What for Joey is a haunting nightmare about the loss of manhood is literally that action—the murder of his wife and children—for which the character, Grounder, is arrested in Mamet's *Homicide*.

16. This remark was made to Mamet. It is of sufficient importance that it appears in *The Disappearance of the Jews* and *Homicide* and recurs, either directly or

indirectly, in numerous Mamet essays, among them "Decoration of Jewish Houses" (1989b, 7-14); "In Every Generation" (1996a).

17. On the subject of "whiteness" see Gilman (1991b, 96-100, 173-74); Pelligrini's essay, "Whiteface Performances: 'Race,' Gender, and Jewish Bodies" is also excellent, though the scholarship on the subject is vast. The allusions to non-white status also find form in Pinter's screenplay for *The Trial*. See my essay, "Peopling the Wound: Harold Pinter's Screenplay for Kafka's *The Trial*" (1997).

18. Macy, interview.

19. Speaking with Barry Davies about those who would disparage the memory of Holocaust victims, Pinter remarks, "People were dying. . . . What the hell were they [non-Jews] talking about" (16).

20. Lynn Mamet's *Lost Years,* directed by Mike Nussbaum, had a staged reading in Los Angeles in 1995. A fascinating play, it inverses the scenario of *Jolly,* delineating the sister as more critical of her sister-in-law and more supportive of her brother trapped in a marriage from which he cannot extricate himself. And whereas the character Laurie, Bobby's wife, is depicted in Mamet's play in a typical minimalist sketch, this character looms large in *Lost Years.* I am grateful to her for the opportunity to read it.

21. Lynn Mamet characterized her stepfather (about whom Mamet writes in "The Rake" [1992a, 3-11]) as a *shegeitz,* "one of those white bread types" (interview, 20 September 1991). The term *shegeitz,* which Mamet uses in his latest revisions of *The Old Neighborhood,* is the masculine form of *shiksa.*

22. See his "Writing for the Theatre" (1990).

23. Mamet spoke with Jay Carr about the Eastern view of decay, which he views as the initial, requisite step in rebirth: "The decay still holds. It's still our life. But confronting it is a way of getting over being frightened by it—admitting rather than denying it" (1988).

24. See Gilbert's monumental study for numerous references to this paradigm, especially in the early years of the Holocaust.

25. Lynn Mamet, interview 20 September 1991.

26. During my interview with Harold Palast, the patriarch of the Mamet family, he recalled that when he was assigned to a base in the United States during World War II, he was taunted in like manner and told directly by several officers that he should go to Europe because it was "his war."

27. See Hertzberg's discussion in *The Jews in America* on the American Jewish need to prove loyalty in service that dates to the American Civil War (136-38).

CHAPTER SEVEN

1. In VerMeulen, "Mamet's Mafia"; and Vallely, "David Mamet Makes a Play for Hollywood," Mamet discusses the work of Frank Capra, Preston Sturges, John Ford, and Stanley Kubrick.

2. See Richard Christiansen, "*Postman* Script: David Mamet's Special Delivery"; Yakir, "The Postman's Words"; Mamet's essay, "The Screenplay"(1996a, 117-25).

3. Mamet disavowed the filmscript of his play *Sexual Perversity in Chicago,* subsequently filmed as *About Last Night,* because the script was altered without his approval and the play's intent perverted (Jones and Dykes 86-87); Brewer's book, *David Mamet and Film: Illusion and Disillusion in a Wounded Land,* is the only full-length study of Mamet's films.

4. See his chapter, "Games Hitchcock Plays" (1-35), esp. 8-10.

5. Mamet's *On Directing Film,* in which he elucidates his views, after Eisenstein's theory of cinematography, on narrative structure and uninflected cuts, is invaluable in this context. "The story," he writes, "is the *essential progression of incidents* that occur to the hero in pursuit of his one goal," and the screenwriter must be "assiduous" in answering a series of "very basic questions: What does the hero want? What hinders him from getting it? What happens if he does not get it?" (1991b, xiv-xv). Taking his lead from Eisenstein, Mamet advocates presenting "*a succession of images juxtaposed so that the contrast between these images moves the story forward in the mind of the audience*" (2).

   Several illuminating essays on specific Mamet films bear close scrutiny, among them Christopher Hudgins's on *Glengarry* (1996); Ann Hall's "Playing to Win"; Steven Price's "Disguise in Love: Mamet, Gender, Narrative" (working paper).

6. Directed by Mamet, *Things Change,* stars Don Ameche as Gino, Joe Mantegna as Jerry, Robert Prosky in the role of the Las Vegas don, and Ricky Jay as Silver. Mantegna and Ameche shared the Volpi Cup for Best Actor at the Venice Film Festival. Although Mamet co-wrote this script with Silverstein, directed by Mamet, it appears to be pure Mamet, a position echoed by Brewer.

7. Professing his attraction to the fable, Mamet maintains that whereas "social drama" may have provided an "appropriate forum/structure in another era. . . . Now movies can be much more powerful dealing with the mythological and the fabulous" (27), a methodology he has employed with great efficacy in his stage plays, such as *The Woods* and *Edmond,* an urban fable, and less successfully in *Lone Canoe.* Ansen posits that *Things Change* "unfolds with the pixilated simplicity of a fable" (1988, 72).

8. Mamet, who writes about codes in numerous essays—"Capture the Flag, Monotheism, and The Techniques of Arbitration" (1987d, 3-11); "Eight Kings" (1996a, 3-5)—recalls Thorstein Veblen linked them to an "endeavor [that] is essentially make-believe" (1987d, 5).

9. Desser and Friedman's study, *American Jewish Filmmakers: Traditions and Trends,* is a capacious, scholarly study of the ethnic and ethical foundations that undergird the cinema of American Jewish filmmakers Woody Allen, Mel Brooks, Sidney Lumet, and Paul Mazursky; with respect to *Things Change,* see their analysis of Woody Allen's "The Schlemiel as Modern Philosopher" (36-104) and Brooks's work, "Farts Will Be Heard" (105-58).

10. In the "Preface" to *Writing in Restaurants,* Mamet writes that he "recognized my state [that of a "lapsed Talmudist"]" when "reading Abraham Cahan's *The Imported Bridegroom*" (1987d, viii).

11. Interview with Lynn Mamet, 21 Sept. 1991; Brewer views the names "Silver" and "Green" as signifiers of money, a theory not without its merit (70).

12. Jewish involvement in organized crime is the subject of Mamet's most recent screenplay. On this subject see Joselit's *Our Gang* and Mike Gold's *Jews Without Money* (1930), which taps into a particularly strong feeling among the members of the Yiddish-speaking ghetto of the Lower East Side that "America has taught the sons of tubercular tailors how to kill" (23).

13. Mamet, *Things Change,* film only.

14. Ibid.

15. For example, "What I am is what you see," Jerry tells Billy; "you can't believe everything you hear," or, as the film illustrates, what you see (18-19). See Malkin's chapter "David Mamet: *American Buffalo* and *Glengarry Glen Ross*" in *Verbal Violence in Contemporary Drama* (145-61).

16. Nan Cibula, interview with the author, 30 December 1995. Cibula, the costume designer of *Things Change* (and *House of Games* and *Glengarry*) suggested to Mamet that the combination of dark shirt and black tie would be "*de trop*"; of course, she said, reflecting Mamet's meticulous sense of design, Mantegna's costume, complete with black tie, was perfect; "it worked against the *GQ* cliché."

17. Brewer also notes the sexual innuendo implicit in Randy's and Johnson's names, which he maintains "sets the tone" (75). But such a reading misses "Johnson" as a fake identity, a coded expression, that permits Gino to enjoy enhanced status and sexual pleasure. Similarly, Desser and Friedman read the double entendre in Brooks's myriad Johnsons in *Blazing Saddles,* as sexual innuendo or "the most gentile name he could imagine" (158 n. 2); see also their treatment of *History of the World, Part One,* the Roman Age scene, (154-55) in this context.

18. See Bettelheim's discussion of this fable in his *Uses of Enchantment* pertaining to "the Reality Principle" and "the Pleasure Principle" (43); Bettelheim's influence finds its way into the film, as well, in Gino's allusion to his family, "Bruno Gato and *little* Bruno Gato" (57). Conversely, Aesop's fable concludes with the (ant's) reality principle rewarded and the pleasure principle scorned.

19. The number twelve, for example, their flight number from Chicago, which Jerry makes a point of remembering and bets, literally turns out to be a winner, not merely by chance but because the number twelve, symbolic of cosmic order and salvation, "is linked to the wheel and circle" (Cirlot 235), further relating it to the other game of chance that Gino plays, the Wheel of Fortune, and the coin, which twice serves as Gino's salvation. And lest we forget Gino's musings on shoes with Don Vincent and lessons on the art of shining shoes, of which he says, "Shine-a shoes like anything else . . ." (48), are not only an emblem of humility, appropriate for this little man, but correlate directly to the Cinderella fairy tale.

20. Gregory Mosher recalls that Mamet and he "were very much influenced by Bettelheim's *The Uses of Enchantment*" (Kane 1992, 235), a point illustrated by Mamet's remark: "In Bruno Bettelheim's *The Uses of Enchantment*, fairy tale (and, similarly, the Drama), has the capacity to calm, to incite, to assuage, finally to *affect*, because . . . we identity subconsciously (noncritically) with the protagonist) (1987d, 13). Likewise, "films," in the playwright's view, "are a symbolic medium," which "succeed when they are symbolic, when we can make the jump between cuts" (Valleley 45). References to Freud and Jung appear in *On Directing Film* and numerous essays. In this regard Joseph Campbell's influence is also writ large.

21. Mantegna recounts in his interview with the author that the inspiration for the line "Hide the Afikomen" in *Speed-the-Plow* came from their discussion of "hid[ing] the sausage" (Kane 1992, 265), a line that similarly finds form in *Things Change*. Mamet contends that "In the movies sex and violence capture our interest because they are what occupies our consciousness: a fear of sex and a desire for violence, so we watch a movie if we're told it will pamper our low desire—including mine—for these low things" (1993a, 10).

22. In "Seventy-first and Jeffrey" Mamet recalls that as a child he went shopping with his grandmother who "spoke in what could have been Yiddish, Polish or Russian" to shopkeepers, "one or two whom she knew from the Old Country, "the town of Hrubieszów, on the Russian-Polish border" (1992a, 125).

23. The echoes of *Waiting for Godot* are especially audible in this scene, reminding one of Didi's and Gogo's efforts to maintain a semblance of conversation, particularly in the early part of act 2.

24. Cohn observes that "Interrogation is [also] prevalent in Mamet, who conveys the insecurity of his characters in flurries of brief queries" as when "characters rush pell-mell into a volubility that is only occasionally short-stopped by pauses" (1995, 64-65). Certainly, interrogatories punctuate the plays: we remember great interrogative rhythms in *American Buffalo, Glengarry Glen Ross,* and *Speed-the-Plow.* In *Things Change,* Jerry's interrogatories are notable in that they are typically directed to himself. Attempting to prepare Gino for his lunch with Don Vincent, Jerry is a schlemiel at a loss for words; when attempting to effect their escape from Don Vincent's heavily guarded estate, he is at a loss for ideas.

25. *Things Change,* film only.

26. Mantegna, who portrayed both Mike Mancuso in *House of Games* and Jerry DeStephano in *Things Change* told the author that whereas Mancuso "is this character however you perceive him . . . Jerry DeStephano thinks he's this character. . . . The reason Jerry winds up shining shoes is that's probably really what he should have been doing from the beginning" (Kane 1992, 260). However, Jerry and Gino's relationship of labor and leisure imbues their collective past, present, and future with new meaning, reminding the audience of what "can be communicated from one generation to the next. . . . [is] Philosophy. Morality. Aesthetics" (Mamet 1978, 20).

27. The American premiere of *Homicide* took place in Boston, Mass., at the 1991 Boston Film Festival. *Homicide,* opened, as well, at the Israeli Film Festival. The film featured longtime collaborators Joe Mantegna as Robert Gold, William H. Macy as Sullivan, Natalia Nogulich as Chava. Also appearing were Marge Kolitsky, Ricky Jay, Tony Mamet, Vincent Gustaferro, and Colin Stinton. Mamet's father appeared in the schoolhouse scene.

28. During a book signing for *Some Freaks* (1989) in Cambridge, Mass., Mamet discussed the reluctance of the studio to fund his forthcoming film on an American Jew. Notably, the masthead of *Homicide*'s production company newsletter was in Hebrew, emblazoned with a five-cent symbol and a bison, possibly the "talismatic beast," as Simon Schama puts it, from the Polish-Lithuanian forest or the American bison of *American Buffalo* fame.

29. The shooting script of *Homicide* (c. 1988, 1990), given to me on the set of *Homicide,* identifies the Jewish detective as Gold. Mantegna told Michael Elkin that Mamet gave him his choice of first name, and the actor, who had just portrayed Bobby Gould in *Speed-the-Plow,* seeing parallels in their victimization and "striving to do the right thing," perceived "'a thread that ties the two characters together'" (ix). The surname Gold (a derivative of Goldberg, also Gould), which Mamet uses in *The Disappearance of the Jews* and *Speed-the-Plow,* was chosen by Mamet as the most common Jewish name in America (interview with author, 12 March 1992).

30. Discussing what he described as a troubling Jewish response to the film in an interview with the author (12 March 1992), Mamet summarized correspondence he received and conversations he held since *Homicide*'s release: "'Why are you bringing this stuff up?'" Representative of this response was a conversation that the playwright held with a police officer whom he surmised was Jewish because the officer was wearing a jacket with the emblem from Shomrim, the Jewish fraternal order of policemen. "I said, 'There's a movie about Jewish cops. Did you see it?' He said, 'Yeah.' I said, 'What did you think?' Was it pretty accurate?' Did you like it?' He said, 'I didn't like it at all.'" The negative reaction by some Jews smacks of what Alan Dershowitz in *Chutzpah* terms "*shanda fur de goyim,*" a Yiddish phrase that means a posture of embarrassment in front of gentiles. Among the one thousand letters that Dershowitz received from anti-Semites and enraged Jews frightened by his outspokenness, Dershowitz, like Mamet, is the most disturbed by correspondence from Jews who would prefer his—and Jewish—invisibility and silence (1991, 98-100).

For an interesting analysis of the Jew in American film, see Friedman who notes that in the 1980s, in particular, movie portraits of Jewish characters lacked "the openness of the 1960s and the sophistication of the 1970s," typically portraying Jews as "clannish," dishonest in business, and more loyal to Israel than America (288-89).

31. Regarding Mamet's "working worlds," see esp. Dorff's "Things (Ex)Change: The Value of Money in David Mamet's *Glengarry Glen Ross,*" and Brucher's "Pernicious Nostalgia in *Glengarry Glen Ross.*"

32. While the candlesticks are a credible prop further establishing the traditional Judaism of this family, they are also profoundly personal. First appearing in the Mamet canon in *Marranos,* in the form of a Sabbath candelabra, religious symbol and family heritage grabbed in haste by the young boy as he flees his family's home in Portugal after the family's capture and murder, the candlesticks literally and metaphorically reappear in Mamet's *Passover,* symbolizing the child's heritage. Mamet owns a set of candlesticks, a legacy from grandparents who escaped from Polish pogroms (Tabor, C15).

33. Notably Mamet makes several changes in this speech from shooting script to text: six thousand is changed to four; reference to *landsman,* a Yiddish word meaning "countryman," is deleted.

34. In *The Disappearance of the Jews,* the first part of *The Old Neighborhood,* Bobby relates a conversation with his gentile wife that parallels Gold's. Mamet told me that such a statement had been made to him (interview, 12 March 1992).

35. In one of the many biographical details that one finds in this film, Mamet's grandmother owned a candy store in Poland (interview with Lynn Mamet, 10 October 1990).

36. See Dershowitz (1991, 121-23) for a discussion of Judeopathy and its distinction from anti-Semitism; Magida quotes Mamet as saying that he applauds the "ethnic assertiveness" promulgated by Dershowitz's book (64). Riveting attention in *Homicide* specifically to American Jewry, Mamet explains that "as a Jew it kind of burns me that the only way that the Jewish experience is ever treated in American films is through the Nazi murder of European Jews. It's the equivalent of *Mandingo*—you know, tie a black man to a post and beat him. 'Oh, my God,' we in the audience say. 'How can they do that?' That is a very good point, but there's more to it than that" (Burnette, 13).

37. Textual changes emphasize the connection between the poster that the reader cannot see and would interpret visually in the film as anti-Semitic, further reinforcing the linkage between ethnic hatred and Mrs. Klein's death.

38. For a study of Kabbalah see the seminal work on this subject, Gershom Sholem's *Major Trends in Jewish Mysticism: On the Kabbalah and its Symbolism;* both the seal of Solomon, the pentagram, with its secular imagery, and the Shield of David, the hexagram, date from the Bronze Age when both, often interchangeable, were "charged" with magical capabilities (1971, 264). Epstein's work on Kabbalah is particularly useful for its analysis of the ten stages of the mystical journey to revelation. Notably, the use of Kabbalah in the seventeenth century corresponds to catastrophic pogroms in Poland, 1648-1655 (Ozick 1984, 140-41).

39. In his monumental *Star of Redemption,* Rosenzweig postulates that the Mogen David may be deconstructed into two equilateral triangles representing heaven, earth, and the essential intersection of both. See, in particular, Rosensweig's Book I: "The Fire, or the Eternal Life"; Book III: "The Star, or the Eternal Truth." Also see Plout, *Magen David: How the Six Pointed Star Became an Emblem for the Jewish People.* Possibly in this scene, the Chasid has

been studying the Zohar, the Book of Splendor, a massive compendium of stories and biblical exegeses that serves as a guidebook to the mystical devotee.

Mamet confirmed that he drew heavily on Joseph Campbell and Gematryia in this scene to synthesize the mythic and the mystical (interview, 12 March 1992). An example of Gematryia is the number seventy-two, which also appears in the margin of this passage of the Book of Esther to which the Chasid refers, and may be interpreted as 2 x 36, the thirty-six righteous ones whom Jews believe sustain the world, among whom Mordecai is believed to be counted; others include the twenty-two citations that Gold has earned corresponding to the twenty-two letters from which the Torah is written. Mamet repeatedly employs variations and permutations of five: the five senses, the five fingers, and the pentagram, to which the Chasid refers, the number of the Books of Moses, the number of the first five commandments enumerating the obligations of the Jewish people to God, and the second five relating to the Jewish people's responsibilities to one another. Permutations on the number five include 212—as police code and name/site of the Jewish defense group—and 203, the number that appears on the door to the Homicide office metaphorically closed to Gold at the end of the film. In a related, interesting bit of arcana Partridge also defines five as an infrequently used euphemism for Jew since 1930, possibly derived from the term "five-to-twos," Jewish shoe-shops (158).

40.   Regarding the etymology of names and their historical significance in the Book of Esther, see *Encyclopedia Judaica* (906-10); and Buttrick, *The Interpreter's Dictionary of the Bible*. Moreover, Wiesel provides a fascinating post-Holocaust interpretation in "Esther" (1991, 133-51); see also Dow Marmur who argues that the biblical Book of Esther is the paradigmatic Jewish experience of persecution, exile, and survival.

When I broached the subject of the story of Esther with Mamet, noting that the majority of his audience would not know the story, his response was to paraphrase the great rabbi Maimonides: "Those that do, do; those that do not, do not." His response underscores the coded nature of the work, accessible on many levels.

41.   See Streicker n. 10. Mamet brought Streicker's article to my attention after he had read my essay on this film. In this regard see Paul Breines, *Tough Jews: Political Fantasies and the Moral Dilemma of American Jewry,* and Mark Zborowsky and Elizabeth Herzog, *Life is With People: The Culture of the Shtetl.*

42.   Mamet made substantial and significant changes in this exchange—which in the manuscript took place before *and* after the bombing of Anderson's Train Store. Notably in fusing these scenes, he frames Gold's action and reaction more clearly, focusing in the now lengthy diner scene on Gold's need to act and to belong, both of which have been building progressively throughout the film as his lessons cumulatively provoke him into action. One speech severely cut is notable:

Gold: I was going to be the fucken Donkey, eh? Pile it on. Pile
it on, huh. Fucken mock me, if you need to, I can carry it, I'm
gonna be the Clown. (1990, 120)

43. Lynn Mamet adds a personal note to this scene: "There are two fine scenes in
     the movie that have nothing to do with action or incident but everything to
     do with my brother. He was the 'donkey'; he was first through the door"
     (interview, 21 September 1991).

44. Brewer's interpretation of this scene is curious. "[D]estroying not only
     previously acknowledged bigotry and hatred," he claims, Gold also explodes
     "the myth of a peaceful, virtuous, domestic America" which is embodied in
     "the toys [that] represent a utopic America, unsoiled, untarnished, full of hope
     and helpfulness" (156, 141). Given that the image of the train is virtually,
     inexorably linked to the Nazi regime's extermination of Jews in the twentieth
     century, Brewer's explication that Gold's discovery of evidence of racial hatred
     in the form of anti-Jewish pamphlets undermines "the illusion of a sparkling
     America" seems to sidestep the film's central themes.

45. Streicker argues that Gold's use of the chain, what he characterizes as a signifier
     "of bondage, of oppression overcome," is used in this scene as "a stark image
     of racism, namely that of a white (and a Jew) attempting to kill a black man
     with the chain of oppression" (64). An interpretation that aligns Gold with
     Jews whose wealth (owning or managing properties in the ghetto), like Mrs.
     Klein's, has figuratively chained the black is not only offensive, it strains
     credulity (64).

46. In the shooting script the term used was the more offensive "[Y]ou're one
     Smart Sheeney, aren't you" (136).
         Commenting on the film noir's pervasive darkness, most reviewers
     found Mamet's conclusion to *Homicide* to be unrelentingly bleak. See Ansen:
     "the bleakness of his ending is a kind of intellectual cop-out"(1991); Rafferty,
     who finds *Homicide* "as alienating and depressing as the local news" (1991);
     and Powers, who claims Mamet "conjures a world in which good intentions
     curdle into disasters. . . . Movies don't come much bleaker than *Homicide*"
     (1991). Brewer similarly reads *Homicide* as "a story of a species' race for
     annihilation—lost, forlorn, imprisoned, without grace or compassion" where
     Gold is denied even the "release of death" (162, 160).

47. See Gilman's "The Jewish Foot" (1991, 38-59) for an insightful study of this
     trope.

48. Speaking about *Homicide,* William H. Macy, who portrayed Sullivan, offered
     the view that the film concerns "a man trying to find his [ethnic] identity,
     trying to find where his responsibilities lay. His fatal flaw, for which he paid
     the dearest price, is that he allowed those Jewish hit men to tell him what to
     do. . . . He allowed himself to be deluded because they got him right where
     he lived. Everything they said was true, but their ends were nefarious. . . . Let's
     face it, he could have discovered his Jewishness *and* made it to Racine and

Third. Because his failed to make his *own* decision—which is what a stand-up guy does—he lost it all." Interview with author.

49. The role of the *Purimspiel* in the development and history of parodic Jewish drama receives an exhaustive examination in Israel Davidson's *Parody in Jewish Literature.*

50. Mamet, interview with author (12 March 1992).

51. *The Edge,* directed by Lee Tamahouri, stars Anthony Hopkins as Charles Morse, Alec Baldwin as Robert Green, and Elle Macpherson as Mickey. It opened October 1997.

52. See "The Story of Noach" (1996f, 59-62). Fluent in Hebrew, Mamet is a recent, avid student of Torah. Undoubtedly he would be familiar with the prophet Isaiah's warnings to the Philistines of the destruction of Israel's enemies in the Book of Isaiah ("a stout one is coming from the north . . ." [Isa. 14:31]). *The Edge*'s reiterated admonitions of danger, such as a gathering storm and a blood-thirsty bear, elicit parallels to the destruction of the northern Kingdom (of Israel's Ten Tribes) by Assyria in 721 B.C.E. Viewed as "the primary source for the Jewish mystical tradition," Ezekiel's writings contain numerous references to north, and, suggests Fass, it is the biblical text where "the concept of north [is] transformed into a full-blown symbol" emerging as: "a source of corruption"; a place "fraught with danger even for the righteous"; and the direction from which both mercy and the messianic future will come (466-68).

  In a scene cut from the concluding moments of the screenplay, Green's question and Morse's correct answer that Nebuchadnezzar was "The King of Ancient Assyria"(112) evoke a key historical referent, inspiring us to ask: "What are they talking about?" In his inimitable way, Mamet links the attack on the bear, the blazing fire, and the powerful symbol of the north in Jewish tradition, reminding us that Nebuchadnezzar wrested the ancient capital of Babylon back from the Assyrians, captured Jerusalem, and established Babylon (located north of Israel) in the sixth century as the largest, most glorious city in the world. Warnings of evil, termination of exile, and revenge are found in Jeremiah: "Out of the north an evil shall break forth upon all the inhabitants of the land" (Jer. 1:14); "[My people] commit adultery, and walk in lies" (Jer. 4:6); "[L]est my fury come forth like fire" (Jer. 4:4).

53. Stewart Edward White's *The Forest* acknowledges the Ojibways were masters of survival who inhabited Minnesota, Wisconsin, North Dakota, Montana, Ontario, Canada.

54. Quotations from *The Edge* are from the unpublished screenplay, *Bookworm* (c. 1995) with Mamet's permission.

55. In 1983 Mamet joined Lindsay Crouse, then his wife, in Churchill, Manitoba, and Stewart, British Columbia, during the shooting of *Iceman* (1984), in which Crouse co-starred with Timothy Hutton. Although the screenplay for *The Edge* was not completed until 1995, Mamet apparently draws upon visual images, phrases, and tropes from that experience in his screenplay. See his

account, "Observations on a Backstage Wife" (1987d, 142-60) for striking analogues.

56. In "Black as the Ace of Spades," Mamet writes that in "American Folklore, the Jack of Diamonds is a trouble card and is known as Jack the Bear," possibly the inspiration for Styles's name (1989b, 173).

57. See Mamet's essay in which he expresses admiration for writers of the Midwest (1996a, 85-91).

58. The screenplay identifies the wildness guide by two different names. In addition to White's book, several others may have served as Mamet's sources: Ellis Edward Sylvester's *Lost in the Wilds* (1840, 1886); Farley Mowat's *Lost in the Barrens* (1956). I am grateful to Lew Foreman for this and others clues to the screenplay.

59. In the screenplay, Stephen, ever deferential, mutters under his breath, " . . . coming . . . coming, Mister Benny . . ." (19), one of the many inside ethnic jokes that punctuate the screenplay, which, like the Yiddish in *Speed-the-Plow, Homicide,* and *The Old Neighborhood,* both establish his cultural connection to Green (or his familiarity with the discourse) and serve as "a wave to the folks back home," as Irving Howe would have it. Jack Benny and his sidekick, Rochester, were a classic television duo. The reference to them was cut from the film.

60. Mamet writes in "The Watch" that he expected a convertible for his twenty-first birthday and received instead a gold watch in a Hunter case (1992a, 31-39); the Hunter also appears in *The Old Religion* (1997b).

61. Stearns/Harrington/Richardson were old-time gun makers and outdoor suppliers, further evidence of Mamet's sense of humor.

62. The epigraph is attributed to Robert W. Service, a British-born Canadian writer of the Yukon.

63. Native Americans or First Nation Indians, among other cultural groups, have long believed there were ritual benefits to be gained from animals, namely, that the power of the beast was transferred to the hunter.

64. Mamet told Yakir that he had *The Blue Dahlia* (1946) in mind, a film noir in which either of two people could have committed the deed.

65. Quotation taken from "Debunking Spiritualism," a lecture presented by Mamet, 21 April 1985, at the Briar Street Theatre, Chicago, during the world premiere of *The Spanish Prisoner* (the one-act play that appears in the *Goldburg Street* collection) and *The Shawl.* With permission of the playwright.

WORKS CITED

PRIMARY BIBLIOGRAPHY

Mamet, David. 1973. *Mackinac*. Unpublished.

———. 1975. *Marranos*. Unpublished.

———. 1977. *American Buffalo*. New York: Grove Press. Originally published in 1977 by Grove Press in a limited book club edition.

———. 1978. *A Life in the Theatre*. New York: Grove Press.

———. 1979. *Lone Canoe*. Unpublished.

———. 1984. *Glengarry Glen Ross*. New York: Grove Press. Originally published in 1983 by Grove Press in a limited book club edition.

———. 1985a. "The Bridge." *Granta* 16 (Summer): 167-73.

———. 1985b. *Two Plays: The Shawl and Prairie du Chien*. New York: Grove Press.

———. 1985c. *The Untouchables*. Paramount. Unpublished screenplay.

———. 1987a. *House of Games*. New York: Grove Press.

———. 1987b. *Three Jewish Plays*. New York: Samuel French. Includes *The Disappearance of the Jews* (1982, 1987), *Goldberg Street* (1985), and *The Luftmensch* (1984, 1987).

———. 1987c. *The Woods, Lakeboat, Edmond: Three Plays*. New York: Grove Press.

———. 1987d. *Writing in Restaurants*. New York: Penguin Books. Originally published 1986 by Viking.

———. 1988a. *Speed-the-Plow*. New York: Grove-Weidenfeld Press. Originally published in 1987 by Grove Press in a limited book club edition.

———. 1988b. With Shel Silverstein. *Things Change*. New York: Grove Press.

———. 1989a. *Ace in the Hole*. Unpublished screenplay.

———. 1989b. *Some Freaks*. New York: Viking Penguin.

———. 1990a. *The Hero Pony*. New York: Grove-Weidenfeld Press.

———. 1990b. *Homicide*. Unpublished screenplay.

———. 1991a. *A Life with No Joy in It. Antaeus* 66 (Spring): 291-96.

———. 1991b. *On Directing Film*. New York: Viking Press.

———. 1991c. *Russian Poland*. Unpublished screenplay.

———. 1992a. *The Cabin: Reminiscence and Diversions*. New York: Turtle Bay Books.

———. 1992b. *Homicide*. New York: Grove Press.

———. 1993a. "Mamet on Playwriting." *The Dramatists Guild Quarterly* 3 (Spring): 8-14.

———. 1993b. *Oleanna*. New York: Vintage Books.

———. 1994. "Why Schindler is Emotional Pornography." *Guardian*, 30 April, 30.

———. 1995a. *Bookworm*. Unpublished screenplay (film entitled *The Edge*).

———. 1995b. *The Cryptogram*. New York: Vintage Books.

———. 1995c. *Passover*. New York: St. Martin's Press.

———. 1995d. "The Room." *Grand Street* 13, no. 4: 163-66.

———. 1996a. *Make-Believe Town: Essays and Reminiscences*. Boston: Little, Brown and Company.

———. 1996b. "Off with the Old Love." *Vogue* (February): 240, 42.

———. 1996c. "Soul Murder." *Granta* 55 (Autumn): 73-76.

———. 1996d. *Spanish Prisoner*. Unpublished screenplay.

———. 1996e. *State of Maine*. Unpublished screenplay.

———. 1996f. "The Story of Noach." In *Genesis: As It Is Written, Contemporary Writers on Our First Stories*, ed. David Rosenberg, 59-62. San Francisco: Harper-San Francisco.

———. 1997a. *The Old Neighborhood: The Disappearance of the Jews, Jolly, "D."* Unpublished manuscript.

———. 1997b. *The Old Religion*. New York: The Free Press.

———. 1998. *Three Uses of the Knife: On the Structure and Purpose of Drama*. New York: Columbia University Press.

INTERVIEWS WITH DAVID MAMET

Mamet, David. 1983. "Donald Sultan with David Mamet [interview with Robert Becker]." *Interview* 13 (March): 56-58.

———. 1987. Interview by Jim Lehrer. *MacNeil/Lehrer NewsHour*. Public Broadcasting System, 12 October.

———. 1992. Interview by the author. Boston, Mass., 12 March.

———. 1994. Interview by Charlie Rose. *Charlie Rose Show*. Public Broadcasting Company, 11 November.

———. 1994. Interview by Melvyn Bragg. *South Bank Show*. London Television, 16 October.

———. 1994. Interview by Terry Gross. *Fresh Air*. National Public Radio, 17 October.

———. 1995. Interview by Susan Stamberg with Felicity Huffman, Ed Begley, Jr., and Shelton Dane. *All Things Considered.* National Public Radio, 6 February.

———. 1996. Discussion with the author. Boston, Mass., 30 September.

———. 1996. Interview by Barry Goldensohn. Cabot, Vt., 26 February.

——— 1997. Interview by Terry Gross. *Fresh Air.* National Public Radio, 29 October.

SECONDARY BIBLIOGRAPHY

Ackerman, James S. 1987. "Numbers." In *The Literary Guide to the Bible,* ed. Robert Alter and Frank Kermode, 78-91. Cambridge, Mass.: Belknap Press.

Adelson, Alan, and Robert Lapides, eds. 1989. *Lód'z Ghetto: Inside a Community Under Siege.* New York: Viking Press.

Allen, Jennifer. 1984. "David Mamet's Hard Sell. *New York,* 9 April, 38-41.

Almansi, Guido. 1986. "David Mamet, a Virtuoso of Invective." In *Critical Angles: European Views of Contemporary American Literature,* ed. Marc Chénetier, 191-207. Crosscurrents, Modern Critiques. Carbondale: Southern Illinois University Press.

Alter, Robert. 1969. *After the Tradition: Essays on Modern Jewish Writing.* New York: E. P. Dutton.

———. 1986. "The Jew Who Didn't Get Away: On an American Jewish Culture." In *The American Jewish Experience,* ed. Jonathan D. Sarna, 269-81. New York: Holmes & Meier.

———. 1991. *Necessary Angels: Tradition and Modernity in Kafka, Benjamin, and Scholem.* Cambridge, Mass., and Cincinnati, Ohio: Harvard University Press and HUC Press, 1991.

Altman, Sig. 1971. *The Comic Image of the Jew: Explorations of a Pop Culture Phenomenon.* Rutherford, N.J.: Fairleigh Dickinson University Press.

Ansen, David. 1988. "An Offer You Can't Refuse: Mamet's Little Treat." *Newsweek,* 31 October, 72.

———. 1991. "Dark Nights of the Soul." Review of *Homicide,* by David Mamet. *Newsweek,* 14 October, 70.

———. 1995. "Phantoms in the Dark." *Newsweek,* 20 February, 72.

Arendt, Hannah. 1965. *Eichmann in Jerusalem: A Report on the Banality of Evil.* New York: Viking Press.

———. 1978. "The Jew as Pariah: A Hidden Tradition." In *Jewish Identity and Politics in the Modern Age,* ed. Ron H. Feldman, 67-90. New York: Grove Press.

Austin, April. 1995. "Mamet Fires Off a Scorching Play." *Christian Science Monitor,* 24 February, 13.

Barnes, Clive. 1985. "Pacino is Back for a Knockout in *Buffalo.*" *New York Post,* 27 October 1983. Reprinted in *New York Theatre Critics' Reviews* 143-45.

Barbera, Jack V. 1981. "Ethical Perversity in America: Some Observations on David Mamet's *American Buffalo.*" *Modern Drama* 24, no. 3: 270-75.

Baumgarten, Murray. 1982. *City Scriptures: Modern Jewish Writing.* Cambridge: Harvard University Press.

Beaufort, John. 1988. "New Mamet Comedy Dreams up a Trio of Hollywood Opportunists." *Christian Science Monitor,* 6 May. Reprinted in *New York Theatre Critics' Reviews,* 2 November, 276.

Bellow, Saul. 1961. *Seize the Day.* New York: Viking Press.

———. 1975. *Humboldt's Gift.* New York: Viking Press.

Beinhart, Haim. 1981. *Conversos on Trial.* Jerusalem: Magnes Press.

Benjamin, Walter. 1969. "The Storyteller." In *Illuminations,* ed. Hannah Arendt, trans. Harry Zohn, 83-109. New York: Schocken Books.

Bermant, Chaim. 1986. *What's the Joke?: A Study of Jewish Humor Through the Ages.* London: Weidenfeld and Nicholson.

Bernstein, Mashey M. 1986. "Whitebread and Whitemeat in Beverly Hills." *Midstream* 32: 42-43.

Bettelheim, Bruno. 1977. *The Uses of Enchantment: The Meaning and the Importance of Fairy Tales.* New York: Random House.

Bigsby, Christopher W.E. 1985. *David Mamet.* London and New York: Methuen.

———. 1988. *Beyond Broadway.* Vol. 3 of *A Critical Introduction to Twentieth Century American Drama.* Cambridge: Cambridge University Press, 251-90.

———. 1992. "David Mamet: All True Stories." In *Modern American Drama, 1945-1990,* 195-230. New York: Cambridge University Press.

Billington, Michael. 1989. "Dream Sequence." *Guardian* [Manchester], 16 February, 21.

———. 1993a. "First Night: Lessons for the Teacher." *Guardian* [London], 1 July, 9.

———. 1993b. "Man Trouble." *Guardian* [Manchester], 12 June, 7.

———. 1994. "Cryptogram." *Guardian* [London], 30 June. Reprinted in *Theatre Record* 18 June-1 July, 799.

Bison Newsletter. 1990. 2, no. 5., 12 October.

Black, Henry Campbell. 1991. *Black's Law Dictionary.* 6th ed. St. Paul: Minn.: West Publishing.

Blau, Zena Smith. 1989. "Strategy of the Jewish Mother." In *The Jewish Family: Metaphor and Memory,* ed. David Kraemer 167-87. New York and Oxford: Oxford University Press.

Blech, Benjamin. 1991. *The Secrets of Hebrew Words.* Northvale, N. J. and London: Jason Aronson.

Bloch, Abraham. 1984. *A Book of Jewish Ethical Concepts: Biblical and Postbiblical.* New York: Ktav.

Blumberg Marcia. 1988. "Eloquent Stammering in the Fog: O'Neill's Heritage in Mamet." In *Perspectives on O'Neill: New Essays,* ed. Shyamal Bagchee, 97-111. *English Literary Series,* 43. Victoria, B.C.: University of Victoria.

Blumenson, Martin. 1972. *The Patton Papers.* Vol. 2 (1940-1945). Boston: Houghton Mifflin.

———. 1985. Patton: *The Man Behind the Legend, 1885-1945.* New York: William Morrow.

———. 1996. Letter to author, 21 May.

Booth, Wayne C. 1974. *A Rhetoric of Irony.* Chicago and London: The University of Chicago Press.

Borden, Diane M. 1996. "Man Without a Gun: Mamet's Mystification and Masculinity." Paper presented at Modern Language Association Convention, Washington, D. C., 28 December.

Boskin, Joseph. 1987. "Beyond Kvetching and Jiving: The Thrust of Jewish and Black Folkhumor." In *Jewish Wry: Essays on Jewish Humor,* ed. Sarah Blacher Cohen, 53-79. Bloomington: Indiana University Press.

Botto, Louis. 1992. "Mamet's *Oleanna.*" *Playbill: The National Theatre Magazine.* Off-Broadway edition, November, 47.

Bourdieu, Pierre. 1990. *Photography: A Middle-Brow Art.* Stanford, Calif.: Stanford University Press.

Brantley, Ben. 1987. "Pulitzer-Power Playwright Takes on Screen Challenge." *San Francisco Chronicle,* sec. Datebook, 30 August, 36, 38.

———. 1997. "A Middle-Aged Man Goes Home, to Mametville." *New York Times,* 20 November, B1, 3.

Breines, Paul. 1990. *Tough Jews: Political Fantasies and the Moral Dilemma of American Jewry.* New York: Basic Books.

Breslauer, S. Daniel. 1980. *The Chrysalis of Religion: A Guide to the Jewishness of Buber's "I and Thou."* Nashville: Abingdon.

Brewer, Gay. 1993. *David Mamet and Film: Illusion/Disillusion in a Wounded Land.* Jefferson, N.C. and London: McFarland.

Brucher, Richard. 1996. "Pernicious Nostalgia in *Glengarry Glen Ross.*" In *Glengarry Glen Ross: Text and Performance,* ed. Leslie Kane, 211-25. New York and London: Garland Press.

Brunette, Peter. 1991. "Mamet Views Cops Through a New Lens." *New York Times,* 10 February, sec. 2, 13, 21.

Brustein, Robert. 1987. "Show and Tell." New Republic. 7 May 1984, 27-29. Reprinted in *Who Needs Theatre: Dramatic Opinions,* 69-71. New York: Atlantic Monthly Press.

————. 1988. "The Last Refuge of Scoundrels." *New Republic,* 6 June, 29-31.

Buber, Martin. 1959. *Between Man and Man.* 4th ed. Trans. Ronald Gregor Smith. Boston: Beacon.

————. 1963. *Israel and the World.* New York: Schocken Books.

————. 1966. *The Knowledge of Man: A Philosophy of the Interhuman,* ed. Maurice Friedman, trans. Maurice Friedman and Ronald. G. Smith. New York: Harper Torchbooks.

————. 1967. *On Judaism,* ed. N. Glatzer. New York: Schocken Books.

Buttrick, George Arthur, ed. 1962. *The Interpreter's Dictionary of the Bible,* 149-51. New York: Abingdon.

Cahan, Abraham. 1896. *Yekl and The Imported Bridegroom and Other Stories of the New York Ghetto.* Reprint, with an introduction by Bernard G. Richards. New York: Dover Publications, 1970.

————. 1917. *The Rise of David Levinsky.* Reprint, with an introduction by John Higham. New York: Harper and Brothers, 1960.

Canby, Vincent. 1991. "Police Duty and Racism in Mamet's Melodrama." *New York Times,* 6 October, sec. L, 56.

————. 1995. "Mamet in a Bleak Living Room of Childhood." *New York Times,* 10 February, sec. C, 3.

Cantwell, Mary. 1984. "The Bulldog of the Middle Class." *Vogue,* July, 216, 281.

Caplan, Betty. 1993. "The Gender Benders." *New Statesman and Society,* 2 July, 34.

Carroll, Dennis. 1987. *David Mamet.* Houndsmills, England: St. Martin's Press.

Carr, Jay. 1988. "Things Change for Mamet." *Boston Globe,* 9 October, sec. B, 77.

————. 1991. "'Homicide': Police Story, Mamet Style." *Boston Globe,* 16 September, 33.

Caruth, Cathy. 1996. *Unclaimed Experience: Trauma, Narrative, and History.* Baltimore and London: John Hopkins University Press.

Case, Brian. 1983. "The Hot Property Man." *Times* [London], 18 September, 72-73.

Chalfen, Richard. 1981. "Redundant Imagery: Some Observations on the Use of Snapshots in American Culture." *Journal of American Culture* 4: 106-13.

Chaudhuri, Una. 1995. *Staging Place: The Geography of Modern Drama*. Ann Arbor: University of Michigan Press.

Chekhov, Anton. 1977. *Collected Plays*. Trans. and ed. Eugene K. Bristow. New York: Norton.

Christiansen, Richard. 1981. "Postman Script: David Mamet's Special Delivery." *Chicago Tribune*, 15 March, sec. F5, 10.

———. 1982. "The Young Lion of Chicago." *Chicago Tribune Magazine*, 11 July, 9-14, 18-19.

———. 1983. "One-Act Goodman Plays Deliver a 1-2-3 Punch." *Chicago Tribune*, 15 June, sec. 4, 12.

———. 1984. "Glengarry Refines Map of Unexplored Terrain." *Chicago Tribune*, 7 February, sec. 5, 2.

———. 1989. "The 'Plow' Boy." *Chicago Tribune*, 19 February, sec. 13, 18-20.

———. 1995. "No Words Wasted in Mamet's *The Cryptogram*." *Chicago Tribune*, 21 February, sec. N, 14.

———. 1997. "Arts Watch." Review of *The Old Neighborhood* by David Mamet. *Chicago Tribune*, 30 April, sec. Tempo, CN1.

Christy, Desmond. 1983. "A Man for the Forgotten Frontier." *Guardian* [Manchester], 16 September, 15.

Cibula, Nan. 1995. Interview by the author. Chicago, Ill., 30 December.

Cirlot, J. E. 1995. *A Dictionary of Symbols*, trans. Jack Sage. 2nd ed. New York: Barnes and Noble Books. Originally published in 1971 by Routledge, Kegan & Paul.

Clay, Carolyn. 1978. "Will Mamet Make It?" *Boston Phoenix*, 28 February, sec. 3, 1,12.

———. 1992. "Power Play." *Boston Phoenix*, 24 April, sec. 3, 10-11.

Clinch, Minty. 1989. "Mamet Plots His Revenge." *Observer* [London], 22 January, 46.

Cohen, Boaz. 1957. *Law and Ethics in the Light of the Jewish Tradition*. New York: Abingdon.

Cohen, Carl. 1963. "Martin Luther and His Contemporaries." *Jewish Societal Studies*, 25: 195-204.

Cohen, Jeremy. 1986. "Scholarship and Intolerance in the Medieval Academy: The Study and Evaluation of Judaism in European Christendom." *American History Review* 91: 592-613.

———. 1991. "Traditional Prejudice and Religious Reform: The Theological and Historical Foundations of Luther's Anti-Judaism." In *Anti-Semitism in Times of Crisis*, ed. Sander Gilman and Steven Katz, 81-102. New York: New York University Press.

Cohen, Richard, ed. 1986. Introduction to *Face to Face with Levinas*, 1-10. Albany: State University of New York Press.

Cohen, Sarah Blacher, ed. 1983. *From Hester Street to Hollywood: The Jewish-American Stage and Screen.* Bloomington: Indiana University Press.

———, ed. 1987. "The Varieties of Jewish Humor." *Introduction to Jewish Wry,* 1-15.

Cohn, Ruby. 1991. *New American Dramatists 1960-1990.* 2nd. ed. New York: St. Martin's Press.

———. 1992. "How Are Things Made Round?" In *David Mamet: A Casebook,* ed. Leslie Kane, 109-21. New York and London: Garland Press.

———. 1995. "Phrasal Energies: Harold Pinter and David Mamet." In *Anglo-American Interplay in Recent Drama,* 58-93. Cambridge: Cambridge University Press.

Colodner, Solomon. 1981. *What's Your Name?* New York: Cole Publishing.

Combs, Richard. 1991. "Framing Mamet." *Sight and Sound* 1, no. 7: 16-17.

Corliss, Richard. 1992. "Sweating Out Loud." *Time,* 12 October, 84.

Csikszentmihalyi, Mihaly, and Eugene Rochberg-Halton. 1989. *The Meaning of Things: Domestic Symbols and the Self.* New York: Cambridge University Press.

Cullick, Jonathan S. 1994. "'Always Be Closing': Competition and the Discourse of Closure in David Mamet's *Glengarry Glen Ross.*" *Journal of Dramatic Theory and Criticism* 8, no. 2: 23-36.

Cummings, Scott T. 1997. "Bobby's Back: Three Plays by David Mamet at A.R.T." *Village Voice,* 6 May, 103.

Cushman, Robert. 1983. "All American Boys." *Observer,* 25 September, 33. Reprinted *Theatre Record,* 10-23 September, 823.

———. 1984. Review of *American Buffalo* by David Mamet. *Plays and Players* (September): 24-25.

Cutter, Irving. 1996. *The Jews of Chicago: From Shtetl to Suburb.* Urbana and Chicago: University of Illinois Press.

Damrosch, David. 1987. "Leviticus." In *The Literary Guide to the Bible,* ed. Robert Alter and Frank Kermode, 66-77.

Davis, Barry. 1991/92. "The 22 from Hackney to Chelsea: A Conversation with Harold Pinter." *The Jewish Quarterly* 38, no. 4 (Winter): 9-17.

Davidson, Israel. 1966. *Parody in Jewish Literature.* New York: AMS Press.

Dean, Anne. 1990. *David Mamet: Language as Dramatic Action.* Rutherford, N.J.: Fairleigh Dickinson Press.

———. 1993. Interview with David Suchet. London, England, 25 November.

———. 1996. "The Discourse of Anxiety." In *Glengarry Glen Ross: Text and Performance,* ed. Leslie Kane, 47-61.

DeJongh, Nicholas. 1993. "Ferocious Attack on the Politically Correct." *Evening Standard,* 1 July. Reprint in *Theatre Record,* 18 June-1 July, 794.

Demastes, William W. 1988. "David Mamet's Dis-Integrating Drama." In *Beyond Naturalism: A New Realism in American Theatre*, 67-94. Westport, Conn.: Greenwood Press.

Dembo, L. S. 1988. *The Monological Jew: A Literary Study.* Madison: University of Wisconsin Press.

Denby, David. 1988. "Small Change." *New York,* 7 November, 102.

Dershowitz, Alan. 1991. *Chutzpah.* Boston: Little Brown.

———. 1994. *The Advocate's Devil.* New York: Warner Books.

———. 1997. *The Vanishing American Jew: In Search of Jewish Identity for the Next Century.* Boston, Little Brown.

Desser, David. 1995. Letter to the author, 17 July.

———. 1997. Letter to the author, 31 May.

Desser, David, and Lester D. Friedman. 1993. *American-Jewish Filmmakers: Traditions and Trends.* Urbana and Chicago: University of Illinois Press.

Diamant, Naomi. 1986. "Linguistic Universes in Henry Roth's *Call It Sleep.* *Contemporary Literature* 27, no. 3: 337-55.

Dinnerstein, Leonard. 1991. "Antisemitism in Crisis Times in the United States: The 1920s and 1930s." In *Anti-Semitism in Times of Crisis,* ed. Sander L. Gilman and Steven T. Katz, 212-26.

Dorff, Linda. 1996. "Things (Ex)change: The Value of Money in *Glengarry Glen Ross.*" In *Glengarry Glen Ross: Text and Performance,* ed. Leslie Kane, 195-209.

Doty, William G. 1993. "A Lifetime of Trouble-Making: Hermes as Trickster." *Mythical Trickster Figures: Contours, Contexts, and Criticisms,* ed. William J. Hynes and William G. Doty, 46-65. Tuscaloosa and London: University of Alabama Press, 1993.

Edwards, Christopher. 1986. "Glengarry Glen Ross." *Spectator,* 14 March. Reprinted in *Theatre Record,* 12-25 February, 179-80.

Elkin, Michael. 1991. "David Mamet's Disturbing Homicide Targets a Jew Cop's Sense of Self-Hatred." *Jewish Exponent,* 18 October, ix.

Ellis, Edward Sylvester. 1886. *Lost in the Wilds.* Reprint, 1916. Chicago: G. M. Hill.

Emerson, Ralph Waldo. 1965. *Selected Writings of Ralph Waldo Emerson,* ed. William H. Gilman. New York: New American Library.

Encyclopedia Judaica. Vol 2., s.v. "Aaron."

———. Vol 5., s.v. "Moses."

———. Vol. 6, s.v. "Esther."

———. Vol. 11, s.v. "Levi."

Epstein, Perle. 1988. *Kabbalah: The Way of the Jewish Mystic.* Boston and London: Shambhala.

Erens, Patricia. 1985. *The Jew in American Cinema*. Bloomington: Indiana University Press.

———. 1987. "You Could Die Laughing: Jewish Humor and Film." *East-West Film Journal* 2: 50-62.

Fass, David E. 1988. "The Symbolic Uses of North." *Judaism* 37 (Fall): 465-69.

Faulkner, William. 1954. *The Faulkner Reader*. New York: Random House.

Feingold, Michael. 1982. "The Way We Are." Review of *Edmond* by David Mamet. *Village Voice*, 9 November, 81-82.

———. 1992. "Prisoners of Unsex." *Village Voice*, 3 November. Reprinted in *New York Theatre Critics' Reviews*, 357.

———. 1995. "Codehearted." *Village Voice*, 25 April, 97.

———. 1997. "Unsaying Substance." *Village Voice*, 2 December, 97.

Fergusson, Francis. 1949. "Oedipus Rex: The Tragic Rhythm of Action." In *The Idea of a Theater*, 13-41. Princeton: Princeton University Press.

Fiedler, Leslie. 1991. *Fiedler on the Roof: Essays on Literature and Jewish Identity*. Boston: David R. Godine.

Finkielkraut, Alain. 1994. *The Imaginary Jew*. Trans. Kevin O'Neill and David Suchoff. Lincoln and London: University of Nebraska. Originally published in 1980 as *Le Juif imaginaire* by Editions du Seuil.

Fisch, Harold. 1971. *The Dual Image: The Figure of the Jew in English and American Literature*. Rev. ed. London: World Jewish Congress.

Fokkelman, J. P. 1987. "Exodus." In *The Literary Guide to the Bible,* ed. Robert Alter and Frank Kermode, 56-65.

Foster, Verna. 1995. "Sex, Power and Pedagogy." *American Drama* 5, no. 1 (Fall): 36-50.

Foucault, Michel. 1984. "The Subject and Power." In *Art After Modernism,* ed. Brian Wallis, 417-32. Boston: Godine.

Freedman, Samuel G. "The Gritty Eloquence of David Mamet." *New York-Times* Magazine, 21 April, sec. F, 32+.

Friedlander, Saul. 1979. *When Memory Comes*. Trans. Helen R. Lane. New York: Noonday Press.

Friedman, Lester D. 1982. *Hollywood's Image of the Jew*. New York: Frederick Ungar.

Friedman, Maurice S., ed. 1955. "Education." In *Martin Buber: The Life of Dialogue,* 176-82. Chicago: University of Chicago Press.

Fredericksen, Brooke. 1992. "Home Is Where the Text Is: Exile, Homeland, and Jewish American Writing." *Studies in American Jewish Literature* 2, no. 1: 38-44.

Foucault, Michel. 1984. "The Subject and Power." In *Art and Modernism,* ed. Brian Wallis, 417-32. Boston: Godine.

Gabler, Neal. 1988. *An Empire of Their Own: How the Jews Invented Hollywood.* New York: Crown Publishers.

Gale, Steven H. 1981. "David Mamet: The Plays, 1972-80." In *Essays on Contemporary Drama,* ed. Hedvig Bock and Albert Wertheim, 207-24. Munich: Max Hueber Verlag.

Galvin, Herman, and Stan Tamarkin. 1986. *Yiddish Dictionary Sourcebook.* Hoboken, N.J.: Ktav.

Garb, Tamar. 1995. "Modernity, Identity, Textuality." Introduction to *The Jew in the Text: Modernity and the Construction of Identity,* ed. Linda Nochlin and Tamar Garb, 20-30. London: Thames and Hudson Ltd.

Geis, Deborah R. 1992. "David Mamet and the Metadramatic Tradition: Seeing 'The Trick from the Back.'" In *David Mamet: A Casebook,* ed. Leslie Kane, 49-68.

———. 1995. *Postmodern Theatric[k]s: Monologue in Contemporary Drama.* Ann Arbor: University of Michigan Press.

———. 1996. "'You're Exploiting My Space': Ethnicity, Spectatorship, and the (Post)colonial Condition in Mukherjee's 'A Wife's Story' and Mamet's *Glengarry Glen Ross.*" In *Glengarry Glen Ross: Text and Performance,* ed. Leslie Kane, 123-30.

Gelber, Mark. 1985. "What is Literary AntiSemitism?" *Jewish Social Studies* 47, no. 1: 1-20.

Gerard, Jeremy. 1995. Review of *The Cryptogram* by David Mamet. *Daily Variety,* 17 April, 45.

Gilbert, Martin. 1983. *Winston S. Churchill: Finest Hour, 1939-1941.* Vol 6. Boston: Houghton-Mifflin.

———. 1986. *The Holocaust: A History of the Jews of Europe During the Second World War.* New York: Henry Holt.

Gill, Brendan. 1984. "The Theater: The Lower Depths." *The New Yorker,* 2 April, 114.

Gilman, Sander L. 1986. *Jewish Self-Hatred: Anti-Semitism and the Hidden Language of the Jews.* Baltimore and London: John Hopkins University Press.

———. 1991a. "Goethe's Touch: Touching, Seeing, Sexuality." In *Inscribing the Other,* 29-49. Lincoln and London: University of Nebraska.

———. 1991b. *The Jew's Body.* New York and London: Routledge, Chapman and Hall.

Gilman, Sander L., and Steven T. Katz, eds. 1991. *Introduction to Anti-Semitism in Times of Crisis.* New York and London: New York University Press.

Gilman, William H., ed. 1965. *Selected Writings of Ralph Waldo Emerson.* New York: New American Library.

Ginzberg, Louis. 1946. *Legends of the Jews.* Philadelphia: The Jewish Publication Society of America.

"Glengarry Glen Ross—Performance." 1983. National Theatre's Education Department's *Background Notes for Teachers and Pupils.* London: National Theatre.

Gold, Michael. 1965. *Jews Without Money.* Afterward by Michael Harrington. New York: Avon. Originally published 1930 by International Publishers.

Goldstein, Patrick. 1987. "Mamet Plays his Directing Card." *Los Angeles Times,* 11 October, sec. Calendar, 27.

Goodman, Walter. 1992. "In Mamet's World, You Are How You Speak." *New York Times,* 4 October, sec. H, 24.

Gottleib, Freeman. 1989. *The Lamp of God: A Jewish Book of God.* Northvale, N.J.: Jason Aronson.

Gould, Joan. 1996. "Midnight's Child." *New York Times Book Review,* 22 December, sec. 7, 23.

Goulder, Michael. 1987. "The Pauline Epistles." In *The Literary Guide to the Bible,* ed. Robert Alter and Frank Kermode, 479-502.

Gross, John. 1993. "The Mouse That Became a Monster." Review of *Oleanna,* by David Mamet. *Sunday Telegraph,* 4 July, 7.

———. 1994. "Tragedies of Good and Bad Manners." *Sunday Telegraph,* 26 June. Reprinted in *Theatre Record* 18 June-1 July, 788.

Gussow, Mel. 1971. "A Conversation (Pause) with Harold Pinter." *New York Times Magazine,* 5 December, sec. 6, 42.

———. 1988. "Mamet's Hollywood is a School for Scoundrels." *New York Times,* 15 May, sec. H, 5.

Guttmann, Allen. 1971. *The Jewish Writer in America: Assimilation and the Crisis of Identity.* New York: Oxford University Press.

Haedicke, Janet V. 1997a. "Decoding (M)other's Cipher-Space: David Mamet's *The Cryptogram* and America's Dramatic Legacy." Paper presented at the annual convention of the Association for Theatre in Higher Education, Chicago, Ill., 8 August.

———. 1997b. "Plowing the Buffalo, Fucking the Fruits: (M)others in *American Buffalo* and *Speed-the-Plow.*" Working paper.

Haggard-Gilson, Nancy. 1992. "The Construction of Jewish American Identity in Novels of the Second Generation." *Studies in American Jewish Literature,* 11, no. 1: 22-35.

Hagerty, Bill. 1994. "Anguish of a Boy Betrayed by Life." *Today,* 30 June. Reprinted in *Theatre Record,* 18 June-1 July, 799-800.

Hall, Ann C. 1992. "Playing to Win: Sexual Politics in David Mamet's *House of Games* and *Speed-the-Plow.*" In *David Mamet: A Casebook,* ed. Leslie Kane, 137-60.

Harriott, Esther. 1988. "Interview with David Mamet [and Esther Harriott]." In *American Voices: Five Contemporary Playwrights in Essays and Interviews,* 76-97. Jefferson, N.C.: McFarland & Company.

Harris, Andrew B. 1994. "American Buffalo." In *Broadway Theatre,* 97-111. London and New York: Routledge.

Hartman, Geoffrey H. 1987. "Numbers: The Realism of Numbers, The Magic of Numbers." In *Congregation,* ed. David Rosenberg, 39-49. San Diego: Harcourt Brace Jovanovich.

Hassell, Graham. 1993. "Call Me Madam." *What's On in London,* 6 July, 59.

Haver, Ronald. 1980. *David O. Selznick's Hollywood.* New York: Alfred A. Knopf.

Hayner, Don, and Tom McNamee. 1988. *Streetwise Chicago: A History of Chicago Street Names.* Chicago: Loyola University Press.

Heinze, Andrew R. 1990. *Adapting to Abundance: Jewish Immigrants, Mass Consumption and the Search for American Identity.* New York: Columbia University Press.

"He Said . . . She Said . . .Who Did What?" 1992. *New York Times,* 15 November, sec. H, 6.

Henry, William A. , III. 1988. "Madonna Comes to Broadway." *Time,* 16 May, 98-99.

———. 1992. "Reborn with Relevance." Review of *Oleanna* by David Mamet. *Time,* 2 November, 69-70.

Hepple, Peter. 1993. "Oleanna." *The Stage* [London], 15 July.

Hertzberg, Arthur. 1968. *The French Enlightenment and the Jews.* New York: Columbia University Press.

———. 1989. *The Jews in America, Four Centuries of an Uneasy Encounter: A History.* New York: Simon and Schuster.

Hinden, Michael. 1992. "'Intimate Voices': Lakeboat and Mamet's Quest for Community." In *David Mamet: A Casebook,* ed. Leslie Kane, 33-48.

Hirshorn, Clive. 1993. "Sex War and a Campus Tigress." *Sunday Express,* 4 July.

Hoberman, J. 1991. "Identity Parade." *Sight and Sound* 1, no. 7:14-16.

Holli, Melvin G., and Peter A. Jones., eds. 1977. *The Ethnic Frontier: Essays in the History of Group Survival in Chicago and the Midwest.* Grand Rapids, Mich.: William B. Eerdmans.

Holmberg, Arthur. 1992. "The Language of Misunderstanding." *American Theatre* 9, no. 6: 94-95.

———. 1997a. "It's Never Easy to Go Back." [Interview with David Mamet] *American Repertory Theatre News,* 18, no. 3: 8-9, 12.

———. 1997b. "The Old Neighborhood." *American Repertory Theatre News*, 18, no. 3: 7-9.

Horn, Bernard. "Jews, Cops, and Jokes." *Midstream* 39, no. 9: 19-20.

Howe, Irving. 1976. *World of Our Fathers*. New York and London: Harcourt Brace Jovanovich.

———, ed. 1977. *Introduction to Jewish-American Stories*, 1-17. New York and Scarborough, Ontario: New American Library.

———. 1987. "The Nature of Jewish Laughter." In *Jewish Wry*, ed. Sarah Blacher Cohen, 16-24.

Howe, Irving, and Kenneth Libo, eds. 1979. *How We Lived: 1880-1930, A Documentary History of Immigrant Jews in America*. New York: Richard Marek.

Hubert-Leibler, Pascale. 1992. "Dominance and Anguish: The Teacher-Student Relationship in the Plays of David Mamet." In *David Mamet: A Casebook*, ed. Leslie Kane, 69-85. First published in *Modern Drama* 31, 4: 77-86.

Hudgins, Christopher C. 1992. "Comedy and Humor in the Plays of David Mamet." In *David Mamet: A Casebook*, ed. Leslie Kane, 191-226.

———. 1996. "'By indirections find directions out': Uninflected Cuts, Narrative Structure, and Thematic Statement in the film version of *Glengarry Glen Ross*." In *Glengarry Glen Ross: Text and Performance*, ed. Leslie Kane, 19-45.

Hynes, William J. 1993. "Mapping the Characteristics of Mythic Tricksters: A Heuristic Guide." In *Mythical Trickster Figures: Contours, Contexts, and Criticisms*, ed. William J. Hynes and William G. Doty, 33-45.

Itzkovitz, Daniel. 1997. "Secret Temples." In *Jews and Other Differences*, ed. Jonathan Boyarin and Daniel B. Boyarin, 176-202. Minneapolis and London: University of Minnesota Press.

Jacobs, Dorothy. 1996. "Levene's Daughter: Positioning the Female in *Glengarry Glen Ross*." In *Glengarry Glen Ross: Text and Performance*, ed. Leslie Kane, 107-22.

Jones, Nesta, and Steven Dykes. 1991. *File on Mamet*. London: Methuen.

Joselit, Jenna Weissman. 1983. *Our Gang: Jewish Crime in New York, 1900-1940*. Bloomington: Indiana University Press.

———. 1994. *The Wonders of America: Reinventing Jewish Culture 1880-1950*. New York: Hill and Wang.

Jospovici, Gabriel. 1987. "The Epistle to the Hebrews and the Catholic Epistles." In *The Literary Guide to the Bible*, ed. Robert Alter and Frank Kermode. 503-22.

Jung, Leo. 1967. *Human Relations in Jewish Law*. New York: Jewish Education Committee of New York.

Kael, Pauline. 1988. "The Current Cinema: Unreal." *The New Yorker,* 14 November, 127-29.

Kaganoff, Benzion C. 1977. *A Dictionary of Jewish Names and their History.* New York: Schocken Books.

Kane, Leslie. 1984. *The Language of Silence: On the Unspoken and the Unspeakable in Modern Drama.* Rutherford, N.J. and London: Farleigh Dickinson University Press.

———. 1990. "Time Passages." *The Pinter Review: Annual Essays,* 1:30-49.

———. 1991. "Interview with Joe Mantegna." *American Theatre* 8: 18-25; 69. Reprinted in *David Mamet: A Casebook,* ed. Leslie Kane, 249-69.

———. 1992. "Interview with Gregory Mosher." In *David Mamet: A Casebook,* 231-47.

———. 1996a. "A Conversation with Sam Mendes and Leslie Kane." In *Glengarry Glen Ross: Text and Performance,* 245-62.

———. 1996b. "American Buffalo". Review of film version of *American Buffalo* by David Mamet. In *David Mamet Review* 3 (Fall): 9, 11.

———, ed. 1992. *David Mamet: A Casebook.* New York and London: Garland Press.

———, ed. 1996. *Glengarry Glen Ross: Text and Performance.* New York and London: Garland Press.

Karp, Abraham, ed. 1976. *Golden Door to America: The Jewish Immigrant Experience.* New York: Viking Press.

Kastor, Elizabeth. 1983. "Playwright David Mamet: The Ups and Downs of His Bustling Life in the Theater." *Washington Post,* 25 August, sec. E, 1, 17.

Katz, Steven T. 1991. "1918 and After: The Role of Racial Antisemitism in the Nazi Analysis of the Weimar Republic." In *Anti-Semitism in Times of Crisis,* ed. Sander Gilman and Steven Katz, 227-56.

Kaufman, Stanley. 1997. Review of *The Edge* by David Mamet. *The New Republic,* 27 October, 26.

Kearney, Richard. 1986. "Emmanuel Levinas and Richard Kearney." *Face to Face with Levinas,* ed. Richard Cohen, 13-34. Albany: State University of New York Press.

Kelly, Kevin. 1988. "Good Mamet, Passable Madonna." *Boston Globe,* 4 May, 77.

———. 1992. "Oleanna Enrages and Engages." *Globe* [Boston], 4 May, 34.

Kepnes, Steven D. 1988. "A Narrative Jewish Theology." *Judaism* 37, no. 2: 210-17.

Kermode, Frank. 1990. "John." In *The Literary Guide to the Bible,* ed. Robert Alter and Frank Kermode, 440-66.

Kerr, Walter. "Verbal Witchcraft Produces Magical Responses Out Front." *New York Times,* 12 June, sec. 2, 5, 22.

King, Thomas L. 1991. "Talk and Dramatic Action in *American Buffalo*." *Modern Drama* 34, no. 4: 538-48.

Klaver, Elizabeth. 1996. "David Mamet, Jean Baudrillard and the Performance of America." In *Glengarry Glen Ross: Text and Performance,* ed. Leslie Kane, 171-83.

Klein, Marcus. 1981. *Foreigners: The Making of American Literature, 1900-1940.* Chicago and London: University of Chicago Press.

Knightley, Phillip. 1975. *The First Casualty, From the Crimea to Vietnam: The War Correspondent as Hero, Protagonist, and Mythmaker.* New York: Harcourt, Brace, Jovanovich.

Kogos, Fred. 1976. *Yiddish Slang & Idioms.* New York: Carol Publishing.

Kolatch, Alfred J. 1967. *The Name Dictionary.* New York: Jonathan David.

———. 1985. *The Second Jewish Book of Why.* Middle Village, N.Y.: Jonathan David.

Kosinski, Jerzy. 1976. *The Painted Bird.* Introduction by author. 2nd. ed. Boston: Houghton Mifflin.

Kraemer, David. 1989. "Images of Childhood and Adolescence in Talmudic Literature." In *The Jewish Family: Metaphor and Memory,* ed. David Kraemer. New York and Oxford: Oxford University Press, 65-80.

Kroll, Jack. 1984. "Mamet's Jackals in Jackets." *Newsweek,* 9 April. Reprinted in *New York Theatre Critics' Reviews,* 5-11 March, 337-38.

———. 1988. "The Terrors of Tinseltown." *Newsweek,* 16 May, 82-83.

———. 1992. "A Tough Lesson in Sexual Harassment." *Newsweek,* 9 November, 65.

———. 1995. "Phantoms in the Dark." *Newsweek,* 20 February, 72.

Kugelmass, Jack. 1997. "Jewish Icons: Envisioning the Self in Images of the Other." In *Jews and Other Differences,* ed. Jonathan Boyarin and Daniel Boyarin, 30-53.

Kushner, Harold. 1994. *To Life! A Celebration of Jewish Being and Thinking.* New York: Warner Books.

Kushner, Lawrence. 1991. *God Was in This Place and I, i Did Not Know.* Woodstock, Vt.: Jewish Lights Publishing.

——— . 1993. *The Book of Words: Talking Spiritual Life, Living Spiritual Talk.* Woodstock, Vt.: Jewish Lights Publishing.

Lahr, John. 1983. "Winner and Losers." *New Society,* 29 September, 476-77.

———. 1992. "Dogma Days." *The New Yorker,* 16 November, 121-25.

———. 1994. "Betrayals." *The New Yorker,* 1 August, 70-73.

———. 1995. "David Mamet's Child's Play." *The New Yorker,* 10 April, 33-34.

———. 1997a. "David Mamet: The Art of the Theater, XI." *Paris Review* 142 (Spring): 53-76.

———. 1997b. "Fortress Mamet." *The New Yorker,* 17 November, 70-82.

Landa, M. J. 1874. *The Jew in Drama*. Reprint, in 1968. Port Washington, NY: Kennikat Press.

Langer, Lawrence L. 1975. "Suffer the Little Children." *The Holocaust and the Literary Imagination*, 124-65. New Haven and London: Yale University Press.

———. 1991. *Holocaust Testimonies: The Ruins of Memory*. New Haven and London: Yale University Press.

Langer, Susanne K. 1942. *Philosophy in a New Key: A Study of the Symbolism of Reason, Rite, and Art*. 3rd ed. New York: Cambridge University Press.

———. 1953. *Feeling and Form*. New York: Charles Scribner's Sons.

Lawson, Steve. 1977. "Language Equals Action." *Horizon* 20, 40-45.

Lazar, Moshe. 1991. "The Lamb and the Scapegoat: The Dehumanization of the Jews in Medieval Propaganda Imagery." In *Anti-Semitism in Times of Crisis*, ed. Sander L. Gilman and Steven T. Katz, 38-80.

Leach, Edmund. 1987. "Fishing for Men on the Edge of the Wilderness." In *The Literary Guide to the Bible*, ed. Robert Alter and Frank Kermode, 579-99.

Leitch, Thomas. 1991. *Find the Director and Other Hitchcock Games*. Athens, Ga. and London: University of Georgia Press.

Lenz, William E. 1985. *Fast Talk & Flush Times: The Confidence Man as a Literary Convention*. Columbia, Mo.: University of Missouri Press.

Leon, Masha. 1984. Review of *Glengarry Glen Ross* by David Mamet. *Forward*, 11 May, 19.

Leograde, Ernest. 1977. "A Man of Few Words Moves on to Sentences." *Daily News*, 13 February, sec. C, 3.

Lerner, Michael. 1994. *Jewish Renewal: A Path to Healing and Transformation*. New York: Harper Perennial.

Lesser, Wayne. 1981. "A Narrative Revolutionary Energy: The Example of Henry Roth's *Call It Sleep*." *Criticism* 23 (Spring): 155-76.

Leviant, Curt, ed. and trans. 1968. "On America." In *Stories and Satires by Sholem Aleichem*, 230-32. New York: Putnam.

Levine, Aaron. 1980. *Free Enterprise and Jewish Law: Aspects of Jewish Business Ethics*. Library of Jewish Law and Ethics, vol. 13. New York: Ktav, Yeshiva University Press.

Lewis, Anthony. 1983. "The Jew in Stand-up Comedy." In *From Hester Street to Hollywood*, ed. Sarah Blacher Cohen, 58-70.

Lieberman, Douglas. 1991. Interview by author, Skokie, Ill., 10 October.

———. 1995. Letter to the author, 22 May.

Lieberson, Jonathan. 1988. "The Prophet of Broadway." *New York Review of Books*, 21 July, 3-6.

Liebman, Charles S. 1973. *The Ambivalent American Jew: Politics, Religion and Family in American Jewish Life.* Philadelphia: Jewish Publications Society of America.

London, Todd. 1990. "Chicago Impromptu." *American Theatre* 4, no. 4-5: 14-23.

———. 1996. "Mamet vs. Mamet." *American Theatre* 13, no. 24: 18-20, 62.

Lopate, Leonard. 1994. "Interview with David Mamet." New York and Company. WNYC, 25 October.

Louvish, Simon. 1993. "Out of the Shadows." *Sight and Sound* 3, no. 6: 18.

Lovell, Glenn. 1988. "David Mamet Keeps His Multifaceted Career Speeding Along." *Chicago Tribune,* 28 October, sec. 7, D, E.

Lyons, Donald. 1995. "To Paris and Back in a '20s Dream." *Wall Street Journal* 14 April, sec. A, 7.

Macy, William H. 1992. Interview by author. Cambridge, Mass., 22 May.

MacLeod, Christine. 1995. "The Politics of Gender, Language and Hierarchy in Mamet's *Oleanna.*" *Journal of American Studies* 29, no. 2: 199-213.

McDonough, Carla. 1992. "Every Fear Hides a Wish: Unstable Masculinity in Mamet's Drama." *Theatre Journal* 44, no. 2: 195-205.

McGinn, Bernard. 1987. "Revelation." In *The Literary Guide to the Bible,* ed. Robert Alter and Frank Kermode, 523-41.

Magida, Arthur. 1991. "Smoking out David Mamet." *Baltimore Jewish Exponent,* 18 October, 64.

Malkin, Jeanette, R. 1992. "David Mamet: *American Buffalo* and *Glengarry Glen Ross.*" In *Verbal Violence in Contemporary Drama: From Handke to Shepard,* 145-61. Cambridge: Cambridge University Press.

Mamet, Bobby. 1991. Discussion with the author [with Tony Mamet and Henry Palast]. Cambridge, Mass., 21 September.

Mamet, Lynn. 1990. Interview by author. Baltimore, Md., 10 October.

———. 1991. Interview by author. Cambridge, Mass., 20 September.

———. 1995. *The Lost Years.* Unpublished manuscript.

Mantegna, Joe. 1992. "Interview with Joe Mantegna [and Leslie Kane]." In *David Mamet: A Casebook,* ed. Leslie Kane, 249-69.

Markfield, Wallace. 1974. *You Could Live If They'd Let You.* New York: Alfred. A. Knopf.

Marmur, Dow. 1991. *Star of Return: Judaism After the Holocaust.* New York: Greenwood Press.

Marx, Bill. 1997. "Mr. Mamet's Neighborhood." *Boston Magazine* (March): 106, 108.

May, Lary L. and Elaine Tyler May. 1982. "Why Jewish Movie Moguls: An Exploration in American Culture." *American Jewish History* 72: 7-25.

Mendes, Sam. 1996. "A Conversation with Sam Mendes and Leslie Kane." In *Glengarry Glen Ross: Text and Performance,* ed. Leslie Kane, 245-62.

Meyer, Michael A. 1990. *Jewish Identity in the Modern World.* The Samuel & Althea Stroum Lectures. Seattle and London: University of Washington Press.

Miller, Arthur. 1995. *Death of a Salesman.* In *Portable Arthur Miller,* ed. and introduction by Christopher Bigsby. Original introduction by Harold Clurman. New York: Penguin Books.

Morley, Sheridan. 1993. "Mamet, Pinter and the Perils of PC." *International Herald Tribune,* 7 July, 792.

———. 1994. "One Long Puzzle." *Spectator,* 9 July. Reprinted *Theatre Record,* 18 June-1 July, 801.

Mosher, Gregory. 1992. "Interview with Gregory Mosher [and Leslie Kane]." In *David Mamet: A Casebook,* ed. Leslie Kane, 231-47.

———. 1994. "Director's Note." Program, *The Cryptogram,* Ambassadors Theatre, London, 3.

———. 1995. Telephone interview by author. Sag Harbor, N.Y., 2 August.

———. 1996. "How to Talk Buffalo." *American Theatre* 13, no. 7: 80.

———. 1997. Telephone conversation with author. New York, N.Y., 27 February.

Movshovitz, Howie. 1991. "Homicide Wrestles with Chicago Ethnic Hostility." *Denver Post,* 25 October, 6.

Mowat, Farley. 1956. *Lost in the Barrens.* Boston: Joy Street Books.

Mufson, Daniel. 1993. "The Critical Eye: Sexual Perversity in Viragos." Review of *Oleanna,* by David Mamet. *Theater* 24, no. 1 (Winter): 111-13.

Nathan, David. 1994. "Glengarry Glen Ross." *Jewish Chronicle,* 1 July. Reprinted *Theatre Record,* 18 June-1 July 1994, 792-93.

Nelson, Jeanne-Andrée. 1991. "A Machine Out of Order: Indifferentiation in David Mamet's The Disappearance of the Jews." *Journal of American Studies* 25, no. 3: 461-72.

Newton, Adam Zachary. 1995. *Narrative Ethics.* Cambridge, Mass. and London: Harvard University Press.

Nightingale, Benedict. 1984. "The Bard of Immorality." *New York Times,* 1 April, sec. H, 5.

———. 1993. "More Aristotle than Hemingway." *Times* [London], 15 September, 37.

———. 1994. "The Sharks Still Have Bite." *Times* [London], 24 June. Reprinted in *Theatre Record* 18 June-1 July, 793.

———. 1994. "No Fiddlers on the Roof." 1994. *Boston Globe,* 29 March, editorial, 18.

Norman, Geoffrey, and John Rezek. 1995. "Playboy Interview with David Mamet." *Playboy,* April, 51.

Novak, William, and Moshe Waldocks, eds. 1981. *The Big Book of Jewish Humor.* New York: Harper & Row.

Nussbaum, Mike. 1995. Interview by author. Chicago, Ill., 27 December.

Nuwer, Hank. 1985. "Two Gentlemen of Chicago: David Mamet and Stuart Gordon." *South Carolina Review* 17 (Spring): 9-20.

O'Brien, Ellen. 1995. "Acting His Age, and More, in a Mamet Play [Interview with Shelton Dane]." *Boston Globe,* 23 February, 53.

Odets, Clifford. *Awake and Sing.* In *Six Plays by Clifford Odets,* ed. Clifford Odets. New York: Modern Library.

Oliver, Edith. 1988. "Mamet at the Movies." *The New Yorker,* 16 May, 95.

Opdahl, Keith. "The Mental Comedies of Saul Bellow." *From Hester Street to Hollywood: The Jewish American Stage and Screen,* ed. Sarah Blacher Cohen, 183-196.

Ozick, Cynthia. 1984. *Art and Ardor.* New York: E. P. Dutton.

Paglia, Camille. 1994. "The Real Lesson of *Oleanna?*" *Los Angeles Times,* 6 November, sec. Calendar, 6.

Palast, Harold. Interview by author. Cambridge, Mass., 21 September 1991.

Panitz, Esther L. 1981. *The Alien in Their Midst.* Rutherford, N.J.: Fairleigh Dickinson University Press.

Partridge, Eric. 1989. *A Concise Dictionary of Slang and Unconventional English.* New York: Macmillan.

Peli, Pinchas Hacohen. 1993 "Responses to Anti-Semitism in Midrashic Literature." In *Anti-Semitism in Times of Crisis,* ed. Sander Gilman and Steven Katz, 103-14.

Pellegrini, Ann. 1997. "Whiteface Performances: 'Race,' Gender and Jewish Bodies." In *Jews and Other Differences,* ed. Jonathan Boyarin and Daniel Boyarin, 108-149.

Peter, John. 1993. "That'll Teach Her." *Times* [London], 4 July, sec. 9, 20.

———. 1994. "Mamet's House of Secrets." *Sunday Times* [London], 3 July, sec. 10, 21.

Piette, Alain. 1995. "The Devil's Advocate: David Mamet's *Oleanna* and Political Correctness." In *Staging Difference: Cultural Pluralism in American Theatre and Drama,* ed. Marc Maufort, 173-87. *American University Studies,* vol. 25. New York: Peter Lang.

Pilpay. "Pilpay." In *The Great Fables of All Nations,* ed. Manuel Komroff, 133-35. New York: Tudor.

Pinsker, Sanford. 1987. "Lenny Bruce: Spritzing the Goyim/Shocking the Jews." In *Jewish Wry,* ed. Sarah Blacher Cohen, 89-104.

———. 1992. *Jewish-American Fiction, 1917-1978.* New York: Twayne.

Pinter, Harold. 1961. *The Birthday Party.* New York: Grove Press.

———. 1965. *The Homecoming.* New York: Grove Press.

———. 1975. *No Man's Land.* New York: Grove Press.

———. 1990. "Writing for the Theatre." Introduction to *Harold Pinter: Complete Works,* One, 9-16. New York: Grove Weidenfeld Press.

Plout, Gunter. 1991. *Magen David: How the Six Pointed Star Became an Emblem for the Jewish People.* Washington, D.C.: B'nai Brith.

Powers, John. 1991. "Murder, He Wrote." Review of *Homicide,* by David Mamet. *New York,* 21 October, 94.

Price, Steven. 1995. "A. T. & T.: Anxiety, Telecommunications and the Theatre of David Mamet." *Cycnos,* "Instants de Théâtre" 12, no.1: 59-67.

———. 1996 "Negative Creation: The Detective Story in *Glengarry Glen Ross.*" In *Glengarry Glen Ross: Text and Performance,* ed. Leslie Kane, 19-45.

———. 1997. "Disguise in Love: Mamet, Gender, Narrative." Working paper.

Prinz, Joachim. 1973. *The Secret Jews.* New York: Random House.

Quinn, Michael. 1997. "Mamet's Performative Realism." In *Realism and the American Dramatic Tradition,* ed., William W. Demastes, 235-54. Tuscaloosa and London: University of Alabama Press.

Radavich, David. 1991. "Man Among Men: David Mamet's Homosocial Order." *American Drama* 1, no. 1: 46-60.

Radin, Charles A. 1993. "An Ivory Cower." *Boston Globe,* 20 January, 1, 12.

Rafferty, Terrence. 1991. "Homicide." *The New Yorker,* 18 November, 122-23.

Raidy, William, A. 1977. "Mamet's Goal is to Change Nature of U.S. Theater." *Syracuse Herald-Journal,* 5 March.

———. 1977. "Playwright with Paid-Up Dues." *Los Angeles Times,* 27 November, sec. Calendar, 72.

Ranier, Peter. 1988. "Plow's Message." *Los Angeles Herald Examiner,* 21 October, 7.

Ranvaud, Don. 1988. "Things Change." *Sight and Sound* 57, no. 1: 231-34.

Raskin, Richard. 1992. *Life is Like a Glass of Tea: Studies in Classic Jewish Jokes.* Aarhus, Denmark: Aarhus University Press.

Ribufo, Leo P. 1983. *The Old Christian Right: The Protestant Far Right from the Great Depression to the Cold War,* 43-63. Philadelphia: Temple University Press.

Rich, Frank. 1984. Review of *Glengarry Glen Ross* by David Mamet. *New York Times,* 26 March, sec. C, 3.

———. 1988. "Mamet's Dark View of Hollywood as a Heaven for the Virtueless." *New York Times,* 4 May, sec. C, 17.

———. 1992. "Mamet's New Play Detonates the Fury of Sexual Harassment." Review of *Oleanna* by David Mamet. *New York Times,* 26 October, sec. B, 1, 3.

Richards, David. 1992. "The Jackhammer Voice of Mamet's *Oleanna*." *New York Times,* 8 November, sec. C, 1.

———. "Mamet's Women." *New York Times,* 3 January, sec. 2, 1, 5.

Rimmon-Kenan, Shlomith. 1983. *Narrative Fiction: Contemporary Poetics.* London and New York: Methuen.

Robinson, David. 1984. *Chaplin, The Mirror of Opinion.* London: Secker and Warburg; Bloomington: Indiana University Press.

Rosenberg, Edgar. 1960. *From Shylock to Svengali: Jewish Stereotypes in English Fiction.* Stanford, Calif.: Stanford University Press.

Rosenfeld, Megan. 1993. "Exit Audience, Arguing: A Poll on Mamet's Uneven Battle." Review of *Oleanna* by David Mamet. *Washington Post,* 30 April, sec. B, 1.

Rosenzweig, Franz. 1971. *The Star of Redemption,* 2nd. ed. Trans. William W. Hallo. New York: Holt, Rinehart, Winston.

Roskies, David G. 1984. *Against the Apocalypse: Responses to Catastrophe in Modern Jewish Culture.* Cambridge, Mass. and London: Harvard University Press.

———. 1995. *A Bridge of Longing: The Lost Art of Yiddish Storytelling.* Cambridge, Mass. and London: Harvard University Press.

Roskolenko, Harry. 1971. *The Time That Was Then: The Lower East Side, 1900-1914, An Intimate Chronicle.* New York: Dial Press.

Rosten, Leo. 1968. *The Joys of Yiddish.* New York: McGraw-Hill Publishing.

———. 1972. *Treasury of Jewish Quotations.* New York: McGraw-Hill Publishing.

———. 1989. *The Joys of Yinglish.* New York: McGraw-Hill Publishing.

Roth, Cecil. 1932. *A History of Marranos.* Reprint, New York: Harper Torchbooks. 1966.

———. 1941. *A History of the Jews in England.* 3rd. ed. London: Oxford University Press. Reprint, Oxford: Clarendon Press, 1964.

Roth, Henry. 1934. *Call It Sleep.* Reprint, New York: Avon Books, 1960.

Roth, Philip. 1966. "Defender of the Faith." In *Goodbye, Columbus and Five Stories.* New York: Modern Library.

———. 1969. *Portnoy's Complaint.* New York: Random House.

———. 1990. *Deception.* New York: Simon and Schuster.

———. 1991. *Patrimony.* New York: Simon and Schuster.

———. 1995. *Sabbath's Theater.* Boston: Houghton Mifflin.

Roudané, Matthew C. 1986a. "An Interview with David Mamet." *South Carolina Review* 19, no. 1: 73-81.

———. 1986b. "Public Issues, Private Tensions: David Mamet's *Glengarry Glen Ross*." *South Carolina Review* 19, no. 1: 35-47.

————. 1992. "Mamet's Mimetics." In *David Mamet: A Casebook,* ed. Leslie Kane, 3-32.

Rousu, Anna-Lis. "Closeness and Unequal Power: Some Aspects of the Teacher-Student Relationship in Shaw's *Pygmalion* and Mamet's *Oleanna.*" Unpublished.

Rubin, Gayle. 1975. "The Traffic in Women: Notes on the 'Political Economy' of Sex." In *Toward an Anthropology of Women,* ed. Rayna Reiter, 157-210. New York: Monthly Review Press.

Russo, Francine. 1993. "Mamet's Traveling Cockfight." *Village Voice,* 29 June, 96.

Ryan, Steven. 1996. "*Oleanna:* David Mamet's Power Play." *Modern Drama* 35, no. 3 (Fall): 392-403.

Samuelson, Robert. 1995. *The Good Life and Its Discontents: The American Dream in the Age of Entitlement, 1945-1995.* New York: Times Books.

Sasson, Jack M. 1987. "Esther." In *The Literary Guide to the Bible,* ed. Robert Alter and Frank Kermode, 335-42.

Sauer, David, K. 1996. "The Marxist Child Play of Mamet's Tough Guys and Churchill's *Top Girls.*" In *Glengarry Glen Ross: Text and Performance,* ed. Leslie Kane, 131-56.

Savran, David. 1988. "Interview with David Mamet." *In Their Own Words: Contemporary American Playwrights,* 132-44. New York: Theatre Communications Group.

Schama, Simon. 1995. *Landscape and Memory.* New York: Alfred A. Knopf.

Schiff, Ellen. 1982. *From Stereotype to Metaphor: The Jew in Contemporary Drama.* Albany, N.Y.: State University of New York Press.

Schleuter, June and Elizabeth Forsyth. 1983. "America as Junkshop: The Business Ethic in David Mamet's *American Buffalo.*" *Modern Drama* 26, no 4: 492-500.

Scholem, Gershom. 1969. *Major Trends in Jewish Mysticism: On the Kabbalah and its Symbolism.* 3rd. rev. ed. Trans. Ralph Manheim. New York: Schocken Books.

————. 1971. "The Star of David: History of a Symbol." In *The Messianic Idea of Judaism.* New York: Schoken Books, 257-81.

————. 1974. "Magen David: Shield of David." In *Kabbalah,* 362-68. New York: Quadrangle/Times Books.

Schulberg, Budd. 1981. *Movie Pictures: Memories of a Hollywood Prince.* New York: Stein and Day.

Schvey, Henry I. 1988a. "Celebrating the Capacity for Self-Knowledge." *New Theatre Quarterly* 4, no. 13: 89-96.

————. 1988b. "The Plays of David Mamet: Games of Manipulation and Power." *New Theatre Quarterly* 4, no. 13: 77-89.

Schwartz, Howard. 1983. "The Aggadic Tradition." *Judaism* 32, no. 1: 84-101

Sedgwick, Eve Kosofsky. 1993. *Between Men: English Literature and Male Homosocial Desire*. New York: Columbia University Press.

Seidman, Aaron B. 1973. "Bar Mitzvah—An Approach to Social Maturity." *Tradition* 13, no. 3: 85-89.

Sessums, Kevin. 1987. "Dammit Mamet!" *Interview* 18: 140-41.

Seuss, Dr. [Theodore Geisel]. 1950. *Yertle the Turtle and Other Stories*. New York: Random House.

Shechner, Mark. 1979. "Jewish Writers." In *Harvard Guide to Contemporary American Writing*, ed. Daniel Hoffman, 191-239. Cambridge: Belknap Press.

———. 1983. "Woody Allen: The Failure of the Therapeutic." In *From Hester Street to Hollywood*, ed. Sarah Blacher Cohen, 231-44.

———. 1987. "Dear Mr. Einstein: Jewish Comedy and the Contradictions of Culture." In *Jewish Wry*, ed. Sarah Blacher Cohen, 141-57.

———. 1990. *"The Conversion of the Jews" and Other Essays*. Houndsmills: Macmillan.

Sholem, Aleichem. 1954. *The Adventures of Mottel, The Cantor's Son*. Trans. Tamara Kahana. New York: H. Schuman.

Showalter, Elaine. 1992. "Acts of Violence: David Mamet and the Language of Men." *Times Literary Supplement*, 6 November, 16.

Shuman, R. Baird. 1983. "Clifford Odets and the Jewish Context." In *From Hester Street to Hollywood*, ed. Sarah Blacker Cohen, 85-105.

Siegel, Ed. 1995. "Mamet's Puzzling, Poignant Cryptogram." *Boston Globe*, 10 February, sec. Living, 47, 50.

———. 1997. "The Talk is Rich in Mamet's Old Neighborhood." *Boston Globe*, 18 April, sec F, 1, 4.

Sierz, Aleks. 1993. "Curriculum Controversy." *Tribune*, 2 July. Reprinted in *Theatre Record*, 18 June-1 July, 740.

Silverstein, Marc. 1995. "'We're Just Human': *Oleanna* and Cultural Crisis." *South Atlantic Review* 60, no. 2: 103-19.

Simon, John. 1981. "Bluffalo." *New York*, 15 June, 66.

———. 1992. "Thirteen Ways of Looking at a Turkey." Review of *Oleanna*, by David Mamet. *New York*, 9 November, 72.

Skloot, Robert. "*Oleanna*, or, The Play of Pedagogy." Working paper.

Smith, Neil. 1994. "Cryptogram." *What's On*, 7 July. Reprinted in *Theatre Record*, 18 June-1 July, 800.

Sokel, Walter H. 1991. "Dualistic Thinking and the Rise of Ontological Antisemitism in Nineteenth-Century Germany: From Schiller's Franz Moor to Wilheim Raabe's Moses Freudenstein." In *Anti-Semitism in Times of Crisis*, ed. Sander Gilman and Steven Katz, 154-72.

Sokoloff, Naomi B. 1992. *Imagining the Child in Modern Jewish Fiction.* Baltimore: John Hopkins University Press.

Solomon, Alisa. 1993. "He Said/She Said." *Village Voice*, 2 November, 110, 115.

Sophocles. 1954. *Oedipus the King.* In *Sophocles I*, ed. David Grene and Richard Lattimore, trans. David Grene. Chicago and London: University of Chicago Press.

Sontag, Susan. 1977. *On Photography.* New York: Dell.

Spears, Timothy B. 1995. *100 Years on the Road: The Traveling Salesman in the American Culture.* New Haven and London: Yale University Press.

Spencer, Charles. 1993. "Hypnotic View of an Epic Power Struggle." *Daily Telegraph*, 1 July.

———. 1994. "Mamet Devastates with a Tale of Growing Pains." *Daily Telegraph*, 30 June, 9. Reprinted in *Theatre Record* 18 June-1 July, 798-99.

Spero, Shubert. 1983. *Morality, Halakha and the Jewish Tradition. Jewish Law and Ethics.* Vol. 9. New York: Ktav.

Stafford, Tony J. 1993. "*Speed-the-Plow* and *Speed the Plough:* The Work of the Earth." *Modern Drama* 36, no. 1: 38-47.

———. 1996. "Visions of a Promised Land: David Mamet's *Glengarry Glen Ross.* In *Glengarry Glen Ross: Text and Performance,* ed. Leslie Kane, 189-94.

Stayton, Richard. 1985a. "A Good Deal from David Mamet." *Los Angeles Herald Examiner,* 30 November, sec. B., 1, 5.

———. 1985b. "David Mamet Turns Out to be a Funny Man." *Los Angeles Herald Examiner,* 27 November, sec C, 1.

———. 1988. "A Mamet Metamorphosis?" *Los Angeles Herald Examiner,* 21 October, sec. Weekend, 6-7.

———. 1992. "Enter Scowling." *Los Angeles Times Magazine,* 23 August, 20.

———. 1994. "The Storm Over *Oleanna.*" *Los Angeles Times,* 30 January, 8, 48.

———. 1995. "David Mamet Meets Alan Dershowitz." Unpublished notes.

Strauss, Bob. 1988. "Speed-the-Mamet." *New York Post,* 17 October, 25, 31.

Steiner, George. 1961. *The Death of Tragedy.* London: Faber and Faber.

———. 1976. *Language and Silence: Essays on Language, Literature and the Inhuman.* New York: Athenaeum.

———. 1996. "Our Homeland, the Text." In *No Passion Spent: Essays 1978-1995,* 304-27. New Haven and London: Yale University Press.

Stern, Guy. 1991. "The Rhetoric of Anti-Semitism in Postwar American Literature." In *Anti-Semitism in Times of Crisis,* ed. Sander Gilman and Steven Katz, 291-310.

Sterritt, David. 1992. "Drama Touches on Political Power." *Christian Science Monitor,* 30 October, 12.

Stevens, Austin. 1975. *The Dispossessed.* London: Barrie & Jenkins.

Story, Richard David. 1992. "David Mamet Raises Outrage to an Art Form in *Oleanna.*" *New York,* 14 September, 58.

Streicker, Joel. 1994. "How at Home? American Jewish [Male] Identities in Mamet's *Homicide.*" *Shofar* 12, no. 3 (Spring): 46-65.

Stuart, Jan. 1982. "Mamet's Reactionary Howl on Sexual Harassment." *Newsday,* 26 October. Reprinted in *New York Theatre Critics' Reviews,* 356.

Suchet, David. 1993. Interview by Anne Dean. London, England, 25 November.

Sylvester, Ellis Edward. 1886. *Lost in the Wilds.* Chicago: G. M. Hill.

Tabor, Mary B. W. 1995. "Mamet on Passover." *New York Times,* 29 March, C15.

Taylor, Markland. 1995. "The Cryptogram." Review of *The Cryptogram* by David Mamet. *Variety,* 13-19 February, 59-60.

Taylor, Paul. 1993. "Dramatically Incorrect." *Independent,* 2 July, 15.

———. 1994. "Brute Strength." *The Independent,* 1 July. Reprinted in *Theatre Record,* 18 June-1 July, 796.

Telushkin, Joseph. 1992. *Jewish Humor: What the Best Jewish Jokes Say About the Jews.* New York: William Morrow.

Tinker, Jack. 1993. "Battle of the Sexists, or How to Put the Boot into Nazispeak." *Daily Mail,* 1 July, 7.

Tomc, Sandra. 1997. "David Mamet's *Oleanna* and the Way of the Flesh." *Essays in Theatre/Etudes theatrales* 15, no. 2: 163-75.

Travers, Peter. 1991. "Homicide." *Rolling Stone,* 31 October, 99.

Tuchman, Gayle, and Harry Gene Levine. 1993. "New York Jews and Chinese Food: The Social Construction of an Ethnic Pattern." *Journal of Contemporary Ethnography,* 22, no. 3: 382-407.

Tuttle, Jon. 1992. "'Be What You *Are*': Identity and Morality in *Edmond* and *Glengarry Glen Ross.*" In *Glengarry Glen Ross: Text and Performance,* ed. Leslie Kane, 157-69.

Valleley, Jean. 1980. "David Mamet Makes a Play for Hollywood." *Rolling Stone,* 3 April, 44-45.

Veblen, Thorstein. 1899. *The Theory of the Leisure Class.* Reprint, New York: Penguin, 1953.

———. 1948. "The Intellectual Pre-eminence of Jews in Modern Europe." In *The Portable Veblen,* ed. and intro. by Max Lerner, 467-79. New York: Viking Press.

VerMeulen, Michael. 1991. "Mamet's Mafia." *New York Observer.* 7 October 1, 20.

Vorlicky, Robert. 1995a. *Act Like a Man: Challenging Masculinities in American Drama*. Ann Arbor: University of Michigan Press.

———. 1995b. "The Cryptogram." Review of *The Cryptogram* by David Mamet, Westside Theatre, New York, 28 May 1995. *David Mamet Review* 2 (Fall): 3-4.

———. 1996. "Men Among the Ruins." In *Glengarry Glen Ross: Text and Performance*, ed. Leslie Kane, 85-105.

Wadeson, Oliver. 1993. "Mamet Guaranteed to Stir the Emotions." *Westminister & South Pimlico News*, 15 July.

Wadlington, Warwick. 1975. *The Confidence Game in American Literature*. Princeton: Princeton University Press.

Wandor, Michelene. 1987. *Look Back in Gender: Sexuality and the Family in Post-War British Drama*. London and New York: Methuen.

Watson, Douglas N. 1991. *Begging the Question: Circular Reasoning as a Tactic of Argumentation*. *Contributions in Philosophy*, Number 48. Westport, CT: Greenwood Press.

———. 1992. *Slippery Slope Arguments*. Oxford: Clarendon Press.

Weber, Bruce. 1994. "Thoughts from a Man's Man." *New York Times*, 17 November, C1, 10.

———. 1997. "At 50, a Mellow David Mamet May Be Ready to Tell His Story." *New York Times*, 16 November, sec. 2, 7, 12.

Weiner, Bernard. 1989. "Whoring in Hollywood." *Tikkun* 4: 77-78.

Weininger, Otto. 1903. *Sex and Character*. Trans. of the 6th German edition. London: Heinemann; New York: Putnam.

Weinreich, Max. 1972. "Internal Bilingualism in Ashkenaz." In *Voices from the Yiddish: Essays, Memories, Diaries*, ed. Irving Howe and Eliezer Greenberg, 279-88. Ann Arbor: University of Michigan Press.

Weintraub, Bernard. 1995. "'Gump' Still Isn't Raking in Huge Profits? Hmm." *New York Times*, 25 May, B1, 4.

Wetzsteon, Ross. 1976. "David Mamet: Remember That Name." *Village Voice*, 5 July, 101-04.

———. 1997. "Altered Faiths." Review of David Mamet's *Old Religion*. *Village Voice*, 18 November, 92.

Wexler, Paul. 1981. "Jewish Interlinguistics." *Language* 57: 99-149.

White, Stewart Edward. 1903. *The Forest*. New York: The Outlook Company.

Whitfield, Stephen J. 1978. "Laughter in the Dark: Notes on American-Jewish Humor." *Midstream* 24, no. 2: 48-58.

———. 1984. *Voices of Jacob, Hands of Esau: Jews in American Life and Thought*. Hamden, Ct.: Archon Books.

———. 1986. "Our American Jewish Heritage: The Hollywood Version." *American Jewish History* 75: 322-40.

———. 1988. *American Space, Jewish Time*. Hamden, Ct.: Archon Books.

Wiesel, Elie. 1965. *One Generation After*. Trans. Lily Edelman and the author. New York: Random House.

———. 1976. *Messengers of God: Biblical Portraits and Legends*. New York: Summit Books.

———. 1990. *From the Kingdom of Memory: Reminiscences*. New York: Summit Books.

———. 1991. *Sages and Dreamers: Biblical, Talmudic, and Hasidic Portraits and Legends*. Trans. and ed. Marion Wiesel. New York: Summit Books.

Winn, Steven. 1994. "ACT Takes Mamet's *Oleanna* to the Edge." *San Francisco Chronicle*, 6 May, sec. 6., 1.

Wisse, Ruth R. 1971. *The Schlemiel as Modern Hero*. Chicago: University of Chicago Press.

Wolf, Matt. 1993. "A London *Oleanna* Deepens the Debate." *American Theatre* (November): 77-78.

———. 1994. "Mamet's Bleak New 'Cryptogram' a Mystery Waiting to Be Decoded." *Chicago Tribune*, 5 July, sec. N, 16 Arts.

Wouk, Herman. 1959. *This Is My God*. Reprint, Boston and Toronto: Little, Brown, 1987.

Worster, David. 1994. "How to Do Things with Salesmen: David Mamet's Speech-Act Play." *Modern Drama* 37, no. 3: 375-90.

Yakir, Dan. 1981. "The Postman's Words." *Film Comment* (March/April): 21-24.

Zborowsky, Mark and Elizabeth Herzog. 1952. *Life Is With People: The Culture of the Shtetl*. New York: Schocken Books.

Zeifman, Hersh. 1992. "Phallus in Wonderland: Machismo and Business in David Mamet's *American Buffalo* and *Glengarry Glen Ross*." In *David Mamet: A Casebook*, ed. Leslie Kane, 123-35.

———. 1994. "Oleanna." Review of *Oleanna* by David Mamet. Duke of York's Theatre, London. *David Mamet Review* 1 (Fall): 2-3.

———. 1997. "Cipherspace: David Mamet's *The Cryptogram*." Paper presented at Mamet at 50: A Conference and Celebration, Las Vegas, 31 October.

Zigler, Scott. 1995. Interview by author. Cambridge, Mass., 30 January.

Zierold, Norman. 1972. *The Moguls*. New York: Avon.

Zinman, Toby Silverman. 1992. "Jewish Aporia: The Rhythm of Talking in Mamet." *Theatre Journal* 44, no. 2: 207-15.

Zoglin, Richard. 1995. "Cryptic Game." *Time*, 20 February, 76.

Zweigler, Mark. 1976. "David Mamet: The Solace of a Playwright's Ideals." *After Dark* 20: 42-45.

INDEX

Acculturation, 26, 38, 43
Ace in the Hole, 116
Achrayut, 56
Aggadah, 4
Aggadic literature, 16, 18, 29, 109,
    121, 247, 271; *see also* Midrashic
    literature
Aggadic narrative, 4, 6, 17, 235, 254
Albee, Edward, 280, 317
Aleichem, Sholem, 146, 192, 196
Allen, Woody, 198, 224, 264, 267,
    268, 329 n.24, 334 n.7; *Radio
    Days,* 108, 205, 224
American Buffalo (Mamet), 2, 4, 5, 13,
    22, 23-56, 65, 77, 127, 150, 182,
    162, 170, 185, 283, 317; abdica-
    tion of moral position in, 26, 28,
    38, 39, 41, 47, 52, 56, 210; fam-
    ily, 24, 26; and *Glengarry,* 26, 48,
    58, 59, 84, 86, 96, 155; land-
    mark production of, 315; and
    loyalty, 24, 32, 38, 39, 41, 47,
    50; obscenity-laced vernacular,
    24, 28, 32, 53, 77, 152; pedagog-
    ical relationship in, 24, 32, 38,
    47, 48, 183; violence, 24, 32, 38,
    47, 48, 183
American Dream, 59, 168; myth of,
    158, 160; attraction for Mamet,
    158; and white middle-class men,
    158
American Jewish filmmakers, 106,
    107, 108, 237, 333 n.4, 335 n.10
American Jewish humor, 35, 76, 82,
    93, 117, 121, 124, 134, 139,
    236, 329 n.24, 334 n.7; *see also*
    Bruce, Lenny

American Jewish immigrant experi-
    ence, 237, 130, 232, 237, 270; in
    Call It Sleep, 25, 192, 193, 222,
    237, 349 n.11; *see also, Disap-
    pearance of the Jews, Rise of David
    Levinsky, Jews Without Money*
American Jewish life, 55, 160, 231,
    232, 243, 276, 339 n.41, 237
American Jewish literature, 59, 96,
    122, 130, 132, 143, 265, 278,
    295, 315, 319 n.2; archetypal fig-
    ures, 323 n.20; Bildungsroman,
    192, 193, 222; urbanals, 266,
    298; *see also;* Bellow; Cahan;
    Gold; Miller; Roth, Henry; Roth,
    Paul
American mythology of violence, and
    the Frontier ethic, 80
Anti-Semitism, 7, 17, 23, 60, 69, 95,
    98, 109, 117, 144, 159, 168,
    175, 227, 239, 242, 256, 258,
    279, 282, 339 n.40, 361 n.36;
    American, 109, 107, 131, 231,
    256, 295; in 1920s and 1930s,
    107, 108, 133, 143, 333 n.4;
    Luther's foundations of, 167, 320
    nn.12, 13, 14; medieval morality
    play, 52, 134, 338 n.39; medieval
    propaganda, 134-5, 338 n.39;
    imagery, 100, 191, 323 n.24, 343
    n.14, 344 n.15; *see* Stereotypes
Apology, 65, 75, 151, 174, 203, 206,
    211, 215, 217, 115, 175, 176
Arendt, Hannah, 68, 145
Argument, modes of, 70, 126, 163;
    pipul shel hevel, 42, 77; slippery
    slope, 118